Flight of the Trogon

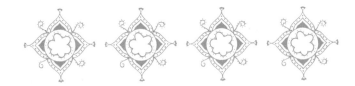

FLIGHT OF THE TROGON

BOOK 2 OF THE MEXICAN EDEN TRILOGY
A Stand-alone Prequel and Sequel to Book 1

Sylvia Montgomery Shaw

**SWEDENBORG
FOUNDATION**
Royersford, Pennsylvania

Library of Congress Cataloging-in-Publication Data

Names: Shaw, Sylvia Montgomery, author.
Title: Flight of the trogon / Sylvia Montgomery Shaw.
Description: First edition. | West Chester, Pennsylvania : Swedenborg
  Foundation, [2023] | Series: Mexican Eden Trilogy : Book 2 | Book 2 of
  the Mexican Eden Trilogy: A Stand-alone Prequel and Sequel to Book 1
Identifiers: LCCN 2023015905 | ISBN 9780877853497 (paperback) | ISBN
  9780877856313 (epub)
Subjects: LCSH: Mexico--History--Revolution, 1910-1920--Fiction. | LCGFT:
  Romance fiction. | Novels.
Classification: LCC PS3619.H3945 F55 2023 | DDC 813/.6--dc23/eng/20230403
LC record available at https://lccn.loc.gov/2023015905

Edited by Meg Tyler
Design and typesetting by Karen Connor
Cover illustration by Samuel Cataño

The scripture quotations contained herein are from the New Revised Standard Version Bible, copyright © 1989 by the Division of Christian Education of the National Council of the Churches of Christ in the USA, and are used by permission. All rights reserved.

Printed in the United States of America

Swedenborg Foundation
70 Buckwalter Road
Suite 900 PMB 405
Royersford, PA 19468
www.swedenborg.com

For my sister Louise, my first friend,
and
for Holland, the love of my life

*To open our eyes to the true nature of the universe
has always been one of physics' primary purposes.
It's hard to imagine a more mind-stretching experience
than learning, as we have over the last century, that the reality
we experience is but a glimmer of the reality that is.*

BRIAN GREENE

*What lies behind you and what lies in front of you
pales in comparison to what lies inside of you.*

RALPH WALDO EMERSON

CONTENTS

AUTHOR'S NOTE

Since *Flight of the Trogon* is both a prequel and a sequel to the first book in the *Mexican Eden Trilogy*, readers need not have read the first novel in the series in order to enjoy this one. *Flight of the Trogon* is a stand-alone novel. Readers who *have* read the first book, *Paradise Misplaced*, may well recognize several short chapters about the Tarahumara prisoner known as el Brujo. I have deliberately included these pretty much *verbatim* so that those readers can see where the two novels intersect.

As for my use of Spanish terms that might be unfamiliar to the reader, you will notice that they are italicized the first time they are used. Typical terms throughout the book include:

- la patrona = the boss
- federales = federal government soldiers
- doña = a prefix of respect (e.g., before Manuela's name)
- don = a prefix of respect (e.g., don Cadwallader)

LIST OF CHARACTERS

The Brentt Family

Cadwallader Brentt ("Cadwally") and granddaughter, **Isabel** Brentt

The Nyman Vizcarra Family

Gen. Lucio Nyman fathered **Rodolfo** Nyman with a mistress

Eva Nyman de Comardo with his first wife

Benjamín Nyman Vizcarra (Isabel's husband)

Father **Samuel** Nyman Vizcarra, with his second wife: **doña Manuela Vizcarra de Nyman**, second wife of the general

The Comardo Nyman Family

Count Francisco Comardo (Pancho), husband of **Eva Nyman de Comardo**

Their three children: **Esther, Emanuela**, and **Evita**

The Tepaneca Family

Rosa Tepaneca (a mother figure to Isabel and former cook for Cadwallader) and her son, **Tomás** Tepaneca, attorney. Isa's friend since childhood.

Key Servants on the San Serafín Plantation

Tacha (confidant of doña Manuela)

Valle Inclán (Head administrator)

Bardomiana (long-time cook to the Nyman Vizcarra family)

Benjamín's Bodyguards

    Mangel, known as Volcán, most feared prisoner in the penitentiary,

    Manco, who lost his right hand in a murderous fight, and

    Vago, who has an inane smile but wields knives all too expertly

Benjamín's Special Friends in the Prison

    Brujo, a Tarahumara shaman

    Caleb Wilkes, young American missionary, known as "el San Juanito" (little St. Johnnie)

Other Characters

    Doña Clemencia, grocer's widow in Samuel's village, who is adopted into the family

    Teresa Gama, Rodolfo's former mistress and mother to their three children: **Teresita, Laurita,** and **Rodolfito** (Lambykins)

    Eufemio Rosarito, the elusive man whom Tomás pursues throughout Morelos

Part 1

THE GRAVE

The day which we fear as our last is but the birthday of eternity.
SENECA

TOMBSTONE

My gravestone bears a simple inscription:

Isabel Brentt

1890–1911

Now that's brevity. Brutal *brevitas*. If ever you find yourself in the south central highlands of Mexico and happen upon a forgotten cemetery in a forgotten plantation, you can see it for yourself. Look for the tombstone that pitches violently to the left, as if grave robbers had been interrupted in their night's work. Pause if you want to but for no more than a few seconds, for what can a mere twelve letters and eight numbers tell you? That whoever I was, I died young? Isn't the real point not how long I lived but *how* I lived? Isn't this the measure of a life? I'd like to share my story, not because its details matter, but because of what does matter: though we die, yet shall we live.

So who was I? Who am I? Let's begin with beginnings. As the name on the stone suggests, I was not a native of Mexico though I felt as Mexican as a maguey plant. I was born in Philadelphia. When I was two my parents decided to start a new life in Oklahoma. A few months later they were both killed by a tornado that scattered our house across a one mile area. Neighbors found me crying but unscathed—not even memories to haunt my nights. A few months later I was transplanted again, this time to a town in Mexico's central highlands, there to be raised by my reclusive grandfather, Cadwallader Brentt.

Cadwally, as I called him, was an American expatriate who eked out a living as an artist. He chose for his self-imposed exile Cuernavaca. In 1910, the fateful year of the Mexican Revolution, the town had fewer than seven thousand people, yet a history so very much older than Boston's or Philadelphia's. This was a place coveted by Olmecs before the times of Christ, and later by Tlahuicas, Aztecs, Spaniards, and Frenchmen. American troops passed through here as well during the Mexican-American War. By a strange coincidence the American commander happened to be a General Cadwalader. No relation to my Cadwallader, but I liked to tease him about it since he was so violently non-violent in his politics.

Cadwally's parenting skills were like his art, fluctuating between the avant-garde minimalism that he preferred and a traditional realism that he could not quite shake off. The one fed his soul, the other our bellies. He used the walls of our home as canvasses for his abstract and stylized paintings. What little money we had came mostly from tourists who wanted realistic renderings of the Tepozteco mountain and the Valley of Morelos as souvenirs of their travels.

My education was just as fractured as Cadwally's art, being both progressive and traditional. Convinced that schools stunt the mind, Cadwally kept me home. He taught me to read in English and then let his library do the rest, which was a fine idea in principle, except that he had brought just a handful of books to Mexico. There were no fairy tales, no Bible, no Shakespeare in our home. No Dickens or Thackery or collected works of poetry to edify the mind. Instead, I had to cut my teeth on John Stuart Mill, Jeremy Bentham, and other like-minded social reformers.

Loosely in the spirit of Mill's utilitarian philosophy, Cadwally encouraged me to better myself by giving me all the freedom of a street dog. From the time I could speak I had the run of the streets in our town. Mexican neighbors cringed at the casualness of the *gringo* artist in the raising of his little granddaughter. American expats, none of whom Cadwally cared to befriend, shook their heads and clucked their tongues at the sight of a disheveled blonde child playing with Mexican street urchins. What could one expect from a Bohemian artist? they asked. The man wore sandals, for pity's sake!

Bohemian or not, Cadwally followed certain proprieties. He always wore vested suits, generally the color of oatmeal, old glories from an earlier era. Though threadbare, they were clean and gave him the air of a gentleman who has been marooned on a distant island—with his trunk, of course. At dinner time, even if we dined on nothing but beans and tortillas, Cadwally always insisted that I clean up before coming to the table, that I sit up straight as a cypress, and that I eat with the proper utensil "in a manner befitting a Brentt."

My grandfather was a contradiction: part rebel, part Boston Brahmin.

In those early years, Cadwally kept a cook. Rosa Tepaneca was a Tlahuica Indian, not a Tepanecan (in spite of her name). Rosa was the closest thing I had to a mother. Likewise, her young son became a brother and constant companion to me. We were fellow adventurers who explored twisting lanes and the neglected gardens of the tragic Maximilian Hapsburg. I learned far more from Rosa and Tomás than from Cadwally's books on philosophy and social reform. The Tepanecas gave me my bearings, grounding me in a culture of mixed heritage—Tlahuican, Spanish, and ultimately Mexican. Tomás filled my head with legends of his ancestors before the Spanish conquest. Rosa took me to churches built by the conquerors and taught me to light candles to the Virgin of Guadalupe.

I had just turned fifteen when my grandfather sent me away to a boarding school in the United States. All expenses were paid by his half-sister, our one living relative. I had never even heard of Great-aunt Delphine Brentt until Cadwally asked her to take me under her wing. I lived with her in Bryn Athyn, Pennsylvania, until old enough to live in the girls' dormitory of the one girls' academy in town. Aunt Delphine's generosity included a new wardrobe each year and a season in Europe. The whole experience opened my eyes to a larger, far grander world than anything I could have imagined growing up in Cuernavaca. By the time I returned home five years later, I could no more step back into my old life than a snake into its shed skin. I had traveled too much, seen too much, changed too much. And what exactly had all that effort and expense accomplished? I was living in penury again, with the difference that now I *knew* it and knew enough to hate it.

That's when Rodolfo Nyman strode into my life.

Rodolfo was a man of the world, twice my age, handsome as a pedigreed race horse, and sired by a general reputed to be the wealthiest man in the state of Morelos and perhaps in all of Mexico. At first I was both thrilled and disquieted by his attentions. After a brief courtship I accepted his marriage proposal, perhaps in the spirit of a materialistic utilitarianism. How could I not accept when Cadwally and I were in such dire straits? Then I met Rodolfo's younger brother.

Benjamín was an officer in the Mexican army. Everyone assumed he would rise to a generalship like his father before him. With his out-going personality and family connections, the presidency itself would not have been beyond his reach someday. Clearly, Benjamín was presumed the most gifted of his siblings. It turned out that he was far more passionate than practical. We both were. We honestly tried not to fall in love with each other— to deny our feelings. But that was like ignoring the bite of a Jalapeño pepper on the tongue, or the scent of a gardenia deeply inhaled. One silver night we whispered to each other all that we had suppressed.

We eloped. Benjamín went a step further, defecting from the army and his family's ambitions for him. Together, we joined the revolution to oust Porfirio Díaz from his thirty-year dictatorship. Benjamín's family disowned him. It didn't matter. We were in love and could handle anything. When the fighting ended a few months later, we entered Mexico City penniless but with all the pride of liberators. Poverty didn't scare us. We had gone to war, Benjamín and I. We had faced the privations of army camps and the distress of a few lost battles before victory. We could make it on our own without anyone's help. We should have known that some enemies are much harder to defeat than others. As for that tilting tombstone of mine—don't let it distress you. It is but one marker on a long journey.

Besides, as a wise old Swede observed, what we call death the angels call resurrection.

FLIGHT

I WAS THE center of the universe. The dead center. This is a little known fact, but I knew it from earliest childhood. All of life revolved around *me,* pulsing to my every thought and desire. My grandfather didn't fully understand that, nor did anyone else for that matter. As I was growing up he would remark with calm detachment: "This may surprise you, Isabel, but contrary to all appearances, you are *not* the center of the universe."

I was all of five or six the first time Cadwally shared this insight with me. I remember pausing in mid-tantrum but only because his words puzzled me. What's the universe? Seconds later the agony of being pried off a carousel pony drew fresh howls of protest from me. By the time I was grown and married, my position in the cosmos had begun to shift. Yet, what is it about an extreme crisis that places us once again in the childish delusion of our centrality?

Early on a July morning in 1911 the very cosmos shrank as never before. Nothing mattered but my anguish, intense and all-consuming. Lying in the dark beside Benjamín, I felt at first like a rape victim, too traumatized to react. Who *was* this man who had come to bed drunk and enraged? Had I ever really known him? Did I want to know him any further? As the night wore on and the initial shock subsided, resentment took hold. While everyone slept, I reached my fateful decision. After six-and-a-half months of marriage I was leaving my husband forever. Staring up into a high ceiling, limitless as the sky in that darkness, I did not even consider the practicalities of how I would support myself, or whether I would return to the United States or remain in Mexico with my grandfather. I just wanted to escape before Benjamín woke up.

I rose before daylight—slowly, ever so slowly so the bed would not betray me, softly so that my feet would touch the Talavera tiles soundlessly, carefully so I could work the pillowcase off the pillow without waking Benjamín. His back was turned, but I could not shake the notion that he would wake suddenly. I struggled to think of an excuse if his eyes should probe the darkness and find me dressing. *I want to make myself a cup of tea, but I can't find my bathrobe. So I need to dress. . . .*

I felt in the dark for a succession of garments. My hands were shaking too much to deal with the stays on the corset, so I slipped it into the pillowcase to take with me. Expediency was vital—to dress quickly and soundlessly before Benjamín woke up. Groping in the dark, I felt the silk of last night's dress. *No, not that one.* My hands found a narrow skirt. *No, I can't run in a stupid hobble skirt. Find the beige suit. Yes, this feels like the skirt. Now a blouse. Any shirt-waist . . . Yes, this will do. Find the jacket. . . .* I found my purse and snatched it up though it had no money. Just the same I slipped it into the pillowcase along with what I guessed was a day dress and one change of undergarments.

Please don't wake up, I pleaded silently.

Even as I remained obsessively attuned to the rhythm of Benjamín's breathing, it occurred to me that I had done all this before. On the night that Ben and I eloped, there had been no time to pack, only to stuff a few things into a pillow case and escape from this very house like thieves in the night. I was running away again, only this time from him.

I felt on the floor for my shoes and on the chaise for stockings, every motion a whisper. *Put them on later, not here.* Just then Benjamín groaned in his sleep and I felt the urge to bolt from the room. Closing my eyes, I forced myself to wait for the galloping inside my ribs to slow to an ambling gait. Only then did I press down on the door knob, slowly, ever so slowly, until it yielded. Then I was hurrying in bare feet down a series of corridors, stairs, and patios. I kept expecting doors to open, heads to poke out, and voices to sound the alarm. Twice I thought I could hear Benjamín running after me on bare feet, arms outstretched to grab me. I paused only when I stood outside under the star-embroidered cloak of night. The back terrace and gardens smelled of damp earth and honeysuckle. It was still dark but I could begin to discern shapes. At best I might have an hour before the sun exposed the dark hills of Morelos. Standing at the top of a stone stairway, I clutched shoes and pillowcase to my chest.

Where is he?

Not Benjamín, but Tomás. Staring down into the darkness of the large garden, I began to discern the contours of my mother-in-law's aviary. The cage rose a full three stories into the gloom. Several of the trapped birds were fluttering their wings.

Where have they stashed him?

The plantation was an enormous complex of buildings that still perplexed me. I knew that my husband's family would never lodge a man like Tomás Tepaneca in the main house. Did they classify him as an unwanted guest or simply as a peasant? A lowly intruder like me, but surely not a servant. So he had to be in the guest quarters.

Hurrying into the lower garden, I passed by the aviary without pausing to look for my favorite bird, the resplendent quetzal—"the greatest of all trogons," Benjamín would have reminded me. I wonder now, did the quetzal gaze at me from his high perch, his long emerald tail feathers blurring into the murkiness of pre-dawn? Did he flutter his wings as if to join in the escape? Or had his long imprisonment robbed him of the desire for freedom? I hurried along until I stood in yet another courtyard. More than a dozen rooms opened onto it, yet I knew intuitively which door to approach.

Go back! This was the final warning, a trickle of doubt seeping into my resolve.

I remember pressing my forehead to the door and shutting my eyes, but I could not shut out the memory of alcohol on my husband's breath and the rage in his words, in his eyes, in his touch. So I let myself into Tomás Tepaneca's room. Now there was no going back.

"Tomás!" He was awake even before I reached the foot of his bed.

"Is it thundering?" He asked with apparent seriousness.

I felt my cheeks burn, in part from his reference to my habit as a little girl to seek safety in his bed during thunderstorms, and in part because the boy was a man now—a bare-chested man—and I had no business being in his room. Yet who else could I turn to?

"Please take me away from here, now, before they all wake up."

Men's voices reached us, muffled by the stone walls. Were Benjamín and his brothers up already? Or was it just the gardeners? Or perhaps some of the guards? Had they seen me enter Tomás's room? With every second that passed, I felt myself slipping further toward a steep incline with no hope of stopping the fearful plunge. I gave him my back as he dressed. He kept the light off but rattled me when he hugged me a few moments later.

"Ah, Isa! Isa!" He used my nickname as only he and Benjamín did, caressing me with the long vowel sound. EE-sah. "Do you realize it's been almost five-and-a-half years!"

I was startled by the rock-like solidness of his body and by his short stature. In childhood he towered over me. Now we stood shoulder to shoulder. Actually, it had been the same in our adolescence. I had simply forgotten. Or perhaps I had unconsciously learned to gauge height by my tall husband. Tomás hugged me a second time.

"What a *relief* not to have to pretend we don't know each other," he laughed.

"I know. I'm sorry, Tomás. It's just that they would have assumed—well, I couldn't let them think that we had connived—"

"I understand." He reached for his suit coat. "So tell me, did they teach you to ride in that fancy boarding school?"

I could have explained that riding classes were not part of the curriculum in Bryn Athyn, but that my Great-aunt Delphine, who was determined to "civilize" me, had engaged a riding master. All that would have required far more conversation than I could handle just then. "Yes," I managed.

"Good. We'll tell the guards at the front gate that we're going for a morning ride. Fortunately, your mother-in-law did not give me time to pack when she ordered us here. So we can travel light. I assume you're not taking anything either."

"Just what I was able to stuff into this."

"Leave it. You can hardly go for a morning ride clutching a pillowcase."

Snatching it from my hands, he flung it over his shoulder, causing me to drop my shoes and stockings. I jumped at the clatter.

"As for you, Miss Brentt, shouldn't you finish dressing?" He bent to retrieve my footwear.

Mrs. Nyman, I was about to correct him. But hadn't I just decided to end my marriage? Wasn't I going to be Isabel Brentt once more? And who better than my oldest and closest friend to help me? Friend or not, I had him step outside so I could slip on my stockings and shoes. It was only then that I realized that I could not hold up the silk stockings without attaching them to the garters on my corset which was now lost somewhere in the dark. And as I didn't dare turn on any lights, the corset would have to remain lost. I jammed the stockings into my pockets and my bare feet into the shoes. Joining Tomás, we headed for the stables. The two buildings were as large as the main house and almost as immaculate. Tomás rousted up a boy who was sleeping in the one empty stall.

"Saddle up two horses."

The boy stumbled to his feet and flicked on a light switch. The sudden brightness blinded all three of us. The boy stared with undisguised curiosity. *I should have looked for the riding habit instead of the suit,* the thought jolted me. *We must look all wrong, Tomás in a business suit, and I in my beige . . .* Holding out my arms, I suddenly realized that I had grabbed the wrong jacket, a blue cheviot. I was mismatched and hatless and glove-less and stocking-less. Now I wonder, why in the grip of the momentous do so many of us fret about trivia?

"Hurry up, *muchacho,*" Tomás prodded the boy with a jerk of his head. "The señora wants to see the sunrise."

After some time, the groom finally reappeared with two white Arabians. Gathering my skirt, I mounted up. Luckily my mother-in-law disliked side saddles as much as I did, so I didn't have to endure that particular challenge. I straddled the horse, thankful that I had not tried to escape in my narrow hobble skirt. Moments later, ill-dressed as we were, we rode into the grand courtyard, *el patio grande.* Tomás was all confidence and authority. With but a few words and a nod from him, the sen-tries opened the wrought-iron gate. We fugitives rode with slow deliberation down a long, tree-lined road. When at last the walls of the San Serafín hacienda were behind us and the first rays of light dampened the horizon, I spurred my horse. Tomás fol-lowed close behind. Fields of sugar cane slowly came into focus, shimmering in the nascent light mile after mile, wet as newborns. Vague, formless shapes became hills dressed in cedars and oaks. After half an hour or so, Tomás rose in his saddle and reached for my horse's bridle.

"Isa, slow down. We're safe now. Tell me what happened."

He brought me to a standstill, angling his horse so that I would have to look directly at him. Again, I was surprised at how much I had forgotten: how bronzed his features; how aquiline his nose; how black his eyes—intelligent and polished with self-confidence. I could still glimpse the boy but I did not know the man.

"I can't talk about it."

Under his intense scrutiny, I reached to tidy my hair, embarrassed suddenly that there had been no time to sweep it up off my neck; embarrassed that my eyes must be puffy from crying, and that by riding in a regular skirt instead of a riding habit, I could not quite cover my legs properly.

"Don't worry," he smiled as if reading my mind. "You've never looked more beautiful. That hair of yours still out-shines the sun."

I had learned across the years how to handle Tomás's teasing but not his compliments. His very next words threw me even more.

"Did he hurt you?" There was no mistaking the menace that crept into his voice, like the low growl of a great cat.

"My husband? No, of course not."

Even then I was conscious of ambivalent feelings. I had made the momentous decision to leave Benjamín, yet I could not bear to have him disparaged by anyone. The slightest hint of censure rankled. So I drew into myself and avoided direct eye contact with Tomás for fear that I would burst into tears. Fortunately, Tomás shifted to pragmatics.

"Last night, after your mother-in-law dismissed me from the table like a servant or a child, did she or that lawyer of hers pressure you into signing anything?"

"No. Let go of the reins." I fixed my eyes on the road, body leaning into it.

"Calm yourself. Just tell me what happened."

San Serafín was far behind us, the road deserted. I could hear the liquid sound of bird calls, moist and fresh as dew. Yet I could not shake my sense of dread.

CADWALLY

"COME NOW. WHEN did you and I ever keep secrets from each other, Isa?" Tomás feigned hurt and stubbornly refused to hand back the reins. "As your accomplice, and the man who may well get himself shot for helping you, don't I deserve at least to know why?"

I glanced at him, darting into his eyes with hummingbird quickness, then away. "I'm leaving my husband. Now, please, please get me home to my grandfather."

Tomás released the reins and let me spur my horse past him. For the rest of our ride he traveled in easy silence. I, on the other hand, continued to glance over my shoulder, my senses attuned for the cavalry of pursuit. There was none. Birds sang from high tree branches. People began to appear along the road: men in the white shirt and pants of the Morelos peasantry, their heads protected under wide-brimmed hats with tall crowns; Indian women carrying large baskets or a baby strapped to their back; barefoot children riding astride soft-eyed burros. If they stared at us I hardly noticed. In my single-mindedness they quickly blurred, like watercolor sketches left out in the rain. *Has Benjamín noticed I'm gone? Is he searching the hacienda grounds? The road? Or is he hung over and still sleeping?* We reined in our horses when we reached the outskirts of Cuernavaca. My heart galloped ahead to embrace my hometown. Small and provincial as it was in 1911, I did love it.

The watchtowers of Cortes's *palacio* were clearly visible now, rising above the treeline. The residence of the famed conqueror was more fortress than palace. Though most people found it downright grim-looking and oddly out of sync with Cuernavaca's lush flowers and palm trees, they were drawn to it. Tomás hated it. When he was no more than eight or nine years old, he would lecture me on the ineptness of the Spanish *conquistadores.*

"They only beat my ancestors because they had guns. But they were so stupid they couldn't even pronounce the name of the place! What's so hard about saying *Cuauhnahuac?* But no, they had to go call it Cuernavaca—Cow's Horn. Duh!"

Then he would rant about their greater crime—tearing down the temple and using the very same stones to build the so-called palace. "But you'll see, the gods will get even!"

I would listen quietly, wondering if the gods were as angry about this as he was. The truth is, I liked the palace that Cortés had built for himself. It used to set my imagination aflame like the blossoms of a poinciana tree. Why couldn't Tomás imagine just for a few seconds a beautiful and gentle queen or a princess gazing down from the upper *portales?* Instead his boyish fancy used to sculpt nothing but fierce Tlahuica and Tepaneca warriors.

We entered the town at a comfortable amble. The tall *jacaranda* trees opened like umbrellas, their lavender blossoms swaying in the morning breeze. Thick vines of bougainvillea spilled over walls, adding magenta and pink to the palette. As we meandered along cobbled stone streets, we passed bushes overflowing with *floripondios,* lovely, bell-shaped flowers that infuse the nights with their scent, a fragrance as strong and assured in the dark as my decision to leave Benjamín, yet oh so faint in the light of day. Had I overreacted? Taken a dangerous wrong turn? *Never touch the blossoms or leaves, child!* Rosa had warned about floripondios. *They are not what they seem!* Yes, but his drunkenness was no hallucination conjured from a floripondio-infused tea. I know what I saw and heard.

Certainty gave way to a new dread: *What do I tell everyone? How do I admit that my marriage was a dismal mistake?* My spirit plummeted.

After a while we entered a part of town where the ruts in the street carved out small ponds; where plaster fell off the facades in great chunks; where decaying brick was exposed like a festering wound. We dismounted in front of several row houses. Tomás knocked repeatedly on one of the battered doors that fronted the street. There was no answer. We both knew the reason, but neither of us wanted to say it. I was home all right.

"I could climb the wall and open it from the inside," Tomás offered.

Just then the door coughed open. A tall, lanky old man appeared in the threshold swaying on long legs, like an egret buffeted by high winds. People say my eyes are just like Cadwallader Brentt's—startlingly blue—only my grandfather's eyes were usually bloodshot. I remember that his scraggly eyebrows shot up. Before he could express his surprise, I rushed forward.

"Oh, Cadwally!" Releasing the tension of hours, I sobbed on his chest with all the abandonment of a child.

He drew me inside. Even as I cried, I was acutely conscious of how tall and bony he was; how he smelled of alcohol, turpentine and oil paints, and that I loved the scent because it seemed his alone, and at this moment I no longer felt quite so alone in the world.

"What's happened?" my grandfather asked in English.

I was suddenly afraid of saying the words that would make my decision final. Crying was easier. Meanwhile Tomás had led the horses into the courtyard, the ubiquitous *patio* of most Mexican homes. Between them and the enormous, blossoming jacaranda tree that dominated the courtyard, the small space was quickly overwhelmed.

"Where's that husband of yours?" my grandfather persisted.

"Oh, Cadwally—"

"Killed?" The old man groaned the word.

No, it's worse than that, I wanted to say but only shook my head.

"She's left him," Tomás answered for me with far less pain.

"Why? What's he done?"

"Please, I'll tell you later. I'm so tired, so very tired."

Cadwally took a long look at me. Then he nodded. "Go rest."

I took the garden stairs slowly, passing his studio on the way to my bedroom. These were the only two rooms on the second floor of our small house. My room had a Dutch door. Longing to shut out the world, I closed both halves and threw myself on the bed. The upper half of the door swung open on its faulty hinges.

"Stupid door!" I muttered under my breath. I'd been cursing it for years. Yet tired as I was, I now appreciated the fact that I could lie on my bed and still hear the conversation going on downstairs.

"What's this about, Tepaneca?" My grandfather switched into heavily accented Spanish. "Why are you with her?"

"She was desperate to get away from her husband, Mr. Brentt."

"Already? And just how do you fit into the picture?"

"I was a guest of sorts in the San Serafín hacienda, on official business. Isabel and Benjamín Nyman were there too. Before sun-up she came to me for help. I've brought her here as she requested."

"You mean, she's quarreled with *Ny-man?*"

It's pronounced NEE-MAN! I wanted to shout down to him. But I realized that Cadwally was deliberately mispronouncing my married name as one more way to show his disdain for the most powerful family in the state.

"I mean that she's left him," Tomás put it simply enough.

I could have gone on listening from the comfort of my bed, but I suddenly needed not only to know what Tomás was telling my grandfather, but also to see his reaction for myself. So I tip-toed into the narrow veranda outside my room. I could see them in profile, the horses standing between them in the small court-yard, Cadwally's hair jutting out in distracted peaks. A streak of indigo paint tinged one of his white sideburns.

"Left him—well, it should come as no surprise," he sighed. "Marrying that—that . . ." He was fishing for a Spanish word. Which one? Arrogant? Jealous? Paranoid? Narrow-minded? Impossible? "Marrying that dreamer and running off like they did, hardly knowing each other, how else could it turn out? What did it last? All of six or seven months?"

"There's something else, sir. Isa's father-in-law died in the earthquake of June seventh."

I was struck by the satisfaction in Tomás's voice.

"General Nyman? What's the old buzzard's death got to do with her?"

"Only that he named Isabel his sole heir. And that, Mr. Brentt, makes your granddaughter the wealthiest woman in the state of Morelos."

I thought I was over the shock produced by the general's will. Tomás's abridgement of the matter, his penchant for cutting to the chase, made it seem raw and terrible again. How could I be the sole heir to the Nyman fortune? I looked at my grandfather. Was he more hungover than usual, or had he grasped the seri-ousness of the matter?

"Come again?" He asked across the backs of the two horses.

"General Lucio Nyman cut his entire family out of his will and left everything to Isabel."

"Everything?"

"Well, not quite. He left all his cash assets to the Church."

"That's illegal."

"Not if you set up accounts in Switzerland and launder the money over a number of years. What matters is that he's bequeathed to Isabel a mansion in San Angel, the San Serafín plantation in its entirety, the sugar refinery, a personal railroad that takes it all to market, Pullman cars for the family's private use, real estate in France, and, oh yes, there are the silver mines, the finest in all of Zacatecas."

"But it doesn't bloody make sense!" In his agitation, Cadwally had momentarily slipped back into English. Tomás, who didn't speak a word of *Inglés* seemed to grasp the gist.

"Actually, there *is* a thread of logic to the general's thinking, sir."

"No. Leaving his wealth to a stranger instead of his family is hardly *logicale*." Cadwally's Spanish was heavily accented and included his own hybrids of English and Spanish.

"Inevitable, then. Everyone knows that the general was estranged from his wife and children. He abandoned them years ago so he could live by himself like a monk—literally like a monk, robes and all—in a drafty old house."

"So he lost his *canicas*." Idiomatically, it made no sense in Spanish to say that my father-in-law had lost his marbles, which indeed he must have. "The family will *contestar* the will on the grounds of insanity, and that will end the matter."

"Oh, they'll contest it all right." Tomás understood immediately what Cadwally was trying to say, being fully fluent in what he called my grandfather's *Cadwalismos*. "But let me assure you, General Nyman was not insane. Eccentric and ruthless, absolutely, but not insane. I think he recognized that he had sired a brood unworthy of the family fortune. Is it really so strange that he would spite them all by leaving the bulk of his fortune, not quite to an outsider, but to someone who had married into the family, one whom he hoped would produce grandchildren worthy of his empire?"

Children. I gripped the veranda railing tighter. When making my fateful decision to leave Benjamín, I had not given our unborn children a thought. Was I guilty of a kind of murder? No, of course not! I snapped at myself. If anyone was to blame, it was Benjamín.

"I know all about the general's religious zeal," Cadwally spoke clearly. If he was at all hungover, the news seemed to have sobered him. "The simple fact is that he would have considered Isabel a *heretica*."

"Not necessarily."

"Yes, necessarily. The man was as *fanaticale* as a grand *inquisadore*." I couldn't help smiling at Cadwally's Spanish, colorful and outrageous as his art. "It doesn't make sense that he would *privy-lay-hee* Isabel over his own flesh and blood. It simply doesn't add up."

"Does it have to?"

"How do you fit into all this, Tepaneca?"

My grandfather had not objected to Tomás when we were children and his mother cooked for us. He had not objected when I played with him in the streets of Cuernavaca, ragged and poor as he was, for weren't we almost as ragged and poor? Besides, playing with him had kept me conveniently out of his studio. The inseparable duo, Cadwally had dubbed us. But over time his smiles for Tomás had turned to scowls.

"Why are you with her?"

"Fate, Mr. Brentt. Fate decreed that I should be the general's attorney at the end of his life, and that I should be the one to make his wishes known to the world."

"Well, isn't fate accommodating these days. Tell me, Tepaneca. Out of all the lawyers in Mexico City, how did the general just happen to choose you?"

"An astonishing coincidence, isn't it?" I could hear laughter behind the words even though outwardly Tomás remained serious, pensively stroking the neck of the mare I had ridden.

"And I suppose he threw in these horses too? Or did you steal them?"

"That's a matter of perspective—and law," Tomás smiled. "The family will say we stole them, but by law everything is now Isabel's, and that includes two stables full of the finest Arabians in Morelos."

"And you really believe that the Nymans won't *contestar* the will, especially now that Isabel seems to have walked out on her marriage?"

"As I said, they'll contest it all right, which is why it's vital that Isabel not fall into their hands again. They almost got her to sign everything back to them last night after the reading of the will. That must not happen again, Mr. Brentt."

"Why? What's it to you?"

You ask him that, Cadwally? You who separated us?

4

TOMÁS

I KNOW THE exact moment that changed Cadwally's perception of Tomás Tepaneca, for it changed mine too. I had just turned fifteen when Tomás kissed me in the shade of our old jacaranda tree, startling me with his ardor. Yet I was even more surprised by the panic that prompted my grandfather to write a "Save Isabel" letter to his estranged half-sister. As noted already, Great-aunt Delphine rose to the challenge, overseeing and financing my education in the United States and in Europe over the next five years. But why Cadwally's reaction?

He had taken special pride in his rejection of the privileged class to which he had been born. From the time I could walk (and he had been saddled with me) he had indoctrinated me to treat all people as equals. He was known locally for championing the rights of the Indians of Morelos. Yet, letting me be romantically courted by one was a far different matter. Free-spirited and penniless as he was, Cadwallader Brentt remained at heart a Boston Brahmin, deeply class conscious and convinced that I had to marry within our own social class. That excluded Tomás Tepaneca. Now as I observed the two adversaries, it struck me that despite my protests when Cadwally packed me off to the United States, I had felt secretly relieved.

"I've known Isabel since we were children," I heard Tomás explain now with quiet dignity. "I'm just looking out for her."

"Thank you, but I can take it from here."

"You don't seem to understand, Mr. Brentt. Isabel is in for the greatest battle of her life. The Nymans are ruthless people. You will need all the legal counsel you can get—"

"From a rookie lawyer?"

"I know enough. And I can help without charging her a cent."

"I didn't think Isabel needed charity. Didn't you just inform me that she is now the wealthiest woman in Morelos, or was that in all of Mexico?"

They were men sparring across the backs of two horses. Watching them, I sensed that much more than horses stood between them and they both knew it.

"Isabel is as cash poor as ever, Mr. Brentt. But once she takes possession of those properties, she'll be a very wealthy woman. Make no mistake about that. So I repeat, I can be of immense help to her."

"Very good of you, I'm sure. But I've never yet known a lawyer who didn't charge fees for his efforts."

Tomás squared his shoulders. "I'll never take a cent from Isabel. Never."

"And you'll help her become a wealthy divorcée, no doubt. How very good of you."

Why does Cadwally bait him so? I wondered. Tomás doesn't deserve that.

"Mr. Brentt, Isabel has been given an extraordinary opportunity, but not if the Nymans take the inheritance from her. You and Isabel must leave here today, this very morning, and go into hiding."

"That's out of the question."

"I can arrange it, only you need to act fast. Benjamín Nyman Vizcarra will soon be pounding on your door. He'll come to claim his wife and take her back with him, whether she wants to go or not."

"It's obvious that they've had nothing more than a marital quarrel, with many more to come. For better or for worse, she belongs by his side. She made her choice, Tomás."

"With all due respect, sir, this is no simple quarrel. When Isabel came to me for help, she was terrified. You must not talk her into going back to that man. Please come away with me now before Nyman gets here."

"I can handle Nyman." (Cadwally was pronouncing it correctly now, long "e" clipped but clear as his mood darkened.)

"He'll come armed."

"Then he'll find he's well-matched. But you'd better get the hell out of here, Tepaneca. If Nyman finds you, he'll feel obliged to shoot you between the eyes. So you get on one of these horses. Better yet, take them both before they muck up the place."

Tomás glanced at his pocket watch. He seemed about to argue, but Cadwally waved him away with a paint-stained hand.

"Go on, now. I won't send her back to the Nymans unless she wants to go. You have my word on that."

Tomás glanced at his watch again, then up at me, and I realized that he had been aware of me all along. Cadwally was only now noticing my presence. He turned back to Tomás.

"If you don't want to leave your mother to fend for herself, you'll get on a horse and stay alive," he urged more gently.

Still Tomás hesitated. The moment he made up his mind, though, his manner morphed. He became the old Tomás, taking charge of everything.

"Isa, I need for you to sell me these horses."

"They're not mine."

"Oh yes they are. Like it or not, it's all yours, and don't you forget it. Now, since I don't care to be arrested as a horse thief, I'll ask you again. Will you sell the horses?" He drew several coins out of his pocket and counted them out. "Since I want to eat this week, I can only offer the grand sum of one peso and twenty *centavos.* Consider the balance I owe you as compensation from your benefactor who had the bad grace to die before paying me for my legal services."

Tomás and the horses disappeared into the hills. I hoped Cadwally would disappear into his studio. He didn't.

"We need to talk, Isabel."

Reluctantly, I slumped into the Adirondack chair that Cadwally had made years ago. It was yellow-green and wobbled side to side like a parrot on its perch. This one chair in the patio constituted our parlor, the kitchen table our dining room. My grandfather reached for a wooden chair. It was painted bright plum and was as solid as his purpose.

"Why are you here, Isabel?"

"I'm leaving Benjamín."

"And why is that?" he asked in the faintly bemused tone that he used so often with me.

"Because he's arrogant and domineering."

"And you've only now discovered that?" I knew my grandfather was smirking under that bristly white moustache of his.

"I refuse to submit to a domineering husband."

"Then why did you marry a Nyman? They're all that way, except perhaps for the priest (meaning Benjamín's twin). Maybe you should have set your cap for Father Samuel. Same good looks but a decidedly blander personality." Before I could think of a retort, Cadwally was shaking his head, "No. I suppose the Church would have objected. So Benjamín Nyman with all his imperfections will have to do. You'll have to love him 'til death do you part, or until you have your next tiff, whichever comes first."

"This is not a joke! And it's not our first fight."

"It won't be your last either." He dropped the banter, his manner suddenly earnest, his eyes glimmering as blue as Arctic water, his bristly brows grayish-white clouds. "Marriage is always fraught with conflict, Isabel. But don't you see? It gives you the choice, to take up arms against each other or to hold each other."

"I don't care. I'm not going back."

"What's this about, Isabel?"

The sound of knocking on the front door made us both start. They were short, civil raps, not a wild pounding, but it set my heart pumping faster.

"That'll be him." Cadwally set the gun down on the table as if suddenly conscious of it at a tea party. "If you want to talk to him alone—"

"No. Not now or ever!"

"Are you certain about this? Shouldn't you at least hear him out? Whatever his faults, Benjamín Nyman *is* a gentleman."

More knocking. I jumped to my feet. Cadwally tried one more time.

"Isabel, we men are awkward creatures. We say the wrong thing. Do the wrong thing. Whatever he has done to upset you—"

"There's a darkness to him—a side I didn't know and don't want to know. He was so brutal last night. Please help me, Cadwally!"

BENJAMÍN

"W<small>AIT UPSTAIRS</small>," <small>MY</small> grandfather spoke calmly.

I hurried up the cement steps but stopped outside my room. I could hear Cadwally opening the one window that fronted the street. Fortunately, it wore heavy iron bars. Benjamín's voice drifted up indistinctly, a polite murmur, an unseen but known ocean splashing the shore. Cadwally's voice reached me more clearly.

"Isabel doesn't want to see you."

Whatever Benjamín replied, his voice was muffled by the wooden shutters that my grandfather slammed in his face. My heart thundered in my ears almost as loudly as the second round of knocking, more insistent this time. I threw myself onto my bed and covered my head with a pillow. When the pounding on the front door finally stopped, I knew that I still had to be on the alert; Benjamín would not give up so easily. My eyelids pressed down heavily. *Stay awake!* I commanded, but in the end the sleepless night and my soft quilt conspired to lull me to sleep.

I awoke with a start. *What time is it?* The long shadows on the wall—a wall that Cadwally had painted years back in bright fuchsia—answered that it was now late afternoon. Somehow, I had managed to sleep several hours, even with my angry husband prowling outside. I hurried downstairs. Cadwally sat at the table prepping his muzzle loader, a relic from his army days. I slumped into the "parlor" chair.

"Do you suppose he'll come back today?"

"Will the neighborhood roosters crow?"

Cadwally shoved the ramrod down the barrel to confirm it wasn't loaded. To test that the ignition hole was clear, and perhaps to send a message to Benjamín should he still be lurking, he put a small charge of gunpowder down the barrel but no miniball. Next came a percussion cap on the nipple. Then Cadwally pointed the gun in the air and pulled the trigger. I flinched. Flames and blue-white smoke blew out of the barrel.

"'Still works," he mumbled to himself. He repeated the process, this time adding a paper cartridge, driving it down the barrel with a ramrod. I knew just enough to recognize that the gun was fully loaded but at half cock until needed.

Rain was beginning to stain the flagstones and some of the furniture. One of my grandfather's eccentricities had been to remove all the downstairs walls that fronted the courtyard. Since half of the dining table and chairs protruded into the patio, they were about to get soaked. Unconcerned, Cadwally simply moved his chair a few feet so it was under cover. I did likewise. He watched the rain. I reflected on another of his eccentricities, which was to use the remaining walls of our home as canvases. Life-size, stylized Indian warriors, maidens, and animals from the Mexican forests watched us in the gathering gloom. Growing up in that house, I had assumed that everyone used the walls of their home this way. Now it struck me more than ever how sharp the contrast, how deep the divide, between my husband's ancestral home with its muted tones and exquisite antiques, and this small house with its garish murals and peasant furnishings.

Why does it seem more crass than charming? The thought slithered. I wondered uneasily if my brief marriage would tarnish everything from now on, including my home.

Is Ben gone? I was about to ask. Lightning streaked across the sky just then, followed by what Mexicans called a "chubasco," a downpour that was both intense and brief. Again, I drew my chair deeper into the kitchen. The wind rattled the clay pots that hung above the stove. I thought about making some tea and remembered that Cadwally only drank coffee and tequila, or cheap aguardiente when particularly low on cash.

"Do you think he's out there?" I had to speak above the storm.

My grandfather walked over to the front door and peered through a long, thin gash in the wood. I joined him.

"Well?"

"See for yourself."

Pressing my face to the crack, I could just make out a tall figure on the opposite side of the street. Even with his hat low over his face, I knew it was Benjamín. With shoulders hunched forward and the narrowest of rooftops to protect him, he was getting soaked. How typical of him that he didn't seem to mind, that his purpose far outweighed all other considerations, especially comfort.

I returned to the old Adirondack chair. Rosa Tepaneca, Tomás's mother, had made the seat cushion for it. Wrapping myself in the small, familiar blanket that always hung over the backrest, I waited out the storm. A darker one brewed within me. *Enough! I'm home now and don't have to think about last night!* But of course, that was as impossible as stopping the rain from drenching the town. Water cascaded in silver sheets. Stairs and *jacaranda* tree blurred into a gray sea, and I at the bottom of it, smothered, drowning in sorrow and resentment thick as kelp.

Then, like all good Mexican *chubascos,* the storm ended as abruptly as it had started. The sun poured itself into the newly-formed puddles in the courtyard, polishing everything within its reach. I left the comfort of my chair and ventured back to the front door. Pressing my face to the crack, I saw Benjamín. He cut a desolate figure, soaked as he was. But when he drew himself straight and started forward with his horse in tow, I drew back— not just because he was approaching the door again, but because I recognized anger in his stride. Seconds later, Benjamín hoisted himself onto the saddle and stood on it, his boots engulfing my thin line of vision.

"He's climbing over the wall!" I cried out. "He's on the roof!"

Cadwally had heard it too and motioned me away. I had just enough time to run back to my room before Benjamín jumped from the roof into the courtyard.

"Isa!" His voice was like the sharp report of a gun.

I slammed both halves of the Dutch door shut, but the upper door perversely bounced open again. Pressing my back to the wall, I heard Cadwally intercept him at the bottom of the stairs. Much as I did not want to face Benjamín, I was ready to step forward at the first sign of violence.

"The gun's primed and still fires," Cadwally observed in a calm voice, as if commenting on the price of beans. "Since my granddaughter does not want to speak with you, I suggest you leave now."

"Not without my wife."

I could picture Benjamín dripping wet, his light brown hair darkened, his chest thrust forward. No. It was worse than a display of arrogance. I could plainly hear the rage in his voice and knew that it was contorting his handsome features.

"Isa!" Benjamín yelled up the stairs. "I'm not leaving without you. Get it straight. I will not allow you or that lawyer of yours to besmirch my honor! Do you hear me? You're coming home now!"

"She *is* home," Cadwally said quietly. Benjamín ignored the observation.

"Isa! How dare you treat me—and my family—in so despicable a way? What did I do to deserve this? Is it because I got drunk last night?"

Drunk and abusive. I could still feel the weight of his body when he woke me, pinning my arms over my head, interrogating me, his questions an assault. *How did you meet my father? I* told you. Years ago, he used to come to Cadwally's studio to buy paintings. *Did he pay special attention to you? Give your grandfather extra money?* More verbal blows to deflect: I don't know. I was a child! I tried to push him off. *But later, when you were anything but a child. He was a notorious womanizer. Maybe he continued to be just as lecherous in his damn monkish years and we just didn't know it. So tell me, did he pay attention to you? Like this?* Benjamín's touch had hovered dangerously between a lover's and a rapist's.

"All right. I probably *was* out of line last night. *Mia culpa!*" Ben quipped now in Cadwally's courtyard. "Kindly bear in mind that I only get drunk when I'm disinherited. I beg m'lady to forget my uncouthness."

Forget your nasty insinuations? I fired another volley of silence. He tried again. "Look, I don't know what I said that upset you. A man who is drunk will say some pretty stupid things. You should know that all too well. No, that's not what I mean."

Don't you dare drag my grandfather into this! I wanted to yell at him. No need. He knew he had taken another wrong turn and grew quiet. I could picture him pushing back the brim of his hat, the way he did when stumped. I waited. What I wanted was an utterly abject apology. Instead he took yet another wrong turn.

"Damn it, Isabel! Talk to me! I know you can hear me."

I heard him all right, but I wasn't about to relinquish the only weapon at my disposal. So I continued to wield silence, clinging to all the details that came flooding back: the smell of his father's room, musty from years of disuse; the green damask draperies and mahogany furnishings; the portrait that Ben dragged me to see though it was the middle of the night. And later his question, his deplorable question.

It had stunned me. Did he know me so little? Trust me so little? Respect me so little? Standing now in the security of my own home, I felt anger gush, dark and ferocious as a new oil strike. So I remained barricaded. Aloof.

"You're coming back with me now, Isabel. I'm warning you—"

"And I'm warning you, Nyman." Cadwally's voice suddenly turned sharp as broken glass. "Get out of my house."

"Forgive me, sir. I'm going up there," Benjamín answered softly with the impeccable courtesy of his countrymen. "Please don't try to stop me."

"I won't kill you, Nyman. But take one more step and it will be the last time you walk on two legs."

Don't! I wanted to shout at them. *We must talk and clear things up.* Yet at that very moment a second emotion surfaced from the depths of my spirit, dark and deeply satisfying: the intense pleasure of revenge. A simple thought came to me. A dictum: *Let him squirm.*

Benjamín left. Shortly afterwards I found Cadwally in his studio. He was splashing splotches of red paint onto a canvas.

"Well, that showed him," I smiled.

Cadwally's face seemed almost as red as the pigment in his brush. Now that the confrontation had ended, a change had come over him.

"The damn war started over words and misunderstandings." Long experience had taught me that when my grandfather spoke of war, he meant the American Civil War, the war of all wars in his life. "They turned us into murderers and mutilators. Words, damn words!"

"He started it with his innuendos."

"Have you left your husband over a petty fight?"

"There was nothing petty about it."

"What the blazes is this about, Isabel?"

"I can't speak about it. What he said was so appalling."

"Isabel, I'll defend your right to leave your husband if you choose to. But you should have talked with the man."

"Why? Do you think words are any better at securing marital peace? Now at least he knows he can't treat me any way he sees fit."

"Like you treat Tomás?" Another splotch exploded on the canvas.

"Tomás was happy to help me."

"Tell that to Rosa when Benjamín Nyman kills her son for the sake of his sacred honor."

I hadn't thought of that.

6

ROSA

THAT NIGHT I was awakened by a boisterous mob and the frenzied screams of their victims. Instinctively, I reached for Benjamín and tumbled instead from the bed. I huddled on the floor,
still in the grip of my recurrent nightmare. Then I heard a whistle, a beacon guiding me out of a hellish reality. *It's all right,* it
told me. *You're home.* Still shaken, I reached for the light on my
nightstand. The garish walls of my old bedroom rushed forward
to reassure me that I was indeed far from Torreón and the massacre I had witnessed.

The nightwatchman blew his whistle again as he made his
rounds on a bicycle. Soft and intermittent, it was a bird-like trill
meant to reassure sleepers. *ALL IS WELL.* I'd heard it all my life.
The whistle diminished as he pedaled away. *All is well.* But how
could it be in a world where nothing was what it seemed? Where
good and evil, right and wrong, love and hatred blurred into each
other? Benjamín and I had joined the revolution against a dictator because we were idealists, only to discover that revolutionary
troops could commit outrages that now haunted my nights. Did
that evil negate the good of our cause? For that matter, did Ben's

drunken episode erase all that was noble in him? What if Cadwally was right? Maybe we could have cleared everything up. Yet certainly his family would have hindered us. I could just imagine what his mother and his siblings were saying—that I had run off with my partner in crime. Did he really think that too?

A more immediate doubt ambushed me: had I endangered Tomás? If so, I had to warn Rosa. It didn't matter that it was the middle of the night. I knew from long experience that Tomás's mother would open her arms to me, her heart more capacious than the whole Valley of Morelos. Yet I couldn't risk running into Ben who might still be out there. I'd have to use the tree that grew along the back wall. Cadwally loved it for its lavish blooms, Tomás and I because it was our "Escape Tree."

"Why use a door when you can climb a tree?" Ten-year-old Tomás had put it plainly enough. Besides providing an exit via the back wall, it was also a shortcut to the shack he shared with his mother.

So there I stood at the base of the magnificent Escape Tree, wondering if at age twenty-one I could still climb it without breaking my neck. It looked formidable—and quite beautiful. Normally it bloomed lavender-blue. Tonight the moon's paintbrush knew only silver. I reached up and grasped the lowest branch. My feet missed the crucial notch. On the third attempt, my limbs remembered the old pattern and I was scampering up the generous arms, climbing higher and higher until I straddled the back wall. Moments later, my feet found the toeholds Tomás had fashioned on the other side of the wall. This had been our secret path to freedom that we had used as children and adolescents.

A narrow dirt road ran behind the houses, all windowless on that side. Across from their stark walls, poverty was even more pronounced but with a distinctly rural character. Instead of more townhouses with chipped plaster, there was a large field on the other side of the dirt path, and further up a one-room shack with a thatched roof. Rosa Tepaneca's hut hunkered down just beyond a big puddle. A solitary duck floated in this temporary pond, its head comfortably pillowed along its back. I began rehearsing my apology.

The front of the shack was bordered by a fence made entirely of branches strapped together vertically. Their purpose was to keep Rosa's hens from straying. Lifting the wire loop that served as a latch on the makeshift gate, I let myself into the small yard. Geraniums scented the night. I knocked on the rough planks that served as the front door. Suddenly, I wanted to run back to the jacaranda tree, but I could sense Rosa eyeing me through the crack in the door.

Sometimes words seem like water pouring down a drain spout. They rush headlong, unoriginal and mindlessly determined. So too was my apology. "Rosa, I'm sorry to wake you." I did anyway. "I have to warn you and tell you how very sorry—"

"*Mi niña!*" No one else in the whole world called me 'my child.' "Is it really you?"

The night could not hide the joy that blazed from Rosa's Tepaneca's face. Her outstretched arms drew me into a tight embrace, the top of her head barely touching my shoulder. Slightly plump, she seemed all softness. An illusion. A tree's blossoms may be tender and fragile, but not so the tree. Bending to press my cheek to hers, I took in the wonderful scent of her. I'd known it all my life and can only describe it as a blend of earth after rain and the fragrance of vanilla.

"Come inside, Isabelita."

As soon as Rosa shut the door on the moon, we were plunged in darkness. She lit a lantern and placed it on the table that doubled as a dining room and kitchen in her tiny dwelling.

"I hear you're a very wealthy woman now. Yet you didn't marry don Rodolfo *Née-man* after all." She pronounced the Nyman surname correctly, emphasizing the first syllable.

"No." I looked down as if to examine the dirt floor that was always swept clean. "Things don't always turn out as we expect."

"True, *niña*. Your grandfather mentioned months ago that you had eloped with a younger brother, a captain in the army, but he didn't tell me anything about him. And now you've run away from him too." She reached for my hand. "What happened, Isabelita? Only first give me another hug. I need to make sure I'm not down there on my *petate* dreaming!"

That second hug undid me. "Oh, Rosa! Rosa! I'm so unhappy!" I sobbed.

"*Ay, mi niña!*" She drew me to the bed so we could sit side by side while she rocked me. "There, there. No man is worth a single tear of yours."

In a flash of memory I was once again a three-year-old child, lost and hungry, who happened to wander into the circle of her arms. Now I desperately needed to be rocked and comforted by the only mother I had ever known, this wonderful woman who taught me how to cook and braid my hair, and that monthly blood is not the blood of death but of life. That night I was a dam bursting, my words an incoherent torrent. Later, when my shoulders stopped heaving, I was able to tell Rosa how I'd thought Benjamín the most wonderful man in all of Mexico, and how his domineering mother had locked him up in one of the rooms of the hacienda when she found out that he wanted to join the Revolution, and then how we had eloped, and now I was sorry because he was not what I thought.

"At first he seemed so loyal. When his father disinherited him for marrying me, Benjamín didn't seem to care. But when the general died and left everything to me, he became insanely jealous and suspicious. Oh, Rosa! He was so horrid last night! He came to bed drunk and so angry. I'd never seen him like that. He yanked me out of bed to see a stupid portrait of his father, pulling and hurrying me along as if the place were on fire."

Rosa listened, as patient as a bird waiting out a summer storm.

"I'll never forgive him, Rosa! Never! I can accept that General Nyman's widow and the rest of them think I robbed them of their inheritance. After all, they hardly know me. But Benjamín—how *dare* he assume such terrible things about me?" Anger dried my tears. "Last night he forced me out of bed to see a portrait of his father. And he kept saying, 'Look at his damn eyes!' which made no sense whatsoever."

"Perhaps because the general's eyes were a blue that startles, like yours," Rosa murmured.

"Blue eyes happen to be extremely common in Scandinavia where the general was born, and they are just as common in the United States where my parents came from."

"I don't know those towns, but I do know that eyes like yours are not common around here, Isabel."

What was that supposed to mean? Yet didn't this echo in part Benjamín, who only the night before had pushed open the chapel door with a single kick of his boot, and had asked me there under the soft stare of the Virgin of Guadalupe his deplorable question?

Were you my father's illegitimate daughter or his mistress?

I cried a *chubasco*. Then I fell asleep on Rosa's brass bed.

PRIEST OR SOLDIER?

WHEN I AWOKE, I could not remember where I was, that is until I smelled *chiles* and tomatoes frying in a pan. Rosa was up, busy in her tiny kitchen. These were the aromas and sounds of my childhood and adolescence—Rosa cracking eggs against the rim of the pan, eggs and oil sizzling at their meeting; her rhythmic alternation between stirring with her wooden spoon and rapping it sharply; the cheerful clucking of hens in the yard; the lusty crowing of her one rooster and the choral response of a dozen others throughout the neighborhood. The front door now stood wide open, inviting sunlight to join us. The growing scent of coffee and cinnamon sticks reminded me that in all the world there was no house I loved more than Rosa's hut.

Rolling onto my side, I tucked my arms under the pillow and gave myself the pleasure of watching her. I had thought her beautiful when I was a child. I still did, though hers was not the classic beauty I had been shown in European art galleries and museums. Rosa's features had a boldness to them, as if sketched in charcoal with a firm hand, the lips and nose unapologetically dominant. She reminded me of the stylized Tlahuica warriors and maidens that Cadwally painted in his murals. Her age was anyone's guess since she herself did not know it. Her skin was coffee with milk and as smooth as a young woman's. Her long braids, on the other hand, were shot through with more gray strands than I remembered.

What else had changed during my ten-month absence, aside from the deposing of our dictator, my elopement and my failed marriage? The intrusion of the monstrous brass bed on which I lay. What had possessed Rosa to let it in? The beast ate up half the living space of her perfect little house. Fortunately, everything else seemed the same: the table with its three brightly painted chairs; the dented aluminum pot with beans soaking overnight; the narrow ledge that held the small *brasero* on which Rosa cooked. An assortment of clay dishes that I had known from earliest childhood stood in neat ranks. Utensils and clothes hung from pegs, herbs from the rafters. And the old print of the Virgin of Guadalupe still stood guard, watching over us.

In short, everything in the tiny home spoke of a delight in continuity and order, unlike my grandfather's house where artistic chaos reigned. I would have to learn to forgive the brass bed. Alongside it on the floor lay the traditional *petate*, the straw mat on which Rosa had always slept. Following my gaze she sighed.

"Tomás bought the bed for me when he started to practice law. He's so proud of it. The truth is, the floor is so much more comfortable, but I don't have the heart to tell him. Every time he comes home he ends up on the floor with a backache, and I on the bed with an even worse one!" she laughed.

"Isn't it time to speak plainly and give each other a good rest?"

She gazed steadily at me. "A man has his pride. A woman should recognize that."

"What about a woman's pride?"

She gave me a lopsided smile and turned her attention back to the coffee she was preparing, her magnificent *café de olla*, brewing it in the clay pot that gave it its distinctive flavor.

"Come to the table, *niña*," she smiled. "I have so many questions! Back when you thought you would marry don Rodolfo, what happened that night that he took you to meet his family? And why did your little grandpa come home on crutches—days later—and without you? The only thing he told me was that he had fallen down the stairs and that you had eloped with a younger brother of don Rodolfo."

I sighed. Why hide the truth that Rosa already suspected. "Cadwally promised not to drink at the dinner party, but he did anyway. He managed to tumble down the full length of stone stairs." My cheeks flushed hot with shame—shame, that old companion of mine since childhood. "The Nymans sent for the hacienda doctor and he insisted that Cadwally not travel back to Cuernavaca. So the family had no choice but to put us up for several weeks while he mended."

Rosa gave my hand several energetic pats. "Never mind. At least your little grandpa is a *simpatico* drunk, not like others who pick fights and get meaner the more they drink. And what about that younger brother? Benjamín, is it?"

I nodded, looking down as if embarrassed.

"That makes you the señora Isabel Brentt de Nyman." She tasted the name. "Last night you told me everything that's wrong about your husband. Tell me what's right about him."

"Very little." I sipped the coffee gratefully. "Well, he *is* tall and very handsome," I conceded, taking another sip. "And he has beautiful eyes. Hazel eyes. Do you know, in a certain light they look green like our hills. And he's fun—when he isn't being stupidly arrogant. Actually, in a strange way, his arrogance suits him. He has such a proud bearing. And I have to admit that he *is* capable of a deep sensitivity. You know—deep feelings."

"Deep feelings—in a soldier?" Rosa tilted her head to one side.

"Oh, he's more than just a soldier. Benjamín has a poet's soul. He sees beauty all around him and finds the words to describe his deepest feelings." Was it the magic of Rosa's *café de olla*? How else was the villain morphing with every sip I took? "He's brave, Rosa, and isn't afraid to act on his ideals. And his eyes! You look into them and find such a rich array of emotions—including a wonderful sense of mischief—a look you would never see in his twin."

"He has a twin?"

"They're identical yet so different. Samuel is a priest and has a gentle disposition to go with his office. Benjamín—well, it's no wonder he's in the military. You know, the night that I went to meet Rodolfo's family, Father Samuel had sent regrets that he would not be able to join us. Then he showed up after all, or so we thought—only it was Benjamín impersonating him. He fooled everyone, even his own mother!" I laughed. "And it didn't end that evening. Benjamín stayed on a few more days, all the while impersonating his brother. Oh, he was all kindness, this charming, fake priest. He even tutored me secretly in Spanish so—"

"What's wrong with your Spanish?"

"Nothing." I reddened at my clumsiness.

"You may have been born a *gringuita*, but your Spanish is as Mexican as a serrano pepper. So why would the *padre* have to teach it to you?"

How could I tell her: *because I spoke like you and Tomás and the street urchins of my childhood, sing-songing my way, clipping words, and over-using the diminutive. No wonder Rodolfo always insisted that we speak to each other in English, for only then must I have sounded educated and perhaps his social equal. His hateful sister knew the truth and insisted at the dinner party that we switch to Spanish for her mother's sake. And I was too confident to notice Rodolfo's panic. Instead I plunged ahead, oh so happy to oblige, so sure of myself because I spoke the language like a native—just the wrong kind of native. So I shamed my fiancé before his family and their guest of honor, Governor Escandón. And I, fumbling through their silent, thick disapproval, became conscious of an enormous inadequacy in me—the terrible consequence of Cadwally's hands off approach to education. Until that night, that awful night, I had been blissfully ignorant of my ignorance of proper Spanish.*

All this flashed through my mind in seconds. Yet how could I tell Rosa?

I didn't have to. I could read in her face the sudden realization that I had been speaking the Spanish of the landed classes, not of the landless *peones,* and she was noticing it only now. I cringed at the momentary look of confusion in her eyes and rushed forward, deliberately sing-songing and clipping some of my words.

"'Seems I'm not snooty 'nough t'please the Nymans."

"Speak like your husband taught you." Rosa spoke sharply.

I felt snagged, caught between two worlds. As I tried to extricate myself, I was struck by the awful possibility that I might not be able to return to Rosa's world any more than to Benjamín's. "I don't want to be like them," I murmured by way of apology.

"You're not. You're better than all the Nymans put together. So is my Tomás. Those schools have changed the way the two of you talk, and there's nothing to be done about that. You can't put the chick back in its egg. Now let me hear the rest of your story the way don Benjamín taught you to speak."

"What—what do you want to know?"

"Tell me why the general, of all the fiends on this earth, was so generous to you."

8

SPOTTED BEANS

"I DON'T KNOW! I don't know!" I was wringing my hands. "I don't understand it either! I met the man only a few times, way back when I was a little girl and he came to Cadwally's studio. He was a tall blond man. Remember?"

"I remember," Rosa murmured, her eyes suddenly hard.

"And that was it. I never saw him again. Years later when Benjamín and I eloped, the old man disowned him. They all did, except for Samuel. Imagine our surprise when the family summoned us to attend the reading of the will."

"And your surprise when you saw our Tomás there, so lawyerly." Her eyes shone with maternal pride, but the hardness lingered a bit longer.

"Surprised? I was mortified. Please don't look at me that way, Rosa. I had to pretend I didn't know him. I couldn't have them think that we had plotted to cheat them out of their inheritance. Oh, when Tomás read the terms of the will, I wanted to die, it was so awful: the stunned silence, the family's pain, and their eyes narrowed with suspicion. I told them then and there that they could have the inheritance; that I didn't want it. That's when my mother-in-law looked at me as if noticing me for the very first time. She even embraced me."

"I'll bet she did."

"Doña Manuela decided that we should all go to San Serafín that very afternoon: the family, her attorney, and Tomás as well."

"Why not settle things there in the general's house?"

"I think she wanted to sort everything out in the security of her own home, far from the general's creepy old house. Do you know, his place didn't have one stick of furniture, except perhaps in his bedroom which I did not go up to see. Anyway, by evening we were having supper in the family hacienda. Then after Tomás left the table—"

"You mean, after the widow dismissed him like a servant or a dog. Tomás told me about that, how superior they all acted. He gave me no details, tearing out of here as if the *federales* were after him. But he did tell me about that."

I winced at the memory. "Doña Manuela *was* rude to him. So was my sister-in-law, Eva, and especially that awful husband of hers. Pancho Comardo may be from the Spanish nobility but there is nothing noble about him."

He's a pompous ass, Benjamín had put it succinctly more than once.

"How about your husband? How did he treat my son?"

"Politely, but he seemed uneasy around him."

"Hmm. I suppose he was still in shock, what with you inheriting everything. How about the twin brother, the *padrecito*—the little priest? How did he treat my son?"

"With kindness."

"Good." Rosa folded her hands on her lap and nodded. "Good."

"In fact, Father Samuel was the one who kept trying to maintain the peace when all the others argued about how the properties should be divided, especially the ones in Europe. When I couldn't take another minute of it, I went to bed. Benjamín joined me hours later, as drunk as Cadwally on one of his benders. Oh, Rosa! I didn't know there's such a mean side to him."

I was crying again in the soft circle of her arms. Rocking me, Rosa sang a lullaby in her native Nahuatl, her voice soft as a cooing dove. After a while she drew back, holding me at arm's length. "Dry your cheeks, *mi niña*—there. That's better. Now look me in the face. Believe me when I tell you that there is no such thing as a truly good man, drunk or sober. Except for the son of God, they're all flawed, like the green beans that I pick in my garden. Some are worm-eaten and good for nothing. Others are spotted but still firm and tasty. Now, if I threw away every bean that has a brown spot, I'd go hungry. So tell me truthfully: is this bean of yours rotten or just spotted?"

The memory of the Torreón massacre leaped at me just then, like a snarling dog.

"First I need to tell you something that I witnessed. It happened to Chinese people who were living in Torreón."

"Chinese? I never heard of that tribe."

Even as I stood on the brink of a dark chasm, Rosa's ignorance of the world beyond Cuernavaca filled me with tenderness. My impulse was to hug her and forget about reliving so wretched a day. But how else was I to exorcize the memory? Would it take one telling? A hundred? A thousand?

"It happened last May toward the end of the revolution, or maybe they had signed the treaty by then. I'm still not sure. Benjamín and I rode into the city of Torreón, up North, and stumbled into a riot. Benjamín rushed me into a nearby church and told me to stay there until he returned. I tried to do as he asked, but I was scared and ran after him. I managed to pull the door open and call out to him, but he didn't hear me. Oh, Rosa, it was like opening the door to hell itself."

"What did you see, *mi niña*?" she whispered, and I could sense that in her mind's eye she was standing alongside me at the church door, her face rigid.

"I saw—I saw townspeople and many of our own troops murdering unarmed civilians. They were killing Chinese men and women. Oh, Rosa! I saw one man dragged by his braid behind a horse. I can't forget his screams and the terror of the other victims."

"Oh, my poor Isabel! You should not see such things! Not you. Not my child. What did you do?"

"Nothing. I was too horrified to move. But you should have seen Benjamín."

When I returned home, I clung to the jacaranda's branch-arms, shutting my eyes tightly as if that could blot out images of the massacre, knowing even then that I would carry them the rest of my life like scars. Yet when I opened my eyes again and looked up into the panoply of Cadwally's *jacaranda*, silvered in the moonlight, I remembered the very reason that I had told Rosa about the killings.

Standing in the church doorway that day in Torreón, I had watched astonished as Benjamín rode into the maelstrom to stop the slaughter. What struck me then and all the more now was that he had wielded his anger, his ferocious anger, like a sword in the hand of a magnificent angel.

9

THE KISS

BENJAMÍN WAS A spotted bean. I knew that now, so I hurried to my room to write and tell him so—well, not quite in those words. My earlier, one-line letter was on the dressing table where I had left it. Crumpling it into a ball, I returned to the courtyard. Still in my nightgown, I climbed the *Escape Tree*, and there, under the dappled shade of its generous blossoms, I opened my heart to my husband, explaining little and forgiving all. Had I written it as a song, the refrain would have been, *this has all been a terrible misunderstanding. I love you,* my heart sang.

Later that morning I dressed in my mismatched suit and walked to the post office to mail my letter. I addressed it to *Capitán Benjamín Nyman Vizcarra/ La Hacienda San Serafín/ Morelos, México,* and kissed the envelope. Then I walked home and waited with a joyously painful kind of hope, then hopelessly as days blurred into each other without a response from him. I wrote several more letters. No response. Staring at the wreckage of my marriage, I concluded that my life had derailed like a train dynamited off its track.

"I'll never be happy again," I confided to Rosa whose solution was to keep feeding me, her philosophy of life leaning toward the gastronomic: "Always eat your sadness before it eats you."

One afternoon while she weeded her vegetable garden, I railed against poverty. "Cadwally gets few commissions these days. I'm sick to death of hiding money from him so we can eat."

"You know you can always help yourself to my garden."

"Thank you, dear Rosa! But we can't keep imposing on your generosity. I've got to get a job, you know, something a respectable woman can do. But there's nothing for me here in Cuernavaca."

"When are you going to claim your hacienda?"

"Claim it? How can I? It isn't mine."

"Tomás says it is, and he should know."

"I have no moral right to it."

Rosa pulled a flea beetle off a tomato plant, crushing it between her fingers. "And you think the Nyman Vizcarras have a moral right to lands they have stolen from others? It's yours now, your turn to benefit or abuse others with your wealth."

"I can't just show up at San Serafín and demand that the family hand it over to me."

"Why not?"

"I just can't, Rosa. It isn't right to throw people out of their homes."

"No, I suppose not." She wiped her sweaty brow, streaking it brown. Her gaze followed the jagged flight of a butterfly. "Tell me about the hacienda's gardens, *niña*."

"Then we might be here till supper time, there are so many to describe."

Her eyes widened. "Just how many gardens does it have?"

"I have no idea." I knelt beside her, and for a few moments felt a dreamy pleasure. "You know, my Aunt Delphine and I visited the gardens of kings and queens in Europe. Wonderful as they are, they just seem oversized and boring compared to the gardens of San Serafín. Each one is extraordinary, no two of them alike."

She wanted to know about specific flowers and vegetables—far more than I could name. So I cut to the chase. "Think of every color and every variety of flower, fruit, vegetable, bush, or tree, and it's all there in the most amazing combinations. Even the grass astonishes you! It's so thick and smooth and soft, that you just want to lie on it and nap. And just when you think there can be no more surprises, you come upon the biggest aviary you ever saw."

"Aviary?" Rosa wrinkled her brow.

"Bird cage, only this one stands as high as a church and is filled with birds from all over Mexico. My favorite of them all is a Resplendent Quetzal. It has an emerald-green tail that must be at least a meter long. Trust me when I tell you that it is truly the greatest of all trogons."

"Gluttons?" she arched her brows. "Do they eat that much?"

I laughed in delight and hugged her, this wonderful woman who was both child-like in her knowledge of the world yet eminently wise. "Not *tragón*, but *trogón*. It's the genus name—the family name of certain tropical birds."

Another time she asked me about Madero's revolution. "So you and your Captain and the other revolutionaries helped to boot out don Porfirio, all so your *señor* Madero could become the next president."

"Yes, but it's not quite that simple, Rosa. We fought for effective suffrage."

"Don't we suffer effectively enough?"

"I mean that we fought so we could finally have real elections. That meant ridding the country of a president who had cheated again and again across thirty years! This fall we are finally going to hold the first honest election that Mexico has ever seen, and Mr. Madero will become our president in a fully legal, honest way."

"If you know he's going to win, why do we need elections at all?"

It was no use talking to Rosa about politics. Yet didn't she have a point? When more days passed without a letter from Ben, I visited her less often, afraid that if I asked her one more time why Benjamín didn't come back for me, she might offer the most logical explanation: he's a rotten bean.

Then one afternoon Cadwally pressed a flat package into my hands. It was crudely wrapped in a rag bound with string.

"I need—I need for you to *reliver* this painting. *Iz* another damned Tepoz— Tepzo-quicko landscape for the tourists. Rosa King will pay you and you can—you can keep four or five *besos* for your trouble." He grinned at his own play on the words *besos*, kisses, and *pesos*. "And don't worry about running into that hus—husband of yours. I happen to know he's out of town."

I looked away.

"If you'd rather, I could reliver it m'self." He swayed on his crane legs.

No, I'd rather you stayed sober for a day, one day, Cadwally! I wanted to yell at him, but I was too disheartened to argue. Besides, I could no longer ignore the fact that our food supplies had dwindled to half a cup of beans and two *tortillas* stiff enough to use as weapons of defense. So I bathed and put on the beige skirt and the blue suit coat that I had worn during my flight from San Serafín. I could only hope that no one would notice the lack of a corset under my jacket. Gazing into the mirror, I carefully worked my hair into the soft Gibson up-do that I had come to accept as requisite before stepping out the front door.

"My hat!" I complained aloud.

It irked me that I had been forced to leave it behind in San Serafín, along with my precious few possessions. By now I had lost two trunks to San Serafín. How could I possibly venture out again without a hat? The thought nagged. On sudden inspiration, I reached for a blue ribbon that matched my jacket and made a wide headband as I'd seen elegant women do in Paris. With my hair loosely swept off my neck, the effect was rather chic. Hatless but otherwise respectable looking, I set off on foot to deliver the painting.

As I negotiated the potholes and cobblestone streets, a refrain sounded in my head. *There's no going back; there's no going back.* To childhood? To Ben? To optimism? The street undulated. My stomach growled its emptiness, and I tottered on the verge of another bout of crying. I walked faster. Within minutes I began to feel less hopeless, whether I wanted to or not. What is it about physical activity that staves off depression? Perhaps the simple act of walking all the way downtown forced my lungs to breathe in sunshine and crystalline sky, bougainvillea and hibiscus blossoms. And that may have been why I did not notice that I was being followed—a fact I did not learn until much later. The consequences would be far-reaching, like the aftershocks of a powerful earthquake.

On reaching the first of the two squares in town, I was startled by the realization that it was already Sunday. Have you noticed how grief swallows days whole? People were strolling. A band played selections from *Figaro.* Parents bought balloons for their children. Indians from local villages spread their wares on the sidewalks: wood carvings, pottery, bark paintings, embroidered blouses, and countless other handmade items. Caught up in that great gathering, I felt a stab of loneliness as I entered the Bella Vista, Cuernavaca's newest and best hotel.

The building was at least two hundred years old, maybe older. As a newly renovated hotel, it had been operating for only a year or so. The *portales,* an arcaded veranda that opened directly onto the street, were cordoned off and decked out with small tables, white linens, mission chairs, and Boston ferns. I cut across the *portales* to reach the hotel's central courtyard. Great swaths of bougainvillea and trumpet vines climbed from urns to the gallery upstairs, reminding me suddenly of the *palazzos* in Venice where Aunt Delphine and I had spent several weeks, back when I should have been in school finishing my senior year.

Ah, school. The very thought of it filled me with a cavernous yearning for the friends left behind; for chatter and laughter; for the preening in Glenn Hall before a dinner party or a ball; for short train rides into Philadelphia for an evening of theater, all magically paid for by some charming suitor, and all so marvelously new for a girl from a small Mexican town. Seeing the well-dressed patrons of the Bella Vista made me long for the touch of a silk ball gown and for gold-leafed evenings. *Where did it all go, that other life?* I wondered. In truth, I hadn't minded Cadwally's penury before going away to school, nor being poor with Benjamín when we eloped. Now I found myself wishing there had been no great-aunt to pay for my education in Bryn Athyn, no trip to Europe, no centennial ball in the National Palace of Mexico City, and no romantic elopement. What had that largesse done but bring my poverty and loneliness into sharper relief? What had my brief marriage to Benjamín Nyman Vizcarra accomplished but to break my heart and to marginalize me in my adopted country?

Ben, Ben. I could feel tears heavy with self-pity threaten to burst free again. Fortunately, I spotted the enterprising owner of the Bella Vista just then.

"Mrs. King?" I hoped I hadn't gasped the name.

"Yes?"

"You may not remember me." I cleared my throat. "I'm Isabel Brentt de Nyman. My grandfather asked me to deliver this painting to you."

Rosa King seemed to hesitate, and for one dreadful moment I had the impression that she was going to ask me to leave her establishment. *Loose women are not welcome,* I half expected to hear, for surely everyone in our small community of English speakers must have heard torrid tales by now about the general's will and that I was no longer living with my husband. Whatever Mrs. King thought, she offered me her hand.

"Miss Brentt—I mean, Mrs. Nyman, it would please me enormously if you would be my guest today for lunch."

"Thank you. You're very kind, but I must get back to my grandfather."

"No. I insist. Please stay," the good woman pressed on. "In honor of the painting that will now grace my office, and because I very much admire your grandfather's art, you really must let me give you lunch, Mrs. Nyman."

I had the distinct impression that she had lowered her voice when she spoke the Nyman name. I chose to take her caution as a gesture of goodwill. My stomach growled again, forcing me to nod.

"Splendid! Would you like to eat inside or in the *portales*?"

"Oh, outside, please. It's so lovely."

As the Bella Vista was particularly busy during the lunch hour, Mrs. King was not able to join me after all. It didn't matter. The scrumptious food was company enough, and there were plenty of people to watch discreetly from the comfort of the arcades. Across the street in the little park, people strolled or bought sherbet or balloons from street vendors. Some had their picture taken by a photographer who had set up his camera equipment directly across from me under the slender limbs of a young jacaranda tree. It was all quite festive and ultimately awful. Sadness soon took the seat opposite me. By the time the waiter offered tea and dessert, I longed for the solitude of my bedroom. I rose to leave.

"Isa!" a voice called out.

My heart leaped at the sound of my name, shortened and softened. EE-sah. Ben called me Isa. Turning around sharply, eyes bright with hope, heart ready to forgive everything, I searched for him. Tomás, who had bestowed the nickname long before Benjamín, was hurrying toward me. What could I do but swallow my disappointment with a shaky smile? I tried to think of something nice to say as he embraced me. *What an elegant man you've become, Tomás.* But I lost the thought when he pressed his lips to mine in a suffocating kiss.

10

TRIAL

I don't know what distressed me more: that Tomás had kissed me on the lips, or that he had kissed me in public. My cheeks burned. I had been fretting about not having a hat. Now I shot furtive glances at nearby tables. Had anyone seen us?

"What were you thinking, Tomás?" I managed in a low voice.

"That it's nice kissing a friend with a beautiful smile?" He laughed good-naturedly.

"You forget that I'm a married woman!"

"No. You're a woman who has had the wisdom to walk away from a bad marriage, which is not the same thing."

I drew back but he captured one of my hands. "I'm sorry, Isa. Please forgive me. I'm just so very happy to see you again. Please, let me treat you to lunch."

"I've eaten."

"Coffee and dessert, then. A client actually paid me, so I can afford this. Come Isa! You are sworn both as a Tlahuica and a Tepaneca warrior to stand by me." He referenced a pact we had made as children. "That means you must at least forgive me when I behave uncouthly."

I stared into Tomás Tepaneca's face with its bronzed skin and aquiline nose. Men who looked like him were squatting on the pavement just a few feet away, solicitously trying to sell their handmade wares. When had he left their world and crossed over into mine? For that matter, when had I made that crossing too? Didn't I used to sit as a child on those same sidewalks with Tomás, barefoot and disheveled? Who was this man who wore the trappings of success and whose Spanish had evolved as much as my own? All this flashed through my mind in seconds, including Rosa's proud boasts over the years: "*My Tomás is the best student in the class. I hear he finished preparatory school in half the time of his classmates; Tomás is studying in the university. You watch. He'll finish law school in half the time it takes others.*" And he did.

Tomás leaned toward me with a mock hangdog look. Glimpsing the mischievous boy who had been my closest companion, I smiled and squeezed his hand. Why did I not notice the photographer across the street? If only I could have heard the opening and closing of the shutter that was to change my life.

"All right. Just mind your manners." As we took our seats, I thought of Benjamín and his insane jealousy. "Is it safe for you, Tomás?" I whispered, leaning toward him.

"Perfectly," he whispered back. "Especially with you to protect me."

"Don't tease. If Benjamín were to find us together—" I started to rise.

"He won't." Tomás stopped whispering. "You can be sure he's at the trial."

"What trial?"

Despite my uneasiness, I glanced at an elegant woman sitting near us, and I confess that I had gone back to fretting about my lack of a hat. Was my blue ribbon enough?

"I forgot about your grandfather's phobia for newspapers. So you don't know."

"Know what?"

"That your brother-in-law—the priest—was put on trial for murdering his own father."

"What!" Several people turned to stare. I lowered my voice. "What are you talking about?"

"It's been the trial of the century," he answered easily. "People talk of nothing else."

"Samuel? You can't be serious?"

"Of course I'm serious."

"But everyone knows that the general died in the earthquake."

"Not according to the autopsy."

"What autopsy?"

"The one that your mother-in-law ordered; the one that got the old buzzard exhumed and onto the table of a team of forensic specialists."

"Doña Manuela ordered it? What for?" I gasped.

Tomás smiled the way I'd seen him do as a child moments before clobbering a bully.

"I think your mother-in-law was hoping to pin it on us."

"I don't understand."

"She's pretty sharp, I'll give her that much. The autopsy strongly suggests that your father-in-law had been dead several hours *before* the earthquake hit. But what she never could have imagined, and here's the delicious irony, is that the very last person to visit her husband late that night was none other than her son Samuel. According to the testimony of the three servants— the cook, her adolescent daughter, and the old porter—father and son quarreled violently. The good *padre* stormed out of his father's room, slamming the door as he muttered words of damnation."

"But Samuel is the salt of the earth. They've got the wrong man, Tomás!"

He studied me closely. "Well, there's little doubt that he'll be convicted. For one thing, the good priest refuses to defend himself. For another, all the evidence points to him. Don't look so downcast, Isa. The Nymans are a brood of vipers and now you know it. The general knew what he was doing when he appointed you as guardian of his properties."

I felt faint. "I need to go home."

Tomás hurried to my side, helping me to my feet. In place of the coffee and dessert he had intended to give me, he hired a cab. The photographer got that photo too.

"Why are you so upset?" Tomás asked as an old nag pulled our surrey along narrow side streets. "Don't let the fate of that patricidal priest trouble you. He's getting what he deserves. We have bigger concerns now. We need to act fast while the Nymans are distracted."

"Not now, Tomás."

"Now. We must act while the wind is in our favor. You need to take physical possession of your inheritance, beginning with the San Serafín hacienda."

The moment I was home I barricaded myself in my room.

Unable to reason me out of my room or away from a new bout of crying, Tomás headed home. Needing to get back to the city, he boarded the train early the next morning. I simply boarded the one to greater self-absorption.

A couple of weeks later I found Tomás leaning over Cadwally. As usual, my grandfather was slumped in the chair where he had slept all night. An empty bottle rolled across the floor when Tomás unwittingly kicked it.

"Wake up, Mr. Brentt. We need to talk."

I returned to my room to dress. When I stepped back into the upper veranda, they were hunched over in intense conversation. Since I had taken to walking barefoot again at home, I was able to descend the stairs noiselessly.

"She's so damn mopey! Don't tell her yet," Cadwally muttered.

"Don't tell me what?"

Both started. Cadwally pressed his lips into a thin line. Tomás shook his head. "Sooner or later, she's got to know the truth, sir."

THE DOUBLE

"You were right about your brother-in-law," Tomás smiled as if conceding a victory to me. "They had the wrong man all right." His very next words were like a knife thrust into my chest, every syllable enunciated clearly and calmly. "I'm sorry to have to tell you this, but Benjamín Nyman was tried for the murder of his father and has been found guilty."

"No. I don't believe it."

"They sentenced him yesterday."

"It's true, Isabel," Cadwally spoke up, his voice as wrinkled as his brow.

"He's to serve twenty-five years in the D.F.'s Penitentiary." Tomás was all neutrality and efficiency.

"Why are you doing this?"

"Don't blame the messenger of ill tidings, Isa. It's all here." He pointed to newspaper clippings that he had brought with him. They spread across the table like blood from a deep wound. "Benjamín Nyman confessed that he visited his father and quarreled with him on the night of the murder."

"No. Benjamín was with me that night."

"Not the whole night. All three of the general's servants testified that he arrived at the inopportune time of one in the morning."

I'll be back late, so don't wait up for me. My mind was racing. "Visiting his father—at whatever hour—does not make him guilty of murder."

"How about visiting his father while impersonating a priest, none other than his own brother?

"It's a harmless prank."

A young priest deep within a labyrinth flashed before my mind's eye: Benjamín masquerading as Samuel a year ago as a joke; Benjamín whose eyes would light up with tender yearning at the sight of me.

"Letting the servants believe that he was Father Samuel and then making sure that they heard him quarreling with his father is hardly a prank, Isa. It's a premeditated strategy."

"No. You don't know him as I do. If he really did pretend to be Samuel—"

"He's confessed to his duplicity."

"Then the masquerade was only so that he could gain access to his father. Yes, that would make sense," I reasoned with swift strokes against a strong current. "The general had disowned him. So it stands to reason that the servants must have had strict orders not to admit him. Benjamín had to resort to this ploy in order to see his father, don't you see?"

"And let the servants think that Samuel was the one arguing with the old codger—violently at that. Forgive me," Tomás crossed his arms, "but I don't see how incriminating an innocent man justifies him, any more than cracking the skull of an old man, however cantankerous—"

"You're wrong! Benjamín wouldn't do such a thing."

"He confessed to trying to silence the old man when he ranted against you."

"He did?"

Did my eyes light up?

"Before you credit Benjamín Nyman with chivalry, you should know that the general died from unchivalrous blows to the skull."

"Caused by the earthquake that dislodged a heavy crucifix."

"Maybe." Tomás tipped his head back as I'd seen him do a thousand times, always in mockery. "But since there were two distinct blows to the general's skull, tell me, how exactly did the dislodged crucifix manage to fall on the sleeping general twice?"

I escaped to my room to cry. *Oh, Ben, Ben! What have you done?* My emotions swirled in panicked flight. *This can't be happening. Oh, my darling, there must be some mistake.*

In my despair I couldn't turn to Rosa for comfort because Tomás was staying with her, Tomás whom I now resented with all my heart, not because he had brought ill tidings, but because he had enjoyed it. Early the next day I packed a small overnight bag. In the kitchen I emptied out the jar that held what was left from the sale of the painting. Eight coins clattered onto the table: six assorted silver pieces and two beautiful five peso gold coins. All told I had twelve pesos and fifty cents, the equivalent of six dollars and twenty-five cents. Would this be enough for a round trip train ticket to the capital, a hotel room, and one or two meals? It didn't matter, only that I get to Benjamín before anyone tried to stop me. I knew that the train to Mexico City ran only once a day. If I sneaked out and caught it, neither Tomás nor my grandfather would be able to follow me and interfere with my plan. A simple note on my dresser could explain that I would be back in twenty-four hours.

I walked to the train station in the outskirts of town. My Oxford bag was small but my arm ached by the time I got there. The round-trip fare cost $7.34 pesos, leaving me with a scant $5 pesos and change with which to pay for a hotel room, transportation to the penitentiary, and one or two meals. It wouldn't be enough. *Oh, why didn't I think to make sandwiches?* I moaned inwardly. *Because there was nothing with which to make them,* the answer came swiftly, followed by the accusation that I had robbed my own grandfather. *Seeing my husband in his hour of need is far more important,* I reassured myself. Besides, I knew that Rosa would look after Cadwally. She still worked for him once a week, even though he often fell behind with her wages. She would see how pitifully bare our larder was and would share something from her garden. *Maybe I shouldn't have taken the household money without discussing it with Cadwally, but he did say I could keep four or five pesos, right?* Guilt and self-justification continued to spar as I boarded. *He might have argued that he had bills to pay, so what choice did I have?*

You always have a choice, Aunt Delphine would have reminded me with a firm nod of her head.

As the train climbed into pine-scented mountains, leaving behind the white walls of Cuernavaca, I re-read the newspaper clippings that Tomás had brought the night before. Some were more than two weeks out of date. I arranged them in chronological order and read every one of them. They were appalling, especially the ones that played up a connection between the murder and Benjamín's disinheritance. The worst one characterized him as a weakling and me as a manipulative woman: "What can we conclude but that the lady in question is of a Macbethian cast, or that once again a man has fallen under the spell of a *belle dame sans merci*?"

The press was having a field day with the whole disaster. There was one article, however, that I kept coming back to: the one in the *Heraldo Mexicano* that described the final day of Samuel's trial. Despite its sensationalist tone, it made me feel a curious blend of sorrow and joy:

Father Samuel Nyman Vizcarra was found guilty of the premeditated murder of his father, General Lucio Nyman Berquist, and was sentenced to thirty years in the Federal Penitentiary of Mexico City. It is worth noting that the accused showed little emotion. His mother, on the other hand, cried out with all the pathos of Hecuba: "No! There's been some terrible mistake! You have the wrong man! My son is the kindest, the gentlest of men! This is all a mistake!"

The condemned man turned around, his eyes brimming with tears. He started toward her but was stopped by the guards. She too, poor woman, was held back by another son, the esteemed Rodolfo Nyman, who was trying to comfort her. Just when the drama had reached its feverish pitch, its tragic dénouement, a tall young man flung open the doors and approached the Bench, buttoning his cassock as he walked. There was an audible gasp. Before us stood a perfect duplicate of the accused! Two identical priests. The intruder spoke in a clear voice edged with bravado and a hint of pride.

"Your Honor, I am Captain Benjamín Nyman Vizcarra, at your service."

I now loved my husband more intensely than ever, not only because I believed his account—that the death had been accidental—but because he had owned up to his guilt and duplicity with such bold honesty. As the train worked its way high above the Valley of Morelos, a band of clouds shrouded the landscape in a thick mist, but not my resolution.

I don't care what they say. I believe you, Ben. You never meant for your father to strike his head against the wall. You only meant to silence him when he began his rant against me. That's what you said at the trial. So you did this for me. For me. I let the thought caress me, ignoring for now the obvious question: if the general disliked me enough to rant against me, why did he leave his wealth to me alone?

12

PENITENTIARY

FOUR HOURS AFTER leaving Cuernavaca the train pulled into the Buenavista train station in Mexico City. Stepping onto the platform, I suddenly regretted my impulsiveness. Everyone around me moved with purpose while I stood like a statue *sans* pedestal. I had absolutely no idea what to do next.

"May I help you, Miss?" a porter smiled.

"Could you please tell me how I can get to—that is, how does one get to—"

"Yes, miss?

"The Penitentiary?"

My cheeks heated up. He studied me ever so briefly, ever so long. "I suggest you catch a tram from here to the Plaza Mayor. From there you can take a second tram. Just ask for the *Peñón de los Baños*. Or you could take a cab."

Having only $5.16 pesos to my name, I opted for a trolley. Fifteen minutes later and six precious *centavos* lighter, I found myself in what is now called the Zócalo, the very heart of Mexico City. This was Tenochtitlán of the Aztecs, Méjico of the Viceroys, and Mexico City of the twentieth century, all converging with the clamor of a collective energy. The massive square teamed with the rattle of electric trams, horse-drawn vehicles, and a few automobiles. As in Cuernavaca, the humble and the elite came together in the plaza. Here in the city it was just on a grander scale. Yes, one still saw lots of men in native white garb and oversized *sombreros,* and Indian women draped in the humble *rebozo*—the thin shawl that often doubled as a carrier for groceries or small children. But here in the city there were far more men in business suits and women sporting the latest fashions from Paris and London. I paused to take it all in, perhaps even to imagine myself in Europe again. Hawkers dispelled the fantasy. Pitching their wares in a high falsetto, they were as distinctly Mexican as tequila. Women's voices added to the cacophony, some urging people to buy lottery tickets, others to purchase certain pleasures without the gamble.

All at once I felt as if I had just plunged into a river whose current was faster and more dangerous than I remembered. I managed to cross over to the park in the center—a park that no longer exists. From there I tried to get my bearings. Large stone buildings from the era of the Spanish empire fronted the square on all four sides. I easily recognized the cathedral with its massive twin towers. *It's on the north end of the plaza. Think of it as the north star,* Benjamín had told me the first time he brought me here. It all came back. Behind me stood the Municipal Palace and Supreme Court; to my left, the *Portales* that sheltered people from the sun, drawing them into shops and cafés, or to the Monte de Piedad pawn shop that robbed the desperate of treasured possessions. The large building along the eastern perimeter was the National Palace. A mere two months before the outbreak of the revolution, I had attended the Grand Centennial Ball there with Rodolfo.

Under better circumstances, I could have revisited that festive evening in flashes of memory, reliving the wonder of seeing the somber Spanish palace transformed by thousands of lights. I might have smiled with satisfaction that I, a penniless girl from Cuernavaca, had held my own in that fashionable assemblage in a gown that was hardly new—my Aunt Delphine's blue silk dress that had been made over for me and had served me so well in Europe. Or I might have reflected that it was there in the court-yard ballroom, under the strange and luminous glow of Halley's comet, that Rodolfo Nyman, one of the country's most desirable bachelors, had proposed to me.

Enough! None of that matters now. Just get to the prison. It's East, somewhere behind and beyond the National Palace.

Another six *centavos* carried me by trolley to the country's largest and newest penitentiary, a parting gift from the deposed Díaz regime. The building sprawled on both sides of the entrance in boring symmetry. A campaign poster caught my eye just then. The bearded Madero stood against a backdrop of the national red, white, and green, his expression benign and intelligent. With revolutionary zeal he had promised us a new, bolder political architecture. Its cornerstone would be true suffrage that would welcome opposition parties in the upcoming fall elections. Democracy at last. Yet reforming the country's political system no longer seemed important to me. What did it matter who gov-erned Mexico or how? My only concern was simply what to say to Benjamín.

Should I begin with our quarrel? I forgive you everything, even that you entertained the notion that I might have been your father's—No. How could I forgive so preposterous a suspicion? Should I begin with the will? Darling, I don't know why your father arranged matters as he did, but it's not important. I'm giving everything back to your family. You're the only thing that matters to me. Or was it crass to bring that up first, as if his present cir-cumstances did not matter so much more? Darling, whatever they say, I believe you. We'll see this through together. My altruism was almost derailed when I remembered yet again his terrible ques-tion: Were you my father's illegitimate daughter or his mistress?

The words still stung because by assuming that there could be no other explanation for his father's bizarre behavior, Benjamín had impugned my very character. This time, however, I also remembered the agony etched on his features and the vow that he had made just seconds before asking his question: Whatever the answer, I swear to love you. To which I now responded inwardly with all the passion of my soul, I'm your wife, not just in this life but in the next one if you and I both will it. So I'll wait for you, Ben, however long.

A pock-faced guard admitted me into the cell with a loud clanking of the metal door. Benjamín jumped to his feet, his eyes wide with surprise. He looked terrible, as if he hadn't slept in days—terrible and wonderful. I took in every detail—that he was wearing dark pants and a white shirt open at the neck, the sleeves rolled up, the hair on his forearms pale in the light; that his hair was disheveled, falling across his forehead, so that I wanted to push it back for him if only to bury my fingers in its silk again; and that he had eyes for me alone, so that for a few seconds the world held only the two of us.

"You have a visitor." The guard gave me a lascivious smile. "As for you," he turned back to Ben, "Get it straight. I'm going to leave the door unlocked, but you can't go down into the courtyard until we ring the morning bell. Got it?"

Benjamín nodded without taking his eyes off me. The moment we were alone, I rushed forward. With the suddenness of a dream that turns nightmarish, Benjamín leaped at me. As he shoved me against a wall, I felt the back of my head strike the hard surface.

13

THREAT

BENJAMÍN'S HANDS WERE rope around my throat. "Was it your idea or his?" He kissed me roughly. Hungrily. With rage. "Is this how he kisses you?" He tightened his grip, strangling my words so that they were nothing but tight gasps. "No, I won't kill you now." His lips brushed my cheek. "But I want you to know that when I get out of here, I'm going to hunt you down, the two of you. No one tramples my honor; do you hear me? No one."

My eyes watered. I made another desperate, tortured sound, but the stranglehold allowed only his words, not mine.

"Spare me the tears. I *killed* my father over you! I sure as hell will have no compunction against killing you and that *indio* you traded me for! Tell that two-bit lawyer of yours to enjoy you and my inheritance while he can. But tell him for me that wherever you go, however much you try to hide, I'll find you, and I will kill you both. Now get out."

Benjamín pushed me out of the cell and slammed the door shut. Alone in the corridor, I staggered to a railing that over-looked a courtyard. Though gasping for air, I refused to believe what had just happened. Why do we cling so stubbornly to what *should* be rather than what is? Still clutching my bag in one hand and my throat with the other, I fled down the corridor, overtaking the official who had just escorted me to the cell. He grasped my arm, "Señora! What's wrong?"

Were my eyes large and vacant with shock? Did I answer him? I don't know. My one thought was to get out of there. I remember running through a series of courtyards until I reached the entrance. No one stopped me. Outside, a line of visitors was forming along the sidewalk. I didn't care about their curious stares. I just kept reliving the moment when Benjamín's touch turned murderous. Tears spilled down my face, tears that I swiped at impatiently with the back of my hand.

Walking briskly, I dodged horse-drawn vehicles and the occasional automobile. The city undulated. *He hates me. Ben actually hates me.* It didn't matter where I went, or how long I walked, or that my Oxford bag felt weighted down by bricks. I could not escape the horrific threat that now stalked me.

Wherever you go, however much you try to hide, I'll find you, and I will kill you.

My God! I halted abruptly. Benjamín *is* a murderer! The certainty stunned me into stillness. Pedestrians worked around me like creek water swirling past a rock in its way, nothing slowing its pace or deterring it from its purpose. Thousands of people surrounded me. Yet in that moment I never felt more alone. It struck me with brutal force that in that great city there was not one single person to whom I could turn for comfort. The creek rushed on, deepening into a river that swept me along, a leaf unable to withstand the forces of a hostile world.

I walked on in a daze, deeper into streets that I did not know. Destination no longer mattered, only that I keep moving, moving until the ache inside stopped. It didn't. By mid-afternoon, as I stumbled across an unfamiliar park, I finally acknowledged that

I was lost. Leg and arm muscles began to rebel. Spotting a park bench, I dropped into it even though it was also occupied by two boys in ragged clothes. They looked surprised.

What are you staring at? I wanted to snap. *Am I breaking some law by sitting next to you?* It occurred to me that my sister-in-law would never stoop to sit with mere commoners—*pelados* as she would have called them. The hell with her, I shrugged. Yet for all my bravura, I became uncomfortably aware that the boys smelled and that they were gawking at me. Closing my eyes, I tried to steady my breathing. When I opened my eyes moments later, the street urchins were no longer on the bench. A cabbie pulled up along the curb.

"Can I take you somewhere, señorita?"

I looked up into the face of an old Indian who doffed his hat. He was driving one of the ubiquitous *peseros* drawn by a horse that looked as bony as its owner. I don't think I answered right away. I was adrift.

"Do you need a ride, Miss?" he repeated.

I rose unsteadily and looked around.

I haven't the faintest idea, I could have told him. Then I remembered a strand of my original plan. "Génova—the Hotel Génova," the only hotel I knew in the city. Ben and I had stayed there a few nights when we returned from the revolution, before we found ourselves forced to move into a tenement. I spoke slowly, deliberately, as if trying to reel myself back from a great distance. The cabbie jumped down with surprising ease for a man his age.

"I know the one. It's on Lucerna Street. Here. Let me give you a hand with that, Miss."

Reaching for my overnight bag, he helped me into the surrey. Then with a faint flick of his whip, we set off. The city drifted past us, yet I hardly saw it. I was desolate. What had happened to my magnificent Benjamín? Had he always been this violent and

I blind to it? Had I ever known the real man? Ultimately, was he only a flawed concoction of my own creation? And when had the world become such a sinister labyrinth?

I need to leave Mexico, reason suggested. 'Begin a new life where he can't find me. I must write to Aunt Delphine. She'll help me with travel expenses. No, it's not that simple. I can't go back to Bryn Athyn. He knows it's the only place in the United States where I have friends and my one living relative. So I have to live far from there. But where?'

I tried another passageway. Maybe Cadwally and I could start a new life in the deepest reaches of North Dakota or Alaska, somewhere far from all this. No, I could never ask him to leave his beloved Cuernavaca. 'Another path that led nowhere. I tried again, my pulse quickening as I sat forward. I won't let Benjamín dictate the course of my life. This is my country too, so I'm staying. Anyway, I'm safe for the next twenty-five years. So why fret now?'

I leaned back into the cracked leather seat, aware of the sun touching my face. Closing my eyes, I let the afternoon drape a warm blanket around me. The dappled light suggested the soothing bath that I would have at the hotel. A bath. A bed. Sleep. My eyelids grew heavy. Yet just as I began to doze, a different thought startled me awake.

What if he escapes?

14

SANCTUARY

What if his family manages to bribe officials to free him? Could they do that? Are the Nymans powerful enough? If so, I'd never know that he was free and looking for me. How could I live with that kind of uncertainty, knowing only that a violent death awaits me? No, don't think about it. But I must warn Tomás—admit that he was right. Warn Rosa again. It's only fair. Oh, Rosa, I wish I were dead, the deed done!

Even then I believed in the afterlife, so death itself did not trouble me. It was the thought of dying violently that horrified me. How had my splendid Benjamín morphed into a murderer? Could despair drive a person to such extreme behavior? I couldn't even blame alcohol for his abuse today. So, who *was* the real man? The gallant poet-soldier who risked his life to save others, or the fiend who nearly choked me to death? How had I been able to love such a complex person? What made me think that I knew him at all? And what were my duties now as a wife? To love him no matter what or to leave him? Weren't we enjoined to love only the good in other people, not the evil that we find in them? So I *could* love his good traits and reject his violent propensities. Hate the deed, not the man. How exactly did one do that? I groaned.

"Did you say something, Miss?" The driver twisted around in his high perch.

"No." I gave him an anemic smile.

The surrey turned onto *Paseo de la Reforma* with its wide boulevards and tall trees. I was aware again of dappled sunlight on my face and folded hands. Yet as the cab rounded a corner, I felt my breath catch. We were passing Rodolfo's house, stately with its blue mansard roof and wrought-iron fence—the house that might have been my home. I shrank into the seat, afraid suddenly of seeing his tall, dapper figure step onto the sidewalk, fearing his derision the most because in spite of everything—the discovery that he had a mistress and children—I still sensed a moral failing on my own part too, not just his. I let him believe that I had forgiven him fully, yet I eloped with his brother.

When the cab finally pulled up at the Hotel Génova, I sighed with relief. The driver jumped down and helped me out. "That will be one *peso,* Miss." He removed his hat and waited respectfully as I opened the small purse that had bobbed merrily on top of my Oxford bag.

*That will leave me with $4.04. I'll need $3.00 for a small room, leaving me with one peso for dinner and four cents for a tip. Or I could skip dinner and have tea and toast brought up. Then I could give him—*The bag opened its mouth wide. *What about the train station tomorrow? I'll need six cents for the tram from the Zócalo—My coin purse! Where is it?*

"Oh, no," I moaned, my hands shaking. "It was here. I had it when I paid for both trams," I found myself explaining to the old man. "I distinctly remember putting it back—"

The train ticket! I couldn't find it either. Pulling off my gloves, I tried to give my fingers eyes as they probed the depths of two inner pockets. Moments later, they surfaced with the return ticket, but the money was gone. I remembered the two boys on the park bench and covered my eyes for a few seconds.

"I think I've been robbed. I can't pay you. I'm so very sorry!"

The cabbie rubbed the back of his neck. "Then, señorita, don't you need me to take you somewhere else?"

Please stop calling me miss! I wanted to snap at him. I'm Mrs. Brentt de Nyman. Then I grasped the import of his words and my hands shot up to my lips.

I can't pay for a room either! There's no train until morning, and I have nowhere to go. What am I going to do?

I balanced on the edge of panic. A second frenzied search inside my purse yielded the key to Cadwally's house and then two more unfamiliar keys, strangers that dangled like men from a gallows. The wind began to blow, disheveling my hair, telling me that I was of no more importance than a leaf swept off the sidewalk. Yet at the very moment when I might have given in to panic, my attention was diverted to the driver who was calmly pulling a dry leaf off the horse's tangled mane. I looked at his gnarled hands. Because he was stroking the mare's neck with a gentle familiarity, and because he seemed in no hurry whatsoever, I felt myself pulled back from a perilous ledge.

Clasping the unfamiliar keys, I remembered that Tomás had given them to me after the reading of the will. They were the keys to my father-in-law's house, San Justín. *I could go there and stay the night. No, what am I thinking? It's a horrible old place.* I glanced at elegant men and women who strolled past the cab, at Indians who went about their business with eyes fixed straight ahead, at street vendors and store clerks and all manner of passersby, all of them unconcerned about me. Conscious of the bustle of a large city, I felt utterly alone again.

A night in San Justín. What choice did I have?

"I need to go to San Angel, sir. I'm afraid that I have no way of paying you, but I do have these." I held out my gloves. "They're kid gloves, very fine. Do you have a wife?"

He nodded.

A night alone in that awful house, the house where Benjamín killed his father.

The moment I handed over the gloves, I knew there was no turning back.

We headed south to what was then the town of San Angel, before Mexico City engulfed it. The mare ambled along, adjusting her footing from smooth streets to cobblestone roads. Leaving behind the wide boulevards and francophile mansions of Reforma Avenue, we headed toward the stark walls and barred windows of colonial New Spain. I sat up straight. Would I remember how to find the general's house? For that matter, would I even recognize it? I had been there only once, the fateful day of the reading of the will. What if I couldn't guide the driver to it? What then?

The wind reared up on hind legs. The sky glowered. Clouds took the sun hostage, but I found the house. There was no mistaking it, even without the plaque that proclaimed its name and the year it was built: San Justín de los Moros, 1568. The cabbie pulled up in front of a massive wall. The front door towered above us like the portals of a cathedral.

"Would you like for me to wait until they let you in, Miss?"

"Yes, please." I was afraid of being stranded should I change my mind.

I went through the sham of ringing the bell though I suspected there was no one there, not even a doorman to guard the place.

I should tell the driver that my aunt and uncle live here, I remember thinking. That way he won't know that I'll be here alone, in case he and others—What was that? I paused. A low rumble mingled with the wind and became gunfire. A mob. A massacre.

Stop it! Don't think about it!

I forced one of the keys into a sullen lock.

Just tell the cabbie that my aunt and uncle live here.

The key jammed.

No. He'll wonder why I don't just ask them for the money I owe him.

I worked the key free and tried the second one. It imitated its partner. I yanked on it. It toyed with me.

I could tell him that they're away just now and that they'll be home later tonight, along with their four or five adult sons, strapping officers all of them.

The key finally responded as if tired of its game.

What rot. Why lie? He's a kind-hearted old man. He's brought me this far, hasn't he? Now the other lock. Careful—there!

Slowly, the great door of San Justín swung open on its ancient hinges. Peering into a dark corridor, smelling a strange dampness, I had the impression that I was about to walk into a long, reptilian throat.

15

NIGHT IN SAN JUSTÍN

TAKE ME WITH you. Anywhere, I wanted to beg the driver. Instead, I forced my voice into a calm, dignified cadence.

"I need to be at the Buenavista train station early tomorrow morning. Would you be willing to drive me there? I could give you—I could give you this ring tomorrow in payment." What did it matter that it was my cherished wedding band? My marriage was over, slaughtered by Benjamín's distrust and brutal vindictiveness.

If I'd known that Benjamín had tossed his wedding band out the window in a fit of temper, I would have thrust mine into the driver's gnarled hand then and there. Instead, I clung to it for a few hours more. For his part, the driver nodded and we had a deal.

"You won't forget to come back for me?" I wanted to grab his arm because he was old and his hair strikingly white like Cadwally's, and I was feeling less and less sure of my decision.

He handed back one of the gloves with a smile. "Now I'll have to come back."

I lingered by the open doorway as he turned the surrey around. Moments later, he vanished around the bend of the street, the clip clop of the horse growing faint. Still I hesitated. All the while the afternoon continued to scribble dark storm clouds across the sky. Taking a deep breath, I took refuge in the general's house, bolting only one of the locks in case I should need to make a sudden escape. Moments later, I stood in the inner courtyard of San Justín.

It's no different from hundreds of thousands of other colonial houses, I told myself. It's simply a stone house built around a courtyard.

And it was. All the rooms, both upstairs and downstairs, opened onto verandas that paid homage to the courtyard. Yet this was no ordinary colonial structure. For one thing, it was far larger than most houses, with multiple courtyards. For another, San Justín was first and foremost a fortress, a bulwark against the world. The tops of the massive walls were lined with shards of glass and barbed wire to keep the unwanted out. It didn't seem much more welcoming inside. The rooms glared gloom. Wind rattled doors and windows. How many deaths had this house witnessed across the centuries? I wondered. And how many murders?

It's only a house. And it's mine. Mine?

I thought about the reading of the will that had taken place right here in the courtyard a little over a month ago—the awful will that had so disrupted my life. That day I had entered San Justín on Benjamín's arm, the two of us in love and united to face his family's disapproval of us. Samuel had been the first to embrace us, Rodolfo following suit, softened perhaps by the sudden death of their father. Doña Manuela had forgiven Benjamín with a fierce tenderness, while offering me barbed words: *So, has my son made an honest woman of you, Isabel Brentt?*

I remembered the touch of Ben's arm around my shoulders as he answered his mother's challenge. *Yes, we're married.*

If you can call a civil ceremony a marriage, the señora had shrugged.

We were also married by the church, Benjamín informed her in as even a voice as he could muster. I could tell that he was seconds from exploding.

Isabel is not Catholic, my mother-in-law observed.

Ben's wonderful response: *She's a Christian, so a priest married us.*

What kind of a priest would do that?

Remembering my mother-in-law's sarcasm, I suddenly wished I had answered, *Samuel, you bigot, that's who. Samuel, the son you're so proud of.* Yet neither Ben nor I had been willing to expose Samuel to her derision, and he had seemed just as eager to skip over the matter. Ben's sister and her Spanish count had remained as aloof as ever until the reading of the will, at which point Eva almost choked to death, quite literally, and Count Francisco Comardo Tejada del Renglón turned tomato-red with rage, his expressionless fish eyes suddenly aflame with emotion.

"I don't know how or why this has happened." He waved a finger in my face. "But I'm going to expose you!"

Remembering that Ben stepped in front of me in a protective gesture and said something deliciously aggressive, I smiled. Distant thunder brought me up short now. Doors and windows rattled.

Wherever you go, however much you try to hide, I'll find you, and I'll kill you both.

I slumped onto the flagstones, drew up my knees and hugged them to my chest. Alone at last I could finally cry—all afternoon if I wanted to and all night and all through the month, and while I was at it, the whole year as well. I sobbed with rage and despair, swaying like the wind-whipped trees of San Angel.

Yet despite the magnitude of my sorrow and anger, physiology overruled both. My poor bladder that I had ignored for hours cut my crying spree short, hurrying me up the stairs in search of a bathroom. I found one at the end of a long veranda. It didn't matter that the light switches didn't work. The toilet flushed and the sink coughed up cold water. Stepping back into the upper arcade, I was assaulted by the next physiological plague: hunger. I had not eaten since that morning. My stomach rumbled like the not-so-distant thunder. There was nothing to do but to venture downstairs again in search of the kitchen. It was growing dark.

I tried a door. It creaked its resentment and glared dusty darkness. I closed it quickly. After a few moments, I took a deep breath and opened the next one, and I realized that I wasn't just searching for the kitchen. I was sifting the growing darkness for something else, for a shape that might materialize in the gloom. A human shape. Stop this! I commanded and made it a point to stare longer into the next room and then to shut the door tightly lest it jabber later that night. A loud sound made me spin around, look behind me, around me. I listened for footsteps from a form, tall like Ben, Samuel, and Rodolfo—an old man with a joyless face.

"Find the kitchen," I remember muttering aloud. "Turn on the lights."

The wind set a door vibrating at the end of a corridor. I opened it. Yet this time I could not bring myself to look into the room. Hesitating on the threshold, I turned my gaze inward. *Go on. Do it!* Taking a deep breath, I plunged as if jumping into a cold lake, gasping as my hands groped the wall for a light switch.

This is just a kitchen. Nothing to be afraid of!

My hand touched a hard object. I pulled back, then returned to it. A light switch! I flicked it on but the gloom sulked its defiance. At the same time a loud thunderclap boomed above my head, instantly plunging me into my old childhood terror of thunderstorms. *Keep looking! There has to be another switch.* Another thunderclap made me stumble to my knees. Something within me, animal and primordial, wrenched guttural sounds as I staggered forward. My hands worked faster along the stone

surface. Searching. Searching. Rain sprang onto the roof on pan-
ther paws. My hands chased down another light switch, but it
clicked like the empty cylinder of a revolver. The rain snarled
and sprinted toward me.

Hunching my shoulders against the downpour, I dashed
across the courtyard and up the stone stairs. Panic stalked me.
Lightning claws tore a gash in the night sky. The stairs vanished
and reappeared. The upstairs arcade flickered into pale form and
vanished; flickered with a new rending of the sky and vanished.
Hide in one of the rooms. Lock it from inside. My God! Which
one was the general's room? Please, not that one!

I threw open a door. Yet even as my fingers clawed the wall
for a light switch, I suddenly remembered something that my
mother-in-law had said in that very house.

"It seems my good husband has played us another trick.
In his monastic zeal, he removed every single light bulb in the
house."

A groan bled into the darkness.

16

THE GENERAL'S GHOST

I LOCKED MYSELF in the bathroom at the end of the corridor. It had a single window that fronted the upper terrace. Instead of glass, it had wooden shutters. When the wind blew them open I screamed. My hands found the lip of the bathtub. The porcelain edge led me to a corner where I huddled like a dog afraid of storms. Thunder shook my body; fear drove my thoughts and emotions—fear of a cadaverous figure that might pause by the open window and look in.

"There are no ghosts!" I sputtered out loud. *Spirits have better things to do than to haunt horrible old buildings. Get ahold of yourself!* I wanted to jump up from my hiding place and close the shutters, but a new dread terrified me as much as the possibility of actually seeing a ghost. Suggestibility. What if the shadows on the floor were to *seem* to take on a human shape? I'd die!

At the very moment when my terror threatened to burst, uncontrollable as an earthen dam rupturing, I closed my eyes and prayed aloud. "Our Father, who art in the heavens. Hallowed be thy name." A thunderclap almost paralyzed me. I repeated the two lines over and over, as if the electricity in the air had short-circuited my memory; over and over until the other lines finally broke free. With eyes shut tightly, I gasped the prayer in a breathy whisper, gasped it until my mind came out of hiding and was willing to *think* about the words, thinking them soundlessly again and again, as the thunderstorm gave way to hail and pelting rain, on and on until I slipped into the mind's shadow world. I slept soundly all night. Peacefully, in fact.

Just before waking up I had one of the most vivid dreams of my life. I dreamed that a wolf was being beaten with cudgels by men in uniform. I couldn't see their faces, but I could feel the animal's terror. Then wonderfully, beautifully, the spirit of the wolf slipped out of his bloodied body and jumped onto a window sill. He was a magnificent animal. Before escaping out the window, he turned to look at me, his eyes brightly intelligent, his stance no longer afraid. I remember feeling an enormous sense of relief for him. And with that strange logic of dreams I realized that I knew him, though I could not place him. Then with absolutely no transition whatsoever, I was inside a sparsely furnished room that held nothing but a cot, a table and a chair. Above the cot hung an enormous crucifix. And I knew. *This is the general's room, and that's the murder weapon that Benjamín used.* Yet I felt more angry at the general than at Ben.

"I'm not afraid of you!" I shouted in my dream in case Lucio Nyman were lurking. "What you did to your family and to me was vile, utterly vile! I don't want your stinking money and I certainly don't want this horrible old house, or prison, or whatever this is!"

For all my bravura my breath snagged just then. In my dream a long shadow crept up the wall in front of me. Without turning around, I knew that a man in a monk's robe was standing directly behind me. His lips brushed against my ear as he whispered, "Benjamín didn't do it. He only thinks he did."

I woke up, heart pounding like a Tlahuica drum. Birds were chirping. Roosters crowed on nearby rooftops. Sunlight puddled on the floor. Gripping the edge of the tub, I drew myself up, slowly unfolding legs and arms from their cramped position. Leaning over the sink, I splashed water on my face and wiped it with my sleeve. When I unlocked the door, I stepped into a morning bathed in translucent light. All along the upper veranda the rain had strung pearls on spider webs. A line I had recited many times in the chapel came to me with all the freshness of this new day.

Weeping may endure for a night, but joy comes in the morning.

Had I tucked away these words for this very moment? What other fragments of scripture or poetry or prose had I stored away without conscious intent? I wondered. And where were they when I needed them last night? In daylight I could scoff at my fear, but the terror had been real, or was it merely a misperception on my part? How did Sophocles put it? *To him who is in fear everything rustles.* So perception *is* everything—all that we know, all that we feel at a given moment.

Just now hunger topped the list. I headed for the kitchen, certain that it would be a cinch to find it now in daylight. I never did. A second impulse took over, even stronger than my slavish hunger: to find the general's room. I was no longer afraid. In the bright light the upper corridors were unmasked. Diminished. Doors were doors. Rooms were rooms, nothing more. I opened and shut each door in steady succession, working my way halfway around the upper quadrangle.

The general's house was an enormous museum that has been robbed of every single object. Its high walls bore the discolorations of religious artwork and family portraits that had once hung there, reaching all the way back to the sixteenth century. The barred windows that rose nine or ten feet to the ceiling had hardware that pined for damask and silk draperies long gone. Generations of feet, furniture, and pets had scuffed up the floors. Electrical wires dangled lifelessly where electrified chandeliers had once lit the cool, dark spaces of an ancient house modernized ever so briefly, and ever so easily plunged back into candle-lit twilight by one man's monastic zeal. Now only spiders contributed finely spun webs to the décor, a snowfall of dust made the floors slightly slippery, and a sorrowful silence amplified my footsteps. In short, every room had been reduced to a warehouse of memories long hushed, empty of even the most minimal furnishings—all, that is, but one room.

Have you ever experienced the phenomenon that has come to be called déjà vu? I did that morning, so I was not surprised to find a cot, a table with a few books, and a chair. I'd already seen them in my dream. Even the crucifix above the cot did not surprise me, only that it should be back again on the wall, for initially, hadn't this very object been considered the murder weapon? How bizarre that it should still be here. Then again, I suppose it ceased to be of interest once Benjamín admitted to thrusting his father violently against the wall. According to the prosecutor, both wall and crucifix had partnered in the crime. How had the man worded it?

I begin to agree with you, Captain, that the crucifix could not have struck the general twice, and I'll tell you why. Because you struck the first blow—not with the cross—but by slamming your father's head against a rough stone wall.

The prosecutor painted the grim picture of a frail old man being brutally assaulted and then left to stagger to his bed with a severe cranial injury. There seemed little doubt that the crucifix was dislodged by the earthquake a few hours later, adding to the head trauma, or perhaps merely inflicting a further blow to a man already dead. The guilt, therefore, lay with the first blow and the duplicity of the accused.

You left his room cursing him, the prosecutor had insisted—*perhaps you had forgotten that you were masquerading as a priest?*

Remembering my own rough encounter with Benjamín in his cell, my heart cried out, *how can you expect me to believe in your innocence after that?*

By unleashing the hellishness of his jealous rage, hadn't he in effect reenacted the murder? Yet even as I stood in the very room where it happened, I felt something stir, and it was not my appetite. As in my dream, I sensed a presence. No, not a presence. This time it was a feeling, an overwhelming sadness, and it was not originating from me. Touching the back of my head, I suddenly grasped the truth, as surely as if the general had whispered it a second time. *Benjamín didn't do it. He only thinks he did.*

17

TRAIN HOME

How often do we make hasty promises and then regret them? When the cabbie dropped me off at the Buenavista Train Station, I clung to my wedding ring. Oh, why had I promised it to him? Just because my husband had threatened to murder me as soon as he is released from prison? Well, yes. That did influence my thinking. Yet now that Ben's father had exonerated him—to me, at least—I very much wanted to keep this most precious symbol of marriage. Surely the driver would see how worthless a thing it was—mere *Alpaca,* the cheapest type of silver. He would take one look at its tarnished surface and scorn it, wouldn't he?

Quick! What can I offer him instead? The night gown in my bag? That would probably shock the old fellow. My jacket then? Yes!

I fumbled with the buttons, speaking fast without quite looking at him. "I know I promised you this old ring, but you see, it's my wedding band and it means a lot to me. Would you consider the jacket instead?"

When I finally dared to look into his face, I found him studying me behind deep-set eyes that almost vanished under great sprouting eyebrows.

"The gloves are payment enough, señora."

I threw myself on him, kissing his cheek. "Oh, thank you! Thank you!"

Did he think me a strange, emotional *gringa*? I thought of him thereafter as an angel sent to rescue me. I don't know if he was then, but he is now, that dear, lovely man. So, with Benjamín's ring safely curled around my finger, I practically floated up the train steps, my heart so light it wanted to ascend like George Meredith's lark, higher and higher. As passengers boarded, I reminisced about the night Ben and I eloped. We had been so ill prepared. No documents. No civil wedding to precede the religious one as mandated by law. No rings. Benjamín laughed that we would have to make off with two curtain rings from his brother's windows. Luckily, the one and only general store in San Gabrielín sold a little of everything, including cheap jewelry. How Ben and I poured over that small tray just moments before the marriage ceremony! We tried on the trinkets with as much joy and anticipation as if they hailed from Cartier of New York or Caldwell of Philadelphia. The grocer's wife, a hefty woman with a strong Castillian accent, lent me a beautiful Spanish *mantilla* to use as a bridal veil. She and her husband stood in as godparents during the ceremony. Several women from the village twisted a vine of honeysuckle into the requisite *lazo* of all Mexican weddings—a figure eight garland that is slipped over the shoulders of the couple, a tradition dating back to preconquest times. Luckily, Benjamín had the thirteen gold coins that he was expected to pour into my cupped hands.

More passengers boarded. Setting aside my memories, I settled in for the four-hour ride to Cuernavaca. Everything was bathed in an ethereal light. What did it matter that I was hungry and penniless? *Benjamín didn't murder his father!* My heart kept trumpeting. That he had attacked me was troubling, I conceded, but it could be explained. Obviously the press and its lies must have triggered his anger. Or perhaps his mother had filled his head with torrid tales. After all, hadn't I run off with the "crooked" lawyer and their inheritance? So wasn't there a logic to his suspicions? Furthermore, wasn't his aggression an outward sign of a deep inner pain? Since he believed himself guilty of his father's death and me guilty of adultery, was it any wonder that he had lashed out against me? From his perspective, wasn't his wrath justifiable, and wasn't its expression the inevitable or at least understandable consequence of the macho culture in which he had been nurtured? With his life in ashes and his honor at stake, he must have felt well within his right to—to what? To practically strangle me to death? To threaten to murder Tomás and me? How exactly was I to excuse that?

You don't, I could almost hear Aunt Delphine say with a shake of her head. You forgive the man if you can, but you do not excuse the bad behavior.

You're right, I would have told her were she sitting beside me, silver hair tucked under one of her no-nonsense black hats. I deplore his behavior and will tell him so someday. But I do forgive him. Isn't my task now to love him and to help him understand his own innocence? Why else did his father come to me in that dream?

A middle-aged man and a small boy took the seat opposite mine. The train lurched forward. Moments later, Chapultepec Castle, perched on its high bluff, drifted by in the distance.

"That's the Castle that guarded the city in 1847," my companion explained to his son. It turns out he was a schoolteacher. "Chapultepec was a military school. Still is. Cadets just a few years older than you fought to the death against the *gringo* invaders." Glancing at me, the man grew flustered. "I beg your pardon, Miss."

"No, that's quite all right. I'm Mexican."

Am I? I suddenly wondered. Before my schooling in Pennsylvania, I would have had no doubt about my nationality, for wasn't that really determined not by the place where you were born, but by the country that nourished and shaped you? How had I come to feel so conflicted about my identity? My traveling companion, however, seemed reassured by my native accent— my genteel native accent. He proceeded to point out *Molino del Rey* to his son.

"We Mexicans fought bravely there and made the invaders pay dearly for their aggression."

He neglected to add that we Mexicans ultimately lost the war, costing Mexico half of its national territory. And I saw then the dignity of Mexicans even in defeat. This father was teaching his son to remember and appreciate, not the outcome, but the brave defense of their country against invaders. I could learn from that, I told myself. Grace in defeat. Blissfully unaware of the battles I was yet to fight, I gazed at the ever-changing landscape, really seeing it this time.

To return to Cuernavaca we first had to ascend higher than Mexico City before traveling several thousand feet down to the Valley of Morelos. I'd made the right decision to sit on the left side of the train as it held the best vantage point to a spectacular scenery. Everything radiated beauty, from the humblest *milpa*, those small plots of land farmed by the poorest of farmers, to the sprawling plantations. The ever- shifting landscape was painted at different points with spiked maguey, Nopal cacti, pine groves, apple and peach orchards, and lava fields long since cooled into black shards—all of it beautiful.

The train zigzagged its way past the volcanoes Popocateptl and Iztaccihuatl, not just once but several times, circling as it climbed higher and higher until we reached the *Cima,* the highest point on the line. The air chilled noticeably. Cadwally had told me once in this very spot that we were now almost two miles higher in altitude than New York or Boston. Seeing the snow-hatted craters so close up, I thought about Hernán Cortés and his armor-clad soldiers. When they plod past the volcanoes in

1520—or was it 1521?—did they tremble with awe or just from the cold?

We began our descent from the *Tierra Fría*—the cold land—to the hotter *Tierra Caliente*. I'd be hard pressed to say what was more wonderful, the volcanoes or the Valley of Anahuac. The valley, steep ledged and vibrantly green, spread out far below us, achingly beautiful. The school teacher and his son would disembark at Tres Marías, but not before they had shared some *biscochos* with me. Breakfast rolls and the kindness of strangers never tasted sweeter.

Tomás met me at the station. He wore a Navy blue vested suit, his hair well trimmed and carefully slicked back, his shoes polished to a bright shine. Remembering a disheveled barefoot boy, I wondered once more, *Who is this stranger?*

"We've been worried sick about you," he snapped as he snatched the Oxford bag out of my hands.

"Didn't you see my note?" I was careful to draw the high collar of my blouse tighter around my throat, in case the bruises were beginning to show.

"Damn it, Isa! A woman shouldn't travel alone. Don't think you're safe just by staying at the Génova for a night. All kinds of unsavory characters stay in even the most respectable establishments. Besides, people can get the wrong impression about a woman who shows up alone at a hotel."

"For your information, I did not stay at the Génova after all. I spent the night in San Justín."

"Where?"

"San Justín de los Moros." I loved the look on his face.

"Alone?"

"Of course alone." I walked on ahead of him. He hurried after me.

"You stayed in that house? It isn't even furnished, except for the old man's room. You didn't actually—"

"Of course not."

"Then where did you sleep?"

I wasn't about to admit that I had crouched in terror next to a bathtub all night. "On the floor." It was a half-truth.

"And you weren't the least bit uneasy?" He stopped again as if he had just remembered something. "That ghost-infested house doesn't even have lights!"

"I know. So I went to bed early."

He shook his head. "You have more guts than sense." I accepted the grudging compliment with a smile. We walked in silence for a while until he asked, "So how is he, that husband of yours? Was he overjoyed to see you?"

"Of course."

"He must marvel at the steadfastness of your heart, even excusing murder."

I grabbed his arm. "He's not a murderer, Tomás. I know that now."

"My mistake. A patricide."

"No. He's innocent. He only *thinks* he killed his father."

Tomás's laughter startled several sparrows into flight.

"Isa, love that aristocratic patricide if you must, but don't give up logical thought altogether."

We argued all along the rutted streets that led to Cadwally's house. By the time we reached his battered door, we were sweaty and breathless. Tomás dumped my bag at my feet and sauntered off to his mother's house.

18

HARD SET HOPE

Tomás and I avoided each other for the rest of the day. It was only after he boarded the train for Mexico City the following morning that I felt free to visit his mother. I knew that in the comforting fortress of Rosa's embrace I could say things that were far too fragile for the hardened scrutiny of Tomás or my grandfather. True to form, she drew me into the gloom of her shack and the warmth of the brazier, where she busied herself scrambling eggs and cooking beans for our meal. As always, she worked silently. When all was ready, Rosa studied me with eyes dark and inquisitive as her son's.

"Tomás tells me that you think your husband is innocent."

"He is." I fingered my high collar, hoping her sharp eyes would not see the faint imprint of Ben's fingers as the bruises began to surface. "It was all a horrible accident. Benjamín never meant to kill his father. I know that now."

"Is that what he told you?"

"No. Not exactly. But I know it."

"How can you be so sure?"

"Well—for one thing, I visited the house where it all happened. In fact, I spent the night there."

Rosa gasped, a primordial fear etching sharp lines on her face. "You slept there? *Madre santísima!*"

"It's all right, Rosa."

"No it isn't. Tomás swears it's full of ghosts!"

"The only ghost I saw was my own terror. Trust me when I tell you that one's imagination can create very convincing hobgoblins." Yet even as I tried to steer Rosa away from the subject of ghosts, I could not ignore the possibility that I might have actually encountered a spirit. Watching my hostess closely, I took the plunge. "I think the general spoke to me in a dream."

Rosa's hand flew to her mouth. Then she crossed herself, kissing the cross she made with thumb and index finger.

"It *is* possible, isn't it, Rosa?"

"That depends. What did he say?"

"These were his exact words: 'Benjamín didn't do it. He only thinks he did.'"

Rosa crossed herself again. *"¡Ay Diosito!"* Once again God in all His omnipotence failed to escape from her predilection for the diminutive.

"Rosa, you've got to help me convince Tomás to prove my husband's innocence. No one else will help me."

"I don't know. The general was the very devil himself, and you yourself had to run away from his son. So tell me again, Isabel, because after listening to Tomás rant against all the Nymans, your don Benjamín in particular, I need to ask you again. Granting that he's as brave as a rooster in a cock fight, and that I need to overlook the fact that he's both a man and a Nyman Vizcarra, curses he can't really help but can't escape either, I still need to know: over all, is Captain Benjamín Nyman a good person?"

Other than the fact that he wants to murder Tomás and me, yes, I could have answered. And despite everything, I laughed, for wasn't it all absurdly convoluted?

"It's not a laughing matter, Isabelita."

At that very moment the memory of Ben confronting the lynch mob flashed again through my mind, so forcefully and in such sharp juxtaposition to his abuse of me in his prison cell, that I flung my arms around Rosa from sheer joy. "Oh Rosa, Benjamín *is* volatile and frightening when he's angry, like he was in Torreón when he tried to stop the massacre. So there *is* a good kind of anger. Believe me when I tell you, there is more of heaven about him than hell."

"Then the blessed Mother must have sent him to the little Chinese Indians that he rescued." Rosa crossed her hands, pressing them to her chest. After a pause she reached for a chile, the kind that turns eyes into waterfalls. She nibbled it pensively, her tongue utterly immune to the pepper's bite. "Now tell me about General Nyman. How did he look in your dream?"

"I couldn't see his face, but I knew it was him. Oh, Rosa, he had such an air of sadness about him."

"Good. You can believe the sad ghosts. It's the ones that are full of themselves that you have to watch out for. All right, I'll talk to Tomás. Now tell me about your visit to the prison. Your husband must have been so happy to see you," she smiled with all the guilelessness of a small child. So I spun an elaborate fantasy about our joyous reunion. Leaving Rosa's house, I felt drained.

Why do I tell lies? I wondered as I climbed the wall and the jacaranda tree. It's such a cowardly impulse. Why didn't I just tell her the truth about my disastrous visit? And have her hate Ben like everyone else does? I jumped to the ground of our patio. No. Besides, it wasn't all lies.

Lying in the dark that night, I let myself return to the terrifying mob scene, but only because I perceived that it put Benjamín's worst trait in a radiant light. Half listening to the night watchman's whistle, I basked in the consciousness of Ben's rage, so dazzling when it was righteous.

Now that Benjamín's essential goodness had been re-established, it followed that he would manifest it by writing to beg my forgiveness. No such letter arrived. The simple truth is that while I believed in his innocence, he believed in my guilt. I struggled to write another letter. What I yearned to tell him was this: I'm appalled by your behavior toward me, but I forgive you. I know that you're innocent of your father's death. Your father as good as told me so himself. You'll say it was merely a dream or a flickering of my imagination. But Ben, I *felt* his presence so palpably. More importantly, it confirmed what I know in my heart: you are no murderer. You just sound like one.

This is absurd! I shouted inwardly, debating the matter as if I were two people, a habit I'd developed growing up as an only child.

Even if he were not able to carry out his threat against me, wouldn't his intent be spiritually damning?

Yes, but Ben wasn't in his right mind that day in his cell. He couldn't have been. Grief and misinformation had distorted his thinking. That wasn't the real Benjamín—or was it?

Ah, doubt, that serpent! I cradled my head in my hands. Do we ever really know the one we love, or anyone else, for that matter? How much do we imagine and how much is real? I crumpled the letter and started again. When it came to trying to explain his father's will and Tomás's role, I felt inadequate to the task. Every one of my attempts ended up a tight ball arching its way across my room. About three weeks after my disastrous visit to the Penitentiary, I finally composed a letter that satisfied me, for it offered a way for me to recoup my good name and thereby save our marriage. After chastising him for thinking me capable of committing adultery and theft, or of knowingly marrying my own half brother, or worse, becoming someone's mistress and then marrying the man's son (as he had implied with his deplorable question), I concluded my letter with a grand gesture.

> As proof of my innocence and good will, I am going to write to your mother so that I can meet with your family's attorney and deed everything back. **I don't want the inheritance.** I never did. Do not imagine that I do this from fear of your threat. I am not afraid to die.

This was a half truth. An exaggeration for rhetorical effect. Death by disease or old age seemed disagreeable enough—events to be endured. But I could not resign myself to a violent death, never knowing when it would strike or how, only that it would be terrifying.

> My conscience is clear. I repeat: I care nothing about the
> inheritance, but I do care very much for my good name.
> If you who have known me better than anyone cannot
> see that I have had nothing but good will toward you
> and your family, then you never knew me at all.

On a sudden impulse I added,

> Oh, Ben, let's love and trust each other again! Together,
> we can face all the hardships that lie ahead, dearest love.

I kissed the letter and folded it carefully into an envelope. I would take it to the post office in the afternoon. Meanwhile, I needed to scrounge up lunch. Cadwally and I were living mostly on beans and rice, the poor man's substitute for meat, and on *tortillas,* the Mexican version of flatbread, only much thinner. Rosa had taught me as a child the art of making tortillas, beginning with how to grind maize the way the Aztecs and her Tlahuica ancestors did. For that they relied on a *metate,* a slab of volcanic rock resting on three short legs. The actual grinding required what looks like a short rolling pin also made of black lava stone. Kneeling in front of the *metate,* I rolled up my sleeves and began the task of crushing the kernels of corn with a vigorous rolling action. I quickly worked up a sweat.

Rosa had also taught me how to turn crushed maize into *masa,* the dough that is needed for making tortillas, how to pat a ball of *masa* between my hands until it is much thinner than a pancake, and then how to bake each tortilla individually on a *comal,* a large flat plate that can withstand direct heat. The *comal* was the Mexican version of a cast iron pan, but it was so much more—a thing mystical and sacred.

Once, when I was about ten years old, Rosa and I were kneeling side by side patting masa dough into tortillas. She was cooking hers on a battered-looking *comal*. I was using a brand new one that Cadwally had just bought for us.

"Wouldn't you like a new *comal*?" I asked Rosa with a touch of compassion in my voice. Ours was so shiny. I remember that she paused and looked at me.

"This *comal* links me to my mother who cooked on it, and to her mother before her, and to her mother, and to a whole succession of women in my family. I'd sooner lose my house and everything in it than part with it."

For the first time in my life I felt truly orphaned. My mother's hands had not placed tortillas on my *comal*. Neither had my grandmother's nor her mother's before her nor any of the women in my family. Did I even have a family? Maybe Cadwally had found me on his doorstep. Or maybe I just sprouted from the weeds. Rosa was watching me as if she knew my thoughts.

"Look at me, niña." She wasn't smiling. There was an intensity about her that I rarely saw. "When you grow up and have a husband and a home with daughters of your own, I'll give you my *comal*."

"You can't. I'm not your daughter," I said softly.

"You are if I give you the *comal*. Then my mother and my grandmother and all the other spirits in our chain will hold you in their heart and call you their own."

And just like that I had a family of Tlahuica ancestors. Oh, that they would enlighten me on how to regain my husband's love again—or at least how to make my meals less boring!

19

INJUSTICE

ONE AFTERNOON I made soup with nothing for stock but water, one tomato, and two Serrano peppers. I was about to ladle it into clay bowls when the mailman's whistle snapped my head toward the front door. Hope made my heart sprint; pride forced me to walk unhurriedly. Again there was no letter from Benjamín. The one piece of mail that arrived bore a Pennsylvania postmark. I sighed. None of my former classmates knew about the terrible unraveling of my life. I had been too ashamed to tell them the truth—that all the fire of my romantic life had ended in ashes. Before I could bolt the door, the mailman knocked again. And again my heart pounded faster.

"Tomás—"; I hoped the corners of my mouth had not drooped.

"What? Not even the ghost of a smile after my long absence? Do you really never think about me?"

"I think a lot about you. No, that's not what I mean. You know what I mean."

He smiled and kissed me on the cheek. Then he followed me into the patio where Cadwally was already seated at the table.

"Good afternoon, sir." Tomás extended his hand.

Noting my grandfather's reserve, the hesitancy with which he shook Tomás hand, I countered with a burst of hospitable energy. "Won't you join us?"

Tomás took a seat and stirred the thin broth that I set before him. "Isa, it's time you were able to add chicken to the pot. Just claim your inheritance. It's that simple."

As always, Tomás Tepaneca stated matters with a directness that circumvented the conventions of polite society: a cutting to the chase, a leanness of speech that viewed most pleasantries as superfluous and innately deceptive. In this he was quite un-Mexican. I saw Cadwally fix his attention on him, but I could not read the raised brow. Beyond astonishment, did it signal approval or disapproval of our guest's bluntness?

"In fact, I've already arranged it." Tomás scooped a Serrano pepper from his soup and bit into it as if it were lettuce. Serving myself last, I fished out the second pepper, slowly biting into it as I looked him in the eye. It was an old game with us, one I had not played in a long time.

"Have you, now?" I managed after a pause. The Serrano made my eyes water but I continued to chew slowly, as if I were trying to bring to mind forgotten lines of a poem. "I'm sorry to disappoint you," I think I was rasping my words by then. "I have absolutely no intention of claiming anything."

"This is no longer just about you, Isa. It's time you started to think about others."

"I am. That's why I'm not stealing someone else's inheritance."

"Then how about helping the truly dispossessed, like the men, women, and children of Santa Lupita de las Milpas?"

Rosa's village. As a child I had heard the sad story on one occasion. It was a tale of dispossession that came by night with the thunder of horses' hooves and the burning of the entire village. At the time of the telling, perhaps because the stoical Rosa had cried as much as the sky—a real *chubasco* of a storm—it had made a deep impression. I had visualized the charred ruins being torn down and the village lands being plowed under to expand the Nyman Vizcarra lands. Rosa never again spoke to me about her village, so my memory of it faded, like Cadwally's watercolor landscapes when he sometimes left them in the rain. Besides, why worry? Wasn't Rosa just about the happiest person alive? Clearly, the present was more important than the past.

"There's nothing I can do for the villagers."

"Oh yes there is. You can take possession of San Serafín, which is legally yours. You can then deed back the communal lands that your father-in-law *stole* from the people of Santa Lupita, back when he was a big general instead of a grim, self-styled monk. Do that and you'll still have more land than you'll ever need."

"I don't know what the general did or did not do years ago, and I don't care."

My letter to Benjamín only needed to be addressed. I could still mail it today if I hurried.

"Well I care, and so did my grandfather who died in prison for standing up to the general, and so does my mother who had to give birth to me in the *streets* of Cuernavaca because our home had been burned to the ground. Small details, to be sure. But do you think you could make yourself care a little?"

I felt my cheeks flush and quickly reached across the table for his hand. "Oh, Tomás. I *do* feel for you and all the other families. Truly I do."

"Then do something about it. Begin by claiming the plantation that the general left to you alone. Release the farmers of Santa Lupita from having to work as field hands in hacienda cane fields that they once owned. Restore their dignity and their livelihood."

"The revolution will do that. When Mr. Madero takes office in November, all those terrible injustices—"

"Your señor Madero is a rich landowner himself, so nothing is going to change. Don't you see? He's one of them. With him it's just talk, intellectual ideals that sound good in speeches. He has absolutely no intention of enacting real agrarian reform at the cost of privileged families like his own. Even if he wanted to, they won't let him."

"You're wrong about him."

"Face it, Isa. He's a one-word parrot: 'anti-re-electionism; anti-re-electionism.' That's all that his revolution was about. Out with the old dictator; make way for younger men like himself."

"You're wrong. He cares deeply. Look how he came here to Cuernavaca to meet with Mr. Zapata and other revolutionaries. Ask your mother if you don't believe me."

"And look what's come of it," Tomás thrust aside his spoon, letting it clatter in his bowl. "Francisco Madero isn't president yet, and he's already exercised his power to select a governor for us."

"That's his right."

"And he's made a colossal blunder in his choice!"

"What's wrong with—"

"If Madero really wanted to institute a government committed to social justice, he would have given the people of Morelos the one man the majority wants, the man who has best championed the restitution of stolen lands: Emiliano Zapata. Instead, Madero has caved in—"

"He's only trying to find the best man—"

"No. He's caved in to the interests of the landed gentry by forcing a man of the old guard on us. So I repeat. *Nothing* will change. Planters will go on squeezing villagers for their lands; the Indians will press their claims in courts that will continue to favor the rich, and the whole bloody revolution will amount to nothing more than a reshuffling of the deck, letting a new set of ambitious men have their turn at becoming rich at the expense of the poor."

"Tomás is right." Cadwally spoke softly, startling opponents who had temporarily forgotten him. "Why do you think I'm a supporter of Emiliano Zapata?"

20

ALLIES

Remembering that Tomás did not speak English, Cadwally switched languages, his Spanish heavily laced with what Tomás called *Cadwalismos.*

"I saw what *pasar* in Yautepec. A rich planter *confiscato* over four hundred *cabeza* of cattle that belonged *collectivo* to the villagers. *Insistare* they had strayed onto his land, but it was Yautepec's land. Yautepec's!" His face seemed all sharp lines, anger carving deep crevices across his brow. "The planter *demando* that they pay *him* to get back their cattle! Greed and lies!" Cadwally banged on the table, making the crockery jump. "The hacienda of San Gabriel *waito* until the villagers *plantar* their *maíz*. Then they *tornar* the hacienda steer loose to *tramplar* the fields. Greed and lies!" The fist thundered a second time, and I realized with a start that he was teaming up with Tomás against me. "There's a *lako* some thirty-five *kilometros* from here," Cadwally was on a roll now. "The town of San Juan Teques—Tetesk—"

"Tequesquitengo," Tomás rushed to aid his unexpected ally.

"That one. Some years ago the villagers complained to the local hacienda for *encrochar* on their lands. The *hacendado's* response was *swifto*. The bastard *emptar* his dikes and *irrigacione* canals into the lako, causing its *bancos* to overflow and wipe out the *pueblo*. All you could see was the church's *doma* sticking up out of the water!"

Cadwally's fist thundered again, but it was his eyes that distressed me more. With every memory that he shared, I sensed that he was shoving me toward a confrontation that I very much wanted to avoid. Yes, I felt sorry for all abused villagers, but what about my marriage? I *needed* to reject the inheritance and give it all back to the Nymans, if only to show Benjamín and his family just how wrong they were about me. It was up to Madero and his administration to right the wrongs of the past. Not me, or so I reasoned with youthful selfishness.

Tomás produced shot glasses from his pockets and a flask with tequila. Cadwally, who normally didn't drink until late afternoon, pounced on that first shot like a cat on catnip.

What are you up to, Tomás Tepaneca? My eyes must have blazed.

"What happened in Tequesquitengo was an outrage," Tomás quickly picked up where Cadwally had left off. "And it wasn't the last one. Our state is blackened with the ruins of villages that tried to fight against hacienda encroachment of their lands, places like Acatlipa, Cuauchichinola, Sayula, and Ahuehuepán." He turned to me, pointing his finger like a gun. "Do you realize that in the last sixteen years the people of Morelos have lost eighteen villages and towns—*eighteen*—to the greed of the planters?"

Cadwally, who had just downed his second shot and was about to accept a third one, turned to me. "It's time you *realiza*, Isabel, that nothing changes for the better so long as people only *hablar* and do *nada* to make it happen." He turned back to Tomás. "But how do we actually *clamo* San Serafín? They have *guardos*."

"We'll have our own and they'll outnumber the hacienda's forces."

"Our own what?" I asked in alarm.

"Guards, a detachment of *Rurales,*" Tomás answered without looking at me, his attention focused on his ally. I may as well have been up in my room.

"How the *diablo* do we get those *banditos* in uniform to help us out?" Draining his shot glass, Cadwally slammed it down, unconsciously switching to English. "They won't do it out of the heart of their kindness. How the hell do you plan to pay them, Tep—Tep-neck-ah?"

Tomás, with his uncanny comprehension of *Cadwalismo,* smiled broadly. "I've informed them that the very wealthy señora Isabel Brentt de Nyman will pay them far more for an afternoon's work than they can earn in a month. They just have to help her take legal possession of her property."

"And how do we *evictar* the Nymans?"

"Evict?" I gripped the edge of the table. "No, Tomás. We can't just throw doña Manuela out of her own home."

"With the law on our side, why not?" Tomás was too busy replenishing shot glasses to look at me.

"Why not? Because it doesn't *feel* right. Everyone thinks I'm a thief, and now I would actually *be* one!"

Tomás turned to me. Spanish has an idiom that expresses perfectly the effect of his stare. *Clavó los ojos en mi.* He nailed his eyes on me, and that's just how it felt—a cold nailing of flesh with that one look of his.

"Isa, listen again and remember. The only thieves in all this are the Nymans. The general swallowed up an entire village, *my* village. Families that used to grow their own maize, fruit, and vegetables as independent farmers are now forced to grow sugar for absentee landowners—"

"Doña Manuela is hardly an absentee landowner. She's always there and works hard running the place. Much as I don't like her, I must tell you that she *is* kind to her people—"

"*Her* people?"

"Look, I've seen the Christmas festivities and the gifts she gives the children—"

"Do you seriously believe that an annual Christmas party and a few baubles erase the theft of an entire village? The burning of our homes? The virtual enslavement of independent farmers? Oh, such largesse!"

I rubbed my brow with both hands. "I can't think right now. Give me time, Tomás."

"The longer we delay, the harder it will be for you to stake your claim. *Act now!*"

"All right. All right. How about this?" I took a deep breath. "We take the hacienda; I sign the village lands back to the village. I then give the hacienda and remaining land back to the Nyman family, and I live out my life here with quiet dignity. Would that satisfy you?"

"No. How many times must we go over this? The moment you place the Nyman Vizcarras back in power, you doom the villagers to dispossession and servitude again. It's that simple. No, *you* must be the owner of San Serafín. The village would be safe with you as their neighbor. I would stake my life on that." His voice softened but his eyes kept me 'nailed.'

"He's right, Isabel." Cadwally rapped the table with his knuckles. "We can't wrong the rights—" he wrinkled his brow. "We can't right the fights of all the villages, but we sure as hell can throw a dart. Make a start!"

"But think of what you're asking me to do. You want me to confirm my husband's ill opinion of me by betraying his family. Admit it. You're asking me to sacrifice my marriage for the greater good."

"What marriage?" Tomás asked bluntly.

I jumped up, nearly knocking over my chair. "Please, Cadwally. Can't you see how very awkward this is for me?"

Looking up into my face, his eyes suddenly intense and brightest blue, he murmured in English with a recall that was miraculous under the circumstances, "'A person may cause evil to others not only by his action but by his inaction, and in either case he is justly accountable to them for the injury.'"

I knew he was quoting John Stuart Mill. When Cadwally taught me to read, he had used as primers his favorite books. Two were penned by Mill. Listening to my grandfather's occasional political rants when I was little, I thought that 'stupid' and 'conservative' were synonymous.

"Oh, Cadwally, you don't know what you're asking." I felt drained. "Let me think about it."

Tomás tapped his forehead just then. "I almost forgot. Mamá made tamales. She wants you to stop by to pick up a plate of them."

"Now?"

"Why not?"

I shot him a grateful look and hurried off to Rosa's house. It was a trap.

21

A TREE-OF-A-MAN

TWO OLD MEN sat at Rosa's table. The older of the two Indians instantly reminded me of the ancient Tule tree of Oaxaca. Not that I had actually seen it myself. Cadwally had made an impressive mural of the famous tree, starting at the foot of the stairs in the patio and climbing up to the rafters outside his studio. *Can we go see the real one?* I had asked as a child, to which he had promptly responded, *I have painted the thing with appalling realism, so there's no need to trouble ourselves.* The enormous cypress now came to mind, not because Rosa's guest was remotely massive, far from it, but because he looked as ancient and as venerable as the famous two-thousand-year-old tree. His skin seemed all bark, weather-roughened, and deeply grooved.

"Ah, Isabel!" Rosa beamed. "I'd like you to meet don Dionisio and his son, don Crispín."

Both men rose and doffed their hats. They seemed discomfited when I extended my hand for a handshake. They were old school and deferential.

"Don Dionisio was the elder of Santa Lupita de las Milpas," Rosa spoke with pride. "He and his son have something to show you, niña."

The son, who looked almost as ancient as his progenitor, reached into a large earthenware jug, the kind that a water peddler would carry on his back. This one, however, was full of straw. Slowly, don Crispín withdrew something wrapped in a cloth yellowed with age. He handed it over to his father as gently as if it were a newborn infant. Don Dionisio laid it on the table with equal care. Then he proceeded to unwrap it slowly, layer by layer of fabric, with a reverence akin to a religious ritual.

"It's rarely moved from its hiding place," Rosa whispered from behind her hand, her eyes luminous. "Very few people have ever been allowed to see it."

Don Dionisio motioned for me to draw closer.

When I returned to my room, I picked up my letter to Benjamín. Bringing it to my lips, I had a fleeting sense of what could have been: reconciliation with Ben and his family, the chance to incarnate wifely devotion, visits to the penitentiary, daily letters, and steadfastness across the years of his sentence. And then at last there would have been a life together in our middle years, our love for each other all the stronger for our shared suffering.

A final possibility streaked across my skies: I could write a new letter to Ben explaining—explaining what? That in order to assure justice for the much abused villagers, I needed to evict his mother and take over the hacienda?

What is false hope but a meteor that vanishes in the blink of an eye?

Still I clung to the letter. Why, oh why does it have to be so difficult to do the right thing? my heart cried.

By day's end fragments of paper leaf-carpeted the floor of my room.

In the hush of night I realized that I had been defeated, not so much by Tomás and Cadwally with their stories of abuse, nor even by the carefully guarded sixteenth-century deed from the Spanish crown that legitimized the villagers' claim to the land, but by a small detail—the *way* don Dionisio had gazed at me with utter benignity and trust. What could I do but claim my inheritance for the greater good?

22

BREACHING THE WALLS

Two days later, Cadwally, Tomás, and I were bouncing around inside a hired coach whose springs had petrified into cantankerous immobility. A squad of mounted and heavily armed *Rurales* rode alongside us. They were crack shots, men in brown with wide-brimmed hats whom the old Díaz regime had commissioned to police rural areas. Skeptics referred to them as legalized bandits. For the promised fee, thirteen of them now escorted us. Rosa, who had intended to come along, had to stay behind to nurse don Dionisio who had suffered a stroke during the night.

"Oh, Rosa! I was counting on you! Why can't don Crispin look after his father?" I complained selfishly.

"Ah! He's as helpless as a child. But don't worry, niña. You're in good hands with Tomás and the *Virgencita.*"

Hours later, when the hacienda's domes materialized just above the tree line, neither Tomás nor the Virgin of Guadalupe could staunch my panic. "I can't do this," I gasped.

"You think this is tough?" Tomás crossed his arms comfortably, like a man settling into his favorite armchair. "Try explaining to our bodyguards that you've changed your mind. Be sure to smile prettily when you mention that you won't be able to pay them and regret dragging them all the way from Cuernavaca for nothing. Of course, as your attorney, I must urge a different course of action since not all men appreciate your smile as much as I do. Trust me, the Rurales are much more pleasant as body-guards than prison guards."

San Serafín was a veritable town protected by high walls. Along with a grand house for the family and its guests, the plantation provided separate housing for workers and their families, a hospital, a church, an electrical power plant, a sugar refinery, a telegraph office, and its own train to get the finished product to market. It also had its own jail house, for how else was one to keep order even in the best-ordered of places? Morning light painted the walls a golden ochre. The yellow-tiled cupola of the hacienda church glistened in the translucent sky. Glorious ivy interlaced with blossoms climbed watchtowers and walls. Colors, especially purple and red tones, seemed sharper. In short, it was all exquisitely beautiful. Yet that's not what set San Serafín apart. It's what one heard: the riotous bird calls of a jungle compressed into doña Manuela's towering aviary. I took it all in with aheight-ened sensibility, terror and admiration colliding. When our small army stopped at the front entrance, I clutched Tomás's arm.

"They'll never let us in!"

"If anyone can talk them into it, it's you, especially in that hat," he winked, referencing the plumed leghorn that he had managed to borrow from the sister of the wife of a friend of his. He deemed it crucial that I look like the heiress he intended me to be. "Never mind. I see in your face that you would prefer to jump over a cliff just now. I'll talk to the guards."

Tomás stepped lightly out of the coach. Having scoped out the security of the place a week earlier, he knew that San Serafín had reduced its number of sentries to eight, freeing up the other men to return to the fields. Several of these guards now stood at the front parapet, looking more curious than fierce. A man with an inverted U-of-a moustache arrived just then and challenged us in a gravelly voice: "Who goes there?"

"Good morning. We're escorting the señora Isabel Brentt de Nyman," Tomás motioned nonchalantly toward the mounted guards at his back. "It's a surprise for doña Manuela."

With a burst of courage or surrender to the inescapable, I leaned out the window, heart thumping so loudly I could barely hear my own words.

"Good morning. Is my mother-in-law home?" I smiled prettily.

When the heavy doors of San Serafín swung open, I thought of the Trojan horse. But I was no intrepid Greek. As we lurched forward into the main courtyard, Cadwally kissed me.

"Well done, soldier!"

23

CLAIMING THE KINGDOM

THE EVICTION PROCEEDED at an astonishing pace. With the *Rurales* at our back, Tomás led the way into the heart of the house. We found Doña Manuela in the central patio of the family's personal quarters. *What's all the clamor?* She seemed about to ask. The moment she saw me, her manner morphed from annoyance to a hatred that distorted her features.

"Out of my house, whore!"

"It is you who must leave the premises," Tomás spoke firmly. "Your husband's last will and testa—"

"Out of my house! Get out!"

Manuela Nyman leaped at me, fingers splayed as if to rip out my eyes. Cadwally shielded me with his tall frame. Tomás responded just as quickly.

"Manacle the woman," he ordered.

Two *Rurales* stepped forward. Doña Manuela ignored them, bent on one thing alone—to shred me as if I were paper. "I'll kill you!" she raged as the men struggled to capture her flailing hands. "Do you hear me? I want you dead, your skull cracked—"

"Gag her," Tomás ordered.

One of the rural policemen untied a scruffy bandana from around his neck and tied it across her mouth with experienced speed. Her eyes grew as round and startled as a yearling's when experiencing a bit for the first time. She groaned. I shut my eyes and burrowed into Cadwally's chest.

Unperturbed, Tomás addressed her with exaggerated civility. "I'm sorry, señora, but you've made this necessary with your abuse of my client. We, on the other hand, have had the courtesy to reserve a room for you at the Bella Vista for tonight. Tomorrow you can board a train in Cuernavaca and rejoin your family in the capital or in Europe or anywhere you choose."

Even now, gagged and manacled as she was, Manuela Nyman still tried to lunge at me.

"Get the keys." Tomás pointed to a large key ring that hung from my mother-in-law's belt. One of our men obliged. "Good. Now put her in the coach and keep her there under guard."

Only when they had hurried her off did I dare to look around, but I wasn't ready yet to let go of Cadwally. Several of the servants and all five of the hacienda sentries ran into the courtyard just then. Guns were drawn on both sides. Luckily, some of our *Rurales* had taken positions in the second-floor verandas and on the rooftop. All told, five hacienda rifles and our thirteen were cocked and ready to fire. Clearly, we had the advantage, except for one detail: Tomás, Cadwally, and I would be caught in the crossfire. Even as my terror escalated, I could not help but admire Tomás's aplomb.

Holding up documents that he had rolled into a scroll, he seemed to me a fierce Tlahuica warrior wielding the law like an obsidian cudgel.

"I hold the documents that make the señora Isabel Nyman the legal owner of the hacienda of San Serafín. She alone is General Nyman's legal heir. Lay down your arms and no harm will come to you." No one moved. No one spoke. Tomás waded fearlessly into the silence. "It is your duty to obey the law and to serve your new *patrona.* Everyone who serves her will still have a job, and through her generosity you will also enjoy higher pay. Now lay down your arms until they are needed to defend her."

The sentry with the ferocious-looking moustache was the first one to obey, laying his rifle at Tomás's feet. The others followed suit.

"At ease," I heard Tomás tell the police.

And just like that, the hacienda sentries morphed back into field hands and our warriors into men slouching comfortably under the *portales,* as if enjoying a respite from the day's heat. Massacre averted, Tomás was all business now.

"You'll get your rifles back shortly," he informed the plantation sentries. "For now return to your posts and await further orders." He then pointed his scroll/cudgel at a young servant. "We need to speak with the family. Are any of them here?"

Too frightened to respond, the girl simply shook her head. Tomás then 'nailed' his eyes on another servant, a stone-faced Indian woman. "You. What's your name?" The woman regarded him without a change of expression and I recognized her immediately as doña Manuela's personal servant.

"I asked you your name."

"Tacha."

"All right, Tacha. You have exactly thirty minutes to pack a trunk for the former patrona. You are to pack only her clothes and a few personal items, such as books and her rosary. Got that?"

"Her jewels too," I whispered hoarsely. "Her jewels and her photographs."

"What? Don't be so quick to—"

"She can have her jewels," I repeated in what should have been a firm voice, only it quavered shamelessly.

"All right. She can take those too, but everything else in this house, in this entire hacienda, now belongs to Mrs. Isabel Nyman. Rob her and you'll have to answer to me and to the law."

Tomás's next step was to commandeer the dining room as his office. Sitting at the head of the long table, with Cadwally and me on his right and our sergeant on his left, he continued to direct the transfer of power. A tall pot-bellied man burst into the room. I had the immediate impression of a bull charging into an arena, not only because of his thick neck and solid build, but because he exuded a raw kind of energy. Tomás had the jump on him as well.

"Are you the administrator, Ernesto Valle Inclán?" he asked him like a judge who knows the answer and is simply following procedure.

"I am."

"You are to travel with the señora Manuela Nyman to Cuernavaca. Your services are no longer required here."

Valle Inclán's fist came down like a rock on the table. "Who the hell are you to dismiss me? I've given more than thirty years of my life to San Serafín!"

"And I'm sure the widow Nyman has rewarded you amply across the years. You are free to continue to work for her, but not here. You have," Tomás drew out his pocket watch, "twenty-two minutes to pack your belongings and join the señora in the coach. But first we'll relieve you of your gun. *Sargento.*"

The big-hatted sergeant held out a hand that said, don't make me wait for it.

Valle Inclán glared at Tomás with almost as much hatred, it seemed to me, as doña Manuela had for me. "You'll pay for this."

Tomás grinned. Couldn't he see that this man who towered over everyone in the room, perhaps over everyone in the whole plantation, was now a dangerous enemy? Dangerous or not, Valle Inclán unholstered his gun and submitted to being escorted to his quarters by two *Rurales.* Twenty-three minutes later the great doors of San Serafín swung open a second time. The coach carrying its two exiles rolled past the plantation guards, none of whom dared to oppose the law, especially when it came so well armed. By then Tomás had also spoken with the hacienda's head accountant and had taken possession of the books. Deploying the rural police so that they were highly visible, he had every man, woman, and child in San Serafín assemble in the largest courtyard, the one that fronted the church. Standing at the top of the church steps, Tomás addressed them in a loud, clear voice.

"General Nyman, the legal owner of San Serafín, bequeathed it upon his death to his daughter-in-law, the señora Isabel Brentt de Nyman. Many of you already know her. Doña Isabel is your patrona now. Your loyalty to her will be generously repaid with protection, better working conditions, and better pay."

There was no reaction. The change had simply happened too quickly. For their approval Tomás could have thrown in the Zapatista slogan of *¡Tierra y libertad! Land and liberty!* However, his passion was even more parochial than Zapata's though no less intense. Spreading his arms wide Tomás Tepaneca cried out, "*¡Viva Santa Lupita de las Milpas!*"

Again there was no reaction, only a bewildered silence. Then an old man with a thin voice answered back, "¡Viva!"

A second old man echoed the viva in a piccolo's voice. Tomás beamed and threw open his arms a second time, his face flushed with triumph: "*Viva la justicia!*"

The younger men who might have been wondering if Santa Lupita de las Milpas was some new saint, joined in the cheering, for who doesn't like justice? Besides, who wants to appear ignorant?

24

GUARDIANS

Tomás proclaimed that a great *fiesta* would be held for the people of San Serafín. All work was to be suspended for the next day and a half. Of course, since he needed for the house servants to prepare enough food to feed over a hundred families, and for carpenters to build an outdoor dance floor, and for the artistically inclined to make a fleet of *piñatas* for the children, and for the pyrotechnically skilled to prepare fireworks, and for everyone else to set up tables and chairs and Chinese lanterns, the people of San Serafín were busier than ever. The feast would take place the next evening in the large courtyard in front of the church.

Having made his magnanimous decree, Tomás wanted to be shown around the hacienda. Agapito, the assistant administrator whom he had just promoted to head *administrador*, was quick to oblige. I, on the other hand, felt emotionally drained and longed to sleep for a century or two.

"All right. Go claim your bedroom." Tomás kissed my hand, his face flushed with victory. "Rest while don Cadwallader and I check things out."

I headed for the grand stone staircase, the one that had broken Cadwally's leg on our first visit. Shoving aside the memory,

I thought instead about Rodolfo, debonair in black tie, escorting me up these stairs to meet his mother and siblings. Was it barely a year ago? I marveled. In that short span I had gone from penniless schoolgirl to Rodolfo's fiancée, Benjamín's wife, bold revolutionary, reluctant heiress, and now the target of a death threat. Why had I been given wealth at the expense of my marriage, if not for some good purpose? Clearly, I was meant to right some of the wrongs of the past, I kept reminding myself. What we did today was necessary, or at least a lesser evil than doing nothing to reverse social injustices. Things will be different now—changed like this venerable old house.

Ben and I were astonished when we saw his mother's renovations. In the few months following our elopement, she had moved all the formal rooms from the second floor to the first. This she accomplished by transforming the ground floor storage rooms into the new parlor, dining room, breakfast room and library—all fitted with wide windows and French doors that provided direct access to the cloister in the heart of the house as well as access to the surrounding gardens. The renovations made sense. Yet Benjamín had hated these alterations to his ancestral home, like a child who stubbornly rejects any change.

Change is unavoidable, I found myself telling him inwardly because I needed to justify the colossal one that I had just forced on his family. Blame your father, not me! He wrote the will. I'm just trying to undo his sins against hapless villagers.

Squaring my shoulders, I started up the stairs, briefly pausing on the middle landing. Here the stairway split off in two directions, like opposing choices in a dilemma. One led to what the servants called the *Condesa's* part of the house, a series of bedrooms and bathrooms that my sister-in-law commandeered for herself and her family on their rare visits. The other stairway led to what the staff termed la patrona's part of the house that included not only doña Manuela's bedroom suite, but the General's former rooms as well as Rodolfo's and the one guest room in the main part of the house. Connecting the Countess and la patrona wings was the *gemelitos'* section where the "little twin brothers" had slept and played and grown to manhood. The fourth side of the rectangle consisted of the former parlors, library, and dining room—all of them recently converted into a new suite of rooms for the exclusive use of Eva. These I had never seen. So it was there that I began the search for a room of my own.

Opening the door to the former parlors, I had the uncanny impression that I had just stepped into a French chateau, or more precisely, onto an elaborate stage set that *suggested* a chateau. Gone were the beautiful exposed beams of a sixteenth-century Mexican hacienda. These had been covered over by a ceiling richly adorned with elaborate baroque flourishes. In place of the elegant simplicity of the former rooms, there now abounded a profusion of mirrors and gold cartouches on the white walls. On closer inspection, I realized it wasn't gold-leaf after all but a kind of yellowy bronze paint that mimicked the look. No doubt, doña Manuela intended to have real gold-leaf added at a more convenient time, sans revolutions. On the other hand, the enormous gilt-edged mirrors, empire furnishings, and crystal chandeliers were the real thing. The overall effect was stunning and stunningly out of character with a Spanish colonial house.

The suite had the cold formality of a museum. I half expected to find portions roped off, guarded by vigilant docents. Scores of framed photographs chronicled Eva from babyhood to middle life. Monogrammed initials abounded. But even more off-putting, the former library had become her dressing room, bookcases replaced by floor-to-ceiling mirrors, wardrobes, and four dress forms fully clothed from head to toe. And I realized that this *was* a kind of museum after all, a mother's monument to a long-absent daughter. In the melancholy stillness, I felt a twinge of pity for my mother-in-law—until I remembered the intensity of her hatred for me.

And hadn't Eva tried to sabotage my engagement to Rodolfo? So the heck with them! I wanted nothing to do with mother
or daughter. Eva's suite could go on collecting silence like dust.
I vowed then and there to protect the venerable old house by
undoing my mother-in-law's decorating sins, starting with Eva's
ridiculous suite.

Returning to the upper corridors, I hurried from room to
room, opening doors formerly closed to me, leaving them ajar
as I moved on to the next. My mother-in-law had the interesting
habit of using full-body, life-size portraits instead of name plates
to proclaim the owner of each room. And not just one painting,
but two per room: a younger version of the person to the left of
the bedroom door and a more recent one to the right. They had
surprised me the first time I stayed in San Serafín. Later, as the
days of Cadwally's recovery ticked ever so slowly, I used to stroll
along the upper verandas, pausing before each portrait, keenly
aware that my grandfather could never have painted them. For
all his talent, he could render the human body only in a flat,
stylized version akin to ancient Egyptian portraiture. The artist
of the Nyman-Comardo menagerie was one Blasco Torres del
Fuego. Working primarily from photographs, he had painted
each member with academic skill, but also with an idealization
that bordered on fantasy. Francisco Comardo, for example, stood
tall and slender, sans middle-aged paunch and his perpetual
pout. His daughter Esther was pretty enough, but the artist had
exchanged the milky film of her blindness for emerald-green
eyes. Likewise, Blasco Torres had gifted Emanuela, the whiny,
pouty middle daughter with a beatific smile worthy of a saint.
Even Evita, the baby, lacked a grounding in reality, bearing more
of a resemblance to the fat cherubs of the chapel ceiling than to
any earthly child. As for Eva, the artist had been careful to deliver
the middle-aged portrait without the fine lines that scored the
corners of her eyes and mouth, her hair stubbornly black.

Since the Comardos rarely visited San Serafin, the collection had struck me as melancholy reminders of absence—lifeless companions for doña Manuela on her solitary walks. It seemed to me that they had morphed since then, their gaze suddenly cold and accusing. Even the children seemed to ask, does our grandmother know that you are poking around in her house?

25

A ROOM OF MY OWN

Running a gauntlet of surly Comardos, I hurried to the *gemelitos'* wing. The Nyman twins stood guard, utterly undifferentiated from each other but for the military uniform and the priestly cassock. The artist had captured the handsome symmetry of their features, the sleek hazel eyes and their boyish charm. But he had completely missed the roguish quality of Ben's eyes and the softness of Samuel's. Focusing on Ben, I found myself pleading inwardly, *Please understand. I had no choice about today!*

You always have a choice, Aunt Delphine's dictum whispered down the long corridors of stubborn memory. I resorted to fantasy, creating my own idealization: Benjamín returning to me one day, his light-brown hair silvered, his spirit chastened but not crushed by twenty-five years of imprisonment. I would search his eyes as I was doing now, for the tenderness and passion that used to ignite the green irises at the mere sight of me. And it would be there! And he would thank me—yes, thank me—for letting his mother keep her dignity.

You gave her independence by allowing her to keep San Justín and the silver mines. You should see how she restored my father's beastly old house to its former glory. She lives there—

Correction: *She lived there to the end of her life,* he would inform me. Yes, that was better. And then Benjamín would kiss me, sweeping aside all the lost years. We would make love all afternoon. And later, when the moon covered us with a silver-threaded blanket, we would lie in each other's arms dreaming of a future together. In the morning I would wake to the steady beating of his heart, my head pillowed on his chest, his arms two guardians.

Yes, I could sleep in Ben's old room, I thought, until I opened one of the wardrobes and found it blackened with Samuel's cassocks. Now I felt just as intrusive as I had in the other rooms, every object proclaiming its rightful owner and me an interloper. On to the old nursery for a momentary escape. There, too, the door was guarded by the twin brothers—five- or six-year-old cherubs with plump cheeks, curly hair, and a wide-eyed look of innocence that made me smile. Yet that day the nursery struck me as the saddest room in the hacienda. Most of it had been rededicated to Eva's daughters. Intricate dollhouses, tea sets, and dolls looked as if just taken out of their boxes, suggesting that doña Manuela's granddaughters had rarely played here. By contrast, Samuel and Benjamín's wooden blocks and hobby horses looked worn, their painted surfaces scuffed through hard play. Tin soldiers bore the wounds of many a battle. A few still stood in ranks. Most lay on their sides, bleeding dust. As I scooped up a forgotten warrior, a couple of lines came to mind: *What has become of our Little Boy Blue/ Since he kissed them and put them there?*

He's walled up inside a penitentiary, that's what! Tears welled up in my eyes. We bring children into the world with such hope. And again I pitied my mother-in-law, and I pitied her tragic child and my own unborn children who might have looked like these two—all those lost children, lost hopes. How did one bear all that?

I hurried out. Don't think about what might have been! Stay focused. Claim a room and be done with it! Moments later a dark, strikingly handsome adolescent smiled at me: Rodolfo as a cadet in dress uniform. On the other side of his door stood Rodolfo at age thirty or thirty-five in formal attire: a man of the world, his dapper moustache outlining rather than obscuring his smile. Sleep in his bed? No. The general's old bedroom then? I paused.

It is worth noting that my mother-in-law had the one and only portrait of her husband removed from the corridor. Even the much-disliked Pancho Comardo had been allowed to stand guard over his own bedroom door. Not so the general. Doña Manuela had incarcerated the General's portrait in his rooms, out of sight, much as she had done with Benjamín himself when he wanted to join the revolution. In place of the portrait, she had hung two landscapes painted by Cadwally years back. In fact, there were a good many Cadwallader Brentts prominently displayed throughout the house, attesting to the fact that both the general and his estranged wife had valued them.

Taking a deep breath, I entered General Nyman's suite. Mahogany furnishings, green damask draperies, and a high dome with eight light-breathing windows urged me to consider it for myself. This was the grandest of the bedrooms, grander even than Eva's. Aside from the family chapel, no other room sported a dome. The general had not slept here in fifteen or sixteen years. Why not claim it?

Slowly, cautiously, I gazed into the eyes of the blue-eyed *vikingo* as he was called in younger years. This was the ambitious Swede who stepped onto Mexican shores penniless and rose to become a mighty general, one of the country's wealthiest landowners, and my benefactor. He stared back benignly enough. Yes, this room was the logical choice for me. Then I remembered

Benjamín's terrible question: *Were you my father's illegitimate daughter or his mistress?* I am no man's mistress! I had retorted when I could speak again. Sleep here? What if I should find traces of myself in that face? No. Definitely not this room.

I resorted to the one guest room in the main house. Benjamín and I had used it during our last night together as husband and wife. Entering, I held my breath as if trying not to wake him. Slowly, I sank onto the edge of the bed. What came to me was a memory of the day Ben had come looking for me at my grandfather's house. I had refused to talk to him. Why? Dismay at the irrationality of his jealousy? Resentment at his resentment? Yes, but more than that, what had I *felt*?

The answer came to me with that snagging of the breath, as if one has just discerned the shadow of an intruder. *Revenge.* I had wanted to retaliate and make him suffer. Yes, fear had also driven my decision to flee from him. Seeing Benjamín drunk for the first time had released a dread that reached all the way to my childhood. But above all, I had wanted to strike back at him for reanimating that old anxiety. Revenge, not just fear, had motivated me to leave my marriage.

Regret pounced. I stumbled out, a jumble of should-haves wrapping themselves around my ankles as if to trip me: I should have stayed! I wrung my hands. I should have waited to see if his drinking was a one-time offense or the first of many. If nothing else, I should have stayed long enough to hand everything back to the family, which would have been the decent thing to do. Then there would have been no awful dilemma, no having to choose between my marriage and social justice. If I'd done the right thing from the start, everything would have been fine between Benjamín and—

The wind blew, slamming a door just then. Startled, I whipped around. To heck with all of you! I railed at the phantoms with their silent disapproval. And then because the house itself seemed to have rejected me too, I tossed my guilt at it and set off to explore the very rooms that were most forbidden.

26

JOAN OF MORELOS

I PAUSED BRIEFLY in front of an adolescent Manuela Nyman Vizcarra. A different artist with an illegible scrawl of a signature painted her. In place of beauty, he gave her youth and soft yearning in her dark eyes. I was in no mood to grant her a gentler persona. Instead, I glared at the middle-aged rendition by Blasco Torres, tilting my chin defiantly at the equestrian whip gripped in her gloved hand, her manner stern as a sentencing judge. *Mother gave the artist a hard time,* I remembered Rodolfo chuckling softly, *telling him to wipe that ridiculous smile off her face. Hence the scowl.* This was probably Blasco Torres's most honest portrait. Glancing over my shoulder, it seemed to me that the Comardos and Nymans were all watching me, judging me, but none as harshly as Manuela Nyman's portrait.

Damn it! I've done nothing wrong. This was thrust on me!

I entered her bedroom. Expecting doña Manuela's suite to be as austere as her glower, I adopted a belligerent posture, shoulders thrust back, hands curled into fists. Instead I was brought to an abrupt standstill. In the afternoon's filtered sunlight, the pale, yellow walls of doña Manuela's sitting room glowed golden.

The room with its white brocades, crystal, and silver-limbed candelabra shimmered in perfect harmony with the Spanish architecture. Pink peonies cloaked in dark foliage spilled over vases, their lush forms highlighted by white linens. A glorious coffee service presided over the room, glorious because it was a work of art, no doubt forged from the family's silver mines and crafted in its workshops. LNB, the general's initials entwined themselves elaborately with MVN, Manuela Vizcarra de Nyman. Wedding silver?

I picked up a gold-rimmed coffee cup. *Limoge,* it murmured when I flipped it over. Wondering how many intimate family gatherings the room had hosted across the years, I felt a stab of envy: envy that the Nyman siblings had each other; envy that they had known both parents; envy that I must always watch other firesides from a distance with yearning unquenchable, ever an outsider. But so help me, I would not be an outsider any more. This was where I would plant my flag. And why not? The law was on my side, and I would wield it to undo the harm General Nyman had inflicted on the villagers of Santa Lupita.

Mixed sounds from the aviary reached me, some imperious, some raucous, and others lyrical. The scent of freshly cut grass wafted from the garden through the open windows. A rose-scented breeze flirted with the sheer curtains, enticing them into a sensuous *pas de deux.*

Can all this really be mine?

I now entertained the idea, not out of defiance, but because it was beginning to appeal to me. Stretching out on a white sofa, I imagined a flurry of letters to my school friends, inviting all of them, parents in tow as chaperones, to stay in San Serafín. I could make up some excuse for Benjamín's absence. Or maybe I could have them not only pity him for his wrongful incarceration but champion him. Yes, I needed their support. With friends and Cadwally by my side, along with Rosa and Tomás who would be given rooms here in the main house, my days would soon fill with laughter and outings and dinners and talk with kindred spirits. So maybe I *could* live here. Yes, why not enjoy myself while doing some good in the world?

That settled, I headed for the bedroom, the inner sanctum.

It turned out to be as plain as Manuela Nyman—downright ascetic in fact. A nun's cell. The room held a dark wardrobe, a small table with a lamp that couldn't begin to light the space, and a bed with a large wooden crucifix hanging above it. There were no bed curtains as in the other rooms. I wandered over to the wardrobe. There were no mirrors or carvings on the doors, no artistry, merely functionality. Empty coat hangers swayed gently when I opened the doors.

The smell of her rushed at me—the clean but distinct mingling of leather, horses, and a fine perfume. My mother-in-law was an accomplished equestrian who could ride all day with the toughest *peones* and dine on Limoge with delicate grace. I closed the doors and turned to the only other piece of furniture in the room: a *prie-dieu*. I had seen a number of them in Italy. For a moment I fancied that I could see the indentations of her knees on the faded purple upholstery and the marks left by her elbows as she knelt in front of a small statue of the Virgin Mary. I could picture my mother-in-law lighting a votive candle and praying daily as one mother to another for her own son's deliverance from the Brentt scourge.

Yet it is this Brentt who will ultimately secure Benjamín's freedom, I told her inwardly. Someday all of you will beg my forgiveness, you most of all for the appalling way you've misjudged me. Until then, rest assured that I have no intention of sleeping in your horrible bedroom. However, I do plan to enjoy the sitting room whenever—

A shadow startled me just then, or perhaps the perception that I was not alone. I whipped around. Tacha, doña Manuela's personal servant, had entered on silent feet, arms limp at her sides and face utterly, horribly expressionless.

Like Rosa Tepaneca, Tacha was of short stature, but rounder and more solid-looking. A woman of indeterminate age, her walk and manner exuded a man's physical strength. I towered over her, yet I sensed that there was something formidable about Tacha. It was not just that she had the build and face of an Olmec warrior carved in stone, her nose large and flat, her lips thick and unsmiling. What I found unnerving was that the servant's face always wore one expression and one alone: none.

"I—I ju—just want to make sure that you haven't for—forgotten anything crucial—for doña Manuela." I stuttered, mortified to have been caught snooping in my mother-in-law's room. The servant said nothing.

Moments later I stood inside the only bedroom that I now felt that I could claim: Emanuela Comardo's small, uninteresting cage. There I was finally able to crumble and pull the bed covers over my head. Tears and exhaustion stupefied me into sleeping.

Perhaps because I was tangled in a blanket that I did not need, I dreamed that I was wearing a suit of armor that was stiflingly hot.

"Why do I need to wear this?" I asked Tomás in my dream.

"To protect you from the Nymans' slings and arrows, of course," he laughed, as if to say, why do you always miss the obvious?

To my surprise, I was on horseback at the head of an army. "What about you?"

"I have to take care of the legalities. The battle is up to you, Isa." With a sharp slap on the horse's rump, Tomás sent me into battle.

As my knights and I dashed across a field of spiked maguey, I thought, *maybe I'm like Joan of Arc obeying the bidding of a higher cause.* Armed with a noble commission, we easily stormed the enemy walls. Moments later, my troops and I were scrambling up ladders and then a spiral staircase to the top of a tower.

My French castle looked suspiciously Mexican. For one thing, the architecture bore all the markings of New Spain; and for another, my knights were wearing large *sombreros*. They busied themselves rounding up prisoners, all of them Nymans. Looking down from the tower onto a high parapet, I easily recognized doña Manuela by the gale-force winds that seemed to emanate from her, threatening to overwhelm my troops. I could see my knights struggling to keep from being swept away. Their hats were no match for her and flew away, literally a flock of starlings. When Manuela Nyman's rage subsided for a few seconds, my knights shoved her over the edge. I distinctly heard her smash on the rocks below. All that remained of Manuela Nyman were pieces of broken pottery, which made perfect sense in the dream.

Rodolfo, Eva, and Pancho Comardo were escorted onto the parapet. Brother and sister had a resigned, dignified air to them. Pancho Comardo, by contrast, was whining loudly.

"You can't treat me like this! Don't you know who I am? I belong to one of the oldest families of the Spanish nobility!"

My soldiers hurled him over the edge. Rodolfo jumped stoically. Eva followed him willingly but with operatic theatrics— Tosca in all her tragic grandeur. With each one, I heard the distinct sound of crockery smashing on the rocks below and saw the fragments. Lastly, they brought Father Samuel to the site of execution. Unlike the others, he turned and looked up at me. He wore the guileless expression that Benjamín was so adept at mimicking. Without moving his lips, his eyes unutterably sad, Samuel told me, Thou shalt not steal, Isabel.

27

TRUNKS AND TREASURES

TOMÁS WOKE ME with his insistent knocking. "Isa! Are you in there?" When I did not respond, he walked in. "I've been look-ing everywhere for you. What the devil are you doing here? The servants have larger rooms than this."

I sat up and rubbed my brow. "What time is it?"

He pulled out his pocket watch that now sported a gold chain. Rodolfo's? The General's? "Half past six. I let you sleep through most of the afternoon and the whole night. Now get up. We have just enough time for breakfast before we head out."

"Head out?"

"To Santa Lupita de las Milpas."

I fell back onto the pillows. "You go with Cadwally. I'm—"

"No. You have duties to perform. It's crucial that the people of San Serafín start thinking of you as their patrona and bene-factress." Gripping my hand firmly, he pulled me off the bed and hurried me down a corridor. "For starters, you need the best room in the house, not a lousy broom closet."

I had a sense of déjà vu: Benjamín dragging me against my will to see his father's portrait and then to the chapel. Now it was

Tomás. Did I have no will of my own? I tried to break free but his hand seemed welded to mine. As we neared Eva's suite, I balked even more. "No, I don't want that one!"

"It's the best one, or at least the fanciest. So you're going to sleep here. If you hope to be taken seriously, you must take charge and act like a queen."

"Well I'm not a queen and I don't want this room!"

"Why ever not?" He chuckled as if I were a grumpy child waking from a nap, which was not far from the truth.

"Because *she's* here," I pointed at a portrait above a fireplace.

Tomás studied the beautiful countess. "Hmm. Very life-like." Still holding me firmly, he called down to one of the rural policemen.

"I need two or three of the hacienda men up here, if you would be so kind."

Moments later three workers entered Eva's rooms. "Take away the portraits, all of them." Tomás was quite adept at giving orders.

"Where would you like them, sir?"

He pointed at Emanuela Comardo's room that I had meant to claim. At least he was good enough to return my hand to me.

"These, too, Tomás," I pointed to the clothes in an enormous wardrobe. *Why fight him? Just get her things out of here.*

"Are you sure? Your sister-in-law has good taste. You might—"

"I don't want anything that's hers. Besides, she wears a ridiculously small size"—which sounded better than admitting that I felt like a towering giraffe compared to her.

When the ridiculously sized Eva had finally been expunged from the rooms, two men returned carrying a trunk that was covered with stickers from various European countries. "Where do you want it, Señora?"

"My trunk!" I had been forced to leave it behind when I eloped with Benjamín, taking nothing with me but one change of clothes stuffed into a pillowcase.

"Set it in the dressing room," Tomás answered for me.

I was soon exclaiming over my lost treasures: clothes that Great-Aunt Delphine had bought for my season in Europe, along with lace fans, hair ribbons, and a silver brush and comb set with ivory handles. Other treasures surfaced.

"My writing materials—and my journal!"

There among the headless forms in Eva's wardrobe room, I rummaged for books, momentarily forgetting that they had all been shipped home when I left school. Then I spotted two stowaways. Instantly I remembered the last time I saw my great-aunt. We were saying goodbye on her front porch just as my ride to the station arrived. She hurried inside and returned with two books.

"You forgot your copy of the Word. And I want you to have my copy of *Divine Providence*—to guide you along your way, child," she had murmured as she pressed them into my gloved hands.

I had started to object that they would be cumbersome on my long journey, though truthfully my enormous plumed hat proved far more burdensome. Luckily, I caught myself. The shininess of her eyes silenced me, or perhaps the intensity of her manner, as if she had just learned that I was going to be marooned somewhere and would need these particular works for my survival. Poor Aunt Delphine. Though I owed her so much, I had grown to distrust her taste in books as much as in fashion. In Europe she would not let me shorten the hem of my dresses a mere two inches as fashionable women were doing.

"If you don't want to be superficial, start by not being a slave to every whim of fashion," Aunt Delphine had observed with the tone she adopted when nothing was going to move her, not even charging water buffaloes.

I had tried to make allowances for her age. But when she refused to let me have Paul Poiret harem pants though they were all the rage in London, I relegated her to the terribly old, stodgy corner of existence. And here she was foisting books on me that I really did not care to drag across two countries—my school Bible and her personal copy of one of Swedenborg's works. Knowing that she cherished them far more than I did, what could I say? Ah! I was such an ingrate in those days! Yet I did embrace her, heeding the silent promptings of a kindly spirit or angel. And for one terrible moment, somewhere between the catch in my throat and the crush of her frail bones against my stronger ones, I felt a rush of love for her, and then the pull of two countries, both deeply important to me, and the agony of having to choose between them. I held my aunt a moment longer. Then I hurried into the waiting carriage.

So here they were again like two stowaways: a King James Bible and Swedenborg's *Divine Providence.* Why couldn't she have given me the collected works of Shakespeare, or *Wuthering Heights* or *A Tale of Two Cities?* My heart complained now as it had then. Even after four and a half years of religious schooling I still did not fancy curling up with the Bible or with Swedenborg's theology. I respected both, but I did not love them. Not yet. Sighing, I set them aside. Moments later, I was kissing a small, hand-painted icon of Christ.

"Good heavens! Have you become *muy mocha* on me?" Tomás quipped.

"Of course not. I'm not the least religious. It's just that the icon brings back happy memories of Paris. I bought it after visiting the Russian Orthodox cathedral. I'll have you know that this little portrait is about two hundred years old. It's so lovely. See?"

It was a mere one inch across and two in length and fit comfortably in the palm of his hand. We studied the stylized, unmistakable face of Christ; the soft glow of the gold-leafed halo; the intensity of the red and blue pigments of his clothing. I flipped the icon over and translated the inscription.

"'Lord Jesus Christ, have mercy on me a sinner.'"

"Since when do you read Russian?"

"Actually, it's old Slavonic." I loved besting him.

"Slavonic? What did they do to you in that school?"

"Don't worry. A guest at a dinner party translated it for me."

"You carry icons to dinner parties? Now I *am* alarmed."

"Well look at the size. It fits so easily in an evening bag."

I remembered sitting next to a silver-haired, bewhiskered Russian diplomat, a lovely old man who spoke to me in French, most of which I was able to follow. He had set aside his wine and his joviality while telling me about the ancient Hesychast prayer—the Jesus Prayer. It would mean nothing to me and then everything. But the time was not yet.

Tomás handed the icon back carefully. He was, after all, Rosa Tepaneca's son and therefore not quite as irreverent as Benjamín. Returning to Eva's boudoir, I set it on the mantelpiece and felt a sense of well-being. With most of my possessions restored to me, I began to feel less homeless. Maybe I *could* claim Eva's rooms after all. She probably hadn't spent much time here since she vastly preferred Europe to Mexico, and Mexico City to San Serafín.

Tomás was watching me again, not teasingly as in our childhood, but with the open stare of a man inviting a woman's attentions. I suspect that his thoughts had made a swift transition from the sacred to the profane.

"For Pete's sake, Tomás. Isn't there some terribly legal legality that needs your attention?"

"No."

Trying to ignore him, I focused on unpacking the trunk. I came across a corset from my school days and remembered the one I had lost in Tomás's room, back when he snatched my pillowcase away from me and tossed it into a dark corner of the guest wing. It was probably still there, for all I knew. He drew closer and picked up this other corset, spreading it open like a fan.

"You must need help getting in and out of this."

I snatched it from him. "In case you don't know it, a woman likes a little privacy when unpacking."

"Does she?"

"Yes. You shouldn't be here. There are proprieties—"

"You didn't let proprieties hinder you when thunderstorms sent you scrambling into my bed," he grinned.

"We were children!" My face burned as if I'd rubbed it with Serrano peppers. "And it wasn't a bed. It was a mat on the floor, and your mother was right there with us."

"More or less. Sometimes she didn't know you were there until morning. Do you remember the first time we woke up together?"

Actually, what I remembered—and it was probably an earlier memory than being pried off a carousel pony—was gazing straight up into a face soft with a mother's tenderness. Smiling up at Rosa, I held out my arms to her and was never quite motherless after that. I remembered vividly how wonderful it had felt to be cuddled by Rosa. Poor old Cadwally hadn't even noticed that I had been gone all night.

A rap on the door announced the delivery of a second, smaller trunk, the one Benjamín had purchased for me on our honeymoon. I had been forced to abandon it too on the morning that I fled from our marriage, without being able to take even a pillowcase as luggage that time.

"Two trunks? You *have* arrived in the world." Tomás followed the servant and me back into the dressing room.

I resumed feeding one of the newly-emptied wardrobes, my clothes a meager snack compared to Eva's abundance. And still Tomás lingered. Reaching into the smaller trunk, he drew out my black dress, the one that Benjamín had bought for me to wear to the reading of the will. It was silk and far more expensive than we could afford, but he had wanted to make a statement to the family that had disowned him. Tomás held it up to inspect it.

"Wear it to the fiesta tonight."

I grabbed it out of his hands. "Really, Tomás. Give a woman some privacy."

He reached for a black veil and draped it on my head. "Yes, black will signal that you are in mourning for your generous benefactor; the silk will tell them that you are indeed a Nyman." Then something in the first trunk caught his eye: a gossamer gown that shimmered when he unfolded it. "What is it?" he asked as he fingered the semitransparent chiffon, his fingers visible behind the folds.

The gown brought it all back: my final quarrel with Rodolfo, the dreadful engagement party, the charade for the sake of appearances, and the awkwardness of our forced smiles, all flashing through my mind as briefly as a shooting star.

"Do you wear this?" Something in the way Tomás asked the question, half in wonder, half in ignorance, let me see past his overbearing intrusiveness and glimpse the boy of my childhood. Had the solitary years of his schooling given Tomás such little experience with women, Tomás the know-it-all?

"Yes, I wear it, but over this." I fished out a long, pale green slip.

"I like it better without it." He grinned and didn't seem quite so ignorant of women.

28

RECLAMATION

THAT FIRST MORNING in San Serafín, Tomás had our breakfast
served in the large formal dining room, though the cozy breakfast room looked so much more inviting. Cadwally was still
sleeping, which suited Tomás. Seating me at the head of the table,
he took the chair at the far end, and I realized he was playing lord
of the manor. Throughout the meal he beamed at me between
the curved arms of the candelabras, his joy spilling over like wine
in the hands of the inebriated. The servants, on the other hand,
seemed skittish. Their forced smiles and quick motions made me
wonder if this was how officials from all conquered cities behave,
trying desperately to please their conquerors. Were we conquerors or just common thieves? Was there that much of a difference?

After breakfast Tomás and I rode in a surrey to the site where
Santa Lupita de las Milpas had once stood. We were accompanied
by two old men and a middle-aged woman, the only former residents that Tomás could find in the hacienda. Most of the villagers had dispersed long ago, like Rosa and the two old men who
guarded the land grant document. The three survivors who still
lived in San Serafín insisted on walking. Since the surrey was a

small one and Tomás wanted me to play my new role of patrona, he allowed them to walk alongside us. Several kilometers later none of our companions seemed the least winded. At length old Justino gazed up at Tomás and pointed with his straw hat.

"That's where your grandfather's house stood, *patrón.*"

"No, it's not," old Camilo countered. "It was over there, more to the west."

"No, you donkey. It was here. I remember."

They argued. A sea of sugar cane undulated in the wind. Not a foundation in sight, or even the hint of one. Tomás intervened. "Never mind. What matters is to rebuild it all."

"What for?" Venancia, our third survivor, had both hands on hips, bringing my ever practical Rosa to mind.

"What for?" Tomás gave her a hard look. "Because it's your land and you have a right—no, a sacred duty, to rebuild."

"When the general burned us out, I cried a *chubasco.* We all did. Then doña Manuela built us better houses, she felt so bad about it."

"So you would sell out for a house made of cinder blocks instead of thatch?" Old Camilo wagged a finger in her face.

"Yes, you nitwit. I like having walls that aren't food for insects. And I like having a cement floor instead of a dirt one."

"Ah, women! You don't know anything."

"I know that a village is not a collection of houses. It's the people, and they've all scattered like chaff in the wind. So this isn't home anymore."

"That's not the point!" old Camilo slapped his hat against his thigh.

"There *is* no point. There's nothing here," she insisted.

The argument would have escalated but Tomás silenced them, his voice a low, menacing growl. "Enough. Burn the field."

"But *patrón,* the harvest," Camilo gasped.

"Burn it." I was still in the surrey when Tomás turned to me, his face more like stone than Tacha's. "Go back to the house. Tell them I want a dozen men to bring all the cans of kerosene they can carry. Go."

I invited Venancia to ride with me in the surrey. I don't know what thoughts or memories tightened her jaw and hardened her eyes. Nor did I ask. She climbed in and sat alongside me. As I turned the surrey around, I heard Tomás exclaim, "Let a new Santa Lupita rise from the ashes!"

A question hopped into the surrey and nagged me all the way back: is this the great liberation for which I gave up my marriage and my integrity?

29

VOLCANO LOVERS

I WAS IN no mood for the grand fiesta that Tomás launched that second evening of our takeover, yet there was no avoiding it. When I emerged in my black silk gown, he twirled me around.

"Even in black you're radiant, Isa."

So are you, I was tempted to respond. But why fan his vanity? Yet he really did look splendid. Dressed in the traditional tight black pants and short jacket of the *charro,* he looked every bit the prosperous planter. The outside seams of the pant legs and the entire jacket were more heavily decorated in silver than the average *charro* suit, and I suspected it was all sterling.

"Where did you get that?"

"Over there," he pointed toward the room that Benjamín and Samuel used to share. "I was tempted to borrow a cassock, but thought better of it," he laughed. As if reading my mind he added, "This wasn't in Benjamín Nyman's wardrobe, if that's what you're thinking. I borrowed it from the priest who doesn't need it anymore."

Since it fit so well, I suspected that my brother-in-law must have worn the suit in early adolescence, before he caught up with the other tall men in his family. I felt the urge to chastise Tomás for taking such liberties with other people's things, but he offered me his arm just then with such an earnest attempt at chivalry, that I didn't have the heart to scold him.

"Isa, there's something you have to see, and we only have a few minutes to catch it."

He led me away from the main house and onto a high cat-walk that ran along one of the outer walls. "Look," he whispered from behind me, his hands on my shoulders where they had rested a hundred times in our growing up together. Why then did his touch feel so wrong now?

Two volcanoes rose before us—Iztaccihuatl and Popocate-petl—gigantic and achingly beautiful. I had seen them many times. Still I gasped. Bathed in the liquid colors of sunset, the snow-mantled peaks were more dazzling than ever. It was Tomás who had first told me the myth about the volcano lovers when I was six or seven years old, opening my eyes to the truth that these were no ordinary volcanoes but really a man and a woman. *They call that one Iztac for short. I call her Iza. Can you see that she's lying on her back?* Tomás had asked me years ago in a child's voice. *That's her head over there, and those are her breasts—like the ones you'll have someday,* he had added with a mischievous grin. Then he had grown serious. *Iza died when they told her that the brave warrior Popoca was killed in battle, but it was a lie. See over there? That's him. When he returned from the wars, he cov-ered her with a blanket of snow and swore that he would never leave her side. He didn't care that snow was falling on him too. He was a brave Tepaneca like my father and me.*

I had not doubted the legend, only the hero's origin. Even in those early years I had noticed that Tomás equated all things glorious with his family's tribe. I remember challenging him on the point: "*How do you know Popoca wasn't an American?*" After all, my grandfather and I had a tribe too. Tomás had ignored the challenge. Instead he had grown very still. And then he had made a solemn vow. Now I tensed as the grown man murmured it again word for word, his lips brushing my ear.

"You're Iztac and I'm the warrior who will always protect you. I only call you Isa to keep others from knowing who you really are." The grown man turned me toward him, his eyes shiny with expectation, his lips seeking mine.

I shoved him back with an awkward smile. "Oh, my gosh! We're going to be late to the fiesta." I escaped down the stairs, seeking safety in a crowd of strangers.

The fiesta was held in the grand courtyard in front of the church. It was plain to me that Tomás had no intention of inviting the humble workers and their families into the house itself or the private gardens. He would maintain the social hierarchy, making it clear that I was the new patrona, the boss whom they were to honor and obey. When I made my entrance, the men doffed their hats and most of the women looked down as I passed. Only the children stared with open curiosity, yet I think they were far more excited by the glow of the newly strung lights. The entire courtyard had become a bay with an armada of candle-lit tables anchored throughout. We would dine al fresco under the stars.

To make sure that I got off on the right foot with the *peones*, Tomás had ordered that a dozen or more turkeys be roasted on the grills. Smoke and aromas rose up like ancient prayers. Women stirred large clay pots filled with hot *mole* sauce—an Aztec concoction of chocolate, tomatoes, peppers, and other spices. Stacks of tortillas rose up like sugar silos alongside cauldrons of steaming rice stained orange-brown from tomatoes and speckled with cilantro. And, of course, there was a beverage table. Tomás served himself a glass of tequila. In a voice loud and triumphant as a brass horn, he made a toast, "To the señora Isabel, with thanks for her generosity and kindness!"

The response still seemed insipid as tepid tea. Certainly, it was more bewildered than enthusiastic. I wanted to run back into the house, but right on cue a mariachi band swept aside all awkwardness. Trumpets, violins, and guitars quickly stepped into all the silent spaces. They were not particularly good musicians.

I had heard better, but they were animated. Tomás led me to a table apart from the others.

"These are your people," he swept an arm like an orchestral conductor inviting applause for the guest soloist. "They love you already."

"No they don't."

He ignored my observation. "Take a good look, Isa. These are the people who will work loyally in your fields and granaries and sugar refineries. And they will love you because you will be good to them."

"My mother-in-law was good to them."

"Not like you will be."

You know, the more the people of San Serafín drank and ate and danced, the more they smiled at me, so that I could almost believe Tomás was right. Perhaps I *could* win them over. Certainly I would try to be a good patrona to them. No, what was I thinking? This fantasy couldn't last. Any moment someone was bound to silence the musicians and point a finger at me. Thief!

"Dance with me, Isa." Much as I protested, Tomás had me on the dance floor. He held me tightly, his eyes shiny with tequila and love, his fantasy as visible to me as the fireworks that torched the night sky: together he and I would govern San Serafín, dispensing social justice while at the same time enjoying the good life, dancing under the stars to love ballads strummed on guitars and proclaimed by trumpets and tenors with thin, quivery voices. The script was clear. When he tried to kiss me I orchestrated a coughing fit that doubled me over.

"Water!" I gasped in my best gasping fashion.

Tomás hurried me to the beverage table. Above us Chinese lanterns tapped to the music. The moment he released me, I bolted for the nearest safe-haven—the labyrinth that had opened its secrets to me more than a year earlier. I knew its every twist and turn. I forgot that it was also a green cage.

30

ORIGINS

I CHOSE THE labyrinth only because it was closer than the house and I was not certain that I could outrun Tomás. Once inside its green walls I slowed to a brisk walk. Even without the electric lights that lit the many passageways, I would have found my way easily to the fountain at its center, having learned to navigate the labyrinth's twists and turns during the heady days when I used to meet Benjamín here, Benjamín who masqueraded in Samuel's cassocks; Benjamín who played the role of priest so adroitly but could never suppress the light that suffused his eyes whenever he caught sight of me. Would he ever look at me that way again? I slumped onto the edge of the fountain.

No. I had finally given him a legitimate reason to despise me. I wanted to cry but sensed it was only minutes before Tomás found me. Even above the loud music, I could hear him thrashing about, cursing each dead end.

"I hope this isn't a preview of purgatory, so close to heaven yet so far!" he joked.

I laughed in spite of myself. After a few more wrong turns, he perched alongside me on the edge of the fountain.

"I see you still like to play hide and seek," he smiled affably. And because he was mildly drunk and had me alone, he drew me tightly into a kiss, this one even more intense than the one in Rosa King's hotel. At first I was powerless to break free. His very body had become granite. And what did I feel? The horror of breaking a taboo. When he finally drew back to look into my face, I sprang to my feet.

"Stop it!" I wrenched free. "I *hate* it when you kiss me, so stop doing it!" And then because he looked so stricken, I took a deep breath and spoke more softly. "Oh, Tomás, don't you see that I love you like a brother? You're all—"

"Well, I'm not your freaking brother!" He took a step toward me, eyes blazing. "If it's a brother you want, then look to that fop you married."

"Stop it, Tomás! He's not my brother!" My eyes must have blazed too.

"Half-brother then."

"Don't be stupid."

He stepped back again, but only so he could cross his arms and throw his head back in mockery, "I'll tell you what's stupid: for you to think that the general, the most land-hungry fiend in all of Morelos, would leave everything he possessed to a stranger out of the goodness of his heart. Such men only love their own. Why would he choose *you* of all people?"

"Next you'll be suggesting that I was his mistress."

"No, of course not. I know you." Tomás grasped my hand.

"Let go."

"Don't you see, Isa? The whole question of your paternity is different. It wouldn't be your fault that the general fathered you."

"That's utterly impossible." I yanked free again.

"No, my blue-eyed one. It isn't merely possible but probable. Of course, he could never claim you openly. Being unable or unwilling to divorce the very Catholic doña Manuela, the blue-eyed Lucio Nyman found it expedient to pay someone to raise his illegitimate child. Why not the gringo artist?"

"Stop it, Tomás."

"No, no. Hear me out. They used to have frequent dealings, the general and your grandfather. Haven't you noticed a predilection for a certain artist around here? You may not remember Nyman's visits to your grandfather's studio, but I do. So here's a general with a serious problem and a simple solution. Why not pay the old gringo to claim you as his orphaned grandchild? Who would question the—"

"That's appalling!" With a single thrust that caught him off-guard, I shoved him backwards into the fountain. "How dare you think such things, let alone say them! I know my origins. I know who my parents were."

"Do you?" He stood up dripping wet from the crown of his head to the tips of his boots, but he made no effort to get out of the fountain. His fine sombrero floated away like a great round barge. "What do any of us know about our origins? All we know is what we're told."

"Well I know that my mother was Emily Valberg and that my father was Joshua Brentt, and that he was Cadwally's only son, and that he was a minister in a small town near Oklahoma City, and that the two of them were killed in a tornado when I was only two, and that I somehow survived. I was found in wreckage near our house, and Cadwally was notified about the tornado and came for me. So you see, I know a lot about my past. So don't you tell me I don't know my origins!"

I was shaking and fighting back tears, but he was far from relenting.

"Well, how convenient. A tornado. And who provided you with the so-called facts about parents who were killed and aren't around to contradict any of this? An old drunk, that's who, an old drunk who could barely make ends meet until he found a rich *patron* in the general."

"How dare you—"

"I dare! I dare because I know what it is to grow up with fanciful tales that your father was a hero, when in fact he was someone that your mother made up, name and all."

"I don't follow—"

"There was no Tomás Tepaneca, Sr. My mother finally admitted it. She made him up after she was raped, and not just by one soldier but by three. So even if I wanted to find the bastard, I'd have no way of knowing which one fathered me. Oh, and irony of ironies, our great benefactor, the *ilustre general,* saw it happen and did nothing as he passed by slowly on his horse. You at least were destined to inherit his wealth. I came into this world nameless and squalling on the cracked sidewalks of Cuernavaca."

"Oh, Tomás."

"Don't pity me—or my mother, for that matter. She at least had the luxury of being able to reimagine the past." Still inside the fountain, he slumped to his knees and stroked the water as if it were a sleek cat. "Think about the power of the human mind to create its own reality, Isa. With no village to return to and only her old father to confront her from behind prison bars, my mother very wisely chose to ignore that she had been raped. She may have even come to believe for a time that it never happened. How? By inventing a husband for herself and a father for me. Just like that." He slapped the water and sat back on his haunches, a lopsided smile on his face.

"Tomás, you've had too much to drink." I spoke gently. "Come out of the fountain."

"She named me and that bastard of a nameless father of mine after a whole tribe, not even her own. Do you know why I'm Tomás Tepaneca instead of Tomás Tlahuica? This is a good one. She told me—she told me it's because the women of the Tepaneca tribe are good weavers and she admired that. Weavers, for cripes's sake! At least when she gave birth to a boy she was good enough to invent some warrior stories. She filled my head

with tales of ancestral valor—never mind the fact that the Tepanecas and the Tlahuicas were mere vassals to the Aztecs. Subjugated—subjected—substantiated—"

"Tomás, you're soaking wet. Let's go back—"

"There's no going back, no changing our origins. But we *can*
reinvent ourselves like she did. Don't you see? That's the chance
we've been given, you and I." His body was becoming taut like
a great cat getting ready to spring. "We can do it, Isa, you and I.
Spit on the bastards who fathered us."

"The general was not my father."

"He knew otherwise. That's why he left it all to you."

"That's a lie."

"Is it? What proof do you have that you're *not* the general's
illegitimate daughter?"

"I don't need proof. And I'm not going to play your little
game anymore, your game of agrarian reform at any cost. I saw
the people's reaction to your great liberation. They didn't seem all
that impressed. Only three of them knew what you were talking
about. Three!"

"There are others."

"Ancient ones like the guardians of the land deed. The rest
are gone, Tomás. Scattered."

"We'll find them and bring them back here."

"I suppose you could force your mother to leave her home in
Cuernavaca. That would bring the population of Santa Lupita to
a soaring what—four residents?"

"They'll find their way back, the disprocessed—the dispossessed. I intend—"

"What? To drag them back to an empty cane field? A burned
one at that. This wasn't exactly the mission of liberation you told
me it would be."

"It's the principle."

"And what principles did we show? Admit it, Tomás. What
we did here was *wrong*, horribly wrong."

"And it wasn't wrong for that madwoman to leap at you like a—like a jaguar trying to rip out your throat? Is that a person worth defending?"

"I don't like Manuela Nyman any more than you do. But to the day I die, I shall regret the way we ousted her from her home. Whatever the general did or did not do, this is *her* ancestral home, Tomás. Not even his. And it's certainly not yours or mine. I'm appalled that I let myself be talked into such a nasty scheme."

"So give her the mines if that will ease your conscience."

"As a matter of fact, that's exactly what I intend to do, along with San Justín."

"Fine. Just have the decadence—the descendance—" Being intoxicated, his mood was tilting toward the humorous, but only momentarily. "Have the *decency,* yes the decency to deed back the land that the Nymans stole from my village, and then have the backbone to stick around to defend—"

"You did this!" It came to me as if he had just confessed his guilt that very minute. "You didn't just *happen* upon the general the day before he died. You went looking for him."

"To thank him for my education."

"No, to tamper with his will."

"That's not true."

"You hated him. You hate them all. I haven't forgotten the glint in your eyes when you informed the heirs that they had been disinherited. You thought your face was a mask, but I know you, Tomás Tepaneca. You were enjoying it."

"Of course I enjoyed it. It was befitting you—benefiting you," he shook his head as if to clear it. "Why should I give a damn about those people who never worked—never worked a day in their lives?"

"So you manipulated a senile old man."

"Lucio Nyman was no more senile than you or me. Ecc—eccentric—but not senile."

"I heard Benjamín and his siblings agree on one thing—that their father had grown old and confused."

"Not that confused."

"But he was old."

"Trust me. The old raptor still had razor-sharp talents—talons."

"But he wasn't sharp enough to outwit you. How could I have been so stupid?" I threw my hands up in the air. "Every newspaper got it right, except that if you and I connived to get the general's money, you might have let me in on the plan, don't you think?" I gave a strangled laugh. "Well, all your schemes were for nothing because I'm giving it all back to the rightful heirs. All of it. Deal with them."

I hurried away as he raged, echoing Cadwally. "Damn it, Isa! You're not the center of the universe! I'm here too! And so are the people—"

I ran, leaving him to find his own way out of the labyrinth.

31

RUBBLE

Tomás and I pointedly avoided each other over the next two days. He had commandeered Rodolfo's bedroom, the one that had become Benjamín's prison nearly a year earlier. I could sense Tomás watching me from the window that opened onto the upstairs *portales,* just as Ben used to do. Cadwally, who seemed less hungover than usual and in high spirits, took over the room next to Tomás's—the general's former bedroom. Musty as it was, he turned it into his sleeping quarters and studio. I thought he chose it because it alone had a cupola which was quite wonderful. It rose straight up into a dome of sky blue tiles. Eight windows invited light in ever-changing angles and intensities. Yet Cadwally ignored that whole end of the room. With an artist's eye for a steadier, more diffuse light, he positioned his studio along the north-facing windows. The conversion from bedroom to studio had been easy. He simply covered the general's mahogany desk with a faded sheet and spread his tools on it: palettes, oils, paint brushes, rags, and a rusty can of turpentine. The few canvases that he had brought with him from home he bombarded with great splotches, bright and garish as his newborn optimism.

I, on the other hand, spent my time wandering aimlessly. The mansion seemed like a museum after hours. Even with Cadwally's "Tepoz-quickos" gracing so many of the walls, the place continued to feel like someone else's house, and I an interloper who would be shamed when the owners came back. My thoughts tangled like the roots of the great trees along the switchbacks on the Tepozteco. Making matters worse, I kept returning to a fragment of memory. I was a small child craning my neck to look up at a tall man with piercing blue eyes, a blond man who stroked my hair and asked my name. Just that, nothing else. Who was he? *What* was he to me?

I went for long rambles beyond the gardens, hands curled into fists, lips smiling at skittish workers while inwardly I seethed against Tomás, not just for destroying my marriage with his reckless scheme, but because he had made me doubt my very identity. The question that now shadowed me all the time was existential. *Who am I?* A more unsettling question added, *Who and what is Benjamín to me?*

Tomás was on an existential quest of his own. Bent on retrieving some lost portion of himself, he wandered through the rubble of the sugar cane field that he had burned. Perhaps he hoped to find a door latch or a belt buckle or a nail, something, anything that he could hold between his fingers and claim as his grandfather's. Or perhaps he just needed to find some evidence that his mother's village really had existed. He did find a few fragments of broken clay pots. My poor Tomás. In truth he had lost more than the village that he never knew. By rejecting him I had deprived him of his dream of us, and that genuinely pained me. There was no denying that I was also depriving him of a shortcut to wealth and power, and that I regretted far less, for hadn't he manipulated the will as much for his gain as for mine? How was I to forgive that?

Anger and despair stalked me. I could have turned to the Bible or to Swedenborg for help, but I had the absurd notion that it would be blasphemous to read such works in my current state of mind. So I combed the house for something secular and dramatic and utterly escapist. It soon became apparent that my mother-in-law only read journals on local politics or agriculture. Samuel was no better, favoring works of theology, most of which were in Latin. I knew that Rodolfo, the only Anglophile of the family, had a fairly extensive collection of British novels and poetry, but I'd sooner struggle through Thomas Aquinas with my dismal school girl Latin than risk entering what was now Tomás's lair. I realized with a pang that Benjamín's favorite books had also been relegated to Rodolfo's room—Ben's former prison and now Tomás stronghold. I thought with longing about my husband's love for Spanish poetry and for birds. Yes, I would have been glad to read his books on ornithology, simply because he loved them. But for now they would have to remain out of my reach.

Is there nothing for me to read in all of San Serafín? I railed.

As a last-ditch effort, I turned to the playroom which yielded several children's books in Spanish and one copy of *Aesop's Fables* in French. Armed with these, I tried to make myself comfortable on Eva's uncomfortable Empire chairs and escape for a few hours. Instead my mind kept slipping into the enigma of my origins. When I finally admitted to myself that Tomás might be right, I rapped on Cadwally's door.

"What's the real reason that you didn't keep any photographs of my parents?"

My grandfather stared at me briefly and returned to his work, directing his paintbrush to make a swirl of purple. "I told you long ago. Scraps of paper do not constitute the person."

"So you tore them up?"

"No. I just didn't burden myself with them."

"Didn't you stop to think that I might want to know what my parents looked like? Look at me, Cadwally. I need for you to tell me the truth, now—before God," I added in unconscious imitation of Benjamín.

My grandfather sighed and gave me his full attention. Furrowing his brow, his bushy eyebrows drew a nearly straight line across his forehead. He waited. I vacillated. Then the questions burst out. "Was the general my father? Were Emily and Joshua Brentt just a convenient lie to protect him?"

"What's this about, Isabel?"

"Just answer the question, because I no longer know who I am. Tomás tells me I'm the general's illegitimate daughter. How can I refute him when I have no memory of my parents, no records, no diaries, no letters, not even a faded photograph?"

"To the best of my knowledge, your parents were Emily and Joshua Brentt."

"Don't you start that, too, doubting what should be rock sure!"

"I wasn't there when you were born." He spread his arms with palette in one hand, brush in the other. "One day I received a letter from Joshua informing me that I had a granddaughter. Two years later a stranger wrote to inform me that you had been orphaned. So I traveled to an orphanage in Oklahoma City and brought you back with me."

"Oh, wonderful! For all we know someone confused the papers and gave you the wrong orphan to raise."

"Of course not," he chuckled. "I knew you were Joshua's from the moment I laid eyes on you."

"How could you be so sure?"

"Because you looked just like him as a child. You have his eyes and so many of his expressions."

"I do?" Hope must have colored my voice. Then I doubted again and grew sullen. "What about my mother? You never talk about her. It's as if you just made her up."

"I never met her, Isabel. We've been through all this before."

"Tell me again. I need to know."

"There isn't much to tell. I was living in Cuernavaca when your father wrote to say he had married Emily. Later, he wrote again to announce that you had come into the world."

"He must have sent photos. Oh, I know. 'Scraps of paper do not make a person.' But those scraps would have made me feel like a more complete person. I can't believe that you would rob me of such a basic right. How could you just toss away—"

"There was no scrapbook."

"Not even one photograph?"

He chewed on his lower lip. "There *was* one. It was of you with your parents, a christening picture. It was framed. Glass and frame shattered, of course. A neighbor found it—and you—in the wreckage after the tornado. At the orphanage I was able to identify you as my granddaughter by identifying Joshua in that photograph."

I tensed. "Where is it?"

He looked away.

"What happened to it? Please, Cadwally, where is the photograph?"

"I lost it," he answered softly.

"How do you lose something that important?"

My grandfather looked haggard as he stared at his hands. His lower lip trembled and I knew the truth.

"You were drunk when you lost it. That's it, isn't it. You miserable old sot!"

I had finally said it, breaking the spell of denial that I had conjured as a child. No more pretending. No more excuses. He was a pathetic old drunkard. I slammed the door on the way out, but I was still uncertain about my origins. Had I been duped by the old sot?

32

THE MISTRESS

LATE THAT NIGHT when the servants had retired to their rooftop rooms or to their small cottages, and when all the birds in the aviary had roosted into feathery stillness, Tomás knocked on my door. I was in no mood to let him in and then have to fend him off. I kept the door bolted.

"Isa, we need to talk."

"Go away. It's late." I drew my bathrobe tighter around my neck.

"Just give me a few minutes. I'll tell you everything, but not out here where Stone-face lurks," he whispered, and I could picture him rolling his eyes. I didn't laugh.

What makes you think I want that Tacha woman to see you enter my room? I thought. Yet, because I desperately needed some truth-telling, I let him into Eva's suite—my suite if only I could let myself believe it, which I could not. Not yet. I took a seat on a sofa near an ornate fireplace. Tenting my legs, I hugged my knees in an attempt to look relaxed. I was a hen watching a weasel. The weasel paced.

"I went looking for the general the day before he died," he began without preamble.

"Why?"

"To thank him for my education."

"So you said. I thought you hated him."

"I do. The bastard destroyed my home and my village. Then he had the effrontery to think he could make amends by forcing four of us boys to be educated at his expense." Tomás stopped and fixed his dark eyes on me. "Nyman never asked us if we wanted to be yanked away from our families. A general gives orders and things get done. No questions. No debate. And yes, they made gentlemen of us. They taught us how to speak, how to dress, and not to wipe our mouth on our sleeve, but they took away our heritage and all that matters."

I didn't know what to say. There was a long pause. "What happened to the other boys?"

"I don't know. One ran away. I lost track of the other two when they graduated. They were older and ignored me. I had to stay on, alone in the rooming house, alone in that city of strangers. I gained a career in exchange for the lost years of my youth. So yes, I hated him."

"Then why bother to thank him?"

Tomás started to pace again, avoiding eye contact. "Maybe I wanted to tell him what I really thought of him. Maybe I wanted the pleasure of spitting in his face. Or maybe I wanted to kill him. I'm still not sure which." He ran a hand through his coarse hair.

"Did you, Tomás? Did you kill the general?"

He dropped into a chair opposite the sofa and looked steadily into my face. "No. But I'll tell you, Isa, under other circumstances I might have. It's just that I was unnerved by what I found."

"What was he like?" I leaned toward him as if we were kids again sharing a secret.

"I expected an officer in military finery, you know, with more medals on his chest than fleas on a dog. 'Or at least a gentleman in an expensive dressing gown or a frock coat. But that's not what was living in that room—the darkest, foulest room you can imagine." Tomás was at ease now that I seemed more curious than angry. "The room smelled as if it had been shut up for years. The only light came from one flickering candle. He had a cot with a log for a pillow—a log, for cripes sake."

"I know. I saw it, remember?"

"Yes, yes." He nodded. His hair which he normally slicked back with brilliantine kept falling across his eyes. "So you have some idea of how the richest man in Mexico lived for fifteen years."

"How did he look?"

"Like a cadaver. Even in that sickly light I could see that his skin was chalk-white. His eyes . . . I've never seen anything quite like them. Restless and tormented. The great tyrant I had hated for years was nothing but a wretched scrap of humanity."

"Was he insane?" I held my breath.

"I'm not sure. He made sense most of the time. 'What did you study?' he asked without looking up from his book. 'Law, sir.' His head jerked up. 'Can you draw up a will?' 'I can.' 'Good! My lawyer high-tailed it to Europe.' And here's where fate stepped in, Isa. Listen and tell me that the hand of providence wasn't involved." Tomás leaned further toward me, resting his elbows on his knees, his face fully animated. "He wanted to leave everything to an Isabela Brentano. Did you hear that, Isabel Brentt? Isabela Bren-ta-no! No doubt one of his many mistresses."

I was on my feet. "No, you must have heard wrong. There couldn't be such a person."

"Oh, I heard right. The old raptor kept repeating her name, and I knew I had him! This was the moment!" Tomás tightened his fist and drew it to his chest as if making a vow.

All the while my thoughts bolted down a different road. A cliff. *Isabela Brentano? My real mother?* Tomás rolled on, unstoppable.

"This was the chance to avenge my family's village and in the process to make you very wealthy." His eyes grew luminous with the memory. "So while the old man muttered and reminisced about his Isabela Brentano—"

"No! You're making this up, and it's evil of you, Tomás. Evil!" My anguish seemed to startle him, as if he had noticed an earthquake only as the roof over his head began to groan.

"It's the truth."

"Swear by your mother. Swear it!"

"By my mother whom I hold sacred, I swear that it happened just as I'm telling you."

Tomás reached for me as I went down on my knees. Then we were both on our knees.

"Oh, God! Oh, God!" I sobbed. "I married Benjamín and I love him so desperately!"

I clung to Tomás as I had during the worst of thunderstorms, body quivering like a newborn chick blown out of its nest. What I was experiencing now, though, was a whole different level of fear—fear mingled with a despair beyond anything I had ever imagined possible. Oh, God! Had I married my own half-brother?

"Oh, Isa, I'm sorry. I'm so stupidly blunt! I should have prepared you for this. Please don't cry. None of this is your fault."

Through the long minutes or hours or decades of that reckoning, I clung to him as I continued to sob. At that point I felt beyond the reach of words. In the labyrinth I had been able to dismiss Tomás's hints about my origins as imaginings sprung from jealousy. Isabela Brentano I could not brush aside so easily. As the full implications of Tomás's disclosure crashed over me, wave after wave, I felt all the moorings of my life break loose. Brother? Husband? Father? Mother? Grandfather? Every relationship uncertain. Scrambled.

I sobbed uncontrollably. When the storm had run its course, I grew still. A drowsy calm settled over me. Tomás helped me to my feet and into the next room.

"Sleep, Isa. We can talk in the morning."

I wanted to protest as he removed my bathrobe and put me to bed, but I don't think I had ever felt more physically and emotionally drained. I muttered something that sounded incoherent even to me and closed my eyes. Nestling into the feather pillows and silken sheets, I dove deep. I did not stir even as I felt his lips on my forehead in a soft kiss. The last thing I remember hearing was the gentle closing of the door.

33

THE PACT

In San Serafín one always woke up with the birds, hundreds of them from the jungles of Mexico and Central America. Some flew about freely. Most were prisoners in the aviary or in assorted cages sprinkled throughout the house and gardens. All of them exercised their vocal cords. So I woke up with them, groggy, my eyelids puffy from my crying bout. Reaching for my robe, I stepped outside. Instantly, the young day rushed to embrace me, sky smiling peach and marigold yellow, tinting the snowy blanket of Iztac. Nearby, the warrior-volcano shifted his mantle over his shoulders as he continued to guard his beloved. I hurried to Tomás's room and rapped on the door, not timidly but with impatience.

What are you doing, Isabel? Aunt Delphine would have gasped. You can't go into a man's bedroom!

Oh, dear aunt, of what use are the proprieties now?

Not waiting, I let myself in. Tomás lay bare-chested, arms clamped over the rumpled bedspread, his hair a wild black forest.

"Wake up." I shook him firmly by the shoulder. A shock of recognition ran through me—an ember-memory fanned to life. The first time I touched Benjamín's bare chest, I had marveled that it seemed both flesh and rock. When Tomás turned toward me I drew back, yet my resolve remained strong. There's nothing like a good night's sleep to reshape the world from dismal to tolerable.

"I need to hear the rest of your confession."

He groaned. "Now? What time is it?"

"Tell me how you manipulated the will."

He groaned again. Then he sat up and smiled. "Should you even be in here? What if old Stone-face sees you leaving my room? You'd be ruined and I'd be forced to marry you."

"Don't be absurd." Yet the thought of that Tacha woman spreading malicious rumors, along with everything that Tomás's smile insinuated, made me less bold. Benjamín was right. I was a rocking horse, easily shifting back and forth between recklessness and caution. "All right. Meet—"

"No, stay." Tomás grasped my hand. "Let the old hag think what she wants. You're the boss here, Isa. La patrona. If she gets the least uppity with you, we—you can toss her out."

"Yes. I suppose so." I perched on the edge of the bed with an eye for the door. "Tell me what happened after the general—" I could not bring myself to say, 'my father,' because I understood that words have a power to make something true or seem to be true. So despite my breakdown the night before, I was not prepared to fully accept the unthinkable, not now in the light of this new day. There had to be some other explanation. "What happened after he spoke that woman's name?"

That woman? Were we talking about my mother? Not Emily Valberg, the school teacher that Cadwally had told me about in his abridged version of my past, but my actual, biological mother? Tomás was watching me attentively now, pocketing his smile for later. Perhaps he was taking in the full damage of last night's revelation. "Are you sure you want to go into this just now?"

"Now!" My anger flared like the sun's rays that suddenly bumped into the dresser mirror. It might have been better to retain my sorrow a bit longer. Tomás understood anger. He could defeat it, outtalk it, outsmart it. Tears bewildered him. Since my tone was testy, he could sit back and calmly cross his arms. But at least he told me the truth.

"I did as the general asked. I wrote a new will, but instead of naming the said Isabela Brentano his sole heir, I wrote Isabel Brentt. For good measure I added the phrase 'granddaughter of Cadwallader Brentt.' Two hours later I returned with a notary public to notarize the document. The general couldn't find his glasses, so I moved the one candle in that dismal room closer to me and read the document aloud, deliberately misreading the name I had written and skipping over the Cadwallader phrase. The general signed it, and the notary public, who kept a handkerchief pressed to his nose the whole time, also signed it without reading it and bolted out of there. It was that easy."

I stared straight ahead, showing neither anger nor sorrow. Tomás uncrossed his arms.

"Isa?" He spoke the name tentatively.

"Oh, Tomás. All that education so you could become a crook?"

"I'm not a crook."

"What else do you call an attorney who deceives his client? You've caused so much harm with that stunt."

"I never meant to hurt you. I swear it. I even thought I was helping you."

"By ruining my marriage? How could you have done that to me?"

"By thinking about my mother's village and the house that was burned over her head; by remembering that my grandfather died in prison when he tried to fight back; by remembering that my mother was raped and abandoned. I thought about *them*, and God help me, I didn't consider for a moment how all this would impact your marriage."

"You've ruined my life, you and the general."

"How can I make it up to you?" He grasped my hands. No sinner crumpled over in a confessional could have looked more penitent. "Tell me what to do."

"Help me prove Benjamín's innocence."

Tomás dropped my hands and tossed his head back in exasperation. "Isa, the man was convicted on the strength of his own confession—"

"Of what? Of having thrust his father against the wall when they were arguing. Maybe that one thrust dealt a fatal blow to the head, but I seriously doubt it. And yes, Benjamín admitted that he had masqueraded as Samuel. But as I keep telling you, it was the only way that he could gain admittance into his father's house after he had been disowned. There was no malicious intent in that deception."

"With that duplicity, and by actually letting his innocent brother go through the ordeal of a murder trial, he—"

"I'm sure he never thought that Samuel would be found guilty."

"Probably not, but he still put his brother through hell. With that alone Benjamín Nyman lost all credibility. I cannot regain it for him, much as you and my mother harass me about it. Case closed."

"No, because Benjamín is innocent. He only thinks that he killed his father, but he didn't."

"So you keep telling me. Just how the devil do you know that? Were you there, quietly reading in a corner of the general's room?"

I headed for the door.

"Isa, wait." I heard him thrust aside the bedcovers and knew without turning around that he was putting on his pants. He hurried to rephrase his question. "I only mean, how can you be so sure of his innocence since you were not there that night?"

I still didn't dare tell him about my experience in San Justín because I knew he would only scoff. When I calculated that it was safe to turn around, I offered the only other evidence in my arsenal.

"I know my husband. He's volatile, but he is not a murderer. Find the real murderer and have the case reopened. That's what you can do for me, Tomás."

He began to pace. "*Por Dios!* How can you still believe in his innocence? Didn't you read the accounts of the trial that I gave you?" I yanked the door open and stepped onto the veranda. He hurried after me. "Well, did you read them?"

"Every one of them." I walked on without looking at him. At the end of the corridor, I stopped and faced him. "It's all circumstantial evidence. You said so yourself."

"A confession of guilt is not circumstantial. Isa, listen to me. I'll fight your fights, but I can't change facts."

"He's innocent, Tomás."

"Prove that to me. Give me something concrete, not just a woman's stubborn love."

That stumped me at first. And then I thrust myself on him as hard as I could, slamming his head against the wall. He shot a startled look at me, his hand reaching for the back of his head.

"I know I had that coming—"

"Are you dead?"

"What?"

"Did I kill you?"

"Not yet."

"Did I crack your skull? I heard your head slam hard. The so-called experts at the trial said the general's skull suffered severe trauma. How traumatized is your skull?"

"It's felt better."

"Is it cracked? Are your brains oozing onto your toes?"

"You're saying it would take more than this—"

"Yes, and Ben shoved his father against the wall only once."

"How the blazes do you know that?"

"Because he insisted on that even while confessing to his outburst. I believe him, Tomás."

"Good for you. I don't."

"Only three people were there the night of the murder: the cook, her adolescent daughter, and the porter. From the newspaper accounts I gather that the cook is a big, boastful woman who is not very bright. Her daughter was just plain weepy and scared at the trial, hardly the murderer type. But the porter, Eufemio Rosarito, the witness who gave the most damaging testimony, was a former soldier, a man who—"

"Eufemio Rosarito is loyalty incarnate. You're talking about a man who allowed French soldiers to torture him during the invasion rather than reveal the general's whereabouts."

"So? That was decades ago. People can change and not always for the better."

"Forget it, Isa. He's not your murderer. He had no motive, whereas your disowned husband had every reason to want to thrash the old man."

"Like you, but you didn't kill him. Neither did Benjamín. I believe both of you. So it has to be Eufemio Rosarito since no one else visited the general that night. In fact, no one could enter or leave San Justín once the door was locked, and only Eufemio had the keys."

Tomás began to pace again. I could see by his scowl that I had blasted a few holes into that formidable skepticism of his.

"You saw the place," I pressed on. "San Justín is a fortress. Don't you see, Tomás? If no one could get in, the murderer had to be inside all along. Who else could it be but Eufemio Rosarito? Find him and reopen the case."

"How? He high-tailed it after the trial."

"I heard doña Manuela say that she had offered Eufemio a home in San Serafín for the rest of his days, but that he had preferred to return to his village."

"What village?"

"She didn't know, only that it was somewhere in Morelos."

"Marvelous. You're asking me to neglect my practice, pitiful fledgling that it is, so I can look for one particular bean in a warehouse chock full of them. How the hell am I going to do that?"

"Morelos is the smallest state in the republic."

"No. That's Tlaxcala."

"All right. Morelos is the second smallest. How many Eufemio Rosaritos can there be? I know you can find him, Tomás. Question him. You know how to get people to talk. Get the courts to reopen the case and I'll deed back the lands to the villagers."

"And keep San Serafín for yourself, as a guarantee. . . ."

"No. Once you've done your part, I intend to deed the hacienda back to Manuela Nyman." He groaned. I pressed on. "I'll give it back but with the condition that she and her children agree *in writing* to forfeit all rights to the village lands. You can draw up the document yourself. I don't know why I didn't think of this sooner."

"They're Nymans and not to be trusted."

"Well, you'll have to start having a little trust. Otherwise, forget about your precious land reform."

Tomás grabbed me and shook me as if I were a rag doll. "Damn it, Isa! How do I make you understand? We could have it all, everything you ever wanted!"

"I *had* everything I wanted, and you took it away from me."

"Isa," he held me tighter. "I won't let you throw it all away. I'll make you—"

"Make me what? Love you against my will, like those men who raped your mother?"

If I had emptied a bucket of Arctic water over his head, he could not have looked more stunned. His lips parted, but no words found their way out. For a few seconds the corners of his mouth plunged downward as if in a silent wail, his pain so palpable that I wanted to stroke his face. I didn't. This was not the moment to show the least sign of weakness. We were standing at a vital crossroad. Or was it more like a rain-slick precipice? Tomás sensed it too. Releasing me, he headed for the staircase, hands clenching and unclenching as I'd seen him do as a boy, clenching and unclenching rather than cry.

When we spoke a few hours later he was all business, as if nothing out of the ordinary had passed between us. As usual, he cut to the chase. "You realize that even if I succeed in finding your Eufemio Rosarito and having the case reopened, there is absolutely no guarantee that your brother . . . ," he caught himself, "that Benjamín Nyman will be found not guilty the second time around."

"I know."

"And it wouldn't solve the problem of your marriage and the probable illegality of it."

I gazed evenly into Tomás's eyes, dark wells that they were. "True, but I need to do this for Benjamín even if our marriage ends up being annulled or whatever." Had I just admitted what only last night was unthinkable? "Just do three things for me: find Eufemio, get his confession, and have the case reopened. We'll leave the rest to divine providence."

"I'm surprised that you're not more interested in having me find Isabela Brentano. With your moral rectitude, I should think you'd be ready to hand everything over to her as your . . . as the general intended."

I stiffened. "Whoever she is, or was, she has no moral right to doña Manuela's property any more than we do. The hacienda came from doña Manuela's family, not the general's. Ethically, it was never his to give away. Our job, yours and mine, is to set the record straight, exonerate Benjamín if we can, and undo the wrong we committed by evicting the rightful owner of San Serafín. The other matter . . ." Here I faltered. Establishing my true identity mattered enormously, but I no longer felt entitled to put my needs first. Our usurpation of the hacienda horrified me the more I considered it. "Oh, Tomás. We need to regain our integrity again, yours and mine. Will you help me? Will you promise to help me?"

He stood without moving a muscle. Then with all deliberation, he brought a closed fist to his heart and struck it twice in the solemn vow that he had devised in our childhood, the vow of a Tepanecan-Tlahuican warrior. I did likewise. We had a pact.

34

DOÑA MANUELA'S LETTER

Tomás set out on his quest the very next day. Before leaving, he had me step into the library. Agapito Alfonso, the young man we had promoted from assistant manager to full administrator of the hacienda, stood by the desk, straw hat gripped in both hands in a respectful stance. The plantation accountant joined us just then and also bared his head. Tomás handed a sheet of paper to me.

"What's this?"

"Our agreement."

Since when is our Tepaneca-Tlahuica vow not enough? I would have asked if not for the two men watching us.

"Please read it carefully, señora. Then sign here, if you would be so kind."

I felt a stab of sadness at his sudden distrust, yet I was careful to read every word on that one-page document. We were no longer children but offspring of a corrupt world. I signed the contract. The hacienda accountant, who was also a notary public, witnessed and signed it as did Agapito Alfonso.

"This copy is for you, *señora*," Tomás spoke with aloof politeness. "Keep it in a safe place. I'll hang on to the second one and will mail a third copy to an attorney friend of mine in the D.F."

When the two employees had left the library, Attorney Tepaneca morphed back into Tomás. "Don't be upset with me, Isa. We no longer live in the world of our childhood. In the adult world vows need to be legalized."

"So you still trust me?"

"Of course."

"Then tear up all three copies." I challenged though we both knew he wouldn't.

He leaned against the desk, crossing one leg comfortably over the other. "Let me tell you something else about the adult world. See this thing?" He held up Manuela Nyman's hefty key ring. "These are the keys to the kingdom. They open every door in the property and this safe. So these more than anything else make you la patrona of San Serafín. Never let them out of your sight. Wear the key ring at all times. Here, clip it to your belt."

"I can do that myself, thank you." I slapped his hands away and for a moment I thought he was going to pull me to him in another kiss. I could see the impulse wash over him and recede like a wave. I took a step back. He smiled affably and I realized he had not given up his dreams. I sensed he was already at work constructing a new scheme. Yes, he would seek out Eufemio Rosarito and reopen Benjamín's case in order to appease me. But he would not forget to play the incest card, which would of course force me to reject my husband. Yet, didn't Tomás know it yet? Whatever Benjamín was to me, Tomás was so very much more of a brother, now and always.

"I've paid the *Rurales* and sent them on their way." He was all business. "The sentries are back on duty and will protect the patrona who will be paying their salaries. Rest assured, the people of San Serafín are with you now, or at least not against you. I've authorized Agapito Alfonso to give everyone the pay raises we promised."

"Like Julius Caesar buying off the masses? Can loyalty be bought so easily?"

"Trust me. In a week, they'll beam every time you smile at them. In a month they'll have forgotten the old dragon."

"Please don't speak of her that way."

"There you go again with the guilt. Isa, you have good work to do here until I return."

"What can I possibly do? What do I know about anything?"

"Do you still remember how to read? Then you could start by replacing the school teacher who quit or died. Give the children the gift they most need: literacy. Leave the rest to Agapito. I know he's young, but he seems bright and capable enough to administer the hacienda. In any case, you've got his loyalty."

"Wonderful. That's *one* who doesn't despise me."

"Everything begins with one," Tomás winked.

The next day he mounted a prized Nyman Vizcarra Arabian. I watched him canter down the long lane of fig trees until he vanished around a bend. Late that afternoon, when strong winds startled palm fronds into wild, futile attempts at flight, one of the sentries found me in the inner courtyard.

"Señora," he panted, "La patrona is outside the gates. She begs you to speak with her."

"Doña Manuela?"

I ran to Cadwally's room and found him passed out on the bed. An empty bottle of bourbon—pilfered from the hacienda *bodegas*, no doubt—glared at me from his bed stand. I wrung my hands as I had done so often in my childhood. "Wake up, Cadwally! I need you! Please wake up."

Oh, why did I let Tomás go? He'd know what to do. Don't we need something in writing from her before I let her in?

A servant found me pacing in the cloistered garden and handed me a letter.

Daughter,

I humbly beg you to forgive me for the way I reacted at my eviction. I have been beside myself with grief over

Benjamín's tragedy and then suddenly the loss of my
home. This is the only home I have ever known. I was
born in this house and became a bride and then a mother
here. I love San Serafín with all my heart. Yet even in my
profound loss, I've come to realize that appearances can
be deceiving and that I may have misjudged you. I saw
your grief the day of my eviction, and I know that it was
genuine. Also, I've come to acknowledge that it is not
your fault that Lucio chose you as his sole heir. In light of
Benjamín's tragedy, everything else pales by comparison,
even my eviction. But I beg you in the name of Christian
charity, do not turn me out. I ask only for one room to
call my own and to be allowed to continue to enjoy and to
care for the birds in my aviary.

Please, let us put aside our differences and begin
again. We live in uncertain times. The revolution is not
over. Fighting will break out again. The road ahead will
be difficult for both of us without Benjamín at our side,
but together we can better face whatever we must.
Blessed are the generous in spirit.

Manuela Vizcarra de Nyman

I read the letter several times. Then I headed for the entrance
courtyard. Sentries watched me from their posts high along the
wall. A sudden gust blew strands of hair into my eyes.

"Open the gates!" My voice shook like a sapling bowing to
the wind.

35

ENTER THE DRAGON

"*YA REGRESÓ LA SEÑORA!*" The call went out, quickly spreading like a bucket of water splashed onto a glass table. "The señora is back!" Servants rushed into the courtyard by the church.

"*Señora! Bendito sea Dios!*" I heard Tacha exclaim with genuine emotion in her voice.

Doña Manuela entered the house with the fanfare of a queen. She strode past me into the dining room, removing her hat and gloves as she went. Tacha took them from her as if they were holy relics. I hurried after my mother-in-law.

"Señora, may I offer you some dinner? Lupe, please bring the señora some soup. It's quite wonderful, señora. And would you like some coffee or tea?" I gushed.

Manuela took my seat at the head of the table. "My servants know what I like."

"Yes, of course." I tried to laugh. Taking a deep breath, I also took a seat at the table, placing myself on my mother-in-law's right. "Señora, first of all, I must beg your forgiveness. Please believe me that we were trying to act for the greater good, but that doesn't excuse our lack of civility. I can't begin to tell you how terrible I feel about all of this. Tomás ... Mr. Tepaneca meant well. He was simply enforcing the letter of the law. But you and I must not let such legalities come—"

I stopped as servants brought in doña Manuela's customary dinner: two tamales served on a dish bearing the family coat of arms, and a *telera,* a crusty roll escorted by small silver bowls with different types of marmalades. A small silver pitcher emitted the unmistakable fragrance of cinnamon sticks and chocolate *atole,* part cereal, part beverage, that no one made better than the hacienda's cook. I waited until the servants had left. Only Tacha remained, Tacha who took up a position a few feet behind doña Manuela's chair, her face an Olmec mask.

"As I was saying . . . well, especially when I read your letter . . . of course you can stay here as long as you want. This is *your* home, and you don't ever have to leave it if you don't want to, señora. You have my word on that."

Doña Manuela thrust a knife into the *telera* and slowly scooped out the hot dough.

"How long have you and your lawyer been lovers?"

"Wha—?" My breath snagged. "No! There has *never* been anything like that between us! Only friendship. Tomás—Mr. Tepaneca is like a brother. We used to play together as children. I assure you, I hadn't seen him in years, not until the reading of the will. Surely you remember that I had been living in the United States for close to five years when I met . . ." I had not meant to go down that road.

"Rodolfo." She spoke his name calmly. "And where was that childhood friend of yours while you busied yourself with two of my sons?"

I felt as if I'd just spilled coffee all over her tablecloth and was scurrying to mop it up with a meager handkerchief. "He was in the D.F. He'd been living there for years. Your husband had chosen him and three others to be educated at his expense."

"And this is how your *friend* repays his benefactor?" She carefully buried a teaspoon of preserves in the hollow that she had carved in her crusty roll.

"No, of course not." But of course, she was right. Yet how could I admit it to her without betraying Tomás? "I know how it must look to you, but Tomás, Mr. Tepaneca, really is—was—your husband's attorney acting on his behalf. Is it really so strange that the general would turn to one of the young men whom he educated, especially the one who had studied law?"

"No. It's actually quite logical. Lucio always made sure to get a full return on every one of his financial investments. And when you come right down to it, it's actually quite logical that you should inherit everything." I had the impression that Doña Manuela was about to pin me to the wall like a butterfly. "With Lucio's attorney as your lover, what could be more reasonable?"

"No. Please believe me. He's a friend. A brother."

"A brother?" Her eyebrows shot up in mock surprise. "Given his Indian heritage, I assume you mean that as in 'the brotherhood of mankind'? Or do you mean it literally, in which case the taboo against incest must not worry you?"

That hit a nerve. I jumped to my feet. "No! You've got it all wrong." I steadied my shaking hands by leaning forward and pressing them to the table. "As I've said again and again, I don't know why General Nyman left everything to me." But that was now a lie and I knew it. Could she read that on my face? "I only agreed to evict you—for which I am truly sorry—because I believed we were acting for the greater good."

"Whose good? Not mine."

"The villagers of Santa . . . Santa . . ." I couldn't think of the blessed name. "I only wanted to restore what is rightfully theirs."

"Vizcarra lands?" Doña Manuela continued with maddening equanimity.

"Just the small portion that legally belongs to them."

"The Vizcarras have owned San Serafín since the sixteenth century. Don't tell me what belongs and what doesn't belong to us, or whose rights have been trampled."

"I'm sorry." Cowered, I sat down again, doubting myself; doubting the deed; doubting there ever had been a Santa Lupita de las Milpas. Perhaps Tomás had made it up and the so-called survivors were simply a few senile old men and one crabby woman. And Rosa too. Remembering her grief, I couldn't help saying: "We both know that the village was burned down."

She pressed a napkin delicately to her lips, then pinned me with her fathomless stare. "Yes, my husband did act harshly with the squatters, but he acted within the law."

The memory of the two old men in Rosa's house, the care with which they handled the ancient deed, surfaced. "I don't mean any disrespect, señora, but law and justice are not always the same thing. If you could see the villagers' documents as I have, I think you'd agree that the Spanish crown gave them clear title to their lands from the start. Mr. Tepaneca, assures me—"

Manuela Vizcarra pushed back her chair. "And I assure *you* that the Nyman Vizcarras only take what is theirs"—*unlike some people.* The phrase hung unspoken but clearly implied.

"Señora, I want you to know that I fully intend . . ."

"Your intentions are of no interest to me, Isabel Brentt." My mother-in-law headed to her room. The interview was over.

36

EL MONSTRO

THAT NIGHT IN Eva's room, I hardly slept. In the morning I felt almost as groggy as my hung-over grandfather. Later that day when he discovered that his stash had vanished and that there wasn't a drop of liquor anywhere in the whole hacienda, he grew as irritable as a wet cat.

"Use that key ring of yours and find me something," he grumbled. "Even some *rompope!*"

But there were no bottles of even mildly spiked eggnog, and no sign of doña Manuela all day. When I knocked on her door that evening, I was answered with silence, loud and unnerving. By the next morning, Cadwally was fully in the grip of *el monstro,* as I had named his darkest mood when I was a child. The monster always spirited him away, leaving in his place a man with feverish eyes who could not see me; a man who rifled through his studio, overturning boxes and tin cans; a man who stormed his way through bureaus and cupboards in his desperate search for a bottle. Here in San Serafín he had to control himself, yet we both knew that he could not last much longer. I hurried after him as he headed for the stables. I could read his intent by the single-mindedness of his stride.

"Wait! Don't go, Cadwally." I grabbed hold of his arm. "You promised you'd stay with me."

"I can't," he said without looking at me, his eyes fixed somewhere far away.

As if the grooms or doña Manuela had guessed his need, his carpet bag and the box with his art supplies had been loaded into a buggy. It was a two-seater. Cadwally climbed alongside the driver.

"Why did you let in the dragon?" my grandfather grumbled.

"I had to. It was a matter of conscience."

"Well, now you can live with her and your conscience."

"Don't go, Cadwally. I'll send one of the servants to Cuernavaca to buy a whole box load of whatever you want. Just stay."

His foot tapped the storm apron with nervous energy. "No," he kept his gaze straight ahead. "It just keeps vanishing here. The servants steal it," he mumbled. "Anyway, you obviously don't need me now that the very culpable—capable—doña Manuela is back."

"That's not true."

He finally looked at me. "I left something for you in my room," he winked like a mischievous boy who offers you a frog as a peace offering. Then he nodded to the driver who flicked the reins. I jumped back as the buggy moved out. "Be a good girl! I'll be back!" Cadwally called out almost cheerfully.

"It's *el monstro*," I muttered aloud, as if being able to hear the words would divert my rising anger. It didn't. Back in my room my own *monstro* caught up with me. *You rotten old sot!* I railed inwardly as I tossed a pillow off the bed, then a second and a third one. *Your liquor always matters more than I do! Always—*

Later, when the storm had run its course and the last raindrops of self-pity crept down my cheeks, I remembered his reference to a gift.

I don't want anything from you, my inner monster snarled. Yet when I stepped back onto the veranda, my footsteps led me straight to the general's bedroom that Cadwally had used as his temporary studio. Lucio Nyman welcomed me from his heavy gilt frame. I gazed into the blue eyes. My father's? *No. Please!* The implications that had so tormented Benjamín assaulted me again. *Incest.* The very word terrified me. I turned my attention to the desk that Cadwally had recently used as a worktable. That's when I spotted it, a sketch of doña Manuela. It had been executed with such realism that I actually recoiled from it. Was it left behind by that portrait artist, Blasco Prieto? I wondered. No, this was no idealization of my mother-in-law. The artist had captured the tightness of her mouth, tight as the hair pulled back into a tight knot. Tight as a blasting primer that waits for the order to obliterate walls and armies. Cadwally drew this?

There it was in the right-hand corner, Cadwallader Brentt's unmistakable circular hieroglyph-of-a-signature. So this is your gift? Very funny.

I wanted to tear it up but couldn't. The wretched thing was so masterfully drawn. This was no two-dimensional, stylized representation of a face like the ones in our home murals. This was photographic in its details. It was all there: the Spanish cast of doña Manuela's features; the austerity of a raven's plumage against the pale, pale skin. Working with nothing but a pencil, he had captured not just the outer form, but the inner person—the eyes with their dark light, implacable as an inquisitor's. No, this was far more accurate than a photograph, for don't people generally project some kind of persona as they stare into a camera? Cadwally had not given her that luxury. Even the thin-lipped compression of a smile was unmasked, that smile of hers that silently sneered, *you poor fool.*

I hated Cadwally's gift, his idea of a joke or the exclamation mark to his reprimand, *why did you let in the dragon?* Yet I had to hand it to him. His talent could not have been clearer here. But what exactly did he expect me to do with the wretched thing? Hang it over my bed? Carry it around for luck?

Folding it several times, I shoved the sketch into my pocket.
General Nyman watched me from his gold-leafed frame, his eyes
smiling like Benjamín's with good-natured condescension, as if
asking, *why do you worry so much?* You ask me that? Just then
I glanced toward the center of the room and forgot him. Heavy
and bright as a waterfall, a shaft of light was cascading from the
high cupola in the center of the room. Wading into it, I found
myself enveloped in a delicious kind of warmth, the sun full
upon my upturned face. It was only when I walked through that
cascade of light to the other side that I found Cadwally's astonishing gift.

Painted directly on one of the walls was a life-size portrait
of a man, a woman, and a baby in arms. Cadwally had only pen-
ciled in the bodies, but he had painted the faces with breathtak-
ing mastery. I was stunned. There we stood, my parents and I.
My mother was holding me and I was dressed in a long christening gown that trailed below her knees. In my elation, my attention jumped with squirrel-like exuberance from one face to the
other and back.

What struck me the most in that unexpected meeting? That
my father's eyes were intensely blue like Cadwally's and mine. If I
had been able to make Benjamín and Tomás materialize I would
have pointed triumphantly at those irises. My mother's eyes, on
the other hand, were a muted blue-gray. I continued to study
every detail. My father was smiling with easy self-confidence,
sans the general's condescension. In build, he was very much like
Cadwally—tall and lanky. Though not handsome in the classical
sense, his nose being a bit long and his face narrow, he appealed
to me instantly. His eyes exuded such intelligence and warmth
that I couldn't help smiling back at him. My mother was decidedly pretty, her features delicate and in perfect symmetry. What
pleased me more was that the expression in her eyes radiated an
intelligence on a par with my father's, and a gentleness to tug at

my heart. Her lips, soft and child-like, seemed seconds from smiling at me. A name floated up from the lake-bottom of memory.

"Mam-mam," I spoke it softly.

I reached to touch my mother's face but pulled back, afraid, I
suppose, of breaking the spell and finding only paint and plaster
instead of flesh. My hand hovered near cheeks, dove-gray eyes,
and hair champagne-blonde as my own. Then my attention went
back to my father. I took in the angularity of his face, the chest-
nut tone of his hair and a second name rose from the depths. A
toddler's remembrance.

"Da Da."

I murmured it, letting sound and sight solidify wisps of
memory—his arms reaching for me, his lips nuzzling my neck,
making me laugh. Hugging myself now, I laughed and cried at
the same time. Later, I would marvel at the speed with which my
grandfather had executed this, his finest painting, his rendition
of the lost photograph. For now I could only stare into faces that
were both new yet wonderfully familiar, finding in them my lost
identity. It was clear now that the sketch of Manuela Nyman was
his way of testifying to the accuracy of the portrait in oils that
he had left for me, glorious even if unfinished. Standing under
the cupola with the young couple, the disjointedness of my life
came together like the pieces of a torn photograph, fragments
successfully reunited. The unfinished portrait gave me something more—the freedom to love Benjamín Nyman without guilt
or dread. If Cadwally had been there beside me, even with his
monstro off its leash, I would have hugged him and not let go for
at least half a day.

I never want to leave this room! The thought spiraled into
the highest reaches of the cupola. I even had a smile for General
Nyman now that I could look into his face without the dread of
finding traces of myself. I could search it instead for suggestions
of Benjamín in the tilt of the head, the athletic build, and the lips,

those lips that I had loved kissing. In short, I could now regard my father-in-law's portrait without fear.

"You can stay, sir. No, I insist." I remember saying aloud with a flourish of my hand.

I finally tore myself away, but only because I intended to move into the general's room directly after breakfast. I forgot that Cadwallader Brentt was not the only one with a *monstro* lurking in the depths.

37

INVISIBLE

THE SAME DAY that I found my true identity, I became invisible. I didn't notice at first. Alone in the breakfast room, I paused to admire once again one of Cadwally's marvelous landscapes. It was executed with the exquisite realism of the Dutch masters. Cadwally dismissed it as just another of his "Tepoz-quickos," such a misnomer since he labored long and hard on them. Even though they had put food on our table, they continued to irk him. Perhaps he felt guilty for betraying his vastly more abstract aesthetics, but I loved them. The lush vegetation reminded me of the times that he had taken Tomás and me as children to explore the Tepozteco mountain, one of many peaks in the Sierra de Tepoztlán. We had loved the steep climb that led to an ancient pyramid; the thick tree roots along the way that stirred imaginings of a prehistoric time; the dark gloom of the canyon that seemed to separate our everyday world from this magical place.

You're a wonder, I intended to tell him when he returned to San Serafín.

Seating myself at the head of the table, I rang for breakfast. No one came. Driven by hunger, I headed into the kitchen. Every single servant, from the old Cook Bardomiana to the adolescent *galopina* at the bottom of the household hierarchy, ignored me. Were they punishing me for usurping the hacienda? Mortified, I grabbed a breakfast roll and retreated into the back garden. Things were no better there. Gardeners who had doffed their *hat* to me just one day ago were now walking past me as if I were a wilted hibiscus underfoot. It was the same with Sinforiano, the man who fed the birds and cleaned the aviary, and with the grooms in the stables and with the men unloading sacks to store in the silos, and with the laundresses whose conversation stopped until I was out of earshot. Even Agapito who owed his new position of administrator to me hurried by without so much as a nod.

I must earn their respect; earn their respect. My intention quickly escalated into a tortuous drumbeat, especially after I discovered that the hacienda already had a perfectly fine school of its own with a school master. I was not needed. Neither was I acknowledged. Students who stared at me ever so briefly quickly turned their attention back to the blackboard as their teacher rapped out times tables with a stick, his gaze sweeping past me. I fled to my parents whom I desperately needed to see again. However, the doorknob to the general's room had frozen into rigor mortis. I yanked on it and shoved my shoulder against the door.

I want this room, blast it! This is *my* house! I raged inwardly at doña Manuela.

The die was cast. I reached for the key ring that I had taken to wearing on my belt. Gone! Had I forgotten to attach it that morning? Was it still lying on my bedside table? Hurrying to Eva's suite, I found myself locked out of it too. In fact, every bedroom door was locked except for one: Emanuela's boring little room. Someone had moved my two trunks there, tossing in my clothes without any care. I might have felt outraged if not for the panic that drove me to empty the trunks onto the floor. Still no key ring.

I had to find it or all was lost. Hadn't Tomás warned me? What was there to do but to retrace my steps, all the way to the stables and beyond to the sugar silos and processing plant? What to do but to check under bushes along garden paths and ask stone-faced people to help me? But would they? The task loomed large and overwhelming. I suddenly thought of Tomás whom I had sent—how did he word it?—to find one bean in a warehouse chock full of them.

It seemed fair that I too should have my own impossible task. Alone, surrounded by people determined to ignore me, I searched the grounds. By sunset I was spent and retreated again to my room, if I could call it such. A dinner tray had been left for me—a clear message from my mother-in-law that she had no desire to share her *merienda* with me. Too tired to eat or to pick up the clothes that still carpeted the floor, I got into my night-gown and crawled under the covers, escaping into a long dark night.

The next morning I awoke to hammering, sawing, and what sounded like the unloading of heavy pallets of some kind. Part-ing the curtains on the one window that fronted the upstairs veranda, I could see a flurry of activity in doña Manuela's side of the house. At least a dozen men were at work. To my horror, they had removed the door to the general's room along with the cas-ing. Worse yet, masons had already bricked up more than half of the entrance. My mother-in-law clearly meant to block me from the mural of my parents. Horror turned to anger. Throwing a blanket over my nightgown, I ran to confront the workers.

"Stop right now. Take every one of those blocks away and restore the door. That's an order."

I forgot I was invisible. The men continued to cement the cinder blocks, one after another. Pushing my way to the gaping hole, the new wall up to my waist, I searched for my parents. Though they gazed back serenely, a galloping started in my chest.

"Take it down! Now!" The work went on. "I'm la patrona here. I give the orders, not my mother-in-law. The law is on my side and you shall have to answer to it if you don't obey me."

More blocks were laid in place. More cement. I hurried off to find doña Manuela, pounding on doors and calling her name loudly. When my blanket slipped off my shoulders I continued my desperate search, night gown fluttering like a sail. That morning I became a madwoman running barefoot past the church and through courtyards and stables and the processing plant and railroad tracks, running and crying out because my parents were being taken from me a second time. Yet, what was I but a phantom that no one seemed to see or hear? What was my pain but a murmuring wind rustling the treetops? When I finally grasped the futility of my search, I returned to the upstairs veranda. By then the doorway to my parents had vanished behind a wall of masonry. Too numb to cry, I locked myself in Emanuela Comardo's room. Only one thing made me stir from my room hours later: that old villain hunger.

Fishing out my dressing gown from the pile on the floor, I headed to the kitchen, my steps so much slower than in the morning. The kitchen door was locked. So too were the dining room, the library, and the breakfast room. In fact, I was now locked out of every single room in the house except my bedroom with its small bathroom. A supper tray stood guard outside my door. And that became the daily routine: one tray in the morning and one in the evening. Tacha was the only servant in the main house, coming and going silent as a shadow. What had become of the others? Where *was* everyone?

Actually, they were still there beyond the confines of the main house, all of them going about the business of the living, for I apparently no longer moved among them. I'd become other. Separate. Invisible. So I spent as much time as possible in the gardens, thankful that at least doña Manuela could not lock me out of those great open spaces. I took to eating my meals near the aviary. Sinforiano and his assistants would go about their work of sweeping and feeding the birds without acknowledging my presence. Being punished by everyone in San Serafín was bad enough, but not as awful as the times when people seemed to see through me, as if I were immaterial, a thing of air. Only the birds noticed me. Heads cocked to one side, eyes round and bright, they alone contested my ever-growing notion that I had died and was now a pitiful poltergeist.

Meanwhile, masons and carpenters continued to work inside the general's room, next door to doña Manuela's suite. What went on, I had no idea at the time. Late one afternoon as the workers were leaving for the day, I heard one of them ask a companion, "Why another chapel?"

"Because la patrona is a pious woman, you moron."

Both seemed startled when they discerned me in the gathering gloom. And because their faces registered surprise and they were momentarily thrown off, I felt alive. *They see me too, not just the birds,* the thought sang. Yet if anyone was invisible, it was my mother-in-law. I knew that it was her habit to ride out early every morning so that she could personally oversee the running of the plantation. Determined to intercept her, I posted myself outside her room every single day, often for hours at a time. Yet there was no catching her. She had become as invisible to me as I to everyone else. One night when I pressed my ear to her door, I heard a stirring, the subtlest swoosh of a robe or perhaps the soft patter of slippered feet.

How the devil did she get past me? With the devil's help, I chuckled in spite of myself.

I didn't know at the time that there was a hidden passage and stairway that linked her bedroom to the new library downstairs. She was therefore free to come and go as she wished, undetected. Perhaps the passageway was another of her architectural innovations, or maybe it was an ancient escape route designed by some grim forbearer. Whatever the case, the woman remained elusive.

When I knocked on her door, her silence didn't even feel stubborn anymore, just indifferent. I resorted to writing a letter of apology and an exhortation for peace, slipping it under her door. The next morning I found shreds of paper outside my room anchored by a pot of geraniums.

Had she at least read it? There was no way of knowing.

Then one day, almost two weeks after Cadwally's departure for Cuernavaca, I rounded a corner and unexpectedly came face to face with my mother-in-law and Valle Inclán, the former administrator of the hacienda. Doña Manuela showed no reaction whatsoever. She simply sidestepped the way one would to avoid colliding with a stranger on a pedestrian thoroughfare. The Spaniard registered the briefest look of surprise. Then he took no further notice of me. On impulse, I hurried after them and blocked their passage.

"I know what you're doing. Pretend all you want, but I exist. Like it or not, I'm here."

It was then that I spotted the missing key ring firmly clipped on doña Manuela's belt.

38

PRISONERS

LA PATRONA AND the foreman walked around me, smoothly resuming their conversation while I dashed to my bathroom to battle wave after wave of dry heaves. When the spasms finally subsided, I slumped onto the bed and curled up, crying and sleeping in cycles until the sun vanished. Waking in the dark, I remembered Tomás's exhortation about taking charge of the keys and thereby controlling the hacienda.

Control? I don't even exist anymore, I tried to laugh.

Then beat the old witch at her game, a more assertive thought counseled. Take everything she dishes out. When Tomás sets things right again, think of the shame she'll feel.

Yes, I could picture the señora's mortification. All right then. Until that day arrived, I would ignore them all: the cowardly servants, the hateful Valle Inclán, and the traitorous Agapito. I could play the same game, looking through them as if they were panes of glass.

I began to cry again.

One sleepless night I dressed and wandered into the back garden. Nothing stirred. The moon was not quite full, but it lit the garden path that led to the aviary. All the birds slept, all but the solitary trogon. I could just make him out high on his perch, his crest nearly touching the cupola, wings opening and closing as if he were exercising them, urging them in the darkness of captivity not to forget their purpose. *I'm like him and all the rest of these poor captives,* the thought struck me. *We no longer have a will of our own.* And then it came to me that there *was* one thing that I could do: I could liberate the birds. Unlatching the outermost door of the aviary, I opened the inner door as well, leaving both fully ajar. Walking to the center of the cage, I gazed up a full three stories to its peak.

"Shoo! Get out of here!" My arms made great sweeping motions as if I were exercising vigorously. Only a few of the captives stirred.

Stepping outside of the cage, I groped in the dark for a stick and found a broom, one of those affairs made from branches wired together. I grasped it tightly and struck the cage from the outside, hoping to startle the birds into flight. They grew raucous but their flight was confused. Only two small parakeets escaped into the night. None of the others seemed to value the chance that I was giving them.

"Shoo! Shoo!" They ignored me like everyone else. "Damn it! Get out of here, you stupid birds!" In desperation or madness, I climbed the tree in the center of the aviary until I was but an arm's length from the trogon, the resplendent quetzal. "Get out! Go!" Electric lights flooded the darkness. People were rushing toward the aviary. The game was up. "Hurry!" I pleaded with the quetzal. But it only fluttered to another branch.

"Get her down from there," doña Manuela ordered.

Two men entered the cage and climbed the tree. By then I was hysterical.

"Ben! Ben!"

"Why is she saying *ven, ven!*" I heard someone ask. "Come where?"

I was dragged up the path struggling the whole way and crying for Benjamín. When we entered the house, doña Manuela slapped me hard across the face.

"How dare you!" La patrona's eyes blazed. She slapped me a second time. "Take her upstairs."

Valle Inclán almost wrenched my arm out of its socket as he dragged me up the stairs and down a corridor. Moments later, he shoved me into Emanuela's room. Even as I pounded on the door, my rage and despair hot as volcanic rock spewing into the sky, I heard the distinctive click of a key coupling with a lock and understood. Like my husband before me, I was now a prisoner in San Serafín.

39

ANOTHER SELF

THE NEXT MORNING, doña Manuela paid me a visit. Crossing her arms and tilting her head back, she smiled in faint amusement but said nothing. I gripped the bars of the one window that fronted the upper veranda and spoke with what I thought was admirable calm and dignity.

"Señora, you cannot keep me here against my will."

"Tacha, tell Bardomiana that our guest is not feeling well. She will not be eating a single bite all day."

"You can starve me all you like, but the law is on my side."

Actually, there was a stronger law at work, but I didn't know it yet. Its dictum was simple: speak without permission and you forfeit all meals for a day. Unaware that my second outburst had just deprived me of food the next day as well, I was about to add that as an American citizen, I was not without protection. But since doña Manuela and Tacha had already vanished down the stairs, I vented my frustration by slamming the bathroom door.

"Witch!"

I ran a bath. Perhaps the hot water would soothe me. Yet how could it? The memory of my mother-in-law slapping me the night before, twice no less, added fuel to outrage. What gave her the right to treat me that way when I had tried so earnestly to make amends? And that arm-wrenching, bull-necked henchman of hers, Valle Inclán, was just as hateful as Tacha. When Tomás got back and set everything right, we would fire the pair. I would also send doña Manuela packing. No second chances, I vowed as the room steamed up.

Just how long would I have to endure this absurd situation? Back when Benjamín had wanted to join the revolution, his mother had imprisoned him in this very house for—I visualized a calendar as I counted on my fingers. At least six weeks. But I'm not her child that she can punish at will. Oh, she's contemptible!

The memory of doña Manuela being manacled and gagged squelched my outrage. Can I really blame her for being furious with me? And maybe I did overstep myself with her stupid birds.

How many women do you know who go around locking people up, all on their own? A thought countered just as quickly.

She's eccentric.

No. She's hateful. Watch out for her.

Throughout that first full day of my imprisonment I tried to keep distracted. Digging into the larger of my trunks, I found my two books and several notebooks that I had used for journal writing during the few years of my formal education. I opened the oldest of these, now dog-eared and water stained. It was full of outlandish glyphs—Tlatepa, Tomás's secret code. It was soon clear that writing *Tlatepa* was vastly easier than reading it. I struggled to decipher three words on a random page. Σ€ μ¥£ μ©∞β . They might as well have been written in Mandarin for all the sense they made to me now. In the next life, angels and spirits have a perfect memory. I was not yet among the so-called "dead," so I had to grapple quite a while with the forgotten glyphs. Then it finally happened—memory and the mind's miraculous capacity to transform symbols into meaning. The mysterious shapes

suddenly made sense. Turning back to the first page, I encountered an earlier version of myself, a fifteen-year-old girl leaving
home for the first time.

September 25, 1905

I'm on a steamer headed to New York!

Was it only yesterday that Cadwally and I took the
train to Mexico City? I never saw so many people! The
downtown is enormous, dwarfing Cuernavaca even
though we can boast two Zócalos. And the traffic! We
must have seen at least two dozen automobiles. We had
to dodge them and lots of noisy trolleys and dozens and
dozens of carriages as we wandered about. Eventually we
bought a meal from a street vendor, sat on a bench in the
Alameda Park to eat it, and then made our way back to
the station to board the night train for Veracruz. I hardly
slept, I was so excited. When we arrived in Veracruz this
morning, Cadwally handed me off to the first respectable
looking couple we saw near the gang plank, a Mr. and
Mrs. Johnson of Rochester, NY.

Would they be so kind as to take me under their
wing during the voyage? And then when we reached New
York, would they make sure that I boarded the train to
Philadelphia? He asked. They very kindly agreed, though
I saw no reason to trouble them. I do speak English and
can make my own inquiries. But he said it would not be
proper for a young girl to travel alone. Since when does
Cadwally worry about what is proper? Meanwhile, since
I didn't get much sleep on the night train to Veracruz,
I know I should be exhausted. But how can I sit on the
deck of my very first steamer and simply sleep? So I'm
writing this down while it's fresh in my memory.

Everything has happened so quickly. Cadwally didn't
even tell me until the day before yesterday that he has

a half-sister named Delphine, and that she is going to undertake my education! I only had a few hours to pack and say goodbye to Rosa. Oh, how she cried. I didn't want to leave her like that. I considered running away. But where could I go? Tomás could have dreamed up some wild escape, but he was back in the D.F. I had hoped that when we got to Mexico City ourselves, that we could stop by and say goodbye to him before boarding our night train to Veracruz, but Cadwally said no. He seemed anxious, not at all like himself. Perhaps he feared the train would leave without us.

No. I looked up from my old journal. The poor man just wanted to get me out of the country, as far from Tomás as he could arrange it. He had recognized the shift in Tomás's feelings for me. Though I never acknowledged it to Cadwally, I was secretly relieved to get away. I read on, listening to the voice of my fifteen-year-old self on the cusp of a new life.

To think that I really did consider running away. Now, as I watch the glimmering water of the Gulf of Mexico and feel the wind on my face, I could burst from joy! How I long for adventure.

It was an adventure, all right, I nodded to my younger self. Such a clash of cultures. There I stood a few days later on Great-aunt Delphine's porch, in sandals no less and a shawl over a brightly embroidered blouse and skirt from the Cuernavaca *Mercado,* and she in a gray silk day dress, corseted, and most properly shod. What must she have thought when she set eyes on me? In another entry I discovered why writing in *Tlatepa* had been so useful.

I'm not sure if I like Aunt Delphine all that much. To begin with she's ancient—at least ten years older than

Cadwally, and he's an old gray fox. But unlike him she's so very proper, this maiden aunt of mine—great aunt, I mean. She's kind but not warm. She took me shopping and paid for all my new clothes. We took a train to Philadelphia to a store with the oddest name, *Wanna Make Her,* or something like that. We came back with a mountain of parcels, but since then I've been fighting the sensation that I am slowly being *axfixiated*—I think that's the word. She insists I have to wear a corset. It's diabolical. And the layers! There's a chemise that goes under the corset, then a short-sleeved thing called a corset cover, and then a slip—all that before I put on a dress!

How would I ever climb the jacaranda tree in this get-up? The shoes for day wear are just as bad. I feel sad every time I glance at my sandals, which I am forbidden to wear.

Another entry read:

Tomás would find my Great-aunt Delphine absurd. When I climbed one of her apple trees, she informed me that a lady only climbs staircases. Such a prig!

A month later I had mellowed:

Aunt Delphine drives me crazy sometimes. But I must admit that without her constant tutelage I wouldn't stand a chance of fitting in. I feel like some wild beast that needs taming, and I'm willing to be tamed. So I must not gripe any more about her. I like her large house with its wide porch and lawns, and I like my room despite the wallpaper. For some reason that I can't fathom, the roses just repeat endlessly with no variation. Such a lack of imagination. What would Cadwally think?

A later entry surprised me; I'd forgotten the sentiment:

I'm so stupid. Given that Cadwally didn't send me to

school until now, that I can read at all is a miracle. What a relief that my teachers don't care about John Stuart Mill and other political philosophers! In English we read *A Tale of Two Cities*. It was glorious! Now we've started *Jane Eyre*. How did I live so long and not know such books existed? As for religion, I'm a Biblical illiterate. On the first day of class I was the only one who fished for *Genesis* in the middle of the book and who thought Swedenborg was a city in Sweden.

Locked as I was in Emanuela Comardo's room, I laughed out loud. How could I have been anything but a Bible illiterate? Cadwally was an atheist and Rosa part Pagan. What hope did I have of knowing Genesis from Revelation or Swedenborg from smörgasbord? I reflected that I still wasn't particularly religious, but at least I was less ignorant now about religion. So I plowed through a few more pages of *Tlatepa* and found more fragments of that younger, ever evolving self. You know, when you come down to it, who are we? Which one of the many different selves we have been or are yet to be? The manifestation now? Which now? The *me* of a second ago, already morphing into the me of this latest split second? And if we are constantly morphing, do we lose all those other selves, or are they curled up one inside the other like Russian nesting dolls? Is it any wonder that we remember some things so vividly and forget impressions and routines that once seemed carved in forever? So I read on to remember again.

Bryn Athyn is not nearly as lively as Cuernavaca, but it *is* a beautiful town. I think I shall grow to like the Academy as well. The Boys' School is on the same grounds, so that keeps things interesting around here. The biggest surprise are the gardens around here. Very few of them have walls around them. I don't know if that's because Americans trust everybody, or because they want to show off what they have. I'll have to observe them a bit longer to decide. Meanwhile, wonderful and strange as it is here in Bryn Athyn, I so miss Rosa and her tamales and her *café de olla*—and most of all her laugh. I miss the night watchman's whistle at night and the sound of the cathedral bells, and the smell of oils and turpentine on Cadwally's clothes.

Immersed in the journals, I spent the first full day of my incarceration rather pleasantly, despite not being fed. By evening, though, the charm had worn off. That night I dreamed about street dogs nosing around trash cans.

40

WINGLESS LETTERS

ON THE SECOND day of my imprisonment, I reached for the most recent of my journals, a richly embossed leather notebook that Aunt Delphine had purchased for me during our stay in Venice. This one was written in plain English. Perhaps I had fewer secrets by then. Still ignoring my books that second day, I devoted the long hours to reading about my travels in Europe during my senior year—the senior year I never completed. Every page brimmed with a young girl's effusion over everything—places, history, food, fashion, young men, and espresso—all deemed equally worthy of ecstatic treatment.

My European travelogue was followed by equally exuberant entries about my return to Mexico in the spring of 1910. Sights, sounds, smells, tastes, and textures were all rendered in opulent detail. I couldn't help noticing though that after Rodolfo Nyman entered my life, the journal entries became noticeably restrained and brief. Truthfully, I was uncertain about my feelings for Rodolfo. It was much easier to focus on externals, so the Centennial Ball of September 1910 received a detailed treatment. I had commented on everything—the women's fashions and my own sapphire-blue gown; the men in black tie or splendid military uniforms; the orchestra with one hundred and fifty musicians; the al fresco ballroom in the central courtyard of the National Palace, the enormous buffet tables and above us Halley's comet, its great luminous tail a startling fixture in the night sky. And the food—oh, the magnificent food!

When is that Tacha woman bringing up a tray for me? I slammed the journal shut.

Because my stomach's grumbling was so plaintive now, memories of the Centennial Ball turned on me, sneering: a year ago you feasted with Mexico's elite. Look at you now, you pathetic thing.

I'm not pathetic. I've lived a life that any one of my friends in Bryn Athyn would envy. I've had several worthy suitors, two marriage proposals—three if I count Luke Lukac's strong hints—ah, "Double Luke" as we called him. And then there was Rodolfo, one of the most eligible bachelors in Mexico, and Benjamín, who topped them all, and my participation in the revolution—all before turning twenty-one. And even now that I am a prisoner, isn't my life all the more like a great novel?

On impulse I turned to a blank page in the journal and dashed off a letter to my closest friend, even though there was no possible chance of mailing it.

Dear Emiline,

I hope all is well with you. I have little to report except that my husband was tried for murder recently and is serving a twenty-five-year sentence in the Federal Penitentiary of Mexico City. His father, an eccentric general who became a self-styled monk in the last years of his life, named me the sole heir to his fortune. His widow is avenging herself by holding me prisoner in her plantation, which is technically mine now. Oh, and my husband intends to murder me when he gets out. What's new with you?

Love,
Isabel

I smiled at my own sarcasm. When my stomach continued to clamor for attention, I set the pen aside.

"Señora! We need to talk!" I yelled out the window. "Tacha! Ta—"

"Keep quiet if you know what's good for you." The servant appeared so suddenly, I felt my heart leap into my throat.

"I want . . . I demand to see the señora."

"She's out. Listen to me, girl. If you want to eat again, never speak to la patrona without permission. Do you understand? Your outbursts have cost you at least two days without food, maybe more. If you know what's good for you, you'll bite that tongue of yours and keep quiet."

"No. I want everyone to hear me."

"What for? They wouldn't come even if they did hear you. You're not la patrona here. You're only a thief, so shut up if you want to eat again."

I was too stunned to respond. After Tacha left, my anger broke free from the pit of an empty stomach, and I kicked a wastebasket across the room. Since not even a plate of humble beans materialized, I sat down and penned the second of my wingless letters, this time to another classmate.

Dear Wertha,

Who says dragons are mythological? A real, live specimen holds me in her lair. She and her slave, a hideous Olmec statue that has been brought to life, are intent on breaking me by starvation. There is no kindness in dragons. No saving grace in stone-hearted servants. They are the stuff of nightmares.

Ravenous,
Isabel

Does life—earthly life—ultimately become nightmarish? I wondered. In the end, before we can have the joys of heaven, aren't we doomed to suffer, sicken, and die? Perhaps we're all like the Chinese immigrants of Torreón, full of hope for a new life, only to be hunted down in the streets? Maybe the whole experience of living can be summed up in one word: struggle. Surely my life bears this out. Haven't I struggled since childhood? To adapt to life without parents; to cope with Cadwally's drinking; to adjust to school when I was so woefully unprepared? And then just when I thought myself happy, didn't my marriage become impossible? Now I'm at the mercy of a woman who is clearly mad or just downright nasty. So am I experiencing a streak of bad luck, or is this the human condition and I just didn't know it until now? I asked the stillness.

Later that night I wrote a wingless letter to Benjamín:

Dear Ben,

I find myself imprisoned like you, pacing the length and breadth of a room that grows smaller each hour. I'm wondering what it is that you and I are meant to learn from our troubles? That passion is dangerous because it incites us to take action before we've thought things out? That people fall in love and marry for the wrong reasons? That no matter how intensely it burns, passion *will* fizzle, like flames in a rainstorm? What about love? Does it diminish or die that easily too? Did I love you, Benjamín Nyman, or merely the thought of being in love with you? I swore to be your faithful wife forever, yet I cut and ran at the first stumbling block. Clearly, intent and deed are not always the same thing, any more than expectation and reality. What is the purpose of it all?

Did you love me, or was I caught in the middle of some long-standing sibling rivalry, a prize to be wrested from your brother? You swore before God to love and protect me all the days of our lives. Yet you've been quick to believe the worst about me and now say you intend to kill me. Is love so flimsy a thing?

Perhaps our marriage was just reckless passion. I should have taken a more rational approach. Marrying your brother would have given me a home, financial security and social standing. You, on the other hand, were sure to be disinherited when you joined the revolution. So given all that I stood to lose by not marrying Rodolfo, wasn't my elopement with you far more genuine and less self-serving?

I cradled my head and closed my eyes.

"I did love you," I whispered, fingering my wedding band.

And then none of it mattered very much—not my failed marriage or my botched attempt at social justice, or my teleological questions. By the end of the third day of subsisting only on water from the bathroom tap, one question dominated my thoughts: *when will they feed me?* I waited well into the night. When no one came and San Serafín fell into its nocturnal stillness, I slumped onto the bed. Too demoralized to undress, I curled up under the covers and tried to sleep. Without Benjamín beside me, the bed grew preternaturally large and empty, my stomach a moaning ghost.

That night I dreamed about skeletal dolls, the kind sold in market stalls during the Days of the Dead festival. In the dream, I was a child again and was trying to carry an armful of such dolls. One by one they squirmed free. Stretching tall, they chased me through narrow lanes, jaws gaping on fleshless faces.

41

A RELUCTANT READER

ON THE FOURTH morning of my incarceration, I was awakened by a gritty voice and the unmistakable scent of coffee. I flew to the window. With a gasp of pleasure I reached for the clay mug that Tacha shoved between the bars. She also brought me a *torta,* that most Mexican of sandwiches. The roll was filled with nothing more than beans, one tomato slice, and a touch of mustard. No cheese. No ham. No avocados or salsa. Yet nothing ever tasted so utterly wonderful. Drinking the hot coffee with greedy gulps, I coughed and dribbled some onto my blouse. Tacha watched me, her features expressionless as a white wall.

"Remember what I told you," she warned in her oddly masculine voice. "Hold your tongue with la patrona."

"I will. Thank you, Tacha." I smiled, forgetting that faces carved in stone do not smile back.

I spent those first days of my imprisonment either obsessing about food—there were only two small meals a day—or reading my journals. Before the week was out, I was both thinner and thoroughly bored with Isabel Brentt. So I turned at last to the only books in my trunk: a King James Bible and Swedenborg's

Divine Providence. There is no greater book on earth than the Bible, I told myself sternly. And it won't hurt to read *DP* all the way through this time, instead of a fragment here and a fragment there. Besides, what else is there to do on a dull day in the dull room of the dull Emanuela Comardo?

What indeed? Plumping my pillows, I nestled into the bed and opened my Bible. Still feeling little inclination to immerse myself in it, I pressed my nose to a page. Instantly its scent flooded me with impressions of high-ceilinged classrooms in Benade Hall, heavy oak desks, friends who spoke English, the novelty of pancakes and maple syrup, ink stains that were hard to wash off my middle and index fingers, bouts of homesick-ness, and my mutinous gaze beyond the school grounds to those strange American lawns without walls. All this and more broke upon me in my prison cell in a matter of seconds, evoked by the simple scent of the pages of a book. What a curious partnership between smell and memory.

I closed my Bible and reopened it at random, alighting on Joshua 8.

"What an appalling story!" I remember venting about this very chapter with Emiline, my first friend in Bryn Athyn. "What is so sacred about this book? The Israelites were utterly barbaric. Frankly, I'm not all that impressed with their god either. Why should we admire that He ordered the deaths of every man, woman and child in Ai? Frankly, I'd rather pray to a volcano or the sun."

"That's because you're reading the story literally."

Red-haired Emiline had deeply intelligent eyes set in a face speckled like a fawn.

"Well, of course, literally. How else?"

"Try reading it like poetry."

"That's stupid. This isn't poetry."

"Sure it is. Think of English class and how often we look past the literal meaning of a metaphor or a simile in order to see the deeper idea hidden within it. When Shakespeare says that the

world is a stage, we know he isn't talking about a physical structure with floorboards, lights, and curtains, right? The metaphor
is a device to point us to something far more profound. The Bible
abounds with metaphors and wonderfully symbolic language."

"All I see is a recounting of bloodthirsty battles."

"All of which correspond to our own inner battles of the
soul."

"Oh, I'm sure that comforted the citizens of Ai as they were
put to death, every last one of them. What kind of a god would
order such a massacre?"

"A loving God who wants us to destroy all the evil *thoughts*
and *desires* that plunge us into darkness."

"The Israelites killed people, not abstractions."

"True. But what if the Bible is more than a history of unre-
mitting violence?" Emiline knew I wasn't a Swedenborgian, or
much of a Christian for that matter. She loved my skepticism,
perhaps because it challenged and solidified her own beliefs.
"Isabel, what if *in spite of* the primitiveness of the Israelites, there
are deeper layers of meaning within the literal accounts?"

"I still don't see how we're going to get past the merciless savagery."

"By probing deeper. Look, what if men throughout the Bible
correspond to ideas, and women to the things that we love? Then
the children that they engender wouldn't be children at all, but
the metaphorical offspring of our thoughts and desires. Don't
you see, Isabel? God wasn't ordering the death of *people*. How
could He when He is love itself?"

I responded with some adolescent flippancy, yet Emiline had
planted a seed. Our studies in English class would germinate it.
By studying poetry for the first time in my life, I was learning that
there are indeed deeper, more meaningful ways to read a text.
Literalism is not the only way. Slowly I came to the realization
that the Bible, like Dante's *Divine Comedy*, does indeed have multiple levels of meaning. Training my mind to venture beyond the
literal, however, was hard work and not particularly to my taste.

Now in my prison in San Serafin, I read the once problematic chapter 8 in Joshua with an eye to a more spiritual meaning and wondered: if this battle and all the other wretched ones in the Old Testament correspond to specific evils that we have to fight within ourselves, how well have I fared so far? Has my decision to abandon my marriage made me spiritually victorious or corrupt? By letting myself be talked into ousting doña Manuela from her ancestral home, have I heeded a divine prompting or merely the dictates of human greed? On a literal level, haven't I acted as ruthlessly as the Israelites grabbing up land in Canaan? But spiritually, am I justified in any way? Then again, what if the zealous Manuela Nyman turns out to be the righteous Israelite and I the Philistine?

Hunger pangs made me groan. Because there was no relief, a wave of loneliness crashed over me. Then fear. I flipped through the pages, hurrying to the New Testament, devouring the Gospels because I needed to feel that in this strange, harsh world, there *is* gentleness and goodness and forgiveness. And though I still wondered back then if the Lord Jesus Christ had been nothing more than a very kind person—not God incarnate—I felt drawn to Him. Above all I loved his voice. It broke over the sterile silence of my prison, like the solo clarinet in the adagio of Mozart's concerto, hauntingly beautiful in its directness. Yes, the Gospels became music in my solitude.

Early one morning, about two weeks into my incarceration, I was bathing when I heard an impatient knocking on the shutters. I had closed them the night before.

"Open these at once!" The voice was unmistakable, the tone dictatorial. Not daring to keep la patrona waiting, I wrapped myself in a towel and hurried to open the shutters. Manuela Nyman glared at me. "Don't you ever close them again."

"No, señora. I won't."

"I did not give you permission to speak. Tacha, see that she gets no food today."

I was about to protest. Catching myself, I slapped a hand over my mouth.

"Good. I see you *are* capable of learning after all."

I stood shivering with damp hair and wet shoulders.

"You needn't be so protective of your modesty. There's no one to see you. No one is allowed to come into this part of the house anymore, only Tacha and I—and the ghost," she added with a tight-lipped smile.

Obeying orders, I left the shutters open all day. Later, the night air wafted in, fluttering the sheer curtains. Lying in bed I watched their graceful dance in the moonlit room.

"Rational people don't believe in ghosts," I had wanted to inform doña Manuela. Since I hoped to eat the next day, I had kept this insight to myself. All my unspoken thoughts lay where they had fallen, like clothes carelessly dropped on the floor.

You hoped to scare me, I told her in another of my silent conversations, bending to pick up the dropped thought. Well, it won't work. I survived a night in San Justín, so you'll have to do better than that.

It occurred to me for the first time that this room had not always been Emanuela Comardo's. For more than three centuries it had housed others. So all kinds of people had slept here, perhaps died here. No doubt San Serafín had its share of ghost stories, ghoulish *leyendas* that attach themselves to every old house in Mexico. Invariably the legends involve murder most foul, skeletons under the floorboards and hideous phantoms that haunt the living. San Sera—

What was that? I sat bolt upright. There it was again, drawing closer to my open window.

Why do we seek protection under a blanket when we're scared, as if that could possibly help us? There it was again, I thought from under the covers—an unmistakable breathing outside my window.

42

HIPÓLITO

Unseen, he crept up the stairway on silent feet, prowling the dark corners, bumping the veranda chairs against the walls and sniffing out the living. Hipólito was an old Irish setter. If there was an actual ghost in San Serafín, I never saw it. What I did encounter was a pair of soft brown eyes peering at me between the bars and a tail that thumped as joyously as my heart.

"Hipólito? Have you come to see me?" I reached out both arms and stroked him. "What a good pooch you are!"

My mother-in-law had an anti-canine decree in place: no dogs inside the house. Dogs belong outside. Do not disrupt the natural order.

"But disrupt it we did," Benjamín had told me once with a laugh. "Samuel and I used to sneak Hipólito into our room after Mother had gone to bed, and we'd let him out before dawn."

The more I petted the old setter, the more connected I felt with the world. *Am I really so lonely?* I wondered, sinking my hands deep into his coat, content to feel the warmth of his body. "What a good old dog," I murmured, my imprisoned voice freeing itself in the dark.

From then on Hipólito sneaked out of the kitchen into the upper corridors nearly every day. He knew intuitively to stay out of doña Manuela's sight. He was bolder with old Stone-face, waiting until she came near but not close enough to land him a kick. "*Sáquese de aquí! Get out of here!*" Tacha would snarl in her distinctive, guttural voice. Hipólito would slink away. The moment she retreated down the stairs, he would be back, wet nose thrust between the bars, tail wagging irrepressibly. At night he was downright brash. And what could I do but share some of my meal with him, my one friend in all of San Serafín?

My food was pared down to the simplest of Mexican cuisine. It didn't matter. Bardomiana was the ultimate cordon bleu chef of beans, tortillas, and scrambled eggs. No one brewed a better *café de olla*, except Rosa. Oh, Rosa! I felt a stab of homesickness every time I thought of her, or of Cadwally with a smear of paint on his face, a brush stuck behind his ear. Yet as my hunger intensified, I'm sorry to say that more than anything else I missed Rosa's cooking.

"Hipólito, old buddy. Would you do something for me?" The red setter lifted his head and tipped it to one side, listening attentively. "Do you think you could go to the kitchen and sneak a *torta* for me?"

I had adopted a tender bantering with him, but inwardly I fretted. How much longer is doña Manuela going to do this? I'm not her child for her to punish at will.

That's right, which is why she'll punish me even more, my inner skeptic countered. Face it. She plans to keep me here for five or six long weeks, just like she did with Ben."

Weeks? The possibility startled me.

Why not months or years? The skeptic rolled on calmly. Who's going to stop her?

Tomás and Cadwally.

And if something were to happen to them, who would know or care that you've vanished?

I began to gasp for air. My hands shot out between the bars to grasp Hipólito. Just the touch of his coat and the warmth of his body were enough to bring the anxiety attack under control. My breathing became less ragged. Tremors followed like the aftershocks of an earthquake, gradually subsiding. The attack passed. I let go of Hipólito. Needing other voices in my head, I retrieved my King James Bible. Returning to sit on the floor by the window, I kept one hand on the page, the other on my companion's head.

In the beginning was the Word, and the Word was with God, and Word was God. He was in the beginning with God. All things were made through Him, and without Him nothing was made that was made. In Him was life, and the life was the light of men. And the light shines in the darkness, and the darkness did not comprehend it.

I felt a jolt. I had expected to find comfort in the familiar text. Instead I experienced the shock of an altered perspective. It was as if the familiar words were stars that I had known all my life but was suddenly staring up at them from a hilltop in Argentina or Chile. From this new perspective, the constellations no longer seemed the same. The metaphors of light and darkness shot upwards like the towering arches of a Gothic cathedral, all to support an idea that stunned me: *If Christ was just a man, then the world has one more holy fool, and it doesn't matter. But if Christ truly was and is God, then nothing else in the whole universe matters as much.*

I don't know where the thought came from. Perhaps I had read it somewhere and was only now grasping it. For a few shining moments, I was keenly aware of the insignificance of everyone and everything beside so monumental a possibility. From then on I read the Gospels for whole hours on end. And when I felt particularly rested, I'd venture into the Old Testament as well, for on a deeper level wasn't it really about Christ? Hadn't he fought deep internal battles like we do, only far more horrific ones? So I read all day every day and reflected on matters that had never mattered to me until then.

On a still afternoon when nothing stirred except Nicodemus having his furtive conversation with Christ, something happened. For a few seconds the walls of Emanuela Comardo's room vanished, and I suddenly felt the cool air of a night-cloaked garden. I was *there* in that garden, far away and long ago, listening to the voices of two men in earnest conversation.

"'How can a man be born when he is old? Can he enter into his mother's womb and be born?'"

Another voice responded but I couldn't make out his words at first, the blood was pounding so hard in my ears. Then I caught up with the conversation and heard, *"That which is born of the flesh is flesh; and that which is born of the spirit is spirit."*

Just as suddenly as it happened, I was back in Emanuela Comardo's room, the walls stubbornly thick again, my fingertips resting on the page, my heart racing. Benjamín would have dismissed the experience as a hallucination brought on by severe hunger. But I know what I saw, or more precisely, what I heard. Believing as I did that we humans live in two worlds simultaneously, the physical and the spiritual, none of this should have surprised me. But it did back then.

I cried and I prayed.

Later, when the experience had been relegated to memory and its immediate reality was no more than a vague impression, like a dream that we try to hang on to, I reflected on the deep connection between the literal and the metaphoric. Like most people who are familiar with the story, I've never had trouble recognizing the parabolic reference to spiritual rebirth. In this instance, the deeper meaning of the literal is quite clear. Yet never before had I *grasped* so clearly the interconnectedness of the literal and the spiritual. I was staggered by the sheer beauty of even a literal reading. With one hand on Hipólito's head and the other on the onion-skin pages of my book, I re-read the archaic King James wording, at once old and ageless, time-locked and time-freed: *The wind bloweth where it listeth, and thou hearest the sound thereof, but canst not tell whence it cometh, and whither it goeth: so is every one that is born of the Spirit.*

I paused. Just then a strong wind blew across the courtyard, fluttering the pages, ruffling my loose hair; rippling over the dog's reddish coat; rustling the fuchsia blossoms of the bougainvillea and the soft petals and leaves of the potted geraniums. Closing my eyes, I could imagine the workers in the fields, their white shirts fluttering like sails, the women in the compound reaching to clamp down their billowing skirts; the manes on the horses dancing—all of them touched by the same wind.

"The wind blows where it chooses, and you hear the sound of it, but you do not know where it comes from and where it goes," I murmured aloud, updating the Old King James version.

Hipólito slinked away.

"What are you reading?"

Startled, I looked up into la patrona's scowl. "The Bible."

"Let me see it."

Doña Manuela inspected it, then tucked it under her arm. "Someone like you has no business reading the sacred scriptures."

"Please, doña Manuela!"

"Pity. Here's Tacha now with your meal. Feed it to the dog."

Tacha set the plate down on the tile floor. Hipólito approached the food cautiously, tail between his legs. Moments later, the plate looked as clean as it had inside the kitchen cupboard. I fought back tears. There was no dinner either. The next morning I whistled loudly. Defiantly. But I had taken one precaution. Closing the lid of the toilet, I had climbed up and hidden my one remaining book high up on the tank. The dragon would not get this one, I vowed. That whole interminable day, I missed my Bible, especially the voice of Christ speaking in the Gospels. I suppose I would have to include the four evangelists as well. I had grown to love their straightforward narratives, those voices that calmly described the wondrous with such a leanness of description. Being able to read the Lord's words had steadied me, giving me companionship and hope. Not being allowed to read the Gospels anymore struck me as a particularly cruel punishment.

If not for Hipólito, the sheer loneliness would have broken me. Yet, so long as he continued to break the house rules for my sake, I could stand it all. I could even settle into a peaceful routine. I had no plan for escape. Tomás would liberate me when he returned with Eufemio Rosarito in tow—for he *would* find him. That was as inevitable as earthquakes in central Mexico, I told myself. Meanwhile, I could count my blessings. The room was pleasantly furnished, the bed comfortable, I had my journals— tedious as they had become—and I had the loyal Hipólito right outside my window. I also had one book: Swedenborg's *Divine Providence,* though at that point in my life I would have preferred a good Gothic novel. Not being quite ready to tackle so theological or philosophical a work, I dashed off another of my wingless letters to Emiline.

Dear Emiline,

I have a champion in my hour of distress: Sir Hipólito. He visits me daily, and since he understands English to a remarkable degree, we are safe from prying ears. I can confide in him and count on his discretion. Hipólito is peace incarnate. Nothing distresses him. I must learn from his example. I just wish that I had his freedom to sneak into the kitchen.

Your hungry Isabel

The attack came by night. Tacha tied my hands behind my back and gagged me. It all happened so fast that I never stood a chance to defend myself. Moments later, Tacha shoved me into the bathroom and locked the door. Later, when I was brought back into the bedroom, all the furniture was gone, including the bed. Only the stripped-down mattress and an old blanket remained. No sheets, no pillows. I cast uneasy glances about the room. Doña Manuela pulled the gag off me but did not untie my hands. Tacha was already in the corridor carrying away the larger of my trunks. She had already absconded with the smaller one.

"My trunks! Please let me keep them, señora!" I pleaded.

"Leave nothing but the mattress," la patrona ordered.

I could see at a glance that not even the light bulbs had been spared. They lay on the floor under a step ladder. Doña Manuela headed to the bathroom, doubtless to steal that light too. That's when I bolted out the door though my hands were still tied behind my back.

"Tacha!" the warning rang out.

I ran down the corridor dodging the furniture. *Should I cry for help or would that only bring the hounds to me?* That in turn allowed me to imagine, however briefly, however impossibly, Hipólito leaping to my defense, teeth bared in a ferocious, protective snarl. But he was nowhere in sight. My jailors pursued me down the dark corridor.

43

WHY THIS ONE?

WHEN I WAS back in my cell, gagged and tied to the window bars, doña Manuela grasped me by the hair. "Try that again or call out for help just one more time, and I'll personally cut out your tongue."

How medieval of you, I was tempted to retort. Yet so intense was her rage that I half believed her, and half believing, grew very still. I spent a miserable night. In fitful dreams I kept struggling for breath. Just before waking up I dreamed I was inside a silo. Millions of uncooked black beans were falling on me, pressing ever tighter on my chest, and Tomás yelling above the din: how the blazes do you expect me to find the one bean? In the morning when Stone-face freed me from the gag and ropes, I actually felt grateful to her. Who would have imagined that one could blur the line between disgust and gratitude so easily? What kind of a dynamic was that? A very real, very frightening one, as I would discover. For now, I was still able to rebel when she muttered, "If you don't want the señora to ram a knife into your mouth, keep it shut. And don't expect any food today."

You stupid cow! I raged inwardly as she locked the door on her way out, leaving me to wonder which was going to be worse: starving or having nothing to do all day. I began to pace, pace and grip the bars, pull on the bars and pace and pace. *How dare she treat me this way! This time the señora has gone too far!* After a while anger gave way to anxiety. Had Benjamín's mother become unhinged? If so, what could I expect but more abuse? A darker thought whispered, what if she's not insane? Wouldn't that mean that she's crossed a dangerous line, deliberately straying from the code of civilized behavior into barbarity—from feigned goodness into overt evil? Once crossed, how does one go back? I sank to my knees. My God, what am I going to do? How will I survive until Tomás gets back? I'll go mad in here.

I became a caged jaguar with a crate for a forest. Back and forth. Back and forth I paced, wishing for mental stimulation if I couldn't have freedom, remembering and bemoaning my Aunt Delphine's steady stream of reading materials—*The Atlantic Monthly, Harpers* and *Scribner's, The Delineator,* and *Ladies Home Journal.* What I'd have given for even back copies of *The Public Ledger.* I would have devoured every word that linked me to the greater world. And then I remembered something. Locking the bathroom door behind me, I clambered onto the closed toilet seat and reached high up on the tank. My book! It was still there! I still had something that was mine.

Climbing fully clothed into the empty tub, I opened Swedenborg's *Divine Providence* that I had been so reluctant to read. I had loved *Heaven and Hell* for the dramatic possibilities that it evoked; I had approached *Conjugial Love* enthusiastically enough, for what young girl doesn't think of love and marriage? But for some reason I had equated *Divine Providence,* perhaps Swedenborg's most philosophical work, with Cadwally's books on philosophical radicalism though they were utterly unlike each other. I had reasoned in my adolescent years that I need read only a minimum to fulfill the requirements of religion classes.

Having discovered Gothic and romantic novels, I had rebelled against lengthy discourses on logic, metaphysics, epistemology or any ology. So I had spent those four and a half years of my schooling only half listening, half registering, half-filling the empty cup. Now that I was marooned with nothing else to read, I plunged into Aunt Delphine's dog-eared copy with a burst of eagerness. And what did I find?

A theological garden.

Sometimes it drew me into an unfamiliar labyrinth, but more often into shaded parks with orderly parterres. Page by page I found my way, to the point that I actually had to force myself to set the book aside. Determined to protect my last possession, I returned it to its hiding place and emerged from the bathroom, in case old Stone-face were snooping around. I wouldn't risk my book. I could sleep during the day and read at night, couldn't I? Oh, but with what light? The dragon had taken every single light bulb.

You stupid cow! I lashed out inwardly at my captor. (I was unfair to bovines in those days.) Just wait until Tomás returns with Eufemio Rosarito. How will you face the world then, huh? Everyone will find out what you've done. Your children will never get over the shame of it and the humiliation. You'll see.

For the rest of the day the book kept calling me back. Reading a few pages at a time was like diving into a lake on a sweltering summer day. When had philosophy and theology become so wonderful? Just two more pages. Two more laps. All right. I'll come out now if I must. Well, after just one more lap, one more page. When it grew too dark to read, I heaved a heavy sigh and hid the book. Returning to the bare mattress, I watched the day grow old. Twilight blurred the edges of things—bars, potted geraniums, the opposite corridor, a patch of sky over the rooftop—the diminishing light lulling me, water lapping on the shore, softly shrugging, sheltering me as I dozed though I had meant to stay awake. Sometime later I woke to night darkness.

Half asleep, I groped my way to the bathroom and flicked on the switch out of habit. Light startled me into full wakefulness, light hidden in the belly of an opaque ceiling fixture. I shut the door quickly.

She didn't get these! The thought vaulted in triumph. The dragon must have forgotten to unscrew the two bulbs when I tried to escape.

What was that? Footsteps? Fear halted the celebration. Switching off the light, I hurried back to my mattress. There it was again. Sitting forward, body taut with listening, I realized that a rattan chair was bumping into the wall outside my room.

"Hipólito?" Relieved, I hurried to the window and reached for him between the bars. "Are you rearranging the furniture again with that tail of yours?" I laughed softly. The touch of his tongue and soft fur were pure joy. Yet I tensed almost at the same moment that he did. Something sent him skulking back into the darkness.

Whatever happens, stay calm, I commanded myself. Don't let the dragon scare you. Stand up to her but be smart about it.

Not a sound. Not a whisper.

"I hope you're getting used to the dark."

I jumped. Doña Manuela stood no more than a foot from the window. *How does she walk without making a sound? It's uncanny and creepy,* I remember thinking, while at the same time forcing myself to keep silent unless invited to speak.

"If my son can live in the darkness of prison life, why shouldn't you?"

Because I didn't attack your hateful old husband! I wanted to retort. *But I won't answer you so that you can starve me. I won't play your game.*

La patrona flicked on a nearby switch in the corridor and studied me from the other side of the bars. *I'm not one of your stupid birds,* I wanted to say. Being too hungry to risk another day without food, I endured the inspection in silence. Then la patrona turned off the corridor light and withdrew from the window. I waited, ears straining to listen to the retreating footsteps. Manuela Nyman was as silent in her departure as in her arrival. Still I waited, listening, listening hard. When I finally felt safely alone, I undressed for bed. With nothing but the clothes on my back, getting ready for bed meant taking off my waist—a high-necked, long-sleeved cotton blouse—that I folded and set on the floor alongside the corset, stockings, and shoes that I no longer bothered to wear. Next I took off my skirt and folded it into a pillow. Instead of a nightgown, I had my underclothes: a long petticoat with a lace flounce, knee-length drawers, a thin sleeveless cotton chemise, and a sleeveless corset cover that I wore for a little extra warmth. Dressed in my petticoat, I slipped off the drawers, washed them in the sink and draped them on the edge of the tub to dry. Retrieving the one blanket that my captor allowed me, a horse blanket from the stables by the smell of it, I draped it around my shoulders and flew to the one place where I felt free—inside my book.

Reading became both escape and subversive activity, which made it all the more delightful. To maintain it, however, required that I reverse day and night in my daily rhythm, making me think more kindly of bats. Doña Manuela became just as much a slave to routine. She visited me every single night before retiring to her room. She would roost outside the veranda window, a vulture approaching on silent wings. Though I grew to expect the visits, I was often startled by the pale face that would silently materialize. Dressed in perpetual mourning, what I came to think of as black feathers, la patrona seemed to merge with darkness itself.

Come, thou sober-suited matron all in black, a half-remembered verse from Shakespeare came to me, a metaphor that I chose to apply literally. Sometimes doña Manuela would flick on the light switch in the veranda and peer into the room. Other times she deemed moonlight sufficient. Either way, she seemed content simply to stare for a few minutes at her caged bird, her "American Blue-thief" as she called me, and then to withdraw to her room. But not always.

"Sit up," la patrona ordered one night in the quiet voice that no one in San Serafín ignored. I was lying on the mattress and obeyed, leaning my back against the wall. "I suppose you think of yourself as a victim, you who seduced two of my sons. You who connived with that Indian lover of yours to—"

"He's not my lover!" I sprang forward, fists clenched.

I suddenly didn't care if she never fed me again.

44

THE CHOICE

"I've never been unfaithful to Benjamín. Never!" I was shouting and didn't care who heard me or what consequences I'd have to face.

"Liar. You and Tepaneca thought you could outwit the witless Lucio Nyman. Well, *I'm* not witless, and I'll never let you take what is mine."

"I never wanted San Serafín or any—"

"Oh, no!" La patrona laughed. "Of course you didn't want it. That's why you rode in here with a band of *Rurales* and dispossessed me."

"I let you come back."

"Oh, and I'm supposed to be grateful that you let me enter my own home, the home that has been in my family for seven generations? Forgive me if I don't kneel in humble gratitude."

"I trusted you and let you back in. Everything you wrote in your letter was a lie!" I cried with passion.

"It's never a sin to lie to the devil," she answered with a saint's serenity.

The very calmness of her manner shamed me. It forced me to speak more softly and with all the earnestness that I could muster.

"Señora, I swear to you by all that I hold sacred, that the only thing I want from San Serafín is to be able to return the land that rightfully belongs to the village of Santa Lupita. That's all. You can keep the rest. I don't want this house nor the sugar mill nor the mines nor the properties in France. I just want to go home to my grandfather." My shoulders slumped forward. "I just want to go home."

"You can. All you have to do is deed the properties back to me."

"Except the village lands."

"No. Everything."

"I can't do that. I promised Tomás Tepaneca . . ."

"So we come to it at last. You promised him the land in exchange for the Nyman Vizcarra wealth."

"No, in exchange for your husband's killer. You and I both know that Benjamín did not kill his father."

Doña Manuela looked as if she had forgotten what she was about to say. "What—what makes you so sure he didn't?"

"Because he didn't shove his father against the wall with enough force to crack his skull. The forensic specialists testified that the back of the general's head—"; I stopped. Was I being too blunt? The look of vivid interest on Manuela Nyman's face reassured me that I could proceed. "They said that the back of the general's head was caved in. Shoving him against the wall in one moment of anger is not enough force. I know that from experience," I added as an afterthought but could not bring myself to explain how I knew this.

"That's the first thing you've said that I agree with."

Hope lifted me to my feet. "Now do you see? Tomás Tepanceca is actually trying to help Benjamín. He's looking for Eufemio Rosarito, the only one who had access to the general after Benjamín's late night visit."

"Eufemio—" She tasted the thought and nodded slowly. "Yes, of course."

"When Mr. Tepaneca finds Eufemio, he'll bring him to justice, and—"

"Finding Eufemio will change nothing!" La patrona's tone flared into white-hot flame.

"It will exonerate Benjamín."

"It's too late for that."

Manuela Vizcarra started to walk away.

"Fine! Then I'll stay right here!" I shouted. "I'll never sign anything. You just go right ahead and starve me to death. I don't care! Do you hear that? I don't care!" Because she hesitated, I wielded what little power I could muster. "You may as well know it: I had a will drawn up before coming here, and it *doesn't* include the Nyman Vizcarras."

It was a lie, a stone tossed at a passing carriage. La patrona of San Serafín turned and took two steps toward me. Crossing her arms, she tipped back her head.

"No doubt you've named Tepaneca as your worthy heir. Or perhaps it's to go to the children that you think you'll have with him. But if after six months of marriage to my son you were not able to conceive—the saints be praised—you are obviously barren."

The remark awoke something dark in me, a monster that lay dormant in a deep cavern. The creature opened its eyes and demanded a greater lie. "It's all arranged and filed with the American embassy. When I die, everything will be sold and the proceeds will go to my school in the United States."

The lie had its intended effect. Doña Manuela was speechless.

The next day Hipólito was tied with a short rope to the railing outside my window—within view but out of reach. La patrona stated the case plainly.

"It's time that we ended this. I've sent for a lawyer. He'll be here on Friday. At that time you will deed all the properties to me."

I said nothing. La patrona clucked her tongue in mild exasperation. "You have my permission to speak."

"Of what use is that, since you starve me whether or not I speak?"

"It is not you who will starve. Listen to me, Isabel Brentt. What happens to the dog is now in your hands. He will not eat a single morsel or drink a drop of water until you deed everything back to me. Is that clear? When you have done so, you can take the mangy beast with you and return to that drunkard you call grandfather."

That day I wrestled with a dilemma. Do we serve God by working toward the good that affects the most people? Or do we serve him even in the least things? In the grand scheme of life, was a dog any less important than a village's land claim? Their lives were not literally on the line. Hipólito's was.

When I held out my arms to him, he lifted his head and wagged his tail. Unable to reach me, he whimpered.

Damn her! I fought back tears. I'll outwit her. I'll sign whatever she wants, take Hipólito away from here and walk to Cuernavaca if we have to. And later, when Tomás comes back, he'll take the dragon to court and they'll revoke the whole thing because she forced me to sign.

"I'll do it," I told her that evening. "In return you have to promise that you'll feed the dog and let me take him home to Cuernavaca as you offered. Swear it by all that you hold sacred."

"Yes, yes. I promise." Doña Manuela handed me a piece of paper. "Now memorize this. It's what you're going to tell *el licenciado* Viscoso when he arrives. Play your part carefully, Isabel Brentt, and earn your freedom. But if that lawyer suspects anything, if there is the least inconsistency in your story or in your manner, I'll have the dog shot, and that too is a sacred promise."

45

PLAY IN ONE ACT

Two days later Tacha delivered a breakfast of *tamales de dulce,* chocolate-flavored *atole,* and a *bolillo* still warm from the oven. I was ecstatic. Just as Tacha was leaving and opened the door, I broke the roll in half and threw it to Hipólito who was still chained outside my room. Tacha scooped it up like a hawk swooping down on a chick in a barnyard.

"The dog gets nothing until you do your part."

I ate the meal but all the gusto was gone from it. By the time the lawyer arrived, I had slipped into my own blue skirt that Tacha retrieved from one of my trunks. It was loose on me so I had to cinch up the belt two extra notches. I was also given one of Eva's expensive Parisian waists, a magnificent silk blouse in a soft cream color. The high collar and yoke were tucked and covered with exquisite lace. I ran my hands over the sleeves again and again.

"Fix your hair," Tacha ordered. "La patrona sends you these pins. There are twelve of them. She wants every one of them back."

During my imprisonment, I had taken to wearing my hair loose or tied back with the one black ribbon that had escaped the ransacking of the room. Now for the first time in days I would be coiffed according to the Gibson fashion, hair scooped up loosely off my neck. Half an hour later, Doña Manuela and Tacha escorted me down the stairs, across the patio and into the back garden. Hipólito was brought on a leash and tied to a pillar in the *portales*. A man sat in the shade of an umbrella table. I had to force myself to ignore Hipólito so I could shine a smile on the attorney. The man jumped to his feet, almost overturning the garden chair. Doña Manuela played the gracious hostess.

"My dear," she draped an arm around my waist. "This is the *licenciado* Rómulo Viscoso, who has very kindly made the trip from Mexico for us." Like most Mexicans, my mother-in-law referred to the capital simply as "Mexico or the D.F."

"How do you do?" I smiled.

The attorney looked more inclined to kiss my hand than to shake it. "I am at your feet, ma'am!" he spoke with the exuberant chivalry of his countrymen.

Attorney Viscoso hurried to hold out a chair for the *grande dame*, though he continued to smile at me. I took a seat opposite hers and breathed in the scent of lilacs. *From now on,* the thought whispered, *lilacs will always make me think of the day I gave away a fortune and regained my freedom.*

"I can't tell you how relieved I am that you're here, *licenciado!*" I delivered the first of my lines with genuine enthusiasm. I was going home at last.

"It is an honor and very real pleasure for me to be of service, señora!" He paused, then added, "To be candid, your request *is* most unusual—and highly commendable, of course!"

"Not really." Here I had to ad-lib, deviating slightly from doña Manuela's script. "First of all, I don't mind telling you, *licenciado,* that I was mortified by my father-in-law's will."

Manuela Nyman hastened to reach across the round table for my hand. "None of that is your fault, dear. Everyone knows that Lucio had grown quite senile in his last years."

"That may be," the play continued. "But I long to set things right. This house is yours, not mine. It's been in your family for

generations. Besides, Rodolfo, Eva and Samuel are just as entitled as Benjamín to their fair share. *Licenciado,* I'm sure you can
appreciate my desire to be just in this matter."

"Of course, doña Isabel." He permitted himself the privilege
of adopting a more familiar, though respectful, stance toward
me. I sensed that his legally trained mind was reeling against my
decision. However, he was Manuela Nyman's attorney, not mine.
"Yours is a most noble gesture."

"Not really. I know nothing about running haciendas, or silver mines for that matter. The señora is so much more competent
than I."

"You're such a dear!" She patted my hand. "Trust me when I
tell you that in the end you will be rewarded for your generous
heart."

"Thank you, señora. You're—"

As Manuela Vizcarra's eyes invaded my own, I forgot my
lines. Fortunately, the attorney stepped in.

"I'm awestruck, señoras! Today I am witnessing a rare and
beautiful love. It is my very great pleasure *and* honor to be able to
assist the two of you!"

"Well then, shall we begin? What do I sign?"

The attorney opened his briefcase. "Doña Isabel, please feel
free to read the document and make certain that it meets with
your approval."

"I've already read it," doña Manuela spoke for me. "Everything is in order."

What can I do but sign?

Yet a spark of rebellion burst into flame. Manuela Nyman's
manner was like a lens angled over kindling, focusing and intensi-
fying the sun's rays. I made it a point to read every word of the document. Patrona, lawyer, and dog had to wait. After a long pause, I
looked up and asked with a honeyed smile, "Where do I sign?"

"Here, doña Isabel, if you would be so kind . . . and then
here, at the bottom of the second and the third pages . . . Perfect!
Thank you very much."

The *licenciado* then hovered over the Nyman matriarch. I glanced over at Hipólito and felt a pang of remorse. What was my rebellion but a show of willfulness? Vain willfulness. Meanwhile, he lay listlessly, his tongue lolling out the side of his mouth, his eyes half closed.

"Excellent!" The attorney scooped up the documents and placed a second set of papers in front of Manuela. "And here is your Last Will and Testament, drawn up as you requested. Please peruse it and tell me if there is anything you would like to add or delete, señora."

Manuela read it carefully, attentive at the same time to the attorney's conversation with me.

"This is the most extraordinary garden I have ever seen." Fixing his eyes on me, he motioned toward a peacock that strutted a few feet from us. "And the aviary is also magnificent, like an open-air church."

"It *is* quite marvelous," I agreed, thinking all along, *When will they feed Hipólito? They should at least give him water.*

Doña Manuela signed the second document without discussing it. Tacha emerged from the shadows, right on cue it seemed to me, and lunch was served in the garden.

The first course was Bardomiana's *sopa de lima.* I breathed in a symphony of aromas: lime, of course, but also cilantro, chicken, oregano, garlic, carrot, onion, and cinnamon. Don't let yourself die without ever having tasted Mexican lime soup.

"Hipólito looks hungry," I commented with studied casualness.

The hint of a frown blew across the dragon's brow. "He'll be fed soon enough. *Licenciado,* can I offer you some fresh ground pepper? Or some avocado slices for the soup?"

"Yes, thank you, señora. You are most kind."

I rose and walked over to Hipólito. Setting my soup dish in front of him, I patted him tenderly.

"*Ay niña, por Dios!*" la patrona scolded with what the lawyer must have taken as mock severity. "Since when does a dog
merit eating out of my Sevres soup bowls, child? Tacha, take it
away. Bring a fresh bowl for doña Isabelita—and a *clay* dish so
the dog can have some soup too," she smiled indulgently. "Now
come and sit down, dear."

I returned to the table. A few moments later an earthenware
dish was set in front of Hipólito and a fresh bowl for me. Much
as I tried to attend to the conversation, my attention was focused
on a tongue that lapped slowly, as if the effort were beyond its
powers. Then Hipólito began to lap up the soup with a thorough-
ness that bordered on desperation. I laughed in relief, the attorney in amusement.

"Well, you were right, doña Isabel. He was hungry all right,"
he beamed at me. "In fact, I'd say he's the hungriest dog I've ever
seen." And then because doña Manuela did not laugh, he reddened. "I mean, I'm sure he's well fed. Over-fed, no doubt."

"The dog never stops eating," doña Manuela observed with
a forced smile.

The lawyer and I ate just as ravenously. The steaks had been
barbecued to perfection. He continued to gush praise, I to nod in
silent, grateful agreement that no potatoes or zucchini or tortillas
or salad had ever been prepared more delectably. Bees droned
in the flowerbeds. Songbirds, whether free or caged, sang solo
and in chorus. The peacocks squawked imperially, adding exotic
instrumentation to the symphony. For the span of the meal, a
festive mood bound the three of us to each other. By the time the
crepas de cajeta and coffee were served, attorney Viscoso had run
out of adjectives.

"Ah, señoras! These caramel crepes beggar the power of language! What can I say?"

The farewell was just as effusive. We stood by the door, Manuela Nyman's arm draped lovingly around her daughter-in-law's
shoulders. The very second that the attorney's coach and armed

escorts rolled past the entrance, the hand on my shoulder tightened.

I followed Tacha up the stairs and entered my room in dutiful silence. Then I waited. The rays of the sun stretched themselves languorously as a cat. The tenants in the aviary grew more raucous as they did every day at dusk, flying about the narrow confines of their prison, unable or unwilling to break patterns ingrained across millennia. Later, when the birds began to roost, I watched the light drop off the edge of the roof on the opposite side of the veranda. Still I waited. The room blurred into the night. Hours later the soft rustling of a skirt woke me. I'd fallen asleep by the window. Straightening, I winced and rubbed my neck. Doña Manuela smiled her mirthless smile, the one that belittled more effectively than words of reproach.

"How odd to prefer the bare floor to a mattress. You know, I must admit that you're not a bad actress, but you certainly are an abominable business woman. You gave away the kingdom for a dog, an old one at that."

I scrambled to my feet and felt unaccountably awkward. Worse yet, I caught myself bowing, almost groveling as I asked, "When can I go home, señora?"

"Home? Did you hear that, Tacha?" Manuela Nyman turned to her Olmec shadow. "This is your home, Isabel."

La patrona started to walk away. For a few seconds I was too stunned to react. Then my outrage spilled like rain water rushing down drain spouts.

"You liar! You're rotten to the core, and I don't care who knows it or what you do to me!" Manuela Nyman paused. Then without looking back, she continued to walk down the corridor, while I shouted all the louder, "Help! Someone help me! I'm being held against my will! Tell the authorities. I'll reward you!"

Tacha entered the cell with rope coiled like a snake.

46

DIVINE PROVIDENCE

I DISCOVERED A simple truth. Bad can become worse. Two days after deeding the properties back to doña Manuela, I lay on the bathroom floor stripped of my finery, feet tied to the pipes of the water closet and arms stretched back over my head, tightly tethered to one of the tub's clawed feet. I had not been fed since my outburst two days earlier. The familiar sound of Tacha's heavy tread made me turn my face in eager anticipation.

I'm like a dog, I remember thinking. I pictured an eager thumping of a tail, ears perked up at the approach of a master, even an abusive one. Well, so be it. For one of Bardomiana's tortas, I'll do doggie tricks and play dead if she asks me.

But Tacha had nothing for me, not even sharp words. Ignoring me, she proceeded to board up the bathroom window with scraps of wood and the well-placed blows of a hammer. The darkish room was plunged into a far deeper gloom. On her way out Stone-face closed the bathroom door again. Stunned, I yanked on the restraints and moaned loudly. And all at once I knew that millions of other human beings across the centuries had reacted with the same disbelief and dread; that all this had happened before and was happening that very moment in numberless prisons across the world. What did it matter whether one's prison was in twentieth-century Mexico or in ancient Babylon? In a great hacienda or in a medieval dungeon? The brutality of isolation and punishing darkness was the same. Timeless. Hellish.

Hours later someone knocked on the bedroom door, softly at first, then more insistently. Though the voice was muffled by thick masonry and two closed doors, I knew it at once.

"Isabel, please open up. Talk to us."

Samuel! I struggled against the ropes and the gag. Instead of the scream that might have incited him to force open the doors, I could only manage the faintest of moans.

"See? What did I tell you?" I heard doña Manuela's muffled voice. "Let her be. She's just being willful and—"

The voices grew fainter, as if chased away by the tormented silence of the cell.

Tacha returned much later to untie me. I groaned when my arms were brought down to my sides. "Don Samuel is gone, so shut up and listen to me. If you don't want to spend the rest of your life gagged and tied up like an animal, practice silence. From now on these shutters stay permanently closed. You're not to touch them. The same with those." She pointed toward the veranda window, "If you know what's good for you, you'll keep them shut at all times, unless the señora raps on the window. Five raps. Got that? Two fast raps, followed by three. Then you'd better fly to the veranda window and open the shutters. Got it?" She shook me by the shoulders.

I would have flung the gag at her but my arms were dead. Separate from me. As they slowly returned to life, they jabbed me with needle pin pricks that left me rocking to and fro. Then my resentment boiled over like unattended milk on a stove.

"You tell the señora that we had a deal. I did my part, and now I expect her to do hers. If she has a grain of decency left in her, she needs to honor her promise to me! You tell her that, do you hear?"

Tacha reached into her apron pocket and tossed a petrified dinner roll onto the floor. I carefully noted where it landed but I had no intention of groveling.

"There's going to be some more construction work in the señora's wing."

"I heard about the new chapel she's building for herself. You tell her she'd do well to start praying, whether it's finished or not. She has a lot of explaining to do to God." I stared defiantly into the expressionless face. "You tell her I won't be silenced anymore."

"No. You listen." Tacha swooped down to within an inch of my nose so that her face became distorted, her eyes merging into one large shiny orb. For a moment I had the uncanny impression that I had just been snagged by a cyclops. "You're to keep the shutters closed from now on and not make a sound. I'll be watching," the guttural voice snarled. "If you try to talk to any of the workers, I'll tell the señora."

"So what?" I shot back, but my voice wavered.

"One sound from you and the *señor administrador* will shoot the dog, and I'll personally drop his carcass here on this floor."

I submitted but I gloried in my secret, carefully guarding the two forgotten light bulbs in the bathroom. I felt a compunction against wasting my precious light just to bathe. Feeling my way into the tub in the dark, I let the hot water caress me. Was it like this in my mother's womb? I wondered. And because the thought of being protected by someone who loved me was so reassuring, I held on to it.

When I was dressed and emerged from the bathroom, I could hear the noise of construction. The racket might have set my nerves on edge. Instead it gave this prisoner an unexpected gift—a small measure of control. I realized that the dragon and old Stone-face would not come near me so long as the workers were out there. I could safely flick on the bathroom light and read all day if I wanted to without being disturbed. Oh, blessed noise!

Sometimes I read while soaking in the tub. In less than two days I had devoured the entire book. By my second reading, I found myself debating interiorly with Benjamín, now that I had stronger arguments to counter his skepticism. When I reached the end of the book, I simply began again on page one. Yet it was becoming harder to concentrate. I was being fed only once a day now, if one could call a petrified dinner roll a meal. Hunger dominated my thoughts and emotions, goading me as I read again that divine providence is "the way the Lord's divine love and wisdom look after us."

Do they now? Anger spewed out of nowhere, ash-hot from the empty depths.

I shot a furious look at the barricaded bathroom window and thought about the miserable rations doña Manuela had reduced me to. How is God looking after me? What love? What wisdom? Why am I locked up like a criminal when I've only tried to do the right thing? Why has God allowed everything to go so utterly wrong in my life? Why has he taken Benjamín and my friends away from me? And while we're at it, why did He take my parents from me, giving me no one but Cadwally to raise me, poor drunken Cadwally? You call that good planning?

There's no plan, Benjamín would have murmured in my ear, sliding into the tub to rub my back. It's all random chance.

No. Divine providence is at work in all things, I would have countered. But that day, as my shrinking stomach launched a particularly pernicious attack, I wasn't so sure. During our brief marriage Benjamín and I had argued about religion almost as often as we made love, which kept us sparring most of the time. He always played the skeptic with maddening precision and wit, while I clung to my fledgling faith with a tenacity that surprised him. The problem wasn't that we couldn't discuss the fine points of theology, but that we couldn't even agree on the most fundamental question of all—the existence of God.

What was it you said when I tried to argue for a benevolent God? I asked him with the internal monologue that had replaced normal conversation with other human beings. Oh, yes, I remember. You sat on the edge of the bed, arms folded, head tipped back, flashing your boyish smile. Then you threw David Hume at me. Actually, you threw both Hume and Epicurus at me:

"Is God willing to prevent evil, but not able? Then he is not omnipotent.

Is he able, but not willing? Then he is malevolent.

Is he both able and willing? Then whence cometh evil?

Is he neither able nor willing? Then why call him God?"

Their logic had seemed stunningly simple and irrefutable. I had Ben write out the argument for me so that I could memorize it. Why? I now asked my husband across the chasm that separated us. So I could figure out how to refute Hume, Epicurus, *and* you. But can I?

My stomach rumbled plaintively.

Hang it all, Ben! I know that your godless worldview makes more sense than my—my 'theistic optimism' as you call it. Yet how could there not be a God? How could everything—the enormous intricacy and beauty of the universe—be random? There *is* a God, Ben. I just can't prove it to you with clever arguments or syllogisms.

Why bother? Bracing my feet, I closed my eyes and let the warm water carry me to Cadwally's sunny patio, sun singing a lullaby, lilting and soft, softly lulling me to sleep. Moments before awakening, I dreamed that Benjamín leaned over me, so close that I could almost feel his lips on mine.

"Say that you're right, my love, and God exists. Why is He letting all this happen to us?"

"To protect our freedom."

"Our freedom, huh?" He smiled sadly. "Haven't you noticed the locks on our doors?"

47

A SECOND DEAL

I WOKE UP shivering. The water was cold now. Worse yet, the light bulbs had burned out. "No! Please!" I cried the words aloud.

It wasn't just a question of how to read without light, but of how to survive mentally without either of these. I was so distraught that I didn't notice how quiet the construction site had become. A distinct, impatient sound made me whip around. Was that four raps or five? Dripping wet, I felt in the dark for my blanket. Making a sarong of it, I fumbled my way to the shutters. On opening them, I was startled by a disembodied face. My captor held a lit candle. The flickering flame and clothes black as the night had reduced Manuela Nyman to a face that seemed more mask than flesh, preternaturally pale and sharply angular.

"What takes you so long?"

It wasn't quite a complaint. La patrona's shiny eyes suggested she was quietly excited about something, "Come closer so I can see you."

I wanted to rail at her for going back on her word, but I was too hungry to jeopardize even a stale crust of bread. Besides, what good would it do? I obeyed, drawing near the candle that momentarily blinded me. There was a long pause. Something dropped onto the floor near my feet.

"Close the shutters," the disembodied voice spoke softly.

Alone again I groped about on the floor. As always, the dinner roll was stale and hard, so I gnawed on it like a dog working on a bone. When I had consumed it, I licked my fingers, determined to scoop up every single stray crumb. Moments later, anger swept over me in great swells—anger at my spinelessness; at lies that masquerade as agreements; at darkness without relief; at light bulbs that burn out. And then the anger morphed into despair. *Oh Lord, please help me!*

Where's your divine providence now? I imagined Benjamín asking with a smile, half-mocking, half tender.

The bathroom light flicked on again. Light, beautiful light! Even as I thanked God I could imagine Ben quipping, Don't get excited. This proves nothing. It's obvious that the power went out and someone got the generator going again. There's no miraculous light.

Oh, shut up. All light is miraculous, I smiled, hugging myself. And I suddenly wished that Benjamín could materialize, arms crossed in a skeptical stance, because then I would reach up and kiss him and concede most gladly: You're partially right, darling. Someone must have gotten the generator going again. I can't prove that God answered my prayer by enlightening that person. But can you prove that He didn't?

I turned to my contraband for another delicious night of reading, of thinking, of grappling with questions that had never mattered to me until my incarceration. What is the nature of freedom? How does one change inwardly? Can we be saved in an instant or is it a process? But above all, why does a benevolent God allow evil? This last question more than the others dominated my thoughts—when I wasn't obsessing about food, that is. In a very real sense, though, reading had become nourishment. So I read *Divine Providence* yet again. When I guessed it was daybreak, I hid the book on its high perch and returned to the mattress to sleep. A few hours later, I was awakened by a rattling sound.

"Remind me to have Rogelio file the key. It sticks," doña Manuela muttered to her stone shadow.

As the two women let themselves into the darkened room, sunlight sneaked in on cat paws, dodging their legs.

"Drink this." Doña Manuela held out a mug with steam rising above its rim.

It was *atole,* the cereal beverage that she and I both loved. Hot as it was, I gulped it down, spilling some onto the mattress. I continued to drink, all the while glancing furtively at my captors.

"Listen closely, Isabel Brentt. Do you remember how you saved the dog's life?" Doña Manuela drew closer. "Don't gawk at me, girl. Answer the question. How did you save the dog?"

"I . . . I did as you told me."

"And you must do that again. Your grandfather is downstairs."

"Cadwally?"

"He's come to visit you. We're going to have lunch together, all three of us, just like we did with the lawyer. You're to speak only in Spanish. Not a word of English, is that clear? He thinks you're in charge here. Keep it that way. I don't make idle threats. I meant what I said about the dog." I felt myself begin to slip into the black, bottomless depths of doña Manuela's eyes. "Make no mistake about it, Isabel Brentt. Your grandfather means even less to me than the dog." I was struck speechless. *She wouldn't. No, not that.*

Manuela Nyman softened her threat with a cliché and a shrug of the shoulders. "These are dangerous times, especially for travelers. Thieves and murderers lurk on our roads again. It's no longer safe to travel alone." Then dropping the mask she added, "If your grandfather suspects anything, anything at all—"

"No! He won't suspect a thing!" I cut her off.

A LANK VISITOR

They had me wear one of Eva's dresses. My own skirts were now so loose that they slid down my hips and puddled on the floor. Though my sister-in-law was of a petite build, her gown fit me. Unfortunately, it was also a good three inches shorter than fashion dictated. Just the same it looked great, from the high collar and yoke of exquisite Swiss embroidery to the lace inserts that ran down to the flounced hem. In spite of my inner agitation, I ran my hands along the pale blue silk, enjoying its smoothness. Ten minutes later, I was walking down the stairs with my mother-in-law, our arms linked affectionately. Actually, I needed to be steadied and leaned heavily on la patrona's arm. Cadwally stood at the base of the stairs in the courtyard, even though doña Manuela had left instructions that he be seated in the drawing room. His eyes, blue and transparent as the Morelos sky above, sparked astonishment. I rushed forward.

"Cadwally! I have so much to tell you!"

Run! Leave now! I wanted to whisper into his ear as we hugged. I inhaled his scent of alcohol, turpentine and soap. *Oh, Cadwally! How could I have forgotten the way you smell and the wonderful touch of your skin—even of your bristly moustache?* For a few seconds I was a child again, secure in the nest of his long scrawny arms.

"What the hell's going on?" he whispered into my ear.

Drawing back, I reached for doña Manuela's hand. "It's all right, Cadwally. You remember. I invited doña Manuela to live with me here in San Serafín." I spoke with slow deliberation in Spanish. "I've been doing a lot of . . . a lot of"—soul-searching, I wanted to say, but the Spanish words took off on me just then, like a dog breaking free of his leash. I dropped doña Manuela's hand as I fumbled in the air, but the expression refused to come. "I've done a lot of thinking. I love my husband, and his family is my family. I can't hurt them."

"Don't be gullible," he muttered in English, his lips a tight line.

I took the plunge. *Make it believable.* "I'm sorry, Cadwally. Please understand. I cannot in good conscience accept an inheritance to which I have no moral claim. None. So I've already deeded everything back to the family."

He groaned.

"I know that you and Tomás had high hopes for the villagers, but we went about it all wrong," I persisted in Spanish, my body half-turned toward my mother-in-law in an effort to lessen the utter unnaturalness of speaking to him in anything but English. "This is doña Manuela's house, and it is she who has shown the greater kindness by letting me live here too. Oh, please be glad for me. I'm so much happier now because I'm at peace with my conscience."

He tried to smile under his shaggy moustache. It was a grudging effort that said, you poor fool. My mother-in-law stepped toward him, craning her neck to look into his face. The contrast between their heights almost made me forget how formidable she was.

"I must confess to you, don Cadwallader, that I *was* furious the day Isabel claimed San Serafín," Manuela shook her head. "I have a bad temper. I've struggled with it all my life. But I hope that you'll consider that I was beside myself with despair over my poor son and then the shock of being evicted. Still, I behaved badly and I humbly ask you to forgive me."

Cadwally suddenly looked as if he had spilled the entire contents of a gravy boat on his hostess's tablecloth. He nodded and mumbled in his heavily accented Spanish, "My apologies, ma'am."

She smiled graciously. All was forgiven. No real harm done. "You know, don Cadwallader," and here she pressed both hands on his crossed arms. "San Serafín was always intended for Benjamín. He has no interest in the other properties, least of all in the mines. He's a farmer at heart. So you see, your granddaughter *will* be the mistress of this hacienda in due course. In the meantime, I can teach her the ropes until my son is able to come home and take his place beside her. I trust that I have your blessing to go on sharing my home with your granddaughter?"

"That's up to Isabel. If she's content . . ." He gestured with his battered old hat.

"I am!" I beamed at him. "In these few days I have found a mother in doña Manuela."

Right on cue we actresses paused for a hug and I almost believed our fiction. In the strangeness of that moment, as I felt my tormentor's body pressed to mine in a warm embrace, I was gripped by an intense yearning. *Please, this doesn't need to be a pretense. We can make it be true.* But of course, the only thing that really mattered just then was that Cadwally believe us.

"Why is she so skinny?" He asked sharply.

"Because she doesn't eat," doña Manuela sighed. "Your granddaughter has a mind of her own, don Cadwallader. She locks herself in her room and weeps for my son, and she simply won't eat."

"It's just that I miss him so much!" I told him earnestly. "You don't know—"

"Hang it all. You've got to eat, do you hear me?" He grumbled in English.

"*En español,*" I wagged a finger in his face.

"You're starting to look . . ." He turned to doña Manuela, scrambling his words in his agitation. "She looks . . . *parecer* like a street dog *calle . . . callajero!*"

I would have laughed at his adulterated Spanish, but I was still too afraid for him. "I'll do better. I promise." I sealed the pact with a kiss on his cheek.

Cadwally chewed the tip of his bristly white moustache. "All right," he shrugged. "Just get her to eat."

"We'll begin with lunch," la patrona smiled. "Come, daughter, let's not leave your grandfather standing in the sun. Let's go in, shall we?"

"Oh, no. Let's go for a walk in the gardens!" I countermanded, drunk on sunlight.

"As you like."

Linking arms with the dragon and my grandfather, I borrowed their energy to step back into the world again. As we strolled through the back gardens, the sheer beauty of the lawns and the sky brought tears to my eyes.

"What's wrong?" Cadwally halted abruptly, causing us all to stumble against each other.

"I'm just so glad you're here," I answered doggedly in Spanish, unnatural as it seemed to both of us. "And the gardens are so beautiful!"

I moved our trio forward. *Don't do that again!* The command went off in my head. Yet I was also beginning to sense that I had to orchestrate my deliverance. Fate—no, divine providence—was granting me a chance through my grandfather. *Give him a clue, but be subtle. Ask him to give Miss Havisham and Estelle my regards. No, they were on the same side; they both hurt Pip. Someone else, some other American or British characters that the dragon wouldn't know.*

"Señora, you must tell my grandfather about your flowers. I still can't identify more than four or five varieties. And the birds: you must tell us all about them."

Doña Manuela obliged. For the next half hour or so she droned on, her voice hypnotic as the ocean. At one point we paused under the arms of an enormous fig tree, the largest of the *amates* on the property. Its limbs shot straight out parallel to the ground, creating a shelter for chairs and tables clustered in its generous shade. We sat for a few minutes. The canopy shimmered and swayed as if humming to the sky.

"This tree is more than two hundred years old," Manuela Nyman explained. "It's a . . . a—" she faltered. "Oh, how aggravating. The name is on the tip of my tongue."

Hester Prynne, the tree seemed to whisper to me.

Yes! I could ask Cadwally to give my regards to Hester and to what's his name—the hypocritical physician who is slowly killing the young minister. That will remind him that people and things are not always what they seem.

When the tree flatly refused to surrender its identity to doña Manuela, she rose with a shrug and we continued our stroll. I did no better with *The Scarlet Letter.* The vengeful physician remained equally elusive. *Dimmesdale was the lover, Pearl their daughter and Hester's demonic husband was . . . Willingworth? Wadsworth? Chadsworth?*

I would have gone on searching for him, but I found myself caught up again in an overload of sensations, an orgy to my starved senses. *My God! Everything, everything is so beautiful!* Dragonflies, blades of grass, the flawless sky, the bright ochre walls, the sun's glint on the chapel's tiled dome, the slow, circular flight of turkey vultures, the gorgeous cracks in the flagstones under our feet—every single thing that my eyes touched rebounded, flowing into me as if newly created and I were witnessing its genesis.

We paused by the aviary, its octagonal dome towering high above us. And I suddenly thought about the blind man in the temple: *When Jesus gave him sight, what must the man have thought? How does the mind take in such an abundance of shapes and colors, drinking it in without drowning? And these birds! Is there no limit to the Divine imagination, to the infinite variety, not just of color patterns, but of wing, neck, head, eye, beak, claw?*

The parrots—lories and lorikeets, cockatoos, and cockatiels—dazzled me. And then there were all the other denizens of the Mexican and Central American jungles, all brought here for doña Manuela's pleasure. Today, this one precious day, they were here for me as well. I gazed in utter delight at a pair of macaws that were preening each other.

"Parrots are monogamous; they mate for life," doña Manuela explained. "This pair has been together for twelve or thirteen years now."

We watched the macaws. After the female was preened by her mate, she closed her eyes and pressed her head to his soft-feathered chest. In a flash of memory, I rested my face on Benjamín's bare chest as we lay in bed. For a moment I could almost feel the contour of the pectoral muscles under the tight skin.

"These are my tanagers," doña Mauela pointed. "I especially like the coloration of those over there. I can't remember what specific type of tanager they are."

Green-headed tanagers, Benjamín would have told her.

"The red ones aren't bad looking, either."

Summer tanagers, Mother.

"And that one on the highest branch of the aviary, that one is my prized trogon. It's a quetzal—not just any quetzal, but the resplendent emerald quetzal."

"Does it have a mate?" Cadwally squinted against the sun.

"She died."

49

DECEIT AL FRESCO

"WOULD YOU CARE to have lunch now, señora?" a servant asked in a soft voice, her manner deferential with la patrona but clearly uneasy with us two gringos. I could almost read her mind: *Am I supposed to look at the señora Isabel or ignore her? What about the old man?*

"Oh, let's eat out here," I preempted doña Manuela. "It's such a beautiful day."

"You heard her. Do as the señora Isabel says."

Moments later we were sitting at a round table on the back terrace, cut flowers, silver candelabra, and fine dinnerware as props. Cadwally took a seat opposite me and reached into an inner pocket of his jacket.

"These came for you." He placed a small stack of letters in front of me. "I've been meaning to get them to you," he mumbled.

I pounced on the letters. Before doña Manuela could contrive objections, I was tearing open one envelope after the other, drinking messages as if I had not tasted water in days.

Dearest Isabel,

For shame! Why haven't you written? Married life must indeed keep a woman busy. So I shall have to forgive you—
    Did you know that Marjorie and Sid are engaged? It's true! Mildred gave a party for them at Cairnwood—

Dearest Isabel,

Carina, Wertha, and I think we should all head south and surprise you with a visit! But our parents won't hear of it until everyone is certain the revolution is really over and that there will be no counter-revolution. Where is their sense of adventure?
    So we must wait and content ourselves with Emiline's accounts of the time she visited you. She swears that Mexico is the most romantic country on earth. What I would give—

Dear Isabel,

I can't believe that it's already been a little over a year since Mother, Father and I visited you in Cuernavaca. As long as I live I shall never forget the Centennial Ball and dancing with dashing Mexican officers under a canopy of stars and comet light. Mr. Nyman and his brother were so kind to us. I think back to those days with yearning. Your Mexico is so marvelously different from our quiet borough. Do you know how lucky you are, Isabel? It snowed yesterday. I'd give anything to escape the cold—

I devoured the letters, each page a magic carpet that carried me high above the walls of San Serafín, back into the world that

I had known as a student in Bryn Athyn, a world that resounded with girlish laughter and the pranks and gallantry of young men; a place of innocent pleasures: dances, the special 'Friday Suppers,' picnics, canoeing, walks in the woods, train rides into Philadelphia for an evening at the orchestra, ice cream and the Ferris wheel in the Valley, classes in Benade Hall, card games with the Whist Club, sledding on winter days—

My God! It's real after all. I didn't just dream up that other life.

"Ah, lunch. Put away your letters, dear. You've neglected us long enough," doña Manuela chastised.

I looked up, startled. "Oh, of course. I'm sorry. I'll finish them later."

"No, no," Cadwally smiled. "Go ahead and enjoy them now if you want. I don't mind."

"No, don Cadwallader. We must get her to eat, remember? Tacha, take the letters to the señora Isabel's room." Bryn Athyn and my friends vanished in steady sync with Tacha's heavy footsteps.

The soup tureen was set in front of doña Manuela, who pushed it a few inches across the small table toward me.

"Well? Aren't you going to serve our guest, dear?"

I stared at the tureen's lid, seeking in its ceramic whiteness the snow-filled fields of a distant place and time. Yet the moment I removed the lid and inhaled the scent of the chicken lime soup, there was only the present with its wealth of aromas, textures, and colors. Oh, the majesty of avocado slices, garlic, tomatoes, tortilla strips, peppers, sprigs of *epazote,* and thick *crème fraiche* swirling together in a new creation. I inhaled deeply. Picking up the ladle, I played my part, serving my mother-in-law first, then my grandfather. When at last I took my first sip, I knew that nothing in the whole twenty-one years of my life had ever filled my mouth with such an explosion of flavors and textures.

I remained in a state of heightened awareness. Colors spoke in a multilayered language, vibrating with a life of their own.

Sounds were amplified, so that there was no less magic in the crowing of the roosters behind the kitchen than in the exotic cry of the peacocks. Most of all, I loved watching my grandfather who sat opposite me.

He has such a beautiful face. I thought, caressing him with my eyes. He in turn was finally relaxing, especially after he drew a small glass flask from his coat pocket.

"I remembered that you don't keep spirits in the house," he commented to doña Manuela. "You don't mind if I spike my lemonade, I hope."

It was not a question. We watched him pour whatever he had carefully stored in the flask. His hands shook as he screwed the cap back on, and I sensed that he was making a great effort to limit his intake. He started to pocket the flask. Then as if he could not bear to have it out of his sight, he set it down alongside his glass.

"I do hope you plan to stay a few days, don Cadwallader—or weeks if you like."

What's her game? I hid my fear on the rim of my cobalt-blue water glass. "Oh do," I managed because that would be in the script, wouldn't it? *But should he? Say no, Cadwally.*

"I'm afraid I've come unprepared."

"We can send for your things. You must stay and help me fatten up our stubborn Isabel."

He looked at me over the rim of his own glass. "Thank you," he said after a pause. "I'll certainly consider it."

I felt myself fluttering in Manuela Nyman's web again. Two swallows flew high above the garden walls just then. I watched them vanish in the high canopy as my mother-in-law gushed hospitality: "I hope you like chicken *en pipián verde*, don Cadwallader. It's baked with a pumpkin sauce with *chiles serranos*, just enough to give it some kick."

"Actually, I haven't found a chile I didn't like, doña Manuela," he nodded affably.

"Then I think you are more of a Mexican than I imagined, don Cadwallader. Here, have some *torta de elote* with it. The way our cook Bardomiana makes it, it's a cross between cornbread and corn pudding. It's quite wonderful, as Isabel can tell you. Do try some. And have some rice with fried *plátanos machos.*"

"Macho bananas, huh? I should have known the state of Morelos could produce nothing less!" he laughed.

I had left my soup bowl bright and shiny, consuming every last drop. However, my shrunken stomach could not accommodate the rest of the meal as easily. I picked at my food, drawing scowls and reprimands from both sides of the table.

"I'll do better at supper. I promise. Feed me more of Bardomiana's tortilla soup and I'll consume two bowls of it!" I laughed because Cadwally was studying me too closely.

"Your grandfather and I will hold you to that."

For a few moments I let myself dream about a series of meals like this one and long strolls in the garden. Why not? I could continue to play my assigned role. It would be such a wonderful reprieve from prison and a chance to simply enjoy being with Cadwally again. And I would gain time, time enough to remember the nasty hypocritical physician in Hawthorne's novel, the one who tormented Hester Prynne's lover, and I would hand it to Cadwally, a clue that he alone in all of San Serafín would understand. *So it's good that he's staying,* I smiled inwardly. As servants began to clear for dessert, the stone-faced Tacha bumped the table. Cadwally's flask shattered on the flagstones. The look on his face proclaimed the fragility of fantasies.

"Damn!" he muttered.

I braced myself, as if the word were an earthen levy, old and deficient, about to let rage crash over its banks. My grandfather clenched and unclenched his hands. As servants scurried to sweep up the shards of glass, he seemed to be struggling to master himself.

"Well, no matter," he waved a large hand. "I have more in my saddle bag."

He smiled. When he didn't insist that the bottles be brought to him, I read in it a magnificent gesture, his gift to me. Moments later, a white-frosted cake was brought to the table. Doña Manuela indicated with the faintest nod of her head that it was to be set in front of me. Taking the hint, I reached for a knife to slice it.

Still caught up in the afterglow of the letters from Pennsylvania, I remember thinking that the cake was like a field covered in snow drifts. I tasted it. "Hmm! This is a three-milk cake, isn't it?" I murmured through half closed eyes as the dessert fork left my lips.

"Yes, and I'll have you know, don Cadwallader, that in this house we have the good taste to spike it with a little brandy," Manuela Nyman nodded so good-naturedly that I almost liked her.

"How very discerning of you," Cadwally beamed.

"Unfortunately, the cake used up the last of my supply."

"Then you must allow me to leave some here with you. Just have my saddle bag brought in."

After coffee and chocolates, la patrona folded her napkin. "Well, Isabel, what do you think? Shall we go inside or take another stroll through the garden?"

"We haven't been in the labyrinth yet."

"That's true. All right. To the labyrinth."

Cadwally jumped to his feet to draw back his hostess's chair. Misplaced Boston Brahmin that he was, his expensive cashmere suit now as threadbare as the yellowed handkerchief in his lapel, he still stepped easily into the old courtesies.

"Oh, thank you, don Cadwallader."

Just then he swayed like a sapling caught off guard by a gust of wind.

50

INTO THE LABYRINTH

"Cadwally! Are you all right!?" Realizing that I had just spoken in English, I quickly translated, "¿Abuelito, estás bien?"

"I'm fine! Fine! *Necesitar . . .* to *fortifica . . .*" I could sense that he was struggling not to ask for alcohol. I poured a glass of water for him, spilling some on the tablecloth.

"Never mind the labyrinth, don Cadwallader," doña Manuela spoke smoothly. "We can sit right here—"

"No, no. I'm fine."

"Are you sure, Cadwally?" I hugged his right arm.

As if to prove the point, he released his hold on the chair back and began praising the famed labyrinth, insisting that he had to see it for himself now that he had two guides. It was obvious that my mother-in-law often caught only the gist of what Cadwally was saying in his outlandish Spanish, but she never let on. She merely smiled or laughed pleasantly. So we set off again, an inseparable threesome strolling into a labyrinth. The hedges towered a full three to four feet higher than our lank visitor. Doña Manuela served as guide.

"I designed it myself," she boasted. "I had full-grown shrubs planted so that Benjamín and Samuel wouldn't have to wait until adulthood to enjoy it. And for a short time it really did stump those little devils!"

We came to a dead end. The dragon laughed. By the third wrong turn her brow was scrunched up and she wasn't laughing. "It's been many years since I ventured in here. Let me think . . . yes, this way, I think." I knew every turn of the labyrinth but said nothing. "No, that's not right. It must be this way." *She's afraid!* I was startled, then elated. *Is it the narrowness of the corridors? The lack of control? Being lost? Should I get us out of here? No. Let the dragon sweat.*

"Maybe it's this way." I deliberately misled them away from the fountain where Ben and I used to meet.

Doña Manuela paused to catch her breath, as if she had been sprinting. I wanted to laugh out loud, but one sidelong glance at my grandfather killed all hilarity. He looked as agitated as the labyrinth's architect, and I knew that he was fully in the jaws of *el monstro.*

"Maybe we've gone far enough," I sighed. "I think I can remember how to get us back."

My companions nodded eagerly.

"I need a drink," Cadwally mumbled as he and doña Manuela stumbled out of the labyrinth. "I want my saddlebag."

We returned to our table on the terrace. Moments later, a servant delivered Cadwally's saddle bag. It hung limp and wet on both sides of her arm. "I'm sorry, señor. One of the grooms dropped it when he unsaddled the mule. All the bottles shattered."

Cadwally's visit had lasted almost four hours, one hour more than doña Manuela would have predicted. I was not surprised either when he announced that he needed to get back to his studio. All my life I had seen him trying to outrun his addiction. But how could he hope to do that? A legion of demons seemed to burn him from within unless he appeased them with an offering.

It didn't matter whether it was with an expensive whiskey or the cheapest *aguardiente*. The demons were undiscerning, their thirst unquenchable.

He gave me a sad, lopsided smile. "I'll be back soon—for Christmas. That's only a few weeks away."

You're doing it again! I wanted to yell at him. *Only this time you're abandoning me to rot in a prison!*

A more urgent thought shoved aside my resentment: *Just get him back to Cuernavaca.* As if reading my mind, my mother-in-law turned to Valle Inclán who appeared just then. The Spaniard stood as tall as Cadwally but overpowering in build.

"My administrator has arranged an escort for you."

"Please don't trouble yourself," Cadwally smiled affably as four heavily-armed horsemen clambered into the courtyard. "I got here just fine on my own."

"No. I insist." Doña Manuela played the benevolent dictator.

"That hardly seems necessary," I ventured. My eyes swept the high walls, where more armed men stood guard, all of them answerable now only to la patrona.

"On the contrary. Zapatista bands have been seen roaming within a mile of our gates. Please, for my peace of mind and Isabel's, let my men escort you back to Cuernavaca."

"No. Thank you, señora," he spoke with sudden firmness. Then he gave her a big toothy grin. "Zapatotes . . . *Zapatatos* have better things to do than to trouble with an old gringo."

La patrona sighed. Cadwally turned to mount his rented mule, his foot missing the stirrup on the first try. He seemed all legs and awkwardness, but he did manage on the third try.

Standing on tiptoes, I reached up and caressed his whiskered face ever so gently.

"Please take care of yourself, Cadwally."

I was aware of Tacha staring with her expressionless face. Stepping back, I watched my grandfather amble alone toward the gate. And then because the forgotten name suddenly rushed out of hiding, I called out in Spanish in a voice as clear as a church bell, "Say hello to all our old friends for me, especially Hester Prynne and Chillingworth!"

He turned in the saddle. "I'll do that!" He smiled from the depths of blue eyes that told me, *I thought so.* "Thank you, ladies!" He tapped two fingers to his tattered wide-brimmed hat. Before clearing the front gate, Cadwally reined in the mule as if he had just remembered something. Turning in his saddle a second time, he called out loudly so that all would hear, "Doña Manuela! Please don't let my granddaughter waste away to nothing! Feed her! Put some flesh on those bones!"

We felt the weight of many stares. "I will!" She called back in a voice that quavered ever so slightly.

I waved. "Have a safe trip, Cadwally!" *Go! Just go!*

He doffed his hat in grand showman style. "See you at Christmas!"

51

THE FAST

THE DAY AFTER my grandfather's unexpected visit, the dragon and Stone-face entered my room. "Set it down there," doña Manuela pointed. Tacha placed a bed tray and a lantern on the floor. "Get up, girl. Write what I tell you."

I was groggy but managed to kneel on the cold tiles. The tray, which was really more like a table with short legs, held several blank sheets of paper and a fountain pen. La patrona dictated the heading, addressing the letter to His Excellency, The Most Reverend José Moral del Río, Archbishop of Mexico. November 26, 1911. The date startled me into full wakefulness. I had lost track of time, and Tacha must have been instructed to keep it that way. Having a sudden fix on the calendar felt like a boon, unintended as it was.

"Now write: I, Isabel Brentt . . ."

I've been her prisoner since September 7th, so that means . . . two months and—

" . . . being of sound mind," la patrona dictated.

Two months and seventeen—no, nineteen days—

"—do earnestly petition—the Holy Catholic Church—"

Twenty-six minus seven is—nineteen. Math had never been my strong point. Scampering after it now while taking dictation was like running after a cat. *Yes, nineteen. So it's been two months and nineteen days. That's almost eleven weeks!*

"—to annul my marriage to Benjamín Nyman Vizcarra. Don't stop, girl. Write it: to annul my marriage to Benjamín Nyman Vizcarra."

I forgot the cat-numbers. I looked up at my jailer. "Do you honestly believe that an annulment has the power to erase a marriage, as if it had never happened?"

"Yes, I do. The church—"

"Well it happened!" I jumped up, overturning the tray with a loud clatter, ink bottle bleeding on the floor. "I was married to Benjamín, in a Catholic church, by the way. Before God and society, I am your son's wife whether you like it or not."

"Hold her wrists, Tacha." Without warning she went for my wedding ring, the humble band that Benjamín had given me.

"No!" I cried out, writhing and biting them. The dragon slapped me hard, as she had the night that I tried to free the birds from the aviary. Much as I tried to clench my fist shut, I felt the ring slip away. "You have no right!" I cried passionately.

"I have every right. Listen to me, Isabel Brentt."

"My name is Isabel Brentt de Nyman."

"Be quiet! If you ever want to eat again, and if you don't want the dog to be—"

"Go ahead. Starve me to death. Shoot the dog. I'm not participating in your colossal lies. Not this time. Benjamín and I are man and wife. And if God wills it, we'll continue to be married for all eternity."

My resolve stunned her. It also enraged her.

Am I dreaming all this? I asked the darkness. I had been fed nothing at all since my refusal to write the petition to annul my marriage. Was it five days ago? Eight? Ten? Without the contrast of light and darkness there was no way to know. Sensation and thought became the only realities. To make matters worse, my mobility had been greatly restricted. Doña Manuela and Tacha had fastened a chain around my waist with a padlock. The other end they secured to one of the clawed feet on which the tub crouched. I could just reach the toilet on one side and the sink on the other. No matter how much I stretched and yanked against the chain, I could not reach the light switch nor the book high up on the tank. So I was in the dark all the time now with absolutely nothing to do. In an attempt to soothe my hunger pains, I could only cup my hands under the spigots in the sink and drink water in great gulps. Then I would ease back into the empty tub or slump to the floor to sleep away the endless hours.

"Do we gag her, señora?" Tacha had asked when they first bound me.

"What do you say, Isabel Brentt? If you scream and rant, no one will come to your rescue. Everyone has been informed that you are insane. But if I hear the slightest sound from you, I'll personally thrust a gag halfway down your throat. So what's it to be?"

I chose silence, but I could not silence the desperate rumblings of my stomach nor fill the loneliness that escalated without Hipólito or my book. I yearned so intensely for companionship that I would have welcomed even Tacha, much as she refused to give me so much as a frown or a scowl. Yes, I would have settled for her indifference or even for Manuela Nyman's barbed remarks. But no one came and thoughts grew claws.

Why doesn't Cadwally come back with rescuers? I know he understood my hints. So why isn't he back? Could something have happened to him? Please, no!

Unwilling to entertain such a horrific possibility, I focused instead on Tomás. Where was he? And then on survival. How long can a person live on water alone? Ten days? Two weeks? A month? No. How could anyone live a month on water alone? What if she means to kill me?

No, she only means to torment me. She's too religious—no, fanatical—to risk damnation.

She could let me die and then confess, not to Samuel but to that pitiful hacienda priest that she employs. She would then think herself absolved of all sin. So she *could* do it.

This isn't happening! Not yet! I haven't accomplished anything with my life. I've done nothing, meant nothing. It's all been such a colossal waste. No one will miss me.

The thought of Cadwally and Rosa grieving for me repulsed my attack of self- pity, routing it thoroughly. All right, I'll ask for the annulment. I'll do it for them. But there was no second chance.

I'm so hungry, Rosa.

Eat your sadness before it eats you.

Only if it tastes like beans with salsa. But what about the pain? Everything hurts.

Endure, my sweetest.

I endured when enduring meant living in a blur between waking and dreaming. Ah, dreams. Such a release but oh so ephemeral, so easily extinguished on awakening or splintering into fragments. Yet as I speak to you, I can still remember two of my recurring dreams with sparkling clarity.

In the first dream I am a child and Rosa is taking Tomás and me to a local cemetery to celebrate the Days of the Dead, our favorite festival. Candy skulls and skeleton dolls fill the market stalls. Their gaping jaws are smiles that render death more whimsical than scary. Marigolds and candlelight give the cemetery a cheerful golden glow. Families sit on the ground spreading out the food that they have brought for their dead, as we have for Rosa's dead father.

"You won't see him," Rosa whispers in the dream. "But listen and you'll know when he is sitting with us."

I listen. There is a squeaking of sandals and a faint ruffling of our blanket as an invisible old man hunkers down alongside us. Seconds later I realize that we have all turned into skeletons. Our clothes hang on us as if pinned to a clothesline. Our bones clatter in the wind. Yet it doesn't matter a whit. We're enjoying the meal that Rosa has prepared for her father and us, laughing because that's what a true Mexican does with death. We laugh, not at it but with it. Embrace it like an old friend—at least during the festival. We can shed all the tears we want the rest of the year, but not during these festive days.

In the second recurring dream, I have forgotten to laugh with death. I'm all anger and clenched fists. It always begins the same way, with me inside a coffin. Anger morphs temporarily into panic. "I'm still alive!" I yell at no one in particular, or at the universe itself.

Striking the lid with my fists, I smash my way out, shards of glass exploding all around, melting into soft-pelting snow. The dreamscape morphs from coffin to the shores of a frozen white lake. A wolf paces on the opposite shore, back and forth on long restless legs. He watches me, hanging back as if he were trying to decide something. In the logic of the dream, I know that it's Benjamín. Yet there is no tenderness in me, only a nursing of old wounds. Old resentments.

"This is all your fault!" I yell at him above the howling wind. "Look what your stupid distrust has done!" The wolf hangs back, pacing on large paws. Pacing and watching. The wind rustles an enormous piece of paper on which I stand—a petition for annulment. "I won't sign it," I yell at the wolf, "but that doesn't mean that I've forgiven you!"

My anger cracks the ice, plunging him into the frigid water. Instantly, the lake seals him up and I wake up gasping.

Oh, Lord! Why can't I forgive and mean it? Why is it so hard?

Then my body clamors with a different question.

How much longer can I go without food?

52

REVENGE

Manuela Nyman visited me days later. I was huddled inside the tub. Her stare, sharp as a wasp's sting, woke me.

"What a foul creature you are, Isabel Brentt." Manuela flapped her hand in front of her nose. "Don't you know how to flush a toilet? You just have to give the chain a good yank. Put some muscle into it."

There's nothing there. My intestines are utterly empty and you know it. So stop your theatrics, I could have retorted, especially since I no longer feared retribution. That I held my peace was simply from a lack of energy.

Manuela Nyman made a show of flushing the toilet. Then sitting on the closed lid, she stared at me long and hard. "Hmm, Tacha's right," she murmured to herself. Setting her lantern on the floor, her face became all sharp lines and shadows. "You look like you have something to say. Go ahead."

"Why?" I gasped the question in a gravelly voice.

"Why what?" doña Manuela answered almost pleasantly.

"Why—"; my throat was a dry valley. Struggling to sit up in the tub, my motions pathetically labored, I reached for the faucet. I could feel the weight of her stare as I gulped water, dribbling on myself. Those few sips quelled my apathy long enough for me to ask, "Why are you doing this?"

"If the blessed saints could fast, severely at times, you certainly can too."

"I've done every—everything you asked."

"How little you understand."

"I understand your anger."

"Do you now?"

"Yes. But this is wrong."

Manuela Nyman crossed her arms. "Don't you know by now that every crime carries its own punishment?"

"Surely—surely, I've been punished enough."

She stared at me with a kind of curiosity, as if she were examining a snake that both repelled and fascinated her. I tried again: "Señora, please forgive me. In the name of . . . of Christ our God." I had to keep pausing to catch my breath. "Let me go home—Everything is now—as it was, and Benjamín—Benjamín *will* be exonerated. The truth will come out—and he'll regain his freedom."

"Of what use is freedom to him?" Doña Manuela uncrossed her arms.

"Everyone cherishes freedom. Why wouldn't Benjamín want his?"

"You really don't know, do you? It's all been so simple for you. Even I helped you, unwittingly betraying my own son to the authorities. My own son! If I'd known all the evil that you and Lucio were going to unleash on us, I would have killed you both with my bare hands. My Benjamín lost everything because of you."

"I didn't ask him—to fight with his father."

"No. I suppose not." She gave me a lopsided smile. "You know, I have to hand it to you, Isabel Brentt. For a short time there you really did have it all."

"So this is about revenge."

"And justice."

Staring into my jailor's stern features, I thought of inquisitors who had tortured hapless victims in the name of Christ and the church that they claimed to serve. How does one reason with such people?

"Get it straight. With or without your cooperation, I *will* get the marriage annulled, because you're not only a thief, Isabel Brentt, but an adulteress."

"That's not true!" Indignation straightened my back. "I never betrayed—"

"Oh! And that's why we found your corset in Tomás Tepaneca's room the day you ran off with him?"

The pillowcase with my corset; Tomás yanking it out of my hands and tossing it over his shoulder. *You can hardly go for a morning ride clutching a pillowcase.*

"Wait . . . I can explain." Why was my breath so ragged? I needed to set her straight once and for all before she killed me, or because I was dying and I wanted her to grasp the extent of her error, her toxic misjudgment. "It isn't . . . it isn't what it seems. I didn't—"

"You didn't anything. That's always the way with you. You didn't connive to cheat my children of their inheritance. You didn't run off with a man who wasn't your husband. And you didn't intend for the guards to beat my son almost to death, but that's what they did!" Manuela Nyman was on her feet now, her body shaking. "Your visit, your little pretense of wifely concern, nearly cost him his life!"

"No. He attacked *me.*"

"Then I wish he had killed you! Then at least the beating would have been worth it."

"What beating?"

"The one the prison guards gave him when he raged against your adultery, as any true man would. They took him into another room and beat him with clubs. Those miserable scraps of humanity cracked his skull."

"No," I shook my head. Why does denial jump to the head of the line?

"They broke one of his legs and his ribs and beat him in the face until his eyes puffed shut, beating him again and again . . ."

"Oh, God! No!" I was sobbing now.

"And they left him to bleed to death, and he would have if Samuel had not visited him a few hours later. When I saw Benjamín, I didn't know him! My own son and I couldn't recognize him . . ." Her voice trailed off. Looking up, I saw the horror of that day carved into her face, her eyes dark and tortured. Then rage propelled her toward me so that her face was inches from mine.

"They took my son's vibrant mind and beat it out of him. Total strangers have to take care of my child because I cannot bear to see what he has become. He sits in a wheelchair unable to walk or to speak. He just stares blankly and drools, my Benjamín!"

"Oh, please, no more!"

"He breaks my heart every single day, every hour, and you ask me why I'm doing this?"

"Ben! Ben!" I shook my head in despair.

"Oh, spare me the act! As if you and your lover cared what happened to my son!"

Manuela locked the door. Neither she nor Tacha would return until nearly a month later.

53

WAKING TO DREAM

THE HORRIFIC NEWS about Benjamín eclipsed the certainty of my death sentence. Because I could see in my mind's eye the guards' blood-splattered clubs, I clutched the sides of my head and let out a long, harrowing wail. Then another and another, despair morphing into rage. In my frenzy I didn't care who heard me or what they did to me. How could you let this happen? I railed at God inwardly. Don't tell me it's for the sake of human freedom. To hell with human freedom! I thundered across the bleakest of landscapes.

For once, Manuela Nyman's anguish and mine cried out in shared pain: "*They took my son's vibrant mind and beat it out of him,*" she had said. "*He stares blankly— drools—doesn't speak—*"

I cried a *chubasco*. When the deluge had run its course, I fell into an exhausted sleep and dreamed that I was cooking in Rosa's kitchen. God was sitting there with me. By that, I mean the demiurgic idea that I'd been given as a child and had not quite shaken—the notion of God as some kind of Father figure who imposes his will and disappoints ours. God, out there, not in us.

God separate from Jesus Christ—which is why I perceived Him in my dream as a shadow, human in shape but otherwise featureless. I was sullen and felt it my duty to make Him understand, once and for all, that His scheme to preserve spiritual freedom at any cost was downright flawed. So I babbled about the right way to cook beans, which made perfect sense in the dream since God and I both knew what I was trying to say. Had I been more direct, it would have run something like this: "Why is the freedom of tyrants and torturers as important to you as the rights of victims like Ben and me? How is the preservation of human freedom worth the cruelty and abuses it permits? What about the hatred it causes in the victims, huh?" I was sorting beans, tossing some away and others into Rosa's clay pot. "Well here's what *I* want in all my blessed freedom. I want to see those prison guards and Manuela Nyman and old Stone-face tortured. See how they like it." I think I was chopping up onions now. "I want to hear them howl in pain and whimper like frightened children."

The dream obliged.

Beans and pot disappeared. Prison guards in tattered uniforms were chained to a stone wall in a dungeon, and I understood that these were the men who had beaten up Benjamín. Manuela Nyman and Tacha were dragged by the hair and chained to the same wall. Men without faces approached the prisoners. Each held a thin metal bar. The faceless men did no more than bend and twist the rods, yet in the logic of the dream this caused the chained victims to cry out, their voices shrill with pain. For a moment, I felt the savage elation of revenge.

Good! Now it's your turn to suffer. Yet how quickly satisfaction morphed into horror. "That's enough," I commanded my avengers. "You can stop now."

They didn't. The torture continued, and mine was to have to listen to the prisoners' cries of agony. Something else was also happening to them. Their contorted faces were growing younger before my eyes, each prisoner reverting to adolescence, then to childhood, and finally to babyhood—all crying, all suffering, and I unable to stop their torment. Isn't that what God sees when He looks at even the worst of sinners? Doesn't He know each of us in our multifaceted, ever-changing manifestations? And knowing us in all physical and spiritual evolutions and devolutions, what if He also loves us even more than we love our own children in all their many phases? Moments before waking from that dream, I remember locking eyes with Manuela Nyman. She was a frightened toddler who held out her arms to me.

I woke up sobbing.

Oh, to be as ignorant as a baby again! To know nothing worse than the discomfort of being wet or cold or hungry rather than this, the knowledge of our worst inclinations; the despotism of inflicting pain; the terrible sense of loss, and the tyranny of regret. Was death the only escape? Yes, and Manuela Nyman was generously providing it for me. She was going to let me starve to death and no one was going to stop her.

I grew still, keenly aware that I had reached the great reckoning that awaits us all, that moment when we grasp the inescapability of our own death, unless we die in a flash of destruction so sudden that we don't even have time to gasp. That was not going to be my case. Like the victims of Pompeii, I would see the end coming as vividly as they saw volcanic ash darkening the sky. Like them, I would have time to feel the physical terror of it, the instinct to flee, and then the stunning realization that there would be no escape. This was it. Everything I had come to believe about God—the Lord as I'd learned to call him in school—everything was about to be put to the ultimate test. Though I was only twenty-one years old, I was going to die. And why not? Wasn't it better this way?

Yes, death would be such a release. I was ready. Then why was I still thrashing like some pitiful shipwrecked survivor clinging to flotsam? Why not let go and sink silently to the bottom? Because it wasn't that simple. As I was beginning to suspect, even when the soul grants the body permission to release it, the body clings to life. So I was as powerless to choose death as to find deliverance. Alone in a blackened, starless, moonless sea, I had no recourse but to hang on and pray. Lines dutifully memorized in school came back to me, murmuring in the frightened darkness: *God is our refuge and strength. A very present help in trouble.*

I sat up and recited what little I remembered of Psalm 46, half gasping, half thinking the words as a manifesto, a promise, a resolve: "God is our refuge and strength. A very present help in trouble. Therefore we will not fear, though the earth be removed, and though the mountains be carried into the midst of the sea; though the waters roar and be troubled, though the mountains shake with its swelling."

I don't know how many times I repeated those ancient words inwardly. Five times? Ten? Nothing changed. And then everything changed when at last I could murmur, "Thy will be done."

I was still chained to a bathtub, the darkness as unrelenting as my hunger, my body an ocean that weeps waves and dashes itself on rocks. But inwardly I could feel a quietude slowly spread across the water—and then the tug of the generous moon drawing me from shore to horizon, back and forth in a gentle, swaying dance. Sea and sky spoke a simple truth: Whatever happens, there is only life. Death is the necessary transition from this world into the next.

Lord, I'm ready.

Having made up my mind to die, I waited stoically.

Sometimes my fingers explored the altered landscape of my face and body as if I were observing the strange angularity of some object on a bookshelf. At such times, I was more intrigued than afraid. Just how long *can* a person live on water alone? Other times I grew impatient. Willing death on my terms, I would temporarily lose all inner calm.

Can't we just get on with this? I want to be with my parents. Why the delay?

I didn't complain all the time. Whenever I thought about the numberless communities of spirits in the next life, and of angels in their heavens, all of them human, all of them fully alive and vibrant, something almost like joy would come over me. Yes, I believed Swedenborg's accounts of the afterlife with all my heart. The immediacy of each person's resurrection made infinitely more sense to me than the notion of a benevolent God stashing us in claustrophobic coffins or crypts, making us wait until He felt good and ready to come back for us. What kind of a monster would do that to his children? Not the Lord who is love itself. *"This very day you will be with me in paradise,"* he told the crucified thief. *This very day.* Was Christ God? Isn't that what John's Gospel says from the very start? Then what about the trinity that Rosa taught me to venerate? Was I praying to the Father or to the Son or to that ghost—whoever, whatever that was? Why did it suddenly seem so confusing when it had been so clear before? Was it because I was having trouble breathing?

Oh, God! Please help me breathe or take me far from here!

And then I remembered: Father, son, and holy spirit: soul, body, and action. One Being. One God. Lord.

Resolved to die, I lay in a fetal position most of the time. The choice seemed obvious. How did Keats put it? *Now more than ever seems it rich to die, to cease upon the midnight with no pain.* When I no longer had the strength to get out of the tub and could barely lift my head to the spigot, I told myself firmly not to drink anymore. *Not a drop. Just end this.* But the body has a formidable will of its own. Despite my resolve, a gnawing thirst drove me to lap water from the spigot, prolonging the death that I longed for. It was maddening.

Sometimes I complained to Rosa. "Why is it taking so long?"

"Everything has its time, *niña.*"

"What if I wake up a week or a month from now and I'm still in this room? What am I going to do?"

"Endure, my dearest. Endure."

"That's your answer for everything." I winced as I tried to lie on my side and felt the collision of knees, ghastly, bony knees. Yet I conceded that Rosa might be right. Chained like a dog, what else was there to do but endure? Maybe I could try laughing. No, that took too much energy. Besides, I was becoming a dry riverbed.

I closed my eyes and dozed. While I waited for the Lord to free me, sleep continued to offer my only reprieve. Dreams, whether fanciful or frightening, were flights into light and color. Awake, I could only moan prayers and shiver in the dark. Asleep, I was articulate and the world vibrant again. Best of all, Benjamín had taken to dropping by, easily stepping through the thick masonry. I loved that despite the beating, he was his old self whenever he visited my dreams or hallucinations. So I wasn't surprised, for example, that he could brush darkness off his clothes with a flick of his hand, as if it were dust. He seemed eager to resume our old debates. I wasn't always sure if we were speaking in English or in Spanish or in some other language neither of us had known before.

"I wish we could die and finally be together in the next life," I told him on one visit.

"Not so fast," he smiled good-naturedly. "What makes you think I want to kick the bucket, as you Americans say? But assuming we did finally kick the ridiculous, proverbial bucket, can you be sure God would let us into heaven? Well, you'd get in easily enough, but a renegade Catholic like me?"

"God isn't some kind of gate-keeper, Ben," my dream responded with all the clarity I lacked when awake. "The kingdom of heaven is *within* you, remember? God doesn't keep people out. We ourselves do that."

"Okay," he conceded. (Now I knew we were speaking in English.) "Assuming you're right and that God were to let in apos-
tates like me, tell me something. How would the joy of heaven
make up for all that we've had to suffer? Why has God let you
starve to death and me wither inside my cracked skull? Don't you
think He has a lot of explaining to do?"

Blast it! How was I to get around that one? "I just need to
sort it all out."

"Well, let me know when you do." Benjamín began to fade
into a wall. "Until then, you'll pardon me if I return to my drool-
ing. There's little else one can do in a catatonic state, or whatever
this is," he joked, flashing his boyish smile.

Sometimes a wolf visited my dreams—the very same gray
wolf I had dreamed about in the general's house. He would break
away from his tormentors. Leaping through the stonework of
my cell, he would land near me, panting, resting his head on my
chest. Other times Benjamín was a disembodied voice that cried
out, as if trying to wake from a nightmare. "Isa! I'm lost!"

"Grab my hand." I would reach for him in the dark.

"I can't. I'm trapped in my head," he would groan.

"Then pray, darling. It really does help."

"Nothing helps. God, I'm so alone."

"You're not. He's with you, Ben, now more than ever."

I sensed that he wanted to believe me, but his skepticism was
as strong as a bull when it first enters the arena. I felt the pain
of his doubts, excruciating as barbed *banderillas* thrust into his
shoulders. Yet there were wonderful moments too. Sometimes
dreams took us to a hotel room. The décor was always wrong,
yet it was clearly the room from our honeymoon. Strong arms
would wrap themselves around me, and I knew without turning my head that it was Benjamín kissing the nape of my neck.
Other times I could stand outside myself and watch us making

love, our entwined bodies dancing to an ancient rhythm. I would have stayed there forever, reliving the sheer joy of our physicality and the eloquence of its language, marveling at a dance that was both physical and spiritual. But I always had to return to dark wakefulness and to the drumming of a heart that beat on and on. Resolving to die was easy. Dying was another matter.

54

DELAYS

So WHERE WAS Tomás while I was slowly starving to death? On a bright September morning I had seen him set off from San Serafín arrayed for battle. To Tomás that meant intelligence clothed in the physical trappings of respectability: a well-cut vested suit, a superb Arabian horse to carry him, gold from the Nyman coffers, and enough self-assurance to puff up three generals. That much I saw. Here's what I've come to know. Though reeling from my rejection of him and what he considered my irrational devotion to my marriage, he was still determined to rebuild and repopulate the village of Santa Lupita de las Milpas. That meant honoring his side of our deal: finding Eufemio Rosarito, bribing local police if necessary to arrest and haul the man to Mexico City with a signed confession, and reopening Benjamín's case. Easy. But it was raining.

It wasn't just raining in the usual manner of rain season, with short downpours in the afternoons. Sunny as it was when he first set out, the day grew irritable, and then downright onerous. Tomás was caught in a downpour of mythic proportions. His prized fedora hat lay limp as wet paper on his head. His wool suit stank almost as much as the horse. Stopping in the middle of a road that had become a muddy creek, Tomás Tepaneca cursed the rain god Tlaloc. Then he cursed himself.

You idiot! Think, Tepaneca! Before Rosarito became the general's personal servant he was his adjutant. Instead of going village to village, you moron, you could be searching for the bastard from the comfort of a dry office. His military record will have the name of his wretched town. Then you can go and collect him.

Turning his horse around, Tomás headed for the state capital and its archives. When he reached Cuernavaca the city hall offices were closed, which was just as well. He was thoroughly drenched and had no intention of presenting himself before municipal employees looking like a waterlogged crow. He headed home. Rosa was feeding her chickens when he rode up to their branch fence.

"Tomás! Did it work?" In her agitation she spilled the feed that was hammocked in her apron. "Are you all right, son?"

Dismounting, he walked the horse inside the small enclosure. His face revealed nothing."My horse needs a drink."

"Forget the drink! You tell me right now, Tomás Tepaneca. Were you able to claim the hacienda for Isabel?"

"Can an eagle snag a mouse?" He flashed his smile with its near-perfect teeth. "Isabel is now fully in charge of San Serafín and living like a queen."

"Was there bloodshed?"

"Nothing that needs prayers to the saints."

"Bendito sea Dios!" Rosa clapped her hands together. Then her eyes narrowed into thin slits. "What about the widow?"

"We sent her packing. She can go live with her children in the D.F. or in hell, for all I know or care. We won."

With a cry of joy Rosa threw her arms around her son. Over a meal of tamales and coffee, she exulted, "So our little Isabel has a home of her own at last! Tell me about San Serafín."

"It's more spectacular than you can imagine. I'll take you to see it for yourself."

"That will have to wait, son. Don Dionisio still needs me. I go to his house every day and sit with him. His son is ailing too."

"All right. When they're both better. Actually, there's another matter that needs my attention."

"And *mi niña*? Tell me again, how is my little girl?"

"As I said, Isa is now living like a queen."

Rosa studied him closely. "And you son, how are *you*?"

He looked away, making her want to stroke his face and warn him, *don't love her so much. It will only break your heart.* Instead she handed him another pepper.

"I'm proud of you. What you've done for Isabel is wonderful. Seeing her happy means the world to me. You and she are my world. My little children."

He pushed away from the table. "Isabel is not my sister."

"She might as well be. From the start she has loved you as if you were the brother she wanted so badly. That kind of love is strong, but it leaves no room for any other kind of love."

He stepped outside to glare at the vanishing day.

At bedtime, Rosa and Tomás had their usual go-around— she insisting that he sleep in the bed, which he yearned to do, and she preferring the *petate*—the straw mat that she found far more comfortable than the too-soft mattress. In the morning Rosa clutched the small of her back, and he woke up cursing *petates, petate*-makers, and the house as well.

"It's time you had a real house, mamá." His back felt out of alignment.

"Do you think we're imagining this one? I don't need another."

"Yes, you do."

"With what money?"

He rummaged through his saddlebag. Moments later, beautiful, heavy gold coins clattered onto the table. "We'll build it with these, courtesy of the Nymans."

She flinched. "Oh, son. What have you done?"

"I didn't steal it. This is my fee for the legal services that I am going to render Isa."

"You charged her?"

"Not her. The Nymans. They owe it to us."

"It looks like you're charging them all right. What does Isabel want you to do?"

"Find her father-in-law's killer."

"¡*Ay, Diosito*!" Like so many of her countrymen, Rosa had a penchant for the diminutive even with God, shrinking him with more tenderness than blasphemy. "Isn't that dangerous? Shouldn't the police do that?"

"I just have to find the man. The police can do the rest."

"So you think Benjamín Nyman is innocent?"

"I don't know." He ran a hand through his coarse hair. "Isa certainly thinks so. Now, about the house."

"I'm not leaving my *milpa*. What would I do with myself if I couldn't plant my corn and beans?"

For all his rhetorical prowess, Tomás was unable to persuade her to give up her hut or her little plot of land. "All right. All right. Stay here for now, but we're going to build a new house on this piece of land."

"I like my little house."

"Well I don't. It's time we each had our own separate bedroom, not a bed and a *petate* crammed into the kitchen. And it's high time the Tepanecas had a bathroom with running water and a sink for the dishes."

Construction of the new house took over three months and ate up most of the money Tomás had taken for his quest. During that whole time he devoted only one day to his search for Eufemio Rosarito's military records.

"I don't know the age or the year that he joined up," he explained to a municipal clerk. "But given that Rosarito served with General Nyman in the 1860s, we should be able to narrow down the years of his enlistment."

Tomás found several potential candidates and carefully noted their date of birth and their towns. He reported his findings to my grandfather, whose only comment was, "I think Isabel is sending you on a fool's mission."

This was right around the time when Cadwally had announced to the Tepanecas his intention to visit me.

"Will you be gone long, don Cadwallader?" Rosa had asked.

"Not sure."

"Oh, stay with her for a month or two, " Rosa had insisted. "Think how lonely *la niña* Isabel must be in that big hacienda. She would be so happy to see you!"

As usual, Cadwally had ended up agreeing with Rosa. He delayed his trip, however, until he could sell a painting, for how else was he to rent a mule and stock up on enough liquor for the visit? With Cadwally considering the option of staying a few weeks in San Serafín, Tomás felt no need to check on me. Neither did he feel the urge to hunt down our suspect until after the holidays. This left him free to focus instead on the construction project that he found so much more satisfying. Benjamín Nyman could rot in prison a bit longer, he decided.

Day by day masons and carpenters built Tomás a house that proclaimed his rising social status. He would have burned down his mother's shack, but they needed a place in which to live until the house was ready. Besides, Rosa would have doused the flames faster than he could start them. He relented. She could have her shack for now and use it later as a stable, he decided. She could also keep her vegetable garden. Someday she might grow flowers instead of food, he told himself.

A chance meeting with a classmate from law school further distracted him from his original quest. The friend urged him to immerse himself in local politics.

"Politics?" Rosa gazed at her son in alarm.

"Don't look like you just saw a scorpion, mamá. We're on the cusp of new times. Tomorrow is the sixth of November."

"So?" Rosa had both hands on hips.

"So Francisco Madero, who won the presidential election by a landslide, takes office tomorrow."

"So what? You told Isabelita and me that you don't trust him; that he was wrong in choosing Ambrosio Figueroa to be our gov'nor instead of the Señor Zapata. That's what you said, and that he's from the *patrón* class and can't understand our needs."

"I may have oversimplified the matter. Look, mamá, try to understand. There are two new groups of reformers emerging in Morelos: those who are law-abiding and those who are rebels like Zapata, Neri, and those other insurrectionists. I want to bring about land reform *legally*. That's why I became a lawyer."

"That's fine, little son. Do what you think is best. But before you get loaded down with politics, don't forget your promise to Isa. You accepted her money. Our house is being built on it. Isn't it time to honor your agreement with her?"

Tomás knew this was one argument he could not hope to win. "All right, but not until after Christmas. The house won't be done until then. Don't look at me like that. You want me to attend Mass with you on Christmas Eve, don't you? After Mass we'll celebrate our new home with friends and more food than any of them have seen on one table."

55

CHRISTMAS 1911

THUNDER SLASHED THE sky open, and I was a frightened little
girl running to Rosa and Tomás. They were downstairs in the
small room off our kitchen because Cadwally had not yet bought
the land that was behind our house—the plot that he would
give Rosa. Nor had he built the one-room cottage for her. So we
were still living together, the four of us. As in so many dreams,
our house looked totally different—recognizable but dream-
distorted. Another thunderbolt sent me scurrying onto Tomás's
petate, the mat on which he slept. I could have gone to Rosa
for protection, but I snuggled into Tomás who was a small boy
again. He gave me a sleepy smile and wrapped his scrawny arms
around me.

I woke from the dream and there it was again: thunder. Yet
it didn't scare me. Nothing did anymore except the possibility of
not dying. But was it thunder? I strained to listen through stone
walls and boarded up windows. No, it was fireworks. My jailors
could have told me that the *posada* season was well under way,
and that Christmas Eve was less than four days away.

In preparation for my death I wanted to pray continually—
a lofty, impossible goal for me. The pain had diminished but

something else was happening. I could no longer say or think the Lord's Prayer without tripping up. Whole phrases would vanish like a chunk of road washed away in a deluge. Then out of nowhere a shorter, simpler prayer came to me. *Lord Jesus Christ, have mercy on me a sinner.* It was the ancient Jesus Prayer, the Hesychast prayer etched on the back of my Russian Orthodox icon. I thought of the stylized face of Christ, his eyes gentle and wise. Compassion itself. *Lord Jesus Christ,* I inhaled, *have mercy on me a sinner,* I exhaled, repeating the prayer with every ragged inhalation and exhalation. For a time, all other concerns dropped away. There was only the prayer, only the Lord, and my ever-growing will to die so I could live again. But my heart beat on and on.

Once, I awoke in Tacha's formidable arms, strong as the limbs of an oak. Old Stone-face was propping me up, forcing me to drink something that tasted bitter. Then she was gone. Later I woke up briefly to the scent of gardenias. She was bathing me. After drying me she drew something over my head. A nightgown? Was I dreaming? No. I was being carried somewhere as if I were a small child again. And then her face with its immutable granite features softened into the smile of a blue-eyed bewhiskered man who winked at me.

"Cadwally!" I murmured in delight, breathing in the scent of him—turpentine and oil paints.

"Hurry. Get her to doña Eva's room," a woman's voice whispered. "I'll lock up."

I was aware of being outside in the cool night air. Patches of a high-beamed ceiling and star-flecked sky flickered by. There was singing in the distance. A *posada.* Have they celebrated all nine? I wanted to ask him, but I was no longer in Cadwally's arms. Tacha set me down in a soft meadow fringed with trees. No, it was a bed with green bed curtains. A harsh light drew moans from me and clamped my eyes shut.

"It's almost time, señora," I heard old Stone-face's gravelly voice.

"I'll go down in a minute. Remember, don't sound the alarm until they've broken the *piñata*. There's no point in spoiling the children's fun."

I continued to struggle against the light. Slowly I was able to focus on a face. Doña Manuela was staring down at me, eyes alert as a crow's.

"You're a tough one, Isabel Brentt." She spoke with a touch of admiration in her voice. Then she giggled like a girl with a secret that she can barely contain. "You do look ghastly. But don't worry. We'll summon the doctor right after the children's *posada*." She drew closer. "Blink if you understand what I'm saying."

I understood, but something else held my attention, something that sent a shiver through me. Two figures hovered behind Manuela Nyman. They were more gargoyle than human, their features sharply angular, their eyes green slits, their skin gray.

"What is it?" la patrona asked in crisp tones, bringing her face closer to mine.

I moved my eyes from the things to doña Manuela. Making a supreme effort, I rasped, "You're already in hell."

La patrona drew back abruptly.

56

HOW DOES IT GO?

THE URGE TO sleep intensified although a strange sound kept intruding. It seemed to be coming from my chest and throat, reminding me of a bad head cold and the struggle to breathe. *This is it. I must be dying.* I tried to say the Jesus Prayer. Short as it was, I suddenly could not remember the second half. In dreams or flashes of memory I turned to my Russian diplomat for help, and I was actually able to glimpse the girl that I used to be, the one who gushed about everything in her journal, making no distinction between the momentous and the trivial. Seeing her again from a distance, as if she were someone in a play, I felt oddly detached from her. There she sat at a dinner party, that other Isabel, wearing the cobalt blue gown. Next to her sat my silver-haired, bewhiskered Russian.

"It's called Christ the Savior." He was examining my tiny icon. .

*Lord Jesus Christ—Lord Jesus Christ—*The dying me kept trying to remember the rest of the prayer.

"Could you tell me what the inscription on the back says?" That other self was asking.

"There's an inscription? Ah, yes. This is highly unusual. Russian artists do not write on icons." He adjusted his monocle. "Ah! It's the Hesychast prayer."

The dinner party shifted to Aunt Delphine's front porch, Russian diplomat in tow. *Lord Jesus,* I struggled to inhale. *Please, how does the rest go?*

"The desert fathers and mothers have been saying this prayer for centuries," my Russian commented between sips of wine. "They repeat the same line over and over, day and night."

"Why?" the Isabel in the blue gown smiled, tipping her head to one side, the little flirt.

Never mind why! I wanted to yell at her.

"They repeat the prayer so that it can become inseparable from their every breath. With time, it's so automatic that they no longer need to say the words."

Lord Jesus, I struggled for breath. A Chinese immigrant was dragged screaming behind a horse. A mob howled in laughter. *Lord Jesus—*

"What's the point of all that repetition?" That other Isabel asked.

"Practitioners say they become more deeply aware of the constant presence of God."

Lord Jesus Christ, have mercy on me a sinner, the words ran to me at last because I desperately needed to feel the presence of God. *Lord Jesus Christ, have mercy on me a sinner.*

In and out of sleep: articulate in dreams yet so utterly inarticulate when awake. In and out the words. In and out of worlds. Candles, prayers, dreaming—dreaming that Benjamín was on his knees by my bedside, Ben dressed once more in a borrowed cassock, no mischief in his eyes, only sorrow.

"Don't leave me, Isa."

Looking back, I can appreciate the universality of the dilemma between the needs of the living and the dying. How many billions of people have cried, 'stay!' while the dying yearn, if not for rebirth, then at least for release? As if sensing the tremendous conflict between my need and his own, the Benjamín of my dream became very still. Then ever so gently, he kissed me on the lips.

"Go," he murmured in my thoughts. "Become an angel."

In and out of wakefulness, in and out, longing only to sleep. A man with a thick double chin and balding head was looking at me, his eyes as round as his spectacles.

"What is it, doctor?" Doña Manuela asked in a tear-stained voice.

"Starvation!" He gasped the word with disbelief. "Your daughter-in-law is dying of severe malnutrition."

"That's impossible. Tacha delivers trays to her room three times a day."

In and out of sleep, the room an ocean, people a blur of sound. Yet there *was* a brief moment of glorious clarity. A man and a woman who were radiantly beautiful appeared at the head of my bed, one on each side of me.

You! Cadwally got it right! I told them soundlessly. *But you're even more beautiful.*

Doña Manuela was clutching my hand. I hardly noticed her, noting instead the breathless moment when the radiant beings kissed me and I remembered the names I had given them as a toddler.

In and out of sleep. In and out of the fast-fading world, Doña Manuela's careful orchestration of my death progressing exactly as expected except for one thing—the unexpected.

57

CENTER OF THE UNIVERSE

IN THE DEAD of night, while doña Manuela made a show of staying at my bedside, even sleeping alongside me, there was a clamor on the staircase. Running feet. Someone bursting into the room. A man standing over me and gasping, "My God!"

Doña Manuela nearly fell off the bed.

My eyes fluttered open. "Ben!" Yet even as I felt myself sink back into the fog, I realized it was Samuel, not Benjamín. I could hear doña Manuela's cascade of words, something about treachery and self-inflicted starvation.

"Why?" I heard the agony in Samuel's voice. Yet I could not muster the strength to open my eyes again, let alone to set him straight. I was sinking inexorably to the bottom of a dark sea where I could sleep, which is all that I wanted to do. Samuel, well intentioned as ever, kept yanking me back to the surface.

"Isabel! Look at me. Look at me."

"She can't hear you, son. She's too far gone."

He took my claw-of-a-hand. Did he shudder? "Isabel! Isabel, would you like for me to hear your confession?"

"You can't give last rites to a non-Catholic!" doña Manuela's voice was sharp-edged. Samuel's was gentle as a lullaby, and I wanted only to slide back into the depths. Oh, to sleep and not wake up in this world! However, my well-meaning brother-in-law would not let me slip away. With his stubborn prayers, he kept yanking me back to the surface, spluttering and gasping. For a few moments I managed to fix my eyes on his stricken face. I wanted to reassure him that I was glad to go, but the struggle just to breathe intensified horrifically just then, and I felt a wave of despair.

"Oh, God!" I gasped in English. "I mattered—"

"Of course you matter," he responded in English.

"—so little." I finished my thought.

"No, Isabel. You matter deeply."

"What did she say? What did she say?" Fear shook Manuela Nyman's voice.

Samuel was not supposed to be there until after my death. Someone had inadvertently messed up la patrona's schedule. A humble stable groom had taken it upon himself to ride in the dark to alert Father Samuel of the family crisis. Now Samuel and his mother were constantly by my side—the one from a sense of *agape,* the other from a dread of exposure. Christmas Eve arrived. Samuel refused to return to his village, sending the hacienda priest in his stead. Throughout the long hours, he and his bleary-eyed mother continued their vigil at my bedside. He had decided that if he could not give me last rites, he could still pray for me and with me. Holding my hand, he leaned closer and whispered the Lord's Prayer in English. At first I tried to say it with him, but the struggle to breathe was paramount. The world, indeed the very cosmos, was fast shrinking into the particularity of my dying. Nothing else existed, nothing, that is, until Cadwally leaned over me and told me once more in the plainest terms: "This may surprise you, Isabel, but contrary to all appearances, you are not the center of the universe." He winked and added, "But by jingo, you matter!"

"There's nothing more any of us can do for her," I heard doña Manuela say. "She will soon be with God. Go, Samuelito. It's almost midnight. You have your duties to perform."

The moment the door closed behind him, I began to choke as if all the oxygen had been siphoned off, and a startling thing happened. I was suddenly outside my body. Hovering above my jailers, I was aware that they were fussing over a pitifully shrunken body. *Is this it?* I wondered, more astonished than afraid. And then with no effort of my own, I was moving quickly through and beyond the massive beams and vaulted ceiling, soaring high above the rooftops of the hacienda compound. Far below I could just make out pinpricks of light: the lit candles of the Christmas Eve procession as it wound its way to the hacienda church. *Misa de Gallo*—Midnight Mass—was about to start. For one terrible moment a wave of regret swept over me.

Oh Lord, forgive me! I did nothing of value with my life, changed nothing, affected no one!

Higher and higher I soared, entering what seemed a canyon of the Tepozteco, only darker and narrower than I remembered—and then I was on the other side of it, soaring into the moon-tinged clouds above the peaks of the volcano lovers, climbing ever higher and higher, so far up that Mexico revealed herself to me as a horn of plenty. And I wondered again with far more awe than fear, *Can this be death?*

Part 2

AWAKENINGS

Let me respectfully remind you—
Life and death are of supreme importance.
Time swiftly passes, and the opportunity is lost.
Each of us should strive to awaken.
Take heed. Do not squander your life.

A meditation often used by Zen Buddhists at day's end

58

GOOD NEWS

BEFORE THE ROOSTERS could crow about it, everyone in the hacienda had heard about my death. Samuel, who had not slept for two days, had left my bedside only to say Midnight Mass on Christmas Eve. By the time he staggered back to my room, half dead himself, my bed had been stripped and my coffin nailed shut.

"Well, it's over." Doña Manuela crossed her hands and gave him a dignified nod that spoke of shared loss, followed by a brave smile.

Doña Manuela was pleased that her plan had succeeded in spite of Samuel. Now a new problem irked her: how to turn what she termed my suicide into an object lesson for her people without damaging the family's reputation? Her instinct was to deny me a Christian burial, but she knew that Samuel would never agree to that—Samuel who had prayed for me; Samuel who had been underfoot, disrupting her schedule, unwittingly protracting the drama all the way into Christmas. Nor could she ignore the fact that everyone in San Serafín knew that I was Benjamín's wife. Like it or not, she had to bury me with at least some of the pomp and circumstance due to a Nyman, even the least of them. None of the gentry were invited. I didn't take offense. There weren't any to invite. Most of her family and friends were observing the installation of the new revolutionary administration from the safe distance of Paris or New York or San Antonio. So it was the humble *peones* who attended my burial. Days later the good people of San Serafín would still be marveling at my mother-in-law's composure, her courage in the face of continual adversity. And yes, I must agree that she took my death well.

Cadwally always said that Mexicans lay their dead to rest faster than a dog buries a bone. Doña Manuela broke records. I was pronounced dead, prayed for and planted in the earth well before mid-morning that Christmas day. I wish I could say that the workers and their families turned out for my sake, motivated by pity or at least by forgiveness for my intrusion. The truth is the men bared their heads and the women draped theirs out of respect for doña Manuela, their beloved patrona. What was I to them but a zephyr that blew briefly and faded with barely a trace?

My coffin was lowered into the earth by four workers, sandaled feet braced against the upturned soil, calloused hands gripping ropes of henequén. True to Mexican custom, the mourners stayed at the grave site until the coffin had been completely buried. Only then did Samuel and his mother lead the procession away from the cemetery. On reaching the hacienda church, doña Manuela stood on the upper staircase landing, crossed her hands on her black skirt, and gave a homily, which as homilies go was uniquely brief and to the point.

"We have buried doña Isabel, not in the heart of our cemetery which is holy ground, but on an edge of it. Never forget that suicide is a mortal sin, and that none of us, not a single one of us, can escape the consequences of sin unless we turn to Holy Church."

She nodded to Samuel to give a final blessing. He cleared his throat, his mind racing. *Why are you doing this, Mother?* He managed an appropriate blessing and sent everyone home to enjoy their Christmas. Then he held out his arm to escort her down the steps. Doña Manuela was not done yet. Grasping his arm, she drew him into the chapel for one more task, for haven't you noticed how a lie begets others?

The chapel was empty except for the stone saints and angels who stared impassively from their niches. La patrona of San Serafín ignored them all, pausing instead before a life-size painting of the Virgin of Guadalupe, that most Mexican symbol of the church. To her she made the sign of the cross. Then she turned to Samuel.

"I want you to promise here before the Blessed Virgin Mother that you will never tell Benjamín about Isabel's death."

He must have thought of the fearful vacancy in his brother's eyes. "Mother, he doesn't understand anything."

"We don't know that. What we do know is how volatile he is and what that volatility has cost him. No, we cannot risk another outburst. Think of what those animals might do to him this time around!" And because she imagined another beating all too vividly, her face contorted. "I couldn't bear it. Do you hear me, Samuel? Another incident like that one would break me. So promise me you won't tell him about her death! Swear to it!"

Her eyes burned with a raw fear that even she did not know how to fake. Seeing such a haunted look, what could Samuel do but take that vow of silence, there under the serene, downcast eyes of the Virgin of Guadalupe?

My mother-in-law tried to extract a similar vow from Rodolfo and Eva. Rodolfo was in Paris at the time and Eva in Naples with her husband and children. Telegrams would have to do. Since the hacienda had its own telegraph office, neither geography nor the holiday would be a problem, only how to strike the right tone. Without revealing her own guilty part, how was she to tell them the news without seeming to gloat? "Isabel is dead! The family's finances are secure again." No, that was too direct.

"I regret to tell you that Isabel is dead . . ." Regret? They would never believe that. "I need to inform you . . ." Yes, and she could relish giving them a tantalizing encapsulation of my bizarre suicide. But how to impress upon them her very real terror of Benjamín's reaction if he should hear of my death?

He must never be told! The telegrams instructed. *Tell no one! I know I can count on you, my dear children.*

Eva and her husband were entertaining two Mexican friends, expats from the state of Veracruz, when the telegram arrived. Eva's daughters Esther and Emanuela were also at the table, a small detail that would have tremendous import later. Eva read the telegram and grew still. *Tell no one!* I'm certain that she would have obeyed readily enough. However, doña Manuela had not allowed for other forces at work. Without warning, Pancho Comardo snatched the telegram out of Eva's hands and read it.

"The news is both sad and good," he declared in the high, piping voice that seemed so mismatched to his great bulk.

"Pancho, no!" Eva gasped.

"It's all right, dear. We're among friends, and the girls are old enough to know the truth."

"My mother expressly—"

"It seems that the fortunes of our family continue to take strange twists. The infamous Isabel Brentt who has caused us such heartache has died, and in my mother-in-law's arms no less."

No one spoke at first. Were his astonished guests groping for the right thing to say—so sorry for your loss—while thinking, hearty congratulation on the death of your swindling sister-in-law? For what else did people think of me? Eva was aghast. She braced herself, half expecting Pancho to follow up with a toast. Certainly it was clear to her that he was trying to strike the appropriate stance. What mattered was *how* one said things, more than what one said, he always insisted. Emanuela, their twelve-year-old daughter whose bedroom had become my prison, turned to her older sister just then.

"Who died?"

"Uncle Benjamín's wife," sixteen-year-old Esther whispered.

"Oh." And because both guests had turned their attention to her, however briefly, Emanuela grasped the moment. "Well I'm glad she's dead. I hated her!"

"Hush! You didn't even know her." Eva snapped. "Never gloat over other people's misfortunes."

"Your mother is right." Pancho struck a pensive look, making a steeple of two fingers which he tapped on his lower lip. "Besides, isn't it God, not we, who must condemn her for her suicide?"

Eva winced. Details of deceit and self-imposed starvation followed. Emanuela lapped it up.

"See, mamá? I'm right to hate her. Besides, I just remembered something. I heard you say that it was her fault that Uncle Benjamín went to prison. So why should we feel sorry that she's dead?"

Pancho laughed. "Convicted by your own words, my dear. What can I say? 'Out of the mouth of babes—'"

He's enjoying this, Eva realized, and she despised her husband more than ever.

After dinner Pancho and his friend Rigoberto withdrew to the billiards room, leaving the ladies to have their coffee in a small salon. Later, when Esther and Emanuela had gone to bed, Eva and her friend donned wraps and stepped outside. A generous terrace overlooked the Bay of Naples. In the darkness the Mediterranean Sea all but vanished.

"I didn't want to say anything in front of your daughters." Eva's friend spoke in a low, conspiratorial tone. "Now that we can speak more openly, I must admit that I keep wondering, how exactly does one commit suicide by deliberate starvation? Can you imagine it?"

"No."

"And how bizarre that this Isabel Brentt who had tried to defraud your family not only changed her mind and gave it all back, but that she should die in your mother's arms! What an extraordinary woman your mother must be. I don't think I could show so much compassion to someone who tried to cheat my children out of their inheritance. On the other hand, I suppose your sister-in-law must have suffered too. To go to such an extreme, she must have been unimaginably unhappy."

"Yes."

Because Eva added nothing, nothing more was said. A stillness came over the women as they listened to the doleful dirges of the blackened sea. Then Eva startled her friend with a half choked sob and heaving shoulders.

Inside the brightly lit villa, Pancho Comardo leaned over the billiards table, a cigar clenched in his teeth as he took careful aim. He had been talking pleasantries with his friend Rigoberto while calculating the consequences of my death. *It's all gone back to doña Manuela now. The old hag has seen to that, no doubt about it, and from her it will go to her four children. A four-way cut.* As his ball slammed two others into opposite pockets, he reflected that it was far from unusual for prisoners to be killed by other inmates, or for priests in lonely villages to be waylaid by renegades. *It's just a simple observation,* he would have shrugged if reproved.

59

HAUNTED

IF IT SEEMS extraordinary that I should know so much about events that I did not witness directly, *it is.* I must ask you to trust my seeming omniscience as I continue to relate all that followed after my funeral. The omniscience is not mine. I narrate what has been given to me to know, along with what I myself experienced and remember.

My brother-in-law, Rodolfo, was living in comfortable exile in Paris, attended by his faithful butler and a bevy of Mexican friends. He and his fellow expats met regularly to enjoy French cuisine and to bemoan the revolutionary politics that had befallen their country. They cursed the newly elected president, Francisco Madero—"that traitor to his own class"—and predicted that his administration would ruin the country in a year if not sooner. One evening when their exploration of a wine list left them particularly *allumé,* they joked about initiating a counterrevolution or at least supporting any general willing to lead a coup détat. In the days that followed, the joke morphed into a possibility, and the possibility into a plot. At first there was far more talk than action. This left my brother-in-law with a lot of time on his hands. Rodolfo suffered in those days from an acute paralysis of the will. He could plot with the best of them, but he waffled back and forth in his determination, much preferring to shop for antiques or to go off on long solitary walks. Destination did not matter on those rambles, only the forward momentum that gave him the illusion of having a purpose in life.

Sometimes he wondered if poverty would not have been the very catalyst that he needed, a rough companion to bully him into action. He did nothing with his life, he told himself, because materially he needed nothing. In spite of having been cut out of his father's will, he was financially secure. The many properties that he had purchased across the years when still in his father's graces, allowed him to live quite comfortably. With agents to collect his rents and a capable foreman to manage his coffee plantation in Chiapas, he could enjoy the freedom of being an absentee landlord. But what to do with his freedom? And what to do with the past, the wretched past?

On the surface, Rodolfo Nyman was the quintessential man of the world—an urbane and seasoned traveler who sailed into middle age with panache and quiet self-confidence. In actuality, he had to fight the impulse to sleep away each day, curtains drawn and blankets clenched tightly to his chin. The optimism that he displayed to friends was the public side of his depression, a cravat to wear with casual flair while trying to ignore its tightening grip around his throat. He had long suffered from the knowledge of his illegitimacy and more recently from his father's violent death at the hands of his half-brother, as he supposed. But above all, Rodolfo continued to agonize over his decision to separate from his mistress of ten years and their three children— all in a disastrous bid to court me.

He had assumed that society—and especially his mother— would overlook my poverty because with my fair looks and education I could pass as *gente decente*: upper class. Unlike his dark Teresa Gama, a humble seamstress from Cuautla, I *looked* like the aristocrat that I was not. Ah, my poor Rodolfo, letting appearances govern his life. Indeed, Mexican society would probably have accepted me as his wife, but passing muster with his mother was a doomed project from the start, as doomed as his determination to make a total break with the one woman he loved. He continued to support Teresa and their children from afar, but this only aggravated the wound of separation.

Spending Christmas with the immediate family in San Serafín was not an option either. My mother-in-law had insisted to her children that they stay away. "It is simply not safe to travel in Morelos. If you love me, honor my wishes on this matter." So there he was, alone in Paris, desperately trying to forget mistress, ex-fiancée, murdered father, imprisoned brother, and the revolution. Yet he could not shake any of us, least of all Teresa. Because he had brought her to Paris early in their relationship, everything reminded him of her. Wherever his ramblings took him, she strolled beside him, a ghost he could never shake. Her unsophisticated wonder at everything had made everything wonderful and new to him. Without Teresa the world tarnished like neglected silver.

After another joyless dinner that even le Grand Véfour could not alleviate, Rodolfo returned to his hotel suite. Drawing a cigarette from a silver case, he let it dangle unlit, his gaze turned inward, his thoughts on the toys that he had shipped to his children. Had they arrived on time for Christmas Eve or would Teresa save them for the Three Kings in January? He had wanted to include a gift for her as well. Yet how to do so without raising her hopes? Wasn't it kinder to keep the break final, his attention focused solely on the children? In the end he had added a slender box with a pearl necklace. Now he fretted. Would she see the necklace as an overture to win her back? Would that be so bad? Why not resume their relationship, whether or not he ever found a more suitable wife? No. What was he thinking? He would not hurt her again. Never. As for the children—*ah, the children. My God! What am I doing here?*

Weston, the English butler whom Rodolfo had employed for years, approached just then on silent feet. "Excuse me, sir. It appears that this telegram arrived this afternoon and was somehow overlooked downstairs. The clerk was indeed most remiss in not bringing it to you before you left for dinner and is highly apologetic. Should I report him?"

"What?" His head hurt. "No. Let it go."

Rodolfo read his mother's telegram, distractedly at first, then with a pounding heart. One phrase stood out above all others: *starved herself to death.* Grabbing his overcoat, he headed back into the rain-spattered night, walking briskly, tears spilling as steadily as the rain from the blackened sky. Whatever unspoken triumph doña Manuela had intended to imply in her telegram, Rodolfo read nothing but his own moral failures: what was my suicide but evidence that he had betrayed the innocence of yet another young girl? As his sense of guilt rushed river-strong to merge with the sea, it seemed to Rodolfo once again that his entire life had been nothing but a series of bad choices that touched off murderous landslides.

60

ABSOLUTION

AFTER MY FUNERAL Samuel and his mother had retired to their rooms—doña Manuela to write her telegrams and Samuel to catch up on his sleep. They didn't meet up again until supper time. Bardomiana prepared it; Tacha served it. Since the other servants had been given the day off, the house was nearly empty, a gray gloom settling over it like dust. Samuel asked that they have their meal in the smaller, more intimate breakfast room rather than in the dining room with its great barque of a table. Doña Manuela acquiesced easily enough. So they sat at a round table, face to face, with candlelight flickering between them. She sighed with inner contentment; he picked at his food, his mind traveling far from his mother's chatter. She in turn became self-conscious and forced herself to take less interest in the meal. Setting aside her fork and knife, she reached for one of his hands and cupped it in both of hers.

"You've been wonderful, Samuelito. I don't know what I would have done without you."

Concern for her drew him out of his abstraction. "No. It's the other way around. You're like a beacon in the worst storms."

Doña Manuela squeezed his hand before releasing it. "You know, you're turning out to be a fine priest, son. You gave the funeral the dignity that was needed for the sake of our people. It was compassionate, yet it also bore a solemn warning to them."

"You added the warning." Samuel gave her a lopsided smile that spoke more to his emotional exhaustion than to reproach.

"When did I do that?"

"On the church steps. You reminded everyone that suicide is a mortal sin."

"Well? It's the truth, isn't it? Do you think that I was trying to upstage you?"

"No, of course not," he shook his head, instantly regretting his observation.

"As la patrona, I have the obligation to give our people additional guidance. You spoke for God and I spoke for the family. Anyway, this whole wretched business has been a good object lesson for them. Suicide is a mortal sin."

"Yes, I suppose so."

"Suppose? There's no supposing about this."

"No, you're right. Now our people know that even a Nyman cannot escape the consequences of sin. That *is* what you want them to take away from all this, isn't it?"

"She was never a Nyman. Don't look at me that way. I do pity Isabel Brentt, but she was never one of us. Her betrayal was too deep."

"Yet she seems to have repented. You said she was anxious to sign over the properties to us. Surely that earned her—"

"What? Gratitude? Why should I be grateful that she gave back what is ours?"

"Didn't that demonstrate good will?"

"No. I'll tell you what she demonstrated—the will to punish her lover."

"I don't follow."

"I'm not certain of the exact details. It all happened during my exile from San Serafín. But from what Tacha and some of the other servants tell me, Tomás Tepaneca and Isabel quarreled. She must have accused him of infidelity. When he stormed off Isabel took the best revenge she could imagine."

"By killing herself? How would that . . .?"

"No. By first deeding everything back to us. Don't you see? With that one gesture she undid her lover's scheme, depriving him of the wealth he meant to enjoy."

"And the slow suicide? What did she gain by that?"

"I've been wondering that myself." Manuela gazed steadily into his face. "I never did understand her. Perhaps she did it out of willful pride or spite. Or perhaps she repented of her revenge against Tepaneca and feared having to face him. Death probably seemed the easier option, and she was too cowardly to do it any other way."

"I should have tried to help her."

"Why? You had no obligation . . ."

"She was Benjamín's wife. He loved her and it's just possible that she loved him too."

"That conniving thief? She never loved Benjamín."

"I'm not so sure."

"My dear Samuel, what do you know of the darkness and the irrationality of the human heart? Trust me when I tell you that the only thing that Isabel Brentt loved was herself and maybe that lover of hers."

"No. I saw how she looked at Benjamín."

"What are you talking about? You had such little contact with her."

Samuel sighed like a man about to open his heart in the confessional. "The night that she and Benjamín eloped, they came to me. I married them."

"You what?"

"I married them."

"How could you dishonor the church that way? She wasn't Catholic!"

"She was a Christian."

"Your duty is to obey the dictates of Holy Church, not to create your own rules for the sake of your liberal notions!"

Samuel winced but held his ground.

"I married two Christians, a tradition that goes back to the very beginnings of the church. Would you have preferred that I turn them away and have them live in sin?"

"Yes! With time he would have come to see that she didn't love him."

"I don't agree. I think that Benjamín and Isabel were deeply in love."

"No."

"If only you could have seen them, how they looked at each other as they made their vows."

"I can't believe what I'm hearing!" She threw up both hands.

"As their priest, I should have done more for them. I had no idea . . ." His voice cracked.

Doña Manuela was startled to see tears trickle down his face.

"Oh, my dearest!" She rose and cradled him in her arms. "I'm the one whom you should reproach, not yourself! Not you with your sweet, innocent heart! I should have been more forgiving." Suddenly she was on her knees, crossing herself and weeping. "Forgive me, Father, for I have sinned! It's all my fault! I knew that Isabel wasn't eating, but the truth is that I didn't care if she starved! All I could think of was Benjamín and what those guards did to him because of her. So this is all my fault, not yours. Please, please forgive me! *Absolve me!*" She wept at his feet.

The astonished Samuel fumbled between roles. As a priest he found himself rushing to say the familiar words of absolution, though he wasn't certain if this was an actual confession or its precursor. As a son he hurried to her defense.

"No one can fault you for having a mother's heart and a mother's pain. Don't blame yourself. You carry enough pain as it is."

Helping her to her feet, he bent his tall form and held her tightly.

⁓

That night doña Manuela slept soundly. Samuel, who had not understood the literalness of her confession, berated himself for having upset her after all that she had been through. Unable to sleep, he stared up into the dark expanse of the beamed ceiling. Two contending images haunted him: one, a bride radiant with love, the other a skeletal face with sunken cheeks, a creature more cadaverous than living.

How could Isabel have been both in such a short time? He kept asking the night. How could she have gone so quickly from a beauty to a grotesque?

The frailty of the human body unnerved him. The gruesomeness of physical death staggered him.

Is this what awaits us all? Samuel wondered bleakly. Did I witness divine retribution for sins too terrible to expiate any other way? Was our heavenly father even there at the deathbed, weeping for his fallen child? Or had he already cast her out for her sin, the unpardonable sin of throwing away her life? After all her suffering, did she awaken in hell?

Tossing aside the bed covers, Samuel flicked on a lamp and began to pace. God is merciful. He'll forgive her. Surely he'll forgive her. Christ in his mercy will wake her, for He is the resurrection, and for all her many faults, Isabel did believe in Christ. God is merciful, he kept repeating to himself. I'm too sinful and too lacking in faith to have seen his mercy in that room.

What mercy? Where were you when she needed you? He hurled the accusation.

That stopped his pacing, for it struck him as clearly as lightning in a field that it was not himself whom he had just accused. With a groan Samuel crumpled to his knees. Ancient words of a desperate father came to him, rushing from the depths of his own desperation.

Lord, I believe. Help thou my unbelief! he wept.

AVIARIES

MANUELA NYMAN PEERED into the aviary at the base of her terraced garden. "What's wrong with that macaw?" she asked Sinforiano, the man who took care of her birds.

"He isn't eating, señora. His mate died yesterday."

"Hmm. Get a new one from the bird peddler the next time he comes around. And don't forget to buy one or two peahens for the peacocks."

"Begging your pardon, señora, but I've coaxed life back into our one remaining peahen." He pointed with his straw sombrero toward a large side lawn just beyond the labyrinth. "She's already out there teasing the males."

"That skanky old thing?" she burst out laughing. "I've never seen a skinnier, more pathetic bird in my life. None of the males will touch her."

Yet even as she spoke, a peacock approached the hen, puffing out his metallic blue neck and fanning out his magnificent tail feathers. The peahen eyed him with quiet dignity, clearly measuring his worth. When at last she made up her mind, she touched her beak to his as if in a kiss. Tenderly, he covered her with his great feathers.

"Males! I'll never understand them," doña Manuela muttered under her breath.

When I opened my eyes, I found myself bathed in a shaft of light.

I've died! I'm in the world of spirits! The thought filled me with a sense of peace and elation. Closing my eyes, I drifted back to sleep, letting the sun kiss my face. *I'm free.*

I woke again and gazed sleepily into an extraordinarily beautiful face.

"Mam mam?" I murmured.

The angel kissed me gently. Then someone else, a figure whose face I could not yet see, grasped me by the chin.

"I'm so glad to be dead!" I whispered happily.

"Oh, no. I'm not letting you off that easily, Isabel Brentt."

I drifted in and out of sleep. When the drug that Tacha had given me finally wore off, I found myself lying on a stone floor in a dimly lit room. There was no shaft of sunlight. No angel, only a voice that made me shiver.

"Well, you've finally deigned to come back to us," doña Manuela spoke cheerfully. "Set it down there, Tacha, then lift her up a bit. I'll feed her."

"Slowly, señora," Tacha counseled. Old Stone-face raised me to a half-sitting position. The moment I felt the contours of a spoon pressed to my lips, I pulled away.

"No!" I rasped.

I tried to fight them off but had about as much strength as a newborn baby. Tacha held my head in the crook of one arm. She easily forced my lips open while doña Manuela doled out sips of a sugary liquid.

"Slowly, señora," Tacha kept counseling.

"I know, I know. Open your mouth, girl. It's only a little sugar water. No, no. Don't spit it out! Pinch her nostrils shut. There. Again—"

I fought, gasping for air. In a brutal reversal, the nourishment that had been withheld was now being forced on me.
When they finally got up to leave, I screamed my despair and
rage at being alive.

"Tie her to the bars and gag her," Doña Manuela instructed
as she rose.

Why am I still here! I railed inwardly against God. *Why didn't
you let me leave this wretched, wretched life!*

I shudder at the memory of my outburst, yet I do empathize
with all my heart with people who have lost their will to live
and are forced by others to continue the struggle. I know their
monstrous sense of betrayal and defeat. Death had seemed my
only escape to a better life. This was the old life and I wanted
no part of it. In my state of mind, I blamed God more than my
captors, for you see, I had no memory just then of my near-
death experience, as such phenomena would come to be called.
Physical duress and mental anguish had temporarily swept it
all aside.

I sobbed until I fell into an exhausted sleep. And there I
would have stayed, deep in that dark, restless realm, but they
were always waking me, forcing me to drink some watery concoction of Tacha's. In those first days of my convalescence no
thought could quiet my sense of outrage. I didn't know enough
words to express my hatred of doña Manuela and her shadow,
but I gave it a go. So they tended to keep me gagged most of the
time and to tie my arms, spread-eagled, to bars that separated
my cell from something behind a curtain. One night when darkness dampened the room and I was slumped on the floor, doña
Manuela walked up behind me. Flicking on a light on her side of
the bars, she unlocked the door with that formidable key ring of
hers and let herself in.

"What a pathetic creature you are," she feigned amusement
as she pulled off the gag. Then her eyes narrowed. "Listen to me,
Isabel Brentt. You can play by my rules or spend the rest of your
miserable life tied up like an animal, urinating and defecating on

yourself. Either way, you're staying here. You're never leaving this room."

"You can't do this. My grandfather—"

"Your grandfather thinks you're dead. They all do. Don't look so surprised. You had the bad manners to die on Christmas day. That's a full two days later than scheduled."

"They think I'm dead?" I was slow to believe her.

"Oh, yes. Every major newspaper in Morelos and the D.F. has printed your obituary. Even though you don't deserve it, we gave you a proper burial in the family cemetery—well, on the edge of it. We even had a Mass for you, but only because Samuel insisted. Too bad you missed it."

Doña Manuela watched me with keen attention, waiting for despair to distort my features. I remained annoyingly slow in responding.

"We brought you to the very brink of death and back," la patrona boasted. "Tacha made one of her drinks that fog the mind. Unfortunately for you, Samuel's unexpected arrival meant that we had to give you heavier doses, which constricted your air passage. You made the most ghastly sounds."

"My grandfather—was he here?"

Because I showed vulnerability, doña Manuela smiled. "We sent word to him, but he was too drunk to make it to the funeral. He showed up two days later and left some scraggly flowers on your grave, which is more than your lover bothered to do." She kept waiting for a burst of emotion. When it didn't come, her lips compressed into a thin line. "Don't expect any dramatic rescues. To the world, Isabel Brentt is as dead as a scorpion under a boot heel. But cheer up. I've gone to the trouble of building you a fine cage, my American Blue-thief. From now on this room is your world. Get used to it because you're never leaving it." She waited for the words to sink in. They merely sank. She tried again. "I want you to have a very long life, longer even than Benjamín's. Isn't it time you showed me some gratitude?"

"Go to hell."

Perhaps these were the very words she had been waiting for. Reaching into a pocket in her black dress, Manuela Nyman pulled out a kitchen knife. With slow deliberation, she dragged the tip along my left cheek. "I would enjoy making you bleed. They made Benjamín bleed because of you." Her eyes were darker than the night-stained flagstones of the cell. "I could so easily have let you die on Christmas Eve, but I chose to let Tacha draw you back from the edge. Don't you know it yet? I have absolute power over you."

The power and the glory—All at once the memory of my brush with death flashed through my mind with startling clarity, like a dolphin leaping from the depths. I remembered that I had hovered over my own body, soaring into the night beyond the hacienda walls and Morelos and the world itself, higher and higher until the very cosmos seemed to lie vast around me. I remembered my final wave of regret: *oh, Lord, forgive me! I did nothing of value with my life!* And now with Manuela Nyman's blade pressed to my cheek, I remembered Light, oceanic in its power, and how it swept away my regrets, granting me a flash of intuition. I was nothing, yet vital. I was infinitesimally minute in the vastness of creation, *yet distinct to God* and distinctly connected to all things and to all beings in the cosmos. All this I had understood then and was grasping again. But it was in the *warmth* of that Light that I had felt a deeper truth. What powered everything, everything in the whole cosmos, was *love*. And I, a mere speck in that vastness, was loved by God, God who is love itself—Christ who enfolded me in his arms!

Caught up in the memory of that encounter, I ignored Manuela Nyman's blade. Some of my wonder, so totally bereft of fear, must have rebounded onto her. When I became aware of her again, I saw that she looked rattled, as if family or friends had just walked in that very moment and their conversation had stopped at the sight of the knife in her hand. Shoving it back into her pocket, she stumbled to her feet and hurried away.

62

A BOON

THE NEXT MORNING I was awakened by the sound of metal clanking against metal: Tacha unlocking the door. She yanked on the ropes as she untied me.

"Drink every drop of this *atole*. I made it with rice instead of *masa*. Your stomach can't handle corn yet. And I put just a touch of *piloncillo*. The raw sugar will give you some energy. We have to go slowly."

You've never given me such a long explanation before, I noted to myself as I sipped the beverage. And strange as it may seem, I actually felt a rush of gratitude that bordered on love for my jailer.

"And don't you go throwing it up, do you hear?"

"I won't. Thank you, Tacha," I smiled.

"Shut up. One more word and you'll go hungry. You know the rule. Just because la patrona let you live, don't think you—"

I burst into peals of laughter. Tacha's face remained rigid, immutable, but something flashed in her eyes. Fear? She left with a great clanking of lock and keys, doña Manuela's precious key ring gripped firmly in her large hands. Alone again, my shoulders continued to heave.

"*She* let me live!" I went into another fit of laughter, wave upon wave carrying me along, salt-rivulets trickling down my face. Then a sobering thought stepped in. After all that suffering, someday I would have to die in earnest. And that didn't seem so funny. And then it seemed hilarious. "Oh, damn," I murmured aloud, awash in a gleeful resignation. All right. Bring it on: death, dragons and stone faces. I've seen God. What is death compared to that?

And, of course, I did die, as we all must. It just wasn't on December 25, 1911. So I have the dubious distinction of having two graves, like Christopher Columbus. Or did he have three? As far as I know, no one on Earth seems absolutely certain which one is truly his. Do you think that matters one iota to him now? But to return to January 1912, I had to wonder: If I was not in the world of spirits—not yet anyway—and certainly not in heaven, where was I? When tied up, I had been unable to explore the cell. It appeared to be large, windowless, and white. It didn't seem to have light fixtures, yet the space was flooded with light during the day, gloriously spilling from the ceiling in the far end. Clearly, I had gone from one extreme to another, from darkness to light, from cramped to spacious quarters, cavernous in fact, and I actually felt another rush of gratitude—not to my captors but to God.

Now that I was finally free to explore my prison, the shaft of light beckoned like a beacon in the night. I started for it, but my legs refused to hold me up, collapsing me like a rag doll. It was a struggle just to return to a sitting position, my back against a half wall that climbed some twelve feet. Wooden bars sprouted from it, reaching all the way to the high ceiling. On the other side and just out of arm's reach, heavy draperies, white as the walls and floor, hid whatever was back there. A corridor? A storage room? What?

Gripping two of the bars, I tried again to stand but slid down to my knees, my ghastly knobby knees. So I began by first exploring the landscape of my own body. That meant confronting once again the ravages of starvation, only now I could see it—stick-like arms and legs, sharply etched rib cage and hips, all reporting that I had indeed become a living skeleton. Even more disquieting, when I ran my fingers through my hair, a handful of it came away. Staring at the clumps in my fists, I began to shudder uncontrollably. Then a thought came to me seemingly from nowhere: *Grass clippings. Grass always grows back after being mowed.*

I had enough awareness to know that the thought had not come from me. Like all good and true thoughts, where could it come but from God—perhaps filtered through an angel or a good spirit. The image of grass clipping comforted me. The loss of my hair was temporary. How could it be otherwise in a world as organic and temporal as ours?

Slowly and painfully, I began my exploration of the cell. Creeping on all fours down the length of the rectangular room, I had to pause often to rest. I estimated that the cell was about sixty feet long and maybe some forty feet wide, making it by far the largest bedroom in the hacienda. Or was it some abandoned storage room? In what part of the plantation was doña Manuela hiding me from the world?

I continued to creep on all fours, discovering a bathroom on my left. It too was an antiseptic white. As it had no door, there would be no privacy when I bathed in the porcelain tub, assuming I would ever have the strength to climb into it, but at least the toilet was tucked just out of the dragon's sight. A small boon. It wasn't until I had traversed two-thirds of the cell that I found myself directly under the source of the only light in the room. I gazed up into a cupola, octagonal in shape. Its peak rose a full three stories in height. As I stared up at the small windows embedded in the dome, the realization hit me like a blow to the face: I was in the general's room, Cadwally's studio!

My parents! Their portrait was gone. Obliterated. There was not a trace of paint, not a hint of eyes peering through layers of plaster to find me. My breath snagged. In my panic I could not bring their faces to mind. *How will I remember you?* Fear drove away enlightenment, calm, and peace. Panic sent me plummeting, so that I cursed Manuela Nyman for ordering the vandalism, and while I was at it I cursed the workers for slavishly slathering paint and plaster over the extraordinary portrait. In those moments I tossed aside all grace and peace, replacing them with a rage that boiled over in scalding waves. Then I caught myself, appalled at how easily hatred can surge like vomit in the throat.

Oh, Lord, what am I saying? My heart cried out.

I murmured the Lord's prayer over and over in a breathy whisper. Gradually, the frenzied pace of the words slowed. My breathing returned to its normal pace. Even as I continued to pray, I was conscious that the effort was changing nothing in physical reality. The vandalism was complete and irreversible. I was still a prisoner, and now everyone thought I was dead. No one would think to rescue me, not even Tomás, still less my poor grandfather. I continued to pray, asking God to give me the strength to accept that I had to go on living in this brutal world. But how? How was I to endure this place when I would so much rather die and be with my parents?

Just then my grandfather came to mind. Because I could picture him in his faded cashmere suit and sandals doffing his hat at my supposed grave, because I could imagine the awkward bending of his tall body, his hands shaking as he set down a small bouquet of flowers, I murmured, "I'll live for you, Cadwally."

Speaking aloud in that great living tomb gave my words more gravitas. And because I visualized Benjamín, battered and silenced, his beautiful eyes as vacant as the tin foil hollows in a skeleton doll, I pledged myself to his welfare too. Much as I wanted an end to my suffering, however much I longed for the beauty and the freedom of the afterlife, I agreed to struggle on inside my emaciated body in that horrible place. I would face it all because Cadwally and Ben needed me—and because I needed to learn so much more and do so much more for others. But oh, it would be so hard! As Seneca observed, *There are times when even to live is an act of bravery.*

I prayed for courage, health and just enough know-how to get me out of there someday. Lying on my back, I listened to the loud silence that seems to punctuate most prayers. Sunlight and a small patch of blue sky caressed me. Calm replaced the frenzy. Then something moved. A whisper of a breeze flitted across my face. Where was it coming from? Still too tottery to stand, I rolled onto my side and half rose. The breeze intensified, kissing my face even as it blew wisps of hair across my eyes. One of the cupola's windows had been left ajar, perhaps by a careless worker. Another missed light bulb? Instinctively, I cast a quick look in the direction of the curtain. It remained closed. Gazing back at the rebellious window—the only one of the eight that had not fallen in line with the others—I realized that it could not be seen from the vestibule.

To safeguard it, I decided then and there to become a model prisoner. I would give my captors no further cause to enter the cell. Nor would I stand under the dome in their presence, in case a breeze should stir my hair or skirt. The window had to remain secret, though what could I hope from it? It was far too high to reach. Yet the simple touch of the wind filled me with hope, irrational and improbable as that would have seemed to my jailers. I promised myself that I would escape through that window. Oh, but it would be vastly simpler if Tomás would scoff at my bogus tombstone and just barge in with an army of Rurales.

63

THE QUEST

So where *was* Tomás back when doña Manuela was cheerfully directing my funeral? He was home. Hungover. News of my decease had not reached him, so his pounding head had nothing to do with me. It was post-celebratory. On Christmas Eve, directly after the *misa de gallo* Mass, he had thrown a dinner party to show off the house that he had built for his mother. It was modest by most standards, but it boasted two bedrooms, a bathroom with a flushing toilet, electrical lighting, and running water in the kitchen sink. Best of all, the new house had a dining room, he would have gloated to me. A small one, but at least there would be no more eating in the kitchen.

"Oh, what have you done!" I would have groaned. "Now there will be no more waking up just a few feet from the cooking with all its enticing smells."

Of course, that would have been eminently unfair of me. Tomás had every right to aspire to material comforts for his mother and himself, regardless of my entrenched nostalgia. Yet it's also true that Rosa was struggling to adjust to the changes. Like me in San Serafín, she had wandered from room to room that first day, trying to shake the notion that she was trespassing in someone else's house. It wasn't until she placed her *comal* and other kitchen utensils in the kitchen that she slowly began to entertain the possibility that the place might actually become her home. Tomás had neither doubts nor regrets, especially about his decision to postpone the search for Eufemio Rosarito.

To appease Rosa, Tomás had spent a couple of hours researching military archives in Cuernavaca. To his annoyance, several Eufemio Rosaritos had surfaced. He jotted down the names of their towns, slipped the list into his breast pocket, and happily set out to enjoy Christmas Eve. Directly after the *misa de gallo,* he invited their closest friends to dinner. Four women and three men entered the new house with a nervous kind of anticipation. They voiced approval of the new formal table and chairs. But when Tomás, the very citified Tomás, drew a chair back for his mother, all conversation ground to a halt. His sandaled guests stared at their plates in awkward silence.

"Come now! This isn't a wake!" He laughed.

He brought out a bottle of tequila that coaxed a few smiles. The second bottle inspired laughter. Rosa's turkey with spicy hot *mole* sauce broke down all barriers. The revelry went on well into the early hours. So with hangover in tow, the earliest that Tomás could have begun his search for Eufemio Rosarito was the day after Christmas. Yet, since it was so close to New Year's Eve, he reasoned that it made sense to postpone his travels a few more days, followed by a second hangover. By the third of January, Rosa was out of patience.

"Show me that list of towns," she demanded. "What's this one at the top?"

"Yautepec."

"Fine. You get on the train tomorrow and honor your promise to Isabel. No son of mine is going to take a woman's money and *defrock* her."

I don't think that Tomás had any intentions of defrocking or defrauding me. He was simply not enthusiastic about the quest.

Chastened by Rosa, however, he set off early on the fourth of January. That very day rebels loyal to Zapata attacked Yautepec. Tomás returned to Cuernavaca two days later, slightly disheveled and happy to tease Rosa that she had nearly sent him to his death.

"Don't give me that, Tomás Tepaneca. So did you find that Eufemio man?"

"Yes and no. The one in Yautepec gave up the ghost six years ago."

"Never mind. What's the second town on your list?"

"Tetecala."

"I'll pack some *tortas* for your trip."

It took Tomás four days to get around to it. Rosa saw him off at the station. Later that very day Zapatistas blew up the Cuernavaca-Tetecala line. Tomás staggered back to Cuernavaca with a dirty, blood-stained bandage around his head.

"Dios mío!" Rosa reached up to embrace him. "I almost got you killed! What times we live in! The search must wait until things settle down a bit. Here, at least, you are safe."

On the twenty-fifth of January, a full month after my "death," it was Tomás who decided to leave the safety of Cuernavaca. Rosa insisted he stay away from trains. He was glad to oblige, resorting instead to the beautiful Arabian mare that he had taken from San Serafín. (He had sold the other one.) Sitting straight in the saddle, his suit newly pressed and a new fedora hat perched at a rakish angle, Tomás grinned that confident smile of his as he saluted her.

"See you in a week or two, *mi coronela.*"

Moments later he was on his way to Xochitepec, blissfully unaware that the very next day the rebel Genovevo de la O would launch the first of many attacks on Cuernavaca. It was a fine, clear day. When Tomás reached a fork in the road, he was tempted to veer off to the left and visit me in San Serafín. My sweet Tomás still dreamed of the day when I would greet him with a passionate kiss. When he remembered my stubborn love for my husband, he spurred his horse along the other road.

"Damn her," he muttered under his breath.

He was morose for the first few miles. Then he began to notice that the *campesinos* whom he passed along the way doffed their straw hats to him. Or was it to the suit? As a child, he often scoffed at the proposition that the clothes make the man, until the first time he put on a blazer and tie. General Nyman, antagonist and benefactor that he was, had provided for Tomás and the other three boys to visit a tailor once a year to be properly outfitted for the education they were receiving at his expense. The school uniforms for the preparatory school were impressive enough, but the suits for university were life-changers.

The first time that Tomás went for a fitting and stared into a three-paned mirror, he took a step back. What startled him was a city dandy whose mouth had dropped open. Shutting it and drawing himself up, he gazed steadily. And that's when he spotted him—a warrior—not like his ancestors armed with stone weapons, but like the powerful men who ran the country, wielding wealth and its power. The longer he stared, the more he despised his former self. He might as well have taken his new satin tie and choked the Tlahuica boy. He wanted no part of him.

From that day on, Tomás had one goal above all others: to work his way up the social ladder and possess its privileges. There was no turning back, no return to the marginalized existence he had known with his mother. Now, dressed in a vested suit with polished Oxfords on his feet, he was pleased to confirm once again how deep a social gap separated him from his own people. The villagers that he met along the road to Xochitepec didn't seem to notice that his features and skin tone mirrored their own. What they saw was his fine horse and city suit. Most doffed their hats to him, which was all quite edifying. And then it all became annoying as people also demonstrated their wariness of him.

"Do you know where I can find Eufemio Rosarito?" he asked more than once. Each time it was the same reply.

"No, señor. Sorry."

Finally, there was one water peddler who set down a heavy clay pot long enough to scrutinize him and ask, "What do you want with him, sir?"

"To speak with him about a very important matter."

The peddler adjusted his headband, slung the pot back up onto his back, and muttered, "No. I don't know him."

"I just want to speak with him. Nothing more. Here's a peso if you can tell me where he lives."

The man glanced at the coin and took it. "Up ahead, about two kilometers."

No one in all of Xochitepec seemed to have heard of Eufemio Rosarito. No matter whom he asked, Tomás met the same resistance, as cold and drenching as rain season in the high central mountains. Stopping a boy on the road, he tried a new tactic.

"Hey, *muchacho*. How would you like to earn twenty *centavos*?" Tomás smiled as he held out the coin. The child, who looked to be about ten years old, glanced from him to the coin, and then at the magnificent horse. "Can you show me the way to don Eufemio Rosarito's house?" Tomás pressed him. "I think he's my cousin on my mother's side. I promised her that I would look him up."

The boy nodded eagerly. "He's in the *cantina*." He pointed to a saloon with swinging doors and peeling paint. "He's the big, fat guy."

Tomás paid him. Two younger boys gathered around to examine the gleaming coin. Dismounting, Tomás walked his horse to a hitching post and carefully tied him.

"I'll give you each ten *centavos* to guard my horse.

The trio nodded and reverently petted what they took to be the most magnificent horse in all of Morelos and maybe in the whole universe. Straightening his tie, Tomás glanced quickly at the sign. *Cantina de los Ángeles Borrachos.* The Drunken Angels Bar. He suspected the drunks he'd meet in there were hardly of an angelic disposition, but in he went. The interior was windowless, dimly lit, and smelled of unwashed bodies. The only man that was remotely fat was a large, unshaven peasant who rested his right hand on an empty bottle of *aguardiente,* rolling the bottle back and forth under a lethargic wrist. His hair was steel-gray, his eyes glazed.

"Don Eufemio Rosarito?" Tomás asked politely.

"*Pos, pos quién lo busca?*" So who's lookin' for 'im?

"Attorney Tomás Tepaneca, at your service."

And though Tomás ordered a round of drinks for the man and two other drunks who joined them at the table, the only thing he got out of the *ángeles borrachos* was a beating. When they tossed him bleeding onto the dirt road, they also relieved him of the effort of carrying gold coins from San Serafín. They returned to the saloon to invest in its stock. Tomás grasped the reins from the startled boys and staggered to the village well. He reached for his handkerchief, but his hands were shaking so badly that he could not unfold it.

An old woman, the ubiquitous old woman of every village, took the handkerchief from him and drenched it in water from the well. Then she proceeded to wipe the blood off his face. "What happened to you, young man?"

"I just asked Eufemio Rosarito if he had ever worked in Mexico City." He winced as she pressed the wet cloth to his bruised nose.

"Eufemio? He's never worked a day in his life."

"How do you know?"

"Because he's my worthless husband," she answered without changing her expression, her hands cold and wet on his face.

Tomás had not lost all of his money. Fortunately, he had had the foresight to hide some of it inside his shoes. After a few more hostile stares, he began to suspect that he needed to trade in his suit for the white peasant garb that he despised. He did so at the very next village. Yet giving up his city persona, in effect giving in to this devolution from lawyer to humble peasant, from success and promise to poverty and servility, frightened him more than a run-in with *ángeles borrachos*. The clothes don't make the man, he told himself repeatedly as he rolled the suit up in a blanket. Trading the fedora hat for a straw sombrero, Tomás set out again to find our Eufemio Rosarito. *The clothes don't make the man. They don't make the man.* The thought drummed as his newly sandaled feet found the stirrups on his horse's saddle. *I know who I am!*

64

IN HIDING

IN A DREAMSCAPE of shadows and dim light, Samuel saw groups of men running through a jungle. They were being pursued by warriors with painted faces and stone weapons. In the logic of his dream, he sensed that if he stood still instead of running like the others, the warriors would not be able to see him. It worked. Pursued and pursuers dashed past him without perceiving his presence. A short distance away a different group of refugees darted by. Suddenly he spotted his brother among them.

"Benjamín!" Samuel called out in a half whisper. His twin paused. Turning, he looked straight at Samuel, eyes rounded, brows arching toward each other, lips stretched thin. "What are you doing, Benjamín?"

"Hiding."

Benjamín's terror-tinged whisper startled Samuel awake.

The dream haunted Samuel for days. Early on the ninth of February—an infamous day for many people in Morelos—he packed a small overnight bag, saddled his horse, and set off to San Serafín. He arrived at the hacienda without mishap. When he didn't find his mother downstairs, he ran up the staircase, taking the treads two and three at a leap and knocked on her bedroom door. Doña Manuela looked surprised and then annoyed when he seemed to want to enter her room.

"I would invite you in, but my chapel has gobbled up my sitting room, remember?"

He'd forgotten. He followed her downstairs to the new parlor that seemed far too big and too formal for comfort. He missed the coziness of her sitting room but refrained from complaining.

"Let's sit outside, shall we?" Doña Manuela seemed to have read his mind.

"Thank you, but I can't stay."

"Nonsense. How long can a cup of coffee take? Tacha, have a tray brought out to us."

Doña Manuela led the way to the back lawn. Moments later, she and Samuel were seated at a stone table under the venerable fig tree. Its ancient arms provided what I still remember as the most generous shade in all of Morelos. In front of them, at the base of the terraced lawn, rose the aviary with its fluttering prisoners.

"I assume you've heard about the recent Zapatista attacks on Cuernavaca?" She asked.

"Led by a rebel chief who calls himself Genovevo de la O. Yes, I've heard."

"So you do get some news out there in San Gabrielin!" She crossed her arms and smiled approvingly. Manuela Nyman made it her business to know what was happening, if not in the world, at least in her world of Morelos. Since delivery of the various newspapers that she read was sometimes disrupted, she paid her attorney in Mexico City to have one of his clerks telegraph her with daily updates of the political situation as it pertained to her family's interests.

"Well, call it rumor more than hard facts. It's mostly word of mouth for us in San Gabrielin. How serious *is* the fighting in Cuernavaca?"

"The actual fighting seems to last no more than three or four hours a day. Fortunately, for now it's mostly in the outskirts of town."

Doña Manuela paused to serve the coffee. "Have an *oreja.*" She handed Samuel a plate of flat, ear-shaped pastries. "Bardomiana baked them this morning. Have you heard that the Madero government, in all its wisdom, has sent us a General Juvencio Robles to crush all the rebels in Morelos?" Delicately biting into one of the pastries, she added with a wry smile, "That includes us as well. The good general stated in an interview in *El País* that everyone in the state of Morelos is a bandit and will be treated as such. I thought you should know that we have been reclassified and lumped together—school teachers, judges, cooks, potters, peons, miscreants, *priests*, and plantation owners alike. We are all bandits."

"It's abominable."

"The coffee?" She laughed, knowing full well what he meant.

"Bardomiana's coffee could never be anything less than perfect." Samuel smiled as he rose. "Thank you for the coffee, Mother. And now I really must be on my way. I assume it's all right with you if I take the train?"—by which he meant the family Pullmans. "I'd like to visit Benjamín."

"No, son. It isn't safe."

"I can be back before nightfall."

"Haven't you heard that the Zapatistas have threatened to blow up every train that enters Morelos? Oh, yes. Three days ago they made it an official proclamation. Since I assume that you would like to return home after your visit, our train will probably be targeted."

"Not if I travel under the banner of our Virgin of Guadalupe. The rebels respect the Church."

"Oh, son, you are far too trusting. Well trust me when I tell you it's too dangerous for you to travel to the D.F. Look what happened to Mr. Brentt."

"What about Mr. Brentt?"

In her maternal concern, doña Manuela played a dangerous gambit. "Don't you know? I meant to tell you, but it slipped my mind."

"Tell me what?"

"He's dead."

"What? When did *that* happen?"

Doña Manuela, slipping seamlessly into another lie, crossed her arms with a heavy sigh. "It happened in early November. He had just been here to visit Isabel, you know, back when she looked thin but none of us imagined that she meant to starve herself to death. We actually had a pleasant lunch together, the three of us, though I couldn't help noticing that she barely touched her food and was beginning to look downright unhealthy. Anyway, at the end of Mr. Brentt's visit, I offered to have some of our people escort him back to Cuernavaca, but he refused—rudely, in fact. But as God protects fools and children, at least temporarily, he did get home without incident. Then two or three days later the old drunk headed for the hills, I suppose to paint or to sketch a landscape, and was waylaid by Zapatistas."

Samuel leaned forward, cradling his forehead with one hand. "Why didn't you tell me?"

"I meant to. It just slipped my mind."

"How does one forget something like that?" He snapped. Because she looked confused and regretful, he reached for her hand. "Forgive me, Mother. You carry too much on your shoulders. What times we live in," he sighed. After a short silence he asked, "How do you know that Zapatistas killed Mr. Brentt?"

"I sent one of the *peones* to Cuernavaca on an errand. He saw the body himself. It was hanging from an oak. They had tied a sign around his neck that read: 'Viva Zapata!' So you see that I'm right. These rebels mean business, as do the *federales*, the devil take them all! Please postpone your trip, son."

"No, I need to go today. If you don't want to risk the train, I certainly understand. I can go on horseback."

"By all the saints and martyrs!" She slammed her cup down so hard that it cracked the saucer in half. "For such a gentle soul, you are horrendously stubborn, Samuel Nyman! Just like your father! Yes, you can have the train. And maybe flying a banner of the Virgin of Guadalupe will give you safe passage with the rebels. But since I am not as trusting as you, I *insist* you take an armed escort. Now have another cup while I prepare a basket for your brother. I assume you can wait a few more minutes?"

Half an hour later, Manuela walked arm-in-arm with Samuel to the hacienda's train depot. "Make sure they're treating him well, and that he still has clean linens and clean towels."

"I will," he smiled.

"And make sure those bodyguards are still doing their job. It's good that they don't know you're coming. Surprise them. See how they treat Benjamín when they think no one is watching." Her eyes misted. Then she looked straight up into Samuel's face. "Remember. Not a word to him about Isabel's death. He may understand more than we think. You know how explosive he is and what those monsters did to him! Remember your vow to our Holy Mother."

"I haven't forgotten." Because she continued to clutch his hand he added in a tone of resignation, tinged with a hint of irritation, "I swear on my life."

"No, not your life. Swear on *my* life, Samuel."

"You know I won't go back on my vow."

When she kissed him, Samuel had the distinct impression that in her mind she was kissing Benjamín. Perhaps it had been that way throughout his entire visit, and maybe long before that. Did it matter that he had become his brother's stand-in? No, he told himself. Not really. Not much.

65

SURPRISE VISIT

A FEW HOURS later Samuel was in Mexico City taking a cab to the penitentiary. With Rodolfo still in France and Eva in Italy, there were no chauffeured cars to meet him. That didn't bother him. Neither did the inspection of his bag and his mother's basket of food. When a surly prison guard jammed his carefully folded stole and missal back into his bag, Samuel gazed at him impassively, his hazel eyes calm as a mill pond on a windless day. Looking at his serene demeanor, no one would have imagined that his inner landscape held the wreckage of a devastating storm. Certainly not the inmates who watched him cross the central courtyard with such steady strides.

Though Samuel knew that this part of the penitentiary housed hardened criminals, not political prisoners, he felt no fear. Some glared at him. *Don't trust the cassock to protect you,* Manuela would have warned, but he would not have believed her. So he moved easily among them. Most of the prisoners doffed their hats to him or murmured a soft greeting. And he blessed them all. In spite of his inner confusion, Samuel was by nature too generous to deny these men the hope that he himself no longer felt. Promising a number of them to hear their confession before he left the prison, he made his way up a stairway and into his brother's corridor. Moments later, he stood once more in the doorway of the most elegant prison cell in all of Mexico.

It was still hung with expensive draperies, carpeted with oriental rugs, and furnished in his mother's impeccable taste. These were the comforts that bribery could buy, mere details that he saw in seconds. The real focus of his attention was Benjamín who was slumped forward in his wheelchair. A bodyguard who had his back to Samuel was spoon feeding him. A second bodyguard who was lounging in one of the wing chairs, a scrawny young man with a shock of hair that stood straight up, jumped to his feet.

"Good afternoon, Father!"

Samuel remembered him for his inane grin and that he was missing at least half of his teeth. "You're the one they call 'el Vago?'"

"Yes, Father. Thank you, Father."

Samuel turned to the other man. The stump of a hand triggered his memory. "And they call you, 'el Manco.'"

"Yes, Father." The man rose. He was older than his companion, perhaps in his mid-thirties with a head of tight curls. Placing his stump over his heart and bowing as he did, el Manco had the look of a man pledging a life-long allegiance.

Samuel turned his attention back to his brother and felt his breath catch. Even though Benjamín's bandages and casts were gone, he looked more damaged than the last time he had seen him. Gaunt. Unkempt. The look was punctuated by a tangle of beard and a mustache that concealed the whole upper lip. Worse, far worse, was the vacancy of the eyes. Samuel took the seat el Manco had been using. Looking directly into his brother's face, he took his hands and forced himself to step into the blank stare.

"Benjamín? It's me, Samuel. How are you?"

The stare remained appallingly fixed and unblinking.

"Mother sends you her love. She's sent you some of your favorite foods, including a jar of Bardomiana's *cajeta*." Benjamín's lips stayed slightly parted as if they no longer remembered how to close, and the other facial muscles sagged as if they too had forgotten their purpose. "Hipólito sends his greetings," Samuel quipped. "When I got home this morning, I could hear that killer tail of his all the way from the main gate. He was rearranging the furniture on the upper veranda with every swipe of his tail." He smiled, but nothing he said drew a response. "I'll feed him," Samuel muttered to the guards.

El Manco handed him a small tin pot with beans.

"Why is he eating these? What about the meal from the Sylvein?"

"It hasn't arrived yet, Father."

"If it's coming, why are you feeding him this?"

"He doesn't like anything else," el Vago offered, then grinned nervously.

"When was the last time you bathed him?"

"He doesn't like to be bathed, Father," el Vago grinned again and quickly glanced out the window.

"Fill the tub."

Vago, who was feared in the prison for his uncanny access to knives and for the way he wielded them in a fight, scurried into Benjamín's private bathroom. Seconds later Samuel could hear water running. He turned to the other bodyguard, the one who never smiled and who killed so efficiently with one hand.

"There's a barber's shop in the prison. So why does my brother have a beard—an unkempt one at that. And don't tell me he doesn't like to go to the barber."

The two men locked eyes. "There didn't seem to be any point."

"To being clean shaven?"

"To getting shaving nicks. The barber is clumsy."

Samuel believed him. "All right. Lay out some clean clothes for him while I undress him on the bed."

Lifting Benjamín in his arms, Samuel was startled by the boniness of his frame. Naked, Benjamín seemed a wraith. Though not as gaunt as I had been on my deathbed, the memory assaulted him.

"Are you starving him?" Samuel exploded.

If Benjamín had been truly present, he would have looked up and whistled, Man, do you look like Father just now! So you *do* have some of his Viking spirit after all.

"He doesn't like anything," el Vago grinned and quickly looked out the window again.

"The truth is, it's almost impossible to get him to eat, Father," el Manco spoke quietly. "He doesn't seem to hear us. Most of the food just dribbles out of his mouth."

"Check the temperature of the water," Samuel glared. "And you," he stared at Vago, "roll back my sleeves."

Both men hastened to obey. Then Samuel set his brother in the tub. "I'll do this today. But so help me, from now on you're to bathe him every single day, do you hear me? Every day." His hands shook as he struggled to master his anger. "Make sure the water is the right temperature and let him enjoy it." Turning to Benjamín, he tried once more to breach the wall of his silence.

"There. How's the water?" He searched his brother's eyes. *Where are you?* Remembering his dream, he whispered in his ear, "Are you afraid?"

Just then a voice in the other room boomed out, "So where's my meal. I'll kill you if you fed it to the idiot!"

Samuel stepped out of the bathroom and found himself face to face with a man he had never met until then, the third bodyguard. For a moment he felt like an Alaskan trapper that he had read about—a man confronted by a grizzly rearing up on its hind legs.

66

MANGEL

THE GRIZZLY LOOKED just as startled. He turned to his companions as if to say, who the hell is this? Why didn't you warn me? His narrow eyes became mere slits from which he scrutinized the visitor. Then they lit up with recognition.

"Are you a brother of the Captain?" Mangel asked though he knew the answer. It was staring him in the face, this uncanny duplicate of the catatonic prisoner.

The visitor ignored the question, firing off one of his own. "Who's the idiot?"

Mangel had the impression that the priest's eyes had become sharp as a bottle smashed in a bar room fight. Needing to throw the first punch, Mangel lunged at el Vago, grabbing him by the throat.

"This idiot is always trying to take my food. Do that again and I'll kill you!"

"Sorry, Volcán. It won't happen again!" the scrawny one gasped, losing his grin for all of eight seconds.

Mangel, known to the prisoners as "Volcán" for his explosive temper, shook his prey one more time before releasing him. With a satisfied air, he turned his attention back to the priest who was watching him with a skeptical air.

"Volcán? What's your Christian name?"

"Jesús Mangel, at your service," the giant smiled from behind a beard and moustache that were even wilder than Benjamín's. "Sorry, Father, but in this place a man has the duty to protect what is his or be trampled."

"Then be careful what you protect. A man can easily find himself out of work."

The delivery boy from the Sylvein Restaurant arrived just then. Mangel watched the visitor reach into a pocket in his cassock to give the boy a tip. Then the priest had the gall to stare him in the face and order him around as if he were some damn official.

"You're going to dress my brother, and then I'm going to show you how to feed him his boxed meal."

When Benjamín was dressed and back in his wheelchair, Mangel spoke in a tone dripping with concern. "Sadly, Father, even a great meal like this won't get your brother to eat. We do our best, but he just lets the food dribble down his front." *The priest isn't buying it, damn him!*

Instead, the unwelcomed visitor was carefully breaking off a piece of chicken smothered in an orange sauce that filled Mangel with murderous longing. And damn if the idiot in the wheelchair wasn't chewing the food, *his* chicken! And the other two were applauding! Bastards!

The final insult came at the end of the visit with the priest's parting shot: "My brother will be receiving guests for lunch on a pretty regular basis. I'll arrange with the Sylvein to double the lunch order on those days. For now he can keep the beard and moustache, but see that the barber trims them. And make sure that my brother is bathed and ready to receive company every single day." Mangel watched the priest head for the door, then stop and tap his forehead as if he had just remembered something. "Oh, and when he gains weight, ten or twelve kilos, we'll celebrate with boxed meals for you too. 'See you soon, gentlemen.'"

67

TZOMPANTLI

BEFORE LEAVING THE penitentiary, Samuel heard the confession of several prisoners. Then he stepped into the brisk February afternoon, aware of how much cooler it was in the higher elevation of the capital than in Morelos. *Why did I leave my overcoat in the Pullman?* Hailing a taxi, he was about to return to the train station. A stronger impulse, however, drew him to the central square of Mexico City—the Zócalo. In one of the many conversations we were to have in the next life, Samuel told me about that visit. Stepping out of the cab, he was struck by a sense of overlapping time and cultures. Twentieth-century electric wires and clattering tram cars spoke of Porfirian efforts at modernization. The sixteenth-century cathedral and government buildings surrounding the massive square proclaimed the glory of Imperial Spain. And then there was that third layer just beneath the surface, the ancient Aztec city of Tenochtitlán. Dismantled stone by stone, most of it had been reconfigured into European forms.

Is Tenochtitlán the soul hidden deep within layers of skin, muscle, and bone? My brother-in-law wondered. Or is it nothing more than decaying bones slowly morphing into dust? Which is the real city? Do these stones remember the cries of human agony? Does suffering somehow imbed itself in the substrate of matter? And what of demonic cruelty? Does it lie just beneath the surface, waiting to blow high like a gush of crude oil?

Walking toward the north end of the great square, Samuel gazed at the cathedral in all its sprawling glory. His father had taken him and Benjamín to see it when they were nine years old. Back then Lucio Nyman Berquist was still a general, tall and manly in his uniform, blue eyes sparked with humor and a touch of mischief. Knowing that they would be visiting the cathedral, Samuel had memorized as many facts as he could cram in two days. His father had listened with arms crossed and feet planted firmly like a conqueror surveying the spoils of war.

"The cathedral was started in 1573," then because he desperately needed to impress his father, he had rattled off a litany of statistics as fast as he could get them out. "It has two bell towers with twenty-five bells, three main portals, five altars, five naves, one-hundred and fifty windows." He had paused for a quick intake of breath before diving back in. "Those statues up there in the clock tower are the three theological virtues: faith, hope, and charity."

"We have an art historian in the family!" His father had clapped him on the shoulder. "Or perhaps a theologian!"

Samuel could still remember how he felt himself swell with pride. Then Benjamín trumped him. "Did you know that right here where we're standing, right here, there used to be a huge rack full of skulls? Millions of them!"

"Millions, huh?" Samuel could still remember his father's laugh, bright and vibrant like mariachi trumpets. And he had wished with all his heart that just once in his life he could make his father laugh like that. But that was something only Benjamín seemed able to do, not him. Never him.

Upon their return to San Serafín, nine-year-old Samuel had hurried to look up the history of the *tzompantli,* the Aztec racks that had shocked even the hardened *conquistadores.* "You got it wrong," Samuel had informed his twin with quiet satisfaction. "The racks held only sixty thousand skulls, not millions."

Benjamín looked at him without the smirk he had expected. "Sixty thousand or a million—what's the difference?"

"Don't you know how to subtract? It's a huge number!"

"And sixty thousand isn't? Instead of worrying about how many bells there are in the cathedral towers, think about what those Aztec priests did in that place."

"I know what they did. Human sacrifices." Samuel spoke from the safe surface of historical facts. His twin, who had read the same accounts and had a poet's imagination, had fallen into a dark place rendered all too real, a fact their father had totally missed when he laughed out loud.

"I'll tell you what those priests did." Benjamín had spoken with a survivor's haunted look. "They took someone like mamá, tore open her chest and yanked out her heart, and no one stopped them. Then they cut off her head and let it become a skull. When they were done with her, they did the same to papá and to Rodolfo and Eva and you and me. And because that still wasn't enough, they did it to every single man, woman, and child in San Serafín. And then because they still couldn't fill their racks, they murdered and skinned all the people in the neighboring plantations and all the villages in Morelos until they had *sixty thousand* skulls. And no one cares anymore! No one. But you know what I hate the most?"

Samuel shook his head slowly, as if suddenly aware that the moment held the end of his own innocence as well, or at least the beginning of a great unraveling.

"I hate that no one stopped them. Not even God." Benjamín fell silent for a few moments, his hands clenching and unclenching. A single tear rolled down his face as he whispered, "Why didn't God stop them, Samuel?"

"I don't know."

God help me, I still don't, Father Samuel sighed.

68

FATHER RAMÓN

Softly, sadly, Samuel entered the cathedral. The lofty expanse enfolded him. He, in turn, embraced ritual, familiar and comforting: fingertips dipping into holy water; right hand making the sign of the holy cross; knees genuflecting; lips praying. When he had completed a full circuit around his rosary, he sat back. Closing his eyes, Samuel silently asked his twin, "That day when you posed your terrible question about God's accountability, was that when you turned away from the Church and I toward it? Did I become a priest, not to please Father in his zealous years, but in order to find the answer to your challenge? Is that why?"

Rising from the pew, Samuel strolled along the edges of the great cathedral, solemnly pausing at each chapel. Sixteen of them, he could have told Benjamín. While stopping at the last one, he was approached by a short, stocky priest who drew him into a tight embrace.

"Samuel Nyman! By all the saints!" Samuel hoped his face didn't betray bewilderment, or worse, his sister's blunt *who-the-hell-are-you* look. "Do you know how many years it's been?"

"I . . . Seven?" He took a wild stab in the hope of a clue.

"Longer than that. I got kicked out in 1901."

Kicked out . . . 1901 . . . boarding school in Maryland . . . Samuel tried to see past the thick neck and mannish square jaw. In a flash of memory a bright-eyed, skinny boy smiled up at him.

"Ramon? Ramón Santos?"

They embraced again like cousins reunited at a family gathering, though Samuel continued to believe that their brief friendship had been founded more on nationality than true compatibility. He, Benjamín, and Ramón had been known to their American classmates as the Unconquerable Mexican Triumvirate. Father Ramón drew him outside where he could untether his booming voice.

"Look at us, cut from the same cloth after all! Who would have imagined that we would both embrace the priesthood? Well, with you it was a foregone conclusion. But me a priest?" Ramón laughed. "Hey, I heard that you actually asked the archdiocese to exile you to the sorriest village in Morelos."

"I escape every now and then."

"So I see. How long are you staying?"

"Actually, I have to get back today." Remembering that Ramón was of a garrulous disposition and that he had promised Manuela that he would return well before nightfall, Samuel hastened to add, "I have a train to catch."

"Don't tell me. Let me put my mystical powers to work." Father Ramón affected to close his eyes and rub his brow. "Yes, I see it now. The Pullman cars are decorated with the Nyman Vizcarra shield, am I right?" He grinned.

"Well, yes."

"Perfect! The train can wait while you and I have lunch."

Samuel was not in the mood to reminisce over schoolboy pranks, but he didn't have the heart to disappoint his effervescent classmate. So he walked with Father Ramon to the nearby Sanborns. The restaurant was housed in a colonial building known to everyone as the *Casa de los Azulejos* for its tile-covered walls.

Sitting in the golden glow of the enclosed central courtyard, secure in the pleasantries of the capital, neither imagined that just one year and six months from then, Mexico City would fall to rebel troops—not only to Zapata's army of the south, but to the fiercely anti-clerical northern troops of Pancho Villa. Blissfully unaware, Ramón Santos reveled in memories of old times in Maryland, while Samuel smiled politely. Ramón's laughter resounded off the high ceiling like a horn that plays its tune and then stops abruptly. With no other transition than a silence to be measured in seconds, he asked, "How is Benjamín?" Father Ramón's voice had grown soft.

"Not well, not well at all."

"I'm sorry to hear it. I read about your father's death. I was stunned when they tried to pin the murder on you. When you wouldn't defend yourself, I knew you had to be protecting Benjamín, like you did in 1901." Samuel winced. Father Ramón continued in a calm voice. "When they kicked me out of school, you knew that your brother had also been in on the prank. You knew, but you remained silent."

"Forgive me, Ramón."

"Forget it. I mention this only—"

"No, hear me, Ramón. When you were brought before the board, it was cowardly and misguided of me to remain silent. I thought that family loyalty had to supersede all else. I'm so very sorry. I've come to realize that silence is a form of complicity."

"Yet didn't you fall into the very same error years later at your father's murder trial? My God, Samuel! You were actually willing to go to prison for Benjamín. Did you think how this would damage not only you, but how it would reflect collectively on the priesthood?"

"I knew he would come forward."

"He didn't in Maryland."

"He was fifteen, spoiled and full of himself back then, but he became a man of great integrity."

"Forgive me, Samuel, but I don't see how letting you go through the ordeal of a trial and a guilty verdict attests to his integrity."

"He never imagined that I would be found guilty. Moments after the verdict was delivered, Benjamín came forward and took the full blame. You must understand, Ramón, that impersonating me was no crime, only a necessity, a ruse to get my father to talk to him."

"And murdering him? Is that not a crime?"

"It was an accident, not murder. Think back. Sure, Benjamín was short-tempered, but he was just as quick to right wrongs."

"Was? Why are you speaking of him in the past tense?"

Samuel tensed. "Benjamín is gone, and I played a role in his destruction." The restaurant morphed into a confessional. "Benjamín's life began to unravel with his marriage. For that I am to blame. I thought I could break ecclesiastical rules when I married him to a woman who is not Catholic."

"The beautiful Isabel Brentt. What did the papers call her?"

"La belle dame sans merci."

"And was the beautiful lady merciless?"

"I don't know any more." Samuel toyed with his food. "Before Christmas I would have pointed to the undeniable fact that she ran off with the very attorney who drew up my father's will just hours before his death—the will that just happened to leave everything to her. But when she signed everything back to us and took her own life—"

Ramón's eyes widened. "I'm sorry. That I did not know."

"No. I shouldn't have brought it up. I tell you this in confidence."

"Of course. Of course."

"I think she was more troubled than merciless. Isabel was a complex person. Right after the reading of my father's will, she returned with us to San Serafín. She seemed genuinely mortified and eager to hand everything over to us, the rightful heirs.

Yet that very night she ran off with her lover. Then a day after Benjamín's sentencing, she visited him in prison. Why? How does one make sense of her behavior? Whatever the reason for her visit, after she left the penitentiary, Benjamín flew into a rage. Guards beat him into submission." Samuel clenched and unclenched his hands. "God alone knows how many hours he lay on the floor in a pool of blood. The upshot is that they crippled him for life."

"Ah, Samuel, I'm sorry."

"The worst of it is that they robbed him of his mind too. He lives in some kind of vegetative state, more dead than alive."

"That's terrible. Terrible." Father Ramon shook his head.

"What's particularly trying is that we can't look after him properly. Rodolfo and Eva fled to Europe, my mother is tied down running the hacienda, and I'm serving in an isolated parish. Visiting him is a rare luxury. Today I discovered that the inmates whom we pay to protect him are eating his food. Well, one of them is—a big bear of a man. My mother has arranged for the Sylvein Restaurant to deliver gourmet meals daily, but it's clear that Benjamín is not getting them. In another month or two he'll look like a skeleton—or be one."

"Fire the guards."

"And how do we make sure the abuse doesn't happen all over again with the next set of inmates that we hire? We can throw money at the problem, but in the end we have to depend on criminals to protect him. The only protection that I could offer him today was a lie."

"Knowing you, it was a charitable lie."

"A desperate, bold-faced one. I told them that Benjamín is going to have visitors on a regular basis to eat lunch with him."

"And he is," Father Ramón smiled. "I happen to have a taste for gourmet cuisine."

"That's very good of you, but I can't ask you to go into the lion's den every day."

"Then don't ask. Just step aside and let me help Benjamín while I can. Unfortunately, I'm being assigned to Puebla in May, but that still gives us about three months. I pledge to visit him daily."

Samuel thought of el Volcán and scowled. Father Ramón thumped him on the back. "Don't worry, Samuel. If it gets too rough I'll bring along some seminarians as bodyguards. They have more zeal and courage than the Mexican eagle. Rest assured, old friend. At least for the next three months Benjamín *will* get his meals. After that, God will provide another solution."

Before parting company, Samuel asked a question he could no longer hold back. "Ramón, tell me honestly, do you ever wonder if you chose the right profession?"

"Every day." When Samuel waited for some elaboration, Father Ramón patted his shoulder. "Don't worry, old friend. All doubts are cleared up for us after we die. Doubting is how we know we're still here."

69

SANTA MARÍA

BOARDING THE PULLMAN, Samuel seated himself in a club chair by a window.

"Would you like some dinner, Father?" the steward asked.

"No, thanks, Reynaldo. I've eaten. But coffee would be good."

"Yes, Father. May I inquire, did your visit go well?"

"Actually, it went exceptionally well." Samuel smiled.

He had a flash of memory: Mangel's look of astonishment and smothered rage when the Sylvein meal went to Benjamín. Reliving the moment, Samuel laughed out loud. Then he turned his thoughts to his unexpected meeting with Ramón Santos, Ramón whom he had been eager to forget. That afternoon they had talked like long-lost brothers joyfully reunited. They talked about everything. And though the vexing problem of evil was not settled in Samuel's mind, something almost as good stepped in. By demonstrating faith in action, Father Ramón gave Samuel hope, if not in God, then at least in humanity.

The ride home went fast. As the hacienda locomotive was pulling only one Pullman car and the caboose where the armed guards traveled, it quickly gained speed. Three of the guards chose to travel on the rooftop, rifles at the ready. The train began the ascent into the mountains before making its steep descent into the state of Morelos. Pine trees darted past Samuel's window as he read. At the very moment when Reynaldo reappeared with crème brulée and more coffee, Samuel glanced out the window. A pageant was playing out in a series of flame-lit tableaux: a town being set on fire; soldiers rounding up people at gunpoint; faces screwed up in silent wails. The locomotive had drowned out all voices but its own. For a few seconds Samuel was acutely aware of the sharp, surreal juxtaposition of his reality inside the Pullman and the horror on the other side of the glass. He struggled to open the window. By the time he was able to stick his head out, the village was out of sight, but he could smell the stench of kerosene and fire consuming everything they touched.

"What was that?" he shouted to one of the guards on the rooftop.

"Santa María! The *federales* were burning it."

When the train pulled into San Serafín, Samuel was met by doña Manuela. "The blessed Mother be praised!" She embraced him long and hard. He could feel her trembling, his mother who was normally so unflappable. "I heard there was trouble in Santa Maria and I knew you would have to pass by there."

"Government troops burned it down."

"Poor wretches. That's Genovevo de la O's town. What did he expect? He attacks Cuernavaca day after day. Then he threatens to blow up trains. Doesn't he know that every sin carries its punishment?" Manuela threw up her hands in exasperation.

～

February 10, 1912, dawned clear and cool in Cuernavaca. In the outskirts of town, de la O's soldiers, those that had survived the Federal attack of the previous night, crept silently past Rosa's new house. Noting the fine front door, several of the rebels let themselves into her garden. Nothing stirred. Moments later, they kicked in the door. Rosa, who had spent the night nursing a sick friend, was just walking up the muddy lane. Pausing to sniff the air, she realized that something was on fire.

My house! My new house!

Running into her garden, she encountered three men about to mount up. Their arms were full of loot.

"What do you think you're doing?" she yelled at them.

A man with a scar across his forehead grinned at her. "Getting even. Tell your masters to remember this. Now they know what it feels like to lose your home!"

"I'm the only master here! This is *my* house, you idiots!"

The three looked at her braided hair and Indian dress. Then they burst out laughing. "Yours, huh? You mean that shack over there."

"No. This one! I'm Rosa Tepaneca, and that's my—" Just then she caught sight of something that enraged her even more. "That's my *comal,* you thief!" Rosa yanked a flat pan out of the hands of a rebel who was trying not to drop the silverware that he had also grabbed. The diminutive Rosa raised the pan menacingly. "You can burn my house. You can steal my silverware, but you cannot have the *comal* that my mother and grandmother used for our cooking! Now get out of here, you thieves!"

The men mounted up. They weren't laughing. The one with the scar turned in his saddle. Speaking like a man whose pride has been wounded, he muttered, "We're not thieves. We're liberators."

"Then the Virgin save us from liberation!"

"We're fighting for the rights of the common people."

The ground shook as the burning roof caved in.

70

A CHAW OF SUGAR CANE

By mid-February, Tomás had visited all the villages on his list plus two more. In each case, he found old timers who could recall that an Eufemio Rosarito used to live there, but that he had long since moved to another village, always another village. So Tomás found himself scouring all of central and southern Morelos. In time, beyond time, he would tell me about his misadventures. Once, he strayed into the state of Puebla, like a sea gull blown off course in a storm. A peddler he met on the road was able to set him back on track. He also sold Tomás an edition of *Diario del Hogar*. The newspaper was almost two months old, but that didn't matter to Tomás who was starving for something to read.

Being so out of date, the *Diario* said nothing about the resignation of the unpopular Governor Ambrosio Figueroa nor about his replacement, a moderate for whom Tomás would have gladly worked, all for the chance of enacting positive, lawful change in his home state. Nor did the old newspaper mention General Juvencio Robles and his army of one thousand Federal troops and five thousand Rurales, dispatched to Morelos to put down the Zapatista rebellion. He would encounter that reality soon enough.

What the old newspaper did offer was the full text of Emiliano Zapata's "Plan de Ayala," a declaration of war against President Madero's government. When it was first published on the fifteenth of December, Tomás had been too absorbed with the construction of his house to read it. He knew about it, but he had dismissed Zapata for being on the other side of the great divide—the unlawful side. Besides, Tomás had been far more interested in deciding on the proper varnish for his new front door and on purchasing a dining room set worthy of his new house.

Now he squatted on the ground, his white pants and shirt covered in mud. Mud under his nails, mud in his hair, mud streaking his face. And though he thought that the text rambled at times and lacked sophistication, Zapata's passion and anger touched something in him, especially the article that declared the justice of expropriating hacienda lands for redistribution among poor farmers. Tomás folded the newspaper carefully and stuffed it inside his shirt. Then he mounted up, doggedly determined to continue his quest rather than admit defeat. By late February, however, he had a far more pressing problem than finding the elusive Eufemio Rosarito. Morelos had become a war zone. To make matters worse, there was no *one* enemy. Federales, Zapatistas, and a variety of non-Zapatista guerilla bands rampaged throughout the state.

A band of masked men relieved Tomás of his horse and bedroll. Now he owned nothing but the clothes on his back and a few pesos hidden inside his folded newspaper. He pressed on, determined to fulfill his end of our bargain. The quest was more than a matter of honor to him; it had become an obsession. He would prove to me and to himself that he, Tomás Tepaneca, had the perseverance and know-how to get anything he set his mind to. Anything.

A few days later Tomás found another Eufemio Rosarito. This one dangled from a tall fig tree, his neck distended to the left at an awkward angle. His pants had been pulled down to his ankles, an act meant to denigrate and to warn others. Another man had been hanged alongside him. Tomás wiped away tears of frustration. Villagers noted the grief and felt empathetic. They simply mistook the reason for his tears. He helped them cut the two dead men from the tree and would have helped carry the bodies back to the village for burial, but there was no longer a village. The federales had burned it to the ground.

"We didn't do anything!" A woman wailed. "Why did they do this to us? Why?"

The hanged Eufemio Rosarito turned out to be a farmer who had never once left his village. Tomás set out again, doggedly determined to find *the* Eufemio Rosarito—a man grayed with years yet still vigorous; a man who had actually ventured beyond his humble farm into the greater world; a man who could serve his master faithfully and then murder him. The one who fit these criteria would help him set in motion his own machine of agrarian reform. So he wandered on, finding Eufemio Rosaritos all over Morelos, ubiquitous as the *ahuehuete* trees that rooted themselves along creeks and riverbeds.

Tomás's sandals blistered his feet. When he had no more than two *pesos* to his name, a small detachment of federales way-laid him. He was now hungry, grimy and totally penniless. As the days dragged on, fever and the monster in his belly howled more and more insistently. Tomás nosed around fields that had been burned or trampled by "the Torch"—as General Robles was dubbed. Hunger drove Tomás into silos where he risked being shot by hacienda guards for a few stalks of sugarcane. No matter. He would break off a piece of stalk and chew it like a dog gnawing on an old bone. Fever made his teeth chatter. Unable to walk any further, he crawled into a ditch. Drawing his knees up to his chest, Tomás shivered with cold and burned up by turns. An old man hunkered down alongside him, bringing the moon with him. Tomás could see him perfectly, an Indian with weathered skin and deeply etched crinkles around his eyes. His hair and moustache were white and stiff as a neglected paint brush. The old man was sucking on a short piece of sugar cane.

"Ah, there's nothing like a good chaw of raw sugar!" he winked good-naturedly. "But it won't put flesh on your bones, Tomás."

"No kidding! You don't happen to have a drumstick on you, do you? Even the toughest old rooster would look good to me." Tomás sat up and studied the old man. "Who are you?"

"Justino Tepaneca. I'm your grandfather."

"Aren't you dead, *abuelo*?"

"That depends on what you mean by dead."

The last thing Tomás wanted as he burned up was a discussion on semantics. "Am I dreaming, *abuelo*?"

"You'll probably think so in a day or two."

Because Tomás could see the old man's face with such clarity, he sat forward with a burst of eagerness. "It doesn't matter. You're real enough now," he told the hero of his childhood. "I want you to know that I'm going to get back our village lands! I can do it. All I need to do is to find the right stalk of sugarcane."

"How will you know it from all the others?"

"By its initials: E.R. Maybe you've seen Eufemio Rosarito?"

"Nope." Justino Tepaneca rose.

"I know he's out there somewhere."

The old man pointed to an enormous cane field, except he wasn't old any more but in the prime of life. "You really think you can find him?" he asked before vanishing.

The field undulated. In seconds it became a lake that swirled around Tomás, engulfing him along with a nearby village, swallowing them whole, and then the whole of Morelos.

A couple of days later Tomás's fever broke. So too did his illusions. Stopping in the middle of a road in the middle of Morelos or perhaps in the middle of nowhere since he was lost, the thought came to him with unapologetic directness: I *am* a damn fool on a fool's mission. Enough.

His grandfather did not need to visit him again to tell him so. Finding Eufemio Rosarito, getting him to confess to his crime, and then dragging him to Mexico City had never been a realistic option. And why bother? Tomás asked calmly. Isa doesn't want me. Why should I help that patricidal Benjamín Nyman get his freedom and enjoy her? Besides, I don't need Isa's charity to get the land back. There are other ways.

He trudged on. That night he stumbled into a camp of Zapatistas. Several men drew machetes. A sentry aimed a gun at Tomás: "Who goes there?"

Because he was desperately hungry, or because he had grasped the absurdity of his quest, or because he shared Zapata's passion for land restitution, or simply because the men looked so startled, Tomás stood with hands on hips and grinned at them.

"Who goes?" The sentry repeated.

Deliberately dispensing with the grammar of respectability, the grammar of the life he had coveted, Tomás shot back, *"Pos yo!"*

In essence he had said, Me, who the heck else? His response, so absurd under the circumstances, drew laughter from the sentries. His fearlessness and ragged clothing gained him a spot around their campfire and tortillas filled with beans and serrano *chiles.* With every bite of the burning peppers, Tomás felt himself divest his persona of *licenciado,* attorney-at-law, and reconnect under the starry sky of his ancestors with the Tomás Tepaneca of his boyhood.

71

A PRIEST'S HOMILY

DOÑA MANUELA DINED in her sanctuary—the vestibule to my prison cell. Opening the great curtains, she seated herself at an antique table with richly carved legs. A banker's lamp gave her enough illumination to read or simply to watch her "American Blue-Thief," as she affected to call me. Leaning into a high backed upholstered chair, a thick oriental carpet under her feet and a cashmere shawl to shield her from the chill of winter and stone walls, she noted once more that I was still wearing nothing but one of Eva's discarded nightgowns. It hung loosely over my emaciated frame.

Doña Manuela smiled as Tacha set a dinner tray on the table. "Tonight I'm having quail the way they cook it in Guerrero." She freed her napkin from a silver napkin ring. "Bardomiana bastes it with a sauce that has a bite to it, then she barbecues it. The potatoes look nice too. Can you smell the *tomatillo* sauce on the rice?" La patrona carved off a small piece of quail and tasted it. "Tacha, give the Blue-thief her *atole*."

Stone-face stepped forward for the key, but her mistress suddenly waved her away.

"On second thought, let's see how an American Blue-Thief walks. On your feet, girl. No more coddling."

I struggled to stand. Weeks after my supposed death, my skeletal legs still wobbled like those of a newborn calf. Both of my captors observed me closely.

"Beauty really is only skin deep." La patrona smiled as if she had just had a remarkable insight. "How grotesque you've become, Isabel Brentt. If your admirers could see you now."

I held my tongue and reached for the cup that Tacha thrust between the bars. *My admirers will see me someday, but not like this.* I drank the milk beverage to the very last drop.

Despite escalating hostilities between Zapatista rebels and Federales, Samuel dutifully visited his mother every other Sunday after he had given Mass to his own parishioners. He would arrive at the hacienda on time for Sunday dinner, stay overnight, and offer matins the following day before returning to San Gabrielín. Though he did not normally offer a homily at matins, I'm told that he gave one that was to have enormous consequences for me. As it was the first Monday of lent, the Lectionary called for a reading of Ezekiel 34:11–16 and Matthew 25:31–46.

Doña Manuela knew very little Latin. Like the humble *peones* who filled the church pews that twenty-sixth of February, she knew the appropriate responses by heart, but of necessity she had always depended on priests to disclose the meaning of the scriptural readings. Latin was therefore more musical to her ears than instructive. Watching Samuel give Mass, she must have listened in a contented kind of haze, watching him with a mother's devotion, maternal pride exulting, he's like an angel! Look at the reverence with which he officiates and how smoothly he reads in Latin, his voice masculine, solemn, and earnest.

Did she remember him as a toddler just then? I'm told that Samuel was always so much more sober than Benjamín, which is probably how most people learned to tell them apart. How could Samuel, with his earnest little face and soft voice, not have inspired tenderness in her? And how could Manuela not adore Benjamín with that look of his that I came to know so well, as if he were holding back laughter from a prank not yet discovered?

That day at matins, doña Manuela fell into a soft melancholia, suddenly missing her tender little twins who had vanished into adulthood. Loving them as she did, she must have mused like so many mothers, where do all those sounds go, the happy prattling and the scampering of small feet? Where are they, the little boys I cradled, the children who thought I was the center of the universe?

Her wistful questions rebounded, unsatisfying as echoes. She was far too pragmatic to pine for the past. Yet I've been given to know that every now and then the past would catch her off-guard, wounding her with longing. *A woman needs to think, not to feel,* she would remind herself fiercely. *It's the emotions that lead to all misery; it's the emotions that deceive a woman into thinking that her happiness depends on a man. I've become a rational thinker, thank God.*

Watching Samuel as he read the second lesson, she did not realize at first that he had switched to Spanish.

What? Oh, yes. The separation of the goats from the sheep. She continued to watch the earnest young man while only half attending to his words about charity and the fate of those without it. She was far more interested in analyzing the differences between her sons. Clearly, she regarded Benjamín a male image of herself, a warrior not afraid to fight to the death if necessary and showing his enemies no quarter. Samuel—ah, Samuel she considered an angel of God, a man not quite of this world.

Manuela Nyman loved them both with a volcanic passion. Sitting under the high dome of the family church, she found comfort, not in the word of God, but in the fanciful notion that here she could see *both* of her sons simultaneously. Doña Manuela became so caught up in the beauty of warrior and angel that she hardly heard the message. It was only when Samuel closed the Bible and finished the lesson from memory that she attended.

"Then He will also say to those on the left hand, 'Depart from Me, you cursed, into the everlasting fire prepared for the devil and his angels; for I was hungry and you gave me no food; I was thirsty and you gave Me no drink; I was a stranger and you did not take me in, naked and you did not clothe Me, sick and in prison and you did not visit Me.' Then they will also answer Him, saying, 'Lord, when did we see you hungry or thirsty or a stranger or naked or sick or in prison, and did not minister to You?

"Then He will answer them, saying, 'Assuredly, I say to you, inasmuch as you did not do it to the least of these, you did not do it to Me.' And these shall go away into everlasting punishment, but the righteous into eternal life."

Samuel made a long pause. "We live in brutal times. Now more than ever we must show compassion for friend and enemy alike."

As Samuel continued his exhortation, doña Manuela had the sudden impression that his eyes rested on her the most, though in fact they swept the room. The homily continued to accuse her. His voice pleaded, but she did not hear the entreaty, only the condemnation from an angel. After Mass, she and Samuel returned to the house for lunch. He hardly touched the meal. His reticence further unnerved her, yet not nearly as much as his sudden anguish. Throwing back his head, he asked in a voice that shook, "What kind of a priest am I? Who am I to presume to guide others?"

"Oh, son, what are you talking about? You're the finest priest in all of Morelos."

"No. I keep failing those whom I should help. What did I do for the people of Santa María when their village was being burned? Absolutely nothing."

"What could you have done, one man against armed soldiers?"

"I should have ordered the engineer to stop the train. I could have offered the villagers shelter here in San Serafín. But I was too slow to react. I just couldn't believe my eyes."

"My dear, the army would not have handed them over to you. We're at war now, and this is part of the administration's strategy to break the rebels."

"And here we sit under our crystal chandeliers sipping coffee while others get burned out of their homes. Where are they tonight, the victims? In some filthy corral or dank prison? And look how I failed my own brother by failing Isabel."

"That's absurd, son."

"I knew she was unhappy. That day that I tried to speak to her and she wouldn't open her door—"

"Samuel, we've been through all this. Isabel was selfish, hopelessly selfish."

"And I was complacent. I should have insisted that you unlock the door. You have keys to all the rooms. Oh. Mother, we should have checked on her."

"I know. It was my fault entirely." Manuela shifted the blame onto her own shoulders, knowing he would quickly relieve her.

He waved away her self-recriminations. "No, no. How could you have guessed the depth of her despair? You have too much on your mind with the hacienda. But my job is to minister to my flock, and in that I failed utterly." Tears rolled down his face in long, sad lines. Manuela rushed to his side.

"Oh, my dearest, she wasn't your responsibility!"

"Wasn't she? I preach compassion, but where was mine?"

He rose from the table.

"Must you go?"

They both knew the answer to that. His next words, however, took her by surprise. "I'd like to stable Chantico here in San Serafín, if that's all right with you."

"No, son. You need a good horse. Your very life could depend on it."

"Every horse and burro in San Gabrielín has been stolen by rebels and federales alike. It's just a matter of time before they take her too. I've had to keep her hidden upstairs in one of my spare rooms."

"Inside the house? But the carpet!"

"I rolled it up and stored it."

"And the floor?"

"It now has a thick layer of hay that I muck out every day."

"But that's absurd!"

"We live in absurd times." He was smiling now.

"Don't go back there, Samuel. You saw what happened in that wretched village. What's to keep it from happening in San Gabrielín?" Manuela clung to his arm. "Think of Mr. Brentt. You're safer here!"

"My parish needs me."

"The people of San Serafín need you."

"No. They have their own priest."

"Well I need you!" she cried with sudden passion. Then remembering her prisoner, she quickly added. "If it's a sense of freedom that you want, you don't have to live in the house with me. In fact, it would be better if you didn't. You're a man now and should have your own place. I could easily have the guest compound fixed up for you. You'd have the whole place to yourself. You wouldn't have to see me except once or twice a week for dinner. So you see, you'd be perfectly free to live your life as you choose at a perfectly safe distance from me!" she quipped.

Nothing she said could persuade him to stay. *How can he be so sweet and so obstinate?* She fumed and marveled.

"Just let me have one of the mules, Mother, an old one that won't attract much attention."

She sighed and walked with him to the door of the house. When he bent to kiss her, she grasped his hands firmly in hers. "Promise me something, Samuel. No more self-recriminations, do you hear? No more sadness about the past. Isn't it bad enough that Eva is so desperately unhappy in her marriage, and that Rodolfo is becoming as glum as your father on his bad days, and that Benjamín—Don't you see? I *need* for one of my children to be happy, do you hear me?"

"All right. No more whimpering. It's time to take action."

"What kind of action?" Now she was alarmed. The set of his jaw reminded her of Lucio Nyman just then.

"We need to get all the planters to petition the President and that new governor of ours. Perhaps we can shame them into protecting the pueblos if we personally vouch for them."

"You're right. I'll draw up the petition today and telegraph everyone."

Samuel kissed her. "That's the spirit, doña Manuela!" Then he headed for the stables with that long, easy stride of his and Benjamín's.

"May God protect you always, son," she whispered.

Returning to her room, Doña Manuela dropped to her knees before a small statue of the Virgin Mary, and prayed aloud. Tacha overheard every word as she paused by the open door. "Blessed Mother, please entreat God to protect my son! He's an angel, one of your own! Ask that He guard him always. Remind God that I have restored and maintained houses of worship, here and in San Gabrielín. You know I've always ministered to His church and to . . ."

Manuela suddenly pulled back startled, not by Tacha whom she had not discerned yet, but by echoes of Samuel's reading: I *was hungry and you gave me no food. . . . Assuredly I say to you, inasmuch as you did not do it to one of the least of these, you did not do it to Me.*

Stumbling to her feet, she hurried down the dark corridor with Tacha now on her heels. Yanking on the cord, la patrona drew open the curtain, taking me by surprise.

LA CALACA

THINKING THAT THE dragon would not return until evening, I was allowing myself the luxury of lying directly under the cupola. A delicious shaft of light enveloped me.

"Get up! Why are you sleeping?"

I staggered to my feet and could see her squinting through the haze of sunlight.

"Take off the nightgown. Go on. This is no time for false modesty. I need to see how you're getting on."

I hesitated. Then slowly I pulled the nightgown over my head. The woman had never seen me completely nude, leaving the heavy nursing to Tacha. And what did she see? A skeletal creature that swayed ever so slightly, like a reed yielding to a breeze. Every rib pressed against my ribcage as if trying to break free. Knees and hips protruded grotesquely. I remember glancing down at the spindles that had once been shapely legs. The sight of my body still unsettled me. I had been telling myself that my thinness was temporary; that it wasn't so bad. But now in the stillness of la patrona's face, under her startled scrutiny, I grasped the full extent of the devastation and felt myself begin to crumble. Then seemingly out of nowhere, or somewhere, a thought winged across my mind.

I have a spiritual body within this one. She can't see it, so she can't hurt it.

Deliberately, imperiously, I met Manuela Nyman's stare head on, forcing her to look away. The dragon closed the curtain as abruptly as she had opened it, and I heard Tacha's gruff voice ask, "Do you want me to feed the prisoner more than *atole,* señora?" Tacha had also attended Mass that morning.

"Yes, yes. Double the food on my trays. Put some flesh back on those bones!" The words tumbled in irritation.

"Fine. But how do I do that without getting everyone suspicious, señora? They're going to wonder why you're suddenly eating so much."

"I don't care what you tell them. Just do it. And put some decent clothes on her!"

Still standing in a stream of morning light, I slipped the night gown back over my head. As it slid past my nose, it released a childhood memory of a doll's satin dress. Cadwally had taken me to the market place to see the many stands set up for the Days of the Dead Festival. When I spotted a stall covered with skeletal dolls, I let go of his hand and ran to it. One of the dolls wore a blue satin gown.

"Buy me a *calaca*! Please, Cadwally!" I remember cradling a ten-inch, papier-mâché skeleton that was wearing a loose-fitting dress.

"Why do you want one of those horrible things?"

"She's not horrible. She's the most beautiful xolotl in the world."

"A *shallot,* huh?" Cadwally could never master the Nahuatl words that Rosa taught me. Aztec *tl* endings stuck to the roof of his mouth like peanut butter. I was forever correcting him.

"She's a sho-lo-*tl,* and she's ever so lonely. Please, can we bring her home?" He laughed but he bought the doll just the same. At breakfast the next morning I set a place for her. "How's Miss Calaca today?" Cadwally winked.

"Her name is Conchita."

For the next few years Conchita joined us at meals and went everywhere with me. I never worried that her ribs protruded outlandishly or that her eyes were mere hollows. Thinking of her now in my prison, I murmured, "*Somos calacas, tú y yo.*" Acknowledging that she and I were both skeletons now, I raised my arms and moaned in mock imitation of a ghost. "Oooooh! I'm the terrible *calaca!*"

Tacha had cracked the curtains apart. She was staring at me, humorless as a cyclops.

Does she even know how to smile? I wondered.

Meanwhile, Samuel had reached the stables. While a mule was saddled for him, he stepped into Chantico's stall. Running his hands along the neck and shoulders of the white mare, he kissed her on the cheek. *When I was a boy I named you after the Aztec goddess of volcanoes,* he could have informed her. His touch told her what he now remembered as a man, that Chantico was also the goddess of personal treasure. Jacobo, an old Tlahuican with hair as white as the horse, stepped up alongside them.

"Don't worry, Father. I'll exercise her every day for you and guard her as if she were my own daughter."

Samuel embraced the old man. Moments later, he was riding a mule through the central gate and down a road fringed with towering fig trees. The February morning chilled his hands. He was just reaching into his pockets for his gloves when he heard a sound that made him rein in. Someone was sobbing. Samuel dismounted on the edge of the family cemetery. A short distance away he spotted a peasant who was kneeling and clutching a tombstone. After tethering the mule to the cemetery gate, Samuel approached the mourner. The man's head whipped around. He was anguish incarnate.

"Mr. Tepaneca? Tomás Tepaneca?"

73

AT THE GRAVE

TOMÁS DID NOT respond. His attention, indeed his very being, was focused on the tombstone. He kept reading the inscription as if hoping that the repetitive act would somehow invalidate it.

Isabel Brentt
1890–1911

Instantly, Samuel was caught between contending emotions—empathy for a fellow sufferer and an irrepressible antipathy toward his family's enemy. His priestly-self wanted to offer comfort; his other self struggled to suppress the urge to pummel Tomás. So Samuel stood, at first neither advancing nor retreating, just watching, watching and waiting, waiting and remembering the palpable pleasure with which Tomás had wielded the infamous Last Will and Testament; the barely contained triumph behind the official mien; the smoldering resentment in his eyes when his mother had snubbed him, dismissing him from the dinner table. Back then Samuel had cringed at his mother's incivility. Yet hadn't her intuition proven true when Tepaneca ran off with Isabel? Wasn't Tepaneca the more contemptible, not just for trying to defraud his family of its rightful inheritance, but ultimately for destroying Benjamín and Isabel's marriage? How did one forgive so much evil?

Perhaps because Tomás was sobbing uncontrollably, or because there was such a sharp disparity between the dapper, social-climbing attorney whom he remembered and the ragged peasant who now mourned with such raw pain, Samuel repeated softly, "Mr. Tepaneca?" When another spasm of pain contorted Tomás's face, Samuel found himself crouching beside him, offering the only words he could muster in the face of staggering personal loss. "I'm sorry."

And because Samuel also mourned me, he and Tomás stared at my tombstone with the silence of a shared loss. Tomás broke the silence with a low moan.

"This can't be real. When I demanded to see her, the guards at the gate said that she had died, but I didn't believe them. I still don't. She was fine in September. How can Isa be dead? This has to be a hoax."

"It's not a hoax. I was with her at the very end, and I officiated at her burial."

"Swear by the Mother of God that you are telling me the truth."

"I swear it."

"Oh, Isa, Isa! Forgive me! Please forgive me!" Tomás was sobbing again. "I should have returned sooner but I was angry, angry and jealous. And I was too busy thinking of myself! Oh, Isa!" Tomás touched the tombstone with aching tenderness, as if caressing my cheek. When he was calmer, he wiped his face with the back of his arm and looked at Samuel. "How did she die, Father?"

Samuel did not respond right away. As he admitted later, he was weighing how much to tell his family's arch enemy. *You don't deserve any explanations*, he found himself thinking as he vacillated again between resentment and pity. *Tell him nothing. Yet isn't silence a kind of lie?* So Samuel spoke the truth as he understood it.

"I'm sorry to have to tell you this. Isabel starved herself to death."

Tomás's head shot up. His eyes narrowed. "She what?"

"She locked herself in her room and deceived us all—"

"Deceived?" Tomás jumped to his feet with surprising elasticity. Samuel, on the other hand, caught his heel in the hem of his cassock, ripping it as he struggled to regain his balance. "Just who exactly did Isabel deceive?" Tomás demanded in a tone that had sprouted thorns.

"The servants, my mother, and—"

"Your mother? We sent her packing to Cuernavaca."

"Well, she returned!" Samuel snapped. "She returned to her rightful home, and Isabel showed a generosity of spirit that you obviously lack."

Rage surged through Tomás. "Your mother tricked Isa into letting her back in. Admit it." He gave Samuel a quick jab to the heart with the tips of his fingers.

"It was not an issue of trickery but of justice."

"And I suppose that Isa deeded the properties back to your family, including the land that your father stole from the villagers of Santa Lupita, and then for good measure she starved herself to death!" This was followed by another savage jab that forced Samuel to stumble back a step.

"Yes. I pray for her soul daily."

"Spare me the piety. You Nymans murdered her!"

"We did nothing of the kind! You should have seen my mother's grief and the care that she gave Isabel to the very—"

"No. I'll tell you what I saw with my own eyes—your mother's rage against Isa the day we evicted her."

"What did you expect?"

"Anger, fear, or pleading, but not such diabolical hatred." It was all coming together for Tomás. "Manuela Nyman did this, God rot her soul!"

Samuel's face contorted as he threw himself on Tomás. The two rolled on the ground, trying to pummel each other. Enraged, Tomás jumped back to his feet, fists at the ready. "Come on! Get up!"

Samuel, who had suddenly remembered himself, held up a hand. "Enough."

"Get up, you coward! Don't think you can hide behind that cassock."

"I should not have struck you. I'm sorry."

"Well I'm not!" Tomás stooped and grasped Samuel by the throat. "Listen to me, priest. I would have given my life to keep the wolves away from San Serafín for Isabel's sake. But now you and your whole family can go to hell where you belong. I swear that I won't rest until I see the hacienda burned to the ground!"

Tomás headed for the cemetery gate. When he reached it, he untethered Samuel's mule. With one swift motion, he mounted up and galloped away in a cloud of dust. Samuel returned on foot to the hacienda stables and had a second mule saddled. He said nothing to the stable grooms about the theft or his bleeding lip. On the other hand, he did alert the guards to be extravigilant. All the way back to his village, Samuel alternated between a sense of outrage toward his family's implacable enemy and shame for his own violent outburst.

74

WINDOWS

THE CLOTHES THAT Tacha retrieved from my trunk hung on
me like shirt and trousers on a loosely stuffed scarecrow. Drawers, petticoats, and skirts puddled on the floor unless cinched
extra tightly. The corset hung uselessly over my emaciated torso;
tossing it across the room I rendered a swift verdict as I'd done
before.

"I banish thee again, foul torturer of women!"

Eating was another challenge. Over the next few weeks my
shriveled stomach had to relearn its function. Stone-face and the
Dragon reintroduced solid food slowly as if I were a baby being
weaned. They were right in not rushing the process. We all knew
it was going to take weeks for my stomach to accept regular
meals, and months for my stick legs and arms to fill out again.
So they fed me, not generously, but at least enough for me to
begin the slow ascent toward health. Isolation and loneliness, on
the other hand, they inflicted most generously. I rarely saw doña
Manuela now, only Tacha. Without saying a word, old Stone-face
would thrust a clay mug between the bars. I knew I was not to
utter so much as thanks, but I did anyway, tossing out the one

word to test her. She accepted it, but then as if in deference to her mistress, she kept the visits all the briefer and chillingly silent.

At first I didn't mind. It was enough that the duo seemed to have lost interest in starving me. Yet isn't solitary confinement an emotional kind of starvation? I soon became so intensely lonely that I was often tempted to risk hunger in exchange for conversation. I usually resisted the impulse, but just barely. Meanwhile, the large theatrical curtain remained closed. Sometimes I thought I could hear a faint stirring on the other side. Had it parted ever so slightly? Was the dragon spying on me? Well, let her. What did I care as long as she continued to feed me real food? What mattered was that I first restore what they had taken from me—my health. Then I could worry about escaping. To that end I focused on small but steady gains, such as walking the length of the cell without losing my breath. One complete lap, then two and three and more. My goal was to be able to run laps instead of walking them. I would achieve it no matter what!

And so we settled into this new phase of my imprisonment. Feeding and clothing me gave the Dragon the illusion of having met her moral responsibility to me, her prisoner. What happened to my mind, on the other hand, she deemed my problem, not hers. If I had challenged her about the cruelty of denying me books and writing materials, she would have folded her arms and explained that she was merely giving me the time to contemplate the enormity of my sins. Had I carped about the mind-numbing sterility of her décor, she would have smirked that only the repentant can appreciate the purity of white.

She means to drive me insane, I realized.

Then don't humor her.

My old self-reliance came into full play. I contrived ways to fill the hours. The moment Tacha left for the day I would launch a full schedule of activities: a brief chapel service in the morning in imitation of the ones I used to attend daily at school, exercise three times a day with increasingly longer walks, a hot bath—my one luxury—and then a long excursion into my imagination.

I became a teacher. No degree required, not even graduation from high school. My brilliance was enough. And since no self-respecting teacher addresses her classes silently, I spoke aloud to mine. No danger of losing my mind, I told myself, because it was all a game of pretend. I just needed to hear a human voice. And in case the Dragon or Stone-face should lurk behind the curtain, I did take the precaution of speaking to my students only in English.

My pupils were dazzled by my erudition and life experience. So were my friends. As soon as classes were over, I would visit them in Bryn Athyn. I remember one such outing with Wertha and Emiline. Walking the length of the cell, I imagined that we had taken off our shoes and stockings, and that we were wading ankle deep in the Pennypack Creek. Pointing my toes, I set in motion ripples that danced in great concentric circles.

"Did you know that people think I'm dead?" I loved the expression on their faces. "It's true. Check out my gravestone if you don't believe me."

I told them all about my incarceration. "What are you going to do?" Wertha asked.

"Escape."

How?

"Through that window up there," I pointed.

"How will you get up there? It's so high up."

"Help me think of something."

They did. Late one night, Wertha and Emiline and some of the other Deka girls from our sorority let down a rope ladder for me to climb. Somehow they had managed to scale the outer walls and to fully open my partially-opened window. Between whispers and stifled laughter, I scampered up. Seconds later we were all on the rooftop gazing up at the stars. I could feel the night's fingers combing my hair. I was free! The only problem was that my friends had chosen to rescue me in a dream. In the morning there was no trace of them or their ladder. I didn't hold it against them.

I did resolve more than once to stop talking to myself, but the silence was so intense that it left my ears ringing. I knew that Rosa would understand, so I often invited her to take a walk with me. Besides, I really needed to hear her opinion on a matter that continued to trouble me.

"Is Manuela Nyman insane or simply evil?" I asked her in English as if she had miraculously imbibed the language with her *café de olla*. It was a particularly mind-numbing day. "Not all insane people are evil. But are all evil people ultimately insane? Can evil be rational?"

Rosa rested both hands on hips and tipped back her head. "The devil is no fool," she said.

"So you don't think she's crazy? Then which is worse, to be in the hands of someone who is insane or insanely evil?"

Rosa threw up her hands the way I'd seen her do a thousand times. "What's the difference? Either way she's out to torment you."

"Well, it won't matter once I'm far from here," I hastened to reassure both of us. "Besides, my job is not to judge the woman spiritually, only to outwit her. Oh but she is hateful and utterly useless."

"Hateful, yes. But is anyone totally useless?" Rosa looked me straight in the face, arms crossed. "Think about it, *niña*. If not for her, you might never have fallen in love with your Benjamín."

"She had nothing to do with it." Sometimes my imagination was downright irritating.

"Didn't she? By locking up her son as if he were one of her birds and then trying to keep you two apart, didn't she simply draw you all the more to each other?"

She had a point. "All right. Then maybe the same positive mechanism is at work and something wonderful will come from this horrible incarceration. In the meantime, I can handle her. I'm going to beat her at her own game. You'll see."

Perhaps because it was growing dark in my white world and loneliness cast its longest shadow of the day, I felt my stubborn self-sufficiency ebb with the outgoing tide of light. I hurried to prepare for bed, a tactic that usually kept depression at bay. Sleep was a sailboat, dreams the wind of a salt-laced escape. So I made a pillow from my rolled up skirt and a bedroll from the old horse blanket. I liked that it still smelled faintly of hay and horse sweat. Too bad it was so scratchy. Still, since I was living inside a cold stone crypt, I appreciated the warmth it provided. Lying under the cupola, I gazed at the night sky in window fragments. And then because the window that could liberate me remained unreachable as the moon, I suddenly gave up all hope. I would live out my days in that one room, and when my captors died, I would starve to death, for who else knew I was there? Cadwally and Tomás thought I was six feet under the ground. Swiping at tears, I accepted at last that the half-opened window was utterly, hopelessly useless.

That night I dreamed about a far different kind of window. In the dream I was lying inside a coffin made entirely of glass. As I stared straight up through the lid, the glass burst into brilliant colors. The coffin sprouted high-vaulted ceilings, and I realized that I was in my favorite church in Paris, the Sainte Chappelle. The stained-glass windows rose about me in all their glory. Mass was in progress. Yet something was not quite right. Heavy incense hung in the air and a choir was singing in Russian instead of Latin. A well-dressed, middle-aged woman stood alongside me.

"Excuse me, Madame," I ventured in my school girl French. "Why are they singing in Russian?"

"Are they?" She smiled pleasantly.

Why do you look so familiar? I wanted to ask her. And then I gasped, "Aunt Delphine! Is it you?" How could it be? My great-aunt was old and wrinkled as crumpled tissue paper. But it was her all right. "What are you doing here, dear Aunt? Shouldn't you be in Bryn Athyn this time of year?"

"I died, Isabel," her eyes fairly twinkled.

"Oh. I think I'm supposed to say I'm sorry, but I'm glad for you!" I hugged her. "'Wish I were dead too. I'm in a prison in Mexico, and I'm worried that I might be losing my mind. I can't reach the window, my one hope for escape."

"Then go inward."

"How do I do that?" Oh, those wonderful eyes!

She dropped a small object into my hand—my Russian icon. "You know how, Isabel." And I realized with a start that I was seeing the face of Christ shining through her.

When I awoke, moonlight had tip-toed into the cell. Silently, I began to recite the ancient Jesus Prayer. *Lord Jesus Christ, have mercy on me a sinner. Lord Jesus Christ, have mercy on me a sinner.* On and on I prayed until slipping into a dreamless sleep.

75

CRUCIBLES

GHOST TOWNS BEGAN to haunt the countryside of Morelos. The wind moaned in the charred remains of houses, churches, and shops, all empty, all silent. The government's war against the Morelos peasants had not yet reached Samuel's village. San Gabrielin's people went about their work quietly, ears attuned for the thunder of horses, eyes scanning the crests of hills and bends in the roads. Frequent glances over the shoulder became habitual gestures. Their priest, on the other hand, had become embattled weeks earlier. Fierce skirmishes raged within him, reason and faith gripping each other in murderous strangleholds.

At the end of each confrontation with his doubts, Samuel felt diminished. Half poured out. Sometimes when he robed for Mass, or when he turned the pages of his missal, or when he held out a wafer to a communicant, his hands shook. He felt his doubts growing like cancerous tumors. At the same time he feared to profane what might indeed be holy. So he continued to say Mass with outer reverence and inner fear. At times he was tempted to take off the cassock permanently and return to San Serafin to live out his days in obscurity. But he could not bring himself to abandon his parishioners, especially now.

For a time Samuel placed my death at the crux of his loss of faith. He recognized that it had affected him far more deeply than his father's death. I think it was because he had found Lucio Nyman lying in cold repose, the battle over and nobly lost, whereas with me the war still raged when he reached me. He had entered the room believing in a merciful god, but he had left burdened with doubt. Nothing had prepared him for the brutality of the process of dying, or of only half-dying. And there too lay another reason to lose faith in God: Benjamín.

One morning while shaving, Samuel stared into the mirror above his bathroom sink and scrutinized the face reflected back to him: the short brown hair that framed it; the symmetry of the features; the light of intelligence that emanated from the hazel eyes. On impulse, he let the muscles of his face go lax, the mouth gape open. And there he was in all his tragic horror—Benjamín staring back at him, Benjamín who had wasted away almost as much as I, a cadaver that still breathed. The soap slipped through Samuel's fingers.

He shut his eyes, opening them again to seek his own face. Yet, because the eyes expressed such inner torment, he remembered Benjamín as a child and his horror at the brutality of human sacrifices. *Why didn't God stop them, Samuel?* Uttered in a child's voice, the eternal question echoed his own bewilderment. Yes, that was it, Samuel realized now, years later. The problem was not death. It wasn't even evil per se. The problem was God's apparent tolerance of evil. How did one justify that?

One night doubt finally morphed into a horrifying certainty. There IS no God, the thought spoke with crushing directness.

Samuel was devastated. He felt adrift in a lifeboat without food or compass, alone at sea in a tempest. When at last he fell into a fitful sleep, he dreamed of a place that had neither light nor darkness. He was aware of people though he could not see them. They stumbled about, all of them looking for a way out, all of them lost and he with them. Someone muttered to an invisible companion, "Are we in hell?"

"No. Even that would be better than this."

"Then where are we?" Samuel asked the voices. "What is this place?" No one answered, so he asked again. "What is this place?"

"You," the darkness groaned.

Samuel woke gasping and crumpled to his knees to pray, to weep, to beg God to forgive his lack of faith. What had he seen in that dream but the emptiness of his inner life without God? So there *is* God, or nothing would exist, not even pain or darkness, he reasoned with a rapturous kind of anguish. But he still needed answers about the problem of evil.

When he wasn't ministering to his flock, or working on the roof of the school house, or jogging along dirt paths, Samuel spent hours rifling through books that he had used in seminary. Back then the whole question of theodicy had been no question at all. Everything had made such perfect sense to him. How had the arguments of St. Augustine and of St. Thomas Aquinas become so unsatisfying to him? What if the Manicheans had it right? What if evil really was as powerful a force as God? Wouldn't that at least let God off the hook, since the two forces, good and evil, would then have an equal share of power? Yes, that would make sense, he reasoned. A benevolent God wills nothing but good, but His adversary, as strong in power as He, foils His plans every chance he gets.

No, that's absurd! He slammed a book shut and paced in his study. How can evil be the equal of God when most, if not all of it, is man-made? Wouldn't that make man equal in power to God, which is patently impossible? So doesn't that bring me back to the same place, the same indictment? Why doesn't an all-powerful, benevolent God intervene and *stop* evil?

This led him back to the free will theodicy. It didn't explain for him why earthquakes killed good and evil people alike, or why diseases killed so indiscriminately. But the free will argument did explain moral evil. The people of Morelos were suffering because of human evil. Pacification at any price was the administration's goal, not the welfare of men, women, and children who were systematically being burned out of their homes and forced to wander the roads without food or the means to earn it. Yet knowing this did little to comfort him or to furnish him with a clear theodicy. In another dream, Samuel found himself trying to explain the free-will argument to Pancho Comardo, of all people.

"There's evil in the world because God has given us free will," Samuel tried to explain to his brother-in-law while wondering throughout the dream, *why has Pancho painted his face like a clown?* "We must be free to make choices, whether good or evil, don't you see? Otherwise, if God were constantly stepping in and keeping us from making mistakes, we would be mere puppets."

"Well, God knows Benjamín got to exercise his freedom, and look where that got him," Pancho smirked, his painted white grin expanding clear to his ear lobes. "So answer me this. When your brother sits slumped in his wheelchair, totally dependent on thieves and cut-throats to feed him and to wipe the drool from his face, isn't he a puppet? How then did free will keep him free?"

"I don't know! I don't know!"

February and March were particularly cruel in Morelos. One afternoon refugees began to trickle into San Gabrielín. By evening dozens sprawled exhausted on the steps of Samuel's church, their lives as fractured as the stone slabs broken by years of earthquakes. Hands reached out to him as he ascended the stairs.

"Please help us, Father! The federales burned our village to the ground. We've had nothing to eat in two days!"

Samuel paused outside the church entrance. In the glow of the electric lights that Manuela had installed in the one paved street of San Gabrielin, he could see human misery in its range of ages, from helpless infancy to enfeebled old age. All looked hungry and desperate. Residents of San Gabrielín approached almost as fearfully. Everyone looked to the young priest for guidance. He hesitated. Then he did the only thing that made sense to him. He took action.

"Welcome, my brothers and sisters in Christ. Come inside. Rómulo! Diego! Fetch beans and rice from the parish granary. Lupe, Rosario, Carmen, please organize the cooking. Manolo and Juvencio, follow me."

After the refugees had been fed, he said Mass. The church overflowed. Inspired by their priest who was quick to share his own food, many of San Gabrielín's families did likewise. More desperate people poured into town over the next few days, quickly threatening to overwhelm it. Samuel sent to San Serafín for supplies. As quickly as they arrived, they would be used up. The starving, bleeding, bewildered masses of displaced people kept arriving as word went out that San Gabrielín was under some kind of special protection.

As Samuel was to learn, it was his mother's letters and bribes that had turned his village into a sanctuary, at least for the present. This made his days longer and harder as he tended to the needs of the wounded, the hungry, the sick, and the sick at heart. But the work did for Samuel what none of his books on theology or his pacing at night had accomplished. The satisfaction of being able to help others gave him a measure of peace. The refugees and those who worked to help them taught him a straightforward lesson—that evil is the corrupt work of human hands, and helping hands, the work of God. He would need to remember this later when war finally claimed San Gabrielín.

In the meantime, it was all Samuel could do to keep the village from becoming a shanty town. Refugees built makeshift shelters from scraps of corrugated roofing, empty crates from the hacienda, palm branches lashed together, or simply a blanket draped over a piece of rope. Drinking water was not a problem. Sanitation was a different matter. When he mentioned in a letter to his mother that his village was seeing a sharp increase in cases of dysentery, she responded quickly. Ever practical, doña Manuela sent masons and plumbers from the hacienda to build public toilets. Ever feisty, she braved the roads to see the refugee crisis for herself. And ever the general, she arrived with a small army at her back. Samuel gasped when he saw her.

"Mother, what are you doing here?"

"¡*Dios mío*! I didn't want to believe it was this bad," she murmured as she dismounted.

When she left the next day, she took over three hundred refugees with her and housed them in a warehouse that she converted into barracks-style living quarters. They blessed her, one and all. Is it any wonder that her children and "her people" all loved her, or at least respected her? Looking back I can admire her spunk, but she was a puzzle to me, this woman who could be as generous as she was brutal. When those two extremes clashed within her, how fierce the battle! Yet as I came to discover, all of us must fight intense inner battles. No one is exempt. It's just a matter of degree that separates the ferocity of one person's struggles from another's. I didn't know yet the full darkness of my own inner landscape. I was too busy being a victim and trying to survive. Samuel witnessed plenty of victimhood in those terrible days and worked tirelessly to help survivors that staggered into San Gabrielín. Fortunately there were lulls in Gen. Juvencio Robles's raids against the *pueblos.* It was during one such lull that Samuel began to dream in red, as he would say later—dreaming because Benjamín was also seeing flashes of red, the color of his awakening.

76

A FLASH OF RED

For months, Benjamín had wandered through a world as bizarre as the Jabberwock's. At best, it was oddly whimsical; at its worst, it was the dreamscape of nightmares. Yet there he had chosen to stay since the beating that nearly killed him. He became so lost in its twisting canyons that he never noticed Father Ramon's daily visits, or the protection these gave him against the voracious Mangel. Neither did he care when the good priest's visits stopped after the promised three months and that Mangel had gone back to his abusive ways, devouring the Sylvein meals and helping himself to anything else that caught his fancy.

El Manco and el Vago, the other two bodyguards, provided what protection they could. But they understood the prison's hierarchy of power all too well and knew better than to challenge el Volcán, as inmates called Mangel. To their credit, they did fulfill most of their duties to Benjamín—bathing, dressing, and feeding him. They also exercised his legs as instructed by doña Manuela's physician; el Vago complained with the regularity of a crowing rooster: "Why don't we exercise the table's legs? We might actually get somewhere!" he would grin his toothless smirk, never varying his attempt at humor.

"Shut up and help me pump his leg! Now the other," el Manco would growl under his sweeping moustache day after day, week after week, adhering to a regimen of physical therapy with fanatical zeal—waiting, ever watchful for a spark in the dead embers of Benjamín's eyes. Throughout it all, Ben remained absent, his legs like malfunctioning pistons that have to be moved by hand, his face as blank as Tacha's. No. It was worse than that, for at least her eyes did register emotions sometimes. I'm told that looking into Ben's eyes was like peering into shuttered windows. No stimulus seemed strong enough to make him open up to the world again despite el Manco's best efforts.

And then it happened.

Benjamín was slumped in his wheelchair in the corridor outside his cell when he spotted a flash of red. Thinking like the ornithology enthusiast that he had been, Ben reached for a name: *a red* breasted—but the word flew away. The next day he saw it again. This time it streaked red and black. A crested doradito. *Pseudocolopteryx acutipennis,* he thought at first. *No. A black-capped lory—lorius lory.* But this was no avian.

As the fog lifted from his mind, a far different word emerged. *Tarahumara.*

Across the courtyard from him stood a man who wore a billowy red shirt, a white loin cloth, and a headband for his long hair. The clothes alone proclaimed the prisoner to be a Tarahumara Indian. One might suspect that the bright color was the key stimulus that guided Ben out of his dark world. And it was to a large extent. But so too was the man's *yearning*—his desperate urge to run for the simple joy of running. Running, Ben would have told you had he the power of speech, is as natural to the Tarahumara people as breathing. Unable to do so in the prison compound, this newest inmate had settled for running in place. Benjamín noted the soft frenzy of legs hungry to break free, and he remembered the flapping of wings in his mother's bird cages. A guard shouted just then, "Hey, you! No running!"

Other inmates shoved or taunted the new prisoner. I can see him now: a tall, gaunt Tarahumara Indian, neither young nor old, pausing until everyone's attention was fixed elsewhere, then starting up again, running in place, eyes fixed ahead, back straight, motions silent and smooth, his bare feet hardly touching the tile floor. The morning wore on, and still he ran in place. And then the Tarahumara prisoner vanished abruptly from Benjamín's view when Mangel yanked the brake free and wheeled him back to his cell.

"Hey, *idiota*! It's time for you to watch me eat your lunch."

When Mangel had devoured the Sylvein's Beef Stroganoff and red wine (despite Samuel's warnings), he threw himself onto Ben's bed and was soon snoring. El Vago drew up a chair so he could spoon feed Benjamín. I'm told that Ben's right arm suddenly shot forward, like a bird darting free from a cage left open. The bowl of rice clattered to the floor.

"What the hell—" el Vago started as if he had spotted a scorpion climbing up his leg.

El Manco was just as startled, "I think he wants to go back to the corridor!"

With a rare burst of energy, el Vago pushed the wheelchair back into the upper corridor; el Manco hurried alongside. "Here? Do you want us to stop here?" Manco asked Ben in a low voice, Ben whose attention was fixed on the Tarahumara prisoner. And then my Dearest spoke for the first time since the beating, his voice softly murmuring three words: "Let him run."

"Did he just speak?" el Vago lost his grin.

Still not looking at his bodyguards, his attention fixed solely on the Tarahumara prisoner, Ben spoke again, his voice just above a whisper, his words a command, "Let him run." When neither of his astonished bodyguards moved, Benjamín turned to them, eyes blazing. "Tell them! I'll pay their damn bribes!"

～

El Manco hurried off to make the necessary arrangements, heart beating fast, eyes tearing up, lips curling into a rare smile.

He spoke! The taciturn bodyguard marveled. *He spoke! And his face! He's another man!*

Manco had no trouble convincing the guards that the bribery money would be paid. Everyone knew that the family of Prisoner 243 could buy half of Mexico if they wanted. Getting over his astonishment at the change in Ben was another matter. Years later, despite his habitual pessimism, el Manco could never think of that day without feeling a lump in his throat. Benjamín's return to normalcy, so sudden and so utterly inexplicable, resurrected something in el Manco that he thought had been killed off.

Hope.

On the rare occasions when el Manco *spoke* about the day of Benjamín's awakening, he would actually wax loquacious, but only if he focused on the Tarahumara inmate. In truth, the runner became a symbol for him of the hope that he could not allow himself to articulate. Hope, in el Manco's life, was a thing as fragile as the Monarch butterflies of his home state. So the tough, one-handed bodyguard stuck to the safer narrative, the one that did not shake him to the core, dragging sobs from hidden depths.

"So I arranged for the guards to let the Tarahumara run," el Manco would begin his version, which was true enough. "First they had to clear the upper corridors: 'Out of the way! Let the damn Indian run!" they shoved and shouted. Then they yelled at the man. "You! Start running!" which of course only made the man grow as still as a rock. Even a new prisoner knows you don't turn your back on armed guards and sprint down the corridors unless you're eager to meet your ancestors. Then pushing aside all other considerations, the Tarahumara gave in to a far more compelling instinct.

"You should have seen the man run!" Manco would still marvel years later. "I never saw anything like it. The man was a jaguar. Fast. Assured. Beautiful though he was one ugly son of a *guayaba.* Of course, seeing a prisoner running like that scared the hell out of inmates who hadn't been cleared off the lower corridors. Some threw themselves on the ground, bracing for the inevitable shot in the back. But no shots were fired. The Tarahumara ran back up the stairs and along the three upper corridors, then down the stairs again and around the perimeter of the spacious courtyard, on and on. We all watched him, guards and inmates alike, waiting to see how long before he bent over to gasp for breath. He didn't. He just kept running hour after hour without stopping.

"When evening came and we tried to move Captain Nyman inside, he, the captain, stopped us by grasping the wheels in a grip that locked them. So we stayed on a bit longer. Vago and I knew full well that Mangel was helping himself to the evening meal just delivered by the Sylvein. Yet we remained just as fascinated by the runner as did our boss. Witnessing such a feat of endurance, el Vago made one of the few intelligent observations of his life.

"He can't be human! The bastard's been running all day and hasn't stopped once, not even to piss!"

"Just then the Tarahumara came to a sudden standstill and locked eyes with Captain Nyman. And damn if the captain didn't jerk to his feet! Remember, his legs had been useless for months," el Manco would remind his son years later, "and now he was standing on his own for a few seconds! When guards shoved the runner back into his cell, we pushed the wheelchair back to cell 243. And sure enough, there was Mangel seated at the boss's table, the wreckage of the catered meal scattered all about him."

"Mangel ordered us to seat our charge opposite him. And I noticed with a start that the muscles in the captain's face had gone limp again. Even his eyes looked vacant. Had I imagined the change? The anger and the sharp commands? What happened next was sweeter than *cajeta!*"

At this point in his storytelling, el Manco's lips, normally so tight, so very grudging, would sweep upward and his shoulders would shake as he went into spasms of laughter, perhaps the only ones in his earthly life.

"That bastard Mangel walked right into the bear trap he himself set. Pointing a grubby finger at the boss, he snickered. 'You, Captain! I want you to know that the meat was particularly good tonight. I left you the dessert. I don't care much for sweets. Here.' He shoved a dessert plate across the small table. 'It's time you started feeding yourself, little man. On second thought, I should at least sample it.'"

"Mangel plunged his fingers into a slice of cake. With no warning whatsoever, Benjamín Nyman, eyes ablaze, jammed a fork into the cake, deliberately grazing Mangel's fingers. By all the saints! I would go back to prison for a month if I could see once more the expression on Mangel's face! And then to hear the captain's warning, low and chilling as the growl of a jaguar: "'If you ever touch my food again, or anything that's mine, I'll kill you.'"

77

BRUJO

IN LATER YEARS when he was a free man, el Manco would tell his grown son about the man they called *el brujo.*

"It didn't take long for guards and inmates to realize that there was something different about the Tarahumara. It wasn't just his endurance as a runner. They're all that way, the men and women of his tribe: endurance runners from the time they can walk. No, I mean that there was something otherwordly about him. People said that if el Brujo chose to, he could cure you, or hear your thoughts, or see one or two of your tomorrows. I don't know."

And then Manco would remember Ben in his former catatonic state, and he would feel a strange stirring—that thing called hope.

"Brujo's escape from the prison became the stuff of legends. But for my money, the most astonishing thing about the shaman was how he changed Benjamín Nyman. First, he guided him out of a dark place."

And here el Manco would gaze longingly into his son's blank stare. After a pause, he would continue his soliloquy, if not for

the boy's sake, then for the stubborn need to remember a phenomenon that he could neither explain nor dismiss.

"You see, in the end Brujo taught Captain Nyman not just
how to walk again, or even how to run like a Tarahumara, but
how to return to his true self. All that took time, lots of time,
and bribes, and persistence, and *iskiate*. That's a strong drink that
the Tarahumara make. The necessary ingredients would arrive
with the captain's food orders. Brujo would provide herbs from
a pouch he wore around his waist. Then heavily guarded, the
two men would run up and down the stairs and corridors for an
hour every morning before the rest of us were let out of our cells.
More bribes bought them two hours of running time. Ah, son!
Never underestimate the power of money. In the captain's case,
it did not let him out of the prison, but it did buy him a certain
kind of freedom."

Manco would cross his arms with a satisfied air as he spoke
about the two people he most respected in the whole bewilder-
ing world. And why not share that with his son? After all, there
was always the chance that his boy understood more than his
face indicated, el Manco reasoned.

"As for Captain Nyman, he took charge easily enough, what
with his military training and a gaze that could burn you if you
provoked him. El Vago was no challenge. Even Mangel, the most
notorious bully in the prison, was suddenly cowed by the fact that
the *idiota* was no idiot after all, but a formidable force. He wasn't
the only one who felt this way. I don't know who unsettled the
inmates more: the man who had returned from hell or the shaman with the power to draw him out of hell. Everyone made way
for them. Even the guards, all but one, that is. As for Mangel, the
volcano as we called him, he seemed particularly rattled. The bastard must have wondered how much Nyman remembered about
his abuse, and would it cost him his cushy job as bodyguard?"

～

Actually, neither el Manco nor el Vago realized at the time
that Mangel had additional concerns: who had more authority?

Mangel wondered. The restored *idiota* or the mysterious Spaniard who had hired him to report on him? Should he alert the
Spaniard that Prisoner 243 had come back to life? Would he now
be ordered to kill him? That part did not bother him. But would
the Spaniard then keep his word? Would he?

In the end Mangel settled on the comfortable half-truth
sprinkled with outright lies. He noted correctly in his report
that Benjamín Nyman could speak now. He added with deceptive intent that Ben raved and talked like a drunkard. As for his
health, he reassured his employer (whom he had never met face
to face, having dealt only with the man's servant, another Spaniard) that Nyman was still a prisoner of his wheelchair—true—
and therefore totally dependent on him and the other two bodyguards—a half truth. He made no mention of the shaman or the
remarkable progress Benjamín was making.

In the early days of his awakening, while he was still confined to his wheelchair, Ben was content simply to watch el Brujo
run. He had no illusions about his own health or his future. He
had served only a few months of his twenty-five-year sentence.
He had been beaten nearly to death and assumed that he would
be confined to a wheelchair for the rest of his life. Worse yet,
my poor Ben lived with the horrific idea that he had inadvertently killed his own father. His sense of guilt often manifested as
nightmares. And me he presumed guilty of adultery. Any one of
these ravenous beasts could have torn him apart. But they didn't,
so strong and wonderful was el Brujo's influence over him.

Again, how do I describe the man known only as el Brujo?
First, I recommend that you pronounce the "j" like an English "h"
and pledge to pronounce the last "o" as a short vowel. Broo-ho.
Ho, not hoe. Broo-ho. The very sound suggests the mystery of
a man reputed to have the power to cross over from our world
to the spirit world and back. No one could begin to guess his
age, for el Brujo was neither young nor old but both. Physically,
he was a tall, ugly wraith of a man, his limbs dark and thin as a

Japanese maple, his skin bark-like. Spiritually, he was as beautiful as a free-wheeling hawk. Few people saw this at first, if ever, distracted as always by appearances. Few could see beyond the wild hair, the loin cloth, and the red shirt that proclaimed his tribe. That he preferred bare feet to wearing shoes seemed to attest to poverty and ignorance. Glancing at his gnarled toenails and calluses, who would imagine that they belonged to an extraordinary athlete, a man who could run barefoot over any terrain for days on end?

Tarahumaras have long been renowned as long-distance runners, and Brujo was one of the best. Elusive as snow leopards, they had managed to evade most of their enemies by living in the high sierras of northern Mexico, some of them in caves. No one knew how he had strayed so far from his homeland, or what he had done to end up in the penitentiary. Brujo was darkly taciturn on the subject, so rumors abounded.

Initially, Benjamín's only interest in the Tarahumara prisoner was to see him run. For this he needed bribe money. Once a month, either the family attorney or the hacienda administrator would arrive at the penitentiary to pay off the warden, certain prison guards, bodyguards, laundry bills, and the Sylvein's tab. Benjamín was grateful for the money, but he was not prepared just yet to let doña Manuela know about his recovery. On some level, he may have wanted to punish her. Certainly at this stage of his recovery, he was bent on distancing himself from her. But in truth he had another, more legitimate reason for keeping his recovery secret from his family. Therefore, he ordered his bodyguards to warn him whenever either of his mother's agents arrived. With impressive theatrical flair, Benjamín could extinguish the light from his eyes and let his face go blank. Neither the attorney nor the estate administrator ever caught on. The attorney would inquire about Ben's health by asking the bodyguards the same three or four questions. Then he would lean into the blank face and mutter a few hurried words of encouragement before leaving. Valle Inclán, doña Manuela's administrator, kept his visits even shorter.

As instructed by Benjamín, Mangel was able to convince both agents to increase the guards' bribes, presumably so Ben could take the morning air before the other prisoners were allowed to leave their cells for the corridors and courtyard. It was arranged. And so began the most unlikely of friendships between the son of one of the wealthiest men in Mexico and a man who lived in a cave.

Every morning just before dawn, a prison guard would wheel Ben to the upper corridor. Only he and the Tarahumara runner had permission to leave their cells a full two hours before the official time. At first they were closely guarded. It wasn't long, though, before it became obvious that the morning routine was nothing more than a rich man's whim and a poor man's obsession. Escape was not the object. It was all about running. Ben was merely an observer. Then one morning el Brujo circled back and leaned toward him without breaking his stride.

"Come with me."

Benjamín looked up, startled. "How can I?"

El Brujo disappeared into the gray predawn chill and ducked into his cell. A few minutes later he reappeared. Without breaking his stride, he pulled up alongside the wheelchair. Running in place, he held out a gourd.

"Drink this."

"What is it?"

"*Iskiate.*"

"Getting me drunk won't change the fact that my legs are dead." Ben handed back the gourd. The Tarahumara continued to run in place.

"It's not what you think. Drink it."

In a flash, the man was off again. He had a way of running that seemed to defy gravity, his feet barely touching the ground, his back straight as a knife, knees slightly bent, feet shuffling in a kind of tip-toeing motion, never punching or pounding. After making another circuit, he returned to Ben.

"All of it." And he was off again.

Benjamín stared into a murky slime and wondered, *What's the shaman put into it? Mouse droppings and frog eggs?* He smelled the brew. It had a faint scent of lime. *Well, what the hell!* Ben took a mouthful and spit it out. The thick custard-like texture had startled him, yet it left a pleasant after taste of lime in his mouth. *Don't think. Just drink it.*

Half an hour later, when el Brujo didn't come back, Benjamín pulled himself out of his chair and peered over the railing into the courtyard below. *Where the devil has he gone?* Benjamín was halfway down the corridor before he stopped and shot a startled look at his abandoned wheelchair.

"Brujo! Brujo!" He half shouted, half laughed the name. A hawk shadow flew past him, then circled around him.

"Run!" the Tarahumara spoke softly.

Benjamín hesitated, yet he felt a rush of energy unlike anything he had ever experienced before. He sprang forward, and just as quickly el Brujo stopped him, facing him with both arms on his shoulders.

"No, not like that. Like this."

Pressing Ben to the nearest wall, he showed him how to run in place, back straight, knees slightly bent.

"No. Don't land on your heels. This way."

And now it was Benjamín who felt the urge to fly and found himself blocked. El Brujo had his method. First he taught Ben to run in place, insisting he do it barefoot for the remainder of their morning run, and then for the day after that and the one after that and after that, on and on for weeks. Then one dark morning el Brujo and the *iskiate* finally released him, and Benjamín flew down corridors and stairs. With the Tarahumara running alongside him, corridors became plateaus with scraggly sage brush.

Stairs rose steeply to cliff heights. Prison walls morphed into the rock faces of the Copper Canyons. The pre-dawn air filled his lungs, awakening not only his body from its sluggishness, but his spirit. From that moment, running became Benjamín's umbilical cord to the world.

78

KUIRA-BÁ

FEW PEOPLE EVER heard el Brujo speak. Fewer still saw him smile. Only Benjamín.

"*Kuira-bá,*" the Tarahumara would speak softly into the morning.

"*Kuira,*" Ben learned to respond to *We are one.*

The notion grew roots. One Sunday the seed sprouted. Benjamín astonished his bodyguards by ordering multiple meals from the Sylvein and inviting them to eat with him—and with Brujo. The three bodyguards sat in awkward silence, but they soon dug into the feast before them. Other Sunday meals followed, each one more convivial than the previous one. El Brujo remained taciturn, but his features seemed less stern. More changes followed. Benjamín began venturing into the courtyard to see the rest of the aviary, as he called it; to smell its smells, to identify its 'birds' by name, to sort song birds from birds of prey, to listen to the cacophony of fellow inmates—their bantering and joking and taunting—and to note vacant stares and bruised bodies.

Kuira-bá. We are one.

The notion grew branches and leaves, and Benjamín perceived for the first time the illusory nature of his sense of self. He saw with startling clarity the fallacy he had scripted for himself, beginning with the premise that he was innately superior to all other mortals. After all, for all the advantages of his social position, he was serving time for murder.

How had that happened? He wondered. What was the precise moment when he started toward this prison? Was it in childhood when he tried to break as many rules as a day held? Or in those years of adolescent hubris, when he believed that he could outdo, outride and out-think anyone? Was it later, when he betrayed the army for an ideal? Or when he betrayed a brother by loving me? Yes. That must have been it, he decided. He had doomed himself when he betrayed his own brother.

79

A SECOND VOW

In the most vivid of his "red dreams," Samuel was running alongside Benjamín as they used to in their boyhood. This time, however, they were not in the hacienda. Instead they were jogging in a deep canyon. Sweat misted their skin. A brisk breeze cooled it.

"Over there," Benjamín pointed.

"Where? What are we chasing?"

"Don't you see it?"

Samuel caught a glimpse of scarlet feathers just as he crossed over from sleep into semi-wakefulness. Slowly, plumage morphed into a red shirt, and the bird into a man. Fully awake now, Samuel sat up and rubbed his face. It felt damp. For a few seconds more, he could still feel the touch of wind on his skin. Yet nothing stirred in his room, not even the filmy white curtains that usually danced to night breezes. So strong was the impression of a new-found vigor, of a nameless excitement, that Samuel decided to brave the trip to Mexico City.

On a bright afternoon he stood outside Benjamín's cell. Peering through the cell door window, he caught a fleeting glimpse of him. The door opened just then, startling him and the body-guard who was stepping out. Samuel recognized el Vago by his brush-like hair that stood straight up in stiff bristles, and by the inane grin. This time the smile quivered and the eyes twitched. Gazing past him through the open door, Samuel had a clear look at his twin.

"Benjamín!"

Caught off guard, Benjamín was not able to fake a blank stare. Samuel was tremulous and radiant as he drew his brother into a tight embrace.

"I knew it! I knew you were back! God be praised!" Words and laughter spilled all around them like sunshine. "For weeks, I've had recurring dreams where you're always trying to break free—from your wheelchair, from boxes, from chairs with restraints, even from Aztec warriors! You name it! But last week was no dream. I saw you running for pure joy!"

"Now how the devil did you manage that, *padre*?" Benjamín crossed his arms in playful skepticism, a stance he often adopted in his brother's presence.

"You know that state between sleep and full wakefulness? It happened just before dawn, when it was still dark. Yet through half-closed eyelids, just for a few seconds, I saw you running alongside a red bird, or a man in a red shirt. I'm still not sure which."

My God! You saw Brujo? The thought jolted Ben. "It was a man, and I want you to meet him, Samuel."

It was not to be. Though the brothers talked exuberantly about Benjamín's recovery, they were headed for a collision. Moments before that impact of wills, Ben was showing off his battle wounds.

"These are my badges of honor, my induction. I'm now a true *asesino convicto*."

"Don't talk that way, Benjamín. You are no murderer."

"Well, I'm here. What does that tell you, Father Samuel?"

"That to err is human, and that we all need God's help and forgiveness."

"Right now it's your help that I need. Please do not tell mamá about my recovery. Not yet. Promise me, Samuel."

"Not tell her? Do you know the anguish she—"

"She'll swamp me. She'll suffocate me."

Samuel drew back. "Do you ever think of anyone but yourself?" he asked quietly.

"Look, I have to learn to live in this place on my own terms. Manuela Vizcarra de Nyman will come here with a team of tailors and order up a dozen suits, so I can strut around in attire worthy of our lofty name. Then she'll reorganize my book shelves and my day, doing all but spoon-feeding me. Don't you see? She'll try turning me into a lap dog—the most pampered of prisoners!"

"You *are* the most pampered of prisoners. How many inmates have a cell like this? Who makes this possible, along with your gourmet meals and personal bodyguards?"

"But it's still a gilded cage! You're free to go where you want, when you want. I can't step out for a walk in the Alameda, or saddle up for a day in the hills, or just step outside to look at the moon. Everything is by their leave, not mine. I have to stay shut up in this room, grand as you think it is! So don't judge me!"

"I'm only saying—"

"That I'm a selfish pig! Well, I am! But I'm begging you to allow me what little freedom I have. Don't tell her just yet."

"It would mean so much to her."

"Give me a couple of months, Samuel. Sixty days! Then I promise to write to her the most eloquent letter ever penned in Castilian, to let her know that I'm back from the dead. Just sixty days, Samuel."

"No. It's appallingly unfair to our mother."

Benjamín was tempted to lean toward his brother and whisper the truth: that he and el Brujo were plotting their escape and needed more time, not more attention. How could he have his mother dropping by any time she pleased, making imperial demands that would only aggravate the very guards that he and Brujo needed to lull into complacency? He could not risk it. Looking back, though, I can see that he should have entrusted his secret to Samuel. Instead, he was evasive, waiting for the chance to resort to artful deception. Ironically, Samuel did the very same thing when Ben asked about me in his own circuitous way.

"What about the will? I suppose we're fighting Isabel in court?"

"No. She signed everything over to mother."

"What? What do you mean, she signed it over?"

"She relinquished her claim to Father's estate."

"What did she keep for herself?"

"Nothing."

Benjamín clenched the nape of his neck and began to pace. Samuel knew that his mind was racing. So was his.

"Then what the blazes did she and Tepaneca gain from all this?"

Samuel thought of a skeletal body. "Nothing."

"But I suppose she's with him?"

A coffin swallowed by the earth. "No."

"What do you mean, no?"

"Look, I don't understand her any more than you do! The only thing I can tell you is that she is not with Tepaneca, and she signed everything back to us."

Benjamín was stumped. "You're sure she's not with Tepaneca anymore?"

"Yes, I'm sure."

Poor Samuel was trapped between loyalty to the truth and a vow not to speak it. He could not suppress a flash of memory just then: my skeletal hand in his as he said the Lord's Prayer for both of us. Benjamín threw his head back and laughed.

"That's rich! She proved too honest for him, and not honest enough for me!" They fell silent. After a pause, Benjamín asked quietly, "Where is she, Samuel?"

"With her grandfather." Now it was Samuel who paced, face growing red, hands clenched. "Now you listen to me, Benjamín. I hate secrets and will not be bound by them; do you hear me? So you're going to come clean with Mother. I won't have you put me under some slavish vow of secrecy! If you don't tell her about your recovery, I will."

"All right. All right. Calm down." Benjamín waited for his brother to resume his seat. When Samuel announced that he needed to leave, Ben dropped to his knees, crossing himself: "Bless me, Father, for I have sinned. It has been months since my last confession."

Though startled, Samuel nodded. Reaching into his bag, he retrieved his stole and draped it around his neck. Moments later, he walked straight into the trap. Benjamín's confession was simple and to the point.

"I am keeping the news of my recovery from my mother for two months, Father. Please grant me absolution for my sin of silence."

Samuel groaned. Then he muttered, *"Te absolvo, in nomine Patris, et Filii, et Spiritus Sancti, Amen."* However, Samuel Nyman Vizcarra, who was not entirely above the sin of revenge, added, "For penance you must say one thousand Hail Mary's, now."

Oh, what a missed opportunity, Samuel! Couldn't you have gotten Benjamín to read the Bible instead? Or St. Augustine's *Confessions*? Or a little Tolstoy or Dostoevsky?

Samuel rode the family train back to San Serafín. The elation that he had felt on finding Benjamín restored physically and mentally had been dampened considerably. Samuel knew he'd been duped. Now he had to uphold, not just one enormous lie, but two of them. Sitting in the mahogany and gilt comfort of the Pullman, he sipped coffee and wondered which was worse: to lie or to violate the sacred confidentiality of confession? In this case, weren't they both forms of deceit? Wasn't it really a question not of doing good, but of choosing the lesser of two evils? He closed his eyes and tried to nap, but he felt ensnared in too many lies. He dreaded facing his mother's eager questions about Benjamín. *Keep the visit short. Hold vespers and leave early tomorrow morning,* Samuel told himself. His mother met him at the hacienda station.

"How is he?" Her voice quavered, and even in the dark Samuel knew she was rubbing her hands as if with lanolin.

"He's fine. He's well treated. Never doubt that. Now please, let's not talk of Benjamín."

"I understand," she patted his hand.

Do you? He almost challenged her. *Because I sure don't.*

80

HOPE

WHEN BENJAMÍN FOUND out from Manco that he had a wife and
a son who had never been to visit him in prison, he pressed for
the reason.

"They live in Michoacán. It's too far and too expensive for
them to come here."

But that wasn't the full reason. Manco deliberately kept them
at a distance, not wishing to expose his son's mental disability to
ridicule. Or perhaps himself. So he had not seen his boy or his
wife in eight years. Then Manco had a change of heart and asked
Benjamín for a loan so his family could visit him. Ben insisted
on paying all travel expenses. When they arrived, he turned his
cell over to them so Manco and his family could enjoy in privacy
the meals that he had ordered for them. Shortly before the visit
ended, Manco sought out Brujo.

"This is my son Gustavo and my wife Gloria," he mumbled.
Then clearing his throat, he bowed to el Brujo. "Please, can you
bring my boy into the world, like you did with Captain Nyman?"

Brujo stooped and peered into the face of an adolescent with
expressionless eyes and facial muscles almost as limp as Benjamín's had been.

"I'll pay you whatever you ask," Manco brought his stump to his heart in pledge. "Just guide him out. Will you do it?"

Brujo continued to gaze into the boy's inner landscape. Time slowed for el Manco and his wife.

"No." Brujo straightened, his eyes sad yet calm. "I can't."

"Please! There's nothing for him—"

"There's everything for him."

"Everything? He goes nowhere. Speaks to no one. Knows nothing but loneliness!" Despair shook the father's voice.

"Don't be anxious for him. His companions are beings of light, and he knows more than any of us."

"He doesn't know squat! He's trapped like Nyman was!"

"Your son wanders through a pine-scented forest. He's there now. You'll go with him when it's your time and he can show it to you."

Manco's wife, a small woman bent with years of grief, grasped Brujo's hand and kissed it. Then she and her son returned to Michoacán. Manco, on the other hand, felt nothing but resentment against the shaman for his failure to perform the miracle that he wanted, and anger at himself for having entertained the possibility of one. Several years later when he was released from prison and returned to his village, he continued to grieve over the extreme slowness of mind that set his son apart from others. And then he grieved the more when the young man drowned and there was no consolation and no God.

Yet sometimes, somewhere between sleep and wakefulness, Manco would see for himself what Brujo had discerned so clearly: his son grown to handsome manhood, wandering through a forest, his face fully animated by the spectacle of monarch butterflies gathering by the millions. For those shining seconds, Manco would perceive that his son was a powerful guardian of a place both physical and spiritual. And he would weep from pure joy. Then full wakefulness would thrust him back into his habitual sadness and skepticism—until the day when no one could wake him and Manco found himself strolling alongside his son, the forest aflame with monarchs.

In life, Manco rejected the notion of miracles. But I believe we are surrounded by the extraordinary. When I think back to Benjamín's rescue from his dark retreat, I marvel even now at the healing power of physical exercise. Brujo unleashed it for Ben, strengthening him not just physically across the months that they trained for their escape, but psychologically and spiritually as well. And just as running became Benjamín's umbilical cord to the world and to his inner life, so too writing—another won-der—wondrous because abstract markings on paper can have the power to change hearts and minds. On July 7, 1912, exactly one year after the fateful reading of his father's will, Ben felt com-pelled to begin work on a memoir—what he called a collection of sketches. After his morning run with Brujo, he would write for hours on end. To ensure some level of privacy from prison guards and bodyguards alike, he wrote it in English and let them believe it was a book on ornithology. He even added beautifully detailed sketches of birds.

Casting me in the archetypal role of Eve the Temptress, he intended at first nothing more than a tongue-in-cheek account of man's eviction from paradise. His Adam happened to be a tall Mexican-Swede: himself. With his beloved San Serafín as the central setting, he might have called it *Paradise Lost,* except that Milton had beaten him to it long ago. He opted instead to call it *Paradise Misplaced,* which is interesting since his initial notions of love and paradise were far more misplaced than he imagined. Working under the assumption that he was just one more poor fool whose wife had made a cuckold of him, he set off with Vol-tairean humor and skepticism—only to discover in the end that he had misjudged me completely and that he was still deeply in love with me. Slowly but steadily, his Voltairean satire morphed into an extended love letter.

What could account for such a radical shift in his thinking? One could credit the process of writing itself with its ten-
dency to clarify our thinking. True enough. Yet I cannot help but
credit a far greater source. Who but God could have redirected
my husband's molten hatred for me back into love? By the time
Benjamín finished the memoir, he was anguishing about the
consequences of his brutal jealousy. Would I ever forgive him?
Would I give our marriage another chance? How could he begin
to explain the depth of his regret except through the pages that
recorded the labyrinthine twists and turns of his thinking?

One day before his planned escape with Brujo, Benjamín
wrapped his manuscript in brown paper from the Sylvein Restaurant. Full of hope, he set off to the prison mail room. But
where to send it? Samuel had led him to believe that I was with
Cadwally, but he had said nothing more, and he wasn't answering his letters. So Ben was suddenly plagued with doubts. What
if Cadwally and I had gone back to the states, even if only for
a visit? He pictured the brown paper package on our doorstep,
soaking up September rains. No. It *had* to reach me! So he sent it
instead to Samuel with instructions that he personally deliver
it to me.

What wouldn't I have given to read Ben's manuscript when I
too was a prisoner? Oh to be disabused of the tragic notion that
he was physically and mentally maimed for life! Oh to know that
he had recovered, that he still loved me, and then to walk hand-
in-hand with him through the labyrinth of his mind and heart!
But by mailing the memoir to Samuel, Benjamín was sending it
to the very man who believed that he had officiated at my funeral.

81

THE BREAK OUT

THE NIGHT BEFORE the escape, Benjamín treated his unsuspecting bodyguards to a last meal from the Sylvein chefs.

"Is it Sunday already?" el Vago squinted.

"No, it's a special occasion." To allay suspicion, he let them think they were celebrating the completion of his book.

While the men laughed and plundered their boxed meals, Ben's sense of guilt escalated. *How can a meal compensate for deceit?* He kept wondering, knowing how utterly betrayed they would feel at not being included in the escape plot. But there was no reasonable way to involve them without jeopardizing the whole thing. That night he hardly slept. For weeks he and Brujo had contrived to carve shallow toe holds on one particular wall, a wall whose plaster had cracked after a recent earthquake. For tools they had nothing but a soup spoon each. Strapped to their right arm and hidden under long sleeves, the spoons would emerge only long enough to strike the wall at the very moment that they slapped it and called out a number, presumably the number of laps. It had been a long, slow-going process to create just two toe holds. Now he fretted, were they deep enough? And could he and Brujo scramble up the wall fast enough?

Benjamín knew the consequences if they failed. At best, they could count on longer sentences; at worst, torture, perhaps death. Yet, throughout that night he fretted more about his manuscript. Would it reach San Gabrielín? Would I get it? Would I believe him? Would I accept his desperate apology? If not, of what use freedom?

Eventually, he did sleep. In fact, he overslept. When a guard unlocked his cell door for the usual morning run, Benjamín was utterly unprepared.

He was still in his pajamas. With heart pounding like an Aztec drum, prisoner 243 slipped out of his pajama bottoms and into the pants he had set aside for his escape.

"Move it!" the guard grumbled. "I can't stand here all morning."

There was no time to get out of his pajama top. Grabbing his jacket and quickly ramming his feet into his shoes, he headed out the door sockless.

It will be all right! The top is blue. It will look like a shirt, Ben tried to reassure himself.

As usual, it was dark and dimly lit at this hour. Cutting back on the lighting saved on the cost of electricity, which savings went into some official's pocket. Benjamín tried to calm his breathing. The chill morning air of the high central plateau crystallized it into soft plumes. He started off at a slow gait, conscious of how strange it felt to run in shoes. He would have preferred running barefoot like el Brujo had taught him, but he could hardly hope to blend into the city in a suit and bare feet. He spotted el Brujo in the opposite corridor. They met halfway and shared a gourd of *iskiate*.

"On the seventh lap," the shaman whispered.

Benjamín nodded. They set off, backs straight, feet barely touching the floor. As agreed, they were both going to make the run with shoes on. Details. It was about the details.

After the second round, el Brujo paused just beyond an orb of light to take off his sandals. He was going to make the arduous journey to the Copper Canyons, hundreds of kilometers away, on bare feet. That's when it dawned on Benjamín that the shaman was not wearing the pants and shirt that he had provided for him.

"What are you doing?" he muttered when he caught up to him inside a stairwell. "Why aren't you wearing the clothes I gave you?" el Brujo ignored the reproach and sprinted ahead.

He sticks out like a damn scarlet ibis!

Their careful planning was already unraveling. By the third lap, Benjamín's sockless feet were as agitated as his thoughts. Removing his shoes, he stashed them in the dark stairwell alongside el Brujo's sandals, but he intended to retrieve them just before the final lap. He would tie them together and hang them around his neck before leaping onto the wall. His agitation grew.

During the fourth lap, Benjamín thought about el Vago with his inane jokes and gap-toothed smile; he reflected that el Manco, thief and murderer that he was, tried living by a code of honor anchored in loyalty to friends; and then there was Mangel, crude and gruff, the epitome of self-centeredness, a man as ferocious as an enormous mastiff that has been long abused. By now Benjamín could no longer pretend to himself that it didn't matter what happened to these men. They were fully implicated in the escape. He knew with the certainty of each footfall that the guards would vent their rage on them.

For reasons that he could not fully understand, my Benjamín Nyman suddenly felt it was as impossible to betray his fellow inmates as to betray his own brothers. By the fifth lap, it was clear to him that he was not going to add more remorse onto his shoulders, but, above all, that he could not allow el Brujo to venture into Mexico City as a fugitive dressed in the white loincloth and the bright red shirt of a Tarahumara.

When they reached a stairwell and were momentarily out of the sight of the guards, he pulled off his jacket and the pajama top. "Put these on," he whispered. "I'm not going."

"Come with me."

"No. I have a debt to pay. Put them on. There's no time to argue."

The shaman pushed his hand away.

"Brujo, go home to your wife and children."

That broke the impasse. El Brujo pulled off his tunic and shirt, but there was only time to exchange tops. They were off again, men in mixed garb—the Tarahumara in a blue pajama top untucked over his loincloth, Benjamín in tailored pants and the Tarahumara tunic and scarlet shirt. At the next meeting in the stairwell, they finished the trade and were off again, each in the other man's clothing.

Halfway down the stairwell, the Tarahumara came to a full stop. Benjamín passed him and stopped a few steps down. They knew they could only pause for a few seconds without arousing suspicion. El Brujo removed his *koyera*, the scarlet strip that kept his hair out of his face. With utmost solemnity, he tied it around his friend's head. Then he bounded across the courtyard with Benjamín a short distance behind.

When they took the stairs for the seventh lap, Benjamín let him get considerably ahead in a ploy to split the guards' attention, assuming any of them cared enough to watch their monotonous run. He reached the far end of a corridor just in time to see Brujo leap onto the wall, his right foot finding the lower toehold, his left foot the second gouge in the wall. It all happened with astonishing speed and agility. Then he was on top of the wall and over it.

No shots rang out. No one noticed. Benjamín ran to the wall and slapped it with his right hand. Then he set off to finish one last lap. The morning breeze fanned him, the ends of the *koyera* rising and falling on the nape of his neck.

They'll probably beat the crap out of me.
Maybe.
It's the last run they'll ever let me take.
True.

"Hey! Where's the rich guy?" a guard called out.

Benjamín realized he had just been mistaken for el Brujo. He couldn't see the man's face, but neither could the guard see his. He slowed his pace but kept his back turned.

"In his cell, puking."

"Then get back in yours!"

Still keeping his back turned, the prisoner waved amiably to the faceless man and obeyed. When he cast a quick look over his shoulder and realized the guards were more intent on their conversation than on him, he ducked into his own cell. Catching sight of himself in the dresser's mirror, Benjamín Nyman paused and took in the measure of the Tarahumara who stared back.

He pictured el Brujo running all that day and for days afterward without stopping, unstoppable as his calloused feet carried him northwest into the sierras, home to the labyrinthine canyons that none knew like the Tarahumaras. He remembered a saying el Brujo had taught him: "When you run on the earth and run with the earth, you can run forever."

What about Isa? How will we ever find each other now?

With the book. She'll read the book, his heart told him.

He suddenly remembered a mating pair of trogons in his mother's aviary, back when he was a small child and his father still loved life. He remembered that the male managed to get out one night, and that he hovered outside the cage to be near his mate. In the morning he was easily recaptured by the keepers. When Benjamín heard about the failed escape, he had run crying to the aviary.

"Why are you crying?" his father had asked, his face handsome with gentle concern, his eyes bright as the Morelos sky overhead.

"Because I wanted the trogon to be free!"

"He is."

"No he's not! He's in there!"

"Where he has chosen to be."

Standing by the open door of his cell, Benjamín Nyman glanced back at the wall that might have led him to freedom, and he felt his spirit soar.

82

AMONG THE TOMBS

Of all physical objects, Teresa Gama loved nothing so much as her sewing machine. Rodolfo had given it to her when their first daughter was born so that she could amuse herself making clothes for the baby. It was a marvel of mechanical engineering, a Minnesota that lodged inside a drop-desk cabinet. The cabinet itself was richly carved black walnut. When closed, it looked like an elegant writing desk. When opened, it revealed a top-of-the-line sewing machine with a large balance wheel and interior drawers with nickel-plated pulls. Teresa caressed it every time she opened it.

Rodolfo had intended the gift as a hobby for his mistress, nothing more. But when he broke up with her back in the spring of 1911 in order to court me, she had had the gumption to let her hobby morph into the respectable livelihood of dressmaker. Not that she needed to work. Rodolfo had dutifully continued to support her and their children, discarded mistress that she was. But Teresa was fiercely determined to achieve financial independence. If not for the children, she would have thrown his money back at him. Scornfully. Proudly. First, though, she needed to establish herself as a dressmaker of fine fashions.

It didn't take long. With her talent for skillful imitation, Teresa could reproduce fashions from the vaunted *Mode Illustré*. For the purposes of her provincial clientele, however, her Sears catalogs provided more realistic models. Sometimes, as she stitched a dress in calico or cheap satin, she longed for the touch of damask or silk between her fingers—and that set her remembering. Don't dredge up the past! She would reprimand herself. Why long for the heady days when Rodolfo had taken her to Paris? Forget it. Live in the here and now.

To that end, Teresa lived quietly, worked hard, and dressed as fashionably as skill and her modest means allowed. My sister-in-law Eva would have sneered that Teresa was always a year or two behind *la dernier cri* of fashion, dismissing her as well for being "a mere Indian, on a par with the servants." Actually, like most Mexicans, Teresa Gama was a mestiza, attesting to the marriage of Spain and the New World. And yes, her dark complexion and high cheekbones did tip the scale more toward her Indian ancestry than her Iberian. It was precisely this that gave Teresa an exotic beauty, a bit battered for wear now, but still evident. She had been a pretty girl when my brother-in-law first discovered her. Cares and disappointment had aged her prematurely, robbing her not only of that earlier bloom, but of softness in her manner. There was a hardness to her now, a crossing of the arms and a tilt of the head that warned the world to back off.

On a day that started out like so many others, Teresa sat hunched over her sewing machine working the foot pedal, carefully guiding the fabric under the presser foot, stitching, thinking, remembering an afternoon that was branded on her soul: the day Eva introduced us to each other, mistress and fiancée. Sewing, snipping the thread at the end of the seam, snipping off all dreams of a life with Rodolfo. Another seam. Eva Comardo's seamless plan to disabuse her of all hope. The truth. The reality. All that she, the jilted mistress, might have said and didn't. A script revised again and again. In the end, what did it matter that Rodolfo had abandoned her for a younger woman, or the delicious irony that this younger woman had then ditched him? Serves him right. There was some justice in the world after all. Divine just—

A loud sound made Teresa stop the wheel and hurry to a window. Horsemen were galloping past her house toward the center of town. A pounding on the front door made her draw back and breathe faster.

The door! Dear God! Did I bolt it?

The pounding continued. The men were shouting obscenities as they attacked the door with their rifle butts.

Mother of God! Don't let them get through! Please let the door hold!

Teresa hurried to her bedroom. Opening the top drawer of her chiffonier, she reached for the revolver that Rodolfo had given her on their last day together. He kissed her and the children as if he meant to return in a week or two. *Rodolfo! I need you!* The pounding stopped. A new terror struck.

The children! Teresa shot a frightened look at the clock that hung on the wall, and realized it was time to pick them up at school. How could she step outside now? Surely the teachers would keep the children inside until the riders left, wouldn't they? They were just passing through, right? But what if they were here to stay? Would the teachers send the children home? Would they?

Teresa reached for a small box of bullets. Box and contents clattered onto the tile floor. Kneeling to retrieve them, she prayed aloud, "Blessed Virgin! Make them go away! Don't let them harm the children!"

A few minutes later, Teresa hurried up a narrow, winding stairway to the flat roof where she had hung laundry to dry. Hiding behind sheets that fluttered in the afternoon breeze, she searched for the riders. There! They had reached the town's zócalo. If she cut across the *Panteón Municipal*, she could avoid the town square and reach the school. But should she risk leaving the safety of the house?

She agonized with indecision until she imagined her little girls running in terror, gripping the hand of their little brother, *el Borreguito*—her lambikins—who would not be able to keep up with his short, pudgy legs. Teresa slipped the revolver into a deep pocket in her skirt. Not bothering to reach for one of her cherished hats and gloves, which she considered the hallmarks of a lady, Teresa Gama set off to rescue her children.

The street was deserted. Nothing stirred as she locked the heavy door behind her. Tightening her grip on the revolver inside her pocket, she hurried toward the municipal cemetery, her footsteps alarmingly loud in her ears. Moments later, she was hurrying past funerary statues and plots with miniature houses in place of tombstones. It was there that two of the revolutionaries spotted her, chasing her deeper into the cemetery. Before she could draw the gun out of her pocket, one of the men wrestled her to the ground. Then he and his companion raped her among the tombstones.

"Rodolfo! Rodolfo!" she cried desperately.

"My name's Rogelio, whore! Rogelio!" The man laughed.

In a Paris cemetery, Rodolfo Nyman paused in front of the life-size statue of a journalist who had been shot to death by Pierre Bonaparte, a cousin of Napoleon III. It depicted a man lying on his back, head tilted back in death, top hat by his feet. Because Rodolfo did not possess that sixth sense of his twin brothers, that uncanny ability of theirs to sense each other's pain no matter the distance that separated them, he never sensed or imagined the desperate cries of a woman who was left bleeding among tombs of a distant place, her head tipped back, her lips, the lovely lips that he still longed to kiss, trickling blood down her neck and cheeks.

REPERCUSSIONS

ONE MORNING DOÑA Manuela opened the curtain of my cell with a flourish. Her every motion exuded a brisk optimism, though she had no idea of Ben's recovery, which is just as well for her, as she might have floated beyond the reach of earth's gravitational pull. Likewise, word of his fateful decision not to escape would have launched her into a murderous rage against me. So we were equally blessed with ignorance that morning. She took her accustomed seat at the desk that faced the cell bars. Tacha set a breakfast tray in front of her arrayed with limoge, crystal, and silver. I waited silently to see if la patrona felt like eating in front of me or with me. That day she deigned to play hostess. Dishing out my portion of her breakfast into a clay mug, she mixed everything together, like a farmer slopping the hogs. Beans, eggs, jelly, fruit, and my half of a *bolillo,* her favorite bread roll—all became one concoction. She even slapped on a spoonful of *nata,* the cream that rises to the surface of boiled milk. The mix was actually quite tasty.

"Well, my American Blue-thief! Do you realize that you have been roosting in my cage for nearly a year now!" she beamed.

I knew better than to respond. I nodded, chewing slowly. Is it late August or September? I wondered.

"It's all right. You may speak." She patted her lips with her napkin. "I'm curious to know what you think of our upcoming anniversary."

"Has it really been that long?"

"Do you doubt me?"

"No, of course not, señora," I replied calmly. "I have no calendar, so it's hard to keep track of time."

"It must be liberating to live without the strictures of time. Well, I suppose you must have a limited idea of it, like a dog who measures time by his meals. I cannot give myself the luxury of such imprecision. Time matters when you have to think about planting and harvesting and getting the produce to market. All of us in San Serafín scurry. But not you." I kept chewing as I met her eyes, my stance fearlessly tranquil. She scowled. Then leaning back in her chair she steepled her fingers. "You know, back in December you were just about the most grotesque creature I've ever laid eyes on. Mere skin and bones. Tacha and I have restored you quite admirably."

I did look more like myself now, some six or seven months after being starved. My limbs had regained muscle and fat. My hair no longer fell out in distressing clumps. And I had grown so much stronger through vigorous exercise. I could see that la patrona viewed me as a kind of unmerited miracle, my recovery from the ravages of starvation affirming God's approval of her, not of me. Clearly it demonstrated His willingness to honor His part of their pact when she had begged him to spare Samuel from the dangers of the revolution, while she, in turn, ministered to her prisoner. Yes, it was all satisfactory, she smiled. But why is the girl always so damnably serene?

Her mood shifted. Pushing back her chair, doña Manuela threw down her napkin and left.

"Thank you, Tacha," I smiled, holding out my empty mug. "It was delicious."

I had trained Stone Face to accept these few words of gratitude without retribution. She grunted in reply while she too must have wondered, *Why aren't you broken by now?* Whereas the question irritated doña Manuela, it unnerved Tacha.

I take no credit for my equanimity. Over the months of nearly continual prayer, I had become aware that my solitude was an illusion. The quiet and emptiness of the cell held immense activity, as invisible to the naked eye as unharnessed electrical energy. Had I the power, or had the Lord willed it, I would have seen the spirits, both good and evil, and the angels that surrounded me. Alone? No, I was not alone. None of us is.

∼

Several hours after Brujo's escape, prison guards kicked open Benjamín's cell door. His personal bodyguards could only stand back and watch. They had been hired to protect him from other prisoners. They could do nothing against the prison guards themselves. One of the wardens, a brute named Calixto Contreras, shoved Benjamín against a wall.

"Where's the damn Indian? Where did he go?"

"I have no idea."

Contreras shook him. "Have you forgotten what we do to *rotos* like you?"

"How could I forget?" Ben smiled.

"Don't get funny with me. Where's your buddy going? Wait until we get our hands on him. Talk or you'll get what's coming to him yourself, right now!"

"We were running together like always. He got ahead of me. Next thing I knew I was running alone."

"That's a freaking lie. You planned the escape with him."

"Why would I want to leave all this?" Benjamín shook the man off. "As you see, I'm here, not out there. El Brujo didn't confide anything to me because he doesn't confide anything to anyone."

"Don't give me that," Calixto Contreras raised his club menacingly.

Touch me and the money dries up. Benjamín didn't say it out loud. He didn't have to. Another of the guards drew Calixto off him. After all, the Nyman protection money was financing his children's school uniforms and books. Calixto Contreras needed the money as well if he was going to be able to continue to support his mistress. Both guards backed off.

Word of Brujo's disappearance spread. Every prisoner in the penitentiary had a version of what had happened. Some joked that he had escaped through his use of witchcraft. Others solemnly asserted that it was precisely *through* witchcraft that Brujo had succeeded. The more practically-minded concluded that his rich buddy must have bribed the guards to look the other way during their run. What no one could understand was why Benjamín Nyman was still there. Why hadn't he escaped too? Calixto Contreras and his superiors wondered the same thing. Yet, as long as the bribery money continued to flow, they were willing to drop the whole matter.

Only Jesús Mangel could not let it go. "Did you know they were planning this?" His question to el Manco was tinged with accusation.

"No."

"You must have known something was up. He confides more in you than in me."

"Captains don't confide in underlings."

Mangel chewed on his lower lip. "No, I suppose not. What about Brujo? Nyman has to have known what he was up to. They were thick as thieves. So why the hell didn't he go with him?"

"Whatever his reason, you'd better get down on those thick knees of yours and thank the Virgin that he didn't. We would have had the crap beaten out of us."

"No. If we'd known, wouldn't we have escaped too? We're here, so doesn't that prove we didn't know squat about the plan?"

"You still think you can reason with them?" el Manco pointed his stump, presumably at the prison authorities. "With

Nyman and his bribes gone, we wouldn't be worth crap to anyone, except as scapegoats."

Mangel's long, unkempt beard and moustache could not
hide the fact that for a few seconds his mouth dropped open.

84

THE MANUSCRIPT

A PACKAGE ARRIVED for Samuel. Little mail reached San Gabrielín, so this was particularly newsworthy. Under the circumstances, it was also short of miraculous to have arrived so quickly.
At the time, he was high up in the church belfry, working on the
roof with two of his parishioners. Samuel climbed down and
wiped his hands on his carpenter's apron. Several of the villagers followed him to the parish house steps where a postman was
waiting. The package was wrapped in brown paper. The handwriting was unmistakably Benjamín's.

"Open it, Father!" a small boy urged.

The child's father swiped at the boy with his straw hat. "That's
none of your business."

"I don't know, Miguelito," the priest smiled. "It feels like a
book."

"Oh." The boy shrugged and scampered off.

Entering his house alone, Samuel set the package on his desk
beside his calendar. He had been marking off the sixty days of
his imposed silence. Just two more days and he would be free to
tell his mother about his twin's recovery. Because he was still irritated with Benjamín who had used confession to trap him into

lying, Samuel deliberately ignored the package and returned to work on the belfry.

That evening, however, he did open it. Dropping wearily into the high-back leather chair at his desk, Samuel picked up the top page from a confederation of loose sheets. The first one consisted of two lines in Latin, which he translated to mean: *Give it to my wife, whom we have judged wrongly.* Instantly, an image of my emaciated face leaped at Samuel. His hand shook as he set the sheet aside.

Have we misjudged her? Samuel was still angry about his confrontation with Tomás, especially the attack on his mother's character. How are we to dismiss the love affair? he reasoned. If Isabel was entangled with such a man, how innocent could she have been?

The title page was next. *Paradise Misplaced: Observations from the Aviary.* Samuel smiled in spite of his irritation. Flipping through the pages of the manuscript, he was surprised by the many sketches of birds roosting in the margins, all drawn with admirable precision. Returning to the dedication page, he could only marvel: *He still loves her!* How had he underestimated his brother's enormous capacity to forgive? Samuel rose to pour himself a glass of wine. Taking several long swallows, he plunged into the prologue:

> I knew the secret as a child before anyone else did—that God planted the Garden of Eden just seventy-five kilometers south of Mexico City, near the town of Cuernavaca—

Samuel read to the bottom of the page and wondered where this Edenic narrative was headed. Did he want to accompany his brother into some irreverent satire? Was this collection of "sketches," as Benjamín was calling his chapters, a mere apologia to justify himself? Or could it be the work of a penitent heart as the dedication implied?

Sketch I

*No one knew what to make of Isabel Brentt. She was as
beautiful as sunrise in Tepoztlán. Her eyes were the blue of
Morelos's skies. Her hair was the color of candlelight—*

Samuel thought back to the first time he and I met. He had
arrived in San Serafín unexpectedly, unwittingly exposing Benjamín's pretense of being the family priest.

Who can blame her for having been furious with us? Samuel
reflected. Yet wasn't she far more deceptive than Benjamín with
his pranks?

He breezed through the first chapter. The second sketch,
"Volcanoes," forced him to pause several times. As Samuel read
his brother's depiction of their parents and siblings, he did laugh
at times. But mostly he felt the intense pain of memories he had
tried to suppress. It was especially difficult to read about the
stroke that had transformed his father from a man in love with
life to a religious zealot wanting only to escape life. Then they
had all been forced to witness Lucio Nyman's gradual descent
into madness, for what else was it? Benjamín's anguish over their
parents' separation brought his own despair back with crushing vividness. Looking up from his reading, he remembered the
brief annual visits to San Justín while his mother waited in the
carriage; the catch in the throat at the sight of a gaunt figure that
was supposed to be his father; the feeling he could never quite
shake that the monk's habit was a good-natured joke; that under
the trappings of a joyless penitence stood a vigorous man in a
splendid uniform, just seconds from laughing and revealing his
old self—but he never did. If anything, he grew increasingly belligerent. Was it any wonder that Benjamín eventually snapped
and roughed up the old man?

Samuel rose and poured himself a second glass of wine.
What's worse? He wondered as he struggled to steady his hand—
that their father had lost his mind, or that Benjamín had just

confessed to the murder in his memoir? Samuel was breathing faster: was Benjamín going to give details of the actual deed? Did he want to know? Why go there?

But how does one not read what one both dreads and yearns to know? So Samuel picked up where he had left off, only to find that confession to murder was not his brother's goal in that sketch. It ended instead with a description of Benjamín's efforts to talk him out of seminary and the priesthood. It was all there, described so vividly that Samuel felt the tension of that confrontation all over again.

Samuel put out the lights and went up to bed. Regret bounded up the stairs with him: *I should have listened to you.* The admission was another sharp blow.

The next morning Samuel checked off another day on his calendar. One more and he could shake off his promise to Benjamín. His vow to his mother, on the other hand, seemed to stretch endlessly across the years of his life. How exactly was he supposed to keep my death from Benjamín? And what about the memoir? Should he tell his mother about it? No, he decided as he paced in his study. Since it was dedicated to me, wouldn't his mother just toss it away or burn it? So what to do with the thing? If he couldn't tell his brother about my death, didn't he at least owe it to him to protect his manuscript? Yes. He could do that much. And Benjamín, for his part, needed the opportunity to atone. Hadn't he made their mother suffer long enough? Let him be the one to tell her about his recovery and his selfish secrecy. Why should he, Samuel, have to risk perjuring himself about how long he had known about all this? No, by all the saints! It was time Benjamín took responsibility for his actions—all of them.

So Samuel remained in San Gabrielín even after the sixty days were up. The summons to San Serafín arrived soon enough via one of the hacienda workers. He was to come quickly.

Doña Manuela greeted him with a feverish luminosity in her eyes.

"Samuelito!" She used his pet name. "A miracle has happened! I've received a letter from Benjamín!" She retrieved it from a pocket in her skirt and gave it to him to read. "Can it be true? Is he back with us again?"

He nodded. Oh yes, and he's back to his old tricks, Samuel could have added. Instead, he hugged her so that he wouldn't have to fake not knowing until that very moment about the recovery. Manuela laughed and cried at the same time. Seeing her joy, Samuel embraced her again, this time with a genuine surge of happiness.

"Please come with me to the prison, Samuelito. I can't face this alone. If it should turn out to be a hoax—"

He agreed to go with her, though in his heart he wanted to distance himself for a while from his twin. Heaven alone knew what new trick he might pull. Yet, how could he let his mother make the journey alone? Not after the massacre at Ticumán, where Zapatistas blew up yet another train. Since there would be no holding his mother back, he set out with her the very next morning, arriving in Mexico City without incident. The reunion was a happy one, even for Samuel since he continued to get swept up in his mother's joy. Doña Manuela was ecstatic, caressing Benjamín with eyes and hands and smiles that softened the hard lines of her face. She laughed like a young girl as her sons seated her at Ben's table with its fine linens. Together at last, they enjoyed a gourmet meal brought in from the Sylvein, laughed and reminisced about better times, painting San Serafín as paradise on earth. Inevitably, serpent discord slithered in with Benjamín's question, even though he posed it with studied casualness.

"Mother, Samuel tells me that Isabel deeded back everything to us."

Manuela shot a quick look at Samuel. "That's right. But please, son, let's not talk about her. The whole subject is so upsetting."

"I just want to know how she is."

"How should I know? She's probably with her lover."

"I don't believe for a moment that Isa ever had a lover."

"You may be right," Samuel jumped in, giving his mother a stern look that carried its own unspoken threat.

She threw up her hands. "She's with her grandfather. That's all I know. Now pass the salt."

For the rest of the visit doña Manuela hid behind a nervous torrent of chattiness. Most of it revolved around her three grandchildren. Eva's baby promised to be a beauty like her mother, she assured Benjamín, only she was blonde like Esther. And why weep over Esther, just because she had been born blind? Reports were that excellent suitors were lining up at the door. Besides, the dear girl was as pure of heart as she was beautiful. As for poor Emanuela, so plain and fractious, she was just going through the awful thirteens. But in time, wouldn't she be all the stronger? Beauty wasn't everything. The world needed strong, capable women too, didn't he agree? And then there was Rodolfo who had not written or telegrammed in a long time. Why were some men so selfish? Just one short letter or message. Was that so much for a mother to ask? She laughed as if describing the latest antics of a mischievous child.

When Samuel announced that it was late, she reached compulsively for Benjamín's hand.

"Oh, my son, I can't believe that you're back!" Did she fear that she was dreaming and would soon wake up? As Benjamín started to escort her to the door of his cell, she pulled him back toward the desk in his room. "Guard the door, Samuel," she whispered. Then she fixed Ben with eyes sharp with purpose. "This was my desk years ago until I bought the big one in my office. It has a hidden drawer." She took his hand and guided it through the mechanism of clever deception.

"The devil himself couldn't have designed it better!" Benjamín smiled with genuine admiration.

"From now on I'm going to have the money delivered directly to you. Hide it here. It's important that you be the one to pay the bribes. The jackals need to see that you have the power now."

"Thank you, mamá." Ben hugged her, a wave of guilt sweeping over him.

She caressed his cheek, her eyes shiny. Then yanking on her gloves, she added. "Never let anyone see you open the drawer, especially those thieves we pay to guard you."

They stepped into the corridor where the bodyguards waited like soldiers guarding the commandant's room. While doña Manuela commended her son to their care, giving orders of her own and a few jars of fig marmalade as her own bribes from the hacienda kitchen, Benjamín hugged his twin goodbye and whispered, "Did you give it to her?"—meaning his manuscript for me.

"Not yet." Samuel grabbed his mother's arm. Breaking off her conversation with the bodyguards, he hurried her away.

Lying in bed that night, Samuel remembered in brief flashes the night that he married Benjamín and me; how Ben and I had looked at each other, and above all the kiss. Benjamín had cupped my face, kissing me with aching tenderness. As Samuel tossed in bed, he also thought about his brother's blundering efforts to talk him out of becoming a priest in the first place. "Don't do this, Samuel. For cripe's sake, you've never even kissed a girl!" At the time Ben's argument had seemed simplistic if not downright adolescent. Why did it not seem so now?

Sleep became a wild bronco that would not be roped. Tossing aside his bed covers, Samuel got up and opened one of his bedroom windows. Moonlight spilled into the silent room. Listening to the night, he wondered if vows of any kind ever brought joy, or at least peace. Meanwhile, federal troops who had been sent to impose peace in Morelos, were encamped less than ten kilometers from San Gabrielín. That very day they had burned another village to the ground, festooning trees with men whose white-trousered legs jerked in sharp spasms and then grew still. A few kilometers further to the west, guerilla fighters had hanged four federales. The night breeze that caressed the face of the priest also stirred the dangling figures, and the moon shone on them all.

PURGATORY

Benjamín missed el Brujo. He missed their morning runs under the watchful eyes of the guards; the *iskiate* drink from a gnarled wooden gourd; the camaraderie of their unlikely friendship. He even missed the silence of the man. Most of all Benjamín regretted that he was no longer in the presence of wisdom, for he knew that of all the men he had ever encountered, Brujo was a true mystic. Yet mystic that he was, it was el Brujo who had initiated the escape plot.

Damn it! Why didn't I go with him while I had the chance? Regret clawed Ben sometimes. By trying to spare his bodyguards from the wrath of the prison guards, he had let Brujo disappear into the dark morning without him. And what had he gained? The question would taunt him sometimes. When all was said and done, of what worth were these three men for whom he had made such an enormous personal sacrifice? What was Mangel but a murderer and a bully, a man as brutal as the prison guards. And el Vago, the laziest bastard in all of Mexico; Vago with his big, idiotic grin and his quickness to slash human flesh at the slightest provocation. No one in the prison seemed more adept at procuring knives or at using them, not to kill, but to scar and to terrify others. And el Manco, with that swooping black moustache that plunged to the jawline, framing lips that rarely smiled; Manco was no invalid. Ben had seen him wield his stump with the violence of a prize fighter. Manco could pack a punch that would make a man like Mangel double over.

Then the doubts would vanish into the horizon like a flock of starlings, and Benjamín would feel at ease once again with his decision. Most of the time he enjoyed seating this trio of unlikely companions at his table, feeding them and laughing at their crude jokes. *What am I becoming?* Benjamín would ask himself sometimes. When he was feeling more benevolent than skeptical, he needed no reasons. He realized that he was simply seeing their humanity under the violence of self-preservation. Like it or not, he had formed a brotherhood with these criminals.

Because they were so closely connected to Ben, they were woven into my own life as well, in that great cosmic fabric that I had glimpsed. Standing at the threshold of death, I had become aware of the numberless life-strands that crisscross every single life. How deeply connected our lives are to others, known and unknown to us!

So Benjamín did care what happened to his bodyguards. Just the same, after Brujo's escape, Ben often felt adrift. Preparing for the escape had filled his days with a sense of forward momentum. Likewise, writing his book had given his days purpose. Benjamín now experienced the emptiness that often follows the completion of a great task without a new one to follow. He struggled to ward off depression.

Compounding this was Samuel's silence about the one question that mattered most to Benjamín. Had he delivered the manuscript to me? Samuel's rare letters talked of everything under the Mexican sun but that. Then he stopped writing altogether. *Fine. May rats gnaw on your communion wafers, padre!* Benjamín fumed. *Hang the book! I should be out there searching for Isa myself. Why do I need you or anyone else for this?*

Alone in his room, Benjamín paced and fretted. One night a thought asked him point-blank: who are you to make demands? You think that you can kill your own father, whether by accident or intent, and pay no penalty? This is the penalty.

He began to dream again in alternating cycles of light and darkness. Sometimes he dreamed about the beating that had nearly killed him; other times he relived the enormous relief that he had felt as he lost consciousness, fleeing through a window that only he could see. In memory and dreams, it hung suspended in mid-air without a structure to hold it. Climbing out the window, he had escaped into a field flooded with sunlight, unearthly in its intensity and beauty. Whenever he dreamed of that field, he felt a deep stirring. Sometimes he woke up weeping, because there was no other way of channeling the powerful emotions that swept through him. Other times he fell back into the old nightmare of being dragged naked up the face of a pyramid to face his father, obsidian knife poised to cut out his heart. Then one night the recurring dream took a surprising turn. The priest at the top of the pyramid was none other than Brujo, his face dark and craggy as the bark of an old oak. Brujo smiled as he held out his wooden gourd.

"Drink this."

Benjamín took the gourd with a laugh. "Now I know I'm not quite in hell, but I sure as hell am not in heaven! So where are we?"

In the dream Brujo ran down the face of the steep pyramid, his feet barely touching the narrow treads. Swallowing the *iski-ate,* Benjamín followed him with an equally reckless disregard for the steepness of the stone staircase. He gave chase, never losing sight of the red shirt that billowed in the wind like a sail at sea. On they ran, Brujo tantalizingly in sight yet out of reach, leading Ben down a wide avenue flanked by Aztec palaces and temples. Moments later, a forest exploded all around them. The tall heads of cypress trees cracked the earth open and soared upward. Benjamín dodged them, his supernatural athleticism delighting him. Gradually, he managed to close the gap between him and his friend. They had reached a narrow pass in a deep canyon when Ben grabbed the shaman by the shoulder.

"Brujo! Where are we?"

Just then the rough walls of the canyon morphed into the smooth walls of the prison, and Benjamín had his answer.

Purgatory. What else was a penitentiary but a place for expunging sins? "What's the point, Brujo? Nothing I do will make things right."

The Tarahumara put a hand on Benjamín's shoulder and asked him without moving his lips, *Are you sure?*

86

EL PALADÍN

WHENEVER BENJAMÍN WALKED down the corridors and out into the courtyards with his bodyguards, the other inmates made way for him. Conversations hung suspended until he had passed. Do they fear me because of the brutes that protect me? he wondered. Or do they respect me because of my family's wealth? What, then, is mine for any man to fear or respect? Of what bloody use am I in this world? The questions haunted him.

On one of his rambles with his bodyguards he came across a man who was being roughed up by a guard. The inmate kept shouting, "This is crap! You expect us to eat crap?" That led Benjamín to investigate what kind of food the others ate, those who had no family to bring them better food; those who had no money for bribes. What he discovered was rice with maggots and tortillas old and brittle as egg shells. Only the ever-sturdy black beans remained immune to age or corrupt prison officials. Benjamín began to write letters to the Maderista administration. In addition, he paid bribes so that at least once a week the destitute inmates in his cell block could eat a little chicken or pork. He even tried to expose some of the corruption. His bodyguards were alarmed. Yet a government agent did show up to inspect the prison kitchen. The food improved. Inmates began to greet Benjamín when he passed by. Within a few weeks, Prisoner 243 had gained a new name: el *Paladín* because they saw him as a heroic leader who championed them. In sharp contrast, they continued to refer to Mangel as el *Volcán,* for weren't live volcanoes unpredictable and dangerous?

"The Volcano" occupied a cell that was as sparsely furnished as el Paladín's was lavish. When he complained one day that he had no writing table or chair, just a lousy cot, el Paladín—my Ben—gave him a small, richly carved table that slumbered between his two wing chairs. Manuela, who happened to be making her second visit since learning of her son's recovery, flew into a rage.

"That was a costly table, Benjamín! It was my gift to *you,* do you understand? You don't give such things to men like that one," she lowered her voice, though not enough. Her eyes watered. Her son apologized. Volcán, who had posted himself outside the opened door, heard every word.

"Bitch," he muttered under his breath.

After the visit—and these were every two weeks now with a banner of the Virgin of Guadalupe to give them safe passage from the Zapatistas—the three bodyguards entered el Paladín's cell and found him slumped in a wing chair, fingers rubbing his temples. He looked spent, but they didn't dare say so. Moments later, he sprang up. "OK, boys. Take the stuff, *pero tienen vuelta,*" he smiled, by which they understood, take everything I've given you to your respective cells, but bring it all back before her next visit. They laughed as they mobilized. The borrowing and gifting also included the smaller throw rugs, spare blankets, pillows, and coverlets that were normally stashed in the great wardrobe. The grandest prison cell in Mexico City began to look stripped down. It was all part of the new, more ascetic life that Benjamín was embracing.

"A man should be able to tell his mother what's what," Volcán muttered to Manco one afternoon. "If he wants to give away his things to his friends, what business is that of hers? Why is he so cowed by the old crone?"

"You don't get it, do you? He simply doesn't want to hurt her." el Manco sauntered off.

Other inmates knew that in a pinch, if they were having a celebration with family and didn't have enough chairs, especially for an aged mother or father, they had only to ask el Paladín respectfully and he would lend them the requisite chairs. Whenever Manuela was due to visit—the second and fourth Saturday of the month—there would be a mad scramble to return all borrowed items. Only the four-poster bed with its bed curtains, the desk, and the wardrobe remained in the cell at all times, along with the largest of the oriental carpets. Volcán insisted on that.

"You need for the bastards in our cell block to believe you're a great man, Paladín." No one called him anything else now, not even the prison guards. "You're not like the rest of us, and they don't want you to be," he added. Manco and Vago agreed. "It's bad enough that you lend out your good chairs. The señora's last visit threw my back out for a week."

All four guffawed.

One drizzly afternoon Manco pointed into the courtyard. "Look down there, Paladín. Since when do they let in stray dogs?" He smirked.

A tall, scraggly boy was being jostled by a group of inmates who had surrounded him. "We don't need your Protestant crap here, gringo!"

Benjamín bolted down the stairs with bodyguards scurrying close behind. "What's the problem?" he asked the group in the courtyard. The men drew back.

"Nothing, Paladín," one of them spoke up. "We were just saying that we don't need his Protestant crap."

The boy stooped to retrieve his wire-rimmed glasses. His hair hung halfway down his chest in long wet vines. "I don't hand out crap," he smiled easily. "I give away Bibles, and that's a whole lot better."

Benjamín liked his aplomb. "What's your name?"

"You speak English!" The boy could not hide his delight as he followed Benjamín out of the drizzle into the cover of the *portales.*

"My wife is American," Ben answered all too simply.

"Caleb Wilkins from Gloucester, Massachusetts. Glad to meet you."

Ben shook the hand that was boldly extended. "Benjamín Nyman—formerly from Morelos, Mexico."

Except for the eyes that were a muted steel gray, the boy reminded him of a younger version of Cadwallader Brentt with his threadbare suit and sandals. Judging from the smoothness of the face, he guessed the missionary to be no more than sixteen or seventeen years old.

"Well, Caleb Wilkins of Gloucester, Massachusetts, what the hell are you doing here?"

"Handing out Bibles. Can I interest you in one, friend?" The boy had switched back into Spanish, a surprisingly fluent variety lightly salted with an unmistakable American accent, his "R's" wet, and his "T's" a tad sluggish.

"No, thanks."

"It might reassure your companions. Besides, don't you want to know the good news?" he asked in the soft, clipped tones of New England transposed onto Spanish.

"That I've been pardoned?" Laughter erupted in the court-yard. The boy-missionary laughed too.

"Even better than that. It's all right here!" He reached into a straw bag that dangled off his hip and retrieved a small Bible. "Take it, brother."

"No, thank you. How much did you have to pay the guards to get in here?"

"Don't worry about it. I only rendered unto Caesar what is Caesar's. Take it."

"No, thanks. You would just be wasting your money."

Pushing back his mop of wet hair, the boy tried again. "If it weren't a sin to gamble, I'd bet all that I have that you'll find something of worth with the very first lines you read. Try it. Open the book to any page. If it doesn't speak to you, brother, I'll take it back and give it to another. Deal?"

"I've played the game before." Ben smiled good naturedly. "Other than being swamped by other people's genealogies or learning how to cut up my sacrificial bull or lamb, I get little else. Thanks anyway."

"Wait. I'll imperil my Baptist soul and gamble this once." The visitor fumbled in his pocket. "I have one peso and . . . thirty . . . seven *centavos*. That's my wealth until Friday. Pick one page. Any page. You can keep the money if only bulls and lambs accost you."

"And if I'm illuminated? What do you win?"

"Your promise that you'll attend my classes."

"What classes?

"The Bible study that I intend to start right here. If I win, you attend the first four of my classes. On the other hand, if the Bible passage doesn't speak to your needs in any way, you keep my money and I beg on street corners until Friday."

Because the boy in his religious ardor reminded him of Samuel, and Benjamín was still annoyed with him, he nodded. "You're on." *Dive into the Old Testament*, Benjamín thought. *Teach the little zealot just how impenetrable it is.*

Flipping the book open, Benjamín plunged haphazardly, landing on the seventh verse of a psalm. He read silently,

Where can I go from Your Spirit?
Or where can I flee from Your presence?
If I ascend into heaven, You are there;
If I make my bed in hell, behold, You are there.

Benjamín felt a prickling of the skin. The group that had gathered around him waited for his verdict. He read the lines a second time.

"When is your first class?" he asked quietly.

"Now," the boy smiled.

And that is how my beloved skeptic found himself in a Bible study group. Since the bodyguards went wherever their master went, the boy-missionary gained another three participants then and there. Caleb Wilkins kept the class short—a smart move. When he left Benjamín's cell some fifteen minutes later, Mangel could no longer contain himself. "So what the hell was that all about, boss?"

"At least the kid won't go hungry," Ben shrugged.

87

STIRRINGS

If el Volcán was some men's worst nightmare, it should be noted that he too suffered from nightmares—one in particular. In his recurring dream, prison guards would burst into his cell in the dead of night and haul him out a back entrance of the penitentiary.

"Wait! Where are you taking me?" he would cry out in a quivering voice. "I do everything you tell me. So let me stay here!"

They would thrust him into a waiting coach. Inside sat a well-dressed man all in black, or was it a giant crow wearing a top hat? A dim light outside the coach revealed eyes, bright and menacing, and the sharp beak-of-a-nose. The thing spoke with a distinctly Castilian accent. In every dream the bird would interrogate him about Benjamín. Interrogation always ended in condemnation, "I don't need you anymore," the crow-like thing would mutter with a faint rustling of his black plumage.

"No, wait! I can write more reports, tell you everything he does and thinks! Please! I can't go back there!"

Nothing he said could move his inquisitor. Seconds later Mangel would find himself being dragged through the dark corridors of a place he knew all too well. A door would open, and he would be shoved into a dungeon crammed with men forced to live in their own filth, men who jostled each other and clawed at him—and he and they would entwine like caterpillars piled on one another, blind in the blinding darkness of Belém Prison.

The most feared man in the Penitentiary would wake up sobbing like a small child.

Before the doors were unlocked in his cell block, el Volcán was already at work writing another of his clandestine reports for the nameless Spaniard who had hired him, not only to keep an eye on Ben, but to kill him if he were to order it. Mangel had agreed readily enough—anything to get him out of the city's infamous Belém Prison with its overcrowded dungeons. The new penitentiary was luxurious by comparison. His one goal in life was to finish out his sentence in the small, clean cell that was his and his alone. It it meant killing el Paladín, so be it. Friendship, loyalty, gratitude—all trailed far below his need for self-preservation. So there he sat, hunched over the very table that Ben had given him. The piece with its delicate tilt top barely accommodated his elbows. That it looked comically out of proportion to his great bulk did not seem to cross his mind. Mangel loved running his hands over the satin-smooth mahogany and the elaborate carving along the apron and legs. The ball and claw legs fascinated him. That morning, however, he was too absorbed in his report-writing to take pleasure in the table or in the elegance of his penmanship.

Jesús Mangel had long taken pride in his fine cursive. Highly legible, it had just enough of a flourish to render capital letters artful. After all, he liked to remind himself, hadn't he been the best scribe in his town back in that other life, back when he set himself up in business at age fourteen? All it had taken was his impeccable handwriting, a small table and stool on a street corner. By the time he turned eighteen he had written hundreds of letters for illiterate peasants who pressed coins into his palm.

Business had boomed, enough that he had been able to marry Albertina. A year later he had hired another scribe to work alongside him, and he would have hired a third if he hadn't felt honor-bound to kill Albertina and her lover. Just now, however, he was not thinking about his dead wife or her lover or the life that he might have lived. He felt no regrets about the murders and held few illusions about distant tomorrows. Only the present and the very immediate future mattered. That meant shaking off the aftereffects of his nightmare. The particulars of the dream itself had begun to burn off like morning mist, but not the uneasiness in his stomach.

He took the dream as a warning. Now that the nosey señora Nyman knew about her son's full recovery, he knew that he needed to be extra careful in his reports. What if she were to broadcast the truth and the Spaniard were somehow to hear that Nyman was no longer talking like a drunkard but like a damned philosopher? No. The news had to come from him, not from her or anyone else. His welfare, his very life, depended on pleasing the Spaniard. So he put extra care into the report. When it was done, he breathed a deep sigh. Folding the paper twice, Volcán congratulated himself on his skills as scribe and strategist.

"This needs to reach the *patrón* today, this very afternoon," he muttered to a visitor who came and went, posing as his brother.

The Spaniard's agent, a small, weasel-like man whose mother had given him the name of Rosito—little Rose slightly altered with the masculine "o" at the end—because she yearned for a girl. Rosito took great pleasure in renaming himself Victoriano for his incognito work. In fact, it pleased him so much to sign his name at the prison guest registry as Victoriano Mangel that he decided to keep the name.

"The report has to go out this afternoon," Jesús Mangel reiterated, scowling for good measure.

The 'victorious' one nodded as he doled out several coins into Volcán's large paw. True to his word, he read the report right away. Perching on a nearby park bench, 'Victoriano Mangel' laughed out loud, enjoying the bodyguard's sarcasm:

> Nyman has made a remarkable recovery, but he isn't quite right in the head. He thinks he's a saint-in-training. He goes about doing good deeds, like complaining to the authorities when prisoners are fed rice with maggots. He even volunteers at the infirmary, scrubbing blood off floors and bedding. The inmates have taken to calling him el Paladín. It all seems to be part of his need to atone for his sins. Confession with a priest would be so much easier, but Nyman seems to enjoy suffering. Adding to his martyr routine, he's even taken to attending Bible classes here in the penitentiary from a gringo missionary.

Taking a pencil from behind his ear, Victoriano Mangel underlined the key phrases that he would telegraph to his boss in Europe. Sending the telegram, on the other hand, would have to wait. First things first: lunch, a haircut, and a rendezvous with Lolita, his latest conquest. Why rush?

While Jesús Mangel's carefully-worded report waited patiently inside a dark pocket, doña Manuela was busy firing off telegrams to Paris and Naples: Good news! Benjamín has recovered fully, the blessed Mother be praised!

Eva Comardo cried for joy as she shared her mother's telegram with her husband and children. Since her vision blurred just then, she did not notice the stillness that crossed Pancho's face, nor the momentary compression of the lips. Hours later, Pancho received a telegram from his agent.

"Wait here," Pancho instructed the delivery boy.

In his study, Pancho Comardo scribbled two questions that were to be telegraphed in reply. Who is this missionary? Could Nyman be hatching a plan to escape?

Volcán wrote a prompt response:

The missionary is a stupid kid named Caleb Wilkins. Everyone here calls him *el San Juanito*. This little Saint Johnny is as harmless as a calf. On his first day here he nearly got himself beaten up. Nyman stepped in. Now the kid comes and goes like *Juan por su casa,* proclaiming the Gospel. He is no plotter of escapes. As for Nyman, if he had wanted to bolt, he could have done it when his closest friend escaped. They were inseparable. Yet Nyman chose to stay and complete his sentence. Why? To set things right with God, which is all that he cares about these days. By my count he's got more than twenty-three years for that. Meanwhile, your humble servant will keep a close eye on him as always.

The abridged version that reached Pancho Comardo as a telegram read:

"Missionary is a gringo. There was an attempted escape. Subject is penitent."

More questions followed. Mangel didn't mind. It meant more tips from "Victoriano Mangel," his so-called brother. A pittance, really. But at least he had enough now to bribe Gómez, the prison guard who procured prostitutes for him.

"Get me a young one this time," Volcán muttered as he plunked down his money. "The one you sent me two weeks ago was so old her breasts hung down to her waist."

Gómez obliged. Her name was Teodora, a young Indian woman who had recently been brought to the capital. She was not pretty, but she had a body that kept Mangel asking for her, and a silence that made him long for conversation. Teodora spoke in low monosyllables. She lay in his arms obediently and turned her face to the wall. In the days between their encounters, Volcán would think of her whenever he paused to let the sun touch his battered face with gentle hands.

⌒

On a sultry night when the moon was nearly full, Benjamín rose from his bed. He could hear the faint strains of a guitar and a man singing. Opening the small window in his cell door allowed him to hear man and instrument more clearly. The lilting melody rose and fell in baritone beauty, sweetly plaintive.

"Zandunga." Benjamín murmured.

Back in 1911, Ben and I had waltzed to it in a victory ball in Chihuahua City. At my request, the soloist and accompanying violinists had shifted briefly from the livelier dances to the gentle, waltz-like "Zandunga." Ben had twirled me around, gently, our motions in perfect synchrony. Hearing the song from his prison cell, he thought about me with such yearning that I in my own stone cell thought of him, both of us remembering simultaneously. Ben scooped up a pillow, holding it close as he waltzed me around the cell. And I, locked in my cage, hummed "Zandunga" softly as I danced in bare feet, imagining the touch of his arm around my waist, swaying with him in the generous moonlight that streamed through the cupola.

88

HAPPINESS

Happiness is a freaking illusion! A rotten lie! Volcán would have insisted to anyone naïve enough to think otherwise, or masochistic enough to contradict him. Following Benjamín into the infirmary for their volunteer work, he was more out of sorts than usual.

What the hell had come over el Paladín? Was this his notion of atoning for his sins? It was all Brujo's fault for bolting like he did. (Thus went Mangel's non sequitur.) Well, let Paladín pursue sainthood. He and the others were being paid to guard him, not to worry about the whole damn place! Besides, what was the point of having power and big money backing them, if they ended up scrubbing bloodstains off the infirmary floor or emptying bedpans for the very bastards that he, el Volcán, had sent there? What kind of justice was that?

"Happiness is freaking impossible!" Mangel grumbled to Benjamín, half hoping to bait him. "The church invented the concept of happiness as a way to control us."

"Just how do you figure that?" Ben smiled with mild derision.

"It's all about control. The church authorities—the head wardens, so to speak—figured out long ago that there is no God, and
there's certainly no such thing as happiness here or anywhere.
But we all want it, so they promise us the happiness of heaven *if*
we obey, confess, attend Mass, and most importantly, if we help
the top dogs live in grand style. You've seen how bishops live.
Deny what I'm saying. You can't because it's the blessed truth!"

"The truth is rarely as simple as you think."

El Manco had been listening to the conversation as he
stripped a bed in the infirmary. Once again it struck him that
el Paladín was the only prisoner who could contradict the most
dangerous criminal in the whole penitentiary and then turn his
back safely. It was rumored that at least half of the men who
ended up in the prison infirmary had been beaten up by Mangel—the Volcano—for slights real or imagined. Furthermore,
there was little doubt that in exchange for favors, Mangel worked
with the guards to soften up rebellious prisoners or those whose
families fell behind with protection money. El Manco didn't hold
that against him. Everyone has to do what he can to survive, he
would have said with a shrug. But he could not understand why
a man like Paladín tolerated Mangel—or him, for that matter.

Everyone knew that Benjamín Nyman—the paladin of the
prison—was the wayward son of the richest man in the state
of Morelos. He had about as much in common with his fellow
inmates as a magnificent quetzal with scruffy vultures, Manco
reflected. Nothing but vultures, the whole lot of us! Granted,
Nyman was no saint or he wouldn't be here. With all his wealth,
he must have been one arrogant son of a bitch. So maybe the
guards did everyone a favor by beating the arrogance out of him.
But, the change in him!

Listening to the contrast between Volcán's badgering tone
and Benjamín's calm responses, el Manco had a flash of intuition:
Mangel is a dog brutalized into viciousness. He hates everyone, yet

he approaches this one man with his tail between his legs, docile and eager to please. Why? Because Paladin is the one prisoner who does not shrink from him.

Rolling up the soiled sheets for the laundry, Manco remembered a bully from his childhood, how he had stood up to him, and later how the bully had cornered him in an empty courtyard. Manco had braced for the fight he could neither hope to win nor evade. To his astonishment, the bully held out a bag of marbles with a tentative, awkward gesture. It was then that Manco understood how deep the loneliness that drove his nemesis to seek his friendship. So too with Mangel, he realized. For what were his desperate attempts at camaraderie but a bag of marbles offered just as awkwardly? Manco watched them a moment longer. Then he left them to their debate about *la felicidad.*

"Tell me something, Paladín." Mangel lowered his voice in an attempt at confidentiality between best friends. "Have you ever experienced even one moment of total happiness?"

Benjamín thought of me but did not answer.

"So? Have you?" Volcán persisted.

"Yes."

"With your woman?"

Ben continued scrubbing the stone floor. He was not about to drag me from the protected fortress of memory and hand me over to Mangel or anyone else.

"Ah, women! Nothing but trouble," el Volcán sat back on his heels. "Still, I'd give up everything for a woman who can make me forget this life—anything except my honor, that is."

Benjamín shrugged and rose to empty his pail of rust-colored water.

"What? You don't believe that a man's honor is sacred?" Volcán followed him to the sink. "Don't tell me it's nothing. I killed my first man because he spit on my honor! He was my wife's lover and I killed them both. Be honest with me, man. Don't tell

me you never think about killing the woman who took everything from you, or the man she chose over you? Everyone knows
that you would be perfectly justified. Honor demands it."

"And this is where it gets us."

"But I made them pay!"

"That was clever of you, except that if the church is right,
then all you did was to set their immortal souls free. Did you do
as much for yourself?"

Mangel slammed his brush down. "Screw freedom! They're
dead! Rotting in the ground! Dust to dust, while I'm still here!"

"Yup. Here."

Later that morning el San Juanito arrived to offer another
Bible class—the ninth by Volcán's reckoning. "Paladín only
agreed to four classes," Mangel complained to the others. "Why
does he put up with the gringo missionary? He doesn't believe
the crap the kid keeps feeding us. So why does he encourage
him?"

Sometimes Benjamín also wondered why he didn't distance
himself from Caleb Wilkins. He disliked missionaries, particularly evangelicals who presumed to think that they alone were
saved. Though outwardly gentle, their zeal reminded him too
much of his father's fanaticism. Yet Caleb Wilkins was different—
comical even with his irrepressible enthusiasm and outlandish
clothes. The boy combined the formal suit of western culture,
if one could call such pitiable rags a suit, with Indian garb such
as sandals and a gaudy blanket over his shoulders instead of a
coat on cold days. On the one hand, Benjamín pitied Wilkins for
being so young, so poor, and so far from home. On the other
hand, he envied the kid's freedom and contentment. Just the
same, Ben often felt the urge to bring the missionary up short;
to wipe the smile off his face and the facile arguments from his
repertoire. One day as they passed by the open cell door of an
inmate who was on his knees praying, arms spread wide before

an image of the Virgin Mary, Benjamín asked pointedly, "Why would you want to take that away from him?"

"To liberate him from a false doctrine. Why should he pray to Mary when he should be praying to God?"

"How do you know he isn't?"

"Look at him. He's obviously praying to Mary, when he should be praying to her son. It's such an indirect path to God."

"Is it? How do you know she isn't the doorway for some people, give or take a billion or so?" Two inmates were yelling obscenities at each other, cursing one another's mothers with language violent enough to start a war. Benjamín nodded in their direction. "You want to help someone? Try reaching people like them, Caleb, and may God be with you, because you'll need all the help and protection you can get."

Caleb Wilkins tasted the challenge, slowly. Then he smiled. "Hm. That *would* be a challenge worthy of the Holy Spirit!"

Benjamín could see in the boy's eyes that he was unafraid, and contrary to Mangel's assertions, absurdly happy. That, he realized, was why he continued to let him hold his Bible classes in his cell. Happiness was as rare in prison as the ivory-billed woodpecker in North American forests.

A DRINK

LATE ONE NIGHT when I was lying under the dome gazing up at a fragment of night sky, a drift of clouds briefly blurring the shape of the nearly full moon, doña Manuela paid me a surprise visit. I could hear her fumbling for the banker's lamp on her table. When she opened the curtain on her side of the great divide, I spotted a wine bottle and two glasses.

"Come have a drink with me."

I drew near, blinking into the light. Her nose looked red and her eyes puffy. Had the dragon been crying?

"Come, Isabel! Let's have a *brindis,* you and I. A toast to lost dreams." It was a large bottle and was already half empty. She poured a glass for me and replenished her own. "Long life!"

I've never been much of a wine drinker, but I was not about to object to this unexpected truce. After a few sips, I took a chance and asked softly, "What's happening out there?"

Doña Manuela's glass stopped halfway to her lips. "You want to know what you're missing, Isabel Brentt? You're missing the chance to be blackmailed by renegade revolutionaries who have no cause whatsoever but to make themselves rich or powerful.

They promise protection if you pay up and war if you don't. You're missing the chance to see villages burned to the ground by Federal troops in the name of pacification. And even better, you're missing the chance to have Zapatistas blow up trains." Her eyes were shiny, but she was fully coherent. "You're also missing the irritation of watching our ineffectual revolutionary government retaliate against other revolutionaries with stupidly vicious tactics. Your Madero may be a good man, but he's surrounded by jackals. His political idealism is wreaking havoc."

She took a long drink, then continued her soliloquy. "Why couldn't you leave it alone? You liberals thought change would be so easy. Just oust the dictator and everything will be wonderful! You didn't stop to think that he was the glue that was holding everything together. Who do you think was keeping the jackals from tearing each other apart and us with them? Without a strong man like Porfirio Díaz, it all falls apart." She waved her glass, slopping some of the wine. "You didn't consider the progress that he brought to Mexico, or that for the first time in decades it was safe to travel anywhere in the nation. Anywhere. Now it's back—back to the old days of highwaymen and murder, only now it's on a scale that we've never seen before."

She had a point. But at that moment I was far more interested in how Rosa and Cadwally were faring. I took a gulp of wine. It burned and warmed at the same time. "Is all this happening throughout Mexico or just in Morelos, señora?"

"What?" She seemed to have forgotten me momentarily and was surprised to find herself talking to me.

"Is all this happening only in Morelos or everywhere in the country?"

"What matters is that it's happening here. Right here. Federal soldiers round up entire villages. They burn the houses and *resettle* people in prison camps. Resettle. Don't you just love the term!" She smirked. "The men are inducted into the army at gunpoint. In exchange for miserly wages and little to no training, they get to be gun fodder up north. Farmers and craftsmen are packed into trains and sent to put down the newest revolt in places they never heard of. Meanwhile their women and children—the women and children are loaded into freight cars and end up as beggars, thieves, or prostitutes in the D.F."

No! You must be mistaken! That isn't what we fought for! I wanted to object.

"To be fair," the monologist continued, "we can't blame the federales for all the—all the atrocities." She waved her glass. Wine spilled like blood. "Revolutionaries of all kinds have turned against your president Madero and commit their share of atrocities. In the name of justice, they destroy property, rape and pillage. Damn your Madero!" Slamming her glass on the table, doña Manuela broke the stem, cutting her hand. She winced and held up her hand as if to inspect it, but her thoughts wandered from it. She seemed unaware of the blood that lay tracks from upheld wrist to elbow.

"Señora! You've cut yourself!"

"Did you know it's my wedding anniversary today? You know, I never expected to marry. My father invited Lucio Nyman to dinner one night, here in the hacienda. Lucio was the handsomest man I had ever seen, tall and blond as a Viking with the bluest eyes—as blue as yours. Back then he had eyes only for me. For me." She thumped her chest.

Looking down just then, she tried to pick glass out of her hand.

"Here, let me help."

Manuela held out her hand between the bars, palm up. "Dig away, you with your younger eyes."

I slipped one hand under hers to steady it. Its smallness startled me. Didn't tyrants have large, stone fists? I focused on my task. Since my nails were long through neglect and I had not bitten them down lately, they were more effective than her closely-clipped nails.

"You and I are like France and England," la patrona observed. "Pity. We can be civil to each other, but we're enemies to the death."

Still supporting her hand, I felt a rush of regret. "Señora, I'm so very sorry for all the distress that I caused you and your family. Please forgive me."

She looked directly at me, surprising me with the forlorness that had crept up on her. "Sometimes—sometimes I wish none of this had ever happened." She waved her other hand in the direction of the cell.

"We can still forgive each other. It's never too late for that." And then I took the plunge because hope is a caged trogon that stubbornly exercises its wings. "Please give me my freedom and I'll never trouble you again."

Her eyes softened, and for one moment I fancied that in spite of everything, she had a kind of rough fondness for me, as if I were a dog that has long annoyed her but that she couldn't help liking on some level. Then she shook her head.

"I can't." Two tears slid down doña Manuela's cheeks.

"Yes you can, señora. Pray for God's help."

"You think I don't know that I could free you and my conscience in one—in one fell swoop? A free conscience. But the price!" Her eyes, normally dark one-way windows, revealed her terror just then. "No! I would lose everything! The love of my children and everyone's respect."

"I'll stand by you." By now I was cupping her hand in both of mine. "I give you my word. I'll explain the horrific stress that you've been under. I'll go back to the United States and never return to Mexico," I added rashly.

Doña Manuela pulled free. "No! The funeral! There's no turning back."

Yanking on the lamp's pull cord, she retreated unsteadily down the dark corridor.

~

For weeks Samuel had neglected his brother's manuscript. It was not anger that held him back. After all, Benjamín had kept his word and had written to their mother. As far as Samuel was concerned, this absolved his brother. His own sin, on the other hand, remained—the sin of maintaining the lie about my death. To read a book dedicated to me was more than he could bear at this time, so he had read only the first two of the twenty "sketches." One evening, however, he read another eleven chapters.

In the nighttime silence, Benjamín's voice skimmed the crests of mountains and pierced the stone walls to reach him. Often, the account made Samuel laugh aloud. Other times it made him wince or nod in agreement about the flaws of the family they both loved. Yet it was the sketch about our elopement and Samuel's role as our priest that undid him, no doubt because the observation came from Benjamín, the family apostate:

> Something else comes back to me [Benjamín wrote]: a flash of intuition that I had while observing Samuel performing the familiar sacrament of marriage. For the first time in my life I sensed majesty in the liturgical Latin and in every aspect of the ritual. Watching my twin, that near-perfect mirror of myself, I became two men at the same time: what Isabel would call a natural man—one who sees only the world around him and cares nothing for the next—and a spiritual man. Moved by the intensity of my brother's devotion, I realized with a start that not only did he believe he was in the presence of God, but that perhaps we all were. I saw in Samuel's demeanor, in his total absorption, the meagerness of my spirit and the amplitude of his. Through him I sensed all that I could be and yearned to be for Isabel's sake.

Alone in his parish house, Samuel sobbed. In part he was unhinged by our tragedy, Ben's and mine. Yet there was something else at work within him. I think it was the startling awareness of his impact on others. Moved by the religious sensibility he had awakened in his brother, Samuel was on his way to finding his vocation again.

90

A TRUTHFUL LIE

SEPTEMBER RAINS HAD washed the hills and fields of Morelos. By November the cane was ready to harvest, but already some of the *peones* of San Serafín were murmuring that there would be no point in harvesting or in processing it into refined sugar. Weren't trains being blown up? Wasn't that why la patrona could no longer visit her son, the *prisionero,* as often as she used to? So how would they get the produce to market? But *la señora* Nyman assured them that the best way to deal with insane times was through the sanity of hard work. They just needed to trust in the Virgin of Guadalupe and to keep on working, *como Dios manda.* They obeyed.

Then came the Day of the Dead festival. As always, la patrona gave generous allotments of sugar for the making of the traditional sugar skulls that would be placed on tombstones and personal family altars. To further boost everyone's morale, she declared that the hacienda kitchen would bake extra loaves of the *pan de muertos* for all three days of the festival.

Doña Manuela took particular pride in two facts: that she ran the hacienda herself, unlike the many absentee planters she knew, and that her workers were loyal to her because she treated them well and protected them within the great walls of San Serafín. Their loyalty and faith in her convinced her more than ever in the power of her compassion, even for the most miserable of sinners. She looked upon my recovery with a certain pride, solid proof that she was doing her Christian duty by me.

On the other hand, she did not feel obliged to make things too easy for me. God punished sinners, she liked to remind herself; so did the church. Was she not simply carrying out justice as divinely ordained? As far as she was concerned, she had stopped a thief from committing further thefts and an adulteress from wreaking further havoc on the lives of two of her sons. If anything, wasn't she teaching me the most valuable lesson of all: that everything we do has consequences?

"Do you know what day it is today?" I looked up from the food crammed into my mug but did not respond. "It's the first of November." Images of the Days of the Dead festival flashed through my mind: cemeteries wrapped in candle glow, marigolds and food offerings placed at the graves. All-night vigils. When I still did not respond, doña Manuela crossed her arms. "This means that you've been under my care now for four hundred and twenty days, if my math serves us."

I thought back to the night when I tried to liberate the birds from the aviary.

"Is the quetzal still alive?"

"Oh, yes. He's like Benjamín, beautiful and strong in spite of his captivity."

"How is he—Benjamín?" I drew closer. She pulled back.

"Do *not* talk about him, do you understand?"

"Please, I just want to know how he's getting on."

"Tacha, the Blue Thief gets no dinner tonight."

The dragon deliberately kept the truth from me—that Ben had made a full recovery. Knowing that he was well in body and mind would have flooded me with light in my darkest hours.

Keeping me ignorant was simply one more punishment that she could inflict. But at least with her boastfulness she had just given me a fix on time. The first of November. From then on I kept track of the days. Having no writing utensils, I resorted to using one of the stays from the very corset that had condemned me in doña Manuela's court of law. When my pillow case suitcase and corset appeared in Tomás's room, she decided that she needed no further proof of my infidelity. The detective's photographs had simply confirmed what she wanted to believe. Now the ever-persistent corset had found its way back into my trunk and eventually into my cell.

Working a long, thin bone free from the corset, I took it into the bathroom so I could make a mark on the one wall that she could not see. Yet I hesitated. Would keeping track of the days help or depress me? Did I really want to know how many months or years doña Manuela was yet to steal from me? I twirled the bone between thumb and index finger. All those stolen days—420 of them. No. Four hundred and twenty days *given* to me to become a better me, the thought countered.

Late that evening, doña Manuela headed to the hacienda cemetery. The family plots stood apart from those of the workers, but close enough that she could enjoy the bright candle glow. It also allowed the *peones* to acknowledge her benevolence to them. The hacienda priest, Father Eustacio, blessed the graves. And because a lot of people were watching her, she placed marigolds not just on the graves of her ancestors, but even on mine. Then she withdrew to the house while the all-night vigil went on without her.

I'm told that in the days that followed, my equanimity continued to amaze and irritate doña Manuela by turns. Does the girl really believe that this is temporary? She would ask Tacha, shaking her head in disbelief, other times in vexation, for what was the point of punishing me if I wasn't suffering enough? More than once she considered cutting my rations. Then she would remember her vow to God and would confront the limits of her power. No, she realized. She would just have to go on feeding and clothing me, at least for as long as she lived. And she planned to live a very long time. So why did the prospect of my long prison sentence feel so unsatisfying? She wondered sometimes.

That made her want to unsettle me by any means. Lying became her principal weapon.

"I've had news about your lover," she told me one morning. "It turns out that he is now married. So you see, he's forgotten you, Isabel."

Could it be true? I turned away to consider the possibility and the consequences of this. She immediately mistook my turning away as sorrow. "How do you know?" I asked softly when facing her again.

"It was in the Cuernavaca papers. In true social climber fashion, he chose a rich girl for his bride. She's quite pretty, by the way." Doña Manuela tapped her riding crop against her boot as if that were the signal for my outcry.

"He's married?"

Because I smiled at the possibility of happiness for Tomás, my tormentor slapped the riding crop more forcefully against the side of her boot.

"Yes. How many times do I have to say it? He's married. So he's forgotten you."

No, I thought to myself. Tomás will never forget me. "You say she's pretty?"

"Very pretty."

"Do you suppose she's nice?"

"What's that got to do with anything? Don't you care that your lover has married someone else?"

"No, because he was never my lover," I smiled.

Her mouth twisted as words snagged on her tongue. Turning on her heels, doña Manuela headed into another lonely day.

The truth is that there was no such report in the Cuernavaca papers. He was not married—yet—and she was not rich. But she *was* pretty, the dark-haired zapatista rebel who now filled his thoughts. The girl he yearned to catch up in his arms smiled whenever she spotted him in the camp. My mother-in-law had spoken far more truth than she knew or intended.

91

LEGION

VOLCÁN WAS SICK to death of el San Juanito, little Saint Johnny with his prayers and Bible classes. That el Paladín continued to aid and abet the gringo missionary long past their agreed-upon four classes was maddening. How many had it been now? Twelve classes? Thirteen? It was time to teach the little bastard a lesson in the realities of life. Mangel decided that he would interrupt the very next class by going down on his knees, clasping his hands in a frenzy of emotion, and crying out for Jesus Christ to save him. After the little bastard went into a fit of ecstasy, he would jump back to his feet and use every profanity that his inventive countrymen had ever concocted, just for the pleasure of seeing the confusion on the boy's face.

Mangel forgot the missionary when Teodora was admitted into his room. He had paid so that she would be able to stay the night for a so-called conjugal visit. She arrived looking down at the floor, her face hidden behind a long sheet of dark hair. He didn't want to use her quickly and simply go to sleep, so he stopped her when she began to undress, drawing her to the cot.

"Lie down," he told her gruffly, adding, "Rest for a while." She lay stiffly in his arms, cramped in the narrow cot. "What part of Guerrero are you from?"

The lights went out for the night. She trembled in the dark and did not answer right away. He touched her cheek awkwardly.

"Cocula," she answered at last.

"Where is that?"

"Near Iguala."

"Oh, yeah. South of Taxco. Why did you leave it?" he asked after another awkward pause.

"To be with my sister in Nexpan, when her time came."

"So what happened? Did she have her baby?"

Mangel could feel the wild pulsations of her heart. It was like holding a small, scared animal.

"*Federales* came into the village," she murmured. The outside lights drew shadow bars on the wall. He waited for her to draw her own images. "They ordered us out of our houses and set fire to them. All of them. We pleaded with them that we were mostly women and children. The general didn't care. He burned down the whole village. Said he was going to resettle us. They made us live in a corral for several days. When they let us go, they told us we couldn't return to the village, not even to see the ruins for ourselves. All the Nexpanos had to check in every day with the Jojutla police. We had nowhere to go; nothing to eat. My sister went into labor."

She was crying now. He held her closer. *You don't have to talk about it,* he was about to tell her, but he remembered his grandmother saying that long-held grief shouldn't be stopped once it overflows its banks.

"She had the baby on the street. Soldiers gathered around. Some laughed. Two tried to help us. They carried her to a barn behind police headquarters. We couldn't stop the bleeding. She died that night. The next morning the soldiers rounded up the young women. They wouldn't let me stay and bury my sister. I had to give the baby to an old woman. They brought the younger ones here to the city to be prostitutes. All the money goes to a colonel. We get beans and rice; they bring us here, and they don't let us go home! They don't let us go home!" she sobbed.

"*¡Malditos cabrones!*" Mangel swore.

He remembered reading about the so-called resettlement policy. One of the guards had left a week-old copy of *El País* within his reach. Stuffing the newspaper into his shirt, Volcán had read it later in his cell. One phrase from an editorial stood out in his memory, a phrase that he had kicked under the cot with indifference: "Resettlement is cruel, yes, but heroic remedies are called for." Now Mangel could feel a murderous rage building up inside him.

"I'd like to beat the soldiers senseless! To pound each and every one of them until their brains ooze out of their skulls! To smear their blood on the walls—"

But the girl, who had stopped sobbing, reached up just then and kissed him.

"*Ya pasó.* It's over. Ssh—" she murmured as if trying to soothe an angry child.

In the morning when a guard came for her to take her to another customer, El Volcán seethed with rage once again. Entering Benjamín's cell for another Bible class, Mangel felt the need to find a scapegoat, especially when he realized that they would have to sit on the floor.

"Where are your table and chairs, Paladín?" Caleb Wilkins asked Ben.

"On an outing." Benjamín smiled. "It's the saint's day of Benito Pérez's mother today." He pointed in the direction of a prison cell across the courtyard.

"Well, your rug looks comfortable enough," the boy smiled, guileless as ever. With that, he opened the class with everyone kneeling for the Lord's Prayer. As always, el Volcán and el Paladín bowed their heads but neither of them joined in the prayer. Volcán glowered as usual so that no one would suspect that something out of the ordinary was about to happen. He'd give them a damned miracle, a conversion to top all conversions.

"Paladín, would you read today's lesson?" The boy asked with that buoyant smile that made Mangel want to strangle him between his oversized hands. "Mark 5. I've marked the passages."

Everyone sat on the oriental carpet. El Vago and Mangel quickly grabbed a wall for a backrest, leaving the others to sit cross-legged, their backs arched forward, elbows on knees. Ben cleared his throat and sat up straight as he faced the group. He read in a voice that spoke majesty and mystery, though not to him. He simply concentrated on being a fine elocutionist.

"Then they came to the other side of the sea, to the country of the Gadarenes. And when He had come out of the boat, immediately there met Him out of the tombs, a man with an unclean spirit, who had his dwelling among the tombs; and no one could bind him, not even with chains, because he had often been bound with shackles and chains. And the chains had been pulled apart by him, and the shackles broken in pieces; neither could anyone tame him. And always, night and day, he was in the mountains and in the tombs, crying out and cutting himself with stones. When he saw Jesus from afar, he ran and worshiped Him. And he cried out with a loud voice and said, 'What have I to do with You, Jesus, Son of the Most High God? I implore you by God that You do not torment me.' For he said to him, 'Come out of the man, unclean spirit!' Then He asked him, 'What is your name?' And he answered, saying, 'My name is Legion; for we are many.' Also he begged Him—"

A desperate, guttural sound startled Benjamín into looking up and losing his place. Mangel sprang up from his sitting position but crumpled forward so that he was on all fours. Groaning, he thrust his arms out, bending his elbows and resting his head on the floor. Great sobs racked him. For a moment no one reacted. Then everyone was speaking at once. "Volcán! What's wrong?" "Are you hurt?" "Quick! Get help!" "Maybe he's been poisoned!" "Get him to the infirmary!"

"That's me!" Mangel gasped. "The demon-possessed man!"

Only el San Juanito understood what was happening. Dropping to his knees beside Volcán, the boy draped an arm over him and whispered, "Pray with me, brother. It's all right! God loves you!"

Mangel struggled to his knees and stared into the radiant face of the boy. "Lord Jesus Christ, receive me!" the boy urged.

"Lord—Lord Jesus Christ receive me!" Mangel sobbed.

"Cleanse me from my sins!"

"Cleanse me—cleanse me from my sins!"

"For with you all things are possible."

Mangel had given the performance of his life. Word spread in the prison, even though el Paladín had urged discretion, especially from Vago. Discretion was a skill el Vago could neither spell nor begin to comprehend. The word was out. The most feared man in the whole penitentiary had been born again, as the *Protestantes* called it—saved right there on el Paladín's fancy rug.

That night, when Jesús Mangel was alone in his cell, he slumped into his chair and rested his elbows on the table that Benjamín had given him. He stared at the small Bible that Caleb Wilkins had thrust into his trembling hands. Finally, he opened it and searched for Mark 5, having no idea whether to look at the beginning, middle, or end of the book. Eventually he found it and read it slowly, beyond the point where he had erupted before the amazed stare of his companions. He read about the legion of devils driving the herd of swine into the sea:

> "Then they came to Jesus and saw the one who had been demon-possessed and had the legion, sitting and clothed and in his right mind. And they were afraid."

The tremors continued in Jesús Mangel's hands. Though there was no one to con or to impress, he burst into tears, his shoulders heaving with seismic force.

92

WHAT THE HELL?

WHAT THE HELL is wrong with el Volcán? He's finally cracked up; the word went out. And why wouldn't the son of a bitch crack up? He's spent most of his life behind bars. Just ask him to tell you about his years in the Belém dungeons. You'll come away thinking this dump is a palace!

Opinions buzzed throughout the prison like flies to unprotected food.

"Paladín, el Volcán keeps to his room, coming out only for the Bible classes or to talk with el San Juanito, *by the hour,*" Manco complained to Benjamín.

"So?" Benjamín looked up from his newspaper.

"So he isn't doing his job. Vago and I keep covering for him, so people around here don't get the idea that he's gone soft."

"Cut him a little slack. It's tough work having to be born again." Ben smiled. "Don't worry. In a few days he'll snap out of it and be as rotten as ever."

When Mangel wasn't conferring with the missionary about his upcoming baptism, he would often stop by Benjamín's cell, Reina-Valera Bible in hand. "Paladín, do you have a minute?" he would begin, and Benjamín would brace for an exegetical challenge.

He wanted to yell at the man, *Do I look like a goddamned missionary to you? Ask the gringo kid, or my brother the priest, if he ever deigns to visit me again.* Yet it was el Volcán, the most notorious bully in the prison, who suddenly seemed like a kid, open and vulnerable whenever he asked about his newfound, fragile faith. So Ben would swallow his impatience and reach for the Bible that his bodyguard was holding out to him. He would read the passage and then do his best to interpret it for him.

Why do I do all this? Benjamín would ask himself. The answer came to him one afternoon, as clearly as if Caleb Wilkins had read it aloud to him. *It's because all of this mattered to Isa.*

Skeptic that he was, a man passionately intent on not falling into the religion trap that had ensnared his father, Benjamín found himself becoming an exegete of sorts. El Manco, on the other hand, was growing increasingly hostile about Mangel's conversion. In one class he finally exploded, intent on shaking Volcán back to his senses. El San Juanito had just read the creation story in Genesis 1, but he got no further than day four when el Manco cut in.

"Hold on a minute. Let me get this straight. The first day we have light. The second we get *el cielo*—sky and heaven," he counted by holding up one finger at a time from his left hand. "Now the third day God made dry land, complete with grass and trees and all that. But he didn't get around to making the sun and the moon until the fourth day? Now how the hell did he get the plants to grow?"

The boy-missionary rushed to battle, ill-equipped but unafraid. "We have to take this on faith, brother. With God all things are possible."

"Well I was a farmer and I'm here to tell you that you can't grow anything without the sun, and nobody is going to tell me any different!"

"Caleb's right. Now take it on faith and shut up." Volcán curled his hands into fists.

El Vago, who was more intent on stuffing his pockets with some of the unshelled peanuts that el San Juanito had brought for the group, caught the menace in Volcán's voice and grinned. *Good. He's back.*

"For a book full of wisdom, God seems a little mixed up about the way things work down here." el Manco wouldn't let it go. "Or else it's all a pack of lies."

El Volcán was seconds from lunging at the attacker of his new faith.

"Or maybe we're reading it wrong." Benjamín cracked open a peanut shell.

"It's all crap!" el Manco glared at Volcán, baiting him. But Mangel's attention had shifted at that very moment to Benjamín.

"What do *you* think it means, Paladín?" The muscles in el Volcán's face had grown taut, and he kept rubbing his thumbs on his index fingers.

Help him out. For all of three minutes, drop the damn skeptical stance. The thought came to Benjamín. "Well—Christ always spoke in parables, right? What if the *whole* Bible is written in parables and in symbolic language?"

"See? None of it is true." Manco crossed his arms and tipped his head back.

"Not necessarily." Ben carefully picked out a peanut from the shattered shell. "What if this chapter isn't about the creation of the world at all?"

"What else can it be?" the boy-missionary asked quietly.

I wish I could explain it to you. Benjamín thought. *Isa could do it far better; sometimes she can even make me doubt my doubts.*

"I don't know what this chapter is about," Benjamín admitted. "But I do know this much. The Bible isn't meant to be a science book, and this chapter isn't about cosmology or geology or any of that."

"Then what the hell is it?" el Manco's stance remained as menacing as the long, black sweep of his moustache.

Benjamín remembered badgering me about this very chapter, using my religious sentiments for target practice. He cringed now at the memory.

"Someone once told me that this is a story about the evolution of the human soul going from darkness to light. It's a process, not an instantaneous thing."

"It's an interesting idea," Caleb nodded. "But where does it say that?"

"'Oh that I were a mockery king of snow / Standing before the sun of Bolingbroke / To melt myself away in water-drops!'" Benjamín murmured the lines aloud in English as they came to him.

"Shakespeare?" Caleb Wilkins asked in English, sucked back suddenly into a world he had almost forgotten.

"*Richard II*, the only Shakespearean play I ever tried to memorize, succeeding only in part."

"What has that to do—"

"Poets don't explain their metaphors and symbols. They leave it to the attentive reader to find the deeper meaning that is hidden within. So maybe every one of those objects—sun, moon, skies, plants, and animals—maybe they all represent something else, something far deeper."

By slipping into English, Benjamín had momentarily distracted adversaries with drawn swords. Volcán and Mangel both stared at him with puzzled expressions.

"I'm no theologian," Ben switched back into Spanish. "I've never understood the Bible, especially the Old Testament. But there must be a reason why it continues to be sacred to millions of people, century after century. Maybe it's like poetry. Read it too literally and you risk missing the point."

"The Bible as poetry? I'll have to think about that one," Caleb Wilkins chewed slowly on a newly released peanut.

Manco left in disgust. Vago scrambled to stuff a few more unshelled peanuts into his pockets as the group broke up. Volcán walked hunch-shouldered into the courtyard as he bent his great frame to listen to Caleb. He and his young mentor discussed his upcoming baptism and the fact that he needed a new name. For the next week or so Jesús Mangel would pop into Benjamín's cell and ask, "What do you think of Daniel? Or is it too vain of me to take the name of so great a prophet? Would Joel be better?"

"They're both good names, Volcán."

"Yes, but I want the name to express, you know—who I need to become. I didn't go far in school, but I did become a good scribe. Aside from that I have no special talents, except maybe now to defend the word of God with my fists."

"Ah, well. How about Sampson?"

Volcán would jot down all suggestions in the back of his Bible and then hurry off. Other times he would go through every name that he could pick out of the New Testament, but he felt no worthier of those names, either. Benjamín finally took Caleb aside.

"Volcán is driving me crazy over this name hunt of his. What the devil did you tell him to make him reject his own name? I'm just curious. Why do you object to Jesús Mangel—Mangel I can understand. In English it has a rather ominous ring to it. But why do you object to Jesús?"

"I don't think anyone is worthy of the name," the boy answered simply. "Protestants reserve it for Christ alone."

"So we Catholics are being irreligious?"

"Well, since you ask, yes."

"Hmm. I see your point. Yet when I was a student in Protestant America, I was astonished at how often the name of Jesus was bantered about. 'Jesus Christ!' a man says when he stubs his toe or is angry that a teammate has fumbled the ball. At least we Catholics give the name in love to innocent babies."

The boy grew pensive. "I hadn't thought of it that way."

Neither of them could dissuade Volcán from seeking a new name. So the hunt was on.

~

On a bright November morning, Mangel greeted his so-called brother, the man who reported by telegraph to the mysterious Spaniard, the not-so-mysterious Pancho Comardo who was carefully weighing the possibilities of increasing Eva's inheritance. Mangel's supposed brother actually bore some resemblance to him, though not in size. The man was only of average height and very thin. The resemblance was in the eyes, deep-set narrow slits dominated by dark pupils and a nose flattened through many battles. They both went through the motions of a greeting in front of guards: a brisk embrace, two energetic pats on the shoulder, and the requisite pleasantries. They sat opposite each other at a long table, the prisoner and the man who wore a suit shiny from wear. When the visitor slid a basket toward him, food that had already been inspected at the door, Mangel slipped the man another of his many reports on Benjamín Nyman.

"Keep it." The visitor spoke in low, easy tones.

"It might interest *father*."

"He has a message for you." The visitor leaned forward and muttered softly. "*Truénalo*."

Kill el Paladín? Mangel's right hand twitched. "But I have news that might interest our father." He fumbled, scrambling for something that might stay the order of execution.

"Forget it. Just do it."

"I need to hear it from him. I need guarantees."

"Nothing is guaranteed in this life: not your health, not your place of residence, and certainly not your life. But if we all do our part, brother, we might actually be rewarded." The man smiled through broken teeth. Rising, he added expansively for the guards to hear, "Sorry I can't stay longer today. I just needed to see you, so I can report to the old man that you're still alive and kicking. Take care of yourself, brother."

The *brother* was plunged into more torment than ever.

93

BROTHERS—OF SORTS

REGRETS WERE MONSTERS that scorched the earth. Jesús Mangel saw his life as a wasteland. In desperation, he read the Gospels daily and clung to the hope that his contrition wiped the slate clean. But did it? One evening before lockdown, right after el Manco and el Vago had returned to their cells, he lingered a few more minutes in Ben's.

"Paladín, do you think it's true what Caleb says, that all our sins can be wiped away in a flash?"

Benjamín studied him. "It's a comforting thought."

"But what do you think?" Mangel gripped the back of a chair.

Benjamín tipped his dining chair back onto two legs. "Are you sure you want to know what I think? All right." He motioned Volcán to sit, while planting all four chair legs on the floor. "If you beat a horse brutally day after day, do the scars vanish just because you're sorry?"

"Meaning what?"

"Meaning we can't undo the past any more than we can make our sins vanish as if they'd never been."

"Then what's the point of trying?" Mangel stared straight ahead as if seeing nothing but darkness. "What can we do?"

"Stop beating horses. Shoulder the past as best we can, even if we stagger under its weight, and begin again. *Now* is all that we have. So we start here. Now."

"What about what happened to me here in this room? Caleb says I've been born again. What do you think?"

"I don't know. Only you know that."

They were silent. Doors were being bolted for the night.

"But if I can never wipe the slate clean, what good is it to want to? What does that accomplish?"

"That we can give you our back and not fear being knifed?" Benjamín smiled. Volcán was startled to his feet.

"It's late. I got to go," he muttered.

Alone in his cell, Mangel continued to agonize about the Spaniard's order. He wanted to warn Benjamín, but that would mean having to admit that he had been in collusion with the very man, whoever that was, who now wanted him dead. How could he admit to such treachery? How could he bear the instant loss of trust that would follow? As for evil deeds, suppose el Paladín had it wrong and all our past sins *could* actually be wiped away in an instant of mercy? Wouldn't that mean that he could kill him, regret it deeply, and therefore be forgiven by an all-merciful God?

So do it and live!

"Why haven't you done it?" Pancho Comardo's messenger challenged Mangel a few days later.

"I'm being watched. When the time is right."

One day in mid-December, the messenger leaned toward him and whispered, "One week, or it's back to Belém."

Jesús Mangel still had nightmares about the dungeons of Belém Prison. Alone in his cell, he fluctuated between his deeply-ingrained instinct for physical self-preservation and his newly-born instinct for spiritual preservation. Just when he would decide on physical self-preservation, Benjamín would look at him as if he were human, or he'd invite him to a meal. Then there would be that twinge in his neck and a throbbing in his head, and a feeling that began as regret and grew into a monstrous yearning that he could not quite name. Only by reading the Gospels could he find some measure of peace—until memories of Belém prison burst in, plunging him into despair.

"*Señor Jesucristo,* help me!" he'd pray. "I am in hell."

94

MURDER

It was a morning like so many others, what doña Manuela affected to call our breakfast together.

"Well, how is my American Blue-Thief?" la patrona quipped, pulling off her gloves and hat. She brought with her the air of the outdoors and the scent of the horse she had been riding since dawn.

"I'm fine, thank you."

That day doña Manuela was in a talkative mood, which meant that she held forth while I listened attentively. She launched into a spirited recounting of the processing of the sugar cane that had been going on throughout most of December. "But the market is abysmal." She sighed. Just as la patrona was leaving, I could not resist asking once more, "Have you any word about Benjamín? Is he happy?"

The dragon turned around sharply, eyes narrowed. "Happy? He's locked away with the most hardened of criminals in the country. He's stuck in a *wheelchair*." Emphasizing the word gave her special pleasure in her lie. "A *wheelchair for life*. He can't speak or walk or feed himself, and you ask me if he's happy? For the record, Isabel Brentt, do you remember how he came to be in that condition? Will you say it or shall I?" By now she had walked away from the table and was pressing her head to the bars. "I'll tell you again, in case you've forgotten. Guards beat him with clubs, smashing the bones in his legs and his arms and his shoulders."

Hearing about the beating still affected me. Great tears streamed down my face as I covered my ears.

"No, hear me. You asked the question. I want you to picture what your casual little visit cost him that day. They struck him again and again. Can you imagine what that must have been like? Because I imagine it vividly every single day of my life. I saw him after the beating, his face was so swollen, so misshapen, that I didn't recognize him. My own son!" Reliving the horror always left doña Manuela trembling, no matter how often she told the story.

"Oh, please don't," I cried. "It's in the past. Please, please leave it there. I only want to know how he is *now.*"

"The past? I carry that day nailed onto my chest. It's always August 17, 1911! You may want to forget, but don't ask a mother to forget!"

Tacha listened silently behind her rigid mask as I tried yet again to breach my mother-in-law's stubborn perspective.

"I live with it too and it hurts me more than you can imagine."

"Ha!"

"How do I make you understand that I love him? That I often wonder about him, how he spends his days; how he—"

"You have no right—"

"I have every right! I'm his wife and he's my husband, whether you like it or not. So I *will* ask about him any time I please!"

All the serenity that I had managed to tap into through prayer, the patience to speak only when spoken to, and the will to be a model prisoner, all of it vanished that morning. Enlightened states of mind are water, sometimes cupped in the hand, other times slipping through our fingers. My outburst surprised her, but she recovered quickly enough.

"You don't fool me, Isabel Brentt, with your attitude of saint. You're still a viper."

"No. You're the viper! You with your hypocrisies! What do you confess to your Father Confessor? Do you tell him, 'Forgive me, Father. I imprisoned my daughter-in-law, nearly starved her to death, and then faked her death? I lied to all of you. Absolve me anyway. I torment her daily. Absolve me.' Is that what you tell him?"

"What I confess is my business!"

The battle raged. Tacha observed.

"You can lie to everyone, but you can't lie to God. Yet I suppose you lie even in the confessional. Your priest gives you a few 'Hail Marys' to say and all is forgiven."

"That's right. The Church gives me absolution every week of my life. But you will die in your own sins."

"And you won't? You think that lying to your priest or withholding the truth makes you blameless? It is you who will die full of sin because you never had the guts to confess honestly, not even to your priest who would carry your dirty secrets to his own grave. So you're a coward and a hypocrite!"

"And you're so pure! Such a victim!"

"A victim, yes. The victim of a mad woman! Who else would do what you're doing? If it isn't wrong, would you stand up at a dinner party with friends and tell them, 'Did you know that I keep a young woman locked up in a cell that I built for my own sick pleasure?' Go ahead. I dare you to tell polite society what you do behind your thick walls! Tell them!"

Manuela gripped the bars. "I'll tell you what they should know. That you're a thief—"

"And you're a liar and a hypocrite! But it will all come out when I'm rescued, for I will be rescued, I promise you that!"

"What rescue? Everyone knows you're as dead as your grandfather!"

The hurricane suddenly stilled. Or more accurately, we had drifted into its eye. I'm certain that she had not meant to tell me about Cadwally, but the need to gore me threw away all other considerations. "You heard me. Your grandfather died months ago," she said triumphantly. "You don't believe me? Ask the Zapatistas who killed him and left his body to rot."

I doubled over as if she had just punched me hard in the stomach. As I struggled to regain my breath, her threats against Cadwally sprang onto my back, like demons let loose. *If your grandfather suspects anything, anything at all—These are dangerous times, especially for travelers—*

I flew at her. Hurling myself at the bars, I trapped doña Manuela's hands between my own and the wooden dowels.

"*You* killed him! You had Valle Inclán do your dirty work for you! Didn't you!!"

It all fell into place—her insistence that Cadwally accept an escort back to Cuernavaca; his refusal; Cadwally waving his hat in grand showman style, unafraid of the men on horseback who watched him leave San Serafín.

"No! Zapatistas waylaid him on the road. Tacha, pull her off." Manuela turned in fright to her servant.

"You liar!" My voice shook with rage. "My grandfather was a Zapatista sympathizer and they knew it!"

"Tacha!"

Old Stone Face tried to pry my hands open, but they had become vices. I didn't care if I broke the dragon's fingers, every single one of them.

"You call me a thief, and I am! But you're a murderer, you and your shadow and your henchmen, and you will all go to hell for it!" As I stared between the bars into la patrona's terror-rounded eyes, I saw an inversion—Manuela Nyman inside the cage—and it dawned on me: "You're the prisoner here." My astonishment stilled the cyclone, but only momentarily. For a few seconds a dark calm settled over me, leaving me pitiless as a judge passing the death sentence. "You're nothing but a slave to evil spirits. You're already living among them in hell and don't know it."

I released her. The sound of Manuela Nyman's footsteps faded quickly down the corridor. Tacha, who could not meet my eyes, hurried after her mistress.

I collapsed to my knees. *Oh, Cadwally! No, no*—Despair rushed over me like seismic waves racing across the surface of the sea. Then a tsunami's rage swamped the land, engulfing, drowning, sweeping away everything in its path, grinding, crushing the inner prayer out of me, so that there was nothing but the violent clash of sea and land, obliterating all living things between them. I wanted to kill Manuela Nyman and her henchman with my bare hands. I wanted—I wanted—I knew not what—only to destroy them without mercy. My hatred was oceanic. Yet even the mightiest tsunami reaches its limit and must recede. So too my fury. When it did at last, I was left quivering in a devastated landscape, sleeping, dreaming, waking only to cry, and making half-hearted attempts to pray, words tottering like survivors. Stunned. Pitiful.

I knew I should pray longer. Deeper. But how could I? I had let hatred pour in, filling me to the brim, leaving room for nothing else. How long was I in that wasteland, muttering, groaning, cursing? I think it was the closest I ever came to losing my mind.

Doña Manuela stayed away. Tacha came and went, her face expressionless as ever, yet her motions seemed tentative and awkward. I ignored her and the food, retreating ever deeper into my despair, rocking back and forth, back and forth between mutterings and tears, back and forth between sanity and insanity.

95

MEMORY GHOSTS

SAN SERAFÍN WAS full of memory ghosts, especially in the Christmas season. Samuel encountered them every year when he attended the children's *posada*. He loved that his mother maintained the old tradition for the sake of the workers' children, long after he and Benjamín had grown up. Though this was a particularly busy time for him with his parish, he made the effort to come home that twenty-third of December to witness once more pageantry parading with memory. He liked watching the children walk into the candlelit courtyard like stiff little soldiers, arms rigid, eyes on the alert, and then how quickly they forgot their bashfulness when blindfolded and handed a thick stick. Every child longed to be the one who finally broke the piñata, forcing the great star to crash onto the flagstones. Samuel loved the commotion. Watching from the comfort of a chair in the *portales*, he could see his own childhood in lightning flashes. The ghost of his eight-year-old-self clamored to be blindfolded again so he could strike the final blow to the piñata—an enormous paper star engorged with candy treats. And strike it he did, square on the clay belly. He could still recall the thud as it smashed on the stone floor; the triumph as he ripped off the blindfold; and then the shock as he watched Benjamín scoop up the broken pot with most of the treasure trove and run off with it, laughing like a pirate. Rodolfo, who was then twenty-three years of age and a spry runner, gave chase.

"Come here, you ruffian!" Rodolfo called out. When he caught the thief, he tickled him mercilessly. Then, grabbing eight-year-old Benjamín by the ankles, he held him upside down, making him squeal in delight.

"Me too!" Samuel had insisted. So Rodolfo had dangled him, swinging him like a bell in a belfry. Seeing those memory ghosts so vividly, the adult Samuel closed his eyes. *You're remembering this too, right now,* he told Benjamín across the miles. *We're taking turns letting Rodolfo swing us by the ankles. Mother is objecting. Father is laughing.*

Benjamín was in his cell for the night. Looking up from his journal, he saw the memory ghosts too. For a few seconds he even felt the sensation of being swung by the ankles, so vividly, that he smiled: *Samuel, I know you're thinking about it too.*

Like so many twins, these brothers could sometimes communicate telepathically, if not in words, then certainly with shared emotions. Of course, both remained utterly blind and deaf to my own despair that very moment. Then again, aren't we all that way? How often do we stroll past strangers, we in our bubble of happiness, they in their calcified shell of sorrow, or the other way around—and all of us ricocheting off one another like billiard balls intent only on our own trajectory? That night of the first posada, Samuel was not that far away from me, walled up as I was on the second floor of his childhood home. Singing drifted up to me dimly, not through the double layer of walls, each a meter thick, but through the one opened window in the dome above my head. Normally, I looked to my precious window to give me hints of life on the outside. Had I looked up that night I would have seen the few bursts of fireworks wandering into my limited view, round like dandelions gone to seed. Firecrackers and barking dogs would have alerted me that a fiesta was underway. A Christmas Posada. In my state of mind little of it registered, only the bleakness of raw grief. So I reacted neither to the commotion of the celebration nor to the exhausted silence when it was over. I had simply stopped distinguishing between sound and silence. I only rocked, back and forth, back and forth.

In the courtyard a gentle breeze roused a troupe of paper lanterns into dance. Doña Manuela took a seat opposite her son. Resting her clasped hands on the small table between them, she smiled. "Well, another posada, another year."

Samuel would have enjoyed sitting alone a bit longer, but the memory ghosts were already withdrawing. He was back in his mother's world. "I'll head out at first light tomorrow, but I'll be back on the afternoon of Christmas day. I want to say a Mass for Isabel."

Her hands tightened. "Why?"

"Because it will be the one-year anniversary of her death."

"So?"

"So, she was Benjamín's wife."

"Don't grace her with that title. She gave up all rights to it when she took a lover."

He rubbed his forehead as if he had not slept in twenty-four hours. "Look, Mother. I don't know if she had a lover or not. However flawed she may have been, in the end she did try to do what was right."

"Right? So were she and her lover right in throwing me out of my own house?"

"No, of course not. But since she did let you return and then deeded back all the properties, isn't it time for us to forgive her?"

"So now you admire her!"

"I admire repentance in action, not merely in words."

"Oh, do as you like! Just don't ruin Christmas. Let her Mass wait. Rodolfo telegraphed from Veracruz. He should be in the city by tonight. I'm going there in the morning to join him.

Come with me, Samuelito!" she reached across the table for his hand. "You want to be a peacemaker? Help me convince Rodolfo to make peace with Benjamín. I've already arranged for our Christmas Eve dinner to be delivered at the prison. Think of it. We could all spend Christmas together—you, Rodolfo, Benjamín, and I! Just the four of us!"

"I can't." Samuel withdrew his hand. "You know what the Christmas season entails. I have two masses—"

"We could send Father Eustacio to cover for you." Her face beamed at the thought.

"He's needed here. Besides, even if you could find a second substitute for me, which is impossible this late in the game, I still wouldn't be able to join you."

"And why not?" She crossed her arms, trying not to lose patience.

"Because I can't go near Benjamín unless you release me from my vow of silence. He'll ask me about Isabel, and I don't want to go on lying."

"And you think I do? I'm only doing this for his sake. You know how volatile he is. No, Samuel. You made a solemn vow and must keep it."

He grasped her hands. "Please, Mother. Don't make me complicit in such a profound lie."

"Do you presume to judge me, Samuel Nyman? I only want to keep your brother from getting himself beaten up or killed. Why is that so difficult for you to understand?"

He rose. "Wish Benjamín and Rodolfo a merry Christmas for me." He headed upstairs without kissing her goodnight.

As Samuel slept in his old room, he could not have imagined our physical proximity. Our rooms actually touched at right angles. Muffled by the additional layers of masonry that his mother had ordered, my brother-in-law and I remained as unaware of each other as if an ocean separated us. Samuel dreamed peacefully. I, on the other hand, fell into an abyss.

In my nightmare I entered a cave. It had a long corridor that opened into a cavernous room. A creature, part snake, part lizard, lay coiled around an enamel bathtub, sleeping. Scooping up a handful of pebbles, I pelted the monster, forcing it to open its eyes. The dragon rose, thrashing its long tail from side to side. Large stones flew in all directions. I could hear them smashing against the rock walls of the cave. Even though the creature's skin was green and scaly, I quickly recognized doña Manuela by the eyes. She didn't scare me. I had come armed with rage. Thrusting my head back, I roared my hatred in flames that scorched her.

I drew closer, teeth bared to rip my enemy's flesh; to expose the evil that hid in sinews and muscles; to gouge out eyes that mocked and threatened; to split open the chest and rip out the vile heart. The dragon roared back. The concussion loosened stones that fell from the ceiling. Fueled by a force that kept expanding in my chest, I felt no fear. Despite the size of the monster, I flung myself at her. The moment I felt the impact of the collision, I glanced at my hands. My fingers had become claws—thick, curved, and razor sharp. The skin of my hands and arms had ossified into grayish-white scales. My tongue burned with the fire that I belched. My nemesis shot back her own fiery hatred. All the while I could feel my body enlarge and distort to meet the enemy on its terms.

With jaws that I did not recognize as my own, I bit into the dragon's throat and tasted salt and blood. The dragon howled and bit off part of my shoulder, which in the odd logic of the dream was a hard-crusted chunk of bread. A man ran into the cave just then. Neither of us paid him any heed. We dwarfed him. Manuela Nyman and I could have crushed him so easily. When we pulled away from each other, he interposed himself between us, falling to his knees. He was a young man whose nose and mouth bled profusely.

"Get out of the way!" I yelled.

Standing on all fours, I roared another blast of fire even though the man was still in the way, his head bowed, his hair growing increasingly gray until it was as white as the moon. He dropped his hands from his face and looked straight into my eyes.

What are you becoming? Cadwally asked me seconds before my fire engulfed him.

I woke up screaming.

Doña Manuela started down the corridor to my cell but had to turn back. Samuel was knocking on her bedroom door. She opened it and quickly stepped onto the veranda, closing the door behind her.

"Who is that?" he demanded.

"What are you talking about?"

I cried out a second time, my voice carrying more clearly in the stillness of the night air. "That. Where is it coming from?" Samuel glanced up at the flat rooftops and then at the cupola.

His mother could not answer. Tacha, who never strayed far from her, stepped out of the dark. "It's one of the servants, Father. She's gone into labor."

"See to her," the dragon waved her off.

Tacha headed for a metal stairway at the end of the corridor, presumably to go up to the servants' quarters on the third floor. In reality, the rooms had been empty for months, the servants having been forbidden to enter that part of the house. Samuel, who knew nothing about this arrangement, cast an uneasy glance in the direction of the dome.

"Go back to bed, son. There's nothing you can do for her. It will be a long night."

After Samuel returned to his room, the dragon hurried to my cell to silence me.

96

FLAME

"Shut up or we'll gag you!" Doña Manuela whispered tensely into the darkness. She was trying to light the banker's lamp on her table, but it refused to cooperate. She yanked on the pull cord several times. "Damn! The power must be out." Even the votive candle had blown out.

Standing in the dark, she realized with a start that she was alone with a creature that groaned and sobbed with unearthly intensity. Her hands began to shake. "Isabel!" She spoke the name sternly to mask her own growing uneasiness. "Stop it!"

Manuela Nyman could not see me, nor could she understand the despair that made me gasp in English, "Oh, God! Oh, God! What am I? Please help me!"

La patrona's hands shook as she fumbled for matches. Striking one at last, she managed to relight the votive candle. What she saw in the flickering flame was a soul teetering on the edge. She could see me at a distance in profile, kneeling with my arms held out in supplication. I'm told that Manuela Nyman perceived the glow of a *second* flame, and she wondered, *how can my candle reflect light into the cell*? So thinking, she blocked the light of her candle with her left hand. At the same instant the flame inside the cell flared up.

Glass shattered on the stone floor as Manuela Nyman fled.

Tacha had just let herself into her mistress's bedroom. "The power is out," she reported. "But at least the *señor padre* believed us. He's . . ."

The sound of my voice silenced her. As my jailors listened to my tortured groans and mutterings, they could not help wondering why my voice sounded so muffled now, whereas it had sounded so much clearer outside on the veranda. How could that be?

"How did she—how did she get a candle?" La patrona's voice quavered. "Go in there and get it from her. And shut her up. Gag her if you have to."

Tacha negotiated the corridor in total darkness. On reaching the cell, she found that she needed neither candle nor electric light to see me. A shard of moonlight spilled from the dome just then. Caught in its silver lines, I rocked to and fro, praying, sobbing, and muttering. Tacha hurried back to her mistress.

"I think—I think the girl has finally cracked up, señora."

"Yes. You may be right. You heard how she ranted all that nonsense about her grandfather, accusing me of murdering the old goat!" doña Manuela coughed up a shaky laugh. "What about the candle? Did you take it from her?"

"I saw no candle."

"She had a candle. I know what I saw." But she wasn't so sure now. "Never mind. Just keep her quiet. Stay with her tonight. We can't risk any more outbursts. In fact, she's all yours for the next few days. I'm leaving in the morning."

"To spend Christmas with don Rodolfo, now that he's back?"

"Yes. He's not expecting me, so I'll be able to surprise him. See to my bird while I'm gone, Tacha. Add some sweets to her diet. That should straighten her out."

"I don't think she'll eat."

"Then ram it down her throat."

"I can't do it from the other side of the bars."

Doña Manuela reached for her massive key ring and unhooked one of the keys. "Take it. And if she lets out as much as a moan, shove a rag down her throat!"

~

Alone in his cell, el Volcán turned the matter over and over. He didn't want to kill el Paladín. That much was clear to him. Yet he reasoned that it wasn't a simple choice between good and evil, light and darkness. If he chose evil and killed the only man he admired, he could go on living in the light of the penitentiary's large, airy spaces. But at what price to his soul? Perversely, if he chose good and spared Benjamín, he would be condemned to live in the darkness of Belém Prison. And what about Teodora? His dilemma revolved around her too. If he didn't kill el Paladín and they sent him back to Belém, he'd never see her again. On the other hand, if he followed the Spaniard's orders and the bastard was true to his agreement and rewarded him, then he could continue to live fairly comfortably in the penitentiary and he'd be able to pay Teodora to visit him from time to time, which would benefit her too since she was destitute.

Still, he didn't want to kill el Paladín. Surely God understood that. Didn't good intentions count for something? Was it so wrong for a man to kill in order to save himself? Couldn't he do more good by staying alive than by dying in some dark dungeon? Maybe he could atone by becoming a *paladín* himself. He could devote his life to the welfare of his fellow inmates. Yes. This way killing one man would benefit a hundred or a thousand others. Sure. And he could do it quickly, sparing him suffering. He owed Benjamín Nyman that much—a clean death.

Good. It was decided. One last crime and then he'd live a lifetime of doing God's work.

Rising from his cot, he reached for his Bible and brought it to the window. Flipping it open at random, he let his finger fall onto a verse and read, *Greater love hath no man than this: that he lay down his life for his friends.*

Mangel stood at the window for a long time staring across the dark expanse. It occurred to him that by reading the entire Gospel of Luke that day, he had seen the whole arc of Christ's life, from advent to crucifixion. What if his own miserable life was a reflection in miniscule of Christ's, complete with advent and certain death? Perhaps, but only if he could make his own death serve a high purpose—the highest, *for greater love hath no man than this.*

When he finally returned to his cot, his tangled beard and cheeks were wet. But the battle was over. *Tell your master the Spaniard to go hang himself,* he would tell the messenger in a calm voice. *I'm done doing the bidding of the devil.*

As for Teodora, he reminded himself that he had never possessed her. *What is it now? Two weeks?* No, two-and-a-half weeks since he had last seen her. What did she care? How could he expect her to care about *him*? Then again, what if she did? He desperately needed to believe that this girl from the state of war-torn Guerrero at least liked him, and that she wasn't repulsed by him with his wiry beard and middle-aged body. He needed to believe that she—

The door to his cell swung open just then and Teodora was shown in. The guard smirked at the prisoner's nakedness. Then he left. Mangel raised himself onto an elbow. The girl hung back shyly. When he held out a hand to her, she hurried to grasp it and kissed it.

"No one sent me. I bribed the guards myself. It took me two weeks to save up, but I got the money together."

"Why?" he asked, astonished.

She answered him with a kiss and a laugh that was pure joy.

While doña Manuela slept, Tacha lit the votive candle and let herself into my cell. Carefully locking the door behind her, she approached me. Apparently I was still muttering and rocking. Setting the candle on the stone floor, she sidled up behind me as she had done countless times as a midwife in the hacienda. She would support the woman in labor, rocking her, keeping her upright to help ease the pains and the birth itself. She now wrapped her arms and legs around me, gently forcing me to slow my frenzied rocking.

"Let's birth this grief," she murmured, rocking gently with me. "Ssh . . . ssh, *mi niña,*" Tacha cooed. After a while she angled me around, placing me on her lap. "Go to sleep."

There are times in life when the only thing we need are arms to hold us—whether they be a lover's, a friend's or even a stranger's. Tacha was none of these. Yet in my terror I found comfort in the very arms that had restrained me so often. My frenzied muttering began to subside. My eyes closed. The moment I felt her try to set me down, I flung my arms around her neck.

"Don't leave me, Tacha! I'm afraid!" I remember whispering as I buried my face in her cotton blouse.

And she, the hated jailor, the hateful Stone Face, murmured with rough tenderness from some place deep within her, "I won't leave you, *mi niña.* Ssh . . . Sleep. I'm here." Throughout the night her flame flickered softly.

97

SURPRISES

A WEEK AND a half earlier, a letter addressed to Benjamín had arrived at the hacienda. Doña Manuela had humphed in surprise. Then, she had smiled.

"How nice that Emanuela should think of her uncle," she had commented to Tacha with a vigorous nod. "I must remember to give it to him on my next visit."

Rising at dawn that Christmas Eve of 1912, Manuela Nyman remembered the letter and slipped it into her handbag. She had no need to pack anything more than that since she kept the wardrobe and bureaus well supplied in her room in Rodolfo's house. With hat firmly anchored in place and kid gloves in hand, she was ready for her trip. Yet there was no hurry. The train could not leave until she gave the word. Time enough to check on the American Blue Thief. But she didn't. She couldn't. Our encounter had left her shaken even now as light poured through her east-facing windows. Tugging on the vest of her black suit, the Nyman matriarch stepped onto the veranda with a firmness of step at odds with the fluttering of her heart.

She met Samuel in the outermost courtyard. A carriage waited to take her to the hacienda depot and a mule to carry him to San Gabrielin.

"So, is it a boy or a girl?" Samuel asked as he mounted up.

"What? Oh, a boy. Born just an hour ago."

Because he smiled the gentle smile she loved, and the sky was aflame with golden light, she returned to her cherished plan for a Christmas reunion. "Won't you reconsider and come with me?"

His smile flattened into a tight thin line, making her think of Lucio Nyman. "So I can spend Christmas lying to my brother? No, thanks."

I awoke to the distant whistle of the departing train. To my surprise I was still cradled in Tacha's sturdy arms. More astonishing yet, she was sound asleep. How had she maintained the same posture all night? Only her chin had slumped forward. I studied her face calmly. I had never seen her asleep. Her features were unchanged, the face round, the lips thick, the nose large and flat. Yet asleep, Tacha looked different. Noble. She was an Olmec statue, serenely immutable. Once again I considered trying to escape, but only briefly. I was all too aware of Tacha's preternatural strength and agility. I wouldn't get much beyond the door. And strange as it may seem to you, something else held me back as well: a reluctance to betray Tacha's unexpected friendship. She had been so kind throughout my night terrors. With the impulse of a child, I touched her cheek. The Olmec eyes opened.

"*Gracias,* Tacha." I smiled up at her.

While in the kitchen sneaking food into the pockets of her apron, Tacha trembled at what-ifs. What if *la niña* had crept off my lap while I slept? What if she had reached for the key in my pocket? She could have made it to the door as silently as a snake. What if she had gotten away, and me sound asleep!

She imagined waking up with a start, the way one does from a nightmare, only to find herself locked in the cell and having to look into doña Manuela's smoldering eyes.

La patrona! Santo Dios! She would kill me! I must never, never be so stupid again! The girl can starve for all I care!

Tacha put back the mango she had just stuffed into her right pocket.

Yes, but Isabel had the chance to escape and didn't.

Tacha looked off as if studying the shiny Talavera tiles that covered the kitchen counters and walls. Moments later, she scooped up the mango again as well as a *concha* pastry baked that morning.

Alone in my cell, I wept for my grandfather. My grief, however, was so very much less raw now, the tears softer. Oh, Cadwally! Be at peace, I prayed. May the Lord continue to grant you the joy of creativity and the freedom you've always loved.

I inhaled the light that cascaded from the cupola. Reflecting on my night terror and Tacha's unexpected compassion, I remembered lines from a psalm, one of many that I had been required to memorize at school. Fragments came back to me, new and intense as the day of their conception.

I will praise You, O Lord my God, with all my heart . . . I could not remember what followed, only the key line: *You have delivered my soul from the depths of hell.*

A few hours later, doña Manuela stood outside Rodolfo's house. She relished the look of surprise that swept across his handsome features.

"Mother?" He bent to hug her, his joy as genuine as his surprise. She reached on tip toe to cup his face in both hands. To her credit, Manuela Nyman had always loved Rodolfo as if he were her own.

"You're looking fine, son. I guess the French were good to you."

"Yes. You should have telegraphed you were coming. I would have met you at the station."

"And spoil my surprise?"

"What about Christmas in San Serafín? The children's posada?"

"We had it last night. This year I have something special planned, and for that I need your help. But first, tell me about your travels. How are you, son?"

They spent half an hour or so in Rodolfo's library while servants prepared brunch. Both seemed determined to speak only of pleasant things. They maintained their light chatter when called into the breakfast room. Rodolfo, who had been in France for the past fifteen months or so, closed his eyes in ecstasy as he tasted scrambled eggs with green *chiles*, salsa, and refried beans. "Oh! I've missed this! I started feasting in Veracruz and haven't stopped!"

"You, the family anglophile? Or have you become a Francophile now?" she laughed.

He leaned back and studied her, noting new lines on her face. "How are you holding up, *viejita*?"

Though she did not think of herself as an old lady, Manuela liked the tenderness this particular term of endearment always seemed to evoke in Rodolfo. "Well, in spite of having a revolutionist for a president and having to fend off federales, revolutionaries, and bandits, I'm fine."

"What can I do for you?" he leaned toward her.

"You can come with me to the penitentiary to visit your brother."

Rodolfo was shaking his head even before she finished speaking. "No. I'm sorry. That I cannot do. Not yet."

"But I had so looked forward to surprising Benjamín. I thought we could bring along the meals that I've ordered from the Sylvein right after Midnight Mass."

"Visit the penitentiary at one in the morning? Absolutely not."

"We could bribe the guards."

"Mother, it's a prison, not a club or a school. It's out of the question. And even if by some miracle you could bribe your way in, which is highly improbable, I would not allow my mother to go into that prison or any prison after dark."

"So come with me and protect me."

"No."

She could see Lucio's face in the darker one. *Why is your father haunting me through you boys today?* She almost blurted out. Looking into her bowl of *atole,* she stirred it peevishly. "First Samuel refused my simple request. It seems his parishioners are more important to him, and now you won't take me there. How easily you thwart my cherished plans. These are the times when I very much regret having been born a woman."

"I wouldn't have it any other way." Rodolfo was quick to smile. "Don't worry. I'll see that you get there safely for an afternoon visit. You'll have a basket brimming with treats from my wine cellar and pantry. Just don't ask me to go with you. I'm not ready to see him."

"Oh, son, I should have thought that you could be more forgiving at Christmas."

Rodolfo's gaze swept beyond the white linens to the mahogany shelves across the hall. "I don't think I'll ever forgive him for depriving me of my father."

"I *marvel* that you can still think of Lucio Nyman as a father!" Her spoon rattled as she thrust it aside. "He threw all of us away. In the end none of us mattered to him. He cared only about his rotten soul—and Isabel Brentt, God alone knows why. As for Benjamín, you and I both know that he did not go to San Justín to murder him that night. Not that Lucio didn't deserve to be throttled. Oh! Was there ever a more exasperating man in all of Mexico? You know that he must have egged your brother on."

"Is that Benjamín's excuse?"

"Lucio went on one of his rants."

"And your son went on one of his, thrashing a frail old man."

"Now you're talking like the prosecutor. But I'm telling you that Benjamín never meant to hurt him. Surely you know that in your heart."

Rodolfo looked away and sighed. "Yes. But that still doesn't change the fact that my father, such as he was, was taken from me. Give me time, Mother." A servant replenished their coffee cups. After another pause, Rodolfo asked quietly, "Tell me how Isabel died."

"Isabel! Why do you and your brothers always come back to her? She was hateful and deceitful, and now she's dead. What more do you need to know?"

"How did she starve herself? How is it possible that no one noticed what she was doing?"

Manuela spun her version. Yet, however much she railed against me, Rodolfo could not shake the notion that he alone was responsible for setting my life on the wrong course, just as he had ruined Teresa Gama. He didn't say it, but the gloom of his silence forced doña Manuela to shift tactics. Dropping all accusations, she let her head droop and her eyes water. This had the desired effect. Rodolfo reached across the table.

"We don't need to talk about this. I'm sorry I brought it up."

She dabbed her tears with the silk handkerchief that he offered her across the table, but she could not staunch the heavy silence that bled into the room.

98

PLOTS

PUTTING HIS CAR and chauffeur completely at his mother's disposal that afternoon, Rodolfo took a taxi to the home of one of his fellow conspirators. Only four gathered that day. The others were still in Paris but would be arriving within the next few days. After effusive hugs and the first round of drinks, they tried to set the date for their coup détat, but no one could agree on *which* day. January twenty-sixth? The twenty-seventh? What about waiting until early February? They needed more time. After all, it would be enormously complicated. They had to spring two generals out of prison—Rodolfo Reyes out of one prison and Félix Díaz out of another—and then coordinate an attack on the National Palace. So how about February or March? The only thing they agreed on was that everyone needed to get home. It was, after all, Christmas Eve. The *coup détat* could wait.

Meanwhile, Tacha had decided to be more generous with lunch. She returned with two mugs for me instead of one, both filled to the top with assorted food. Hunkering down on her haunches, she watched me from her side of the bars. I knew what she was thinking. *Why didn't Isabel try to escape when she had the chance? And why is she so calm now?* When I had finished my meal, she reached for the empty mugs.

"Oh, stay a while, Tacha."

"I have work to do."

"Please! It's Christmas Eve, isn't it? Just stay a while. Tell me about your home. Where are you from, Tacha?"

"Tepoztlán." She spoke the name without a hint of emotion, her face a perpetual mask.

"I've been there! Cadwally—my grandfather—used to take me there sometimes. He liked to paint the Tepozteco hill with the pyramid." My throat tightened. Tears slid down my cheeks. "Oh, Tacha, she killed my *abuelito*. Why did she have to kill my grandpa?"

"I don't know anything about that. Now stop asking me questions."

But it was Tacha who now had a burning question of her own. That evening, when she found Valle Inclán, the hacienda administrator, she turned her question into a fish hook.

"That old gringo was a thorn in la patrona's side. Someone had to stop him. Good for you!"

Valle Inclán started. Then he slapped his forehead as if he had just remembered some vital task that needed his attention and hurried off. He had said nothing, but Tacha had her answer: *Santo Dios!* She murmured.

That afternoon Rodolfo's chauffeur drove doña Manuela to the penitentiary. He followed her inside so that he could carry the basket that Rodolfo's butler had put together for Benjamín. Armed with gifts and a helper, Manuela Nyman arrived at the prison with a mounting sense of anticipation. *Benjamín will be so surprised!* she thought happily. The place was mobbed. Waiting in line, it seemed to her that at least a third of the city's population had a criminal to visit. By the time she was hugging Benjamín, she was physically and emotionally spent. However, since he seemed in high spirits as he set up a fresh tablecloth for their lunch, she began to perk up.

"The bottles are from Rodolfo's cellar. He sent them to you." Instantly she regretted her comment.

"I suppose he's not quite ready to spend Christmas with the criminal element." Benjamín spoke without rancor as he continued to empty the basket. "What's this?"

"A letter from Emanuela. It came to San Serafín a few days ago. I don't suppose she knows the address here." He slipped it into his pocket to read later. "As for Rodolfo, give him time, son. He's so much like you, stubborn as a wild mule."

"Actually, I don't see that we're all that alike. Can you see him fraternizing with the element here?"

Both smiled at the thought. "No, you're right," Manuela conceded. "But you've both been wronged by the same woman," she added almost against her will, or perhaps very much according to her will. So strong was her need to discredit me to Ben, that she risked arousing his anger. *How else is he ever to free himself from her spell?* Doña Manuela reasoned even as she braced for his reaction.

"No. It's Isa who has been severely wronged," he answered calmly. "Rodolfo behaved badly when he courted her while he was still involved with Teresa Gama, and I behaved even worse."

"As I recall, Isabel repaid you by running off with that lawyer of hers."

"I drove her away. That night at the hacienda, I acted despicably. I was drunk and—"

"And with good reason."

"Don't make excuses for me, Mother. Whatever my feelings, my behavior was reprehensible. I don't remember everything that I said—just bits and pieces. But I know that I was every bit as abrasive as Father at his worst."

"No one could be as hateful as Lucio. No one."

"I am, Mother, only I'm worse. He never laid a hand on you, never, whereas I tried to choke my wife the day that she came to see me."

"You mean the day that they beat you to within an inch of your life? And you think that *you* are the despicable one?"

"Yes! See me as I am, Mother." He spread his arms.

"How can you not hate her?" Doña Manuela asked with genuine puzzlement. "Isabel Brentt took everything from you, including your honor."

"I'm here for what *I* did. Isa did not kill Father. I did that. As God is my witness, I never meant to harm him, only to stop his rant against her."

"Ah! So you admit that she was at the bottom of it all."

"No."

"Of course she was. You never would have gone to see Lucio if she hadn't put you up to it."

"Isabel had absolutely no idea that I was going to his house that night." No matter how he tried to explain it to her, Benjamín could see that his mother was entrenched in her own version of an event that she had not even witnessed. He sighed.

"What is that sigh? You keep acting as if she's the victim in all this, not you."

"She *is*."

"That's absurd! How does a man of honor forgive his wife for infidelity, Benjamín?"

"Because she wasn't unfaithful!" He was shouting now.

"Of course she was! We caught her red-handed. The photographs! Have you forgotten the one of her kissing Tepaneca on the lips? They prove—"

"That *he* kissed her. Yes. But have you never noticed how her arms are limp, not around his neck? Does it ever occur to you that she may have been taken by surprise? That the passion was one-sided?"

"Don't you trust your eyes?"

"No, as a matter of fact, I do not. If there is one thing that prison has taught me it's that things and people are not always what they seem. How do I make you understand?"

"Where is your sense of honor?"

"A man of honor would have treated his wife far better than I did."

"How can you men be so superficial? You trade everything—family, personal freedom, and honor—for love, you say, when all along it's simply for carnal pleasure."

"No." In an unconscious gesture, he reached for the envelope in his pocket and pointed it at her. "The true superficiality, the real absurdity, is to believe a photograph, a mere scrap of paper, instead of the living person! I'll tell you what's unforgivable: that I who know her better than anyone did not believe her." His voice cracked.

"Open your eyes, Benjamín."

"No, open *yours*. Understand once and for all that Isabel is not capable of the deceit we all accused her of. I have to face the fact that I married an angel and then drove her away."

"What rot! Forget her! She's dead!" And then, because an awful stillness came over him, she hastened to add, "To all intents and purposes, she may as well be dead. I want nothing further to do with her. If you do not want to ruin the holiday for me, I ask that we not speak about her at all."

"Fine. But like it or not, Isabel is my wife. Never forget it."

Doña Manuela busied herself by unpacking their Christmas lunch and filling the sullen silence with superfluous chatter. She told him about Eva and her children and about Rodolfo who never wrote to her any more. And weren't men selfish?, she chuckled with dogged determination. When Benjamín did not eat a single morsel of their Christmas lunch, his hands clenched, his gaze pointedly avoiding hers, Manuela threw down her napkin and left. And because Rodolfo was not expecting her until dinner, Manuela Nyman spent the next hour pacing rooms that were as silent as the Borda Gardens after dark.

99

DEAD A YEAR TOMORROW

BACK IN SAN SERAFÍN a revolution was slowly gaining momentum. Tacha unlocked the door to my cell with a loud clanking. She carried a small rug rolled up under an arm.

"Set it up." She tossed it at my feet. "I'll be back with our Christmas supper." And sure enough. About half an hour later she returned with a large tray. As she unlocked the door I had the impulse to push past her, perhaps knocking her backwards, tray and all as I bolted down the corridor. Yet I knew from experience that she could easily outrun me. "Today we're going to eat off plates," Tacha announced proudly. "Look. They're the good ones."

"You just took them?"

"There's no one in the kitchen. They all know that the señora plans to stay in the city for two or three nights."

"At don Rodolfo's, I suppose." *The servants are gone for the night.*

"Yup. He's returned from Paris." Tacha reached into one of the deep pockets of her apron. "All I could find for dessert were a few *pastelitos de boda*. Bardomiana baked them two days ago."

"Oh, I love her cookies! And the tamales smell heavenly," I sighed as I removed the layers of corn husks, still hot. I could plan my escape after eating.

Tacha sat crossed-legged across from me. "I have a gift for you, *niña.*"

"Because it's my one-year anniversary of being dead?" I quipped. "No, I didn't mean that the way it sounds." I reached and patted her on the knee.

The keeper's face remained disconcertingly neutral. Reaching into another of her prodigious pockets, Tacha drew out a book.

"My *Divine Providence!* Where did you get it?"

"I found it in the niña Emanuela's bathroom when I removed the boards in the window. I've had it in my room all this time. I can't read a word, and I thought you might like it back."

"You're a wonder, Tacha!" I laughed, hugging the book to my chest.

When we had eaten our fill, she scooped up tray and dishes. "I have to go now, but I'll be back soon."

What was happening? I kept wondering. Marveling. Tacha's attitude toward me was morphing faster than an ice cube puddling in the sun. She had offered neither explanation nor apology, and I had asked for none. Why risk breaking the magic spell? Was it merely my mother-in-law's absence that was causing this show of kindness? Would it fade the moment doña Manuela returned? If so, didn't I need to act now? Hit Tacha over the head? With what? Use my shoulder to knock her down, then grab the key, lock her in my cell, and escape? Oh sure. That would be as pointless—and painful—as ramming the stone walls with my head. Besides, after Tacha's unexpected compassion last night, I could not bring myself to betray her. How was I to forget the tenderness with which she had held me throughout my night terror?

What is it about human touch when it is gentle, whether from lover, friend, stranger or enemy, that can comfort us as nothing else can? Is it a throw-back to earliest childhood, a need to be held that we never quite outgrow? I wondered. Last night, as my terror escalated, I had clung to Tacha—Tacha of all people! Who *was* this woman who could torture me one moment and hold me with a tenderness that bordered on the maternal? Was she tormentor or healer, monster or slave to someone else's will?

I thought back to my explosive confrontation with doña Manuela. Fixing my hatred on the dragon, I had pretty much ignored Stone Face—but not completely. After I accused doña Manuela of having Cadwally murdered, a dreadful fact that I grasped as clearly as if I had witnessed his death, I noticed not only my mother-in-law's dread of being exposed, but an agitation in Tacha as well. For once, I had stripped Manuela Nyman of all her pretensions to righteousness. By revealing the depth of her evil to the woman herself, had I also made it known to her faithful servant? It now struck me that Tacha, like most human beings, had a moral code. Could it be that hers allowed torture if administered to thieves and usurpers like me, but balked at murder? Though Tacha had maintained her mask throughout my unmasking of her mistress, I had the impression that she was stunned by my accusation. When I had finally turned to her, glaring my hatred of her for the servile wretch that she was, she had been unable to look me in the eye. Could it be that murder went a step too far for Tacha? Why else had she seemed so cowed then? Why else was she falling all over herself to be kind to me now? Did she fear retribution from the law or from God?

Whatever the reason, I sensed that Tacha had reached a crucial crossroads in her life.

What to do? If I tried to escape and failed, which was highly likely, Tacha would never trust me again and I would lose my one ally in the hacienda. But if I befriended her enough and could work my way around to it, I might be able to persuade her to let me escape. I wouldn't rush her. After all, I still had two or three days before doña Manuela returned. The trick was to gain Tacha's trust while tapping deeper into that surprising conscience of hers.

Go slowly, I told myself. For now, just enjoy the truce. See where it leads. One thing was certain: change was in the air, tangible as the transitions that I had learned to discern in Pennsylvania, like September mornings that suddenly turned brisk, announcing the coming of fall, or the graying skies in winter that coughed snow flurries in soft warning of an approaching storm. Or perhaps this change in Tacha was more like the longed-for appearance of crocuses pushing their way through the snow—crocuses, those startling harbingers of spring renewal.

Tacha returned with coffee and more cookies. Better yet, she let herself into the cell.

"I have something for you." She kept substituting presents for apologies. And again she looked away, unable to look me in the eye. "There's something you should know. Don Benjamín is no longer wandering lost in the spirit realm of the insane."

I stopped in mid-chew and grew very still. "What are you saying? Is he—has he—" I couldn't bring myself to say, is he dead?

"He's recovered."

"Recovered? Physically or mentally?"

"Both, I think. Doña Manuela says he's no longer in a wheelchair and hasn't been for many months now. And I think he's all right in the head now." Tacha looked down at her hands, one more gesture of unspoken regret.

I threw my arms around her neck. "Oh, Tacha! This news is the very best gift you could have given me! Benjamín has recovered fully! Oh, Cadwally will be so—"

His name triggered another deluge. Well, no apologies. Grief must have its outlet. After a while the storm began to subside. Struggling to pull myself together, I tried to consider the matter of my grandfather's death from *his* perspective, not mine. The real challenge was not to dwell on how he had died, but on the fact that he had made that astonishing crossing into the next life;

I needed to imagine all that Cadwally was gaining—to picture his reunions with those whom he had lost long ago: his parents, his wife, his son, friends lost in battle, and who knows how many others. Instead of dwelling on my loss, I should be glad for *his* joy. In short, in spite of my overwhelming sadness, I wanted to be happy for *him.* I would grieve later, long and hard if necessary, because how else can we begin to heal? Meanwhile, my heart was singing joyfully that Ben had recovered, and I thanked God for such a gift. At the same time, I was keenly aware that I needed to keep my wits sharp, dulled neither by despair nor joy. Just nurture my startling, fragile friendship with Tacha. Pragmatism demanded it. So too did my emotional hunger for human companionship.

So I wiped away the tears, sat cross-legged with her on the throw rug, and munched cookies (And this time they did taste a bit stale. No matter.). We chatted like school girls who have sneaked food into their room against the rules. Throughout it all I sensed that she was enjoying it too. Yet her face remained maddeningly serious.

"Oh, Tacha. Just once, give me a smile, one glorious smile."

"I can't."

"Sure you can."

"No." Tacha crossed her arms. "When I was born a *nahual* stole my smile."

"What's a *nahual*?"

"A sorcerer who can change shape as easily as the wind blows. My mother told me that a *nahual* frightened away all the happiness and the anger and the sadness that were supposed to show on my face. So I can't move anything there, just my mouth."

In spite of my not knowing the medical term for her condition, and not being acquainted with thieving *nahuals,* the emotionless mask suddenly made sense. "Oh, Tacha, I'm sorry."

"It doesn't matter," she shrugged. "Toci, the grandmother goddess, made me into a great midwife. I've brought many *chilpayates* into this world."

"You're a midwife? I had no idea!"

"I've birthed most of the *chilpayates* in the hacienda, including don Benjamín and don Samuel."

"You helped bring them into the world?"

"It was a difficult labor. The señora always said I saved her life. She trusts me more than anyone in San Sera—"

Her voice trailed off. I hurried her along a different path. "And were you a midwife in your hometown?" She nodded. "Then they must love you in Tepoztlán."

"Actually, they used to call me *Cara Muerta*—Dead Face."

Her features remained expressionless, but I heard a hint of sorrow in her gravelly voice. Rising to my knees, I cupped Tacha's face. "Did you know that your soul smiles? It smiles in a beautiful face that no *nahual* can hurt."

She grew very still. Then two tears crept down the bronze mask.

She left abruptly. Had I offended her? Was she angry with me? She returned a little while later with a bundle and a mug. I stared into a dark concoction that smelled of lime, coffee, and something pungent. "What is it?"

"It's for your hair, to make it black."

"Why would I want to do that?"

"So that you can come with me tonight to birth a child. The smell only lasts a little while. Take off the dress so we don't stain it."

My mind was racing. Had I heard her right? Go with her out there somewhere? I obeyed, not daring to ask questions for fear that I had heard wrong, or that she might change her mind. Some twenty minutes later, I stood shivering in my chemise and petticoat, my hair hanging in dark, wet strands. Tacha removed the towel from my shoulders and worked vigorously to dry my hair.

"We'll need to take the towel with us since it's stained. We don't want to leave any hints of your disguise. All right. Look up." Tacha pulled a comb out of one of her hard-working pockets.

"We have to wait until dark." She spoke quietly as she worked the comb. "Bundle up one change of clothes. Tonight you'll have to wear these others." She motioned to a small pile on the floor. "You can't be a grand *señora* tonight, only a pretty Indian. When your hair is dry, cover it with the *rebozo*. Do you—"

I hugged Tacha, inadvertently smearing some of the dye onto her cheek.

"*Guah*! I'm dark enough already!" she growled. "I'll be back soon."

She left without locking the cell.

While waiting for Tacha's return, I braided my new black hair even though it was still damp, tying off the ends with the scraps of string that she had given me. Slipping on a plain blouse and the grayish-white skirt of the Morelos peasantry, I twirled about the cell as if preparing for a ball. Tacha had even brought me a pair of sandals. Two pairs, actually. The first pair was too small. The second one cradled my feet like an efficient nurse bundling a baby for a nap.

"Whose are they?"

"Never mind." she snapped.

I could see that Tacha was wound up taut as a violin string. *Please. You won't change your mind, will you?* I almost asked. Instead, I kissed her cheek. Tacha stared back expressionlessly.

"You look too excited. That will draw the attention of the guards."

"I'll look sad! I promise!"

"Practice humble. And while you're at it, practice walking with smaller steps, Isabel. None of that swinging of your arms. You're a *campesina* of Morelos now, and you're afraid of leaving the safety of the *hacienda* to help birth a child. Don't say it in words. Only your body can do the speaking tonight. I want them to think you're that girl Genoveva assisting me. So you'll need to hide most of your face with the shawl and keep those blue eyes lowered, do you hear? I'll be back when it's dark."

Oh, I'll be humble and frightened all right! I thought as I walked up and down the length of the cell, practicing smaller steps. But every now and then my feet would remember the waltz or the polka. I'm going to be free! I'm finally leaving this place! But where will we go? Will Tacha come with me? She has to. La patrona will never forgive her. Oh, can this really be happening?

Going to the cell door, I turned the handle and swung the door open. Closing it quickly, I let my joy burst loose again, making me laugh out loud and pirouette across the room. When I dropped down onto the carpet again, I opened my book and delved happily into it until the light faded. Sitting in the growing darkness, I marveled that my deliverance should come from Tacha of all people. That set me crying. *How great and wondrous are your works, O, Lord!* Wiping my face, I slipped into the smooth cadence of the ancient Hesychast prayer, linking words to breath, breath to words, with the lengthening shadows.

When night draped me in darkness, I continued to sit on the small carpet from doña Manuela's room. Unable to read now that even the votive candle had sputtered out, I hid the book in my bundle. Sitting in the dark, I listened to the whistle calls the guards sent back and forth as signals during their watch. The birds in the aviary and in the treetops had long since settled down. Is the trogon sleeping? I wondered. Or is he keeping watch with me? If only I could set him free.

Just then Tacha ran up to the grille. "She's back! Quick! Give me the rug!" she gasped.

Part 3

APOCALYPSE

*"These bodies are perishable, but the dwellers in these bodies
are eternal, indestructible and impenetrable."*

THE BHAGAVAD GITA

EPIPHANIES

"You're back early, señora!" Tacha greeted her mistress on the lower staircase landing, grateful for once that her face did not know how to portray emotion. The trick now was to keep her voice from betraying her. "I thought you were going to spend Christmas with don Rodolfo and don Benjamín."

"Oh, don't talk to me about those two!" doña Manuela growled as she started up the stairs with Tacha hot on her heels. "They're impossible! Just like their father! Since they don't seem to think that I matter all that much, they can spend Christmas without me."

"Didn't don Rodolfo try to talk you into staying?" Tacha asked, feeling the need to stall her mistress.

"He conveniently made himself scarce, so there was no opportunity to discuss the matter." They had reached the upper landing. Doña Manuela was breathing heavily. She paused to catch her breath. When calmer, she turned to Tacha, her one confidante in the world. "If he had accompanied me to see Benjamín as I begged him to do, I'm certain that the visit would have gone so much better. But they're both selfish, like all men. When

I left the penitentiary, I had Rodolfo's chauffeur take me straight to the train station."

La patrona could not seem to catch her breath. "Are you all right, señora?"

"Yes, yes."

Tacha followed her into the bedroom. "You should get some rest, señora. I'll make some tea."

"I want to see the Blue Thief. Did she miss me?"

"She's feverish, but it's nothing serious. She'll be fine in a day or two."

"The key." Doña Manuela held out her hand. Tacha handed it over.

I, with my damp, darkened hair, lay huddled under my blanket, listening as the dragon inserted the key into the lock.

"She's been throwing up all afternoon," Tacha spoke in a flat tone. "I finally got her to sleep, señora."

There was a pause. "What is it? Indigestion?"

"No. It's something more than that. But she'll be all right in a day or two."

My heart was pounding in my ears. A dragon stood on the threshold of my life. Or maybe it was just a very tired woman.

"It's been a long day. I'm going to bed. Bring me a cup of chamomile."

Tacha obliged. She also added an herb to make her sleep.

Over the next hour or so, Tacha kept a vigil outside la patrona's bedroom door. When she calculated that her mistress had finally dozed off, she opened the door a crack and listened. Then she let herself into the room and down the corridor. Motioning to me, Tacha whispered, "She's asleep. Take off your sandals."

Clutching my bundle in one hand and the sandals in the other, I followed Tacha along the corridor that I had never seen until this moment. It was longer and darker than I had imagined.

A monster slept at the end of the passageway. *Lord Jesus, have mercy on me, a sinner*, I prayed. I could not see the dragon, but I could plainly hear her snoring. Then suddenly, miraculously, Tacha and I stepped into the night air. Taking my hand, she whispered sharply, "Hurry now."

We moved quickly and silently in our bare feet, down the stairs, across the central courtyard and into the kitchen.

"Put on your sandals. Remember to keep the *rebozo* over most of your face. Look down at all times, and no swinging of the arms. Let me do the talking."

I nodded. Tacha looked cool as ever, but I noticed that her hands shook as she bent to strap on her own sandals. When we let ourselves into a smaller courtyard behind the kitchen, we stumbled across a dark form.

Hipólito! With a burst of joy, I dropped to my knees to stroke the warm head. The old dog's tail thumped away.

"Forget him! He belongs to Bardomiana now. Hurry!"

I hesitated. Why not take him with us? At the same moment a strong intuition urged me to leave him in Bardomiana's care, at least for the present.

"Goodbye, Hipólito." I kissed the noble face.

Moments later, I climbed into a wagon that was hitched to a mule. To my astonishment, Tacha suddenly traded stealth for boisterous vigor. Taking the reins, she called out to the guards, "*¡Abran paso, que viene un chilpayate al mundo!*"

And because they believed her that a new child was coming into the world and needed to be birthed, two guards with rifles slung over their shoulders ambled over to the gate and swung it open.

I sat alongside Tacha, head bent downward, shawl firmly clutched so that it covered most of my face. Grasping the seat rail, I felt the wagon lurch forward. We were rolling past the sentries into a night shimmering with stars and no one was stopping us.

⁓

In the *penitenciaría*, the electric power was being shut off in all the cells for the night. Yawning in the darkened room, Benjamín set aside his reading and started to undress. That's when he felt the contours of the forgotten letter in his pocket. Reaching for it, he tore open the envelope. There was only one way to read young Emanuela's letter now. Opening the small window in his door, he let in a thin shaft of light from the corridor. Seeing the childish handwriting of his sister's child, Benjamín smiled.

December 5, 1912

Dear Uncle Benjamín,

Everyone is fine. Father had a portrait done of all of us here in Naples. I hate it. He had the painter pose me sideways, so I can be seen only in profile. He didn't do that with my mother or my sisters. It's not fair. Plus everyone who sees the painting is going to think that Esther has lovely blue eyes, but that's only because Father and Mother took her to Paris where a surgeon removed her eyes and gave her glass ones. Father says that glass eyes, especially blue ones, will make her more appealing to suitors than her dead blind eyes. I think that's cheating. I suggested brown eyes for her, but no one listens to me.

I'm sorry I haven't written to you before. I need to tell you something that everyone has been keeping from you since forever. I think it's wrong of them not to tell you the truth. You'll be glad to know that your wife Isabel can't hurt you anymore. She died about a year ago. *Abuelita* Manuela wrote to tell us that she starved herself to death, right there in San Serafín! Mother and Father made us swear not to tell you, but I think that was wrong of them. So I'm telling you now.

I hope you have a nice Christmas. Write soon.
Your niece,
Emanuela

Far away in the village of San Gabrielín, Samuel was climbing the church steps. There was still time, almost two hours to
rehearse the choir before the midnight mass. Halfway up the
flight of broken stone treads, he suddenly doubled over. Clasping an arm over his stomach, he started again and stumbled. Two
men rushed to help him to his feet.

"¡Padre! ¿Qué le pasa? What's wrong, Father?"

Samuel gasped as if the air had been knocked out of his
lungs. The alarm went out. Something was happening to the
priest! A crowd gathered. Two men carried him to his bed;
women rushed about to fetch water or herbal teas or compresses.
¿Qué le pasa, padre? They watched their priest cover his face with
the crook of his arm. When he could finally speak, he gasped:
"He knows!"

Alone in his cell, Benjamín was struggling to catch his
breath. When he could breathe more evenly, he slumped slowly
to the floor. A bit of moonlight broke through the barred window, cold and skeletal white.

"No—no—!" He groaned, deliberately striking the back of
his head against the door with each denial.

His hands found a soft tangle and gripped it tightly. It did
not register right away that it was his mother's knitted cape that
she had left behind in her haste. Burying his face in its folds, he
sobbed his oceanic despair. Yet even in the grip of such overwhelming emotion his mind was racing. It was all beginning to
make sense now—my lack of response to his letters; Samuel's
evasiveness about me and his silence about the manuscript; and
today the confession that had escaped from his mother's lips:
Forget her! She's dead!

Benjamín tugged on the cape, tearing a hole in it as if it were
the universe and he had the power to rip it. Everyone had known
the truth, even Emanuela, and they had dared to keep it from
him? And then he was tearing the cape because the betrayal
had been perpetrated, not by the vast, impersonal cosmos, but

by his own mother. *Forget her! She's dead!* His fingers pulled and tugged, unraveling lies and a careful design until nothing but a long strand coiled in his lap. Then a poisonous thought hissed, *What's the point of going on? Join Isa.*

A deadly calm came over him. Getting to his feet, Benjamín cast about the darkened room for a weapon. He had no knives or scissors or razors. He could use a belt, but would it be long enough? A better idea came to him, drawing him back to the door and its slit of light. Layered strands of yarn could be twisted into rope. So he set about his task, growing ever calmer, ever more determined to end his life.

When he had his rope, Benjamín climbed onto his dining table and made a hangman's noose. The other end he carefully tied to the long light fixture that dangled from the ceiling.

101

FORK IN THE ROAD

THE LANE OF San Serafín stretched into a pewter-edged darkness. Giant *amate* trees linked arms, creating a leafy ceiling that temporarily obscured most of the sky. Tacha and I rode in silence, letting the formidable hacienda walls shrink far behind us. When we rolled at last beyond the shaded lane onto the public road, I dared at last to look up. A near full moon stared back, glazing everything with a silver wash.

"The sky, it's so big!" I gasped.

Tacha grunted. Did she smile inwardly? We rode on. After a while I asked the question that had climbed aboard with us and wouldn't leave.

"Why are you helping me, Tacha?"

She was silent for so long that I thought she had dismissed my question. She stopped the wagon and turned to look at me, her face emotionless as a rock. "Thieves deserve to be punished, and you were a thief, Isabel, no matter what that last will says. So I was willing to help la patrona punish you for trying to take San Serafín away from her. But I know that to commit murder is a mortal sin. So I was scared when we almost killed you. I kept praying to the Virgin Mother to have pity on all three of us—you, la patrona and me. And she did! The Virgin let you live and later she made la patrona want to feed you again."

So she could go on torturing me? I couldn't help thinking, but I didn't say it.

"I can't tell you, Isabel, how glad I was when I could finally serve you real meals. I had promised the *Virgencita* that if you lived, I would treat you better. I did, didn't I, Isabel?"

"Yes, you did, Tacha," I patted her hand.

"Everything was fine for a time. But *la Santa Iglesia* is right: you can't serve God and the devil. You have to choose between them. I've had no peace since the day you confronted the señora about your grandfather's death. That's when I knew that she had gone too far, and I was even more scared. Would her sin become mine too? Yet I owe so much to her. How could I betray her?"

She looked up and studied the sky, as if to probe the exact boundary of moonlight and darkness.

"But you know what really convinced me to leave la patrona? It's a small matter, a memory I can't get out of my head. That day that your grandfather showed up so unexpectedly, when you said goodbye to him, you had to stand on tiptoes to kiss him. I used to do the same with my own grandpa. I loved that old man because he loved me. He loved me even though the Nahual had taken away my face. My *abuelo* had white whiskers, like . . . like your grand . . . pa." Her voice began to crack, slowly at first, like earth in a landslide. "And then one morning . . . one morning . . . I couldn't get him to wake up! He wouldn't wake up!"

For the first and only time, I saw Tacha sob. Now it was my turn to hold and gently rock a hurting soul. Deep within that formidable body of hers was a frightened, heart-broken little girl with a frozen face. Though she had not asked directly for my forgiveness, I forgave her everything then and there.

"You'll see him again, Tacha, just like I'll see Cadwally someday."

"Not if I go to hell!" Another sob racked her.

I brushed hair off her damp forehead. "Only hellish people want to be in hell. Listen to me, Tacha. You're a midwife. A good one. That makes you a healer. Use your gift, not because you're afraid of going to hell, but because you *want* to help women who are in pain. *That* desire to help others will build you a road straight to heaven."

She embraced me and there was nothing more to say. Flicking the reins, she coaxed the mule forward. We traveled a long way, each of us in our own separate but overlapping worlds. When we came to a fork in the road, I broke the silence.

"Stop! I know this road. It goes to San Gabrielín! Benjamín and I took it when we eloped."

Tacha reined in the mule and turned to look at me. "Well, it's not the one we want, niña. We need to go toward Cuernavaca."

"Isn't that the first place they'll look?"

"Yes, which is why we will veer off before we get there and go instead to Tepoztlán. I have family that can shelter us, and they will since I have *clacos*." Tacha thumped her chest with the palm of her hand, indicating where she had hidden her life's savings.

My thoughts were traveling along a different path. "Tacha, I need to go to San Gabrielín. Come with me."

"No! That's Nyman Vizcarra territory. We need to push on. When la patrona discovers we're missing, she'll send her two-legged hounds after us. We need to get to Tepoztlán."

"I can't, Tacha."

"You're going to Father Samuel, aren't you? Don't trust him, Isabel! He's one of them. They'll look for you there too and he'll turn you over to his mother. Ties of blood always win out."

"I have to risk it."

We argued under the impartial sky. Tacha growled her discontent but was not able to dissuade me. "I can't take the time to take you there, Isabel. In a few hours this road will be thundering with horses. I have to keep moving."

"I know. So this is where we must part company."

"How will you find your way in the dark?"

"There's plenty of moonlight to guide me." Far in the distance we could hear church bells tolling. "Do you hear that? Those are the bells of San Gabrielín. I'll just follow them to the town."

"You're making a big mistake. Come with me, Isabel."

For one terrible moment I almost agreed with her. Why *was* I putting so much trust in Samuel whom I hardly knew? Mistaking my silence for stubbornness, Tacha sighed. She opened up my bundle and added a second, smaller one. "Here's some food. The herbs are for your hair. Brew them like you were making tea. Make it dark. Let it cool just a little, then wash your hair with it if you want it to stay black." Making a kind of backpack with my shawl, she tied it around my shoulders and back. "All right. Go."

"Oh, Tacha, how can I ever thank you?"

We embraced one last time. "*Adiós, mi niña!* May the dear Virgin Mother forgive me and bless you always."

I cupped her face in my hands. "Goodbye, my lovely Tacha."

Fighting back tears, I watched my former tormentor vanish into the night. And it struck me once again how little we know the innermost soul of anyone. How often had I judged her to be a demon-in-the-making, and with good reason? Yet now I felt nothing but love, her harshness and collusion with Manuela Nyman—not forgotten—but truly forgiven. I vowed never again to judge anyone spiritually, no matter how vile they seemed, for who but God can know the true person? I set off along a narrow, unpaved road. Everything went well until clouds drifted across the moon, leaving me in near darkness. I kept going, arms outstretched in temporary blindness. Whenever I felt my skirt catch on brambles, I knew I had strayed off the path and corrected my course, guided all along by the distant bells of San Gabrielín. Groping my way, I could have felt my heart shrink. But I had my prayer and those bronze voices to steady me. I lost my focus only once. Letting my imagination run off the leash, I visualized la patrona waking up and sounding the alarm. Instantly, I stumbled to my knees. How often do we trip ourselves up with our own worst imaginings? Brushing myself off, I breathed deeply and began again. *Lord, Jesus Christ, have mercy on me, a sinner. Lord, Jesus Christ, have mercy on me, a sinner—*

～

Benjamín did not lack the resolve to hang himself. He needed only to jump off the table and let the rope snap his neck. He thought of his mother and felt a grim satisfaction, then a twinge of guilt. How could he do this to her? Yet wouldn't his suicide make her life easier? He reasoned. Wouldn't he be freeing her from the enormous expense of the bribery system? Yes, she would mourn him intensely, but she would move on with her life. She was strong. Of that he had no doubt. Samuel had his faith to comfort him, Eva, her daughters and her fashionable life. As for Rodolfo, perhaps this would bring about their reconciliation. Clearly, everyone would benefit in the long run, went the rationalization.

He thought of his other family—Volcán, Manco, Vago, and Caleb—and he felt genuine pity for them, especially for the three who had to go on enduring prison life, whereas he could finally escape into the void. All of these thoughts sped through his mind in seconds. He tested the rope one more time, letting it support the full weight of his body for a few seconds.

Tasi, a voice whispered in his head.

He slipped the noose around his neck. No prayers came to him. Instead he remembered something I had said the night that we eloped—that a good marriage does not end with death.

"If that's true I'll find you, Isa." Benjamín whispered as the night held its breath.

How perverse that my belief in the afterlife should be the very catalyst to push him into suicide.

Tasi! The word came to him again, more insistently.

Even as he remembered that it was the Tarahumara word for "no," Benjamín prepared to jump. Skeptic that he was, he crossed himself and solemnly kissed the cross that he made with thumb and index finger. Then he thrust his hands into his pockets to keep them from flailing.

A deep voice rushed at him like wind through a canyon. *Tasi mukúame!*

"Brujo!" Benjamín's hands flew up to the rope around his throat as he continued to balance precariously on the edge of the table. His eyes darted about the darkened room searching for the tall, willowy form of his friend. Though the warning had come in the Tarahumara language, he understood the command not to kill himself. There was no sign of Brujo, but two thoughts jogged alongside him now, challenging him.

What if there are many heavens, not just one? Have you learned enough, lived enough, to fit into *her* heaven?

"Brujo!"

A sudden dread took hold of Benjamín—not a fear of the preternatural. He would have welcomed seeing his friend just then, as ghost or man. What came to him instead was a dread of consequences that he had not considered. Could it be, was it possible, that by killing himself now, by tossing his life into the vast unknown, he might launch himself along a trajectory that would totally miss mine? The possibility terrified him.

"Damn it to hell!" Benjamín muttered in a broken voice, great tears streaming down his face. Other choice words erupted from his desperation. Yet they—and a shaman—led him to a different resolution on that crucial night. Freeing himself from the noose, he jumped down and leaned heavily against the table.

How do I get to your heaven, Isa?

The kingdom of heaven is within you, he remembered from childhood lessons long ago.

I have no kingdom, only ruins.

Grasping both sides of his head, Benjamín slumped to his knees. This time he prayed a more fruitful prayer: Oh God, I don't know if you are real or not. But if you are, please help me! Show me how to live, so I can find her someday.

102

MISA DE GALLO

THE BELLS OF San Gabrielín had stopped tolling. Fortunately, I no longer needed them to guide me. I found myself walking along the only paved road in the village. I should explain that despite my long imprisonment, I was not especially fatigued. After my captors started feeding me adequate meals, I had made it a point to exercise rather rigorously in my large cell, running and dancing to melodies in my head. It paid off. I reached San Gabrielin no worse for wear.

The entire village seemed both deserted and haunted by ghosts. Disembodied voices broke the silence, chiming responses in Latin. Everyone was inside the church where the *misa de gallo* was well underway. With a pang of regret, I realized that I had probably missed a midnight procession of Roman soldiers, shepherds, angels, wise men, and the holy family—a pageant that I had loved since childhood. Generous candlelight drew me inside the small colonial church. Remembering what Rosa had taught me, I dipped my fingers into a font with Holy Water and crossed myself. An old woman smiled as she handed me a candle. I must have stared stupidly, being so unaccustomed to interacting with people other than my jailors. When she lit my taper with hers, I managed to nod by way of thanks. Was I dreaming? What if I should wake and find myself alone in the cell? No, the press of people was real. Since every seat was taken, I joined the many who had crowded whispering and watchful along the side walls.

Several hundred candles suffused the church with a golden glow. And there he stood, Benjamín impersonating his brother! Of course, I knew it was Samuel. Yet for a few moments I needed to pretend that it was Ben so I could relish a rush of impressions: his tall, well-proportioned body; the eyes that would turn hazel when he stepped back into direct light; the manly cut of his jaw and his lips, those wondrous lips; even the familiar side part of his hair delighted me. I had to remind myself sternly that the man who was holding up his arms to heaven as he prayed could not possibly be Ben, my skeptic. Tell me, why do we persist in thinking that we know anyone at the deepest level? As for Samuel, little did I imagine how emotionally drained he was, even after he perceived that his twin's anguish had grown less acute and therefore less self-destructive.

Unaware of Ben's close brush with death, I continued to stare at my brother-in-law from the safety of my head covering and darkened hair, eyes caressing him as if he *were* Benjamín. Yet when Samuel glanced toward me, I cowered, afraid suddenly that his eyes might register surprise before I was ready to be recognized. Fortunately, he looked past me, no doubt too intent to notice an escaped prisoner trembling like flickering candle flame. When he gave us his back, which was most of the time, I focused on the people around me. Instantly I had a sense of déjà vu—an overload of impressions for my starved senses. It was like that day more than a year past when Cadwally had shown up unexpectedly, and I had been allowed to stroll in the gardens with him and the vigilant doña Manuela. Everything, from the humblest blade of grass to the emerald glint of the trogon's feathers, had overwhelmed me with its beauty. Now it was happening again in that small crowded church.

I was awestruck by the many faces in candle glow, all of them beautiful to me: old men and women with age-sculpted features, hair silvered by the many cycles of moon and sun and harvest, hands gnarled by long labor, and hearts gladdened by tradition upheld. I loved the young couples, their attention divided between the mass and each other, fingers entwined, lips smiling when not praying. Others were holding small children in their arms, or they were gently hushing those who fidgeted. And the children, especially the babies! Was there anything more wondrous in all the earth than eyes still bright with newness?

The Mass was coming to an end. Just before the recession, Samuel surprised me by addressing the crowd in Nahuatl. Blessing them, he offered up an ancient prayer that praises the Virgin Mother. That my brother-in-law chose to include it in the Christmas mass spoke to his knowledge of church history, his awareness that early efforts of evangelizing the conquered people had often made use of their languages. Yet in the early twentieth century when Latin was still the ruling language in church, this prayer in Nahuatl attested to his sensitivity for his parishioners' heritage. He was reminding them once again of the marriage of Aztec and Spanish cultures, a linking together that had merged the goddess Tonantzín with the Virgin Mary centuries ago. Thanks to Rosa, I was able to understand most of the words that Samuel tossed like confetti into the joyous crowd: "Her garments are like the sun, so that she shines in rays of resplendence. . . . And the mesquite, the prickly pear cactus, along with the other small grassy plants, are there adoring her; like the green plumes of the quetzal bird, like precious turquoise their coloring appears—"

Samuel caught sight of me just then and fumbled his carefully memorized Nahuatl. I am certain that he did not recognize me, but I did disconcert him. Clearly, I reminded him of the woman he believed he had buried. In that faltering, I realized how deep a wound I was going to inflict on him, and I could not bring myself to do it. Not yet. How could I bear the look on his face if I knocked on his door—I, a ghost in the flesh, and his mother whom he loved, a monster?

The Christmas procession that I had missed became a recession: Mary, who seemed to have lost her traditional burro, walked cradling her infant son with Joseph at her side. Roman soldiers with large *sombreros*, innkeepers, shepherds, a couple of stray dogs, and triumphant angels with straw wings, all filed out of the church to the drumbeat of Aztec *huehuetls* and *huilacapitzl* flutes. Above them tolled the bells of San Gabrielín, their bronze throats trumpeting the advent of Christ.

I hurried into the cool December night. Pausing on the church steps, I was keenly aware that I needed to prepare my brother-in-law for my presence. But how? I needed to think this out, beginning with where to spend the night. I had no home. No family. No friends. Church-goers poured through the doors. A well-dressed woman in a formal black suit and a white veil of exquisite lace brushed past me. The grocer's wife! I could have hurried after her, identifying myself as the young bride whom she had helped by letting me borrow her beautiful *mantilla* as a bridal veil. But how to do it without frightening her to death, for surely she must have heard of my decease? Aware that Samuel would step into the night any minute, I crossed the street and hid in a stable. To my surprise, it was empty. There were no horses or livestock of any kind, not even a few clucking chickens, only scatterings of hay and manure. Peering through a crack in the rough-hewn door, I saw Samuel hurry out of the church. He appeared to be searching the crowd and only half attending to his parishioners' greetings.

103

DEMONS

"She's dead!" doña Manuela told him again, boasting in the fog of a dream. Her triumph was a pyrrhic one. Holding a sharp blade to his left wrist, Benjamín cut a deep slit. "No, son! Don't!" she cried aloud, waking herself.

Sitting bolt upright, doña Manuela shuddered uncontrollably. Her heart hammered a strange rhythm, snagging her breath, tangling it as with wire. A cacophony of bird song blew through the open windows—a thousand singers all performing their own tunes at the same time without a thought to harmony. Yet the exuberant confusion from the aviary cleared her own confusion. It was just a dream, a nasty dream!, she chided herself.

Doña Manuela reached for her bathrobe, then rang for Tacha.

Yes, but the stillness, the awful stillness that came over him when I let it slip—Mother of God! What was I thinking!

She had scrambled to take it back, to laugh it off, her words spilling over Benjamín in a nervous torrent. But what had she said? She wondered desperately.

That Isabel might as well be dead. Something like that. But did he believe me?

She rang more insistently for Tacha. *That look on his face—it was irritation. Yes. That's what it was,* she told herself with each stroke of her hairbrush. *He's always annoyed whenever I attack his precious Isabel. I should have let her die when I had the chance.*

Manuela Nyman fell into her own stillness, her eyes wide with dread. *¡Madre santísima! What if he should find out about the funeral? He'll hate me for keeping it from him and then lying. Where is that Tacha!*

Benjamín's mother started down the hidden corridor to my cell. Before she could turn the key in the keyhole, the door swung open. *What ails Tacha!* She muttered. Then she noticed it—an emptiness that frightened her voice, shaking it as she called out my name. Had I escaped? No, how could that be? Doña Manuela felt a sharp pain in her head. Gripping the nearest wall, she struggled to understand. Was she inside or outside the cell? Flailing her arms, she managed to stagger back into the corridor.

Tacha! Who but Tacha could have helped her escape?

Doña Manuela made her way to the upper veranda. She wanted to call out to the servants, but her head ached as never before. Gripping the wide top rail, her body bent over it, she dragged and stumbled her way down the stairs and into the kitchen.

"Fetch Valle—Valle—!" she gasped to a startled servant girl, her words thick as mud. "Go!"

The administrator of the hacienda took his time answering the summons. Close to an hour later, Valle Inclán sauntered into the library.

"What kept you! Close the door," doña Manuela motioned, her words a little less thick now.

He obeyed, again without hurrying. Then he stood feet wide apart, hat firmly planted on his head—a stance he had adopted with her since killing my grandfather. The fact that she did not reprimand him for this impertinence spoke to the power of the dark secret that linked them. She was about to lay a second one at his feet. Valle Inclán listened, all the while wondering why the señora was slurring her words. Could she be hung over?

"Wait," he interrupted. "Are you saying the señora Isabel is not dead? Then who did we bury?" He asked, astonished.

"Rocks and a few bags of beans. It's time we buried her in earnest."

He was to find Tacha and me and kill us both, just as he, and he alone, had been entrusted to murder my grandfather. He could do as he pleased with Tacha's body. Mine he was to bring back and bury after nightfall in my supposed grave.

Valle Inclán noticed that la patrona's mouth drooped slightly on one side. A mild stroke? To play it safe, he demanded full payment in advance this time. He got half, along with something else that might prove useful in smoking me out: an intercepted letter of reconciliation that I had written to Benjamín long ago, along with a second letter that Ben had written to his mother a few years back.

"Copy his handwriting. Add it to Isabel's letter to lure her out. Write what you like."

Touching the brim of his hat, Valle Inclán left the room. Moments later, he mounted up armed with his whip, revolvers, the letters, and Manuela Nyman's promise to make him a very rich man.

There's no other way, she kept telling herself. *I can't have her turn up alive with nasty stories to tell.* The very possibility terrified her. *¡Dios mío! I must remember to fetch the wretched wedding ring out of my jewelry box and have Valle Inclán bury it with her.*

That same morning, el Volcán was led by three guards into a nearby cell. They were carrying clubs. His body tensed.

"I'm needed—I'm needed at the infirmary," he stammered.

"You're needed here."

He tugged for a moment on his beard, afraid to let them see that he was afraid. It was not his own fear that he encountered, but the look of stark terror on the face of another prisoner, a thin balding man. One of the wardens handed Mangel a club. "Soften him up."

"No, please!" the man pleaded. "My family will come up with the money. I promise you!"

"*Dale duro!*" Thrash him hard!

Mangel had obliged in the past, brutalizing fellow prisoners without any qualms. This time he felt his stomach tighten.

"Is this necessary?" He tried to smile. "The bastard is already scared shitless. He's yours without you having to lift a finger."

"Get out of the way, *cabrón!*" One of the guards shoved past him.

Mangel cringed as the man screamed in pain and terror. A second guard joined in the beating. Volcán yanked a club away from the third guard, striking him a vicious blow. Then he turned on the other two men, engaging them in ferocious combat even as reinforcements rushed through the door.

Caleb Wilkins, the little St. Johnny as he was called, had just arrived when prison guards dumped Mangel and the other prisoner on the floor of the infirmary. Volcán was covered in blood from the top of his head to his tattered shoes. The other man lay unconscious.

"Jesús!" the missionary gasped. "You!" he pointed to el Vago, who had just strayed in. "Get the doctor."

"He doesn't come on Sundays," Vago grinned though his lower lip trembled.

"I didn't let the demons back in!" Mangel cried like a child. "I didn't let them back in!"

"It's going to be all right, Jesús." Both knew that Caleb was according him the sacred name as a desperate salve. "Vago, help me get him to the bed!"

"No! Don't move me!" Mangel cried.

"Hold my hand, Jesús," the boy offered through his own tears.

"Don't call me that! I've trampled his name all my life."

"Don't talk. Rest." The missionary wanted to help the other man too, but he could not free his hand from Mangel's grip. "Vago, find el Paladín! Hurry!" The man on the floor was not moving. "Pray with me, Mangel." Caleb began reciting the Lord's Prayer. *"Padre nuestro que estás en los cielos, santificado sea tu nombre—"*

El Vago ran to Benjamín's cell. A guard was just unlocking it.

"Paladín! Come quick! It's—" Vago's voice trailed off as he stared at the noose dangling from the ceiling, and then at Benjamín who was asleep on the floor. "Paladín!"

Benjamín sat up and rubbed his face. The guard pointed to the noose. "What the hell is that?"

Ben rose, calmly brushing himself off. "That's for hanging my socks to dry."

The guard and el Vago stared at noose and man. Then Vago remembered his mission. "Hurry, Paladín. Volcán needs you. They've beaten the crap out of him!"

Benjamín and el Vago hurried to the infirmary. Mangel lay in a bed whose linens had not been changed from its previous occupant. Not that it mattered. He was bleeding profusely, creating puddles on both sides of the narrow bed. The other man was still unconscious.

"My God!" Benjamín clasped Mangel's flailing hand.

"Paladín!"

"I'm here."

"Some Spaniard wants you dead! He paid me to do it, but I told him to fuck off! I'm a piece of crap, Paladín!" He sobbed.

"Fetch Doctor Rodríguez Siqueiros!" Benjamín ordered the guard as if he were still an officer with privates to command. He remembered to add, "I'll make it worth your while."

The guard shrugged. "Go to hell! Mangel messed with my companions. He can damn well bleed to death for all I care."

"I'll go," Caleb offered.

Benjamín applied compresses to Mangel's numerous lac- erations. "Vago, do the same for him!" he motioned toward the other prisoner. "Like this, Vago!"

"I'm a worthless piece of shit!" el Volcán raved.

"No, you're not. Vago! Reach for more compresses!"

"I'm going to die without my true name—" Mangel's anguished voice trailed off. The wide, desperate eyes started to roll back into the head.

"Mangel! Mangel! Look at me!" Benjamín ordered him back from the precipice. "Do you know what your name means in English?" Ben had to think fast. Creatively. "*Hombre Angel*. Man Angel. You've had the right name all along!"

For a fleeting second light emanated from Volcán's dark pupils. Energy surged from his fingers as he pressed Benjamín's hand. Then he sighed and closed his eyes.

"Look at me, *Hombre Angel!* Look at me!" Benjamín insisted. The eyes opened reluctantly, puffy and glassy. "Mangel, don't you know that to become an angel you must first be a man—a good man? *Stay* and become that man. Stay and we'll figure this out together," he murmured, pressing Mangel's hand to his forehead.

104

TRUTH AND DENIAL

THAT SAME CHRISTMAS morning, I woke up feeling stiff, cold, and hungry in an empty stable. Sitting cross-legged on the ground, I opened the small bundle that Tacha had given me. Along with herbs for my hair, I found two *bolillo* rolls filled with mashed black beans, tomato and avocado slices that were no longer their earlier green. I devoured one roll and carefully wrapped up the other. Now I was thirsty and had no water. Should I leave my hiding place? Knock on Samuel's door now that it was daylight?

The church bell began to toll, urging parishioners to Mass. My thirst escalated. What to do but to endure, as Rosa would have urged?

No. Turn to doña Clemencia, the thought whispered. Drawing my shawl tighter, I headed for the general store that was attached to the stable. I knocked and waited, glancing nervously over my shoulder, then rapping a second and a third time. Finally, the grocer's wife opened the shutters of a window that fronted the street.

"What do you want?" she asked in the Castilian accent that I remembered. The voice that I had thought husky when I first met her, seemed greatly softened. Compared to Tacha with her oddly masculine growl-of-a-voice, doña Clemencia seemed, if not a soprano, at least a melodious mezzo-soprano.

"Please, may I come in and speak with you for a few moments, señora?"

"I'm sorry. I'm closed today."

I let the shawl slip to my shoulders and drew closer, allowing the woman to study my face. I could almost hear the questions. *Why does she look so familiar? And why does this Indian girl have such blue eyes and pale skin?*

"Come back later, *muchacha.* I don't want to be late for Mass." The woman started to close the shutters.

"Please, doña Clemencia. I'm so thirsty."

"How do you know my name? Do I know you?" She narrowed her eyes.

"Yes, señora, you do. Please, I must talk to you. It concerns Father Samuel."

She unbarred the door and admitted me into the dark, cool interior of the shop. Doña Clemencia had not changed since the night of my wedding. She was tall and hefty, a few defiant streaks of red nestling in her gray hair. She was probably the only other woman in the whole village, this Spaniard, who could afford a black taffeta dress. A rosary made from delicate crystal balls dangled from her belt, and the remembered veil from her right hand.

"What about Father Samuel?"

"Don't you remember me, doña Clemencia?"

She drew closer. On impulse, she draped her veil on my head. The rich lace with its scalloped edges cascaded gracefully to my shoulders and halfway down my back.

"It can't be!" she gasped. "You died!"

Doña Clemencia was late to Mass that Christmas morning. There had been simply too much to discuss: my elopement nearly two years earlier; the happy memory that she and her husband, don Gustavo, had stepped into the role of godparents when rousted out of bed by their priest; the startling fact that I had been imprisoned in San Serafín for over fifteen months and had finally managed to escape, and then the tragic revelation that a band of renegades, neither Zapatistas nor federales, had murdered don Gustavo simply because he spoke with a Castilian accent and they hated Spaniards. And wasn't life both dismal and wonderful? She asked, wiping her tears and hugging me.

We devised a simple plan on how best to deal with Samuel. That afternoon, when we calculated that we had given him enough time to fortify himself with his Sunday lunch, I headed to the empty church and doña Clemencia to his house. Her task was to tell him straight out that his sister-in-law was not dead; that the whole thing had been an elaborate hoax, and that he could see me for himself in the church where I was waiting.

I stood in the center aisle in front of the altar, keeping my back to him even when I heard him come in. The flame of the votive candles flickered with the sudden draft of air. His footsteps sounded hollow in the emptiness of the church—hollow and hesitant. He stopped halfway down the aisle. When he did not approach any closer, I turned toward him and saw in his face a spectrum of emotions, as if he were in the presence of a disembodied spirit both dreadful and wondrous.

"Who are you?" he gasped.

"You know who I am, Samuel."

"No. You only look like her," he muttered, his mind stubbornly clinging to the darkness of my hair and my peasant clothing.

"I'm Isabel," I insisted gently. When he shook his head and dropped his gaze to the floor, I switched to English. "Samuel, you married Ben and me here in this very church nearly two years ago."

His head shot up. "I gave you last rites! We buried you!"

"You buried an empty coffin."

"But I was with you to the very end!"

"Were you?"

"Yes—No—" He gripped the nearest pew, remembering that his mother had insisted that the end was near, and that he needed to leave my side to say the midnight Christmas Mass.

Samuel sank into the pew. His shoulders slumped as he clutched both sides of his head. His lips quivered in their search for a prayer that would address this moment. "*Santo Dios—Dios todo poderoso—Señor Jesucristo—,*" he gasped, unable to go any further. I drew closer. Only two pews stood between us now. I faced him silently, deeply cognizant of all that he was about to lose. He looked up at me, a spark of anger in his eyes.

"I want the truth. As you stand in the house of God, I exhort you to speak nothing but the truth!"

"I will, whether I stand here or out there."

Taking a deep breath, he motioned for me to proceed, bracing himself for the first incision without morphine, but I began with a confession of my own.

"I did try to claim the hacienda, as granted to me in your father's will. I thought I was acting within my legal rights. But I was wrong to allow others to oust your mother from her home, for which I am so very ashamed. I swear here before God that I thought I was acting on behalf of villagers whose lands your family—appropriated." I drew back from the word *stole*. "I tried to make amends to your mother by letting her come back. She, in turn, locked me in Emanuela's room for weeks."

"No. Wait a minute. I go home frequently. I would have known if you were locked in there." His eyes narrowed with suspicion. "She was worried about you. I remember calling to you to open the door and how pointedly you refused."

"Because I was tied up and gagged. That's right. Your mother and Tacha tied me up in the bathroom. Many days later, probably right after the funeral, they moved me into the cell that she built next to her bedroom."

"What cell? My mother turned my father's suite into a chapel."

"No. She turned it into a prison cell."

His mind must have been racing as he thought about the mysterious chapel and the fact that after she had it walled up, it could be accessed only through her bedroom.

"How long—how long did she—"

"Keep me prisoner? Four hundred and seventy-four days."

He flinched. Did the exactitude of my answer betray bitterness? I had hoped to be kind. He looked away. Was he grappling with the math? One year and how many months?

"Oh, Isabel! You must excuse my mother. She is not herself, not since Benjamín was beaten to within an inch of his life. I admit that she can be overly harsh sometimes." I could see that he was mortified, but he had not yet grasped the extent of her crime. "Don't forget that she also imprisoned Benjamín to keep him from joining the revolution."

"For a few weeks, not months."

"Yes—well, I can certainly understand that you must have despaired. But to deliberately starve yourself—"

"You think that I did *that* to myself? For weeks your mother fed me nothing but a little stale bread. One roll a day, to be precise. Toward the end she simply stopped feeding me altogether. I had to subsist on nothing but water."

"That's impossible."

"Oh, I assure you it is more than possible."

"You would not be the first young woman to try to kill herself over love gone wrong," he insisted with a single-minded stubbornness. "The failure of your marriage and problems with your lover must have overwhelmed you."

Did I stomp my foot? "Tomás Tepaneca was never my lover! But I could never make your mother understand that. So she punished me unmercifully."

"Yes. She overreacted. But can you blame her when the circumstances pointed to greed, collusion, and infidelity? You did run off with the very man who wrote that bogus will. Can you blame her for protecting—"

"I do not blame her anger. I blame her cruelty."

"Yet here you stand looking healthy again. Whatever disturbance, whatever it was that happened to my mother earlier to cloud her judgment, it's obvious that she resumed feeding you. Her actions may have been—" he groped with outstretched fingers for the right word, "extreme at times, and for that I apologize. But as you must admit, she is not without compassion."

"She locked me in a dark room and left me to starve! Don't you dare call that compassion!"

Did he remember my cadaverous face just then? "My God," he moaned.

Neither of us spoke for a long time. When he could finally bring himself to look at me, he spoke with utter weariness. "Why did you come to me?"

"Because I have no one else I can turn to. You can be sure that her henchman, that detestable Valle Inclán, will be out looking for me."

"He's hardly a henchman, Isabel. He's simply—"

"—the man who was ordered to *murder* my grandfather and then spread the lie that Zapatistas had killed him." My voice flashed a glint of steel.

"Why would he do that?"

"You'll have to ask your mother."

Samuel was jolted to his feet. Stepping out of the pew, he headed for the door. I hurried after him and grasped his arm tightly.

"I came to you for protection. Tacha warned me that you would hand me back to your mother, that blood runs thicker than water. Does it, Samuel?"

"I need to hear the truth from her own lips."

"Truth from *her* lips? Who told you that I was dead? Who gathered the whole hacienda together for my funeral?" I continued to hold on to his arm. "Please help me, Samuel. You *saw* what she did to me. Do you think that she wants anyone to know the truth about her abuse and the funeral that she faked? Don't you know in your heart that she will be scouring the countryside for me? If she could have my grandfather killed—"

"No! I'll never believe that!" he yanked free. "Yes, you've been wronged, Isabel, and for that I am so very sorry. Clearly my mother had become unhinged. But to accuse her of murder— What gives you the right to make such outrageous allegations?"

"My body—the body that she tortured for months; my funeral that she orchestrated and that you carried out, or have you forgotten that she deceived you too? The tomb that bears my name though you won't find my body there. But most of all, the terror in her face when I confronted her with the truth: that she had my grandfather murdered."

"She must have been appalled that you could make such an accusation."

"No, Samuel. She knew that I had discovered her crime, which is why she couldn't look me in the eye."

He slumped into the nearest pew, desperately massaging his brow as if to rub away the whole terrifying conversation.

"Oh Samuel, I know this is so very hard for you. Ask the Lord for the strength to cope with the truth. And understand once and for all: if your mother could bring herself to have my grandfather killed—"

"No," he shook his head. "Call her emotionally demented. Call her a liar if you will, but not a murderer. She would never sanction murder. Never!" His denial remained entrenched. He was a knight fighting on, his sword no match for the cross bows aimed at his heart.

"Believe what you will. Lie to yourself here before God if you dare. I am not afraid to speak the truth. Your mother had my grandfather killed. Maybe God can forgive her. I cannot. My escape poses the very real threat that I will expose her crimes, as I am doing now with you. Don't you see, Samuel, that she'll try to silence me? Will you stand by and let her further endanger her soul with a second murder?"

That got his attention. So I pressed on: "If not for my sake, then for the sake of her soul, will you protect me? I need for you to tell me here before God, are you first and foremost her child or *His*?"

"I know my duty."

"To whom? Are you clear about that, Samuel?"

"What do you want from me?" His fists were clenched, his voice both angry and despairing.

"Your solemn promise that you won't betray me to your mother or to anyone else. Let me stay here for a time. Hide me from that henchman of hers. Please, Samuel."

"I'll go see her today and call him off."

"It's too late for that. You can be sure that he's already out there looking for me."

"I'll have my mother recall him."

"How? Even if she agreed to it, how do we know that word would reach him in time not to kill me? Besides, if you confront her she'll deny everything to justify herself."

"Oh, for pity's sake, Isabel!"

"Precisely! For *pity's sake,* stay and protect me. You owe it to me Samuel, you and your whole family. After all that she's done to me, the very last thing that I want is for her to know where I am. Can you understand that? Can you?" I was growing increasingly agitated and afraid, because, you see, states of enlightenment come and go like light and shadows. I still had so much more to learn about trusting divine providence.

Samuel hung his head. After a long silence, he nodded and he made me a promise: I could stay in San Gabrielín under his protection, and he would not confront his mother until I felt ready for him to do so. He rose, signaling that our conversation was over, but I was not done yet. Struggling to regain my composure, I asked softly, "Is it true what Tacha told me, that Benjamín has recovered fully from the beating?"

A small smile escaped Samuel. "Yes."

"Oh, thank God!" I burst into tears. Samuel watched me. Was he surprised or was he trying to gauge my sincerity? Then I asked because I had to know: "Does Benjamín ever ask about me?"

"We'll talk about him later. Right now I need to walk you back to doña Clemencia's."

Hearing the tightness in his voice and seeing the tremor in his hands, I sensed that he desperately needed to be alone. He held the door open for me, his manner at once polite and brusque. It remained so when we stood before doña Clemencia. Dispensing with pleasantries, Samuel came straight to the point.

"Señora, would you allow my sister-in-law to stay with you until I can make other arrangements for her?" He spoke in a flat tone, as if he had not slept for days. The grocer's widow was watching him attentively.

"Of course, Father."

"I will pay for her room and board."

"There's no need for that. I'd be honored—"

He raised a hand and shook his head. "My brother's wife is my responsibility, not yours. I do need to ask for your indulgence in one more matter." He cleared his throat. "For now, we must keep her presence a secret. No one must know that she is here."

"You can count on my discretion, Father."

So it was arranged. Essentially, I was to be a prisoner in a homier prison and to be guarded by kinder guards. It wouldn't be long before I rebelled.

105

THE BOUNTY HUNTER

Ernesto Valle Inclán was an adept tracker. That Christmas afternoon, with the sun high above the *barrancas,* he was carefully examining track marks at a fork in the road. Yet he did not head to San Gabrielín, for it was obvious to him that the wagon had proceeded toward Cuernavaca. Further down the road he did note that the wheel marks had veered off.

Dead Face and the girl went to Tepoztlán, he reasoned, or they parted company and the girl is traveling alone to Cuernavaca. And why not? Even with her grandfather being dead, wouldn't she want to go back to the house to look for money, or clothes, or things of sentimental value? Besides, she must have friends—which could complicate matters—but not too much. She won't be able to hide for long, not in a small town.

The first thing Valle Inclán did on reaching Cuernavaca was to stable his horse. Traveling on foot the rest of the way, he reached Cadwally's front door with the lengthening shadows of afternoon. The door was locked, which was hardly an impediment. Going around to the back, he climbed the wall with its convenient toeholds and the jacaranda tree. Standing in the courtyard, feet wide apart, he listened for sounds of occupation. The house breathed emptiness. Thick dust coated everything, like a forest that reclaims an abandoned cabin. Empty bottles of *aguardiente* and *tequila,* their labels illegible under the film of dirt, were strewn about like the pages of a diary to prying eyes.

The old wino! Valle Inclán sniggered.

Whatever food the kitchen had once held had long since imploded on itself or been carried off by zealous ants. He did find a tin of spam hidden behind a curtain of spider webs. And why wouldn't the place have enough dust to choke a pig? He smirked. How long has the old gringo been dead now? Thirteen, fourteen months?

He sauntered into each of the rooms: Cadwally's bedroom with its sagging mattress, the small tiled bathroom, then up the stairs to the studio. Dozens of canvases listed against the walls, their vibrant colors muted in the dust-fog. The stylized people who inhabited the murals were more subdued now, silver-grayed. Valle Inclán paused in front of a painting perched on an easel. It was a mass of blue and gray tones swirling, churning, a work of abstract art but for one important detail—a soldier in blue uniform rendered with utmost realism, from the musket in his right hand to the buckles on his knapsack. The soldier stood in the foreground, his back to the viewer as he looked up, his cap perched far back on his head and seconds from falling off. All about him masses of blue and gray clouds rushed, roiling.

The bounty hunter shook his head. A monkey can paint better than this!

But I would have known right away that Cadwally was depicting a memory that had long haunted him. I was about ten or eleven years old the first time that he shared that memory with me.

"See up there?" Cadwally had rested a hand on my shoulder while pointing with the other at a massive formation of clouds that stretched from horizon to horizon. "Once, just before a battle when Blue and Gray were seconds from blasting away at each other, a flock of wild pigeons flew overhead. There were so many, millions upon millions of birds, that they completely blocked the sun. I'd never seen anything so terrifying and so wonderful!"

"What's so scary about pigeons?" I had challenged with a child's skepticism.

He didn't answer at first. When he finally looked into my upturned face, he seemed to be struggling for the right words. How to convey the power of a sound? Analogy would have to do.

"Isabel, you know the first time I took you to the train station here in town? Do you remember how frightened you were by the racket of the approaching train? I want you to remember the deep rumble as it rattled toward us. Can you hear it?"

I nodded.

"Good. No, no. That doesn't begin to describe it." He began to pace, distractedly twirling one end of his moustache until another analogy came to him. "You remember that time in the Tepozteco when we were caught in a storm? It came on so suddenly that we had to take cover in an abandoned shed. The roof was a sheet of corrugated metal. Do you remember how the rain and hail pummeled it, so loudly that you screamed?"

Yes. I remembered my panic. I had thrown myself on him and would have climbed inside his breast pocket if it were possible.

"The sound of those flocks of pigeons was even louder than that, a roar so intense that many of the men threw themselves on the ground. Mind you, these were battle hardened soldiers who had faced artillery shells without shrinking. Others dropped their guns so they could cover their ears."

"Were you scared too?"

"Yup, because we tend to fear the unknown. But then I stood up on that hilltop and just stared. By jingo, that was a sight to behold and to hear! Millions, maybe billions, of wild pigeons sped overhead like meteors. After a while some of the Rebs took off their caps and cheered them on. So did I, cheering though we couldn't hear our own voices. My God! I'd never seen anything like it. If there's a god, Isabel, that was Him drawing on the sky's blue canvas."

That was the one and only time that Cadwally ever spoke to me about God.

"What about the battle?"

"What? Oh, yes. We got around to it."

"Did you win?"

"I don't remember."

Yet he never forgot the blue meteors. Across the years I'd see him watching certain formations of clouds that would set him remembering and fashioning them into one of the last great flocks. Now, as the year 1912 edged toward its end, so too did his beloved passenger pigeons. In all the earth, there was only one left—one out of the billions that had haunted his imagination. She was imprisoned in the Cincinnati zoo where she would die on September 1, 1914. Oh, Earth! Did you weep at the whole-sale slaughter of birds in the skies and men in the trenches and fields of Europe? Did they not mirror each other, those killings on a scale never-before seen? And yes, the guns would finally be silenced after four years of slaughter. Soldiers would clamber out of the trenches. Nations would stagger to their feet again. But oh, the ravaged skies of North America! The wounded skies were robbed forever of their blue meteors. There would be no survivors. Not one passenger pigeon—only memories like Cadwally's.

Valle Inclán stood with hands on hips and hat tipped back. Even if he had known what he was looking at, I doubt that he would have sensed anything mystical about those vanished flocks, sharing as he did the world's indifference and the greed of opportunism. Grabbing a brush whose bristles had petrified into immobility, he affected to improve Cadwally's painting. When the bristles refused to yield any paint, he tossed the brush across the room. And standing there in the space that most aptly described his victim, he reviewed the murder as dispassionately as he analyzed his moves after every hacienda rodeo. With the pride of championship, he remembered the exact toss of the lasso around my grandfather's neck; the quick looping of it on a thick branch; the spurring of Cadwally's mule so that it lifted my grandfather clear off the saddle, and the sharp snap of the neck.

Stepping out of the studio, my grandfather's killer headed for my room. The Dutch door amused him. Pretending that I might actually be crouching in a corner, he flung open the upper door and peered in, doffing his hat with a gallant gesture.

"*Muy buenos días,* doña Isabel!" He greeted with his heavy Castilian accent.

He knew, of course, that the room was empty. Kicking open the lower half of the door, he let himself in. One entire wall had built-in cubbies, each filled with some childhood treasure. Reaching into one, he pulled out a doll, a skeleton dressed in a pale blue dress. Conchita smiled her toothy grin. Tossing her into a corner, he dropped onto my bed. Cupping his hands behind his head, Valle Inclán settled down to wait for me.

106

GUARDIANS

THAT SAME CHRISTMAS day Dr. Rodriguez Siqueiros, a longtime friend of the Nyman family, was able to stabilize Jesús Mangel and Rómulo Pérez, the other prisoner. Standing over Mangel as he wiped his hands, the doctor marveled.

"The man is strong as an ox."

Mangel had suffered broken ribs, but the real damage had been inflicted by a cudgel fitted with a point, sharp as a razor blade. Dr. Siqueiros lost count of the stitches after the hundredth one, compared to the twenty-two of the other victim. The wounds of both men would heal with time. The possibility of internal injuries, on the other hand, posed a more serious threat, particularly for Mangel who had been beaten far more severely than his companion. Both patients would need to be kept under observation. Benjamín assured him that he could stay with them until lock down. Paying the doctor, on the other hand, would not be nearly as easy. The family attorney who normally delivered funds had not been to the prison and was not likely to make his monthly appearance now or at least until after New Year's.

"I must apologize, Doctor. We will, of course, pay you."

"I can wait, don Benjamín," the good doctor smiled. "But I do hope that you will give yourself some rest." His attention had switched to Ben's haggard face.

"Rest? Prisons are as noisy as rookeries," Benjamín smiled, hands in pockets.

"Yes, I suppose so. Well, Merry Christmas, don Benjamín."

"Doctor! A question. Is it very painful to die of starvation?"

The physician narrowed his eyes. "Initially, yes, and less so toward the end when lethargy sets in. Do you see much of that here?"

"What? No."

"Well, Merry Christmas."

Benjamín spent the day in the infirmary at Mangel's bedside, in effect the guarded guarding the bodyguard who slept through it all. When Manco offered to take over for him, Ben shook his head. "No. It's Christmas. Take the day off." Manco hesitated. "Go on. Vago already has the jump on you. Sit this one out."

Alone with the sleeping patients, Ben spent that Christmas grieving over me and tormenting himself by imagining how I had died.

Starved to death! God in heaven!

He had to keep brushing away tears. Often they were quicker than his hands. Later that night when he was back in his cell, exhaustion and despair whispered: There *is* no God. You only prayed because you were terrified of never seeing her again. That's what drove you to your knees, but fear does not make God real.

He thought about Mangel's religious conversion. It had burst suddenly, like a meteor that makes a tear in the night sky. He remembered the groaning and the sobbing that they all mistook at first. For illness? For black comedy? And then the shock on realizing that Mangel's emotional outburst was real. And didn't he leave the room that day of his conversion a different man? What could have changed the most notorious bully in the prison so completely that he let himself get beaten up rather than betray—what? A mere illusion?

Seconds before the lights were shut off in the cells, Benjamín glanced up where the hangman's noose had dangled the night before. A new thought struck him: Could it be, was it remotely possible, that Mangel with his vast store of ignorance and brutality, had perceived what he, Benjamín Nyman, with all his education and poetic soul, had not?

That night Benjamín dreamed that he was home in San Serafín, climbing the stairs by threes. The house was dream-distorted, but he recognized his old room easily enough. Opening the door, he felt a chill all the way to his fingertips. Samuel was standing on his desk, a noose around his neck. He turned to look at Ben for a moment. Then he leaped.

"No, Samuel!"

Running up to his brother, Benjamín struggled to support him by the legs. "Not you! Not you! Someone has to believe!"

Benjamín woke up in a cold sweat. And once again he found himself on his knees.

God in heaven. I don't know who or what you are, but I trust *them*—Samuel, Isa, and even Mangel. I don't know what to do with my skepticism and my yearning. I don't know how to love you. But this much I do know. I love *them*. Please protect them. Let my love for them be my prayer to you.

That same night Valle Inclán had a dream of his own. It came after a day of fruitless waiting. Since I didn't seem in any hurry to go home and be strangled, he had idled away the long hours eating what food he had brought with him, scrounging up half a bottle of *aguardiente* from under Cadwally's bed, and using the men and women in the murals for target practice. Not wanting to make noise with his revolver, he had contented himself with his knife until the blade grew dull. Using the sharpening stone that he found in our kitchen, he then took aim at the furniture. Shadows lengthened. Sunlight dimmed. Night came on. Acting on the chance that I might creep into the house under the protection of nightfall, he returned to my room, carefully leaving the upper half of the Dutch door open.

Nothing stirred that night, not even the birds in the treetops. The late December air chilled just enough that he draped my old comforter around his shoulders. Though he had meant to stay awake, Valle Inclán succumbed to sleep like human and beast alike. He dreamed about an old man dangling on the end of a rope, his legs twitching as he choked to death. I suppose it was meant to be Cadwally, but he looked different in the dream—different yet unmistakable. The old man suddenly stopped struggling. Reaching into a pocket, he pulled out a long Bowie knife and cut himself free. Then with supernatural strength he leaped at Valle Inclán.

The bounty hunter was startled awake, not just by the nightmare, but by a sound. Was someone walking in the upper corridor? Sitting up, he looked through the open half of the Dutch door. In the gloom of a night lit only by a moon not quite ripe, he thought he saw a figure, tall and lank. It was standing outside the studio at the top of the stairs blocking his escape—a man with white hair, a man who turned slowly and stared directly at him. The formidable *señor administrador* of San Serafin slammed the upper door shut with a deep groan.

A MESSENGER

Morning brought calm in her sturdy arms. Daylight murmured that he had dreamed the specter. Or maybe some homeless person had let himself into the abandoned house for the night. Yes, that made more sense, Valle Inclán told himself. A vagrant. Just the same, before creeping softly past the studio, the bounty hunter unholstered his gun. The moment he reached the stairs, he hurried down to the patio. And though he refused to run, he wasted no time in leaving his victim's house. Leaving the door ajar, he left it to rattle in the wind. My sweet Rosa noticed it later that day and closed the door with a deep sigh. How she mourned my grandfather and me! Valle Inclán, on the other hand, had walked briskly down the steep hill, rubbing the back of his neck as he wondered, *What now? Tepoztlán?*

He knew it was Tacha's hometown and therefore the next most likely place for me to be hiding. He also knew better than to venture into such a nest of revolutionaries, he with his hated Spanish accent. Everyone had heard the stories of hacienda administrators being strung up or nailed to the front door of the plantations they ran. No. He wouldn't risk going to Tepoztlán himself, but he could send a messenger. In fact, he could distance himself, Castilian accent and all, by hiring someone who in turn would hire the messenger. Finding men to do his bidding would be easy enough. Qualifications? Hunger and unemployment. His first messenger was a fugitive from Guerrero with a family to feed. The second one was a farmer who had lived a few kilometers from Tepoztlán before federales torched his village.

There were delays. The first messenger got lost. Guerrero was not Morelos. And the second messenger, a man who had lived near Tepoztlán, could not find anyone who fit my description. So he searched instead for 'the woman with the dead face.' After more inquiries, he found Tacha standing outside a hut rubbing the small of her back. The sun was just starting to scale the steep hills, spilling orange and pink above the treeline.

"Are you the midwife Tacha?" the messenger asked, his eyes shifting from her face to the ground.

"I can't come with you. I'm in the middle of delivering a baby."

"I'm looking for the señora Isabel Nyman. I was told to come to you."

She swooped down on him, her eyes narrow slits, her nose almost touching his. "Who are you?" She rasped in her masculine voice.

"Juan—Juan Pérez Rubio, *pa' servir a usté.*" He took two steps back. She stepped forward.

"What do you want with her?" Tacha's voice must have intimidated him as much as her stone features.

"I have—I have a message from her husband."

"What's the message?"

"I—I need to give it to her myself."

She held him in the grasp of her skepticism a few seconds more, then turned to go back into the hut.

"Please! I just need to tell her that her husband has escaped and is in hiding. I can take her to him if you'll just—"

Tacha swung around to face him. "Prove that you're telling me the truth. Prove it!"

Unnerved by her ferocity so at odds with the utter blankness of her face, he almost forgot the proof that he carried tucked in his shirt. Feeling its contour against his now sweaty chest, he reached for it and held it out to Tacha, like a white flag in a battlefield. Struggling to steady his voice, he managed to remember his lines: "This is a letter that she wrote to her husband. He's carried it with him ever since. And see here at the bottom? He's written a message to her and signed his name."

Tacha snatched the letter from his hand and studied it. She couldn't read but wasn't about to admit it. Neither could the messenger who was simply following instructions. In truth, the letter *was* mine. As I learned later, Ben never saw it. Doña Manuela had intercepted it, keeping it locked in a desk drawer with all my other letters.

While waiting for me in Cadwally's house, Valle Inclán had added a message, carefully copying Ben's handwriting from the second letter. Perhaps because Tacha could see two distinct hands at work, or because she had been up all night with her midwifery, or because she was too proud to admit her illiteracy, she allowed herself to be hoodwinked.

"She's in San Gabrielín. Talk to the village priest. He—"

A woman in labor cried out just then, ripping the conversation like paper. Tacha vanished inside the hut. The second messenger reported to the first one, and that one, the man from Guerrero, reported to Valle Inclán.

San Gabrielín. Of course! The bounty hunter would have set off that very day, much as he was enjoying his stay in the best hotel in town. But Ernesto Valle Inclán was as mortal as the next man. Having eaten tainted meat from a street vendor, he had to fight for his life for a number of days before he could think of taking mine.

108

REFUGEES

THE DAY AFTER Christmas stretched endlessly, like a desert without hills. As I listened for Samuel, minutes died a slow death. Hours became epochs. Glaciers formed. Tucked away as I was in the house behind the grocery store, I could hear the occasional tinkle of a bell as customers opened or closed the shop door. I could hear their chatter, a sea-murmur of indistinct words, but not a hint of Samuel's voice. When would he return? He had promised to talk to me about Benjamín. Why, then, the long, agonizing delay? Had he betrayed me? Had he sent word to his mother? No. Samuel Nyman was a man of his word, I insisted to myself. So I waited in the gloom of doña Clemencia's house, a small one-bedroom cottage. The little parlor had to double as guest room. Since her love seat was far too small for my tall frame, I slept on blankets on the floor. I didn't mind a bit. If anything, my incarceration had taught me to prefer a hard mattress to a soft one, and the floor to any mattress.

At lunch time doña Clemencia hurried in to offer me a simple *comida* of rice and beans. No, the padre had not visited the shop, she told me. That evening she commented that no one had seen him all day. Had my revelations cut him so deeply? Doña Clemencia and I ached for him. Two days into my own confinement I also ached for me.

Much as I appreciated doña Clemencia's hospitality, I was like a dog tugging at its leash, yearning to break free. Early on the morning of the twenty-seventh, while my hostess snored softly in her room and the day bathed itself with dew, I tiptoed across the small patio behind the shop. Ever so quietly, I slipped into the grocery store and let myself out, knowing that I would be locked out. No matter. I had to feel the sun full on my face, to walk swinging my arms if I so chose, and to kick small stones into flight.

The sun was still trapped behind the hills, so the night's chill lingered a bit longer. No matter. I draped my *rebozo* around my shoulders and headed into the new day. Oh, the birds! Was that a mockingbird joining the chorus, sweeping in and out like a virtuoso soloist? I started down the street and happily sent a pebble into low flight. Almost immediately I came to an abrupt standstill. What had happened to the village? It was not quite the way I remembered it from my wedding, or even from my arrival on Christmas Eve. In daylight, dozens of makeshift shacks emerged clearly. Some people were sleeping with nothing more than a piece of burlap for a roof; others had found shelter under a hat or a shawl. And the litter! When had San Gabrielín become so squalid—and so silent? I cocked my head to listen for the ubiquitous roosters and chickens of every town. Not a sound. And where were all the horses and donkeys, for that matter?

Moments later I stood across the street from Samuel's house, a two-story structure with a flat roof. Architecturally, it was unremarkable—the ubiquitous Mexican home built of cement and stone and encircled by a high wall. Here in the humble village of San Gabrielín it seemed a mansion. I remembered Benjamín's observation that his mother had built the house for Samuel even though he would have preferred living in a simple cottage with a thatched roof—or a monk's cell for that matter. Yet Samuel had acquiesced to his mother's wishes. Was he always that way? How would he handle the crisis of my sudden appearance? Would he bend the knee to her will once more? Would he—Good grief! What was that thing sticking its head out the window?

Shielding my eyes from the sun that had just climbed above the tree line, I squinted up at the second floor of Samuel's house. A mule with jaunty ears stared back at me. With his upper lip curled back, he seemed to be giving me a toothy grin. I burst out laughing. "Well, good morning to you, *señor Mula*."

I knocked on Samuel's door. No answer. After several more tries, I walked on. Villagers began to emerge. People on the street—refugees, as I would soon learn—began to shake out blankets and shawls. Some people carried clay jugs to fill with water from the well in front of the church. Others headed for fields that they farmed communally. Some of the women carried bundles of laundry to a nearby creek. And some, I was glad to see, were busy sweeping up the street with makeshift brooms— thick branches with smaller ones lashed to them. Every single person that I passed along the way greeted me with a nod or a cheerful *buenos días*. It was all I could do to keep from gawking, my hunger for human companionship bordering on rudeness. People! How glorious to be among them again! I drank it all in with the gulps of a deep thirst. When I came to the end of the one street in town, I sighed and turned back. Yet how could I bear to incarcerate myself inside doña Clemencia's house? Making my way instead to the church, I entered its walled garden.

The church garden was minuscule compared to the ones in San Serafín—an acre at most. Instead of expansive velvet lawns, it was crisscrossed with narrow paths paved in earth-colored gravel. Sprinkled along the winding paths were a few flower beds, several large fig trees and a majestic old sycamore. Thick green vines cloaked the garden walls. And there on a stone bench sat Samuel, elbows on knees, eyes fixed on the ground. I coughed. He jumped to his feet. For a moment he reminded me of Benjamín that dreadful day that I visited him in his cell. He had looked far more surprised than pleased. So now Samuel.

"Should you be out and about?" my brother-in-law asked without preamble.

"I won't stray far."

He had the disheveled, sagging look of someone who has not slept. "Do you need anything?"

"No, thanks. Yes. Samuel, did I see a mule at one of your windows or did I imagine it?"

He gave me a crooked smile, and I felt emboldened to sit alongside him on the bench. "That was don Pepino, as the villagers call him. He too is a refugee, the last of his breed here."

"Why is that? And where are all the other animals?"

"Serving the nation. Pepino and I were in San Serafín when a detachment of federales helped themselves to all the mules and donkeys in San Gabrielín. A week later some unnamed rebels without a cause had cause to appropriate all the chickens, roosters and goats in the village, for how else were they to help the people of Morelos?"

"They couldn't have been Zapatistas."

"No, I suppose not. They at least seem to be fighting for the pueblos. No, these others were just shameless bandits."

After a pause I asked the question that mattered most to me: "Please, does Benjamín ever speak of me?"

Samuel, who despised lies, chose his words carefully. "*Speak* of you to me? A little."

He seemed to prefer the sin of omission to the sin of lying. His motive was straightforward. Before handing over Benjamín's manuscript that spoke extensively about me, my brother-in-law needed to decide: was I purely a victim or the guilty cause of my victimhood? That I may have been responsible for his mother's moral deterioration hardened him against me to the point that he could barely stand to be in my presence. He seemed anxious to leave. I detained him with another question.

"Samuel, does Benjamín still think that Tomás Tepaneca and I—" I hated the very words. "Does he think we were lovers?"

"Were you?"

"No! A thousand times no!"

"Then why was the man so devastated at your grave?"

"He was at the funeral?"

"No. I came across him long afterwards. He was sobbing and clutching your tombstone."

"Ah, Tomás," I murmured, stricken at the thought of his pain.

"Now, if you'll excuse me." Samuel rose, using the courteous phrase dismissively.

"No, we need to talk. Why can't any of you understand that I love Tomás like a brother and only like a brother? We grew up together, played together, ate together. His mother is the only mother I have ever known. So to all intents and purposes, he is my brother."

"Well, he doesn't seem to love you quite like a sister. His anguish was too extreme, too passionate. Do you deny that the man is in love with you?"

"No, but that does not make me guilty of adultery, only of hurting him by my rejection. Shouldn't you of all people pity him?"

"Pity Tomás Tepaneca?" Samuel's hands flew to his hips. "Whatever that man is to you, lover or brother, he has sworn to burn down San Serafín and to destroy my family. No. I do not pity him."

I was too shocked to respond. Samuel stomped off, entering the church through a side door. My stomach was churning because I believed Tomás was all too capable of carrying out his threat. I had to find him and set him straight. But how? I didn't dare leave San Gabrielín yet. I knew intuitively that Valle Inclán was out there somewhere, waiting to drag me back to San Serafín, or worse, to kill me. For pity's sake! Was I doomed to go through life inspiring men to murder me?

Lord, please help me! I cried inwardly.

My face had grown hot. The gentlest of breezes rustled the leaves overhead, large sycamore fans with cooling touch. Almost imperceptibly, then ever more surely, I felt the rustling of the Hesychast prayer as it breathed for me, with me, in and out, in and out. And I understood again what my imprisonment had taught me: that praying was not about having our way in the world, this transient world, but about strengthening our spirit. Those formidable mountains of Christ that we're supposed to be able to move by prayer and belief—are they literal mountains of earth and stone, or metaphors for *spiritual* obstacles, massive as mountains? Not my will but Thine be done. So I prayed that morning for spiritual strength to live that day well. I even tried to pray for doña Manuela and Valle Inclán, for weren't they also children of God who had strayed onto hazardous paths? Weren't they to be pitied for surrounding themselves with hellish spirits?

I told myself that if Valle Inclán *were* to kill me, then so be it. He could only destroy my body, not my soul. So why fret? Yes, but would it be terrifying? And would it hurt? Stop thinking about it! My job, I reminded myself firmly, was to take common sense precautions and to have faith that whatever happened, even my murder, God would turn to good purposes. In the interim between now and my death—whether that happened soon or in my dotage—I needed to make myself useful in the world. But doing what? Of what use was I to anyone?

Well, I could begin by returning to the shop to reassure my hostess that no harm had come to me. Then I could start repaying her kindness by sweeping the floors and doing her laundry or any other task she cared to give me. Yes, that made so much more sense than fretting about the future with its gray-faced phantoms.

I opened the garden gate just as Samuel stepped out the front entrance of the church. Both of us came to an abrupt standstill, our attention fixed on a woman who was dragging a goat cart piled high with bundles. Two little girls walked alongside her, all of them dressed in rags. A third child slept on top of the bundles. Samuel should not have been surprised at the sight of another desperate refugee fleeing with her children. Yet, when the woman paused to wipe her brow with the back of her arm, did he and I both gasp her name?

109

TERESA

TERESA GAMA! I took a step back, hoping to retreat into the garden before she noticed me. How could I face the woman whom Rodolfo had betrayed and discarded in the hope of marrying me? That I had known nothing about her until the day, the awful day that Eva brought us together, did nothing to lessen my rising sense of awkwardness. Fortunately, Teresa had not seen me yet. Her attention was fixed on Samuel. Before he reached her, she clasped her hands together and gasped, "*Padre!* Please help us!"

And of course, he did. While he led them down the street to his house, I ducked into doña Clemencia's store. It did not surprise me to learn shortly afterwards that Samuel had turned his house over to them and himself out of it. After all, legitimate or not, were they not Rodolfo's children? While he was at it, Samuel reasoned that he also had a moral obligation to me as Benjamín's wife, whether or not I deserved such consideration. He had not yet made up his mind about me, but he was quick to embrace duty. So after installing Teresa and the children in his home, he headed to doña Clemencia's store.

"You know that your sister-in-law is welcome to stay in my humble house as long as you say, Father," my hostess objected, her Castilian accent lisp-like to my ears, with th's replacing all s's and z's.

"I appreciate your kindness, doña Clemencia, but there is no longer any need for us to impose on you. Isabel will now be sharing my house with my brother's—"

He wanted to say *wife* but could not bring himself to lie. Neither could he denigrate Teresa by allotting her the title of *discarded mistress.* I hurried to fill the breach and to save myself.

"I don't mind sleeping here on the floor," by which I meant, *please don't make me live in the same house with Teresa Gama,* not because I blamed her in any way, but because I could not shake my sense of guilt, guiltless as I was.

"Is there room for everyone, padre?" our grocer asked.

"Once Pepino and I move out, yes."

"There's no need," I tried again. "I really don't mind sleeping on the floor."

"But where will you live, Father?"

"There are two empty classrooms in the school. Pepino and I will be quite comfortable there."

"I actually prefer the floor to a bed," I tried yet again. "So I'm fine right here."

Samuel finally looked at me. "That may be, but it's time we relieved your hostess of further inconvenience."

It was arranged. Of course, he first had to muck out the guest room that don Pepino was occupying. Since Samuel was fastidious and cleaned it two or three times a day, it didn't take long to prepare it for me. The barn-like scent would linger for days, but I didn't mind it half as much as Teresa's reaction on being reintroduced to me.

"I believe the two of you have already met, so introductions are not necessary." Samuel made a half-hearted attempt to adopt a light tone. Actually, I think he was even more uncomfortable than I. Teresa's eyes narrowed as she inspected my darkened braids and peasant dress.

"It's you," she murmured.

"Yes. It's me," I answered with a definite lack of imagination, fingering one of my braids. "I had to color my hair in order to—" I caught myself, but not before Samuel's face flamed and I began stumbling over my words. "I had to escape, that is, that is, I'm a refugee too."

My fumbling explanation did not keep Samuel from hurrying out the door any more than it erased Teresa's scowl. Taking hold of her children, she herded them up the stairs. Moments later, she closed the door to her bedroom, keeping the children in and me out. Two of the village men carried her sewing machine up the stairs, and Samuel's library to the school, basket-load by basket-load, over a two-hour period. I, on the other hand, with nothing but one change of clothes and a book, was able to move into my new residence in a matter of minutes.

The only one who was pleased with the arrangement was Samuel who finally had his monk's cell. Teresa, who had been careful not to mention the rape to any of us, considered my presence in such close quarters one more indignity to be endured. Throughout that first day, she pointedly avoided me. When our paths crossed outside the bathroom, she sidestepped to let me pass, as if we were strangers occupying the same sidewalk. Her children, who must have been under strict orders to have nothing to do with me, walked past me with eyes obediently fixed on the floor. Only the little boy peeked up at me. He was all eyes and chubby cheeks, making me break into a big smile every time I saw him. That evening I sat alone in Samuel's dining room while Teresa had supper upstairs with her children.

The next day I rose with the first light and went for a walk. Then I read in the church garden for an hour or so. When I returned to my room, I dragged a chair to the window that had framed the mule only the day before. There was a knock on my door. Opening it, I found myself gazing into the upturned face of Teresa's little boy. The rags were gone. Dressed in a smart sailor suit and with his hair slicked back with brilliantine, he made me think of Rodolfo as he must have been at that tender age.

"This is for you." The child held out a bundle. "The lady who talks funny told me to give this to you."

I knew he meant doña Clemencia. I crouched down to his level. "Thank you. What's your name?"

His small shoulders shot up once by way of answer.

"Don't you know your name?"

"I'm not *asposed* to talk to you."

"Ah. Well then, you'll have to whisper," I murmured ever so softly. "What should I call you?"

"*Borreguito*," he whispered back. Oh, he was a lambykins all right. "You know what?" he added a little louder. "I have another name too. *Wodolfo,* like my daddy."

Again, I could see the father's face in his son's rounder, softer features. And for a moment I felt a stab of envy. Would I ever have a child of my own? Would I have to endure nothing but privation? Teresa stepped into the hallway just then. Faster than a hawk protecting its young, she swooped down on her child and hustled him down the stairs. The little girls hurried past me, their gaze dutifully fixed straight ahead. I endured the shunning for about thirty seconds more. Then I followed them downstairs.

"Señora, we must talk." I addressed Teresa respectfully. She had her back to me as she set about to light the stove.

For all the modern touches that Samuel's mother had put into the house, including plumbing, the stove was a quaint wood-burning affair like the one that Cadwally and I had used back home. Teresa kept her back turned. I waited, knowing she could not stare at kindling all morning. I noted that she too had traded yesterday's rags for a beautifully tailored skirt and waist trimmed in lace. Like Tomás, Teresa fiercely believed that the clothes make the man—or woman. When she finally turned to face me, she took up a defensive posture, arms crossed and lips pressed into a tight line. She reminded me of a hibiscus bloom at dusk. You know it was lovelier when it first unfolded to the morning sun, yet it still retained traces of vibrant color.

"Señora, we are not enemies, you and I." Why not come straight to the point? "We were lied to, both of us. As God is my witness, I did not know about you and the children until that awful day at the Bella Vista, when Eva brought us together. Please believe me."

Though Teresa Gama was much smaller and shorter than I, she projected more strength than I felt at that moment. Tipping back her head, she gave me a hard look. After an eternity, she nodded.

"I believe you, señora."

"Isabel. Please call me Isabel."

The crossed arms and scowl told me we were far from forging a friendship or even a purely diplomatic alliance. However, when she grudgingly allowed me to help her make breakfast, I knew that she had withdrawn the border guards from the wall that she had built between us. We sat at table together, the children glancing uneasily from their mother to their plates. I sailed into a silent sea.

"You may remember that we met a little over two years ago," I commented to the children.

"At a westwant!" little Rodolfo crooned.

"Yes, that's right! What a good memory you have. How old are you now?"

He spread out the fingers of his right hand and held up a sixth finger with a mischievous grin.

"No, you're not!" His sister Laura's rebuke came quickly. "He's still five. I'll be ten in two and a half weeks."

"Then we must celebrate that." Smiles were melting the ice. "And you?" I turned to the oldest child, a demure girl who looked so much like her mother. "Teresita, right?"

"She's twelve," her sister rushed to inform me. "How about you?"

Teresa Gama rapped on the table with her palm. "That isn't a polite question."

"Why not? Isabel asked us our ages?"

"Mrs. Nyman," Teresa corrected.

"Oh, call me Isabel."

"*Señora* Isabel," Teresa looked firmly around the table.

I suddenly realized that I was the children's aunt. Orphan that I was, I had a family at last! One look at Teresa warned me to tread carefully. Illegitimacy. Social classes—oh, hang them both!

"I'm your Aunt Isabel. Call me *tía* Isabel."

"*Tía! Tía!*" little Rodolfo clambered. Teresa would have no choice now. She would have to drop her defenses and call me by my first name. Is that what she was mulling over so seriously? Lambykins jumped down from his chair and rushed to my side. "*Tía*, did you like your *pwesent*?"

"My present? Oh, yes. Doña Clemencia was kind enough to give me two dresses that she no longer needs," I explained all around.

The next day I came to breakfast in one of doña Clemencia's cast off gowns. The shoulders hung halfway down my arms. "I know it's a little big."

Teresa's laughter burst free from its cage. "About four sizes too big!"

Because she continued to laugh, and the children and I joined her so eagerly, Teresa began to accept me. That I had embraced her children so readily also helped her to forgive me. The world, on the other hand, she regarded with mounting suspicion. As I was to learn, she kept a revolver carefully hidden from the children but fully available to her anxious musings.

Lying in bed that night and many nights afterward, I would hear the distinct snap of the chamber as she loaded and unloaded it, again and again.

110

WHENCE EVIL?

Samuel had his own obsessive musings. What could explain his mother's abuse of me but a complete mental breakdown? Or perhaps she was suffering from some dreadful pathology that crippled her judgment? He could not deny that I had been made to suffer terribly. Yet he could not help wondering how much of that suffering I had brought on myself. Didn't my own nefarious role exculpate his mother to some extent? But how to excuse her brutality? He was so absorbed in this thorny problem that he did not notice me sitting in the church garden.

"Good morning," I spoke in English, looking up from my reading.

He approached hesitantly as if weighing his options: to escape into the church or to practice civility. "Good morning. I trust everyone is comfortable at the house?" His English was as fluent as Ben's.

"Yes indeed. We can't begin to thank you for your generosity, Samuel." He shrugged it off, as if handing over one's comfortable home to go live in an empty classroom with a toothy-grinned mule were an everyday occurrence. "Please thank don Pepino for giving up his room to me. He's being such a good sport about it."

Samuel gave a short laugh. "The mule should have offered it sooner." He drew closer, his tall form momentarily blocking the sunlight. Sitting beside me on the bench, Samuel smiled such a sad smile, so like Benjamín, that I had to suppress a sudden urge to hug and kiss away his sorrow.

"What have you got there?" his gaze shifted to the book on my lap.

"Swedenborg's *Divine Providence*."

"May I?" He fanned the pages. Then he turned to the table of contents. "Now why on earth would a young woman want to read something like this?" He handed it back.

"Why not? Do you imagine that only men care about such things? Didn't Sor Juana Inés de la Cruz and Teresa de Avila hold their own with the best theologians of their time?"

He put up his hands and laughed. "*Mia culpa!* What I mean is, why are you reading *this* particular book? Wouldn't Swedenborg's *Heaven and Hell* offer more dramatic reading?"

"You know the work?"

"Portions. I came across it in seminary, though it was not in the curriculum. So why this book?"

"The truth is I didn't choose it. It was an unwanted gift that I had to accept. But you know, during the first phase of my incarceration, it became my most precious possession. I had to keep it hidden after your mother confiscated my Bible."

He looked away, embarrassed, and I almost wished that I had not mentioned it. Yet, how else was he to understand what had happened or might yet happen? Still, I did try to soften the matter a bit.

"To be honest, I would have preferred to be marooned with a good English novel. Isn't it strange how easily we prejudice ourselves against something about which we know so little or nothing at all? This book that I had not cared to read, astounded me."

"Oh? How so?"

He even arches his brows like Benjamín. "Because it speaks so powerfully to my deepest concern."

"And what is that?"

I hesitated, then plunged ahead. "Why God permits evil."

"Ah." He looked off. "So, did Swedenborg's theodicy resonate for you?"

"Much to my surprise, yes."

"Then perhaps I should have a go at it."

"Please do." I held out the book to him.

"Oh, I don't mean to deprive you of it."

"It's all right. I've read it more times than I can count," I laughed. "Please feel free to borrow it if you care to."

"What can I offer in return?"

"A Bible."

"Which one?"

"Why, the King James. There is no other," I answered naively.

Samuel's eyebrows shot up. Later that afternoon he approached me with three books.

"How's your Latin?"

"Nonexistent."

"I was afraid of that. So the *Clementine Vulgate* won't help." He tucked it under the other two tomes. "As I do not own a King James edition, my humble library can offer you only two options in English: the 1582 Douay-Rheims translation of the New Testament, and the 1752 revised Douay-Rheims-Challoner version."

I accepted the 1752 edition. Setting down the books on the stone bench, we strolled through the garden. As the afternoon sun drew patterns of light and shadow, Samuel disabused me of the notion that there is only one definitive translation of the Bible into English. I listened astonished as he listed a sampling of them, his voice calm and pleasing as the garden itself. Names rolled off his tongue as easily as the names of bird species from Benjamín's lips. Bishop's Bible, the Coverdale, the Darby, Ferrar Fenton, Geneva, Tavener's, Thomson's, Tyndale and so many others. Walking with his hands clasped behind his back, my brother-in-law then told me about variations in the Biblical canon. I stopped abruptly.

"Oh, but surely they all have the four Gospels!"

"Yes."

"Oh, good!"

He was watching me closely. "Which one will you read first?"

"The Gospel of John. I love it."

Catching myself, I braced from habit against an onslaught of skepticism or a condescending smile. But Samuel was not Benjamín, much as he looked like him down to the whites of his fingernails, and much as I kept wanting him to be Ben, wanting it except now in this garden, in this sun-dappled space where I could speak about God so openly.

"That's my favorite one too," my brother-in-law smiled. "The opening lines in particular have such an understated profundity."

As we discussed the metaphors of light and darkness, I was conscious that Benjamín and I had never had a conversation at that level. Since we always snagged on the starting point, the existence of God, we could never get very far. With Samuel I felt a sudden burst of freedom. I hadn't realized quite so forcefully how very exhausting Ben's skepticism had been, and how great my spiritual hunger. Chatting with a kindred spirit, how could I not feel drawn to Samuel? How could I not relish his love for Scripture, his spirituality, and even his sadness, little imagining the scale of his inner struggle—or my husband's for that matter. How little we know each other! And how easily we misjudge one another.

111

INSANITY?

DENIAL IS A stubborn force that borrows the cloak of rationality. Having decided that there had to be some hidden pathology to explain his mother's abusive behavior, Samuel launched a campaign to persuade me to accept his version of the whole unfortunate business of my incarceration. Having apologized on her behalf, he seemed to prefer to ignore the details of that dark past and to concentrate solely on the present. Getting me to forgive her was crucial. Our theological chats seemed the very tool he needed. Yet he genuinely enjoyed our discussions. Having close to no experience with women other than his mother and older relations, he was surprised and then delighted with the fresh perspective that I brought to our discussions. And since I was his sister-in-law, he reasoned that there was nothing unseemly about our walks in the church garden.

"Your Swedenborg is a scientist all right," he told me the next morning, his smile part mocking part admiration. "His theology is painstakingly methodical. No poet, he! Yet I admit I prefer his rational approach to rapturizing. Shall we?" Samuel motioned toward the gravel paths. I nodded and strolled alongside him.

"Swedenborg's notion of love is far more expansive than our commonly held conceptions of it as romance or altruism or affection for other human beings. Correct me if I'm wrong, but as he uses the word, love is the very essence of our life."

"We are what we love."

"Yes, I suppose so." After making a full circuit of the garden paths, we seated ourselves on the stone bench and our conversation took a different course.

"Isabel, my mother loves nothing so much in this life as her family. To put it in your terms, that is her ruling love. To protect her family's interests, she would do anything, no matter how tragically misguided." Samuel leaned into the warming day, elbows on knees, hands rolled tightly over his lips as if in prayer. Then he sat up. "I don't know how to explain my mother's behavior. Something has impaired her thinking. I'm mortified about your incarceration. I take solace that you were housed most of the time in the best room in the house—my father's former suite. It has particularly nice furnishings and a sizable library. I hope these gave you comfort and distraction."

Ah, my poor Samuel! I don't want to hurt you, but I will not cover up the truth.

"The cell was spacious, but it was not comfortable." I looked up into his face, so earnest in its hopefulness that I hesitated, but only momentarily. "There were no furnishings and certainly no library. Your mother had the room stripped. For a full year I had to sleep on the stone floor with nothing but a horse blanket for a bed. In all that time, she never let me have books or writing materials. And lest I find the tiniest bit of mental stimulation in the colors of walls or ceiling or floor, she had everything painted white."

Samuel left abruptly, but I saw the fierce contraction of his face as he fought back tears. And it struck me once again that I was witnessing the death throes of a cherished perception. What were my assertions—as well as my very presence among the living—but assaults on the mother he adored? Was it any wonder that he kept trying to rationalize, even justify, the horrifying truth that I was unleashing on him?

Early the next morning he sought me again in the church garden where he knew I would be reading. "There's a lot that I appreciate in Swedenborg's theodicy," he observed without pre-amble. "In some ways he is quite original; at the same time, his foundational premise is quite traditional. Like most theologians, he asserts that God is goodness itself. Therefore, it is patently impossible for evil to come from Him. Evil is from us." His eyes wandered restlessly about the garden. Theodicy was not upper-most on Samuel's mind at that moment. Then his gaze sharp-ened. "I also agree with the distinction he makes between inten-tional evil, which is ultimately the greatest form of insanity, and biological insanity which cannot be held against the victim." I saw where he was going with this. "Isabel, I fear for my mother's sanity. I hope you can learn to see her harsh mistreatment of you as a symptom of her illness, not as evidence of evil per se."

I did not answer right away. Samuel was watching me intently, and I wondered again, is my truth-telling constructive or punitive? Should I spare him by sparing his mother? No. No lies. No justifying the unjustifiable.

"When your mother first imprisoned me, I used to wonder if she was insane or just plain evil. I cannot presume to know the state of her soul. I can only speak about her actions. This much I know: she spoke lucidly with the attorney when I signed over the properties; lucidly when giving orders to servants, and just as lucidly when she threatened to have poor old Hipólito shot unless I signed over the properties. When my grandfather showed up unexpectedly, she implied ever so calmly that she would have him killed if I let him suspect what was—"

"Ah! She implied it! That is not the same as ordering it."

"When I confronted her about his murder, she could not look me in the face."

"That's not a confession of guilt. Give me proof. As for lucidity, let me remind you that insane people are perfectly capable of sounding rational. What happened to you—the funeral—these things were not done by the Manuela Nyman I've known all my life. Clearly, she has become mentally unhinged."

"I suppose the Romans who enjoyed watching people suffer in the colosseum were all unhinged?"

"That's not the same thing at all! They were patently evil—or just acculturated to cruelty. She is not!" He was shouting now. I responded in kind.

"She sealed me up in a dark room and left me to die of starvation! Don't tell me that was not evil or cruel."

He paced, his face contracted in pain. "For pity's sake, Isabel! Isn't all evil a form of insanity?"

"I don't know. Maybe. Yet didn't you just tell me that there are two essential types of insanity? One is a biological pathology that befalls people through no choice of their own."

"As in her case," he insisted.

"The other is a spiritual sickness, self-inflicted through a series of conscious choices. I know that you need to believe that your mother is insane, but is she?"

"What else could explain her behavior?"

I gazed at the swaying treetops. My long silence accused louder than words. He took a deep breath.

"All right. Suppose, just for the sake of argument, that she is not insane. Then wouldn't you agree that she has imperiled her very soul? Isabel, I beg you, let me go to her and begin the work of redemption."

"She'll just deny everything. Besides, what if Valle Inclán should find me while you're busy saving her?"

"Then come with me if you're uneasy."

"Back into the lions' den? No. Not a chance. You promised not to confront her about me until I feel ready. You promised, Samuel."

He rifled through my book. "Here," he pointed to a passage. "In paragraph 276 Swedenborg states the matter in four succinct propositions. 'One. We *are* all involved in evil and need to be led away from it in order to be reformed.' Would you deny that?"

"No."

"Two. And this is the crucial one, Isabel. 'Evils cannot be set aside unless they come to light.' If we do not make my mother aware of her mistakes and we allow her to remain blind to them, how can she free herself from the evil forces that have entrapped her? Tell me Isabel."

Blast it! He didn't need to read the other two propositions. I had given him the very ammunition that he needed. I hurried away.

112

PETITIONS

Morning—and a good night's sleep—calmed and chastened me. I resolved to be kinder and more patient with Samuel. No more flair ups. I would also try being more helpful. Hearing the tolling school bell, I decided to ask Samuel to let me help him, perhaps by taking the younger children off his hands. Besides, that would give my days purpose. I waited until the pupils had gone home. Then I walked to the school. He wasn't there. Something or someone had called him away. Taking a seat in the courtyard, I waited for close to two hours. The empty school seemed preternaturally quiet, save for don Pepino who was munching fodder in his new stall. Samuel entered the patio so silently that I jumped, startled, startling him. "Isabel?"

"I need to ask you for a favor." And then I suddenly felt awkward. Who was I to ask anything of him who had given so much while I stubbornly refused his one request?

"What can I do for you?" He stood by a thick vine of red bougainvillea that climbed to the flat rooftop. I approached, lacing and unlacing my fingers.

"I've been wondering, could I help you by working with the younger children?"

He thought about it, then nodded. "I *could* use the help. Have you ever taught before?"

"Yes. No."

His lips curled into a smile. "Which is it?"

"I've taught many classes in my imagination, which is a training of sorts. I know I could do it."

"I thought you wanted to remain incognita."

"I do. They could call me . . ." I thought of my skeleton doll. "Conchita. Miss Conchita."

He agreed. And to his credit, he did not try to pressure me into forgiving before I was ready to do so. The very next day Samuel handed over fourteen children under the age of nine—fifteen when Teresa dropped off little Rodolfo. He alone wore a spiffy navy suit, which made his companions laugh more from surprise than malice. His sisters, on the other hand, entered Samuel's class under a glare of suspicion, they with their city clothes, they whose shyness was taken for aloofness. Teresa could have eased her children's transition by dressing them more simply, but that she was not prepared to do. Ever. Like it or not, they were to remember their more exalted heritage, and that was that. If not for their uncle's presence, school would have been an ordeal for them. As for me, by noon I knew that teaching imaginary students was infinitely less challenging. Yet what exhilaration! I loved every one of those bright little souls and they loved me back so generously.

When school let out and quiet was let in, I dropped onto the one bench in the courtyard. Samuel laughed when he saw me. "So, Miss Conchita, are you sure you want to come back tomorrow?"

"Maybe I can talk Teresa into taking my class so I can take yours."

"Taking my job, are you? Well, there's gratitude for you." He plunked down next to me and stretched his long legs.

"Well someone needs to cover for you while you're visiting your mother."

"I'm not due there for nearly two weeks."

"Go to her, Samuel."

He took back his smile and sat up straight. "What are you saying?"

"Help her find her way back. Just don't ask me to go with you. I won't go back there."

"I can confront her about you?"

Oh, this was a calculated risk. "Yes," I nodded resolutely.

With an impulse of joy, Samuel hugged me and kissed me on the cheek. Because that sudden contact unleashed memories of a face just like his, or because the happiness that animated it could only be, had to be, Ben's, I turned and kissed him on the lips, and he kissed me back with all the longing of our souls.

113

ERRARE HUMANUM EST

I FELT THE full impact of his body pressed to mine, the lips that I knew so well, loved so well, pressed to mine at last, the scent of his skin washing over me like the sea. For a few seconds time doubled back. Benjamín was masquerading as a priest, teaching me to love poetry and the poetry of his love. And then as we spiraled into the exhilaration of passion set free, it was not Ben whom I continued to kiss. And then I caught myself.

"I'm so sorry!" I gasped pulling away.

Samuel looked utterly stricken. "Forgive me!"

I didn't answer. Coward that I was, I hurried back to the house. When I had slammed my bedroom door shut and had pressed my back against it, I was assaulted by a terrifying thought: *My God, I love the wrong brother!*

I cried inconsolably. Teresa listened at the door, uncertain whether to intervene or respect my privacy. When the storm did not abate after an hour, she stepped in with her large sad eyes and softly murmured questions. I could only shake my head and swim out deeper into my anguish, so deep and so unreachable that Teresa had to cast a line longer and stronger than her past jealousy. Recognizing the intensity of my suffering because it mirrored her own, Teresa hugged and rocked me, while I clung to her as I sobbed. My conscience accused me: *don't pretend you thought he was Ben.*

After Teresa had gotten me to lie down and had tip-toed out of the room, I fell to my knees and covered my face. *Oh, Lord, help me! Please help me! I don't want to commit adultery, physically or in my heart. Help me to see clearly. Forgive my selfishness. Please help me!*

Samuel was just as devastated. Hurrying to his room in the schoolhouse, he prostrated himself, his head touching the cold tile floor, tears burning his cheeks.

Father in heaven! What have I done? How could I have betrayed Benjamín? And how could I have betrayed you? I offered you my chastity. Yet I came so close to forgetting my sacred vow.

Separately, alone, Samuel and I prayed throughout the night, two souls as shattered as the beleaguered villages of Morelos. Doña Manuela had her own desperate prayers. Unable to sleep, she paced the empty prison cell. Returning to her bedroom, she knelt before a statue of the Virgin Mary: *Mother of God! Help me keep the love and respect of my children! Protect me from vile slander. Help Valle Inclán find the girl, and I will build a church to your glory!*

Benjamín peered into the patient's face. "Well! I see you decided to come back to the Penitentiary Suites. I trust you enjoyed your little excursion."

"How da look?" Mangel murmured, surprised that his words slurred so shamelessly.

"Like a raccoon that got into a fight with a badger. Can you actually see out those slits?"

Mangel tried to grin with lips too swollen to command. "Da still haf . . . ma bes body part?"

"Yes, it's still there. But after the licking they gave you, you'll be able to father only ten or twelve kids." Benjamín grasped Mangel's hand. "You're made of tougher stuff than I. For all the blows, they only broke a few ribs and some skin. You're one tough bird!"

He kept up a gentle banter, but the incident with Mangel and the other wounded prisoner had awakened in Benjamín a rage intense as flame but controlled and focused. Once again Benjamín wrote letters to men in high places, beginning with the president of the republic:

Dear Señor Presidente,

I am a revolutionary who had the privilege of fighting alongside you in Chihuahua. I am also a murderer who must pay for his crime and find redemption within the walls of the penitentiary. All the ills that you hoped to eliminate in our country are magnified here, where the simplest rights must be purchased with bribery, where order is replaced with corruption, compassion with brutality. I entreat you to extend your visionary gaze to all Mexicans, even to the lowest, that if we enter the penal system as animals, we may emerge from it as men.

Benjamín was a realist. He knew from newspaper accounts that the Madero regime was fighting several rebellions, not just the Zapatista revolt in Morelos. So it was unlikely that Madero would make time to give penal reform the attention it merited. Benjamín could picture his revolutionary hero stroking his trim beard pensively, eyes dark and sad, shoulders stooped from the lofty expectations he had inspired in his countrymen. Yes, there were still enormous flaws in the system, but Ben needed to believe that the Maderista revolution could still foster an era of social reform, however slowly or imperfectly. So he mailed his appeal.

And indeed, the President did read his letter with interest. He even added the appeal to his list of items needing his attention.

But Madero was running out of time. His enemies had allotted him less than a month and a half of life. The country would soon revert back to the old pattern of military dictatorship. So there would be change and no change. Meanwhile, Benjamín resorted to the very system of bribery that he had decried. Within half an hour of a visit by a clerk from the office of the family's attorney, Ben paid a bribe on behalf of Mangel so he could smuggle Teodora into his room for a few hours. My Paladín made no attempt to reconcile his inconsistency. Love needs no justification, he would have insisted. We must live meaningfully in the present and attempt to improve one life at a time. To that end he wrote to his cousin and childhood friend, Federico Casamayor.

Dear Cousin,

Congratulations on your promotion! I hear that you are distinguishing yourself up north as you fight *Orozquistas* and other troublemakers. Your mother and stepfather visited me in my gilded cage last week, which I thought was extremely kind of them. Your step-father looked stunned to find an antique Isfahan Persian rug on my floor. Aunt Sofía, for her part, was delighted by everything—my mother's wing chairs, tables, and dinnerware. We had coffee and enjoyed the pastries that they brought from *el Globo.* For the duration of their visit, I actually forgot that I live in a prison. Samuel says I'm the most pampered prisoner in Mexico. He's right.

How can I begin to atone for my sins unless I use my family's resources and connections for a greater good? To that end I've been writing to people in high places to denounce the policy of resettlement in our long-suffering Morelos. Resettlement! It's as hypocritical a euphemism as it would be to name a plague after a rose or a saint. I am gladdened by your report that the brute who was handling "the Morelos problem" has been replaced by

General Felipe Angeles, the man you deem the most honorable officer in the Federal Army. I'm relieved to hear that his policies are far more moderate than his predecessor's. May he succeed in appeasing the Zapatistas and restoring a semblance of peace to the pueblos.

I've enlisted your good mother in one of my smaller efforts. I am determined to free at least one young woman from abuse. Teodora Molina, a gentle soul, was taken from her family and forced into prostitution. One of my bodyguards is deeply in love with her and she with him. If Teodora can escape from the officer who has profited by prostituting her, your angelic mother has agreed to give her a position in her household. I've met Teodora and can vouch for her character. Believe me, Federico, when I tell you how often the high-born are low, and the lowest have true nobility.

114

THE SOUL'S LABYRINTH

THE MORE I thought about Samuel, the greater my turmoil. I loved his gentleness and his spirituality. Did that mean that I loved the man or just his traits? And when all was said and done, what was there to love about Benjamín? His jealous nature? His religious skepticism? His volatility? Was it enough that he dabbled in poetry and ornithology? Oh, why did I marry him?

I felt myself falling into a frightening vortex until I reached for prayer, a sturdy limb keeping me from the abyss. It alone pulled me back to safety. By morning I felt calm enough, not only to resume my duties at the school, but to seek Samuel before the children arrived. I found him in the courtyard, pitchfork in hand as he mucked out don Pepino's stall.

"How are you, Samuel?" I asked softly.

He looked awful. No doubt I did too. Propping the pitchfork against a wall, he opened his hands as if to say, what can I say? Then he said it. "What happened yesterday was not your fault. I beg you to forgive me. It was vile and perverse of me."

"No, it wasn't. Your reaction was the utterly normal response of a young man. Attraction between the sexes is a gift from

God—the normal order of things. Perpetual celibacy is a man-made dictum that runs counter to natural and spiritual order."

His eyebrows arched in surprise. "One could argue that, I suppose, but that does not justify the breaking of sacred vows."

"Ah, that's different." Engulfed as we were in a shaft of morning light, we were people struggling out of the dark.

"Isabel, I took such flagrant advantage of you yesterday. You needed Benjamín and I usurped his place."

"That was as much my fault as yours."

"No. The sin is mine. The duplicity, mine alone. I don't know what came over me. I betrayed not only you and Benjamín, but the Church."

"I'm at fault too."

"For what? For needing to be comforted by your husband? How is it your fault that I happen to look exactly like him and that for a few moments I seemed to be him?"

"We did cross a line yesterday, and it will never happen again. After today neither of us will speak of this. But today I need to speak honestly. I need to confess that as much as I have longed for Benjamín, I kissed *you*, Samuel."

"No." He began to pace, shaking his head. "You needed Benjamín and I took advantage of that."

"Look at me, Samuel." He stopped pacing. What anguish in those eyes! Mine glistened too as I made my heartfelt confession. "I kissed the man that you are and the angel that you are becoming. Maybe I'll be allowed to love you in the next life. Or perhaps there is another woman whom you will meet and love profoundly in the life to come, the two of you completing one another. I don't know. I just know that if I were not married, and if you were not a priest, I could love you so easily, Samuel Nyman. But I *am* married and I *must* be true as long as I'm married to Benjamín."

"And I'm a priest and I must work to be true again."

"So there we have it." I tried to smile. "Oh, Samuel! Be the finest priest you can, if that is your choice, and I'll honor my marriage as best I can, even though marrying Benjamín was the most dreadful mistake of my life."

"Don't think that way about your marriage."

"Why not? It's time that I faced the truth. Benjamín and I married impulsively, out of youthful passion. We confused the romance of elopement and of the revolution for real love, when all along it was only infatuation. That's why it was so easy for his passion for me to turn into hatred."

"Hatred? He adores you, Isabel."

"No, Samuel. When I visited him in prison that one time, he grabbed me by the throat and wouldn't let me say a word in my defense. Not one word. Before throwing me out of his cell, he—" My voice began to crack like plaster in an earthquake, "He vowed—he vowed to kill Tomás and me."

Samuel thrust his head back. "Oh, the hot head! But surely you know how quickly he flies off the handle. He didn't mean it, Isabel."

"Oh, he meant it all right. He intends to kill Tomás someday, though he is totally innocent, and me, though I'm not so innocent after all," I tried to laugh as I wiped my face with shaky hands. Samuel handed me his carefully folded handkerchief.

"You're wrong, Isabel. All right, I'll concede that in the heat of the moment he probably did mean his threat. Trust me when I tell you that he's had a complete change of heart."

"Don't you understand? He doesn't love me. Perhaps he never did."

"And you, do you love him?"

"I don't know anymore. All those months when I thought he was so damaged, I felt—I felt such pity for him."

"Just pity?"

I remembered my imagined dance with Ben, on a night when I could almost feel his arms around me as I waltzed barefoot in my cell. Were longing and love dance partners? "Maybe I just love an idea, a notion of what my marriage could have been but never was."

"Or may yet be. Isabel, believe me when I tell you that Benjamín is deeply in love with you. He knows that he was wrong about you and regrets it deeply."

"Please don't try to make me feel better."

"Don't take my word for it. Hear it directly from him. I don't know if trains are running this week, but I do know that we could travel to San Serafín and use the hacienda train."

"No. I won't go back there."

"Nothing will happen to you. You have my word. Come with me, Isabel. Think of it: by this time tomorrow you could be reunited with Benjamín—not the maniac who threatened you, but the husband who loves you deeply. And today you and I could confront my mother and begin a great work of redemption."

"If she's insane as you keep insisting, what good can we do in a day?"

"Well, you're right about that," he sighed. "How about this? We'll go straight to Benjamín. We could go directly to San Serafín's depot and take the hacienda train without my mother knowing about it. I can authorize it to take us to the D.F."

"How can she not know we're there? Won't my sudden appearance cause a commotion?"

"With a little luck no one will recognize you with that dark hair."

Now I was pacing. I had let fear drive out my inner prayer. "I don't know."

"What are you afraid of, Isabel? If it's being held against your will, I swear by all that I hold sacred that I won't let it happen."

"I think I'm more afraid of false hope."

"Yet isn't hope our true life-blood?" When I didn't respond, he gave me that boyish smile of Benjamín's that always disarmed me. "Then believe your Martin Luther if you won't believe this Catholic priest. 'Everything that is done in the world is done by hope.'"

～

When Samuel informed Teresa that we would be gone for two or more days to see Benjamín, she smiled at me and volunteered then and there to cover for Samuel at the school. So it was settled despite my uneasiness, and then unsettled when we stopped at doña Clemencia's and found her in bed with a high fever.

"I'll stay with her." Did I betray a selfish kind of relief? Samuel mentioned several village women who could stay with her, but I insisted on staying behind. He tried to mask his disappointment. Or was it exasperation smoldering like lava beneath a grassy volcano? Benjamín would have erupted at that point. Samuel remained all grassy slopes, outwardly calm. Teresa merely shook her head but did not try to talk me into anything.

"All right. I'll be back the day after tomorrow." Samuel explained to both of us. "I've asked Timoteo and don Gustavo to be on the alert, though I don't think you need to worry. San Gabrielín has become a kind of unofficial neutral territory. No one will trouble you."

"I'll see to that." Teresa thrust a hand into one of her pockets. Then she added almost cheerfully, "Well, then I must be off too. I have a school bell to ring. Have a good trip, Father."

Before mounting don Pepino, Samuel handed Benjamín's manuscript to me.

"This is for you."

"What is it?"

His face softened. "One soul's labyrinth. Don't let the sarcasm and false assumptions of the first pages put you off. Follow the twists and turns to the very heart. They lead to you, Isabel."

As priest and cantering mule disappeared around a bend in the road, I suddenly regretted my decision to stay behind. Any of the village women could have done a better job at nursing doña Clemencia than I. Why, oh why was I such a coward? What had I accomplished but to put off the inevitable? Confronting doña Manuela with Samuel by my side would have given me a sense of justice. And seeing Ben again—Oh, but could I bear it if he were to reject me again? No. I was right to stay behind, I insisted stubbornly.

Tucking the manuscript under my arm, I hurried to my nursing duties.

115

APOCALYPSE

SAMUEL FOUND HIS mother in her office downstairs. He noted that she looked both surprised and annoyed by his unexpected visit.

"Samuel!" she tried to smile. "I wasn't expecting you for another two weeks."

"Yet here I am." He stooped to kiss her on the cheek.

"Well, I'm almost finished here. Then we can have a late breakfast. Or is it lunch that you'll be needing?"

"Call it what you will," he smiled, taking a seat in a corner.

From there he observed her interactions with the assistant administrator and with the hacienda accountant. Though she seemed a little distracted at first, she soon focused on the tasks at hand, including accounts from the Zacatecas mines. Watching her carefully, he was struck by her enormous managerial skills and her mental competence. His shoulders slumped.

Twenty minutes later, he and his mother were having lunch in the small dining room that I liked so much, as it was far cozier than the formal dining room. Halfway into the soup course,

Samuel began his work of redemption. Making a steeple of his fingers, he leaned back and asked, "Were you with Isabel to the very end?"

Doña Manuela started at the mention of my name. "Yes, of course."

"So, you saw her die?"

"Yes. It was pitiful. Why are you bringing this up?"

"What were her last words?"

"I don't recall."

"Did she struggle, or did she slip away quietly?"

"I don't know. What does it matter now?"

"I never saw the corpse, so I can't quite believe that she's dead and that Benjamín is a widower."

"Well, he is. Tacha and I washed her and laid her in her coffin."

"Try to remember. Was the end peaceful?"

"Not especially, now that I think about it. She carried too many sins and no possibility of confession and absolution. I'd say she got what she deserved. Now let's have no more talk of Isabel Brentt."

Samuel pushed back his chair and rose. "I want for us to pray at her gravesite."

"Now? Don't be absurd."

Samuel pulled her chair out for her and forced her to her feet.

"*Ay, hijo!* The meal will get cold," she complained. Since he had a firm grasp of her arm, she had no choice but to walk with him, scurrying to keep up with his long, determined strides.

"Ring the outside bell," Samuel ordered one of the servants. "Have everyone assemble in the cemetery."

"For pity's sake, son! Why are you pulling people away from work? Pray for her to your heart's content, only let the rest of us get on with our work!" He kept her walking briskly, past the church and into the hacienda cemetery, stopping at last at the foot of my grave.

"Samuel, this is very inconsiderate," she muttered. A crowd began to gather, answering the summons. When three men arrived with shovels as previously instructed by Samuel, doña Manuela grasped his arm tightly, pinching him. "What's this about?"

An apocalypse. A revelation, he could have answered as he pulled free. Reaching into a pocket in his cassock, he withdrew three short candles and a box of matches. Bending over my grave, he plunged the candles into the ground until they stood upright. When almost two hundred men and women had assembled, Samuel lit the candles.

"In nomine Patris et Filii et Spiritus Sancti." Everyone made the sign of the cross. Then he switched to Spanish. "We are gathered here not just to remember our sister, Isabel, but to pray for the gifts of repentance and redemption." Samuel reached for a shovel and plunged it into the grassy sod. "Our Lord Jesus Christ is the light of the world. Every time we commit a sin and do not repent, it is as if we were throwing dirt on that light," he explained, tossing soil onto one of the lit candles until he extinguished it.

It's a sermon against Isabel's sins and her suicide! Doña Manuela breathed a sigh of relief. She would have smiled had it not been unseemly.

Samuel plunged the shovel into the soil several more times, a mound growing in front of my tombstone. "If we continue to do this, sinning without ever repenting, we smother the light of heaven that should shine through us. It is only by the grace of God that we can be saved from our many sins, but *only* if we repent from the heart. It is written: 'Repent and turn to God, so that your sins may be wiped out, that times of refreshing may come from the Lord.'"

His gaze swept over the crowd, resting briefly on his mother whose head was dutifully bowed.

"We read in Ephesians," he continued from memory, "'Get rid of all bitterness, rage and anger, brawling and slander, along with every form of malice. Be kind and compassionate to one another, *forgiving* each other, just as in Christ, God forgave you.'"

Manuela Nyman looked up long enough to make the sign of the cross and then to cast her eyes down again, for wasn't it her duty to lead the common people by example?

"But what if our sins are buried so deeply that they remain hidden even from us?" Samuel asked, his gaze now fixed on her alone. In the long pause that followed, he seemed to hesitate, as if he had lost the thread of his homily. There was still time to back away from his plan. Still time to say an appropriate blessing and send everyone away. A light breeze rustled his hair and cassock. A dragonfly landed soundlessly on his sleeve; sunlight burst free through a cirrostratus cloud, thin as a bridal veil. Taking a deep breath, he turned to the men with shovels: "Dig up the coffin."

There was a collective catch of breath.

"Dig it up," he repeated as he returned to his mother's side.

"What are you doing! I won't stand for this desecration—" she whispered, her words halted by the fierce grip on her arm. While the digging proceeded, he intoned the Lord's Prayer. The onlookers joined him, eyes darting from priest to grave and back again. When the coffin was visible, he ordered it brought up and lain perpendicularly across the hole. Speaking softly to his terrified mother, he murmured Isaiah's gentle exhortation.

"'Come now, let us settle the matter,' says the Lord. 'Though your sins are like scarlet, they shall be as white as snow; though they are red as crimson, they shall be like wool.'"

She tried to pull free.

"Open it," Samuel ordered the men with shovels. Again, an audible gasp convulsed the group. "Don't be afraid," the priest reassured them. "Pry it open."

The crowd pressed forward, simultaneously afraid and morbidly curious. Doña Manuela closed her eyes as the wood protested sharply. A crowbar was sent for, but there was no need. The gravediggers used the tips of their shovels and pried the lid open. There was another collective gasp. Samuel, who had been holding his mother captive, pulled her toward the open coffin. Inside were several rocks and sacks of beans that had been stitched together to form a primitive figure.

"Don't be afraid," he murmured in her ear. "Repent of your deception and be healed."

"It's all part of my plan—my plan to hide food for us to use later!" she told the murmuring crowd in a loud, clear voice. "Famine is sweeping across Morelos. It's vital to store and to hide food by whatever means!"

Samuel released her arm and headed back to the house. Her first impulse was to run after him, but a second, stronger one asserted itself. "I should have told Father Samuel about my plan. My daughter-in-law is not dead. When she left with Tacha, slinking away in the middle of the night without telling anyone, she was as good as dead to me. To us. I used their defection as a God-given opportunity to further safeguard you and your children. I have hidden away food for you against the famine that is coming. Granaries are being burned to the ground by federales and rebels alike. You," she pointed to the men with shovels. "Bury the sacks again. I know that I can trust each and every one of you to keep them secret and safe until we need them."

No one moved. Rattled, doña Manuela hurried after her son who was well ahead of her. If he heard her calling his name, he made no attempt to slow the pace that drew him up to the second floor of the house. When she caught up with him at last, he was standing in the middle of my cell, her supposed chapel. In the stillness of his heart, he was taking in the bleakness of the walls and the coldness of the space.

"Samuel, I can explain everything!"

He stared at a tattered blanket on the floor. When he turned toward her, his eyes were like Lucio Nyman's, torched with an anger that could melt rock.

"So it's true!" he muttered between clenched teeth.

He knows! He's talked with her!

"Don't believe everything you hear, Samuelito. Nothing is ever quite what it seems."

"You imprisoned her *two* Septembers ago! It's January now!" His voice kept rising. "Count the months!"

"I'm sorry! I suppose I shouldn't have kept her here so long. But I couldn't just let her and that man take everything from us, could I?" He drew closer, tall and menacing. She had never seen him like this. "Calm yourself, son. I can explain everything."

"Don't explain. Confess! Confess right here before God! You can lie to everyone else, but not to him! Not to him! You didn't just lock her up like you did Benjamín. You starved and tortured her for your own sick pleasure!"

"No! Is that what she told you?"

"It's what my *eyes* told me. My God, Mother! She was a wraith! Even the most sadistic guards at the penitentiary don't torture their prisoners like that. And the old man, you had Valle Inclán murder him, didn't you? Didn't you!"

He towered over her, his face contorted. When she didn't meet his gaze, he knew, and the truth was a boulder crushing him. "*What* are you?" he gasped.

Manuela Nyman felt a tremor run through her as he pushed past her. Massive tectonic plates deep within her heaved violently against each other.

"No! Wait, son!" She hurried after him. "Samuel!" She staggered down the stairs, then out into the back garden just in time to see him vanish into the labyrinth. "Samuel! Please, son!"

The day was perfect, all clouds banished now, the sky flawlessly blue. Manuela Nyman Vizcarra stumbled along green corridors that swallowed her whole. Every turn led to a dead end or to further deception.

"Samuel!"

He ran to the heart of the labyrinth that he knew so well. When he reached the fountain, he slumped down onto its scalloped edge. For a few more seconds he fought back the flood that threatened to wipe out that part of him that was child, adolescent, and idealist. For some reason, he thought of her just then as she had been years back when her hair was black as obsidian and his blond and curly; back when he could reach up to sit on her lap, hide his face on her fragrant, soft chest and cry. She would rock him and soothe him with the soft, steady voice of a mother's love. Remembering with equal vividness my starvation in all its grotesqueness, he felt the last of his earthly defenses swept away, wrenching sharp sobs that startled the birds in the aviary and those that nested free in the garden treetops.

Manuela Nyman stopped to listen. Servants in the house and in the courtyard and in the cemetery became silent. All heard the sound of agony itself—a man's agony, enormous and uncontainable. Hearing it, she preferred the sharp pain that dropped her to her knees. Even the paralysis that was spreading throughout the left side of her body was infinitely easier to bear. She wanted to call out to him, to soothe him as if he were a child again and she a mother worthy of his love. Staggering to her feet, every corridor of hedge looked identical to her confused mind. Even in the midst of dying brain cells, one thought pushed past the obstructed pathway: *I'm lost.*

116

DEAD AND ALIVE

SAMUEL HAD GONE to San Serafín prepared to accept that his mother had suffered some kind of mental collapse, or even that she was insane. But not this. Not such blatant, unrepentant evil. He wrung his hands. Hadn't he struggled to accept his father's insanity? Yet now, how he longed for the same illness to explain his mother's behavior. How had insanity become the lesser of evils? Holy Mother of God! What now? Hide the truth from his siblings?

No, by all the saints! I won't lie for her. Samuel jumped to his feet, anger energizing him. I've got to see Benjamín. He, more than anyone else, deserves to know the truth.

Getting out of the labyrinth was no problem for Samuel, who could navigate its elaborate twists and turns as easily as he did the *Missale Romanum*. Striding resolutely, he remained unaware that he had passed within a few feet of his mother who lay paralyzed on the ground on the other side of a green wall.

The *peones* of San Serafín doffed their hats to the priest. No one spoke. It was as if the entire hacienda were caught in the spell of a fear that was utterly new. A holy fear, Bardomiana would call it. It was more unsettling than bodily fear. Samuel boarded the train. The great rear gate swung open on its massive hinges, and the locomotive nosed out. He arrived at the Penitentiary shortly before lock-down. He was shown into Ben's cell with the admonition to keep the visit brief.

"I see you've let your beard grow back," Samuel commented as he went to hug his brother. Ben yanked free.

"I know about Isa, how all of you kept her death from me. I could expect as much from Mother, but not from you, Samuel. Not you."

My poor brother-in-law sighed, dropping heavily into a wing chair. *Confess one sin at a time.* "I'm sorry. It was wrong of me. Mother—" He choked on the word, coughing it up as if it were a morsel of fish turned treacherous with unsuspected bones. "She swore us all to secrecy. She was so sure that you would rampage and get yourself brutalized again or killed. In that sense, I suppose she meant well. Can you ever forgive me, brother?"

Benjamín shook his head in grim amusement. "That's rich! You're asking *me,* of all the worthless scum of the earth, to forgive *you?*" Ben seated himself opposite his brother, his eyes shimmering. "Just tell me: how did Isa die? Did she really starve herself?"

Gazing into Benjamín's bearded face with its Christ-like beauty, Samuel had a sudden insight. *Knowing they would crucify you, oh Lord, you still let yourself enter Jerusalem with the joy of the moment. You fill each moment, live each one.*

"Isabel is alive!" Samuel beamed.

Ben was slow to react, as if his brother had spoken to him in a dead language that he had learned long ago and needed to extricate from dusty memory. Then the muscles in his face shot through a repertoire of shock, incredulity, and cautious joy, as if afraid he had heard wrong.

"Alive?" he gasped.

"She's probably reading your book as we speak." Samuel reached over and clapped him on the knee.

"Where? Where is she?"

"In my house. She and Teresa Gama and all three of Rodolfo's children threw me out!"

"What?" Ben wanted to laugh even as tears began to trickle down his face.

"I've had to take up residence with a mule in the old schoolhouse. But I'm making Isabel and Teresa reward my chivalry by helping me teach the village children."

"She's alive!" The brothers embraced and laughed. "Then she's all right?"

"Well, aside from the fact that her hair is black now, yes."

"Black?" Benjamín looked bewildered, then radiant. "I don't care if it's purple or green!"

"And she's as beautiful as ever." Samuel knew they were drawing inexorably closer to the fearsome, dark truth that he still had to disclose. So he lingered a few more moments, as if joining in a great, joyous procession into a walled city carpeted with palm branches. Crucifixion still lay ahead. But then, so did resurrection.

"So why did Mother blurt out that Isa is dead? And why did Emanuela write to tell me that Isa had starved herself to death, and that no one was supposed to tell me the truth? What the hell was that all about?"

Samuel saw himself as an archer, arrow aimed at his brother's chest. "The suicide was a lie. A fabrication. Mother deliberately led all of us to believe that Isabel had willfully starved herself."

"But—the body? Surely you saw her?"

"The coffin was nailed shut when I returned to the sickroom."

"What sickroom? Samuel, look at me. How was Isa sick?"

Samuel felt himself release the arrow. "She was dying from starvation. Mother—Mother—" There was no recalling the shaft speeding toward its target. "Mother and Tacha had kept her locked in Emanuela's room. God knows how long she had to subsist on nothing but tap water."

"And no one stopped them?" Ben sprang to his feet, his voice rising.

"No one knew. I arrived unexpectedly, just before Christmas. By then Isabel was dying. They had moved her to Eva's old room, I suppose so that some of the servants could see her and bear witness that she had starved herself to death. Even I was fooled."

"Did she speak to you?

"She was too far gone. All I could do was hold her hand and pray. What they had done to her—I've never seen anything like it."

Suddenly both brothers were crying, clinging to each other. When they could speak again, their eyes swollen, their reddened faces mirrors reflecting devastation, Samuel found a small reserve of hope.

"Be at peace, brother. By the grace of God, Isabel is fine now. Sometime after the funeral, Mother went back to feeding her again."

"So she came to her senses and released her?"

"No. She kept Isabel imprisoned for almost a year more."

"But you say she's in San Gabrielin now. So Mother—"

"No. Tacha helped Isabel escape. Blackening her hair was necessary, as a disguise. She walked into my village around midnight during the Christmas Eve Mass."

"Starved her. Starved her—" Benjamín murmured as if he needed to say the words aloud before he could believe them. "Has Mother lost her mind?"

Samuel began to pace, rubbing his face with a shaky hand. Another reckoning. "No. I don't think our mother is insane, not like Father."

"So she knew what she was doing?" Rage supplanted all other emotions, contorting Benjamín's face. "Then it's Manuela who is dead, God damn her!"

"Try to forgive her, Benjamín, for your own sake," Samuel implored as he was being ushered out the door for the nightly lockdown.

"You tell that viper that she is never again to visit me." Ben spoke with deadly calm. "I don't want a cent of her bribery money. Not a cent. You tell her I hope she rots in hell."

ROPE

I WASN'T ABLE to get to Benjamín's memoir until late that afternoon, around the same time that Samuel was visiting Ben, as it turns out. Seating myself in the one arm chair in doña Clemencia's room, I untied the bundle. The title page read: *Paradise Misplaced: Memoir of Captain Benjamín Nyman Vizcarra*. For all my misgivings, I found myself touching his name gently. The very next page, the dedication, took me totally by surprise.

Beloved, if as your Swedenborg notes, birds are like thoughts,
  Accept these as the flocks I have gathered for you alone.

Hope leaped out of the depths, joyous as a spinner dolphin. Leafing through the loose pages, I smiled at Ben's pen-and-ink drawings of birds. They strutted along the bottom of pages, or nested in the tops, or roosted along the margins. All were skillfully executed, these thought-birds.

Doña Clemencia called to me just then, her voice uncharacteristically feeble. The manuscript had to wait. Filling in for her at the shop kept me hurrying from her bedside, across the

small patio, into the store, and back again. At night, when doña
Clemencia dropped off to sleep, I was finally able to read unin-
terrupted, sitting cross-legged on the floor that was so much
more comfortable than the lumpy old love seat. What I found in
my husband's memoir was a candid narrative full of humor and
pain. It soon became clear that as he struggled to understand me,
he was coming to know himself.

As I followed the gradual shifts in Benjamín's thinking,
I realized that he was allowing me to peer into his heart. On I
read as stars tiptoed across the night sky. I had to blink back
tears whenever I felt the power of his despair. Other times my
spirit soared as he expressed the depth of his love for me and
the intensity of his remorse. By dawn, a light was shining within
me, bright and riotous as my grandfather's art. The conclusion
turned out to be a three-paragraph letter for me. This I had to
save for a special place. Taking a quick peek at doña Clemencia
who was sleeping peacefully, I slipped away to the church garden. Only the great open sky could begin to contain the joy that
surged through me as I read:

> Beloved, I love you and always will, yet I have wronged
> you every step of the way. That day in my cell, you came
> to me with nothing but generous intentions, and I repaid
> you with brutality. I was half crazed with jealousy and
> despair, but that neither explains nor justifies my despi-
> cable behavior when I do not fully understand it myself.
> Yet here I am begging you to forgive me. Only that, Isa.
> You owe me nothing, you who gave me everything.
>
> I have been wrong about everything, but most of all
> about you and Tomás Tepaneca. I don't know how long
> you have known him or under what circumstances, and it
> doesn't matter. It's clear to me that he loves you, perhaps
> even as much as I do.

I paused. *Oh, my poor Tomás!* Since Samuel had told me
about their confrontation at my grave, I had grieved for Tomás's

anguish. Now I begged his forgiveness inwardly. *Forgive me, Tomás, for never being able to love you as you love me. And forgive me for sending you on such an impossible quest. Wherever you are, drop it. Please, please be happy, Tomás.*

I returned to Ben's letter:

> I don't know why the fates made him [Tomás Tepaneca] my father's attorney, or why my father left everything to you.

I felt my cheeks burn at the memory of Tomás's confession that he had meddled with the will. And again I had to wonder, since my father-in-law had apparently intended to leave everything to the mysterious Isabela Brentano, had we defrauded her? Or was the old man so unhinged by then that he didn't know what he was doing? Had he scrambled my name with someone else's? Should I tell Samuel and Benjamín the truth at Tomás's expense, or keep silent? Why compromise Tomás now that the inheritance had been straightened out? I returned to Ben's letter, re-reading the lines about Tomás:

> I don't know how or why the fates made him my father's attorney, or why my father left everything to you, or why Tepaneca kissed you on the lips. No, that's not true. I know all too well why he kissed you. I see it in that grainy photograph: *his* longing, not yours; *his* desire, not your betrayal; his arms around you, not yours around him. *Dios Santo!* Why was I so blind to what I knew in my heart? I know what marriage means to you—its sacredness, its eternalness. That is why you were willing to try again, to come to me even here in this wretched prison. Ah, my love! What would I give to take back that day and recast it for you with love and the most profound gratitude!

Samuel was right. The memoir was a labyrinth that led my husband back to me. Benjamín loved me more intensely than ever. And I? What did I feel? A rush of love and a fierce determination to resume our life together, no matter how many years I had to wait. Oh, to see him again! Oh, to forgive each other fully and start again!

Lifting my face, I let the sun kiss me as if its warmth were the touch of his lips.

That same morning, Samuel left the hotel where he had spent the night and returned to the penitentiary for one last visit before heading back to San Serafín. One look at Benjamín and he knew that he had had as sleepless a night as his own. Disheveled hair. Puffy eyelids. Dark circles under the eyes. Yet Ben was in buoyant spirits.

"I've written a letter to Isa. A dozen, actually. This pitiful thing can't begin to tell her all that I need to say, but will you give it to her?"

"Of course."

"Now tell me everything about her, black hair and all! Does she ask about me?"

As if by mutual agreement, neither spoke about their mother. Samuel made it his mission to reassure Benjamín that all would be well in the end, never imagining as they laughed over coffee that a new drama was unfolding in San Gabrielín.

Less than two kilometers from the village, a bay horse pulling a cart stopped in front of an abandoned church. Valle Inclán dismounted. Taking care not to scuff up his newly polished boots, he sauntered up to the battered door. When the door resisted, he used his shoulders to force it open. The church was empty. Cobwebs and thick dust suggested it had not been used in decades. He nodded and stepped outside again, leaving the door slightly ajar. The rug that he had purchased in Cuernavaca lay rolled up in the cart. Taking hold of the reins, he guided horse and cart behind the church, securing them to a withered fig tree. Then he set out to find the messenger he needed. The dirt road was deserted, except for a small boy who was hurrying toward the village. The spire of Samuel's church rose above a green canopy of swaying trees.

"Hey, muchacho!" The bounty hunter smiled. "Are you going to San Gabrielín?" He enunciated his words carefully, trying to minimize his Castilian accent. He judged the boy to be around six or seven years old. The child looked as wary as a deer that has sensed the presence of a hunter. "Listen, how would you like to earn a peso?" Valle Inclán reached into his vest and pulled out a small gold coin. The boy took the bait, drawing closer. "Tell me, do you know a lady with blue eyes?"

"Like my new teacher?"

The boy, whose name was Jacobito, arrived at the schoolhouse moments before Teresa began her second day as a substitute teacher with all the children assembled in one classroom.

"Where's Miss Conchita?" Jacobito struggled to catch his breath.

"She isn't teaching today. Now go and sit with the others."

"No, I have to give her an important message!"

"What message?"

"I can't tell you. It's a secret."

"Oh. Well, in that case you have to whisper it in my ear," Teresa murmured conspiratorially, consciously adopting the very tactic she had overheard me using with her little Rodolfo.

As her suggestion seemed eminently logical, the boy cupped his lips and whispered, "Her friend gave me a letter for her. He's waiting for her in the broken church."

"Show me the letter."

Teresa could see that I'd written it to Benjamín, and that I'd signed it—not Isabel, but Isa—clearly a nickname, which implied a special familiarity. Not wishing to snoop more than she had already, she refrained from reading my letter but could not help reading the postscript that was in someone else's handwriting.

Beloved. I've escaped. Tell no one. Come to me. B.

"Did the man say his name?"

The child chewed his lower lip and scowled. Then he remembered. "Ben-amín!" he crooned with satisfaction.

"All right. Give it to Miss Conchita. She's in doña Clemencia's house, behind the grocery store. Knock loudly so she hears you, then hurry right back for your lessons."

He darted out the door, running as fast as his short legs and tattered sandals would let him. Moments later, he delivered the letter. I knew it at once, my breath catching as I recognized Ben's handwriting on the bottom.

"Who gave this to you?" I gasped.

"Ben-amín. He's in the broken church. He says to hurry!"

"*Gracias!* Jacobito, right?" He gave me a big *chimuelo* smile, unabashed by his missing front teeth. I couldn't help hugging him. "You've done a very good job, Jacobito. Now promise you won't tell anyone else about this. It's our secret."

"Well, I sorta told the señora Teresa. Bye!"

My heart was racing. Ben escaped? How on earth? The place was a fortress. Was he hurt? No. He would have said something about needing medicines or a doctor. Clearly he was in hiding. Perhaps because my head was full of Benjamín's memoir, his words soaring inside me, I stupidly threw aside all caution, believing what I wanted to believe. Seeing that doña Clemencia was sleeping peacefully, I locked the front door with her key ring and hurried up the deserted road, straight into Valle Inclán's trap.

The abandoned church stood near what had once been a main thoroughfare. Time had littered the dirt road with an assortment of weeds, cacti, and pines. The building rose nearly three stories high. Its adobe façade was chipped and stained as if from rust tears. All its outdoor niches were empty, its bells long gone, perhaps to take up residence in Samuel's church in the center of town. A portion of the roof had caved in, victim of earthquakes and revolutions. Peering through the door that stood ajar, I noticed that the narthex and a portion of the nave still had some protection from the weather. The rest of the church was exposed to the elements. For some reason, I felt the impulse to look up at the sky before entering.

The abrupt contrast between searing sunshine and cool darkness blinded me momentarily. Squinting, I stepped cautiously into a space that smelled of dampness and neglect. The sanctuary at the far end had long been exposed to the weather. A bird fluttered from beam to sky unopposed.

"Ben?" I murmured.

A single column of sunlight bathed the sanctuary. Dust motes danced in the shaft of light. Only a handful of the church pews remained. I imagined Benjamín sleeping on one of them.

"Ben?" I spoke louder.

Valle Inclán stepped through the front door and closed it behind him. I bolted toward the sacristy on my left.

"I've blocked the rear door," he told me in his thick Castilian accent. "You know, dark hair suits you. I like it."

"I'm not going back with you!" My eyes darted from him to the rubble as I searched for a weapon. "Father Samuel knows the whole truth. He's confronting his mother right now and he's alerting others."

"Is that so?" The hacienda administrator had rope in his hands, which he was calmly working into a lasso. "I bought a cart and a rug so you can travel in style." He seemed deeply amused.

"I'm not going with you. You'll have to kill me first."

"That's the plan," he grinned. "See that beam? I'm going to hang you from it until I hear your neck snap."

"Is that what you did to my grandfather? Is it!"

"Pretty much, except I had to use a tree."

"Do you think killing old men and defenseless women makes you *muy hombre*? You're a rotten coward!"

Holding out his arm, he began to work the lasso. "Which beam do you want? How about that one?"

118

EXECUTIONERS

I LEAPED TO the left, narrowly escaping the lasso. He drew it in and whipped it out a second time with ferocious speed and aim. Yanking on it, he easily dragged me to him. With the lasso still around my throat, he threw me to the floor. Tearing my blouse open, he began hiking up my skirt.

"I like my women warm, not cold and stiff!"

When I started to scream, he covered my mouth. And then a shot rang out.

"Get off her!"

He turned in surprise to face Teresa Gama.

"I was just having a little sport." He said with a forced laugh. Rising, he noted where the bullet had grazed a pillar. Her shot had missed him by a full meter.

I pulled free of the noose and scrambled to get away from him. Valle Inclán's lasso shot out again, this time snaring Teresa. The moment he dragged her toward him, she fired a second shot, hitting him in the left thigh. Valle Inclán dropped down hard, swearing and stirring up clouds of dust. Without the slightest hesitation, Teresa fired another shot, this time into his chest, and another and another and another until the cylinder was empty. Then she rushed to my side.

"Did he hurt you, Isabel?"

Unable to speak, I shook my head, then burst into tears. Teresa hugged me tightly.

Taking the hacienda train back to San Serafín, Samuel reflected that he had asked his brother to do what he himself was not yet willing to do: to forgive their mother. As a man of the cloth, hadn't he extended God's forgiveness to numerous people? Why could he not extend the same mercy to his mother? Was it because she had not asked for forgiveness? Instead, she had chosen to justify herself. True. But above all, he admitted to himself that he simply didn't know how to forgive such monstrous crimes as hers. Should it matter? He asked himself. As a Christian, wasn't he enjoined to forgive seven times seventy?

Samuel tried to pray, to little avail. When he looked up from his prayer book, the charred ruins of a village darted past his window. The work of government troops or of a rebel band? he wondered. When had the forces of good and evil become so blurred? He recalled that when he had asked his mother about the payments that rebel bands were extorting from her, she had responded without hesitation, "To save San Serafín, I'd make a bargain with the devil himself. Practical necessity compels us to take distasteful measures."

Distasteful measures. The memory of my cadaverous face rose to haunt Samuel once again. Leaning forward, he clutched both sides of his head. *Oh, Mother, Mother! How did you stray so far from the light?* By the time he arrived at the hacienda depot, he felt overwhelmed. *Only God can help her,* he told himself as he mounted up and galloped away, unaware of the cook's desperate waving of arms. Old Bardomiana's cries were no match for the thunder of his heart and his mule's hooves.

Samuel's one goal was to get back to San Gabrielín where the world still made sense; where good and evil dressed plainly, lacking subtlety or guile. His wish was granted. Teresa's confession in the doorway of the now empty schoolhouse was simple and to the point.

"I killed a man this morning, Father, and I am not the least bit sorry. The man was trying to rape and murder Isabel."

Teresa and most of the village escorted him to the abandoned chapel. I stayed behind with her children, keeping them in doña Clemencia's parlor since Teresa did not want them to see the bullet-riddled body. I didn't need to be there to see it again. Valle Inclán's blood-soaked corpse was engraved in my memory, there to lodge for many years. Samuel recognized him at once and groaned.

"Tell me what happened." He turned to Teresa with soul-weariness, for wasn't this further proof of his mother's treacherous nature? Who else would have ordered Valle Inclán to murder me?

"I overheard a small boy—I think his name is Jacobito—I heard him boast to his friends that a man had given him a gold coin to deliver a letter to Isabel, I mean Conchita," Teresa glanced at the crowd that had gathered. "I insisted on seeing it. It was addressed to Benjamín and was signed, Isa. I didn't read it," she added defensively. "But I couldn't help reading the postscript. The handwriting was different from hers. It said that he had escaped and that she was to come to him. It was signed "B," which I assumed to be Benjamín. So I was glad for her until I heard the boy imitating the stranger's accent." Teresa crossed her arms and threw back her head. "I never met your brother, Father, but I very much doubt that he speaks with a Castilian accent. So I grew suspicious." The crowd nodded and murmured its approval. "I told the children to stay inside the schoolhouse until I returned, and I ran all the way. When I got here, Isabel—Conchita—was screaming. The man was on top of her and had a rope around her throat. So I shot him."

"Where did you get the gun?" Samuel asked, but only to give himself time to think.

"I always carry it with me."

At this point one of the villagers removed his hat and stepped forward. "*Padre,* we didn't know whether to burn the body or just toss the devil into a hole out back. If the authorities come looking—"

"No crime has been committed here." Samuel spoke firmly. "In the sight of God, it is never a crime to defend oneself or someone else from evil. What the señora Teresa did was right. It is also right to give the man a proper Christian burial."

"In our cemetery, Father?"

"No. Right here, out back."

Several men dug a hole behind the abandoned church, where it would not draw the attention of federales or rebels. There was no coffin, and no one offered to make one. Samuel prayed for the man's soul—and silently for the man's accomplice.

As soon as Teresa picked up her children, I hurried to find Samuel. I caught up with him halfway to his house. He looked haggard.

"Samuel, I'm sorry to trouble you, but I must know. Did you see Benjamín? How is he?"

My brother-in-law seemed to study the cracks in the pavement. Then he looked directly at me. "He's like a man who has gone through a terrible death and a joyous resurrection." Samuel managed a smile as he retrieved Ben's letter from a pocket. "This is for you."

That night Teresa knocked softly on my bedroom door.

"Are you all right, dear?" She draped an arm around my shoulders. I turned and hugged her close. Ben's letter had restored calm, even joy. Now it was Teresa who shivered in my arms. Pulling away, she tried to strike a defiant stance: "I'm still not sorry. He got what he deserved, what all rapists deserve!" And then she was crying desperately, as if she had used up the very last of her reserve of anger. "I was raped."

"Oh, Teresa!" I hugged her. "I'm so sorry! When?"

"In Sep—in September. Two men raped me. I'm pregnant, Isabel. Oh, God! What am I going to do? What am I going to do?"

I thought of Rosa's answer, *endure,* but didn't say it. Teresa needed consolation and the chance to vent her fear and anger. Enduring would come soon enough. So we sat on the edge of my bed, like sisters telling all, confronting one of the oldest dramas in human history. Then the practicalities.

"So, you're at least four months along, maybe five?"

"I suppose."

I drew on Rosa's strength. "Ah, Teresa! What happened to you and almost happened to me was terrible. Valle Inclán paid the price. So will the men who did this to you when they have to face God. None of us can escape the consequences of our misdeeds. Sooner or later there is a reckoning, if not in this life, in the next. But you know, maybe this baby will be a joy to you."

"A joy? How can I look at the child and not remember those thugs?"

I took her hands in mine. "You may have to remember those men for years to come. But what you'll *see* is an innocent little child who will adore you, because you are its mother, its true mother. God can bring good out of evil."

She pulled away, "Can he now?" She began to pace, anger spewing from her eyes. "Why should I trust God? If He's all powerful, why didn't he protect me from those men? Look what Valle Inclán almost did to you. Why does a benevolent God allow such blatant evil?"

The answer came to me with stunning force. "So that you can be you, and I can be me."

The next morning Teresa visited Valle Inclán's grave. It pleased her that he lay in a cemetery overgrown with weeds, without so much as a pile of rocks to mark his grave. And yet, because it was peaceful there and the morning so ripe with promise, she bowed her head and asked God to forgive her for taking a life, and then she didn't feel quite so angry anymore. But she could not bring herself to pray for Valle Inclán or for the men who had raped her. That was simply a step too far for her. Gazing at a hawk drawing ovals on an azure sky, she wondered yet again, wistfully this time, Oh, why doesn't God stop people from hurting each other? Wouldn't it be infinitely better if He simply stepped in like a strict father who is looking out for us, and kept us from making bad choices in the first place?

Since neither sky nor hawk offered answers, Teresa headed back to the village. Walking briskly, she paused at the crest of a hill. Before her lay San Gabrielín glistening in the morning light. As she told me later that day, "Suddenly I understood your answer, Isabel!"

"To what?"

"The question of evil. I asked you why a benevolent God allows it, and you answered, 'So you can be you and I can be me,' which made no sense. But standing on the hill that overlooks San Gabrielín, I got it, and I wanted to shout: I'm Teresa Gama, the woman who chose to kill a killer and to love Rodolfo Nyman!" Her face was flushed with excitement. "Right or wrong, I made my own choices, and I would have it no other way. And then I thought about what you said—that God can bring good out of evil. I'm not proud of having been a man's mistress instead of his wife, as the Church would have it. But my children who are everything to me *are* a great joy and a gift from God. So why couldn't it be the same with the child growing inside me?"

119

BIDDEN OR NOT

EARLIER THAT SAME morning, while Teresa was visiting Valle Inclán's grave, I was sitting in the church garden. Having re-read Ben's letter yet again, I had turned to the last pages of Ben's memoir. Though Samuel spoke softly, I jumped.

"Still working your way through the memoir?"

"No. I'm just reading my favorite passages again."

He joined me on the bench. Pleased that the manuscript seemed to have done its intended work, he smiled and stretched his long legs. It was a comfortable stance, but it could not mask his sadness.

"How did it go with your mother?"

He drew in his legs. "I gathered everyone, and we dug up your grave."

"Goodness!"

"I forced her to watch as we exhumed you. I had them pry open the coffin."

I actually felt a stab of pity for her. "How did she react?"

"Like a fox with a chicken in its mouth. 'A hen? What hen?'" He gave me a wry smile. "I succeeded brilliantly in revealing the truth to the people of San Serafín, but not to her."

"Wasn't her deception painfully obvious?"

"She wasted no time in justifying herself to everyone. She arranged your funeral, she told them with admirable composure, so that she could hide food inside the coffin as a safeguard against the coming famine."

"That doesn't make sense."

"Tell *her*." He rose, signaling an end to the conversation. Yet something kept him rooted to the spot. "I saw the cell. My God, Isabel! How did you keep your sanity?"

"I almost didn't."

He began to crumble. "I'm so ashamed for her! For my family! And most of all for me."

"None of this is your fault, Samuel. Please don't blame yourself." He slumped onto the bench, bending over in a spasm of pain. I sat alongside him, not daring to touch him. "Samuel, what your mother did was terrible. And yet, I wouldn't trade what I learned from it. Strange as it must sound, I feel grateful now for the very hardships that opened me up to perceiving more inwardly. The kingdom of heaven really is within us. I found that out the hard way, but for that alone I'd endure incarceration all over again."

Anger and pain intertwined in his tortured soul. "How can you still believe in God?"

"Because all-powerful as your mother seemed, she could not keep Him out of the cell. How does Goethe put it? 'Bidden or not, God is with us.'"

"Where was he when you were starving to death? You almost died, Isabel!"

"I think I did die, delusional as that must sound to you. One moment I was struggling to breathe and the next I was outside of my body hovering high above it. I could actually see it lying on Eva's bed, a pitiful shell-of-a-thing. Tacha and your mother looked rattled as they worked to revive it while I, the real me, felt nothing but *exhilaration and freedom*."

"How long—how long did that go on?"

"I have no idea, only that I was suddenly soaring high above the hacienda grounds, then higher yet above Morelos and the whole of Mexico. And then I saw Him."

"God?" Samuel crossed his arms, his stance suddenly as skeptical as Ben's would have been. "Now how exactly does one see omnipotence and omnipresence?"

"You don't. I think we see only what we are capable of perceiving or enduring. I saw—I saw—"; suddenly I felt the angst of a translator struggling to render exalted poetry into the colorless prose of a primitive language, all nuances lost, a higher reality crammed into straight-jacketed words. "Light. Light. Brilliant," I gasped, my hands clenching and unclenching. "Fire—fire that does not burn. *Love. Love above all!* Tender. Overpowering!" I paused to swipe at my uninvited tears. "He's human, Samuel, and He embraced me!"

"Christ!" He murmured the name, making of it neither curse nor expletive but something tentatively sacred. "Then the Church has it right," he murmured in astonishment. "Tell me exactly what you saw."

"I saw Jesus Christ. Perhaps others experience God differently—as an angel, or as Krishna or Buddha or a woman or—"

"No," Samuel shook his head emphatically. "The omnipotent God is absolute! He does not need to morph for our sake."

"Why shouldn't the creator of universes manifest himself in billions of ways?"

"Because then what is all this for?" He tapped his chest with both hands, invoking the cassock and all that it represents. And I sensed his need for the absolutism that I could not give him— absolute answers to justify his vocation and his very faith.

"Christianity might be the most direct path to God," I conceded. "It is for me. But surely the Lord has provided many other ways for humans to connect with Him. Consider the world's different religions—"

"They can't all be right."

"True. But maybe they each have their portion of truth as do the arts and sciences."

"Truth is one," he insisted with uncharacteristic stubbornness. Or was it desperation?

We fell silent. After a while Samuel cocked his head to one side. "So, have you seen Him since your brush with death?"

Does he believe me? "No. I saw the Lord just that one time. When I regained consciousness and found myself still a prisoner, He faded back into invisibility—a fair trade."

"How exactly is his invisibility fair? I'd say it's the crux of the problem for those who doubt the existence of God."

"It is precisely his invisibility that offers us the freedom to believe in Him or not—*and the freedom to be ourselves,* Samuel. My brush with death—my encounter with the Lord, astonishing as it was—did not *force* me to believe. I've been free to rationalize it away. In fact, when I found myself a prisoner again, I didn't remember the experience right away."

"How could you not?"

"I don't know. In a way it was like waking and chasing an elusive dream."

"Perhaps that's all it was," he said gently. "After all, didn't Tacha drug you?"

"True. When they revived me, I railed against God. Despair would have destroyed me, but then I remembered everything! Well, probably not all of it, but enough of it. And all I could do was weep with gratitude and pray in my own stumbling way."

"How can you be certain it wasn't all some ecstatic delusion induced by your severe malnutrition?"

"Because I have *felt* the Lord's presence several times since then."

"Simply by praying? Then clearly He favors you over most of us."

"No, by learning to link my breathing to prayer."

So I told Samuel what little I knew about the Hesychasts and the Jesus prayer. And though he said nothing, I sensed from the expression on his face that this was a spiritual practice—a discipline—that he could respect. During the silence that followed, we let the garden have its say through the drone of cicadas and the call of grackles. After a while Samuel interrupted them.

"My God, Isabel! What is it like to feel that presence?"

"The first moment of awareness draws a gasp from me, a shaking of the body, and then tears that are both joy and ache."

"Holy tears. That's what Eastern Christian mystics call it," he mused.

I don't know how long we talked. When we realized how late we were for school, we ran all the way, both of us laughing as we gathered up skirts and cassock to keep from killing ourselves on the uneven road. We arrived out of breath, sweaty and smiling. It was but the beginning of a long process of healing. So here is another lesson I would share with you: when life seems bleak, run—if not from the peril itself, then for the sheer pleasure of your physicality. Run. Let your heart pound and the blood surge through your body. Never underestimate the power of good physical exertion. It carries God within it too.

CAMAXTLI

SEVERAL DAYS LATER, Teresa and I were in the school when more than two hundred Zapatistas rode into town. They were peasant men and women whose rallying cry had become *¡tierra y libertad! Land and liberty!* Samuel was in the church. So it fell to Teresa and me to protect the children, most of whom had rushed into the courtyard. Bolting the gate shut, we could see the troops while keeping them on the other side of the iron bars. Teresa reached into her pocket, fingering her revolver. I turned to the children: "Let's sing to our our visitors! Who knows a good song?"

"*Cuatro Chivos Pintos!*" a small girl called out.

So we launched into the "Four Spotted Goats" song, timidly at first, with increasing gusto the more we repeated its all-too-repetitive lyrics. We added other childhood songs with their nonsense jingles and then the one revolutionary song that most of us knew: "Adelita." Our voices slid between the bars and leaped above walls and treetops, spilling onto the street. Emiliano Zapata, riding at the head of the column, paused outside the school. I recognized him at once though I had seen him only one

other time: the very night that Benjamín and I eloped. He and
several of his men had stumbled into us on a deserted road, all of
us startled. Benjamín was gallantly prepared to fight them all. Yet
it was Zapata, eyes and moustache dark as the night, Zapata, the
man destined to be the revolutionary hero of Morelos, and perhaps the only true hero of the Mexican Revolution, who offered
us protection the night of our elopement, escorting us to the outskirts of Cuernavaca, where we boarded a train North.

So here I was, seeing him for a second time from the safety
of the school's gate, wondering if he would remember me. He
didn't seem to. Pushing back his large sombrero, he crossed both
hands over the pommel of his saddle and listened a while longer
to our impromptu performance. The whole column of horsemen
waited patiently. When our repertoire ran dry and we resorted
to singing the goat song again, he nudged his horse forward. He
and his troops dismounted outside the church. Samuel met them
on the steps.

"Have you come in peace, son?" he asked Emiliano Zapata.

"Of course, padre," The rebel leader nodded.

"Then you are welcome."

"Some of my people would like confession before we ride
out to meet our fate today. Others need supplies." He motioned
toward the grocery store.

"I trust that you will pay doña Clemencia. She's a good
woman, a widow who helps the villagers with free food when
they cannot pay."

"Then she won't mind feeding my hungry people."

Samuel heard close to fifty confessions that morning. Most
sounded as if scripted from the same tired playwright. He listened, absolved, and prayed with each. They followed one after
the other in nameless succession. Then one stood out from all
the others.

"Bless me, Father, for I have sinned. *Perdonando,* but I allowed a murder to happen." The penitent used an odd phrasing

for "pardon me," that seemed familiar to Samuel, though he could not place it at first.

Most of the penitents that day had readily confessed to killing in the line of duty. Three had confessed to crimes of passion for the sake of a woman. This one was different.

"*Perdonando,* padre, I was the doorkeeper to a powerful general. I served him faithfully for over forty years. I was supposed to keep the house safe, but I let a killer in and he killed my master."

Samuel felt a jolt. Drawing closer to the grille in the confessional, he gazed into the wrinkled face of a man with a scraggly white beard and a mole on his left cheek.

"Eufemio?" Samuel asked, blatantly throwing aside even the pretense of anonymity. "Eufemio Rosarito, is that you?"

The man drew closer. "Padre Samuel!" He hesitated, but only for a few seconds. "Father, what I tell you in holy confession remains secret, right?"

"Yes."

"You can't tell anyone else?"

"No. This is between you and God. I am only an intermediary. Don't be afraid to speak the truth, my son. God already knows it, but He must hear it from you if you wish forgiveness." Samuel had made such assurances to many a fearful soul. This time he could feel his own heart racing. "Who did you let into the house?"

"The killer." Eufemio Rosarito brought a trembling hand to his mouth and cheeks.

"Who is he, my son?" Samuel's face was breaking into a sweat. "Who killed my—Who killed the general?" he asked again.

"Me."

"Why?" Samuel groaned the Word that Spanish bifurcates into two: por qué?

"*Porque—*" And here Spanish reunites the bifurcated *why* into *because,* merging question and answer. "Because I had to. I loved him, Father. Don't you see? He was a man's man, a soldier who wasn't afraid of death. But later, the señor general became afraid of life. Day after day I had to watch him wither away, body and mind, padre."

There was a long silence.

"Tell me about the night you murdered him, Eufemio."

"I knew it wasn't you who was visiting so late at night. I knew it was don Benjamín pretending to be you. I've always liked his mischievous ways, so I played along. I've always said I could see the devil in Captain Benjamín's eyes. But the devil was in me." Eufemio Rosarito swiped at tears that slowly dampened his cheeks. "After—after your brother left, I ran up to check on *el señor general.* He was agitated, talking to himself about his will. Just a few hours earlier he had some young lawyer write a new one for him. *Perdonando,* but my master was always making new wills. In this last one he cut off everyone in his family and was leaving everything to some Isabela Brentano, but there was no such woman, padre. Maybe he meant Isabela Orentano."

"A mistress from long ago?"

"Sí, padre. But he forgot that she died years ago. In those last months he ranted against some Isaura Brentt for marrying don Benjamín without his consent, and because she was a *protestante.* Other times he called her Anabel Brentt. *Perdonando, padre,* but in those last months the General mixed up names and people like he was scrambling eggs, shells and all."

"What happened after my brother left the house?"

"I found your father talking to himself, shouting that all of you were worthless, even his Isabela Brentano, though I think he meant Isabela Orentano. So he was going to write a new will in the morning and leave everything to the Holy Church, and I was to go fetch the lawyer again and the notary public at first light. I finally got him to bed, but he was still swearing and muttering. The last thing he said to me was, 'Straighten the crucifix. It's crooked.'"

Samuel closed his eyes. He could visualize the heavy bronze cross that hung above his father's bed, and he trembled as if he were about to witness the murder.

"When I shifted the cross to straighten it, the nail came off. I caught the crucifix. It was heavy as a sledge hammer. I would need to fetch a bigger nail in the morning. I meant to prop it against a wall, but I looked at the General just then. Such pain in those eyes, like he was suddenly remembering his old self, like he knew that he was trapped. I looked at his shrunken body and remembered how your father used to look in his uniform, tall and manly in the saddle, so unafraid. I tell you, those eyes were begging me to free him! Don't we show mercy when we kill a horse in agony, an animal that can no longer be itself?"

Great tears rolled down Samuel's face, even as Eufemio's voice hardened.

"So I picked up that bronze crucifix and I put the horse out of his agony."

Neither spoke for a minute or two. Several Zapatistas grumbled that they wanted their turn in this life, not the next. Eufemio sighed.

"Please give me my penance and absolution, Father."

"No." Samuel shook his head. "True penance requires that we deal justly with each other. My brother Benjamín is in prison paying for your sin."

"I know. But Father, I did try later to make it look like the earthquake knocked the crucifix down onto your father."

"That wasn't enough. Your testimony at the trial implicated Benjamín. So I repeat: an innocent man—"

"Hey! Old man!" someone grumbled loudly. "You don't have to confess every damn sin you've committed since you stopped wetting your pants!"

"Listen to me, Eufemio. An innocent man is paying for your mortal sin," Samuel spoke quickly. "But it's never too late to speak the truth."

"I have, padre. I've told you and God. Now bless me, Father."

"No. If you do not confess your crime to the authorities as well, then you are immersed in the sin of deception."

"What deception? I stayed in the house all night. I was going to turn myself over to the police the next morning, I swear it, Father! But God had other plans, don't you see?"

"No, I don't."

"*Pardoning,* but He sent the earthquake so that no one would be blamed for freeing your father from his torment."

"But someone *was* blamed! An innocent man! Eufemio, you *must* return to the D.F. and turn yourself in, or your sin remains!"

"*Perdoñando,* padre. I never meant to hurt your brother, but I cannot give myself up like you want. I have my own fight here in Morelos."

"Please, Eufemio!"

"*Perdonando,* padre. Please give me my penance and absolution."

"It's not enough to be sorry! True penance needs deeds from the heart!"

Eufemio Rosarito left abruptly. Samuel hurried out of the confessional. The next Zapatista in line intercepted him.

"Bless me, father," the man asked, humbly bowing his head.

Samuel made the sign of the cross over him. Others clustered around him.

"We're heading out, Father. Please bless me."

By the time Samuel stepped outside, most of the troops had mounted up. They were an army rendered faceless under large straw hats, their backs turned to him as they rode out of town.

"Eufemio!" Samuel shouted.

Eufemio Rosarito had vanished into *la revolución.* As Samuel watched the riders blur into clouds of dust, he tried to remember what the ancient Tlahuica tribes of Morelos had called the god of war. The memory of it rode away. Another came to him: Camaxtli, God of War of the subjugated Tlaxcala tribe. Camaxtli, a god who promised faithful warriors that they would rule the world. Camaxtli, a deity who dressed in yellowed human skin.

GENTE DECENTE

SAMUEL DID NOT mention Eufemio to Teresa or me. For the next
two days he kept to himself, wrestling against the intense desire
to tell the authorities what he had heard in the confessional. How
else was his brother to be exonerated? What was more important? Keeping his vow to honor the confidentiality of the confessional, or speaking the truth to ensure that justice be carried out?
Wasn't his duty to the truth? On the other hand, didn't a vow to
the church have to supersede all other vows? Wasn't it spiritually
higher than civil or fraternal duty?

What did it matter? No matter what he chose to do, Samuel
was faced with the indisputable fact that in the chaos of revolution, it was highly unlikely that Eufemio would ever be appre-
hended, much less be put on trial. And then there was his ecclesiastical duty. In refusing to give Eufemio absolution, hadn't he
failed as a priest?

The questions vexed him like bee stings.

If there was one person in San Gabrielín who was fast shed-
ding her sense of personal failure, it was Teresa Gama. She went

about her day with quick, assured steps, smiling to herself. Helping at the school only in the afternoons, she spent her mornings designing and creating. The wheel of her sewing machine whirred; her hands maneuvered fabric with a dexterity at par with a nascent self-assurance. Several days later she surprised me with a beautifully tailored suit and a waist that she had made from doña Clemencia's cast-offs.

"Oh, Teresa, they're beautiful!"

"The skirt is gabardine taffeta, which is really better suited as lining, but it has a nice color, and I think that adding the cording enhances it. I hope you like it."

"You're amazing!" I twirled about in my new outfit. "You didn't have to do this. I don't mind wearing—"

"No, Isabel. You cannot go on dressing like an Indian. Though you do make a very pretty one when you braid your hair, the simple fact is that you're not one of them."

"Of course I'm one of them. We share the same humanity."

"Humanity, yes, but you are not one of them. Even I am no longer one of them."

"Clothes make us that different from them?" I crossed my arms.

"I don't know how it is in the rest of the world, but I do know that in France and in Mexico—and probably everywhere else—you are judged according to how you dress. It determines your station in society and—"

A commotion in the small plaza cut off her words.

Federal troops had just ridden into town. With alarming efficiency, they were herding the villagers of San Gabrielín into the central square in front of the church.

"This is an outrage! We did not aid the enemy!" Samuel insisted firmly to the federal colonel. "They took most of our food, and I see your troops are taking what little is left!"

"I'll tell you what's an outrage, padre." The pockmarked officer spoke with slow deliberation. "That in the last two weeks rebels have burned fields in Atlihuayán, Chinameca, Tenango, Treinta, Santa Inés, and San José. They also attacked a train with civilians."

"But not these people! I can personally vouch for every one of them!"

"I have my orders."

The villagers were arrested. The colonel had been ordered to spare all *gente decente*—higher-class people. He doffed his hat to the fair-skinned doña Clemencia, to me in my new outfit, and to Teresa—mestiza, dark-haired, fine-featured, and decidedly elegant in her tailored clothes and upswept hair. Firmly holding onto her well-dressed children, she returned the colonel's greeting with a curt nod.

The cries of the village women and children drew tears from us, survivors who could only watch helplessly. We knew that the younger men would be conscripted into the Federal Army, but what would become of the rest? Teresa reached into one of her pockets, but she did not retrieve the revolver. Bitterly, she had to acknowledge to herself that there *were* severe limits to her self-reliance. This was a battle she could not fight.

The Federal troops set fire to all the houses except ours. Then they mounted up. Doña Clemencia and I scrambled to provide blankets to the prisoners. Having no food to give them now that the federales had confiscated it, we pressed coins into their hands. Women and children sobbed as they were marched out of town. Samuel walked alongside the prisoners.

"I'll talk to the right people and get you back home!" he promised the many who reached out to him in desperation: Venancio and Bonifaz, who had helped him with his roofing projects; Rigoberta and Gustavo, who had lost their son when he joined the Zapatistas; Jacobito, the little boy who had run into Valle Inclán; Trini, whose irreverent humor always made us laugh; and so many others, all tied to each other like inmates charged with crimes they never committed.

Samuel walked with them for several kilometers. At first he tried bargaining with the sullen colonel who rode at the front of the column. The man ignored him, keeping his eyes fixed straight ahead. Samuel's anxiety grew with each kilometer that separated him from San Gabrielín. He knew he had to get back to us now that we no longer had food.

When he staggered back into the town, the wind was whipping through the ruins of scorched houses. A few timbers, the last of the resisters, crackled as they succumbed to the flames. Ash swirled like snow. Thick smoke assaulted his lungs, doubling him over in a coughing fit. Pressing a handkerchief to his nose and mouth, Samuel stared in disbelief at the devastation of his village. Only the church and his house had been spared. Even don Pepino was taken. Only a small canary had escaped the ransacking. It perched in yellow mourning on the rooftop of the school, a solitary figure in the cold clarity of a February sky.

Samuel had returned to a ghost town.

ON THE ROAD

SAMUEL STOOD IN the middle of the deserted road. His face was sweaty and grimy, his spirit desolate. Then he heard a child's voice ring out: "Uncle Samuel!"

The door to the parish house flew open and little Rodolfo scooted past us. Samuel scooped him up into a tall embrace. We all stayed together in the parish house that night. Across the long hours, Samuel tossed and turned on the sofa. Dark thoughts convinced him that he was hopelessly inadequate—that as a priest, he had failed Eufemio just as he had failed to protect his parishioners. What was the moaning emptiness of San Gabrielín but a mirror of his own soul?

Morning brought light and resolution. "We have to leave," he informed us.

"Leave?" doña Clemencia's voice quavered. "They're out there on every road, in every town. Killers every last one of them!"

"We must take our chances. They've taken everything. If we stay, we'll starve. I suggest that we go either to Cuernavaca or to San Serafín. They're about the same distance from us."

"But we have no horses or mules, Father." Doña Clemencia wrung her hands. "If you insist, then you'll have to go without me. I cannot walk all that way. My legs—"

"We still have my goat cart," Teresa brightened.

"And I'm a good goat," Samuel winked at the children. "So doña Clemencia and Rodolfito will ride in style. I suggest we pack lightly."

"Perhaps we should each bring only what we can carry inside a single pillowcase?" I suggested.

Teresa glanced up the stairs, as if she could see her sewing machine. Then she nodded.

"The question remains, do we go to Cuernavaca, which is in Federal hands, or to San Serafín which could fall any day to either camp?" Samuel was looking directly at me. "Both offer the possibility of a train to the D.F. I've prayed all night for a sign, and the only thing that came to me is that you should decide for us, Isabel."

"Me? No. This is for all of us to decide together."

"No," he answered firmly. "You've earned the right to choose for us."

Homesickness swept over me. I longed to walk through the rooms that Cadwally had painted so garishly; to smell the fragrant honeysuckle and orange blossoms; to cook again in a kitchen that spilled into the small garden patio, and to climb a tree that promised lavender-tinted freedom. Above all, I yearned to see Rosa who would open her heart and her home to us. But would it be fair to impose on her like that? We were seven refugees now. Seven mouths to feed and very little money of our own. Returning to San Serafín, on the other hand, would impinge on no one but doña Manuela. Whether or not she had been chastened by Samuel's exposure of her grand deception, she was in a far better position to help us with shelter, food, and her own personal train to get us out of Morelos—and to Ben!

"I think we should go to San Serafín," I answered at length. "Besides, I'm sure you want to see how your mother is faring."

He did not, but he nodded anyway.

As we filed out the front door an hour later, Teresa had to suppress the urge to hurry upstairs to run her hands on her sewing machine one last time. Samuel locked the door. It was a symbolic gesture of hope. Then he placed a heavy jug of water into the cart. Silently, as if making an offering, we added our bulging pillowcases. Each was stuffed with a single change of clothing and a treasure or two. Aside from the barest essentials, my own pillowcase held Benjamín's manuscript and my edition of *Divine Providence*; Teresa's held photos of the children as babies and a framed photo of herself with Rodolfo in Paris in another life. I remember that doña Clemencia packed a candlestick from Toledo and the exquisite lace *mantilla* that had once served as my bridal veil. The children were each allowed to take two favorite toys that their father had sent from Paris. Ah, our treasures! Samuel helped our elderly companion arrange herself on top of the stuffed pillowcases. Last of all, he lifted six-year-old Rodolfito, as he was starting to call himself, (*Lambikins* no more) and placed him on doña Clemencia's generous lap.

"You can be the driver, Rodolfito," Samuel offered. "I'll be the horse."

"No, Uncle. You're Billy got grof," the boy answered in heavily accented English.

"Isabel has been telling them fairy tales at bedtime," Teresa explained.

"Right. I'm the Billy got grof," Samuel agreed, grabbing hold of the cart's wooden handle.

Nine-year-old Laurita slipped her hand into mine. Eleven-year-old Teresita, her back very straight and her eyes grave, walked alongside her mother. With treasures on board, we set off on foot.

"I'm hungry. When do we eat?" Little Rodolfo asked with a regularity that helped us gauge how far we had gone.

"About one fourth of a kilometer per question?" Samuel quipped.

We soon lost track of time. The road to San Serafin seemed endless, especially on empty stomachs.

"At least it isn't hot or rainy," doña Clemencia tried to comfort us in her lovely raspy voice. "It's so much better to feel a little cold than hot!" She wrapped her shawl more tightly around her ample figure. Rodolfito fell asleep on her lap. Whenever the wheels became trapped in deep ruts, Teresa and I helped to push it free. So we trudged on—a priest, a grocer's widow, a discarded mistress, three children, and an escaped prisoner. The few people we passed on the road cast furtive glances our way, but they did not trouble us. When night came on, Samuel pulled the cart off the road and hid it in the thick vegetation. We too hunkered down in the undergrowth and slept with the glorious abandon of exhaustion. Late the next day we finally reached the gates of San Serafin. A guard's challenge rang out.

"Halt! Who goes?"

"Father Samuel! Open up!"

They knew his voice. Moments later, the great door swung open, and I had a sense of déjà vu—that I had come to claim once again what was not mine. The thought passed quickly. This time I focused on something far more enticing than claiming a plantation: how wonderful it would be to eat something, anything, from Bardomiana's kitchen.

HOMECOMING

SAMUEL PUSHED THE cart the last few feet. His face and back were drenched in sweat. Since he was busy helping doña Clemencia down, he did not notice the curious, almost amused glances of the guards. I did. Before I could alert Samuel, he was striding into the house like a man entering his front parlor, except that the parlor had vanished. It was instead a stable. Hay bales were stacked along the walls, obscuring antique tapestries; dung coated the oriental carpets; horses and mules flicked their tails at flies. Samuel whipped around.

"Where's my mother?" he asked the nearest man. "Where's the señora of the house?"

The man, who was grooming a horse, cocked his head indicating upstairs. Samuel took the steps at a gallop, with us close at his heels, afraid to be alone with the intruders for even an instant. Assorted laundry hung on the balcony railings to dry. Chickens scurried out of the way. Grungy children ran in and out of the bedrooms. Entire families had moved in, each claiming a room as a home. When we reached his mother's bedroom, we found a tall, stout Indian woman leaning over the bed. Turning, her hand flew to her chest.

"Padre!" the old cook exclaimed in relief.

Samuel embraced Bardomiana. On the bed lay a woman who resembled his mother. Her face was ashen, and she lay so still that we thought her dead.

"She's sleeping, Father."

"What's happened, Bardomiana?"

"The poor señora had a stroke. Two, actually. She's paralyzed and can't speak. She can only move her eyes."

"When did this happen?"

"I think the first one happened the day you dug up the grave, padre." Bardomiana shook her head sadly. The stricken look on Samuel's face cried out, *I did this! I caused it!* Sensing the weight of his regret, Bardomiana quickly added, "The señora wouldn't let us send for you, and she did seem to get better at first. The second stroke was far worse. It happened the day those bandits broke in here. You remember Jesusita, my *galopina*?"

Samuel gave a vague nod, but I remembered the youngest of the kitchen maids. How could I forget that she had carried letters so willingly between Benjamín and me, back when we were first falling in love in this house and he was the prisoner.

"The day those *miserables* demanded to be let in, that Jesusita walked up to the gate, as cheeky as can be, and said—" Bardomiana lowered her voice. "Pardon me, Father, but she said, 'The señora is a devil! We can't serve her anymore, not after her lies about doña Isabel.' *Santo Dios!* It's you!" The old cook had just recognized me as I uncovered my head.

"Hello, Bardomiana."

"Jesusita and Tacha said you looked like a skeleton!"

"I did, but I'm fine now. Please, continue."

The old servant scrutinized me closely before turning back to Samuel. "Jesusita let them in. No one tried to stop her. The bandits and their women poured through here like a river in a flood. Then the looting started. A lot of our own people joined them. I hurried up here and found people fighting over your mother's jewelry, *padre,* with her lying right there in her bed. Two others were going through her desk, emptying the drawers onto the floor."

"My God! Did they hurt her?" I could see that Samuel was beginning to drown in guilt.

"No, padre. I kept them away from her. I told those thieves that this was the one room that neither God nor the devil would let them have." She reached into a desk drawer that no longer closed properly and handed him a small stack of letters tied together with string. "This is all that I managed to save."

He nodded but took little notice of them. "And they obeyed you?"

"Yes, Father. I threatened to curse all the men with impotence," she nodded matter-of-factly. "They haven't troubled us any further. They know to stay out of this room. Now, if you'll excuse me, I'll go prepare some food for you."

"God bless you, Bardomiana."

When the door closed behind her, Samuel glanced at the letters in his hands.

"I think these are yours." He sighed, by way of apology, as he handed them to me.

Many of them had Pennsylvania return addresses and were clearly from my former classmates. A few were in my own handwriting, letters that I had written to Benjamín, back when I had hoped to reconcile with him. The envelopes had been ripped open. Given that they had been stored in his mother's desk, it was obvious that she had intercepted them.

He never saw them, I understood with a pang of sadness.

Doña Manuela opened her eyes just then. Samuel returned to the bed and peered into her face. Thinking about it later, I realized that he did not kiss her. He did speak gently, the way he would with any dying person, but with a marked stiffness. "How are you?"

She answered with a garbled sound and frightened eyes.

"It's all right. We're here. We're going to take you to Rodolfo's house as soon as you're strong enough to travel. Can you understand me? Blink once for yes, twice for no."

She fixed her eyes on his and blinked once with slow deliberation.

"Good. Meanwhile, look who I've brought to see you!" He turned and reached for the children. As he did so, his eyes met mine. Doña Manuela had not noticed me yet, since I was standing by the door. I shook my head and mouthed the word no to Samuel. He must have wondered whether I simply did not feel ready to face his mother, or if I was trying to spare her another shock. It was both, I suppose.

"You remember Rodolfo's children?" I heard him ask, doggedly refusing to address her as Mother. "This is Teresita, and this is Laura, and—"

Closing the door behind me, I stepped into the secret hallway, a secret no longer. The door that had kept me a prisoner stood ajar. I paused, afraid to enter; afraid the door might slam and lock behind me. Afraid I might drown in old fears, I reached for the Jesus prayer. Moments later, I stood calmly under the cupola, the renegade window unreachable as ever. The last rays of the day cast my shadow on a wall. Instantly I remembered my skeletal figure, the *calaca* that used to sway on unsteady stick-legs. Memories of hunger and loneliness encircled me. I continued to pray, breathing the words in and out, in and out with steady deliberation. The phantoms softly faded into the fading light.

That night my old cell became the family's sleeping quarters. Large as it was, none of the intruders had wanted it when they heard about the ghost that haunted it—the ghost of the girl who had climbed out of her tomb; people said that the victim had been murdered by her evil mother-in-law. Everyone in the hacienda had a story about hearing the ghost singing or lamenting at night. Some swore they had seen my pale form wandering among the graves. Few ventured into the cell in daylight, none after dark.

So far, only Bardomiana had recognized me, primarily because I had kept my *rebozo* draped over most of my face until I reached doña Manuela's room. The old cook had looked shocked at first. However, she soon looked relieved by my presence, perhaps because it exonerated her mistress from the sin of murder. Bardomiana returned with two blankets from her own room and pillows for the children.

"I'm sorry, padre. These are all I have. They sacked all the linen closets. I'll have to see what else I can find to make you comfortable. Meanwhile, Rosaura and I have brought you beans and tortillas for your supper." She indicated a pleasant, round-faced young *soldadera,* one of those self-sacrificing women of the revolution, women on all sides of the conflict who traveled with their men, cooking, binding up wounds, sometimes fighting alongside the troops, and burying their dead. The *soldadera* carried a clay pot in both hands. A small basket dangled from one wrist.

Just then a wild bronco-of-a-man barged into the cell. Unlike his sandal-clad companions, he sported sharp-pointed boots and an intricately decorated black *charro* jacket that he could not button over his enormous belly and white pants. A self-styled uniform in process. I suspected that the jacket hailed from the wardrobe in Samuel's old room. The intruder swaggered as if to say, *I'm not afraid of any damn ghost!* Like most Tlahuica Indians, he was a large, dark man with singularly white teeth. Unlike the majority of his people who were slight and nimble like Tomás, this individual lumbered with a heavy tread. And then there was his moustache, extraordinary for its very failure. Most of his upper lip was as smooth as a child's. To compensate, the man had settled for verticality. No more than five or six strands of hair sprouted from the corners of his mouth, swooping down to his chest. These he tugged on as he spoke, alternating between the right and the left.

"I'm General Contreras Agustín! I'm the man in charge here!" he thumped his chest, causing the cartridge belts that crossed his chest to rattle. "This isn't your house anymore! I claim it on behalf of my people!"

"Welcome. *Mi casa es su casa,*" Samuel smiled, fully aware of the literalness of the *my house is your house* pleasantry. Contreras Agustín grinned.

"That's right, padre! Your house *is* my house! What are you going to do about it?"

"Say Mass tomorrow."

"And then what?" Agustín tugged on the right side of his moustache.

"And then I'm going to ask a great favor of you as a Christian."

The man narrowed his eyes and leaned forward. "What favor?"

"General, I respectfully ask that you allow us to borrow the hacienda train tomorrow morning so that—"

"What do you want with my train?"

"With all respect, General, to get my mother to a doctor in Mexico City."

The man's laugh startled like a blast from a shotgun. "Now why would I let you do that?"

"Because I'm going to pray for you every day of my life, Contreras Agustín, to thank God for your mercy and to ask him to extend his mercy to you."

The bandit general tugged on the left side of his moustache. "'*Stá bien!*" He agreed, his Spanish as rough as his manner. He left with scowl and swagger. The next visitor entered with a gentle knock and hat in hand. Agapito Alfonso, the assistant administrator of the hacienda, bowed and kept his voice at a respectful volume.

"May I speak with you, padre?"

"Agapito!" Samuel embraced the shy young man.

"I just wanted to pay my respects and to see how the señora is doing today."

"Bardomiana tells me that she sleeps most of the time now. I suppose that is a mercy." Samuel lowered his voice. "Tell me, who *is* this Contreras Agustín?"

Leaning in, the young man murmured, "A cutthroat. Some of our people here in the hacienda call him General *Asustín*."

"And is he as scary as the name implies?"

"Oh, yes. He's dangerously unpredictable. He's also a peacock, loud and vain."

Samuel cocked his head to one side. "Speaking of peacocks, why don't I hear them squawking away?"

"The general had them killed and cooked up for dinner a few nights ago. Then he complained about their toughness."

Samuel sighed. "And you, Agapito. How are they treating you and everyone else?"

"All right, padre. They want all able-bodied men to join them, but I'm not about to follow an ignorant man like this *Asustín*." Squaring his shoulders, Agapito added in a firm voice: "However, I have to tell you that I believe in the cause of land for the dispossessed. I think Emiliano Zapata is the only man in all of Mexico who really cares about his people. So I need to ask you, to tell you—you know I've always been a loyal servant—"

Samuel placed a hand on his shoulder. "Follow your conscience, Agapito. Do what you believe to be right. It's all any of us can do."

When Agapito had left, Samuel gazed at the fields from his mother's window. His family's land stretched to the distant horizon and generations back in time. Lines from Ecclesiastes came to him just then: *"The profit of the land is for all; the king himself is served from the field."*

Land redistribution? Maybe it was time.

124

FEBRUARY 9, 1913

THE VERY NEXT day, Caleb Wilkins did something he had never expected to do as a Protestant missionary: he attended a Catholic mass, a bold step for an ardent Baptist from Gloucester, Massachusetts. And though he knew his folks back home would have turned quite pale at the mere thought of it, he would have rushed to assure them that he had not fallen under the spell of the papacy, but of a girl with hair blacker than Ipswich Bay at night and a smile to guide ships home. So on the morning of February 9, 1913, Caleb Wilkins was happily seated between Carmelita and her widowed mother. Carmelita's two younger sisters giggled every time they leaned forward to stare at the couple. The cathedral was packed.

After Mass, Caleb, Carmelita, and her family stepped into the tree-lined park that used to front the great Cathedral of Mexico City, and from there into the wide-open spaces of the Zócalo. Brushing against Carmelita's hand, however briefly under the eagle eye of her mother, he tingled with the thrill of that contact. Both felt the pleasure of young love, morning sunshine, the mingled scents of flowers and food from the stalls, and the excitement of being together in a large crowd. People of all economic classes strolled in their Sunday best where Aztec pyramids had once risen to the sky. Where tens of thousands of human skulls had once gazed from enormous racks, men in tall, peaked hats and colorful sarapes now sold balloons, fruit drinks, and religious trinkets. In place of long lines of slaves for the day's sacrifice, electric trolleys brought in visitors bound for the Alameda Park where the police band would play Verdi and Bellini alfresco.

Caleb laughed at something Carmelita had just whispered in his ear. Then looking off to the right, to the far end of the great square, he caught sight of a white-bearded officer on horseback, splendidly arrayed. Cavalry and foot soldiers marched behind him.

"What luck!" he smiled at Carmelita. "I think we're about to see—"

Though he didn't have time to say 'parade,' the word hung suspended in his mind, so oddly out of sync with the loud, mechanical bursts from machine gun nests in front of the National Palace. Tenochtitlán, city of human sacrifice, ran red again.

Meanwhile, as Samuel prepared for Mass in the hacienda church, he discovered that every one of his chasubles had been stolen from his old room, which was now inhabited by several bandits who were sleeping off a night of heavy drinking. Yet one chasuble did make its way back to Samuel that morning. A woman of indeterminate age with a face as weathered as the hacienda's front door, pattered up to him on bare feet. Kneeling before him, she murmured, "I've brought you a vestment, *padre*. Forgive me for taking it!"

"Thank you, *hija*. May God bless you for your honesty." He made the sign of the cross over her. The woman reached up and kissed his hand.

When he had robed in the returned vestment, Samuel took his mother's hand. He wanted to bring it to his lips, knew that he should, but could not bring himself to. Not yet. Her eyes opened.

"I'm just stepping out to say Mass," he felt compelled to tell her. "I've asked Isabel to sit with you. It's all right. I want you to make your peace with her, and through her, with God. I'll hear your confession when I get back."

He set off with Teresa, doña Clemencia, and the children, all of whom stayed almost as close to him as Hipólito, who had bounced happily between Samuel and me, tail wagging with newfound energy. I think that for Samuel, Hipólito was the one joy in that joyless return to his home. Priest and dog soon became as inseparable as in his boyhood. I didn't mind Hipólito's preference for his 'boy.' Besides, he was generous with his affection, pausing to greet me with canine elation. He moved about the hacienda as fearlessly as Samuel.

My brother-in-law knew that with the possible exception of the self-styled General Agustín, or *Asustín* as we called him in private (the made up word implying 'the Scary One'), the rebels in Morelos revered or at least respected the church and clergy almost as much as they hated the haciendas and their owners. Though he straddled both social institutions, Samuel was regarded first and foremost as a priest. Therefore, most of the men doffed their hats as he passed by. Samuel nodded or blessed them, his face solemn as he walked through the wreckage of his family's home. Every room was smoky from cooking fires that scorched carpets, tile, and parquet floors alike. Samuel Nyman Vizcarra showed no emotion as he walked past the portraits of his ancestors now riddled with the bullets of an afternoon's sport; past the library whose books carpeted the floor; past the mahogany desk whose contents spilled out like guts from a butchered animal. Entering the church, he made a deep genuflection before the altar. Hipólito took up his position at the far side of the altar steps, and I approached my former tormentor.

We each had our duty to perform that fateful Sunday.

125

FORGIVE US OUR DEBTS

MY ALL-POWERFUL captor lay before me, too helpless even to turn her head away. She was my captive. My prisoner. Like it or not, she would have to hear me out. Sitting sidesaddle on the bed, I looked into those fathomless wells of hers.

"Doña Manuela, it's me, Isabel." I fingered one of my braids. "I darkened my hair the night of my escape, but can you see that it's me? Blink once for yes; twice for no."

She blinked once. How to begin? I tried to take the high ground.

"I'm very sorry about what's happened to you."

I stopped, conscious of all that the sentence implied, physically and spiritually. There was so much that I needed to say. Confront or confess first? *Forgive us our trespasses as we forgive those who trespass against us.* I remembered a carriage ride in a borrowed hat and mercenaries riding alongside me. I took a deep breath.

"We've hurt each other, you and I. Do you think we could try to forgive each other?"

She stared through me, her eyes expressionless, then at me. With slow deliberation, she blinked twice. Manuela Nyman was not completely helpless after all. I waded deeper.

"I thought I was acting within my legal rights. But to my dying day I shall regret that we evicted you from your home. I believed, or tried to believe, that we were acting on behalf of the villagers of Santa Lupita whom your husband had dispossessed. We were going to right his wrongs. Yet how were we any different from him? Please forgive me."

Manuela Nyman's eyes remained dark pools, absorbing light, giving back nothing, her features immutable as Tacha's. Yet I sensed that she was listening closely.

"There's something you need to know about your husband's will. Before I tell you, you must understand once and for all that Tomás Tepaneca and I were never lovers. Never. He is simply my oldest and dearest friend, a childhood companion that I shall always cherish—but it's Benjamín whom I love with all my soul."

A stare, opaque as hematite.

"After we evicted you, I struck a bargain with Tomás. I told you about it, remember? I agreed to deed back the stolen lands to the villagers of Santa Lupita, but only if he had Benjamín's case reopened and brought Eufemio Rosarito to justice. You and I both know in our heart that Benjamín did not kill his father. So you see, we don't disagree about everything."

Déjà vu. How many times would I have to rehash the past before she believed me? There was no reaction, only a surge of regret on my part.

"Oh, why didn't we work together instead of against each other? We could have given each other the moral support we both needed so desperately!"

She was unmovable. A colossus half buried in desert sand. The moment had come: "Doña Manuela, I have not been totally honest with you. After we evicted you, Tomás admitted that he tampered with the will, just as you suspected."

At last a light flashed from the depths of her eyes. Her mouth twisted grotesquely. Was the sharp, garbled sound the broken voicing of triumph?

"I did not tell you sooner because I was trying to protect Tomás. But I swear to you by all that I hold sacred, that I did not know about his tampering until after I claimed what I thought was my inheritance. Please forgive him for the wrongful way that he sought social justice, and please forgive me for me for my part—and for covering up for him. Can you do that?"

She watched me, neither blinking yes nor no.

"Well, I forgive you." I crossed my arms with more impatience than love, my tone suddenly corrosive. "I forgive you for locking me in a dark cell and leaving me without food for more than a month. We don't treat our worst criminals that way, but then again, maybe you're just criminally insane. So what can I do but forgive you for pushing me to the very brink of death!"

I admit it felt good to tell her off. How deeply we all need to expose those who have wronged us; to voice our outrage, especially when it is justified. "And thank you for that spiffy new cell. It was so very kind of you to stick me in that white coffin of isolation and loneliness and—"

How else but through isolation and loneliness? The thought whispered unbidden, stopping me in my tracks. A sense of awe seeped in: a trickle. A creek. Then a stream.

"Do you know what's strange, señora?" I confided in a softer tone. "Looking back on my imprisonment, I can see that I gained far more than I lost. I didn't know it then, but I do see it whenever I think with hindsight—and if I don't cloud my thinking with anger. It was precisely because of my isolation and loneliness that I found God. So I forgive you. I forgive you everything, even—"

No. Not everything! Dropping her hand, I drew back, keenly aware that I had reached the limits of my humane impulses, or that perhaps I had blocked whatever goodness I had encouraged to flow through me. I could genuinely forgive all the harm that she had caused *me*. Only that. A second wave of anger hit me, stronger and more destructive than that first one, thrusting me toward her, my face inches from hers.

"What I do *not* forgive is that you had my grandfather murdered—that poor, dear old man. There was no need to do that! None! I had already deeded everything back to you." Manuela Nyman shut her eyes, locking me away. I drew closer and spoke into her ear so that she would not miss a word. "Valle Inclán boasted to me about the murder the day that he tried to kill me." The eyes flew open. "That's right. You may not have bothered with the specifics—how he was doing your dirty work. Do you want to hear what you sanctioned? The hanging of a helpless old man. You ordered it, so before God you are as guilty as Valle Inclán."

I had said all this before, that day when I confronted her, trapping her hands between mine and the prison bars. But victimhood needs more than one opportunity to cry out against injustice and criminality. Because I suddenly pictured the dreadful twitching of Cadwally's legs as he dangled from a rope, his death was *now* and my outrage now. So I gave in to the sweet pleasure of revenge, satisfying and poisonous.

"You got away with your crime in this life, but you will soon be facing divine justice, like your miserable henchman. Your Valle Inclán is dead now and probably in hell where you both belong! There are no verses of contrition and no number of Masses that will save you or him unless you repent from the heart. But you don't have one. Do you hear me, Manuela Nyman?" I shook the pillow on which she reclined. "You stand on the brink of death, and you chose hell long before this!"

Forgive us our trespasses as we forgive those who trespass against us.

How? I began to crumble. How does one forgive the unforgivable? What do I do with my just rage? I can't forgive her. I can't. Who but God can forgive so much? Who but God—Oh Lord, please help me! This is beyond me.

I don't know how long I prayed. When I opened my eyes, I was no longer a warrior bent on bloodletting. Seeing the paralyzed, mute Manuela Nyman, I felt the compassion of a war-weary soldier who pauses to help a mortally-wounded enemy.

"Oh, Manuela," I spoke with soft urgency, softly taking her hand. "Don't you see that we're nothing, you and I? We're just empty vessels that accept or reject good impulses or bad ones. What made us think that our conflict was about your husband's will? Oh, it was about the will, all right—the will to choose; the will to do; the will to *be*. When all is said and done, what are we but our choices? Even now, we can still choose! All that anger in us—"

She squeezed my hand weakly. Was I reaching her at last? I leaned closer.

"Squeeze my hand again if you agree that we should forgive each other. Please, Manuela."

Inert. Deliberate stillness. I tried again.

"I thought that I had the largesse of spirit to forgive you entirely from myself, but I don't have it. Neither do you. This *is* beyond our meager power. Only God can help us now. Please, will you pray with me, Manuela?"

Was ever a stare so fixed? So intransigent? Still holding her hand, I knelt by the bed and prayed aloud in Spanish: "Lord, you who creates universes, you who have known Manuela and me since you formed us in our mother's womb, forgive our sins, both intentional and unintentional. Help us to perceive your love; let it flow into us unimpeded. Grant Manuela and me the strength to forgive each other, that our souls may be freed from the hellish forces of hatred and revenge. Heal us, oh Lord, through your love."

Still on my knees, I moved into silent prayer, Manuela's cold, limp hand in mine. I don't know how long I prayed, only that at some imprecise moment, time stopped. Something shifted.

There was no *me*, no *I*—only the will to love. A surge, warm and bright as the sun, flowed through me. It did not *come* from me, only *through* me, flowing as freely as my tears. Rising, I kissed the dying woman and whispered, "Be at peace, Manuela."

Clamping her eyes shut, Manuela Nyman locked me out of her orb one last time. Her chest rose and fell as if she were sleeping fitfully. I remained at her side, my emotions soft—swooping like a bird in flight.

Gradually, I felt myself slip back into the familiar world—the world of concrete needs and the habitual reliance on the appearance of things rather than on the hidden substance. What then of those brief flashes of enlightenment? Are they fireflies that glow for the blink of an eye and then disappear into the dark opaqueness of daily life?

Long experience has taught me that spiritual progress is not linear. It's spiral. A sudden gift of enlightenment, as powerful as it is brief, propels us upward along that spiral. Yet even the saints among us backslide at times. That is the human condition. Still, the more frequent our efforts to atone or to better understand or to better love another being, the closer we draw to God. I suppose the same is true in reverse. The plunge into spiritual darkness also spirals, with short upward thrusts of diminishing goodness, the inexorable downswing moving a life into ever-increasing degrees of evil, all freely chosen, until the soul comes to rest on the plateau of its choosing. Where was Manuela Nyman in that long spectrum? I dared to wonder. Did she regret anything? Had my words opened up the possibility of peace or had they entrenched her all the more? I knew only that it was not for me to judge her spiritual condition—only her deeds in this life, and that life seemed to be sputtering like a tired machine.

After Mass, Samuel and the rest of our group hurried back to prepare for our trip to the D.F. They need not have rushed. The feckless General *Asustín* had changed his mind about the train. No explanations offered. Apparently, the mighty need not explain themselves to mere pawns. Similarly, the mighty *Asustín* had not bothered to consult anyone when he ordered the cutting of the hacienda's telegraph wires and the destruction of the telegraph office, back when they first took over the plantation. So no one in the hacienda knew about the momentous events that were unfolding in the nation's capital.

Ignorance is not bliss. It's dangerous. My little group, as homeless now as the beleaguered peasants of Morelos, yearned for the safety of Mexico City, never imagining the name that historians would assign to this period in our nation's history. Had we known, we would have chosen to remain a bit longer in the overcrowded, vandalized hacienda with *Asustín* and his gang, for it is with good reason that the military coup of 1913 has come to be called *la Decena Trágica*—the Tragic Ten Days.

126

BEDLAM

Seventeen-year-old Caleb Wilkins drew amused stares wherever he ventured. Six feet two inches tall, skinny as a young sapling, and with scraggly auburn hair that plunged halfway to his elbows, he was readily recognized as a foreigner. The fact that on chilly days he draped a colorful Indian sarape over his vested suit and that he had a predilection for Indian *guaraches* instead of socks and shoes, made him seem eccentric. Armed with his guileless smile and sturdy sandals, Caleb walked everywhere, covering prodigious distances. On the morning of the third day of the coup d'etat, he was back on the streets again. The guns had been silent all Monday and now into Tuesday morning. So why hide like a frightened dog?

Normally, Caleb Wilkins would have whistled as he walked, pausing to greet street vendors and to pet stray dogs—but not after Sunday's massacre; not after what he had witnessed. Now he walked with shoulders hunched forward and mouth drawn tightly as he struggled to forget what could not be forgotten. When he was about half way between the Cathedral and the Ciudadela, the city's old fortress, an artillery shell exploded nearby, shattering the morning calm. A second shell struck a building a block from where he stood. Caleb ran, not stopping until he reached his destination.

He was sweating profusely when he entered the city's infamous Belém prison. He often went there as part of his prison ministry. Every time he entered its dark throat, he reeled from the stench of its overcrowded dungeons. There was no getting used to it. How could they have named it Bethlehem? He used to wonder. So what that it had been built to shelter women in the seventeenth century, or that it had been a school. Now it was the closest thing to hell: a warren of dark, overcrowded dungeons; a place smeared with urine and feces; a pestilent hole that drove many prisoners to suicide. Yet that day, as Mexico City became an urban battleground, Caleb felt a rush of relief to be able to shelter within Belém's thick walls. Besides, he was carrying a message that he very much wanted to deliver.

The din inside the prison was almost as bad as the chaos in the streets. Since the prison guards knew him well, they allowed him a brief visit.

"Ten minutes. Then get out!" a guard snarled, flinching as another shell found its mark somewhere out there, out there where the corpses of people and horses were piling up.

Caleb had no idea which of the dungeons held his friend. He could have shouted out the name, but he liked the new one that Benjamín had dreamed up in the penitentiary hospital. So he shouted that one.

"Man Angel!" Caleb deliberately pronounced it in English. "Man Angel!"

"Cah-léb!" Mangel shouted in the gloom, shoving his way forward to reach between bars. "Bless you for coming!" he grasped the missionary's hand. "How did you know where to find me, Cah-léb?"

No one in all of Gloucester says my name like that! The boy smiled with tender amusement. How often had he heard Mangel say it that way without giving it any thought? Yet here in the putrid darkness of Belém, the Mexicanization of his name was like a match that lights the darkness, even if only for the blink of an eye.

"Paladín told me they came for you in the infirmary. I figured you might be here. How are you?" Caleb squinted as he peered into the battered face.

"I'm all right. Tell me what's happening out there? We heard gunfire on Sunday, nothing on Monday, and today this."

"Some generals are trying to take over the government. I saw one of the leaders killed. What you heard on Sunday was a gun battle right in the Plaza de Armas."

"You were there?"

"Yeah, with Carmelita and her family."

"What happened?"

Caleb sighed, wanting both to talk and not talk about it. After a long pause, the need to unburden himself broke through. "We were just coming out of Mass."

"You went to Mass? Catholic Mass?"

"Yes. Yes, I did." The boy squared his shoulders as if owning up to a fault. "I think God was there too. Anyway, the cathedral and the square were packed. After Mass we started across the square, and I happened to look across the plaza. There was an old man on a big white horse. Even from where I stood, I could see that he was wearing a fancy uniform and that he had a long white beard. He was leading his men forward, and I thought—" Caleb gave a short laugh, derisive and pained. "I thought we had lucked into a parade. Everything happened so fast and so slowly. You know what I mean? I saw the old man draw his sword and lead a cavalry charge. For a moment, he looked the way you imagine battles when you're a boy, you know? Gallant. Noble. Moments later, he flung his arms out and fell dead. Federal troops must have been alerted, because they were waiting for them. I've heard of machine guns. Now I know what they sound like and what they do to a human body. Mangel, there were women and children trapped between the armies, but that didn't stop the shooting."

"Bastards!" Mangel swore, adding a few choice words before he caught himself. "*Dios mío*," he added apologetically, for he was a man who genuinely longed to be a new man, someone other than the old Jesús Mangel. "What happened next?"

"Panic. People ran in all directions. In the confusion we got separated from Carmelita's little sister, Ricardita."

"Is the child all right?"

The boy closed his eyes. "She was trampled to death."

"Oh, Cah-léb. I'm sorry."

"We buried her yesterday. She was only seven years old! Seven! One moment she was a little girl giggling in church; the next she was lying face down like a broken doll. And those armies—those soldiers—they just kept firing. I heard that more than four hundred people died in those first minutes, and more than a thousand were wounded!"

Much as Caleb tried not to think of the bodies he had seen strewn all over the city's central square, it would be years before he would be free of the memory of a collective terror.

"You know what they never tell you about battles?" he murmured. "The books don't tell you about the cries of the wounded. And they don't tell you how to brace yourself from the cries of a mother who finds that her child has been killed."

They fell silent. Outside the walls of Belém, it continued to thunder though it was long past rain season.

"What's happening today?"

"More fighting in the streets. My God, Mangel! On my way over here, I saw two people blown right out of their home! A man and a woman. I think they were dead even before they landed on the sidewalk. Their clothes were on fire, and the man's head—" Caleb shoved the memory away. "You know where the rebels are holed up? No more than a block from here," he pointed. "They're in the old citadel. You know the place?"

"I'm not from around here," Mangel shook his head, half smiling. "I don't know the city. I've spent most of my life here in Belém."

Caleb blinked into the pestilent gloom. "My God," he murmured. And he understood for the first time how a bear-of-a-man like Jesús Mangel could be both damaged and ferocious, bullied and a bully.

"Why did they bring you back here? Why didn't they let you stay in the Penitentiary?"

"Ah, Cah-léb! I deserve this. I've done terrible things. Terrible things," he shook his head. "I would give up my life right now, this very minute, if I could undo all the harm I've done. But I can't bring back the dead. I can't heal those that I beat up, and I can't unwrite the reports I wrote about el Paladín."

"What reports?"

"The only reason they moved me to the penitentiary in the first place was because some rich *magnate* with a lot of connections hired me to keep an eye on Paladín. The bastard knew that he wouldn't have to pay me much. He knew that anyone lucky enough to get out of Belém would do anything to keep from being sent back here. I had to promise to kill Benjamín Nyman if ordered to."

"Who hates him that much?"

"I don't know. I never got the name of the man. A Spaniard, I think. When the order came, I couldn't do it. I won't be the demon-possessed man anymore. Never! So I'm here where I belong. This is my graveyard, Cah-léb, but Jesus has found me. So I'm not alone."

"Thank you, Man Angel!" the boy managed in a choked voice. A criminal had just validated his very reason for being so far from home. He had found one lost sheep. One! And that made it all worthwhile.

Mangel reached into a pocket and drew out a small book. "I carry it all the time, the *Santa Biblia* that you gave me. But it's so dark in here, I can't read a word. Could you recite something from memory?"

With utmost reverence, Caleb recited the twenty-third Psalm.

"Thank you, brother! Tell me again the part about walking through the shadow of death."

"'Though I walk through the valley of the shadow of death, I will fear no evil. Thy rod and thy staff, they comfort me.'"

Mangel repeated the lines several times. Then he turned his thoughts in a different direction. "There's one more thing I need to know."

"If I were a betting man, which I'm not, I'd bet my last peso that you're wondering about Teodora."

"Have you seen her?"

"Yes. I'm here with a message from her. She wants you to know that she's run away from the colonel who forced her into prostitution."

"Where is she? Is she safe out there?"

"Calm yourself, brother. El Paladín got her a job as a servant with a relation of his."

"So she's safe? Are they treating her well?"

"She told me herself that the señor and the señora are a kindly old couple and that you're not to worry about her."

"Where is she?"

"In a house on Lucerna Street, in a swanky part of town. You can be sure she has far better living quarters than you and I do."

"Lucerna. Where's that?"

"Not all that far from here. It begins one or two blocks west of the citadel."

"The citadel?"

"The old fortress I told you about—where the insurgents are holed up. She was planning to visit you yesterday after we buried her sister, but her employers insisted that she return to their house and stay inside. As it turned out, it was calm all day, so she could have come after all. Today it's a battleground again."

"Out!" a prison guard yelled at the few visitors who had ventured into Belém that day. "Visitations are over! Everybody out!"

"Take heart, Man Angel. Teodora asked me to tell you that she will come to you as soon as it's safe."

"No! Tell her *not* to come until the fighting is over. Tell her, Cah-léb!"

Early the next day, on the fourth day of the *Decena Trágica*, Mangel and his cellmates were startled awake by a renewed artillery barrage between the two enemy camps. His immediate response was to go down on his knees to pray, and there he stayed for the next hour or so. Later that day a shell hit the prison. The force of the blast threw him against a wall, momentarily stunning him. Before the smoke had cleared, a second blast hit Belém, setting the building ablaze. Mangel staggered to his feet. Instantly he was swept up in a mad scramble, unstoppable as giant ocean waves. He and many of the inmates stampeded out of the inferno, running from pestilent confinement into an urban battleground. Many more died in the blaze.

Horses, soldiers, and civilians lay dead or wounded in the streets. Mangel and most of the escaped prisoners ran toward the rebel-held citadel. No one stopped them. Those who reached the old fortress begged the insurgents to accept them into their ranks, which they did. Others, like Mangel, kept running. In his confusion, he could not remember the name of the street where Teodora was working. Utterly disoriented, he ran through the streets of an embattled city that was as alien to him as Paris or Buenos Aires.

127

SACRAMENTS

In San Serafín, a different drama was playing out. Doña Manuela was dying. The hacienda doctor assured us there was nothing anyone could do for her. Samuel was not so sure, but he could not persuade General *Asustín* to allow us to transport her to the city. In truth, she was far too fragile for the trip. All we could do was to try to keep her comfortable. Once Samuel accepted the futility of trying to save her life, he returned to his obsession to save her spiritually. Having performed the Sacrament of Healing, he turned now to the Sacrament of Penance, offering to hear her confession. The rest of us stayed in the large cell so that they could have privacy. Laurita and Teresita played hopscotch. Rodolfito grew fitful.

"Mamá. Why can't we go outside to play?"

"Because there are nasty men out there who might hurt you. We're safe here." Teresa's tight-lipped smile attempted to warn and reassure at the same time, a tricky proposition.

Rodolfito patted the pistol in her pocket. "Couldn't you just shoot them?"

~

Since doña Manuela could no longer speak, Samuel devised questions to which she could blink once for yes, twice for no. After a prayer he asked, "Do you wish for me to hear your confession?"

She blinked a deliberate once. Crossing himself, he knelt by her bed and murmured softly, "Do you repent of the sin of deception?"

After a long pause, she blinked yes.

"Do you repent of your cruel treatment of Isabel?"

A fixed stare.

"Do you repent of the sin of torture?" The eyes remained defiantly wide. Samuel's voice grew sharp. "Do you repent of the sin of murder—if not by your hand, then by your will?"

At that point, she shut her eyes tightly. Exasperated, Samuel slammed his book shut. "Without true repentance, confession avails you nothing! Nothing! Even if I could bring myself to forgive you—" But he hadn't. He couldn't.

When she remained unresponsive, her eyes fluttering under their lids, he stormed out of the room, conscious as he gripped a railing and stared unseeing into the patio below, that he was on a collision course with his faith, for didn't the Church teach the forgiveness of sins via confession and absolution? Wasn't he empowered to forgive sins? Forgive? Why? Because he had received Holy Orders? Who was he to give her absolution? What if sins cannot be wiped out in an instant of divine mercy? What if our life can be changed only gradually through sincere repentance and effort? Wasn't it too late for her?

No. Not while she breathes, he told himself. So he doubled his efforts to stir her to true contrition, that she might partake more meaningfully of the Eucharist. But she seemed to be sleeping most of the time now. Later that afternoon she opened her eyes and seemed alert. Samuel rushed to her side. The rest of us hurried away, again to give them privacy. Speaking gently, Samuel urged his mother to unburden herself for the sake of her immortal soul. When she shut her eyes in rebellion, Samuel broke out of his role yet again, the priest becoming a son full of sorrow and fear.

"Oh, Mother, I tremble for you! How could you have taken pleasure in torturing a young girl, whatever her sins against you? When did you become so utterly heartless?" Dropping into the chair by the bed, his shoulders heaved as his voice broke. "Oh, Mother, Mother! You were the light of my life."

She groaned just then.

"There's still time, mamá. Do you want the solace that only the church can give you?"

She blinked yes.

"Then tell me, do you regret ordering Valle Inclán to murder Mr. Brentt and Isabel? Do you acknowledge that you have sinned most grievously?"

Her stare became fixed, her silence a razor that slashed him.

"You've imperiled your soul! And for what? For a house that has been turned into a den of thieves? For land that will swallow your bones and turn them to dust? Look to your soul!

"Whoever you are, whatever you've become, I will not allow you to drag my mother to hell! Do you hear me? My Manuela, the Manuela I loved, was all kindness and wisdom. What have you done to her? Tell me that you regret the harm that you've done to all of us. Are you sorry? Blink just once, damn it!"

Manuela Vizcarra de Nyman opened her eyes desperately wide as her body convulsed, wrenching her spirit free.

Samuel was devastated. He hurried down the stairs, Hipólito at his heels.

"Stay!" Samuel snarled. Then he was gone, leaving the safety of the hacienda walls for the fields; ignoring the stares of the curious as tears spilled down his face; running, running until his calves ached and sweat stung his eyes.

～

While he was gone, Bardomiana, Teresa and I did what women have done since time immemorial. We washed and dressed the body in preparation for burial. Doña Clemencia helped by offering to take the children into the garden to gather flowers, for wouldn't it benefit them to remember years later that they had done something for their grandmother, stranger that she was to them? Teresa agreed, but only after handing her gun to our Spanish friend.

"Do you know how to use it?"

"As surely as I love España," doña Clemencia answered in her heavy Castilian accent, smiling as she shoved the gun into her own pocket.

"But would you have the nerve to use it if necessary?"

"How do you think we conquered the Aztec Empire? Don't worry, *muchacha.*"

After we saw the children and their protector out, we focused on bathing the body. I was startled by its smallness and vulnerability. This was the fearsome Manuela Vizcarra de Nyman? And it occurred to me that all of history's most feared men and women must have seemed just as pitiful—defanged and childlike in death's repose.

"What is this?" Teresa pointed to a ribbon around Manuela's neck. Two keys dangled from it.

"I don't know, señora," Bardomiana scowled. "When those thieves broke in here and took everything, including the keys to every door in the hacienda, they must have missed these, maybe because she kept them hidden under her clothes, as you see."

"What do they open?"

I leaned over the body. "I think they're the keys to her husband's house."

"How do you know that?" Teresa straightened.

"Because for a brief time they were mine."

The old cook who had been trying to brush la patrona's hair with nothing but her gnarled fingers as a comb, untied the ribbon.

"These keys must have been important to her. You take them, señora Isabel." Then she turned sorrowful eyes to her mistress. "Those *malditos* barged in here and helped themselves to all of the señora's clothes. It doesn't seem right to bury her in her old nightgown. It isn't right!"

"She could have my new skirt and waist," I offered. "That is, if you wouldn't think me ungrateful," I turned to Teresa. "I still have the outfits Tacha gave me. What do you think?"

Teresa, though she had long endured Manuela Nyman's disapproval, didn't seem inclined to begrudge her children's grandmother a little dignity. She nodded and I changed into my peasant clothes. The blouse that Teresa had so skillfully made for me from doña Clemencia's cast offs, looked elegant on Manuela with its high collar and Chantilly lace. The skirt trailed several inches beyond her ankles, which was good since we had no shoes for her, plus it added to the grace of the figure. Before leaving the room, I gazed at Manuela Nyman one last time. She looked peaceful, and thanks to Teresa's nimble needle, every bit the *gran señora* that she had been.

Feeling an urge to be alone, I ventured at last into the garden. So far only Bardomiana had recognized me, and I preferred to keep it that way a little longer. I needed solitude without curious stares. Covering most of my face with my shawl, I kept my eyes downcast and my motions unhurried. *No swinging of the arms,* Tacha would have growled.

Several of *Asustin's* people glanced my way, but no one bothered me. Moments later, I was in the gardens behind the house. The grass needed mowing and the hedges trimming, but the flowers were perfection itself. Smelling their fragrance, I remembered the intense pleasure that these gardens had given me the day of Cadwally's unexpected visit. For a few hours, I had been allowed to reconnect with the world and with beauty itself. I had strolled arm-in-arm with my grandfather and my jailor. The real boon had been more than that taste of freedom. I had been given the chance to see at last past the disease of alcoholism, discovering nobility in a silver-haired old man.

Even now I cherish the memory of our last day together. The very extremes of the experience as we strolled—Manuela on one side of me, Cadwally on the other—seems like life itself: terrifying and wonderful, tragic and beautiful. At the end of the visit, my grandfather had ridden fearlessly past armed guards, waving his hat in grand showman style, only to hang by the neck from a tree before nightfall. Even now I could weep if I dwell on the violence of his death. Cadwally won't have it. All bad things pass, he tells me like a woman who dismisses the intense suffering of her labor as she joyously cradles her baby.

HEART OF THE LABYRINTH

As I entered the labyrinth, my thoughts flew to Benjamín. Samuel had told me about Ben's reaction on learning about my imprisonment. Would news of his mother's death soften his just resentment and ease his soul? More than ever I longed to see him. Samuel had promised to take me directly to the penitentiary as soon we got to the D.F. What a reunion it would be! Yet were joy and sorrow ever so entwined?

Ah, my love! Don't hate your mother, I intended to advise him. Love what was good in her. Leave the rest in God's hands.

I was almost in the heart of the labyrinth when I remembered a conversation with Benjamín, back when we were falling in love and didn't know it yet. He was strolling alongside me disguised in one of Samuel's cassocks, hands behind his back as he struck a priestly stance.

"To the ancient Christians, labyrinths were vivid metaphors for sin and the powers of hell," he had intoned solemnly. Then he had slipped up, becoming Benjamín for a few seconds, his eyes bright with the irreverent brand of his humor. "Now that I think of it, Miss Brentt, I don't know if it's advisable that I lead you into the perils that await at the heart of our labyrinth."

"Why? Does your mother keep a minotaur?"

No, I now answered my own question. She kept birds and a scraggly American, but not here in these twisting paths. So, what *does* lie at the heart of a soul's labyrinth? God or the minotaur-self?

After facing a revolution, imprisonment, starvation, isolation, and now the death of my nemesis, which of the two had I found in my innermost being? God or self? Both. Yes, both at different times. And now, at this moment? Sitting on the fluted edge of the fountain, I felt such peace. Looking up, I spotted two small birds flying overhead. Escaped parakeets? I wondered. Lovers like us, Ben? I smiled, dipping my fingers into sun-dappled water, blue as the sky.

Samuel returned hours later. He had the look of a man who has narrowly survived his first battle. During the short time that I lived in revolutionary camps, I had seen that dazed look more than once. Here it was again. We all hurried to Samuel's side, each of us giving him a hug and a *pésame,* words of condolence that couldn't begin to encompass his loss. General *Asustín* had his own brusque *pésame.*

"I heard that your mother kicked the bucket. I guess we won't need to go to the D.F. now."

"But we do, General."

"And why the hell is that?" *Asustín* pushed his large sombrero off his forehead. "What good will that do your mother now?"

"It won't, but I have work to do there, just as you have work to do here in Morelos." Samuel answered evenly. "For one thing, I intend to light a candle for you in the cathedral and to pray for you, General."

Asustín tugged on his right whiskers. "What about *la muer-tita?*"—the little dead one.

"My mother should be buried in the home she loved." Samuel didn't miss a beat. "If that is agreeable to you, General," he thought to add, just as the General thought to think about it, chewing the inside of his cheek as if weighing battle strategies.

"*¡Stá bien!* But you'll have to bury her at first light tomorrow and keep it short. We leave as soon as you drop her in the hole." If Samuel cringed, he didn't show it. "And it's going to cost you. Fuel for the locomotive is expensive, padre."

It cost us all right: every last peso that we had collectively. We would have to travel without a cent, but we agreed to it. The goal was to bury Manuela and get away to the city before "*the Scary one*" changed his mind again or lived up to his nickname.

We held a wake that evening in Manuela's room. As there was only one chair, which of one accord we gave to doña Clemencia, the rest of us had to sit on the edge of the bed or on the floor. Samuel spent a good portion of that night on his knees praying, his voice a hypnotic murmur. The children soon fell asleep, the two younger ones pillowed on Teresa's lap. Resting his head near the foot of the bed, Samuel finally dozed off. Only Bardomiana and I seemed as sleepless as the night sky. Halfway through our vigil, Samuel roused himself. When he stepped into the terrace, I followed and stood beside him, staring down into the blackened depths. The February night was cool but not cold. Nothing stirred.

"How are you, Samuel?" I murmured.

He didn't answer right away. "I failed her." He said in English. Was it in case anyone else were up at that hour? Or perhaps because he needed to confess in a language other than the one rattling his thoughts. "I forgot that it was not for me to judge her, but to minister to her."

"You were trying to help her."

"By bullying her? I railed against her when she wouldn't show remorse. Tell me honestly, Isabel. Have you forgiven her? I don't mean in words, but in your heart?"

"Yes, Samuel. I have."

"How in God's name did you manage it?"

"I didn't. I couldn't. So I asked God to forgive what I could not." I pressed his hand as it rested on the railing. "Mourn her, dear Samuel. Reject her evil deeds and love her good ones. Above all, ask God to help you both. Believe me, He alone can give you peace."

At the first sign that the sun was scaling the steep *barrancas* of Morelos, I slipped away to see the aviary one last time. I found General *Asustín* astride his horse, gun unholstered.

"Open up them doors!" he ordered Sinforiano, Manuela's bird-keeper.

The man clutched his straw hat in both hands in a gesture of appeal. "Please, *mi general,* the birds are skittish."

"So is my trigger finger. Open the damn doors!"

I looked for the trogon. He sat perched on the uppermost branch of the tree in the center of the aviary, his long emerald green tail giving proof to his name—the Resplendent Quetzal. The general cocked his revolver and fired randomly into the cage. There was a panicked flapping of wings as a hundred birds flew back and forth. The quetzal remained in his high perch. Three birds escaped from the cage. The others remained inside. *Asustín* fired off a second bullet, killing a white cockatoo. The bird-keeper groaned. The general fired a third time, missing when his newly acquired horse reared up.

"Stop it!" I yelled at him.

Contreras Agustín turned in surprise. "They're just chickens with fancy feathers."

"No, *mi general.* They're like the people of Morelos. They all have a home they love and want to get back to. You're the head of a liberating army. Set them free, *mi general.*"

I had slipped into the gentle sing-song cadence of my early years, the Spanish that Tomás and I had spoken as children. *Asustín* studied my country clothes and dark braids. Then he studied my eyes as I stepped closer.

"All right, girlie. You can have them buzzards, but I want that one for my woman. She's wanting green feathers for her hair."

I grasped the bridle and yanked the horse to the right.

"*No, mi general!* That quetzal is our Mexico," I urged, even though I knew it to be the national bird of Guatemala. "He's been trapped for so long, he's forgotten how to fly free. But if you give him the chance, he'll learn like the rest of us!"

I smiled up at him, my face full of hope. Did he think me bold, guileless, or stupid? A crowd had gathered at the aviary. "That's right, mi general," someone said. "That bird is our Mexico!"

I shall never forget *Asustin's* next words.

"*Bueno! Bueno! Saquen a esos pajarracos pa que volen libres pues!*"—which translates roughly as, "All right! All right! Get them buzzards out of there so's they can fly free!"

For the next hour or so Sinforiano and several of *Asustín's* men managed to shoo most of the birds out of the aviary. I watched anxiously as the cage emptied. The trogon remained stubbornly on his high perch, afraid or incapable of grasping his chance for freedom. The great bells of San Serafín began to toll for my mother-in-law's funeral Mass. Reluctantly, I pulled myself away from the aviary and the solitary quetzal.

129

TOMBSTONES

FOUR PALLBEARERS CARRIED Manuela's open coffin into the church. All along the way, the men of San Serafín doffed their hats as if they had chosen to remember la patrona's protection rather than her guile; the women draped their shawls over their heads and bowed; the children watched in awed silence. Many of *Asustin's* people also attended the funeral Mass. Samuel kept it brief, as ordered. Afterwards, we processed to the cemetery.

"That's her!" I heard a San Serafín woman gasp. "That's the daughter-in-law that went missing!"

"Don't be stupid," her companion scoffed. "She's dead. Lots of people have heard the ghost wailing at night. This one doesn't even look like her!"

Doña Manuela was laid to rest next to her parents' tomb. At the end of the ceremony, Samuel grasped a shovel and threw in the expected first shovelful. He didn't stop there. When two other men stepped forward to help him, Samuel waved them away. Everyone sensed his desperate need to defuse his personal anguish through physical action, or perhaps to perform this deed as a kind of penance. I think it was a son's final gift to his mother. When the grave was filled in, Samuel looked up at the sky. Still gripping the shovel, he added a prayer not in his book.

"Lord God, who knows all our innermost thoughts, have mercy on your humble servant, Manuela, for she was much loved. Pardon her sins, which were many, for she also knew how to love. Have mercy on us. Guide her, however long it takes, from the pit of sin with all its delusions into the radiant light of your heaven. *Gloria Patri, et Filio, et Spirítui Sancto. Amen.*"

The train whistle blew.

General *Asustín* slapped his hat back onto his head. *"Bueno, ya 'stuvo, padre! Vámonos!"* Enough already, Father. Let's go! "Everyone, pack up, and don't keep me waitin'!"

How long would it take his people to gather their belongings and loot? Fifteen minutes if they really hurried? As I had already packed my pillowcase, I knew I could take a few moments to look for my own tombstone. I found it on the edge of the cemetery. The ground was torn open like a knife wound. The coffin lay perpendicularly across the hole, the lid tossed to one side, its cache of beans gone. The headstone pitched to the left.

Isabel Brentt

1890–1911

What will my real tombstone read? I wondered. Will it look this desolate someday when I am long forgotten? Does it matter?

I hurried back to the aviary. Samuel stayed behind, taking a few moments to walk alone through the cemetery of his ancestors. Did he sense this would be the last time he would pause by their headstones and read their names? In truth, he hardly noted them. Samuel remained haunted by his mother's fall from grace.

Oh, Mother, Mother—his wounded soul cried out, to her and to heaven. Doubts assailed him. *If I who knew you best knew you so little, how can I presume to be able to help anyone? Of what use was I to you?*

Sometime after he and I had both died, Samuel shared with me what had pulled him back from the abyss of despair that day: lines from the Peace Prayer attributed to St. Francis.

Lord, grant that I may not so much seek to be consoled as to console; to be understood as to understand; to be loved, as to love; for it is in giving that we receive; it is in pardoning that we are pardoned, and it is in dying that we are born to eternal life.

"That said it all," he told me with a radiant smile.

As *Asustín* and his people prepared to leave the hacienda, I continued to fret about the quetzal. During my incarceration, I had associated the bird, the grandest of the trogons, with Benjamín. Eventually it came to symbolize inner freedom to me. Train or no train, I hurried back to the lower garden. The aviary was almost empty now. The quetzal, however, was still perched on the top branch of the leafless, lifeless tree inside the aviary.

"Go! Go! You're free!" I waved my arms.

There was a second blast from the train whistle. Agapito, the assistant administrator, came running to fetch me. "They won't hold the train much longer! Please hurry, señora. Another band of men has been spotted heading this way."

"Does the General know?"

"I don't think so. One of our field hands saw them and hurried to warn me. They could be friends or enemies of *Asustin*. Don't wait to find out, señora."

I gazed longingly at the trogon one last time. Then I hurried with Agapito to the depot at the far end of the hacienda. The locomotive sported a banner of the Virgin of Guadalupe, that quintessential emblem of Mexico, and more specifically of the Zapatistas. Our little party was assembled on the platform along with many of *Asustín's* people. Samuel was urging old Bardomiana to travel with us.

"No, Father. This is my home. Thank you just the same."

Where was Hipólito? I searched the crowd. No sign of his ever-wagging tail. The engineer blasted his whistle again, so we clambered aboard. The family Pullmans were crowded with armed men, women, children, horses, and chickens. None of

General Agustín's people seemed to worry about the carpeting or the upholstery. Passengers who didn't fit inside simply perched on the rooftops of the cars. A holiday mood had boarded the train, a festive air so at odds with the subdued and respectful tone of the funeral. Samuel helped Teresa's children into the top bunk of a sleeping-berth. Teresa and doña Clemencia quickly claimed the lower one so they could stay close to the children. I still hoped for a glimpse of the aviary, but now I also felt an urgency to see Hipólito one last time. More people got on, blocking the windows. I followed Samuel into the smoking car. *Asustín* and a buxom *soldadera* with gun belts criss-crossed over her breasts sat on a sofa. The general was tugging on his left whiskers. When he saw us, he growled at two of his men to vacate their chairs and to take their chickens with them.

"*Séntense*," he ordered us, his hospitality as questionable as his grammar.

I had my window. And yes, I could see the cupola of the aviary. But where was the quetzal? And where was Hipólito? As if he had read my thoughts, Samuel ignored the chair vacated by bandits and fowls, and worked his way back to the open door. The train lurched forward. Less than ten feet from me two horses reared up. Chickens squawked in a flutter of feathers. And a dog with a beautiful red sheen ran alongside the slowly departing train. Seeing him, I caught my breath.

"Come on, boy!" I heard Samuel urge.

In one of those stupendous moments of sheer will, the old dog leaped onto the stairs. Samuel reached for him and pulled him safely onboard. Even Asustín clapped.

"Bravo!" our bandit-general applauded dog and priest.

Flying our banner of the Virgin of Guadalupe, we were finally on our way. Several *soldaderas* squatted on the carpeted floor and started up the *braseros* that served as small stoves. The car soon filled with the mingled scents of beans, chiles, tortillas, horse manure, and unwashed bodies. I peered out the window, and there it was! A streak of green in the silver-blue sky, a streak that settled in the swaying treetops, its tail feathers a resplendent emerald green.

What none of us witnessed was the takeover of San Serafín by the second band. Its leader, a young colonel loyal to Zapata, dismounted in the cemetery. A pretty woman with long dark hair rode beside him, her belly round and fecund. A band of fifty or so fighters paused behind the couple.

"Wait here," he instructed the men. Turning to his companion, the colonel reached up and pressed her hands. "I'm just paying my respects to an old friend."

Tomás walked a hundred feet or so to the spot he remembered. When he saw my grave, he recoiled as if struck by a jolt of electricity.

"You, there!" he called to one of the hacienda *peones* who had just finished raking the soil over the newest tomb. The man looked up with large frightened eyes. "You! Come here!"

"*Sí, mi jefe,*" the gardener muttered, grasping his straw hat between hands that shook.

"Who did this!" Tomás pointed to my empty coffin, rage shaking his voice.

"Father Samuel ordered us to dig it up. But—"

Tomás did not stay to hear more. Leaping onto his horse, he galloped toward the house. His companions rode after him, the thunder of their horses' hooves terrifying the people of San Serafín. Tomás strode into the house, yelling: "Samuel Nyman! Show yourself!" Several servants, their arms full of loot, huddled by the library door. "Where's the priest?" No one answered. "I asked you a question," Tomás turned murderous eyes on the youngest one in the group, a girl of about fourteen. "Where is he?"

"He's not here, sir." Her voice squeaked with fright. "They— They all left."

Tomás looked about him and saw the ruin of a proud house: overturned furniture; piles of horse manure on carpets and tile; mahogany surfaces stripped bare of valuables; portraits pockmarked by bullets. Smashed china and glassware crunched their despair under his boots.

"Everyone out! Out!"

For what he imagined to be the deliberate desecration of my tomb, Tomás burned the hacienda house to the ground.

130

INTO THE FIRE

WHAT MADE US forget that General *Asustín* was first and foremost a bandit? He took our money readily enough. Yet instead of taking us to Mexico City as promised, he had the train stop in the middle of nowhere.

"You'll have to walk the rest of the way, padre. I have other business to attend to."

Banditry further up the line? Samuel was tempted to ask. Instead he looked *Asustín* in the eye and spoke with him man to man, lowering his voice as if confiding in him. "I can appreciate that, General. Likewise, since you are a born leader and a man of his word, I'm sure that you'll want to honor our agreement, especially where children and the elderly are concerned."

No dice. Moments later, all seven of us stood clutching our pillowcases as the train pulled away. *Asustín* stuck his head out a window and waved. "Don't forget them daily prayers you promised, Father!"

We watched the train round a curve, bound for who knows what new raid. *Asustín's* cause was opportunism. Doña Clemencia sputtered for all of us. Then she nodded to Samuel as if to say, enough! Lead on. We walked along the tracks, Hipólito trotting along beside us. A couple of miles later, we found a footpath that led us to a place of tall eucalyptus and narrow waterways. The water, green like the trees and vegetation, sparkled in the morning sun. A white heron spread its wings and glided across the shiny surface.

"We're in Xochimilco," Samuel smiled in relief. And because he loved teaching, and because he wanted to keep the children distracted, he offered them a history lesson. "The Aztecs built these waterways more than four hundred years ago. See over there? And there?"

"Are we going to see Aztecs?" Rodolfito asked round-eyed.

"Sure. Here comes one now." Samuel nodded toward a canoe far ahead of us. A man was paddling in the gentle silence. Samuel lifted his little nephew onto his shoulders and resumed the lesson as we walked along the water's edge. "At the peak of their power, the Aztecs had built a whole network of canals—over seven hundred and fifty kilometers of them. Today only a fraction remains, maybe a hundred and seventy kilometers at best." He stopped. "Take a good look, everyone. These are the last remnants of the hydraulic engineering of a lost civilization."

"What were the waterways for, Uncle Samuel?" Teresita asked in her usual serious tone.

"To transport people and food to Tenochtitlán. The Aztecs built their city in the middle of a lake."

"In a lake! That *solly*!" Rodolfito laughed uproariously. "Evwee-thing would get wet!"

"Can we go there, *ple-ea-se*, Uncle Samuel?" Laurita grasped one of his hands.

"Sorry. It's gone now. But we're going to a bigger, friendlier city that was built from its ruins."

"I know! Mexico City," Laurita crooned. "Papi told me all about it once. He has a house there, isn't that right, mami?"

"That's right." Teresa smiled, though it still cut her to the quick whenever the children mentioned their father. How long could she go on letting them believe that he was away on a very long business trip in *Francia*? How long before they realized for themselves that he was never coming back to them? Yet here they were, stragglers headed for his house, uninvited and unexpected. She knew from Samuel that Rodolfo was back in the city. Would he be pleased to see the children? Was it good for them or simply a deepening of the wound to see their father again? And how should she react when she saw him? Did it matter, so long as the children were safe? They need stay only a day or two under his roof. She would find a way to support her family.

"Most of the canals are gone now," Samuel continued in his pleasant manner. "They were drained long ago. But see over there?" he pointed to a vegetable garden and then to a lush flower garden just beyond it. "Those are man-made islands called *chinampas*. The Aztecs built them as floating gardens where they could grow crops and flowers and then transport them to their city. Farmers still work their *chinampas* and take their produce to market by canoe. See them over there?"

More canoes appeared. Men with enormous *sombreros* doffed them to Samuel; the women nodded or wished us a good morning. Up ahead on the path we spotted men carrying heavy burdens on their back, leather straps tied to their forehead for added stability. Except for the straw hats and trousers, everything else conjured the world of the ancient Aztecs: the waterways, the eucalyptus trees, the *chinampas* overflowing with fruit and vegetables, and the stooped figures hard at work. Several kilometers later, we came upon the Mexico of our own times: a busy town with commerce, a trolley station and a fleet of *trajineras,* flat-bottom boats with flower-bedecked arches.

"If today were Sunday you'd see families hiring these gondolas," Samuel told the children, even as we adults noted that it was too quiet, even for a weekday. "You'd see vendors sidling up in canoes to sell cooked meals."

The trolley station was open for business, yet it was practically deserted. Out of breath, both doña Clemencia and Teresa dropped into benches outside the ticket office.

"What now, padre?" doña Clemencia gasped as she fanned herself.

"If we had any money at all, which we do not, we could take a trolley to Rodolfo's house, or at least within a short walk of it." He rubbed the back of his neck. "As it is, we seem to have no other option than to walk."

"How far?" The fan stopped fluttering.

"About twenty-five kilometers, I would guess."

Everyone groaned. Samuel turned to the children. "Who knows what it means to barter?"

A few minutes later, he returned from the ticket office with seven one-way tickets. The price was exorbitant: the medallion of the Virgin Mother that he wore on a gold chain under his cassock. We boarded the near-empty trolley with sighs of relief. Hipólito curled up and napped at our feet as we headed into the city. Within half an hour we could see a trickle of people carrying large bundles. The trickle became a mass exodus. Samuel walked to the front of the trolley.

"What's going on?" he asked the driver.

"It's the twenty-four-hour truce, Father."

"What truce?"

"Between the armies."

"What armies?"

"*Federales* and—I don't know. I guess you could call them *Insurgentes*."

"What are they fighting about?"

"God alone knows, padre. Someone wants to be president, I suppose. They've been blasting away at each other, making a shambles of the *Centro*. People say the armies rarely hit each other's strongholds, but God help anyone caught between them!"

Samuel was stunned. Shelling in the city itself? He might have doubted the man's account but for the growing masses of people who were fleeing. Then he noticed a strange, coppery smell and a bonfire on a street corner. Teresa seemed to recognize what it was before any of us.

"Children! Get on the floor!" she cried out, throwing herself down, dragging them with her. "Find my ring!" She pretended to search under the seats, hoping they wouldn't notice its outline under her glove, watchful so they wouldn't see the charred bodies. "Keep looking!"

The driver muttered to Samuel, "They can't bury the dead fast enough, Father. To prevent a plague, they burn the bodies. They've taken a lot of them to Balbuena Park. They just pile them up into huge stacks, douse them with kerosene, and burn them."

The trolley stopped several blocks from Rodolfo's house. Fortunately, there were no bodies along those streets. Perhaps they had already been burned in Balbuena Park. We did see a lot of civilians with bundles in their arms or with their belongings piled high in every kind of vehicle, both automotive and horse-drawn, all of them traveling in the opposite direction from us. When we finally reached Lucerna Street, we passed a well-dressed elderly couple in a square landau. In their hurry to leave the city, they had heaped odds and ends into the center of the carriage: clothes in a pile, gilt frames with paintings and photographs, and a bird cage with several small parakeets. Because most of us were well dressed, the old gentleman doffed his hat to us, but with a distracted look. His wife, on the other hand, focused sharply on our little group.

"Samuel? Is that you, dear boy?" she cried out.

"*Tía* Sofía!" Samuel reached up into the carriage to kiss his aunt. As he explained later, he had called her *tía* since childhood when she and her son, Federico, lived with them for several years in San Serafín. The actual familial relationship was nebulous. Second cousins once removed? Third cousins slightly removed? The fortunes of the widowed and homeless *tía* Sofía had improved only when Federico made a good career for himself in the Federal Army and later when she married a wealthy Chilean.

There was a round of introductions, while the old gentleman drew a gold watch from his vest pocket, opening and closing it with nervous clicks.

"Aren't you leaving like everyone else?" the *tía* asked.

"No. We're headed to Rodolfo's house."

She glanced at the children and at our elderly companion who was struggling to catch her breath. "Well, we could get out and let you borrow the carriage just to Rodolfo's house. Then the driver could come back for us."

Her husband winced visibly, his walrus whiskers twitching.

"That's very kind of you, *tía,* but please do not trouble yourself." Samuel pressed her hand. "It's only another two blocks from here."

"Well, if you're sure. You tell Rodolfo not to delay. This cease fire is only until tonight. Goodbye, my dear. Give your mother my love."

Making no mention of his mother's death, Samuel graciously let his relations get on with their exodus. We resumed our own journey, the children pulling us along in their excitement to see their father.

"*Tío* Samuel, is that my papi's house?" The girls kept pointing to different mansions. "What about that one? Does he—?"

An explosion behind the houses on our right cut into questions, bricks, and mortar. For a moment we stood motionless and alert as deer. Did we all look back with regret at the aunt's landau now a block away? We could see her horses rearing up on their hindlegs, the driver trying to calm them. While the adults in our group were calculating the odds of our survival, trying to decide whether to retreat to the carriage or to find cover in Rodolfo's house, I was transfixed by the voice of a man who cried out with such anguish and joy: "Teodora! Teodora!"

Even as our group hurried toward Rodolfo's house, I paused long enough to look back at the landau. A servant who was sitting next to the driver, jumped down from the high seat. As a second shell exploded a block or two away, she ran to a large, bearded man who caught her up in his arms. I watched them for a few more seconds, sketching them in memory: love and joy in the midst of chaos.

Years later I learned that Mangel and Teodora made a life for themselves and their children in Mazatlán, on the shimmering Pacific coast.

131

CONSPIRATORS

THE SHELLING GREW more ferocious. Samuel pounded on Rodolfo's door until he thought the bones in his hand would break. By then the children were screaming in terror, Teresa and I were struggling to calm them, and doña Clemencia was gasping for air. The only calm one was Hipólito, which is how we discovered he had gone deaf in his old age. A boon under the circumstances. Suddenly the door coughed open, and there stood Rodolfo in shirt sleeves, unshaven, and disheveled.

"Samuel? What the hell—" And then Rodolfo saw the rest of us and gasped, "No! You're not safe here!" even as he drew us inside.

The children rushed him, sobbing as he drew all three into his arms. Rodolfo's face contracted as he struggled to stifle his own tears. After a few moments, he focused on civilities too ingrained to be totally ignored despite the circumstances. Rodolfo gave Samuel a brisk hug, doña Clemencia a chivalrous bow when introduced to her, and Teresa a kiss that glanced off her cheek as she pulled back. And then he saw me, black-haired and alive.

"Isabel?" His startled look asked, *how can this be?*

Just then two men hurried down the stairs, one of them cursing the *federales* for breaking the cease fire earlier than accorded.
At the sight of us they halted. For a moment I half expected a
second round of introductions, but a blast shattered windows in
the dining room. Rodolfo's expression, indeed his very posture,
changed drastically. The determined set of his jaw and the squaring of his shoulders reminded me just then of Benjamín, and I
wondered, had their father worn the same look when he led men
into battle against the French?

Rodolfo ushered us into a large room. Enormous bookcases
stretched mahogany arms to touch the high ceiling. Books by the
thousands stood in disciplined ranks.

"There's only one window in here. Stay clear of it, and keep
the draperies closed. There's a water closet over there. You are
not to leave these two rooms. Is that understood?"

We all nodded, our teeth chattering.

"Papi, I'm hungry!" Rodolfito whimpered.

There was no indication that Rodolfo heard him since he
left so hurriedly. Moments before the door closed behind him,
though, I did hear him mutter to Samuel, "I thought she was
dead!"

"Long story."

We settled in, nestling into a tufted leather sofa and big wing
chairs. Rodolfo's library had the look of a London gentleman's
club, at least as I imagined such places, with rich wood paneling,
a fireplace with a beautifully carved surround and mantlepiece,
humidors for cigars and crystal glasses fronting decanters. All
that was missing was an English butler. Less than fifteen minutes
later one stepped into the room! A tall, thin man with a pinched
face and a brisk manner delivered sandwiches and tea, the silver
tray so at odds with the rifle slung on his shoulder.

"Thank you, Weston," Samuel spoke with easy familiarity.

The butler gave a slight bow. Without fanfare or explanations, he left as quietly as he had arrived. And though the barrage did not let up and we should have been scared witless, we wolfed down our meal, the first in more than twenty-four hours. Spam sandwiches and tea never tasted better. Several hours later an eerie stillness descended, silent as snow. Teresa and I cracked the door open but did not venture out of the room. There was a commotion on the stairs, a hefting and shuffling of feet.

"Watch his head," someone said.

"Any chance of flagging down a Cruz Roja?"

"Not likely. Just get him to the American embassy."

"Take my motor car," someone offered.

At that point, Samuel set aside the book he was reading. "I'll see what's going on."

Moments later the power went out, leaving us in sudden blackness. One of the girls yelped. We sat closer to each other. Before long, the butler returned with two lit candles, his long face preternatural in the gloom.

"Was someone hurt, Mr. Weston?" I asked in English.

"Just Weston, madame." Did the man flinch at my small breach in etiquette? I suppressed a smile. "One of Mr. Nyman's friends was wounded."

"Oh, I *am* sorry!"

"He's in stable condition. Regrettably, we lost two other gentlemen earlier this week."

"Why not take him to a hospital?" I couldn't help asking. "Why the embassy?"

"Several doctors have volunteered their services there. Now, if you'll excuse me—"

"Thank you, Mr.—Thank you, Weston."

Sometime later, Rodolfo and Samuel joined us. "We need to get you away *now*."

"Why can't we stay here?" Teresa seemed to have forgotten how much she had not wanted to be in Rodolfo's house.

"Because it will just start again tomorrow."

Exhaustion flattened Rodolfo's voice. His glazed stare betrayed a soul-weariness. No general now with a set jaw, only a man pushed dangerously to the limits of his endurance. Even the children sensed it. So no one argued about staying on. Since the hotels downtown were now unsafe, and the safe ones further away were overrun by panicked citizens, the brothers decided that we should seek shelter in their father's house in San Angel. Obediently, we followed Rodolfo to his waiting car.

The soft glow of a lantern revealed a magnificent hybrid of a vehicle, part automobile, part carriage. To this day I remember that shiny red wonder. It had wooden wheels with white tires, a black tufted leather seat up front, brocade upholstery for the back seat, lanterns with brass trim, and a partial roof. (No roof deemed necessary for the chauffeur.) It was Rodolfo's latest acquisition from the Paris Motor Show. Under normal circumstances he would have enjoyed explaining that it was a 1912 Renault Type CB Coupe DeVille. Then as now I knew close to nothing about motor cars, but this one has lodged deep in my memory, perhaps because it was to be our ark in troubled waters. I could imagine the great care it required, and then all care undone, flying debris denting its elegant body and shattering the windshield. Climbing into the front seat, I first had to remove a shard of glass that had been missed during the quick clean-up. As Rodolfito settled on my lap and Hipólito at my feet, I was startled to see Samuel at the wheel. Did he know how to drive? Where was Rodolfo's chauffeur?

"Nicolás was killed two days ago," Samuel whispered in English as if he had read my mind. The girls, doña Clemencia, and Teresa piled in the back, fully enclosed as in a carriage with generous windows. Pillows and blankets had been hastily thrown onto the floor. Weston strapped two hampers to the trunk.

"Do you remember the basics that I taught you?" Rodolfo asked his youngest sibling. Samuel nodded with less confidence than I wanted to see. So Rodolfo launched into hurried instructions: gears, instrument panel, electric self-starter, roads to use, and roads to avoid. Above all, Samuel was not to stop for anyone or anything until we were safe inside their father's house.

"Drive slowly. She can do 40–50 miles per hour, but with so many unlit streets and fleeing pedestrians, you'd better—" His words trailed off as he caught sight of me again. What baffled him more, I wondered? That I was alive or that I had black hair? No time to explain anything.

Samuel started up the coup. "We'll need light bulbs!" I called out above the motor's din.

While Weston fetched them, Rodolfo turned to the children. "I need for you to continue to be brave. There will be no beds or furniture in your grandfather's house, but you'll be safe. I'll have furniture sent over in a day or two. Tonight, your mother and aunt will make bedrolls for you out of blankets."

"Like we did when Grandmother was dying?" Laurita asked. And the proverbial cat was out of the bag.

The blood drained from Rodolfo's face. "What's this?"

Samuel got out and steadied his brother. "She suffered a series of strokes. She died last night. We buried her this morning." The news tumbled out with a staccato cadence. The brothers clung to each other. And this time Rodolfo was not able to pull himself together as he had that afternoon.

132

SAFE HAVEN

At night, San Justín looked more forbidding than ever. Armed with nothing but a candle and a box of light bulbs, Samuel led the way from the front gate, through the dark tunnel-of-a-foyer—the so-called *zaguán* of colonial buildings, and into the inner court-yard. The wind blew out the flame twice. Each time, everyone instinctively drew closer. The wind moaned, rattling windows and doors.

"This was my other home when I was a child." Samuel put on a cheerful persona for the children. "Listen," he cupped an ear, "Do you hear that? That is one of the most magical sounds in the world. It's the sound that only a talking house can make. Hear it?"

"What's it saying?" Rodolfito whispered, wide-eyed.

"It's saying, 'Welcome. I'm sorry I have no lights. Would you send Samuel upstairs to install a few light bulbs?' Would you like to come with me, Rodolfito?"

"No, thank you." The little boy pressed closer to his mother.

"I'll go!" Laurita always needed to prove herself and did.

They vanished up the stairs. Waiting in the dark, I thought back to my lonely night here in San Justín, and then to my father-in-law's desperate sadness as he attempted to vindicate Benjamín. I could almost feel the touch of the general's lips whispering in my ear. I vowed then and there that I would tell Benjamín about it, even if he were to scoff and brush it aside. Oh, to see Ben again! When would that miracle finally happen? How long before the fighting would cease and we could travel safely to the Penitentiary?

A light filled one of the upstairs rooms. A couple of minutes later, a second room sprang to life, and a third. Down in the courtyard, we cheered and hurried up the stairs, guided like ships by a lighthouse on a moonless night.

The next day Hipólito and I entertained the children by exploring the house with them. Even in broad daylight the place was intimidating. Lugubrious, doña Clemencia called it; a grim network of high-beamed rooms that had witnessed too much sorrow across centuries; dust balls and cobwebs like festering wounds; corridors and staircases that challenged courage or simple curiosity. I tried to steer the children away from a mural outside the General's room because it depicted the martyrdom of saints with such graphic detail. They found it and were both horrified and titillated. I would have taken them to play outdoors, but the gardens of San Justin were a tangled jungle. The children, who were used to town life, preferred playing tag in the courtyard and even in the grim corridors rather than risk tangling with the spiders and snakes of their imagination. Actually, they were not totally off. Their only regret was that poor old Hipólito increasingly preferred napping to playing.

When Teresa called them to lunch, I took a moment to visit General Nyman's room. I found Samuel standing in its gloom. He turned momentarily when he heard me come in.

"This is where my father was murdered," he murmured, squinting as if searching for the faded outlines of a killer and his victim. "Just like they said at the trial," he hastened to add, careful not to betray Eufemio's confession.

"'Benjamín didn't do it. He only thinks he did.' Those were your father's exact words."

Samuel turned sharply. "What do you mean?"

When I told him about my encounter with his father—vision, intuition, whatever it was—he believed me.

"Thank you, Samuel."

"For what?"

"For not thinking I'm crazy or a liar."

"I've encountered stranger things, like finding my dead sister-in-law waiting for me in church," he smiled solemnly.

The next night Rodolfo arrived with Weston and two hired wagons piled high with furniture from his house. The children rushed into his arms with cries of pure joy. Teresa smiled, but she kept her distance. It was so out of character for Rodolfo to look the least bit disheveled. He was still unshaven and his hair in open rebellion. More tellingly, his eyes were bloodshot, grief and sleep deprivation marking their assault. Nonetheless, he had just enough energy to take off his jacket and start to unload the wagon. We all helped. The men carried the heavier pieces. In passing, I heard him mutter to his brother, "Federico is dead."

"What?" Samuel gasped.

"Papi, can you help us carry this table?" Teresita and Laurita were attempting to haul a mahogany side table up the stone staircase.

"I want to help too!" Rodolfito chimed in. And for good measure, to further stress the stressed, he jumped down from the wagon cradling a lamp that was all glass and crystals. Rodolfo exploded.

"Get away from there, all of you! Upstairs! Now!"

The unexpected reprimand, so unlike Rodolfo, set off a volley of tears. Later, when the unloading was better organized,

Rodolfo hugged the children and let them help, but he remained aloof, his mind far from them. Even his courteous behavior with our elderly doña Clemencia had a detached, automatic quality.

"Where would you like your bed, señora?" he asked as he and Samuel paused on the upper landing with a heavy headboard.

"In that nice big room. Thank you, Mr. Nyman."

When Teresa and Teresita and Laurita and Rodolfito all asked that their beds be placed in the same room, Rodolfo startled us with his laughter—no doubt his first in many days.

"You don't have to sleep like nomads in the same yurt! The house has rooms to spare."

"And ghosts to spare," doña Clemencia muttered under her breath.

Had it been daylight, they might have claimed separate rooms. But it was dark and the old house unnerved them. Not that they had seen the phantoms that they feared. It was the imagined *possibility* of encountering a ghost around a corner or emerging at the end of a dark corridor that made the others insist on sleeping in the same room, like wolves bedding down with their pack: doña Clemencia in one bed, Teresa and Rodolfito in another, and the two little girls in the third bed. At night, no matter the hour, they escorted each other to the bathroom. Samuel and I, on the other hand, wandered through the house untroubled and claimed our own rooms, preferring privacy to communal sleeping.

When the wagon finally stood empty and the children were being tucked in bed by their mother and their "Aunt Clemencia," we returned to the parlor, now grown warm with lamp light, a red Persian rug, a sofa and one of the wing chairs from Rodolfo's library. Samuel and I flopped into the sofa's leather embrace. Weston headed to the kitchen to organize our modest pantry. Rodolfo started to unpack a box of books. Suddenly he slammed one down.

"All right. I want to know right now, what gave Mother the idea that Isabel died in her arms?" He glared at his brother, then at me. "And why is your hair black? What the hell is going on?"

The moment had come. I let Samuel handle it. As he told Rodolfo about my incarceration, starvation, and funeral, I saw Rodolfo lose his mother a second time. I don't think I've ever seen a man more undone. Certainly, his physical fatigue was a factor. However, this was the death of an ideal that bordered on the sacred. Samuel caught Rodolfo as he crumpled to his knees, sobbing and swearing. What could I possibly say to staunch such a hemorrhage? I left quietly, giving the brothers privacy to mourn and comfort each other.

The next day dawned crisp and cold: a typical February morning in Mexico's high central plateau. While everyone slept, I draped a blanket around my shoulders and headed to the kitchen to make coffee. By now it was clear to us that Rodolfo and his companions—civilians all—were deeply embroiled in the conspiracy to oust President Madero. If they succeeded, the revolutionary government that Ben and I had so ardently supported would be overthrown. If they failed, then Rodolfo and his fellow conspirators could be shot as traitors.

Oh, Ben! Why is it all so complicated? I need you!

ERUPTIONS

EVERY TIME RODOLFO could get away to visit us—always after dark—I would chime the same two questions: is the penitentiary still within range of the shelling? When can we visit Benjamín? Rodolfo's answer never varied: Yes, and not yet.

On the tenth day of the coup—I remember it was a Tuesday—we Morelos refugees ventured into the streets of San Angel to pray for peace in the nearby *Iglesia del Carmen*. We were slow at first to notice that something was different. Then we heard it. The silence. The distant thunder of artillery shells had stopped. That evening Rodolfo looked tired but like his dapper old self again: clean-shaven, his moustache trimmed into a thin line, and the fragrance of expensive cologne wafting in his wake.

"It's over. Madero and Pino-Suárez were arrested yesterday."

I was both relieved for Rodolfo and furious with him. "Let me remind you that Francisco Madero and José Pino Suárez were duly elected as this nation's president and vice-president! Disagree with them politically all you like, but do not gloat over their downfall, not to me."

"I'm sorry, Isabel. I forgot that this would be painful for you."

"Not just for me, but for everyone who fought to make our Mexico a better country, a truly democratic republic."

His eyes blazed as suddenly as a match flaring into flame. "My companions fought and died to make this country *safer* and more stable."

"By killing who knows how many innocent civilians?"

"To save us from anarchy!" Rodolfo yelled, his face contorted with rage.

You're the anarchist, you and your stupid conspirators! I wanted to shout back, but I caught myself, for I saw far more pain than anger in his eyes. So I tried to shift the conversation away from the politics that so deeply divided us. Unfortunately, he wasn't willing to drop the matter. He was a man desperate to justify himself.

"We had to take matters into our own hands. Your Madero has been a disaster from the very start. Look at the mess he's made in Morelos. And why do you think there have been rebellions against him throughout the country? For all that he's put us through, he deserves to be shot!"

"He's speaking metaphorically, Isabel." Samuel jumped in. "What he means—"

"Metaphors be damned! Madero and his cronies deserve to be shot, every last one of them!"

"Is that what's in store for the president and vice-president?" My eyes welled up. "Are we back to *la ley fuga*? Murder political adversaries and claim they were shot trying to escape?"

"We are not barbarians." He spoke with slow deliberation, his manner reproachful as if I were offending his sense of honor. "Even though they don't deserve any special consideration, *Misters* Madero and Pino-Suárez will get the same treatment that they gave don Porfirio and his family: exile. They can go to Europe, or the United States, or to hell for all I care."

Rodolfo returned two days later. Samuel was up on a ladder unscrewing a faulty light bulb in the courtyard. My job was to steady the ladder and hand him a new bulb. Both of us paused as Rodolfo shut off the engine of his motor car and got out.

"We have a new president," he announced without fanfare, neither exulting nor lamenting.

Samuel climbed down. "Our Foreign Minister is third in the line of succession. So I assume you mean Pedro Lascurain?"

"Congress swore him in today." Rodolfo removed his gloves with unsteady hands.

"Well, he has the education and diplomatic experience to—"

"He resigned."

"What? You said he was just sworn in today!" Samuel's fists flew to his hips. I watched Rodolfo fidget with gloves and driving goggles.

"He was duly sworn in."

"As President for a day?" Was this a joke?

"Forty minutes. Maybe less. I suppose Lascurain will be remembered for having the shortest presidential term in history." Rodolfo gave us a crooked smile. "Before resigning, he named General Huerta Interior Minister, fourth in the line of succession. So that makes Victoriano Huerta our interim president until we can hold elections and vote in Félix Díaz."

I followed Rodolfo as he started up the stairs. "Wait. What about Mr. Madero and Mr. Pino Suárez? Are they safely out of the country as promised?"

Rodolfo paused, one foot on a higher step than the other, his gloves gripped so tightly that his knuckles turned white. He kept his back to me for what seemed a long time. When he finally turned around, his gaze flitted from my face to a vague spot over my shoulder. "They were killed during a bungled attempt to escape."

"You mean they were executed!" I shouted. "You said they deserved to be shot."

"I didn't mean it."

"Yes you did! You said it twice! Don't lie about this!"

He stepped down so that our eyes were level. "This wasn't supposed to happen. The decision was in the hands of the military, not of civilians like my comrades and me. As God is my witness, we played no part in their death."

"Oh yes you did! You and your friends willingly joined the conspiracy to overthrow our duly elected government. You allied yourself with people willing to blow up the heart of our city, killing God knows how many innocent civilians. And for what? So that we can have one more military dictator?"

"I admit that Victoriano Huerta is far from ideal."

"An astute observation, given that he's a traitor and a murderer."

"Rest assured that Félix Díaz is cut from a far different cloth. Huerta is only a temporary measure."

I hurried to my bedroom to sob tears of despair and to pray for the poor families of Madero and Pino-Suárez. They had been promised exile. Instead, they had to bury their loved ones. Oh, the wanton treachery! Once again I had to pray for the Lord to help me forgive what I could not forgive on my own. As for Huerta accepting his interim status, I knew like everyone else how very unlikely that was. People in the streets were soon asking, "Whoever heard of a conquering general willingly giving up power? Maybe in the United States with that Washington fellow, but not in Mexico."

Early the next morning, when the newborn day was swaddled in first light, I took the narrow stairs to the flat rooftop of the house. In 1913, Mexico City's air and sky had a crystalline quality, making all things stand out with unusual clarity. Beyond the tree line and rooftops, I could see a range of volcanoes. And I remembered something Cadwally told me back when I returned from my first night here in San Justín.

"How were the ghosts?" my grandfather had quipped as he daubed a blob of vermillion on a canvas.

"They send their regards," I had shot back. "Very courtly, those sixteenth-century Spaniards."

"I meant the indigenous ones. Most of San Angel sits on a lava flow that swallowed a whole city. Xitle erupted only once, as far as we know, but that's all it took to destroy the ancient city of Cuicuilco, long before your courtly Spaniards arrived to pillage and baptize." Turning to face me, palette in one hand, brush in the other, he switched from teacher to philosopher. "Life is all about cycles of destruction and construction. New things are born from the ashes of the old lost things. Nothing endures. Yet there is always newness. A fresh canvas!"

Nothing endures, yet there is always newness, I echoed now as I breathed in the cool morning, the brightening sun, and the arrogant, absurdly cheerful crowing of roosters. Rodolfo found me in my high perch and stood quietly beside me, both of us gazing beyond San Angel's rooftops to a string of tree-studded volcanoes.

"I want to be honest with you, Isabel. I still do not regret that we removed Madero and Pino Suárez from power. It had to be done. But not the assassinations. What I said the other night when I wished them dead—I didn't mean it. For my crass comment, for all of it, I am sorrier than you'll ever know."

The roosters went on crowing with joyous impunity, oblivious to human traumas.

"Madero's administration had its glaring flaws," I conceded. "Idealist that he was, he was no judge of character. Some of his appointees were utterly vile. Yet I still believe that we were far better off with a flawed idealist at the helm than with a general who so easily betrayed his president and then had him murdered." Rodolfo started to protest. I held up a hand. "You and I will never agree on politics, Rodolfo. Believe if you can that Huerta will keep his word and step down. Pin your hopes on your Féliz Díaz if you must. I cannot and will not. So let's promise each other something—that we will not let our political differences, deep as they are, divide us as a family. Let's agree to disagree and not discuss it any further."

"Agreed." He spoke solemnly. A flock of finches—the common *gorriones*—flew overhead, the males adding delicate touches of red to the morning palette. "Isabel, would you allow me to drive you to the Penitentiary? I suspect there's a certain Captain Nyman who would love to see you."

134

DESAPARECIDOS

Sitting next to Rodolfo in the roofless front seat of his Coup DeVille, I felt the exhilaration of sun and wind on my face. I was going to see Ben at last! Rodolfo sensed the intensity of my joy, for every so often he would turn and smile at me without saying a word. However, as we drove through the battered downtown our mood darkened. Block after block of damaged buildings cried out against the recent carnage. An acrid smell clung to charred walls and blood-stained streets.

No one knew for certain how many people had been killed. Some would put the figure at three thousand, others at over five thousand. The need to incinerate so many of the corpses during small breaks in the fighting, had made it difficult to get an accurate count. Oh, the pity of it! All those men, women, and children who had been reduced to ashes, their remains unclaimed. Unmarked. These were the latest *desaparecidos*—the 'disappeared'—the vanished who would never be accounted for. How were their families to cope? I wondered as I fought the urge to weep for them. Yet, what is it about hope that is so irresistible? As we pulled up in front of the Penitentiary, I could not suppress the surge of joy that coursed through my body.

~

"Prisoner 243—" A prison official scanned the roster. "Benjamín Nyman Vizcarra—Yes, here he is. He's not here."

"Of course, he's here!" I insisted. "Please check again."

"It says here that he's been transferred."

"Where?" I felt my chest tighten.

"I don't know, señora. He's been transferred. That's all I can tell you."

Rodolfo stepped in front of me, setting down his top hat and some money on the man's desk. The bribe helped the official locate more information. "Tlatelolco. The Military Prison of Santiago Tlatelolco."

"When was that?"

"Tuesday, 11 February. The order was signed by General Aureliano Blanquet himself." The official slammed the log shut. "That's all I can tell you."

We hurried to the Tlatelolco Prison. Officials there insisted they knew nothing of a transfer. Bribes could not change the fact. Rodolfo had to steady me as he walked me back to his motor car.

"We've got to find him!" I gasped.

Rodolfo expanded the search. Yet neither bribes nor his political connections could break the silence that surrounded his brother's disappearance. None of the prisons in the country, those that were still controlled by the Federal government, had any record of Benjamín. He had vanished without a trace, joining the mournful ranks of Mexico's *desaparecidos*. We, in turn, experienced the agony of families desperate to know the fate of their loved one.

Victoriano Huerta, our new president, began his administration with purges against supporters of Madero. In his paranoia, he had hundreds murdered. Thousands went into hiding or headed north to join revolutionaries pledged to avenge Madero and Pino Suárez. Perhaps Huerta's distrust had extended even to Maderistas in prison, we speculated. More alarmingly, a trusted source of Rodolfo's informed us that General Blanquet, the man who had ordered Ben's transfer, was deeply implicated in the killings of Madero and Pino-Suárez. Was Benjamín another of his victims? Had he vanished without a trace because his killers had tossed his body onto one of many funeral pyres in Balbuena Park?

I tried to dismiss such a possibility, focusing instead on the present reality. As we all grew increasingly wary of General Huerta, we failed to recognize a dangerous enemy within our own ranks: Eva's husband. Since 1911, Pancho Comardo had been watching the Mexican situation from the safety of Europe. On many an idle hour over brandy and cigars, he had entertained fantasies of a telegram announcing Benjamín's death in prison, and maybe a month or two later, news of Samuel being waylaid on a lonely, nameless road. Such misfortunes, he reflected, would let Eva inherit *half* of the Nyman wealth. Yes, he could live with that. And maybe Rodolfo could humor him by falling off a cliff or drowning at sea—

Before long, Pancho's fantasies had morphed into an obsessive need for specific information. Was Benjamín still in a vegetative state? Had he been pardoned? Was he being cared for by his damn mother? Was she going to favor Benjamín, her own child, over Eva who was only an adopted daughter? Or would the old crone funnel her love into the oh-so-pious Samuel? Was he still saving souls? Shouldn't the rabble have caught up with him by now? Damn them all! Pancho would glower over the rim of his brandy glass. Of what use is a damn revolution if it doesn't kill the right people?

Pancho ranted inwardly, but he had taken no action beyond reading the boring reports that his agent sent on behalf of Mangel and of the Rural Policeman who kept tabs on Samuel. In 1913, when he celebrated New Year with expat friends, Pancho Comardo still had qualms about giving the order that would give Eva a greater share of the inheritance after Manuela died. Then on a gray afternoon that wouldn't stop weeping, he made up his mind. *Kill them now, now while we can blame the current unrest.*

So Pancho Comardo gave the order to his agent, who then passed it along. But things do not always go as planned, even for the most Machiavellian of us. Pancho had not counted on one of his murderers becoming a born-again Christian. Nor had he imagined that in the melee of a coup d'etat, Benjamín would vanish beyond his grasp and ours. Nor did he foresee that the sergeant who could so easily have blamed Zapatistas for killing the priest of San Gabrielin, would himself be killed by the rebels. We would not know the full extent of Pancho's treachery until after our own deaths, when so many things are made known to us.

That winter of 1913 we mourned Benjamín's disappearance, each in our own way. Truthfully, I could have borne news of his death far better than the nagging uncertainty of his fate. If dead, I would have found comfort in my conviction that he was enjoying the freedom and beauty of the afterlife. But *desaparecido*— what exactly did that mean? Was he languishing in some dreadful prison? Was he being tortured?

Oh, Lord! Where is he? How is he?

For a short time, I fell back into my old self-sufficiency— writing letters, obsessively pouring over newspaper obituaries and the daily lists from the Red Cross and White Cross, pinning my hopes on Rodolfo's bribes and inquiries—all of which would have been fine had I also made time for internal prayer, keeping spiritual and physical needs in balance. Unfortunately, I did not. Despair led me into a bleak inner desert where I wandered utterly alone, until at last I recognized my aloneness for what it was: an illusion as fictive as the taunting waters of a mirage. How could I have forgotten that it is precisely in our times of deepest tribulation that God is closest to us?

One morning, as sunlight tinted my bedroom walls, I found my prayer again, and then the Lord's prayer. A calm settled over me, and calmly I set about to *do* for others. It was time to stop obsessing over my own sorrow; time to trust in divine providence. Whatever had happened or was happening to Ben, in the long run only good would come of it, I told myself. So I joined Samuel on his rounds of the Red Cross and the White Cross to see if I could be of help. Despite not being a trained nurse, there was much I could do as a volunteer—simple things like helping patients sit up, writing letters for them, reading to them, praying with them, smiling or simply touching them gently. All of these small things did as much for me as for them, not eliminating our mutual pain, but certainly sanding down its sharp edges.

Samuel and I also made it our mission to comb the city streets for his former parishioners. Most days we returned empty-handed. Then late one afternoon we found old don Gustavo begging outside a church. With his help we were able to locate a few other villagers of San Gabrielín: seven women, five children, and two more men who had been rejected for conscription—Encarnación Gómez because he dragged one leg as he walked, and Pío Corral because he was missing fingers in his right hand. All ten adults begged us to employ them in exchange for housing and protection. We agreed while also insisting on paying them fair wages, which we did thanks to Rodolfo's generosity.

We located more San Gabrielinos, including little Jacobito who had inadvertently acted as Valle Inclán's messenger. The servants' quarters and guest wing filled up quickly, so we converted some of the downstairs storage rooms into further housing. The upstairs rooms of the main house continued to be used only by our own immediate family. Even Rodolfo was living with us while his house underwent major repairs. With his income and the help of the San Gabrielinos, San Justín was transformed into a bustling, almost joyous place. Rodolfo, on the other hand, fluctuated between gloom and jitteriness. He often draped himself in a moody silence or exploded over the children's trivial infractions. We breathed easier whenever he left the house to campaign with fellow *Felicistas* for their man, Félix Díaz. At least for now the Pact the Citadel, facilitated by American ambassador, Henry Lane Wilson, had placed several members of the Felicista party in Huerta's cabinet. A start. A safeguard. But was it? Huerta was becoming ever more ruthless with perceived enemies to his "temporary" presidency—and that included supporters of Felix Díaz.

CAMPAIGNS

RODOLFO BEGAN TO focus more on campaigning for Teresa's love than for a presidency that would never happen. Her refusal to be his mistress perplexed him, especially now that she and the children needed his protection more than ever. *What's gotten into her?* he wondered. She had mastered her qualms long ago, entrusting her fate to him completely. She had always understood that they could never marry, but that had not mattered to her. Why the sudden obstinacy? It was her duty to let him fulfill his obligation to their children. Besides, with all the peasants that Samuel had brought home like stray cats, wouldn't she vastly prefer a quiet home of her own?

As it happened, Teresa was quite happy in San Justín. In me she had found a sister, in Samuel a brother, in doña Clemencia a doting great-aunt for her children, and in the displaced San Gabrielinos a village. Her children were safe and well fed. What more could she want? As her belly slowly expanded to make room for new life, as she felt mysterious stirrings within her, Teresa began to experience the familiar pangs of maternal love. Still, she continued to keep her pregnancy secret from all but me. In the meantime, more protective of her children than ever, she opted to teach them at home. And though she included the San Gabrielín children in her classroom, sewing clothes for them, she still insisted on maintaining clear boundaries between social classes, dressing her children in crisp Navy-blue, sailor-style suits in sharp contrast to the white outfits of the humble San Gabrielinos.

Samuel left us for a few days to search for San Gabrielinos in nearby towns. He returned alone but to a shriek of delight from Laurita: "*Tío* Samuel!" The child rushed to kiss him. "Come see all the pretty furniture Papi has brought us!"

"Admission is free, the tour obligatory!" Teresa laughed.

Taking the hand of his little niece, Samuel let her lead him upstairs right up to my bedroom. He stood hesitantly at the door. It was his father's old room.

"You can go in. Aunt Isabel won't mind. You've got to see it. It's such a pretty room!"

"It's all right, Samuel!" I called from the courtyard downstairs.

The cook announced lunch, prompting Teresa to issue orders. "Children! Go wash your hands!"

Laurita stomped her foot, but she ran off to the bathroom at the end of the corridor, totally unaware that her aunt had cowered in it one stormy night. Samuel took a deep breath before entering his father's former bedroom. Thanks to Rodolfo's unstoppable generosity, I had been able to transform the one room that no one wanted to use. I, in turn, had become fond of the old gentleman despite his flaws. Perhaps because he had reached out to me, I felt a certain connection with him. Adopting his room felt right. Besides, it sported fresh paint, new furniture, and light pouring through the open windows. A spring breeze fluttered the sheer curtains and pale green drapes. A vase of white peonies decorated my desk. It was all beautiful and restful—all but the one object that made Samuel flinch: his father's bronze crucifix.

Surprisingly, it had been returned by the authorities after Ben's trial. Long afterwards, I found it carelessly stashed in one of the storerooms. I could barely lift it, but I was quick to appreciate its artistry and subject matter. So I hefted it one morning and had it hung in my room. I did take the precaution of not placing it over my bed—a prudent move in earthquake country. It now lodged over my desk. I thought of it primarily as a sacred symbol, but also as a beautiful work of colonial art. Samuel knew it for the weapon that it was. Glaring at it, his lips a tight thin line, he could almost hear his father muttering to Eufemio, *Straighten the crucifix! It's crooked!* And he could visualize all too clearly the servant's gnarled hands reaching for it to bludgeon his father to death.

Samuel's fingers drummed on the desktop as he wrestled down the impulse to grasp the cross and hide it in the farthest, darkest corner of the house. But it was bathed in light, that bronze crucifix, and a thought came to him unbidden. *Would you throw away the most sacred of Christian symbols because someone has abused it? Do you reject the church because a succession of Torquemadas have made a cudgel of it?*

Slowly, reverently, the priest crossed himself. Holding out his arms, he felt a prayer flow into him.

Heavenly Father, bless and protect those who live within these walls. Help your children see beyond appearances to the true essence of all things. Help us to learn from the horrors of the past, to see clearly in the present, and to do your will now for the sake of the future. May it be luminous as your love. Amen.

One evening Rodolfo joined Teresa in the veranda outside her room. Neither moon nor constellations could stir him to romance. "We've turned this monastery-of-a-place into a damn beehive," he grumbled. "We're all so busy, so content with our busyness. But that doesn't change a thing. Benjamín is dead and

we'll never know where he lies. Our rebellion has utterly back-
fired. We succeeded in killing thousands, including a cousin of
mine, all so that a vindictive drunkard could install himself in
power."

"What about the election?"

Rodolfo gave a strangled laugh. "Election! 'Lord! What fools
we mortals be!'" He gazed at Teresa through a haze of tears.
"Worst of all, the mother I loved became so unspeakably monstrous, it's better that she died. But damn it, I do miss my *viejita*,
the old Manuela Nyman."

POST-MORTEM

Mexico City slowly returned to normal. Construction crews began the process of demolishing buildings beyond hope and repairing those that could be salvaged. Stores and restaurants swept up the debris and opened for business. Even my hair reverted to its former color when I ran out of Tacha's dye. Yet we were all changed—Rodolfo most of all. Outwardly he looked the same in his dapper London-tailored suits and top hat. Inwardly, he was a warrior suffering from wounds that we could not see. Only his courtship of Teresa kept him from sliding into total despondency.

In yet another attempt to win her over, Rodolfo took her and the children on a picnic in a nearby park. While the children climbed into the inviting arms of a tree that had met Teresa's guarded approval, he reclined on one elbow, his long limbs stretching across the picnic blanket. Studying her as she watched the children, he forgot for a short while the savagery of machine gun fire and what it does to human flesh.

Teresa sat opposite him, her legs tented, arms draped around them. It seemed to him that she had gained weight, but there was a flushed look about her that he liked. *La India bonita*—the pretty Indian—his mother had called her, intending it as a backhanded compliment and a warning to him. As he studied Teresa with her thick, black hair and aquiline nose, her full lips and vibrant eyes, Rodolfo wanted to caress her cheek with the back of his hand.

'Has anyone else ever pleased my eyes so much?' He loved the way she did her hair up in the gracious Gibson style and the way the high collar of her blouse emphasized the slenderness of her neck. But most of all, he loved the fact that they had experienced the grand adventure of love and parenthood together, back when the world made sense to him.

Teresa, for her part, struggled daily to maintain a distance. Yet she had felt it her duty to accept his picnic invitation for the sake of the children. Sensing that he wanted to talk to her on a more personal level now that they were alone, she groped for something to divert his attention, unthinkingly reopening a wound perhaps never to heal fully. "Isn't it strange how quickly people get over their sense of outrage?" she mused. "Everyone was so shocked by the deaths of Mr. Madero and Mr. Pino-Suárez—especially because no one believes that ridiculous story that they were shot while trying to escape. I don't care what you say, the whole business was handled badly."

"You don't believe I had a hand in their deaths, do you?" His face went rigid.

"No, of course not. I know you didn't mean what you said—that they deserved to be shot."

"Oh, I meant it all right in that moment of anger and frustration. So I ranted like Lucio Nyman. But I swear to you, Teresa, I never thought for a moment that Huerta and Mondragón and the others would stoop to assassination."

"What was it all for, Rodolfo? So many innocent people died."

"There seemed no other way to restore order."

"You mean the old order. Don't you know by now that we can never go back to the way things were?"

He reached for her right hand and kissed it. "Why not?"

"Because the past is an illusion. It isn't real."

"Then let's make a fresh beginning. I need you near me, Teresa. Leave San Justín and come back with me! We could take the children and go wherever you want: Paris. Rome. Venice. Name it, Teresa."

"As your mistress? No, thank you." She yanked her hand free. He trapped it again.

"Marry me, Teresa." Saying the words that he had withheld for so long sparked in him an unexpected sense of freedom. He was a ship that had been moored far too long, tied to his mother's expectations as much as to societal ones. "Marry me, Teresa" he entreated joyfully as he felt the heaviest of anchors finally lift off the seabed. "Let me be a true father to my children and a true husband to you."

Teresa tried to pull away again as he angled himself so that he could look directly into her face. She could feel his thigh pressed against hers. "I'm very grateful for all your help, Rodolfo, and I'll continue to need it a while longer until I can fend for myself again. You can visit the children any time you want. But please—"

"I don't want to be a damn visitor. I want you in my life every day."

"Well it's too late for that!" Her voice rose sharply, causing the children to pause and look in their direction. Rodolfo smiled and waved while asking, "Why is it too late? We're here together." The children went back to playing.

"Society will never accept me, any more than your mother ever did. You said it often enough."

"Hang society. I don't care anymore what others think about our union."

"Oh, and why such a change of heart?" She could not repress the sarcasm that crossed her arms and thrust her head back.

"Because I've seen death up close, Teresa, and it dwarfs all other considerations. I've watched friends die. I've killed more men than I had a right to. And I saw my cousin Federico cut down by machine gun fire in a suicide attack. Our insurrection-ists cut him down! *Our* guns! Do you think I can ever again care about something as superficial as class distinctions?" He drew closer. "I want to wake up with you every day. Be my wife."

"No. I need to be independent. I want to become Mexico's finest couturiere. If you want to help me, lend me the money so I can have my own dressmaker's shop."

"Done! I'll get you a shop on Reforma Avenue or wherever you want it."

"And I'll accept gratefully and pay you back every cent. But don't ask me to marry you."

"Why not?"

She looked off and for the first time grew flustered. He repeated his question, murmuring it gently. "Why won't you marry me, Teresita?"

Her eyes sparked as suddenly as summer lightning. "Because I'm pregnant! That's why."

He drew back as if she had struck him in the face. "How— Whose—?"

"I did not take a lover, if that's what you're wondering!" She startled him with the force of her anger. "I was raped by soldiers."

He seemed unable to speak for a few moments. Horror, anger, and anguish contorted his face. Tears sprang to his eyes. "Ah, Teresita! I should have been there to protect you! This shouldn't have happened to you. Not to you! What horrors this revolution has spawned."

She draped an arm protectively across her abdomen. "This child may seem like a spawn of the devil to you, but it's mine, Rodolfo, and I'm keeping it."

He knelt in front of her and murmured ever so gently, "I meant nothing against the child. How could I not love a child of yours, Teresita? Let me be its father."

"No." Two tears slipped down her face, glistening like paral-lel seams. "Noble intentions are fine, Rodolfo. But will you be so quick to love a child that might look darkly Indian? What if you only see the father in his eyes and grow to despise—"

"No. I'll see a defenseless child who needs my love and protection."

Teresa struggled to her knees. "Children! Time to go home!" she called out as she began to pack up the picnic basket.

"But we're having such fun!" Laurita whined. The other two joined the chorus.

"All right!" Rodolfo called out. "A few more minutes!" Fresh grass clippings stuck to his knees as he turned back to Teresa. "I'm Lucio Nyman's illegitimate son. Who am I to reject an innocent child on the grounds of illegitimacy?"

"Rodolfo—"

"No, hear me out. My father made many mistakes. I was one of them. But I'll say this much for him: he didn't throw me away. He brought me as a toddler to his first wife who was pregnant with Eva. When she died and he remarried, he had Manuela raise me along with Eva and then the twins that they had together. Growing up, it always seemed to my young eyes that he loved all four of us equally—as did Manuela to her everlasting credit. Everything that happened later, his insanity, his rejection of us, and that damnable will of his, I forgive in light of his magnificent gesture of giving me life and then nourishing it. Likewise, for all her faults, Manuela Vizcarra loved me like a son." He turned to her. "Let me do the same for your child."

"You don't need to marry me out of a sense of moral obligation. I've learned to fend for myself. I don't need you!"

"But I need you! I'm lost without you!"

"Mami! Papi! Look what I can do!" Rodolfito called out as he hung from a tree limb, his feet dangling a foot or so off the ground. Both parents waved absently.

"Maybe you *are* better off without me," Rodolfo's shoulders slumped as he clutched both sides of his head. "My god! What if I turn out like my father, more cracked than the sidewalks of San Angel?"

"You are not your father, Rodolfo!" Teresa spoke firmly because the thought frightened her too.

"Then why do I see his face every time I look in the mirror?"

She drew nearer. "Looking like someone and being like someone are two very different things."

"I was with him, you know, that last night. I got there some two hours or so before Benjamín. All this time I've blamed him for killing the old man, even though he didn't mean to. But I'll tell you, Teresa." He turned to look at her, his eyes bleak as coal slag. "The sacred truth is that I *wanted* to throttle the old man when he went into a rant against you and the children. And I would have done it too if Eufemio had not walked in just then. I came *that* close to killing my father just to make him shut up. Damn it! Damn it to hell!"

Rodolfo's shoulders heaved.

"Please, Rodolfo! You'll scare the children."

"I'm the one who should have been charged with the murder. I *wanted* him dead." The more he remembered, the more Rodolfo stumbled as if lost in a labyrinth. "What if I become like him, mad and hateful? How could I bear to inflict that on you and the children?"

How can I bear it? The old man had asked abruptly in the middle of his tirade, his eyes large and stricken. Those had been his very words, Rodolfo remembered now, echoing his own fear.

"He was sick, my love." Teresa's voice was a string guiding him out of the labyrinth. "What you really wanted to destroy was the disease, not the man."

How can I bear it? Rodolfo sat very still, his mind fixed on an old man's face that had suddenly contorted with more grief than venom. "My father was trapped inside a decaying brain. I know that now. That maniac wasn't him, Teresa. That last night, for a few brief moments, he tried to tell me that, and I wasn't listening."

The general's firstborn son broke down and sobbed.

Teresa embraced him, rocking him gently. "Don't cry my dearest. Don't cry. Isabel says we are all spirits temporarily housed in material bodies. We're spirits living in bodies that *have* to fail us if we are to be free in the end. I think she's right, Rodolfo." She pulled away and searched his face. "The spirit is not the brain; it's not the body. Your father, the *real* man, is very much alive and well somewhere."

"But you don't know what he put us through. How could I bear it if at some time in the future—if I were to subject you and the children to the horror of insanity?"

"None of us knows the future, Rodolfo. What matters is now, because only now is real. The rest is memory or speculation."

By the time the children ran back with stories of their physical prowess and daring exploits, their parents had agreed to the most daring of all adventures.

137

EXILES

TERESA AND RODOLFO were married quietly in the home of his best friend and fellow Felicista, Roberto Iturbide Blas. They decided to say nothing about the wedding to the children, for the simple reason that the children assumed their parents had been married all along. Neither Teresa nor Rodolfo wanted to dispel the illusion, at least not until they were older. So they married in secret, inviting only two guests: Iturbide Blas and me. That spring day in March we traveled in Rodolfo's car to the nearby town of Coyoacán, to the ancestral home of Roberto Iturbide Blas. It was a large colonial mansion furnished with history, antiques, and the inevitable legends about ghosts. Doña Clemencia had insisted on helping by staying in San Justín with the children. But she had placed her beautiful lace *mantilla* in Teresa's hands.

"Wear it if it suits you, my dear."

Rodolfo paid a magistrate to perform the civil marriage in Iturbide's house. Before the signatures were dry, our host had uncorked bottles of champagne. After a round of toasts, Rodolfo and Roberto escorted the judge to his waiting coach. Then the group walked across the inner garden to the chapel where Samuel would perform the religious ceremony. It was a small structure designed to seat no more than ten or twelve people comfortably. Its walls were white and stenciled in elaborate gold leafing.

The bride had made her own dress. Using the new sewing machine that Rodolfo bought for her, Teresa had worked her magic on a bolt of exquisite silver-gray silk. She wore doña Clemencia's beautiful *mantilla* as I had done when I married Benjamín and carried a bouquet of pink roses laced with sprigs of baby's breath. I saw our host studying Teresa, who was definitely showing signs of her condition, and he must have reached the logical conclusion that the baby was Rodolfo's. Acknowledgment and marriage. A happy revision of *The Scarlet Letter,* I thought with a smile.

I watched through a happy shimmer of tears as I remembered a scene so similar to this one. *How extraordinary that both of Samuel's brothers have had to marry in secret!* The thought hit me. *Their family's hold has been that strong. No, it was doña Manuela's hold. She tried so hard to do what* she *considered best for her children and made them utterly miserable. Can we continue to impose our will on our children once they're adults and expect a happy outcome?*

I loved how bride and groom gazed so serenely into each other's eyes. And I loved watching Samuel. *Samuel as stand-in for Benjamín?* Only in part. After all, this was one of the few occasions when I could stare at him without self-consciousness and see Ben in the well-proportioned features, in the eloquent hazel eyes, and in every gesture. As I watched the earnest young priest, I was conscious of my deep love for him—not in any sense that would adulterate my love for Ben—but the way one loves a good person or an angel if one is lucky enough to encounter such a being. Just that. No more.

Two days later we saw Teresa, Rodolfo, and the children off at the train station. As the pain of separation became inescapable,

Rodolfo explained again that they would live in France only until Félix Díaz was elected president, which we all knew to be as likely as snow in Tabasco. Or, he added, they would return when peace was restored once and for all in Mexico, a hope we all needed to embrace.

"By then the children will be more French than Victor Hugo!" Samuel tried to joke.

As we waited on the platform for the train to Veracruz, Teresa threw her arms around me.

"Please come with us, Isabel!" she begged again. "And you too, doña Clemencia. There's still time to purchase train tickets and passage on the ship."

Doña Clemencia shook her head. "Heaven forbid, my dear. I'm too old for such a journey. I'm staying here where I belong. But perhaps Isabel—"

"Isabel is staying where she belongs too," I tried to laugh. "But thank you, dear friend."

"It doesn't feel right to leave you behind!" Teresa fretted. "Don't you want to see Europe again?"

"Not as much as I want to see Benjamín. I *must* wait for him here."

Oh, my dearest! He's dead. Don't you know that yet? Teresa's eyes told me. "Then just come with us for two or three months," she pleaded.

"I can't, Teresa."

"What will you do? Oh, I don't mean for money. You know that Rodolfo and I will always see for you and doña Clemencia. I mean, *how* will you live in a city where you have no friends, no family?"

"I have my new family, our people of San Gabrielín. Besides, I have plans. I'm going to open my own school in San Justín—my own *Jardín de Niños*. That will keep me busy and out of trouble, and I'll wait for reports from the detective Rodolfo engaged."

"But what if —"

A train whistle cut her off. With eight of us on the platform, there was a furious round of hugs. "Be happy, Teresa! Send photos of the children and of the baby!"

Rodolfo and Samuel helped Teresa and the children into their compartment. Then the brothers returned to the platform for a final goodbye. A second whistle blew.

"I've left instructions with Romero." Rodolfo spoke quickly to Samuel. "I'll cable money to your account every three months. If you need anything, if you—"

"Thank you, Rodolfo. Now get on the train and begin the life you've wanted for so long!"

The brothers embraced. Then Rodolfo hugged me tightly. "*Que Dios te bendiga,* Isabel!" God bless you, Isabel!

Rodolfo jumped onto the moving train. Standing on the steps, he waved one last time. He had begun his trip toward a safer, saner country, unaware, of course, that World War I loomed less than a year and a half away, out there on the other side of the cerulean Atlantic.

138

RECALLED

Despite its dark history, I loved my room in San Justín. It never once inspired a nightmare, but it did host a recurring dream that I was home again in Cuernavaca. The house looked totally different, as happens in so many dreams, yet I knew it by the garish colors of the walls and by the warriors and maidens who waved at me from their murals. Shading my eyes from the sun, I looked up just as Cadwally stepped out of his studio. He was dressed in one of his cream-colored suits and the colorful Indian tunic that he used when he painted. In the bright sunlight, his hair was radiantly white, his eyes a stunning blue, his smile outrageously wonderful. The dream was so vivid that I could smell turpentine and the ever-evocative scent of oil paints. And he spoke so clearly that he woke me.

"Come home, Isabel."

Oh, I wanted to. I longed to see Rosa, but Zapatistas, bandits, Felicistas, and Huertistas kept blocking my way. The dream became more insistent.

One night I lay in bed rereading the last letter Benjamín had written to me. He had penned it a few hours after Samuel told him the truth about their mother and my incarceration. It was a long letter that I read and reread.

My astonishing Isa,

I believe at last in the Resurrection because God has seen fit to bring you back to life! I thought you dead and myself with you. There is no force in nature, no volcanic eruption, no upheaval of the earth that can rival the force of Samuel's words when he told me you are alive! He promised to pick up this letter before returning to San Serafín. So I will not sleep tonight. How can I when my sorrow has turned to joy so uncontainable that it erupts in laughter? Sleep? How can I when shame and rage wrench cries from me in alternating cycles?

Dawn: I have crumpled thoughts into misshapen orbs, wept words, raining them across night's fields. The sky is casting its flame-warning now. Samuel will be here soon. So I must finish what I cannot begin. How to express the profound shame that I feel for my mother's abuse of you? When Samuel told me about your imprisonment and the starvation that you endured, I lost my mother irrevocably. How does one forgive such monstrous evil? Yet who am I to condemn her cruelty and not mine as well, I who gave in to my inner demons?

I know no words in Spanish or in English that can convey the *depth* of my own regret and shame, Isa. What right have I to ask for the consolation of your forgiveness, I who cannot forgive Manuela Nyman or myself? Without you I am an asteroid aimlessly wandering the darkest regions of space. Yet, just knowing that the light of the sun still enters your eyes, fills me with wonder and hope.

Throughout the night I keep remembering those first days of ours in Zacatecas—oh, sparkling jasmine days! The wonder of your body. Forgive me! I always reveled in it with a man's passion. I am also recollecting just as clearly your sense of wonder and of appreciation for everything—whether I had roses sent to our room or simply plucked a sprig of honeysuckle on our rambles.

Isa, you are the great gift of my life. I shall never stop loving you. I admit that my lust and love for you are as tightly interwoven for me as light and sight. The memory of us as husband and wife—lovers—will always burn in me with all the force of a prophet's vision of heaven.

I live for the day that I can see you again and beg your forgiveness in person.

Ben

Carefully folding the letter, I turned off the light. "I'll find you," I whispered into the darkened room. That night, Cadwally visited me again in my recurring dream.

139

RETURN TO CUERNAVACA

THE DAILY TRAIN to Cuernavaca was running again. Samuel and I took it one bright morning with doña Clemancia as our chaperone. She had insisted on accompanying us, for how could a priest be seen in the company of a young woman—"and a pretty one at that?" she had spoken firmly, allowing no further discussion. Personally, I did not care what people thought of me. But why compromise Samuel? Federal troops also boarded our train. Clearly, the new president intended to continue the war against the people of Morelos. A few hours later, Cuernavaca rushed to greet us. Our hired cab bounced us along uneven roads to Mrs. King's hotel downtown. Familiar buildings, some of them scarred but otherwise unhurt by recent skirmishes between *federales* and *zapatistas,* winked in greeting. Bougainvillea, tabachin, and jacaranda trees waved, and the neglected, romantic Borda Gardens where Tomás and I had played as children, smiled bright and lush. The cathedral whose midnight bells had always made the night safe, stood ramrod straight, ever guarding. Hawkers in the two central squares serenaded all passersby with their bird-like calls, and the solemn *Palacio de Cortés* offered its stony scowl. I could barely contain the impulse to jump out of the cab and touch every remembered site like a long-lost friend. When we arrived at the Bella Vista hotel, I stayed in the coach. Samuel, who had just helped doña Clemencia down, held out a hand to me.

"No, thank you, Samuel. Please help doña Clemencia get settled. Have lunch. I can't wait another minute! I've got to find Rosa. Then I'll go over to my grandfather's house."

"All right," he smiled. "When should I send a cab for you?"

"I don't know how long I'll be. To tell you the truth, I'd rather walk back if it's all the same to you."

"With all these soldiers on the loose? No. I'll meet you later at your grandfather's house and escort you back, say around six o'clock?"

It was settled. I could have the solitude that I needed to visit my old life.

The cabbie seemed surprised when I directed him along unpaved streets into one of the poorest neighborhoods in town.

"Please stop here."

"*Here*, senorita?" We were halfway up the hill with the back walls of houses on one side and Rosa's field on the other side. Did she think I was dead? If so, I didn't want to give her too much of a shock. So I turned to the driver.

"I need you to do something for me. Please knock on that door up there." I pointed past the charred ruins of a house that I had never seen before, to Rosa's front door.

"That one?" The man studied my clothes and hat.

"Yes. Please tell the señora Rosa that you have good news for her. Tell her that Isabel is alive; that I'm here to see her."

He smiled a great toothless grin and jumped down. Then he ambled off to deliver my message. I fidgeted in the coach. Unable to stand the tension as he neared the door of Rosa's shack, her wonderful shack, I stepped out and patted the horse absent-mindedly, careful to keep my back turned. The man's words were indistinct to my ear. Rosa's gasp was clarity itself. Turning, I saw her hike up her skirt as she ran toward me. I ran too.

"*Mi niña! Mi niña!*"

"Oh, Rosa! Rosa! I've missed you so much!"

We cried and laughed as we hugged. I had almost forgotten how small she was, yet how strong and marvelous her arms felt, and how her skin smelled of vanilla and earth after rain. I paid the driver and hugged her again before entering the one-room house. As always, it was immaculately clean.

"Tomás said you were dead! He stood right here with tears like rain, and he said that he saw your grave with his own two eyes. He said the Nymans dishonored it."

"They what?"

"They dug up your coffin and dumped your body, who knows where!"

'Well, not quite. Here I stand. So it doesn't matter, Rosa."

"Oh, but it does. That's why my Tomás—¡*ay, Diosito!*" She clamped a hand over her mouth. Her eyes widened.

"What's wrong?"

"I swear he only meant to get even with the Nymans. Promise you won't be mad at him, at least not forever."

"All—right."

"He told me—that is, he mentioned—admitted—"; Rosa was strangling her apron with white-knuckled fists. "He burned down the house."

"He burned San Serafín?"

"He told me it's as charred as the wood in a baker's oven. *Ay, mi niña.* I'm so sorry that he destroyed your house."

I slumped into the nearest chair. All that artwork and antiques! All that beauty! And more than three centuries of history! I felt a staggering sense of loss. Not just my own, but a collective one, as if a great museum had been destroyed, cheating all future generations from knowing its treasures. Yet hadn't Tomás simply finished what Asustín and his gang had initiated?

Seeing Rosa's stricken face, I reached for her hands. "Please don't fret on my account."

"Not fret? You could have lived in the finest hacienda in Morelos!" She covered her eyes with her apron.

"But it was never mine, Rosa, no more than the cathedral or the *palacio*. Don't you see?"

She uncovered her face slowly as she tasted the thought. "Yes. I suppose so. Like the house that Tomás made for us. It never felt mine."

"What house?"

"The one that looks like a bonfire the day after."

I glanced over the top of her head at blackened rubble. "That was yours? Oh, Rosa, I'm so sorry!"

"Don't be. It was a humble place, not like your beautiful hacienda!" Her eyes welled up again and her lower lip trembled.

I cupped her face in my hands. "Don't cry, dear Rosa. What matters is that *we're* here!"

We hugged. After a while, she drew back and wiped her eyes again with her trusty apron. "We've got to be like my tough old rooster, Robustino. Full of fight. When those no good rebels tried to grab him along with the hens, you should have seen the way he drove them off, the cowards!"

And though she preferred not to talk while she cooked, Rosa broke her rule and told me about the skirmishes between Federales and Zapatistas, and how some of Genovevo de la O's rebels had burned her new house by mistake. Her hands grew still when I told her about Benjamín's disappearance. She hugged me again, getting some of the masa dough in my hair. We laughed with nervous energy, our emotions stretched tight. Then I told her about my incarceration, and *that* she could not laugh off.

"Oh, Isabelita! She *starved* you? May God rot her soul!"

"No, don't say that. I'm not angry anymore. So please, don't let yourself feel all that turmoil. It's all in the past now."

"But no food at all? What did you do?"

"I did as you told me. I endured," I smiled. "With God's help, I endured."

Rosa plied me with food.

"Tell me about Tomás," I asked between bites of warm squash *empanadas*.

"He's a colonel now with men of his own to boss, and he's fighting alongside Emiliano Zapata," she told me proudly. "And he's going to be a father soon."

"Oh, Rosa! How exciting! Do you like his wife?"

"I think so. She's a strong girl and pretty enough. It's just that she fusses over him like a hen with her chicks. It will turn his head."

"But think of it: you're going to be a grandmother! How wonderful!"

And it was, all of it: her cooking, our storytelling, and even the grave that she showed me later in her field. Instead of the standard headstone, Cadwally's grave had a small house-like structure made from scraps of wood. It was painted in bright pink and royal blue, with touches of parrot green that he would have loved.

"The church wouldn't bury your little grandfather because he wasn't a Catholic, and I didn't have the money for the Protestant cemetery, so we laid him to rest here in my field. And see? I had his name painted right there."

Cadwalader Brent. It was missing an "l" and a "t," but it brimmed with love and smiling geraniums.

"It's beautiful. Thank you, Rosa." And yet again I got weepy, for that whole visit seemed designed to grant us the catharsis of tears. "I miss him so much, Rosa!" And I smiled too because on some level he *was* there, and we all need to feel a physical connection with someone we have loved and lost in this life. We need to be able to do something, even as simple a thing as placing wildflowers on the grave, which I did. And then I was crying for Benjamín, and Rosa was comforting me. When I was calmer, I told her what I should have said years ago.

"What would I have done without you, Rosa? I'm very grateful to Emily Brentt for giving birth to me. But you are the only mother I have ever known and the only one I want in this life. Please come back with me to the D.F. My brothers-in-law are letting me live in their father's house."

"That dreadful place where his ghost wanders?"

"It's beautiful now, and he has better things to do than haunt it. It even has a small village now! I know you'd love it."

"And leave my *milpa*?" She waved a hand to encompass her tiny portion of paradise.

I know. That's unthinkable. After all, isn't this what Zapata is fighting for? Land and liberty!

"All right. I won't argue for now. Stay here if you must. But so long as people don't start blowing up the trains again, I promise to come back every month to visit you. Now I need to go home to my grandfather's house, even if just for a few minutes. Do you mind if I go alone?

"Go, *niña*. Stay as long as you need to. We'll have coffee when you get back."

Rosa told me that she had bolted Cadwally's door from the inside, back when she first found it blowing back and forth in a strong wind. She had then exited by climbing the jacaranda tree. So I also availed myself of it. Taking off my dressy boots and anchoring them around my neck by the laces, I climbed the wall up to the magnificent old tree, high up into the expected past, and down into the altered present. The small courtyard still held the orange tree, bright bougainvillea vines, and the Morelos sky above. Though the house was silent and empty, it was not as dusty or as neglected as I had feared. Instead, it gave me the impression that I had entered a sacred space.

Are you here, Cadwally? I did as you asked. I've come home. Gazing up at the studio, I hoped to see him step out and wave to me as he did in my recurring dream. So I waded into the afternoon light, waiting, listening. Dark-eyed men and women and jungle animals stared back at me from their muralled world, all so silent, the house so empty.

Please, Cadwally. Let me see you one last time. I know that's why you urged me to come home.

But there was only longing and memory in short flashes: Tomás and me running down the stairs as children, our voices young and shrill; Cadwally coming down to dinner, his white hair tinted with a streak of blue or magenta or whatever pigment dripped from the brush tucked behind his ear. I remembered myself, a married woman fleeing from marriage up those same cement stairs, slamming the Dutch door, and Benjamín standing tall and arrogant and worried as he called up to me, awkwardly trying to induce me to return to him, and I so hurt, so willful, so vengeful.

Oh, Ben, if only I could turn back time! Will we ever again hold each other in this life? Please, if you no longer walk on this earth, let me feel your presence, even if only for a few seconds!

The veil between worlds remained stubbornly fixed.

Sighing, I climbed the stairs and entered Cadwally's studio. The scent of oil and turpentine only reinforced the notion that Cadwally had to be there. Paintings, some of them unfamiliar to me, leaned against the walls or lay stacked on shelves. And then I saw on the easel, as if just left to dry, his depiction of a massive flock of passenger pigeons—the blue meteors that he had loved all his life, and a young Union soldier staring awestruck at one of nature's greatest spectacles. It was then that I felt my grandfather's presence, not as the physical sighting I yearned for, but as a *felt* connection, as deep as it was comet-brief.

When I could bear to pull myself away from the studio, I entered my old bedroom. The bed covers looked smoothed over. I could picture Rosa's hands at work. Conchita, my skeleton doll, sat grinning at me from the pillows. The touch of her blue satin dress triggered more impressions of a lost world.

Oh, God! Oh, God! Where has it all gone?

Shutting my eyes tightly I fought the urge to sob like a child.

It's all in you, a thought murmured.

I went back to Rosa's house, a pilgrim returning from a holy site where one senses far more than one sees.

140

WHICH ONE?

ROSA SET DOWN her clay mug. "I've been meaning to ask you, how did you get here, Isabel?"

"By train. I traveled with my brother-in-law and an elderly friend of ours."

"Oh? Which brother?"

"Samuel."

"The priest?"

I nodded, swirling a short stalk of sugarcane in my coffee.

"Then you won't need the letter he wrote for you."

"Why would Samuel write to me?"

"I don't know, *niña*. He just stopped by and asked me if I was Isabel's Rosa. And when I said yes, he introduced himself— such a handsome priest he is—and asked if he could come in and speak with me. So of course I said yes. He looked famished, so I fed him. He was most grateful, especially when I told him to help himself to vegetables from my garden."

"That was kind of you, Rosa. But you know, he wasn't supposed to come for me until 6:00 this afternoon."

"I don't mean today. He stopped by two—no, three days ago."

"But we just got here." Then I remembered that Samuel had been away for two nights before our trip. Yet why would he venture here without telling me?

"Well, he wanted to know where you were, and I had to tell him about your death."

My heart sprinted. "Quick! Show me the letter!"

Rosa grew flustered. "I wasn't trying to lie. It's just that the truth that Tomás had told me wasn't any kind of truth after all. The priest didn't believe it either."

"Please, Rosa! The letter!"

And precisely because she could see my urgency, her memory bolted. "Now where did I put it? I know it's here." She checked under a pot of beans, behind her Virgin of Guadalupe picture, under her pillow, and all the while my heart beat harder than a runner's. A century and a half later she held out a folded sheet of paper. It had neither envelope nor signature, only the handwriting that I knew so well. A poem? And in English? No, not quite a poem. A message disguised within the form.

> *I am a bird newly freed from its cage,*
> *now hunted while searching for its mate.*
> *Nests and forests burned to ash, you and the flock vanished,*
> *I must migrate. Yet we can both write to a great-aunt*
> *where first you learned of angels and spirits. I'll find*
> *you—if not through her—then in a flower's home*
> *on the day we first flew from our cage.*

"He was here!" I gasped.

"That's what I said. Father Samuel—"

"No. Benjamín!"

My mind was racing. I reread the letter. Clearly, Ben had not dared to write in straightforward prose about his escape. Instead, he had left clues. He had searched for me, no doubt in San Gabrielín and probably in San Serafín as well. Not finding me or any of his siblings, and now being hunted by Federal authorities, he was *migrating.* Heading up north, no doubt. By both of us writing to a third party *where first [I] learned about angels and spirits*—Aunt Delphine in Bryn Athyn!—we could establish a way to communicate. And if all else failed, Ben would brave being captured by returning to *a flower's home*—Rosa's house—on *the day when we first flew free from our cage:* our flight from San Serafín when we eloped! Oh, but that anniversary was months from now! How could I stand it that we had missed each other by a mere two or three days?

Yes, but he's alive and free and he's devised a way for us to communicate! Hope burst like sunlight. I kissed his message, my heart a hawk soaring on thermals. Yet almost immediately the image of his homecoming pierced me. What bitter disappointment to have braved who knew how many dangers only to find his beloved home in ashes and us gone. Then there was Cadwally's house, steeped in mournful emptiness. All dead ends. Oh, my poor darling! How could you have known that I—that most of your family—would seek refuge in San Justín of all dreary places?

"Is it good news, Isabelita?" Rosa asked timidly.

"Oh yes! He's free, Rosa! Free! But he's had to go into hiding. God willing, we could be together by no later than December and maybe a lot sooner!"

"If that makes you happy, niña, then it makes me happy too."

"Thank you for everything, dearest Rosa!" I kissed her. "Now I must go and tell Samuel the good news!" I started out the door then hurried back. "And please don't tell a soul about Benjamín's visit. Not even Tomás. Promise me!"

I hurried down the lane, my feet barely touching the ground. Before I'd gotten very far, I spotted Samuel on the street corner at the bottom of the hill. At the very same moment an enclosed coach rolled by. I waited impatiently for it to pass, then started across the street.

"Samuel! He's alive!" I whispered none too softly in English, though the road was deserted again.

He stood motionless as I hurried toward him. A strong wind rustled his long cassock and nearly made off with my hat. Reaching up to save it, I started to tell him about the cryptic note. Before I could get half a sentence out, he startled me by kissing me on the lips. I yanked free. Then because his eyes glinted with mischief and irrepressible joy, I was just able to gasp his name before returning the kiss.

"Ben!"

141

FEDERICO

HEARING THE CLIP-CLOP of an approaching cart, we pulled away from each other.

"Meet me at Cadwally's." I spoke breathlessly and turned resolutely away, afraid someone would see us and the cassock for the ruse that it was. Or maybe our inflamed faces would tell a torrid tale. I walked fast, not daring to turn around because I might not be able to resist running back to him. He followed, at first keeping a discreet distance. However, by the time I was climbing the jacaranda, I knew by the creaking branches and his laugh that he was but a shadow's length behind me. And then, though we balanced on high limbs, he caught me up in another passionate kiss and another and another, all under the swaying blossoms and dappled light. And then he was gasping, his eyes shimmering regret deep and punishing.

"Oh, Isa! I'm so very sorry about your grandfather, about my mother; about me! Oh, God! How do I begin to undo so much harm? Can you forgive me? Not right away, of course. Someday?"

I kissed him softly. "Only if you forgive me too."

We went up to my old bedroom and rediscovered each other, body and soul in rapturous dance. When at last we lay back, arms and legs deliciously entangled, fingers intertwined, words could not begin to encompass all that we needed to say. So we held each other in a silvered silence. When afternoon light sketched long swaying shadows, Benjamín rolled onto his side like a Roman at table and grinned.

"It's a good thing you didn't run into me three days ago. You would have fled in horror. I was desperately in need of a bath, and my cassock was so caked in mud it could actually stand by itself."

"Well, you certainly cleaned up nicely, Captain Nyman." I pressed my nose to his cheek, inhaling the wonderful scent of him. "How ever did you manage it?" I asked in a teasing tone.

"By being a shameless interloper. I've been hiding here making ample use of your grandfather's bathtub and—"

The mere mention of my grandfather nearly derailed the light heartedness that we were attempting. Ben's face grew rigid; my eyes watered. But we caught ourselves and stayed the course.

"So you shaved and cleaned up before visiting Rosa?"

"I had to or she might have fled for the hills."

I sat up, tucking my legs under me. "She said you were a very handsome priest. So tell me, *padre,* how did you escape?"

"Do you remember my cousin Federico Casamayor?"

"The Federal officer who tried to have you recommissioned after the revolution?"

"The very same."

The memory of that missed opportunity flickered briefly into flame: a post in the coastal town of Mazatlán; employment to alleviate our poverty; the fresh start we might have had. Instead, we got sidetracked with the reading of my father-in-law's will, followed by the whole tragic chain of consequences.

"How on earth did your cousin free you? The prison is a fortress!"

"Right in the middle of an artillery barrage, the kind that shatters windows and nerves, I was called into the head warden's office. And there stood Federico, bold and cocky as a matador! With him was a picket of two soldiers and an order that I be handed over for transfer to another prison. He even had the gall to forge General Blanquet's signature."

"And the warden released you? Just like that?"

"The artillery discouraged conversation."

"So you and your cousin didn't plan this together?"

"Nope. And there was no hint of it in his letters. I knew that he had been up north putting out fires against the administration, and that he had recently been transferred to Cuernavaca to deal with Zapata. His most recent letter gushed with praise for his commanding officer. Federico declared on no uncertain terms that General Felipe Ángeles is—and I quote—'the single most capable and honorable officer in Mexico.'"

"No. That honor goes to your wonderful cousin. He's helped us twice now. I *must* meet him to thank him in person."

"God knows when that will be. We're fugitives now, Isa. We'll have to leave Mexico, maybe for good." He looked at me as if to say, could you stand it?

"All right," I nodded resolutely. "So tell me more about that clever cousin of yours. How did he happen to be so conveniently in the D.F.?"

"When the city came under attack, the President sent for Ángeles and his men to help defend it. Taking advantage of the chaos, my ever-resourceful cousin found the opportunity to pull his stunt at the Penitentiary. It was outrageously simple!"

Federico is dead. I suddenly remembered a fragment of a conversation that I had overheard between Rodolfo and Samuel. And later they had talked in low voices about an aunt whose only son had been killed in the fighting downtown. Could this be the same Federico? Seeing the animation in Benjamín's face, I could not bring myself to raise the possibility. Let sorrow prowl like a cat out there somewhere, not in here. Not just yet.

"I don't know if my cousin bribed the escort to keep quiet or if they are astoundingly loyal to him. In any case, they hurried me into a waiting car. Two blocks later, he had the cab pull over. The men climbed out. Before joining them, Federico slapped some money into my hand and a black bundle—the soon-to-be-abused cassock. He told me that the driver would take me to the Toluca Station so I could head north. I told him I needed to head south to find you. We argued briefly, shouting above the din of artillery."

Can it be? Were we in the city at the same moment, yet we missed each other? The thought clawed me.

"I told Federico, yelled it, that he was an idiot for jeopardizing his career for me. 'Too late,' he grinned. And you know, Isa, for a moment it felt as if we were kids again plotting some great adventure. Even with a moustache, Federico has one of those faces that retains the clear imprint of childhood: round, pug-nosed, and wide-eyed, which makes him seem almost as guile-less as Samuel. But Federico has grown cunning. I have to hand it to him. His scheme went without a hitch."

Break it to him now?

"Isn't fate strange?" Ben looked off. "Here we were, child-hood friends who grew up to fight on opposite sides in 1910. Yet now in 1913 we are devoted to the same leader."

"I guess we can thank Mr. Madero for not disbanding the Federal Army after our victory."

"Which seemed madness at the time. Whoever heard of dis-banding your own army and leaving the enemy one intact?"

"Mr. Madero was certainly generous in victory," I mur-mured.

"And it's paid off. Now the Federal Army is defending our revolutionary president, incredible as that seems!" Benjamín chuckled with satisfaction.

Oh, Ben! You really don't know!

"You know Isa, as the cab pulled away, I turned and had a final glimpse of Federico. He was calmly unholstering his gun as he prepared to go back into the fray. And I envied him—envied that he had a noble cause besides self-preservation." Benjamín's tone was wistful. "Plus I couldn't help admiring his aplomb. The chauffeur, on the other hand, was shaking like poor old Hipólito when firecrackers boom. The man drove as if demons were pursuing us."

"So he took you to Toluca?"

"If I hadn't threatened to choke him, I think he would have kept going all the way to Texas. Since he refused to drive me south, I got out, put on the cassock, and started walking."

"Was it awful, Ben?"

"For the terrified civilians, yes. No one knew what was happening. Why was the city under attack? But for me, the very thought of finding you filled me with exhilaration. At times I ran like a Tarahumara friend of mine taught me. Other times I had to walk in my best Father Samuel manner."

"And we both know you've mastered *that*," I smiled, still stalling.

"So tell me about the attack on the city, Isa. I'm still pretty much in the dark about it. There was neither time nor calm for Federico to tell me much. Since then I've been dodging Federales, Zapatistas, bandits, hunger, and illness."

"You were sick?" I drew closer to him.

"Only for a few days." He shrugged.

"You must tell me all, Ben. How sick were you?"

"To the borders of Valhalla," he admitted. "When I staggered into the ruins of San Serafín, I couldn't tell if I was dreaming or if that hellish landscape was real. And then I blacked out. I awoke in a primitive lean-to and Bardomiana was hovering over me. If not for her, I don't think I'd be here speaking with you. Let me tell you, that dear old woman is so much more than a good cook."

"I'll second that."

"I'm living proof that she is also quite savvy with folk medicine. Politics is another matter. She confines the whole world within the limits of San Serafín. Your Rosa Tepaneca doesn't know much either beyond the limits of Cuernavaca. When I ran into you, I had ventured out to see if I could scrounge up a newspaper from a park trash bin. So tell me, who were the renegades this time?"

"Officers of the Federal Army," I answered quietly. "It was a coup d'état, Ben. The generals who fought to overthrow the government—" I hesitated, then gave it to him straight. "They killed President Madero, his brother Gustavo, and Vice-President Pino-Suárez. In a mere ten days the two enemy camps killed thousands of civilians who were caught in the crossfire. Then one of the generals, a man named Victoriano Huerta, forced his way into the presidency."

"Damn it to hell! Does nothing change?" The veins in his neck throbbed.

What could I say? In 1910 we had joined the revolution with such hope, all to end up with a dictator who was making Porfirio Díaz look benign by comparison and certainly more enlightened. We discussed the matter further. Then came the hardest part: telling him about the Federico whom his brothers had referenced.

"There are lots of Federicos." The deliberate shrug of his broad shoulders defied the very possibility. "What makes you think they were talking about my cousin?"

"Because I also heard them say that your Aunt Sofía lost her only son in the fighting downtown. I'm so sorry, Ben."

He looked away trying to hold back tears. "It should have been me, worthless me." His voice cracked.

"Oh, darling! You are not worthless!" I tried to reach for him but he pulled back.

"For God's sake, Isa! Love me if you can, but see me as I am! I killed my father! My own father!" Such anger. Such anguish.

"No! Your father himself told me that you are innocent." And so I waded into the broiling waters of Benjamín's despair and innate skepticism. As I recounted my strange experience in San Justín, he did grow calmer but no less skeptical.

"You dreamed it, and I thank you for it." Benjamín stroked hair away from my face, his touch a gentle apology.

"Benjamín Nyman! For once in your life open your heart to other possibilities, other realities!"

"Isa, I know you need to believe I'm not a monster. I'd like nothing better than to believe it too. But without proof—"

"No. You prove that he didn't speak to me! Go ahead, oh you who knows all the workings of the universe. Prove it!" I glared at him across the old chasm, ever wide, ever deep, a wave of anguish washing over me.

"Forgive me, Isa I don't mean to upset you."

"You demand proof. But how does one apply physical laws to a higher reality that has its own laws? It can't be done. But I *can* assure you that I was not sleep-walking or dreaming, and I am not lying when I tell you that I *felt* your father's presence. I still don't understand it myself. Did I hear the words out loud like I'm speaking to you now, or inwardly? I just know that he told me with such urgency: 'Benjamín didn't do it. He only thinks he did.'"

142

A BRAZEN SCHEME

BEN AND I clung to each other. Throughout that afternoon we used our lovemaking as both a salve and a passionate manifesto to life. Later, when we lay in each other's arms, I wondered if he truly believed me or simply loved that I believed in him, Benjamín Nyman, condemned patricide. We lay in bed listening to raucous grackles as they roosted in the treetops. The room began to fade into the retreating light. And then he told me about the extraordinary Tarahumara who befriended him in prison, how they plotted to escape together, and how he had felt compelled to stay behind, giving Brujo a better chance to seek freedom without him. As for his bodyguards who would have been scapegoats had he escaped, Ben downplayed his altruism.

"No. That was wonderful of you!" I kissed him. "And brave."

"I'm not brave, Isa. When I thought you were dead, I tried to kill myself."

My heart sprinted like a runner. I hugged him closer. "Oh, darling!" I gasped.

"Brujo stopped me."

"You said he escaped."

Benjamín gave me a lopsided smile. "Skeptics can have strange experiences too." And so he told me about the night that he tried to hang himself. "Like you, I don't know if I actually heard his voice or if I imagined it. But I'll tell you, Isa, it stopped me cold." He shook his head. "I can't explain it. So who am I to say that you didn't hear my father's voice?"

"Then you believe me?"

"God help me, I think I do."

Eventually Ben fell into an exhausted sleep. Shadows climbed the walls like vines. Pewter twilight covered us in warm fleece. And I might have slept too if not for insistent knocking on the front door. Dressing hastily, I tiptoed down the stairs and found Samuel and Rosa, both of them worried and both of them overjoyed when I told them about Ben's escape.

"Have you eaten, child?" First things first with Rosa. "Then I'll be right back with dinner. No more starving for you!" Remembering Samuel and his mother, she clapped a hand over her mouth. "I mean—"

"Why don't we all eat here?" I draped an arm around Rosa's shoulders. "Let's celebrate."

"Good idea." Samuel reached for his wallet, and Rosa was off to shop for food. In the meantime, he helped me finish the cleaning that Benjamín had begun. When I found old paper lanterns in the back of a cupboard, my brother-in-law was off to buy candles and string.

It was dark when Ben awoke—dark yet magically alight. Naked, shielded only by the half wall in the upper corridor, he stood staring down onto gaily-lit lanterns strung across the patio. Rosa was stirring her delectable *pollo en cuñete,* chicken cooked in a large clay pot with herbs from her garden; I was cutting up onions, tomatoes, and cilantro; Samuel was uncorking bottles of wine, and doña Clemencia was smiling up at Ben, her arms crossed over her generous chest, her head thrust back.

"The groom awakens at last!" She laughed her deep laugh. "Get some clothes on young man and come join us!"

Moments later two identical men in black cassocks were hugging and clapping each other on the back in that ever-so-Mexican way. Doña Clemencia, who had not seen Ben since the night when we were married, approached the brothers, hands on hips.

"Blessed Mary! Have I hit my head? I'm seeing double!"

Sitting at the table with its brightly painted, mismatched chairs, we filled the night air with the laughter and talk of people who care about each other, love drawing us into its golden orb. And for a few seconds, I thought Cadwally was sitting with us, glass raised as we toasted Benjamín.

Early the next morning, Samuel dropped off his travel bag as agreed the previous night.

"It has two changes of clothes and toiletries," he told Ben. "Help yourself. I would have asked for your bag when I checked out, Isabel," he turned to me, "but I thought it would look suspect, especially as the staff must consider it doña Clemencia's."

"That's all right. As you see, I can still fit into some of the clothes stored in my old wardrobe." And indeed, I was wearing once again the loose-fitting blouses and plain skirts of the Morelos peasantry.

Samuel gulped down some coffee and was off to catch the one and only train out of Cuernavaca. "I'll be back in two or three days. Until then, do *not* leave the house, whatever you do."

Leave our paradise? Not a chance. For the next two and a half days Benjamín and I enjoyed a second honeymoon. It was glorious! To be truthful, we were disappointed when Samuel returned. We would have preferred to go on living as lovers suspended in time, free of the world's perils and demands.

"I've checked back into the Bellavista," Samuel told his twin. "Tonight we swap identities."

And so was launched the plan for our escape from Mexico.

143

INTO THE LION'S DEN

IT HAD BEEN decided that the fastest route to freedom was via the port of Veracruz, and the surest route to Veracruz in those troubled times was via train from Mexico City. We would travel on the night train. Once in Veracruz we could board a ship bound for Europe or the United States. Expediency would decide that one—that and Samuel who was making all the arrangements while in Mexico City. On his return to Cuernavaca, he handed out envelopes, one for me, a separate one for Ben.

"It's all there: train tickets to the D.F., night train to Veracruz, and your passage on the *Ypiranga*. She sails for Europe the day after tomorrow."

"To France?" I was eager to see Teresa, Rodolfo, and the children.

"Spain," Benjamín cut in. Narrowing his eyes, Ben drew closer to his twin. "You're packing us off to La Coruña." Samuel didn't answer right away. When he smiled and nodded, I felt my skin prickle. So these brothers *could* read each other's minds sometimes. Benjamín gave the *mariachi* cry of triumph. "I can still read your mind, brother, but you can't read mine."

"Don't be so sure." Then Samuel turned to me. "Don't worry. From La Coruña you can make your way to Paris. Rodolfo and Teresa are expecting you. But we're getting ahead of ourselves. First you need to get to the D.F. Once there, doña Clemencia will accompany you as far as the Santa Clara Station. You and Benjamín must continue to be strangers to each other. *Strangers,* Benjamín." Samuel gave his brother a stern look.

"We'll need to kill time between trains," I observed. "Where can we go during those long hours and not draw attention from the authorities?"

"That *is* a problem," Samuel conceded. "I suppose you could go to Palacio de Hierro to buy a few items for your trip—discreetly of course. You could eat in some small, inconspicuous restaurant. All the more reason for doña Clemencia to stay by your side, Isabel, at least until you board the night train."

"I'm not letting Isa out of my sight," Ben draped an arm around my shoulders.

"Fair enough. Just keep a dignified distance, *padre*. Remember you're a priest."

"You forget, brother, that I have played this role to the acclaim of a few discerning souls." Benjamín quipped, his tone in sharp contrast to Samuel's.

"Then make this your best and final performance. Everything depends on it. Above all, guard how you look at Isabel. Don't—"

"I know, *padre*. No gawking at her. No hand holding and no sneaking into her sleeping compartment. Trust me. I am the very image of the very reverend Father Samuel, though I must warn you that he has morphed lately from mild-mannered servant of God to shameless smuggler." And then Ben dropped all jocularity, drawing his brother into a tight embrace.

That night Ben began his impersonation of Samuel by spending the night in the hotel. Samuel moved into Cadwally's house, where he would remain for several days until certain that we were safely out of the country. And I took the opportunity to stay with Rosa one last time.

Early the next morning Benjamín and doña Clemencia checked out of the hotel. Rosa and I walked to the station, giving ourselves plenty of time. I was dressed once again in formal travel attire with Rosa acting as my servant. People, especially soldiers, stared at us but no one gave us any trouble. A long tearful hug later, I was on the train bound for Mexico City. As planned, Benjamín did not sit with me. Instead, doña Clemencia sat alongside me. Since she slept through most of the bumpy, rattly ride, I gazed longingly at the hills and mountains that drew me ever further from my dear Rosa and home. Would I ever see her again, or would I return all too soon, tearfully telling her how the police had seen through our masquerade?

The problem wasn't that Benjamín would be returned to prison. If caught, he was far more likely to be executed for his well-known support of the slain President Madero. General Huerta, our new dictator, had begun terrifying purges against supporters of his predecessor. A mere ten days after usurping the presidency, Huerta had ordered squads to machine-gun over a hundred *maderistas* in the suburb of Santa Julia. Political assassinations were becoming horrifyingly common. My poor Mexico was plunging into ever greater chaos.

We arrived in Mexico City without incident. Hours later we headed to the Santa Clara Station for the next leg of our journey: the trip to Veracruz. While waiting for the night train, doña Clemencia and I sat on a bench and talked trivialities, wishing we could say instead all that fluttered within us. We could see Benjamín a short distance from us. Then a wall of uniformed men came between us. Federal soldiers crowded the platform, weapons slung casually, all voices homogenized as the train lumbered into view. My companion embraced me tightly.

"God be with you, my dear!" She choked out the words in her lovely Castilian.

I held her close. "Thank you for everything, dear doña Clemencia! I promise to write!"

Two army officers gallantly stepped aside to let me board first. In the sleeping car, Benjamín walked past me without a second look. The officers, on the other hand, smiled and tipped their hats to me. One of them, a tall, thin man with a moustache waxed into upward peaks, added a wink. More passengers boarded. Closing my door, I sat on the edge of the narrow bed. *Why all these soldiers?* Imagination, that capacity we tend to praise, momentarily drove out my much-needed inner calm, sketching an image of Benjamín being led off the train in handcuffs. *Why aren't we leaving?* At last the final whistle blew and the train lurched forward.

I would have sat by the window during the whole trip, my eyes caressing the country I might never see again, but the night's ink blotted out the landscape. Flicking on the light above my berth, I reached idly inside the large envelope that Samuel had given me. Tickets spilled onto my lap, along with a folded piece of paper. Rodolfo's address was written on one side, on the other a note from Samuel, some of which was configured in a geometric shape—a quadrilateral.

Dear Isa,

Whence evil? If we accept the proposition that only good flows from God, then the fault must lie, 'not in our stars,' but in our *reception* of what flows into us from God. *Our willful inversion of good.* Given the reality and the persistence of evil, how then are we to cope? Humbly, I venture a suggestion: that we make our life into a joyous wind-blown kite with God—not ourselves—at the top, and that we freely choose to live by the Lord's injunction, counter-intuitive as it seems. It begins with a negation, and that makes all the difference:

But I say to you,
love your enemies, bless
those who curse you, do good to those
who hate you, and pray for those who spitefully use you
and persecute you, that you may be children of your Father in heaven; for
He makes his sun rise on the evil and the good, and sends rain on the just and on the unjust.
MATTHEW 5:45

In hell, the goodness that flows in from the Lord is turned into evil and the truth into falsity.
Surely, though, anyone can see that the evil and falsity do not come from
what is good and true and therefore from the Lord. They come
from the receiving subject or object that is focused on
what is evil and false and that distorts and
inverts what it is receiving.
DIVINE PROVIDENCE 294

Dear Samuel! I read it twice. Then kissing the note, I tucked it back into the envelope, my heart full of gratitude that my brother-in-law had made his peace with God.

The train barreled into the night, swaying rhythmically like a dance partner. Balancing on bare feet, I prepared for bed, intent on playing my role of normal passenger. And though I lay wide-eyed in my berth for a long time, the train's rumble and motion did in fact rock me to sleep.

Sometime in the night the train came to a shuddering stop, throwing me to the floor.

144

THE BEST LAID PLANS—

DAZED, I STAGGERED to my feet. A fierce barrage of gunfire sent me running into the corridor.

"What's happening!" I asked a porter who seemed almost as white as the towels in his hands.

"We're being attacked! Please stay in your compartment, señora."

But I want to be with my husband! I almost blurted out. Only Samuel's stern admonition that we play our roles consistently— only that kept me from searching for Ben. The lights went out just then, and I could not see my hands in front of my face. Groping my way, I sat motionless on my berth and listened to an invisible battle. Moments later, there was the distinct scurry of feet as soldiers rushed into my compartment. Someone cursed the window that was stuck. Glass shattered as they smashed it to return fire. Yelling and swearing. So much yelling. So this was combat! Not men gritting their teeth and fighting in stoic silence as I had imagined, but cursing and shouting above the din.

Two things became clear: that the soldiers had not yet perceived my presence though we were only a few feet apart, and that the only sensible thing to do when you are under attack in total darkness and have no weapon of your own, is to pray. On that occasion, my prayers were a form of meditative practice. A calming emptying of the mind.

At some point the shooting stopped. The soldiers in my compartment, three by the sound of their voices, laughed and yelled a volley of profanities at our invisible enemy. Their banter seemed artificially careless, their laughter an attempt at bravura. And still I prayed, my breathing soft and controlled. When the lights blinked on for a few seconds then out again, one of the men let out a yelp, startling the other two. My sudden appearance spooked him more than the din of gunfire. Someone lit a match and held it near my face. I prayed on, eyes shut.

"Say one for me too, Miss," one of the soldiers murmured.

Then I was alone again. Gazing calmly into the dark, I waited for signs that the attack was definitely over so we could be on our way. Above all, I listened for Ben who would knock softly under the guise of concerned priest checking on all passengers in our car. *Yes, I'm all right. Thank you, Father,* I would assure him cheerfully, letting him proceed to the next door. But there was no knock, only a gust of voices. Still I waited. *Any minute now.* Still he didn't come. Then a man called out, "Over here! A priest has been wounded!"

A priest! Jumping to my feet, I threw open my door. At that very moment the lights were switched back on, momentarily blinding me. Running in the direction of the voice I had heard, I came upon our car attendant who was hovering over someone. When the man became aware of me, he turned and I had a quick glimpse of Ben on the floor. He was bleeding from the head, his eyes shut, his body stillness itself.

"Oh, God, no!" The words escaped me because I had dropped my prayer and was fully in the grip of fear. And then another man was telling me to step aside, a man carrying what looked like a doctor's satchel, "Oh, please! Can I help?" I begged.

The doctor gave me a cursory glance, half concern, half annoyance. "No, thank you. I suggest you return to your compartment, señora." And he closed the door in my face.

That's my husband! I wanted to yell and pound on the door. And then I realized that I was a woman in a nightgown who had hastened to a priest's sleeping compartment. Was it fair to Ben for me to soothe my fear by blowing our cover? Play your role no matter what! Yet wasn't it more important to be by Benjamín's side now? Before I could decide, we came under fire again. Seconds before the lights were deliberately extinguished a second time, the officer with the waxed moustache grabbed my arm and hurried me along.

"Lock your door, señorita, and stay clear of the window." He spoke tightly without a hint of his earlier flirtation.

I felt my way in the dark. A sharp pain sent me limping to my berth. This time I had stumbled onto some of the shards of glass that carpeted the floor. Was I bleeding a lot? A little? I didn't care, only that Benjamín had suffered a serious head wound. After all that we had gone through, was this how it was going to end? I thought I could handle death with grace. My own did not scare me. But the death of my beloved—ah! That was a far different matter. I could not bear the thought of him suffering, or of me living the rest of my life on Earth without him. How I longed to go to him! *Lord! Will this trip never end?*

That night as I prayed, I dove into a dark ocean of yearning. Its currents plunged me into depths that began with supplications for Benjamín and for the safety of my fellow passengers, and then for the deliverance of my country from the violence of revolutions and counterrevolutions. I prayed for our troubled world with all its ravenous wars and suffering. So much suffering! On I prayed, yearning to encounter God whatever the cost. Like the prophet Elijah, I would have confronted nature in all its raw power—the rending of mountains and the roar of wind, earthquake, and fire—if only to hear the still small voice of God. But first I had to quiet my own voice.

I don't know how long I linked my breathing to the Hesychast prayer. Gradually, the metallic clamor of machine guns and rifles grew fainter to my hearing, though the fighting whirled all around me. At some moment outside of time, I felt a surge of warmth like no other. And I knew it to be the presence of God, neither seen nor needing to be seen. *Felt*. Exhilarating. Frightening. Astounding. And I an empty vessel. Love poured into the emptiness, coursing through me like a mighty river. Yet what was it but an infinitesimally minute portion of Divine love, for how else could the very force that creates and sustains the universe flow through us without destroying us? I felt God's love extend to attackers and defenders alike. And in that stunning moment, I knew that whether any of us survived or died that night didn't matter ultimately. There is only life, ever changeable but unstoppable in its trajectory into eternity.

What are souls but comet-voyagers? Pain and terror, all powerful as they seem to our physical senses, are mere particles deflecting off the soul's flaming ice. We hurtle briefly through this world and then into a spiritual vastness that dwarfs the very cosmos.

I became aware once more of my cabin with its floor of shattered glass. Gunfire rumbled. Shouting and cries rained their downpour. And then like all storms, the fighting wound down, fading to a few sporadic shots. A trickle. And then the dewy silence. Nothing stirred but the stirring birth of a new morning. Daylight, still clothed in early gray, began to usher darkness out with slow, gentle motions.

After a while someone shouted orders to clear the track. Something about a tree. Though the lights remained off, I could now see my blood-stained bed covers. Sitting cross-legged, I pulled out several small shards of glass from my feet. Yet even as I winced, I could not shake a delicious sense of well-being. A skeptic might say it was because I was alive and relatively unhurt. True. I did want to live on a bit longer if possible. But I knew once more what I had been shown when I nearly died in San Serafín, and what the ancient *Bhagavad Gita* had asserted centuries ago: *"These bodies are perishable, but the dwellers in these bodies are eternal, indestructible, and impenetrable."*

At last the train lurched forward and we were on our way. The cool morning air that wafted through my smashed window grew noticeably warmer over the next hour. Dawn lit up the sky and a giant came into view: majestically tall Orizaba. The magnificent volcano glided past my window, its snowy shoulders tinted in shades of hibiscus pink and orange-yellow.

Without further incident, we finally pulled into the station in Veracruz. Stepping down onto the platform, I felt the shock of tropical heat and its smells. I'd forgotten how different they were from Mexico City with its high altitude and cooler climate. Pulling off my gloves, I hobbled on sore feet over to a car attendant.

"Please, is everyone all right? I heard that a priest was wounded."

"Yes ma'am. Several passengers and soldiers were wounded. One died."

"You! Get over here!" someone yelled at him.

"Excuse me, ma'am," And he was off to help carry a litter off the train.

A blood-soaked sheet covered a body. Someone had tied a rope of coarse *henequén* around the body, presumably to keep it from sliding off the litter. I walked toward it with deliberately unhurried steps. *Thy will be done. Thy will be done.* Other passengers gathered around. An official reached down to uncover the face. If not for the crimson stain on his carefully waxed mustache, I might have assumed that my officer was napping peacefully after a long night.

"God bless you, sir," I murmured as others crossed themselves.

And then I knew to glance back at the train. The wounded were being helped out. A tall man in a cassock, his head bandaged with torn strips of bedding, stood on the top step, his eyes searching the crowd. I ignored a voice behind me that asked politely in the unmistakable accent of Veracruz: "May I have the ticket for your trunk, señora?" When the porter repeated his question two or three times without the least sign of impatience, I finally looked at him.

"My trunk? Actually, I don't have one." And I laughed from sheer elation, my heart embracing the porter with the kind face, the morning with its rising heat, and above all the priest whose eyes met mine so joyously.

THE END

ACKNOWLEDGMENTS

My protagonist Isabel Brentt came to me on a commuter train to Boston. I had but a glimpse of her—a nameless young woman locked in a white room. She may have entered my mind unbidden, but she was fleshed out through my interactions with a number of key people who were willing to read the various manuscripts across nine years.

Lisa Hyatt Cooper and my daughter Alex Shaw were my first two readers. Thank you for your enthusiasm that kept me writing. Dr. Stephen H. Smith valiantly read every page of one of the manuscripts. His feedback usually came via emails or texting—always insightful, enthusiastic even when he didn't particularly care for Isabel's personality in the early chapters. (Like all of us, she had a lot to learn.) Thank you, Steve, Lisa, and Alex for your love of literature in general and for your belief in me as a novelist.

My neighbor John Crane, an avid reader who loved the first novel, urged me across nine years to finish the second book of the trilogy. His appreciation of Brujo, the Tarahumara prisoner in the first book, inspired me to bring him back briefly in this second novel. Thank you, John. I had forgotten that some literary characters can take on a life of their own for readers who would like to encounter them again.

A special thanks to Dr. Gerald Lemole and Star Silverman who read the manuscript in the spring and summer of 2020. Thank you, dear friends, for your enthusiasm for my project and for the generosity of your time.

Ninety-six-year-old Father Daniel Binney Montgomery, Orthodox priest and Buddhist scholar extraordinaire, blind as he was in one eye, also read every word of the 2020 manuscript. His feedback was Socratic. Asking me a few questions, he prompted further reflection and fine-tuning on my part. Many, many thanks to you, my ever-loyal Dad. May your wisdom ever increase as you now explore the world beyond this one.

And of course, the final product would not have been possible without the skill and patience of my editors: Morgan Beard, Prof. Meg Tyler, and John Connolly. Early on, Morgan read every single line of two separate versions and inspired me to do two things: to opt for a first-person narrative instead of the omniscient voice of the earlier drafts, and not to end the novel so abruptly. Thank you, Morgan. I hope the four chapters that I added will satisfy readers who may want to know more about the two lovers of our story beyond the moment when they are finally reunited.

Prof. Meg Tyler, my official fiction editor, combed every line of the 2021 final version and gave me invaluable feedback via Google Docs. Her literary acumen, her keen eye and her poetic soul were crucial in this long-awaited, final phase of the novel. I am grateful to Samuel Cataño for the beautiful cover images that he created for all three books. And my thanks to John Connolly, the editor at the Swedenborg Foundation, as well as to Chelsea Odhner and Karen Connor, who ushered the book into full publication.

Last and first of all, I thank God for his love that gives life, not only to all things in the physical cosmos, but also to all good things in the spiritual expanses of the human soul.

SYLVIA MONTGOMERY SHAW (DECEMBER 2021)

KEY SOURCES

I was born in Mexico twenty-nine years after the end of the Mexican Revolution. From childhood, the firsthand accounts of my maternal grandparents took deep root in me. For my doctoral dissertation many years later, I focused on 1910 to 1914, four crucial years in the decade-long conflict. My dissertation bibliography cites one hundred and fourteen sources. For the purposes of my novel, I am citing a small sampling of the many writers who have given me a solid sense of the history of the period.

Above all, writing *Flight of the Trogon* over the course of nine years has given me the opportunity to reflect on the spiritual dimension of prayer and on a problem that has vexed me for many years: why our benevolent God permits evil. The Eastern Orthodox Church of my childhood taught me much about prayer, which would sustain me during my rebellious years when I declared myself an atheist while paradoxically praying to God whom I stubbornly denied. The works of Emanuel Swedenborg gave me a theodicy that restored my faith, along with a new appreciation for the deeper meaning within the literal texts of the Bible. In the exultant words of John Bigelow, nineteenth-century citizen extraordinaire of New York City, Swedenborg's astonishing works gave me "the Bible that was lost and is found."

On God, Prayer, and Spirituality:

Anonymous. *The Way of a Pilgrim*. Translated by R.M. French. New York: Harper & Brothers, 1925.

Bigelow, John. *The Bible that Was Lost and Is Found*. New York: Swedenborg Press, 1893.

Bloom, Anthony. *Beginning to Pray*. New York: Paulist Press, 1970.

Mathewes-Green, Frederica. *The Jesus Prayer: The Ancient Desert Prayer that Tunes the Heart to God*. Brewster, MA: Paraclete Press, 2009.

Swedenborg, Emanuel. *Divine Providence*. Translated by George F. Dole. West Chester, PA: Swedenborg Foundation, 2010.

_____. *Heaven and Hell*. Translated by George F. Dole. West Chester, PA: Swedenborg Foundation, 2010.

On the Mexican Revolution:

Brenner, Anita, and George R. Leighton. *The Wind that Swept Mexico: The History of the Mexican Revolution, 1910–1942*. Austin: University of Texas Press, 1971.

Calvert, Peter. *The Mexican Revolution, 1910–1914: The Diplomacy of Anglo-American Conflict*. Cambridge: Cambridge University Press, 1968.

Casasola, Gustavo, ed. *Historia Gráfica de la Revolución Mexicana 1900–1960* (10 vols.). Editorial trillas, 1970–71.

Cumberland, Charles C. *Mexican Revolution: Genesis under Madero* (Texas Pan American Series). Austin: University of Texas Press, 1974.

De Bekker, Leander Jan. *De Como Vino Huerta Y Como Se Fue*. México: Librería General, 1914.

Fernández Rojas, José. *De Porfirio Díaz a Victoriano Huerta*. Guadalajara: Escuela de Artes y Oficios del Estado, 1913.

Flandrau, Charles Macomb. *Viva México*. New York: D. Appleton & Co., 1908.

Fontana, Bernard L. *Tarahumara: Where Night Is the Day of the Moon*. Tucson: The University of Arizona Press, 1997.

Frankl, Viktor E. *Man's Search for Meaning: An Introduction to Logotherapy*, 3rd ed. New York: Touchstone Books/Simon & Schuster, 1984.

Guzmán, Martín Luis. *Febrero de 1913*. México: Empresas Editoriales. S.A., 1963.

_____. *El águila y la serpiente*. Antonio Castro Leal, ed. *La Novela de la Revolución Mexicana*. Madrid, México: Aguilar, 1958.

Henderson, Peter V.N. *Félix Díaz, the Porfirians, and the Mexican Revolution*. Lincoln and London: University of Nebraska Press, 1981.

Johnson, William Weber. *Heroic Mexico: The Violent Emergence of a Modern Nation*. Garden City, New York: Doubleday & Co., 1968.

King, Rosa E. *Tempest over Mexico*. Boston: Little, Brown, & Co., 1936.

Knight, Alan. *The Mexican Revolution: Counter-revolution and Reconstruction*, vol. 2. Cambridge: Cambridge University Press, 1986.

MacHugh, R.J. *Modern Mexico*. London: Methuen & Co., LTD, 1914.

McDougall, Christopher. *Born to Run: A Hidden Tribe, Superathletes, and the Greatest Race the World Has Ever Seen*. New York: Alfred Knopf, 2009.

Márquez Sterling, Manuel. *Los Últimos Días del Presidente Madero*. Habana: El Siglo XX, 1917.

Martínez Fernández del Campo, Luis. *De Como Vino Huerta y Como se Fue: Apuntes para un Régimen Militar*. México: Librería General, 1914.

Mellado, N. Guillermo. *Crímenes del Huertismo*. México: Privately printed, 1913.

Meyer, Michael. *Huerta: A Political Portrait*. Lincoln: University of Nebraska Press, 1972.

Moats, Leone B. *Thunder in Their Veins: A Memoir of Mexico*. New York: The Century Co., 1932.

O'Shaughnessy, Edith. *A Diplomat's Wife in Mexico*. New York and London: Harper & Brothers Publishers, 1916.

_____. *Diplomatic Days*. New York and London: Harper & Brothers Publishers, 1917.

Ross, Stanley R. *Francisco I. Madero: Apostle of Democracy*. New York: Columbia University Press, 1955.

_____. *Fuentes de la Historia Contemporánea de México: Periódicos y Revistas*. México: El Colegio de México, 1965.

Simonds, Louis. "Victoriano Huerta: A Sketch from Life." In *Atlantic Monthly* 113 (June 1914): 721–32.

Tamborrel Suárez, José. Personal interviews, 1971–1988.

_____. *Páginas Sueltas*. My grandfather's unpublished memoir. Mexico City, July 1972.

Terry, T. Phillip. *Terry's Mexico: Handbook for Travelers,* 2nd ed. Revised. London: Gay and Hancock, Ltd., 1911.

Toro, Carlos. *La Caída de Madero por la Revolución Felicista*. México: F. García y Alva, 1913.

Velázquez, Victor José. *Apuntes para la Historia de la Revolución Felicista*. México: Librería de la Viuda de Ch. Bouret, 1913.

Vera Estañol, Jorge. *La Revolución Mexicana: Orígenes y Resultados*. México: Editorial Porrua, S.A., 1957.

Womack, John, Jr., *Zapata and the Mexican Revolution*. New York: Alfred A. Knopf, 1971.

Zepeda, María Luisa. Letters and interviews with my maternal grandmother.